Stuck in Her Teens

A Lesbian Ageplay Spanking Romance

Stuck in Her Teens
A Lesbian Ageplay Spanking Romance

By Clarine Klein

http://clarineklein.com

Pretending to be her adoring (but super strict) mommy-dommy's niece while out in public has become just a normal part of life for petite and oh so sassy college junior Rhen Mathews. With her small frame and bratty attitude, it's not exactly a hard fit, and she knows that when she gets out of line she can expect to find herself being taken across her partner's lap for a good old-fashioned bare bottom spanking.

But, what happens when her "aunt" starts giving others permission to discipline her?

Surely that nice old lady from down the street or her best friend from the dorms wouldn't ACTUALLY spank her, would they?

Well, as her partner is fond of saying: "If the panties fit, they might as well come down for a spanking!"

Chapter 1

Captain Rhen's Crash and Burn

It was the perfect afternoon in early May, and Rhen Mathews was pedaling her way back home with a huge grin on her face. She'd just finished the last of her finals for the spring semester (not doing quite as well as she'd hoped she would, but still passing) and was now very much looking forward to spending the next three weeks sleeping in and not having to stress about keeping up with homework or making it to lectures on time for a change.

"God, it feels good to finally be done!"

Pushing herself up into a standing position on her pedals, the petite junior gave her arms and back a much-needed stretch as she coasted along an empty stretch of road. She'd just spent the last two hours hunched over a scantron sheet in her university's exam hall, and all she wanted to do now was bask in her new-found freedom and the simple pleasure that came from riding her bike on a quiet afternoon. The sky was clear, the sun was shining, and there was even a cool breeze blowing through the trees around her that whipped her dark ponytail and the tassels on her handlebars back behind her as she flew through the quiet neighborhood where she lived with her partner (and no-nonsense disciplinarian), Dana Johnson.

Oh man, we should totally go out for dinner tonight, she thought to herself with a spike of excitement as she cut across a jogging path and back down onto the street. *It's been way too long since we went anywhere fun...*

Reaching the top of the steep hill that marked the last couple of blocks on her journey home, Rhen beamed to herself and started pedaling as fast as she could. After a few hard pumps to get herself moving, she shifted into high gear and closed her eyes, allowing gravity to take over from there as her imagination took flight.

"Phrooom! Here comes Captain Rhen!"

As she hurtled forward down the hill, feeling her front tire starting to wobble as her speed continued to build at a slightly alarming rate, she swallowed her fear and forced herself to keep her eyes shut tight. Reveling in the spike of adrenaline that came as a result, she felt the boring sidewalks and houses of the suburbs around her fall away, being replaced instead by the cockpit of an advanced space fighter that she was maneuvering through enemy territory, a pair of plasma missiles hot on her heels!

"Heh. Nice try, you federation scum," she smirked, picturing herself performing a daring aerial maneuver with all of the accompanying sound effects as she avoided the incoming attack. "But you'll have to do a lot better than that if you plan on capturing *me*."

At first these impromptu space battles had terrified Rhen (riding with your eyes closed was apt to do that, after all), but over the course of the last few weeks she'd found herself growing more and more bold as she'd gotten used to navigating blind. And, feeling particularly daring that afternoon, she decided to let go of her handle bars entirely, forming twin finger-guns that she used to shoot down her pursuing attackers.

"Pew, pew! Take that! You'll never defeat the Ancillary Alliance, Admiral Sloan! Pew!"

This bout of intergalactic heroism lasted for all but a moment, however. She wasn't actually *that* reckless (not to mention she could feel her bike rapidly slipping out of her control), and as she once again took hold of her handlebars, she decided to crack one eye open just to make sure that she was still on course for Home Base.

Which was exactly the moment when she noticed her neighbor pulling into her driveway just a few yards in front of her.

"Oh crap!"

On instinct, Rhen squeezed the break lever on her handlebars just as hard as she could, hoping against hope to avoid a head-on collision with the side of the silver car closing in on her way faster than she was comfortable with. But, rather than engage her inertial dampeners like such a move might in the books she read, it instead just proved to be the final bad decision in a long list of them she'd been making over the course of the last minute.

"Crap, crap, crap! Watch out!"

SCREEEEECH!

As her front tire came to a sudden stop, squealing loudly in protest against the asphalt beneath it and leaving one heck of a skid mark in its passing, she lost control of her bike entirely. Veering sharply to her left, she hit the curb with a sickening *CRUNCH!* that halted her forward momentum all at once and sent her flying headfirst over the top of her handlebars as her back tire kicked up like a bucking bronco.

From there, the next few moments passed by in a terrifying, bone-rattling blur.

By some small miracle of fate in that split-second before she was sent flying, Rhen managed to at least angle herself in the general direction of her neighbor's front yard, rather than her unforgiving concrete driveway. However, that didn't do anything to prevent her arms and legs from getting scraped up to high heaven by protruding roots and the occasional loose stone as she tumbled head over heels across the grass. Denim shorts and a cute t-shirt were hardly the most robust safety equipment in the world, and as she finally came to a stop, landing on her side with a heavy *THUMP!* that knocked the wind out of her, it felt as if her poor right arm had very nearly just been wrenched right out of its socket.

"Oooh…"

For several long, agonizing seconds after rolling over onto her back, head spinning and heart pounding like a jackhammer against her heaving chest, all she could manage to do was stare blankly up at the crystal clear Iowa sky above her while she moaned pitifully at the all-encompassing stinging, throbbing, aching pain that was every inch of her body just then.

And then the tears came.

"Oh god…" she croaked, unable to articulate herself any more so than that as she began to sob in earnest. "Aunt D-Dana… H-Help…"

Had she been in a clearer frame of mind just then, Rhen might've laughed at having her first reaction to taking a major spill on her bike be her crying out for her tough but loving mommy-dommy. But, just then such feats of self-reflection were entirely lost on her, and instead she simply allowed herself to be overtaken by the need to have a good, hard cry.

"Blimey, child! What on earth were you thinking?"

"Wha-?"

Blinking away tears, Rhen's brows knitted together in momentary confusion as the silhouette of Missus Hastings (the retired English woman whose car she'd just narrowly avoided plowing headfirst into) suddenly obscured the pounding glare of the sun above her head, looking equal parts terrified, relieved, and furious.

"You could have broken your fool neck zipping about like that!"

With a low groan and an audible popping of several joints, her elderly neighbor eased herself down onto the grass beside her and began gently prodding and poking at her bruised and battered frame in search of any major injuries or broken bones.

"Well, everything seems to still be where it's supposed to be, so that's good," she eventually declared with a stoic frown. "Are you hurt anywhere I'm not seeing?"

Suddenly feeling more than a little embarrassed about crying like a five-year-old in front of the woman she waved hello to on her way to campus in the mornings, Rhen bit back on another sob as she dragged a dirty forearm across her eyes, sniffling in spite of herself as she tried to pull herself back together.

"N-No, I think I'm okay…" she groaned, pushing herself up onto her elbows and gasping at the sharp stinging sensation that produced in them. "Kind of."

"Easy now," admonished Missus Hastings gently, helping her

the rest of the way up into a sitting position and busying herself with brushing away some of the stray bits of grass and dirt clinging to the back of her t-shirt. "You took quite the spill, you know."

"Tell me about it," agreed Rhen, attempting to shrug the whole thing off with a rueful grimace.

Only to hiss in through clenched teeth and whimper as her shoulder gave an alarming twinge of pain in protest.

"Oh no. Oh no, no, no. This will not do at all. Not at all."

Clucking her tongue in worried disapproval, looking the very picture of a fretting mother hen, Missus Hastings shook her head and then pushed herself back up to her feet. Then, after brushing off the front of her skirt and knuckling some of the stiffness from her lower back, she leaned forward and hoisted her up after her. Seizing her with a surprisingly strong grip under her armpits and hauling her up with only a slight grunt as she deposited her back onto her feet as if she were a small child.

"Come along, love," she ordered then, draping an arm around her trim waist to avoid her shoulder and turning to half lead, half carry her toward the front of her house. "Let's get you inside and cleaned up, and then I'll ring your auntie to come collect you. I dare say you've had enough bicycling for one day."

"Uh-huh…"

It wasn't a request, Rhen noted with some small amount of annoyance, but by then she was well-used to people mistaking her short stature, petite frame, and youthful looks for those of a young teenager and bossing her around accordingly, so she didn't bother trying to assert herself. Besides, it wasn't like she had anything on her just then that would be able to back up her claims that she was *actually* a twenty-year-old college student even if she'd wanted to.

Dana had seen to that long ago.

Part of the stipulations for moving in with her partner the year before when she'd been on the verge of being kicked out of the dorms on campus had been that when the two of them were in public, she had to pretend to be the older woman's teenage niece from out of town. Which meant handing over her ID, her debit cards, and anything else tied to her "adult" identity to her for safe-keeping just in case anybody started asking uncomfortable questions like, for instance, why a supposed adult was being put across someone's lap in the middle of public for a well-deserved spanking. And, while it was certainly true that their romantic relationship had evolved and deepened since that fateful day last summer when her then boss had mistaken her for one of her disobedient charges who just refused to stand in the corner like she'd been told to, that hadn't done anything to lessen the other side of their dynamic in the slightest.

Which, combined with the nauseatingly adorable outfits she insisted that she wear every day, and her own natural penchant for sass and disobedience, meant that to the world at large, she was indeed little Rhenny Mathews. The precocious and head-strong thirteen-year-old living with her strict "aunt" while she went to school away from home.

And she wouldn't have had it any other way.

But, even if that weren't the case and her neighbor knew *exactly* how old she really was, Rhen had to admit that she wasn't at all in the mood to argue with her just then. Her head was throbbing, her shoulder was aching, and the scrapes and scuffs all across her arms and legs stung like crazy. So, instead of pitching a fit and insisting that she could walk just fine all on her own thank you very much, she allowed herself to be shepherded inside the neat and tidy Hastings residence, past the walls of smiling grand-children and wedding photos, and into the equally neat and tidy kitchen at the other end of the house.

"Right then, now you just sit your little botty here," ordered the old woman in a brisk, motherly fashion as she deftly pulled a chair away from the table with one hand and turned it around to face the rest of the room, giving its seat a perfunctory pat. "And I'll be back in just a tick with some antiseptic for those cuts."

Not seeing much choice other than to do as she'd been told, Rhen tamped down on the urge to roll her eyes and instead set-tled herself gingerly onto the proffered seat with a meek nod and a quiet "yes ma'am" while her host disappeared off down the hall they'd just come from. Thankfully, by then her head was starting to clear up a bit, and the dull, all-over ache that she'd been experiencing ever since wiping out was easing somewhat as well. Though, that didn't seem to be doing much for the sharp stinging sensation still throbbing away in her elbows and knees where she could see now she'd scraped them up quite a bit.

"Geez, yikes…" she said to herself with another wince, tearing her gaze away from her torn up legs and casting it about the kitchen in search of something to distract herself with.

Looking around, she couldn't help but feel the corners of her lips quirk up in a fond smile. Missus Hastings's kitchen was very much a reflection of the woman herself. Clean, meticulously tidy with everything in its proper place, and with a sense of style that was several decades out of date. Heck, she even had an honest-to-god rotary-dial telephone mounted on the wall beside her back door.

Holy cow! Talk about retro.

Rhen was just in the process of climbing back to her feet, wondering if it would be rude to start digging around in the freezer to make herself an ice pack for her aching shoulder, when the old woman came bustling back into the room.

"I thought I told you to *sit*?" she huffed, punctuating her question with a firm but gentle push against Rhen's uninjured shoulder that sent her backside plopping back down onto her hard, wooden seat.

"I was just-" the younger girl tried to explain, her voice coming out a lot whinier than she'd meant for it to, before being cut off by an admonishing finger-wag from Missus Hastings.

"None of that now, love," she said with a shake of her head. "You don't want those cuts to get infected, do you?"

"I- Um, I guess not ma'am…" answered Rhen, not bothering to hold back her eye-roll this time.

"Good," chirped her neighbor, ignoring the attitude she was giving her as she eased herself down onto her knees in front of her. "Right then, you just hold still and Nana Hastings will have you right as rain in a jiffy.”

Blushing all over at the patronizing, motherly tone Missus Hastings was using with her, Rhen bit back on pointing out that she was perfectly capable of taking care of herself and instead did her best not to squirm too much as her neighbor pushed the legs of her shorts up her thighs and began wiping away the bits of dirt and grass still clinging to her scraped knees with a damp rag.

“Now this might sting a bit,” she warned a few moments later as she soaked a cotton ball in something strong smelling that she poured from a brown bottle with a worn label.

Rhen was just in the middle of reassuring her that she’d be fine, when an involuntary yelp escaped her lips and she found herself springing up out of her seat as if it had just tried to bite her.

“Ah! Hey, watch it!”

SLAP! SLAP!

“Oh hush, you little turnip,” tsked Missus Hastings, giving the embroidered flowers adorning the tops of her thighs a couple light swats. “And hold still! It’s just a tad of peroxide, you’ll be fine. But if you keep squirming around like you’ve got ants in your pants, it’s going to ruin these pretty shorts of yours.”

“But it stings…” Rhen found herself whining with a sullen pout, flopping back into her chair again and rubbing absently at her legs while blushing even brighter at the childish way she’d been reprimanded and her equally childish reaction to it.

“That just means it’s working,” the other woman reassured her with a gentle smile.

“If you- Ack! Say so…”

Continuing to pout at her neighbor while she worked, Rhen grumbled under her breath about everything and nothing in particular as she watched her finish applying the stinging antiseptic to her scrapes before then spreading a generous amount of antibiotic ointment across each of them, followed by a bright pink band-aid to keep them clean. Try as she might to focus on being indignant, however, she found that she just couldn’t keep it up for very long. There was something about the retired woman's wry but friendly demeanor as she kept up a running commentary on how silly she'd been and how glad she was that she hadn't been hurt too badly that soon had her smiling right along with her despite how embarrassing it was to be treated like a little girl who'd hurt herself while playing in the yard.

"Well, I can see that that cheeky attitude of yours is doing just fine," observed Missus Hastings with a low chuckle, her tone admonishing while her eyes remained teasing. "I'd say that's a fairly good sign that you're well on your way to a full recovery, wouldn't you?"

"Heh. Yeah," agreed Rhen with a chuckle of her own.

By the time her neighbor finished cleaning her up and covering the rest of her scrapes in seemingly half a box's worth of band-aids, she'd all but forgotten about her sour mood, and instead was simply grateful that she'd come away from her accident with so few injuries. Well, other than the sharp twinge of pain her right shoulder produced whenever she tried to move it too much.

That was definitely more than a little concerning. But, since she *could* move it at all, she figured that it was probably fine.

Hopefully.

"There we are," cooed Missus Hastings, patting the top of Rhen's left thigh with a warm smile before using her for support as she levered herself back to her feet. "All better."

"More or less," agreed the younger girl with a chagrinned smirk. "Thanks, Missus Hastings. I owe you one."

"Oh, never you mind," replied the other woman with a dismissive wave of her hand. "Taking care of each other is what good neighbors do. Now, you just stay put while I put the kettle on. I dare say you could use a pick-me-up after all that."

Truth be told, Rhen had been hoping that she could just slip out the back door and limp her way home as soon as the other woman had finished patching her up. But, by the time the last band-aid had been applied, a heavy weight of fatigue had settled down around her, and anything that delayed having to make the two-and-a-half block walk home (there was no way she was getting back on her bike that afternoon, assuming it was even still rideable) came as a huge relief.

"Tea or cocoa?" prompted Missus Hastings, pulling her thoughts back to the present as she held up a pair of decorative, tin containers.

"Um…" replied Rhen with a frown. "Do you have any coffee?"

A shot of caffeine sounded *really* nice right about then.

"Not for little ones like you, I don't," replied the other woman with a disapproving shake of her head, her lips tightening at the corners as she repeated herself with a bit more steel in her voice this time. "Tea or cocoa?"

"Cocoa is fine, thanks!" squeaked Rhen with a blush.

She hadn't *meant* to reply quite so quickly (or quite so nervously), but there was something about the look Missus Hastings was giving her just then that had the words tumbling out of her mouth before she could stop them.

"Uh, ma'am."

"There's a good lass."

Despite the offer of a hot beverage and her neighbor's motherly smile at her response, however, Rhen was still far from being out of the woods just yet. As Missus Hastings set about retrieving a shiny metal kettle from a cabinet above a truly antique looking microwave and filling it with water from the sink, she began to give her an earful and a half about how totally irresponsible she'd been while she went through the motions of making their drinks; her movements clearly second-nature to her by now after decades of practice.

"You could have been hit by a car or cracked your damn head open, you silly girl!" she huffed, sounding more worried than actually angry as she banged her kettle down onto one of the stove burners with more force than was strictly necessary. "There's absolutely no excuse for it whatsoever! No excuse. You're just lucky that you were able to tumble onto my lawn like you did. I can't imagine what might have happened had someone hit you while they were coming up the street!"

Rhen opened her mouth to argue, more so out of habit than because she actually felt the woman was wrong, but the only thing that she could think of to say just then was that *technically* it was she who had hit a car, not the other way around. Which, given the way Missus Hastings was muttering under her breath about irresponsible and disobedient kids these days, probably wouldn't have gone over very well. So, instead, she wisely chose to keep her mouth shut and simply nodded along with her lecture.

"Yes ma'am… I'm sorry, ma'am…"

Missus Hastings was having none of it, though, and rounded on her with a glare hard enough to cut through diamonds as she pressed the attack.

"I should hope *so*, young lady!" she growled, nostrils flaring as her lips drew down into a hard, thin line. "What would your auntie say if she knew that you were riding around like some sort of crazed maniac with your eyes closed like that, hmmm? Oh yes, my girl, don't think I didn't happen to notice *that* particular bit of foolishness!"

It was clear that her neighbor was working up a head of steam just as her kettle started doing much the same and Rhen was at a loss for what to say next.

"I… I wasn't- I mean-"

"And not even wearing a *helmet*!" she fumed with a disbelieving scoff, steamrolling over her feeble attempts at an excuse before she could make one as she took half a step forward and jabbed an angry forefinger at her. "What on earth were you thinking, girl? What if you'd really gotten yourself hurt? You could have been killed!"

Now *that* shut Rhen up in a hurry.

Staring forlornly down at the dirt and grass stained tops of her shorts, she deflated and just nodded while doing her best to hold back the tide of tears that were suddenly threatening to overwhelm her.

"I… I guess I wasn't really…" she started to croak, her voice and lips quavering as a single fat tear trickled its way down the side of her cheek. She tried to wipe it away, but that just seemed to make things worse, and soon two more were there to replace it. "R-Really thinking about… about…"

Seeing that she'd thoroughly made her point, Missus Hastings let out a long sigh and shook her head in exasperation.

"There, there, child," she soothed, closing the distance between the two of them and leaning down to wrap her in a warm embrace. "That's all in the past now. You're safe, and that's all that matters…"

Grateful for the physical contact just then, the reality of how close she'd come to seriously injuring herself (or worse!) hitting her way harder than she'd hit the ground, Rhen let the last of her dignity go for the moment as she clung to Missus Hastings and sobbed her heart out, soaking the front of her blouse with her tears. The old woman, for her part, simply continued to cradle her against her chest while she cried. Rubbing her back and murmuring gentle words of encouragement against the top of her head until she'd at last calmed down enough to get herself back under control, letting go of her only when the kettle on the stovetop finally started to whistle.

"Cheer up now, sunshine," ordered Missus Hastings with a gentle tsk as she bustled her way back over to the stove and moved the kettle off of its burner. "A spot of cocoa and a couple ibuprofen for those bumps and bruises ought to have you feeling better in no time."

"God, that *does* sound nice right about now," agreed Rhen as she wiped away the remaining moisture from her cheeks with the backs of her hands, inadvertently smearing them with dirt in the process.

She sniffled again, and then flashed the other woman a watery smile as she watched her set about pouring their drinks.

"Language, young lady," chided Missus Hastings, almost as an afterthought and not bothering to look back at her as she scooped dark brown cocoa powder into a blue ceramic mug, followed by a handful of tiny marshmallows, before pouring some of the water from the kettle on top of it all and giving it a quick stir.

"Sorry," apologized Rhen, blushing faintly as she accepted the warm mug with both hands, blowing on its steaming contents before taking a tentative sip. "Oooh, this is *yummy*."

"I thought you might say that," smirked the other woman as she turned back to the counter, poured water into her own mug, and began to dip a teabag into it. "Now then, you just sit tight and nurse that while I ring up your auntie, alright?"

Hearing that, Rhen's stomach lurched and she very nearly choked on the sip of cocoa she'd just been in the middle of taking. She'd completely forgotten that her neighbor was planning on calling her partner.

Oh crap.

If Missus Hastings's reactions to her two-wheeled daredevil antics were anything to go by, her Auntie Dana was going to be absolutely *pissed*.

"Um… Do you *really* have to do that, uh, ma'am?" she asked, bringing her most endearing smile to bear.

"Why, whatever do you mean, child?"

Turning back to face her with a confused look, Missus Hastings set her mug aside to let it steep.

"Of course I have to call her! I can't have her wondering why her niece is coming home looking like she just got back from a trip to the ER!"

"I mean… I guess that's true," conceded Rhen with a reluctant grimace, trying desperately to think of some way that she could possibly spin things so as to keep this just between the two of them and drawing a blank. "It's just that…"

Rather than elaborate further and embarrass herself, she instead made a vague gesture in the air with one of her hands.

"You know…"

That seemed to be clear enough for Missus Hastings, though, whose eyes lit up with understanding as her lips quirked into something approaching a sympathetic smile.

"Yes, I do imagine that you're in for *quite* the sore botty when you get home," she agreed with a sage nod, not sounding sorry for her in the slightest. "From what I've seen peeking in through that big window your aunt likes to leave the curtains drawn back on whenever I take my walks around the neighborhood at night, she tends to keep you on a rather short leash, doesn't she?"

It wasn't really a question, Rhen knew. Especially not if Missus Hastings had already seen her standing there in the corner of her and her partner's front room with a freshly-spanked bare bottom on full display (as was so often the case for her). And the sudden strawberry flush in her cheeks, not to mention her inability to meet the other woman's gaze, all but confirmed it for her if there was any lingering doubt.

"Well, good," sniffed Missus Hastings, deftly plucking her tea bag out of her mug and tossing it into a nearby trashcan with a sharp flick of her wrist. "After the way you've been behaving today, I dare say a damn good hiding is *exactly* what's needed to sort you out."

"Humph. Agree to disagree, thanks."
Huffing at her neighbor's smug satisfaction, Rhen directed her attention back to her mug of cocoa and took a nice, long (and intentionally loud) sip to distract herself. It was hard to keep pouting, though, when the stupid stuff tasted so dang good.

Well, I guess it has been a few weeks since I actually had to sleep on my stomach, she mused to herself with another half-hearted harrumph. *Oh well. It was a good run while it lasted…*

Seeing that she'd made her point for the time being, Missus Hastings took an experimental sip of her tea, nodded to herself, and then stalked purposefully over to her wall-mounted telephone. Cradling its handset against her shoulder and dialing with her free hand while her other continued to hold her tea, she waited patiently for the call to go through. Which it did after only a handful of rings.

"Hello, Dana? Yes, this is Olivia from down the way, how are you?"

Rhen continued to scowl into her mug while doing her best

to eavesdrop on the conversation happening just a few feet away from her, unable to help but notice the distinct difference in tone her elderly neighbor used while talking with her "aunt", compared to with her.

Stupid double standards.

"Oh, I'm fine, I'm fine. I've got Rhen over here, actually…"

She paused then while Dana replied, balefully eyeing her over the steaming rim of her mug with a very "you've got nobody to blame for this but yourself" kind of look, before continuing.

"No, she's alright, but it *was* rather a close call, that…"

Continuing to maintain a disapproving frown in her direction, she gradually began to fill her adoptive auntie in on all that had happened in the last half hour or so, framing her tale of downhill daring against the evil forces of the Federation in the most unflattering light possible as she painted an uncomfortably detailed picture of a very bratty teen who'd been acting completely irresponsibly. Unfortunately for her, though, none of what she said was in any way a fabrication, and as much as it irked her to admit it, Rhen was hard pressed to deny that she *had* messed up pretty badly. Which only made the sinking feeling in the pit of her stomach that much worse.

And then Missus Hastings got to the part about her not wearing a helmet.

"She *what*?!"

Wincing, able to actually *hear* Dana's shrill and tinny squawk of disbelief blaring out from the worn bakelite handset, Rhen ducked her head to hide behind her bangs.

Uh-oh… That's definitely not a good sign.

"I know, I know, it's completely beyond the pale," agreed Missus Hastings with the fervent nod of one outraged caregiver to another. "Could've cracked her silly head right open, she could've."

Oh god, the thoroughly mortified twenty-year-old turned teenager moaned to herself, sinking down in her seat with a self-pitying roll of her eyes. *I am so very, very screwed. Why didn't I just wear that freaking helmet she bought me?*

Well, because it was bright pink and sparkly enough to make sure that not a single person could miss her coming, obviously. But, looking back on things now (and her near miss with serious head trauma) that suddenly seemed like a pretty dumb reason to needlessly put herself in danger.

Dang it. I really stepped into it this time, didn't I?

Snorting as a morbid grin tugged up on the corners of her lips, Rhen took a pouty pull from her cocoa.

Well, more like launched myself headfirst into it.

"Humph."

The two older women continued to chat amiably for a while longer after that, apparently not in any particular rush to get off the phone even with her near-constant glowering and silent pleas for them to do so.

Eventually, though, Missus Hastings *finally* hung up after a cordial, "Of course, of course. I don't mind in the slightest, love. I'll keep her snug as a bug until you can get 'round to collect her…. Uh-huh… Uh-huh… Oh, I have just the thing for that, don't you worry… Right… Right. I was planning on doing just that, so I'm glad we're in agreement there… Alright then, cheers."

Geez. Took you long enough.

"Well now," her neighbor said after taking a moment to enjoy a prolonged sip of her tea, savoring its taste and aroma before setting it aside on the counter with a light *clack* of ceramic on tile as she turned to face Rhen with her hands planted firmly on her hips. "I think it's fairly safe to say that you're in for quite the smacked bottom when your auntie gets hold of you, my dear."

"Is that right?" deadpanned Rhen as she drained the last vestiges of lukewarm cocoa from the bottom of her mug and scowled. "I'm *shocked.*"

"Quite," sniffed Missus Hastings, either not picking up on her sarcasm, or else choosing to ignore it as she continued. "But, on the bright side, you're at least safe from her wroth for the time being."

Unable to stop herself from perking up just a little bit at this unexpected good news, Rhen asked, "Uh… I am?"

She'd honestly been expecting Dana to come storming over just as soon as she'd hung up.

If not sooner.

"Indeed you are," nodded her neighbor with a faint chuckle, gathering up her tea for another sip and continuing to act as if they were discussing the weather, rather than her impending doom across her irate partner's knee. "She's still tied up with her daycare duties and has asked me to keep an eye on you until she can come collect you later this evening."

"Phew," sighed Rhen with an over-exaggerated swipe of her hand across her brow, deciding that since getting a spanking from Dana was already a foregone conclusion that she might as well make the best of an unpleasant situation by injecting a little levity into the mix. "I guess that means I'll still be able to sit down for dinner, at least."

"Well… Not exactly," corrected Missus Hastings with a rather insincere looking apologetic frown, heading off her next question before she could ask it. "You see, in addition to keeping an eye on you, she *also* asked me to, and I quote, 'warm her bratty butt up something fierce.'"

"She *what*?!" demanded Rhen, mirroring her partner's own righteous indignation from earlier as she sat up stalk-straight in her chair, all of the color draining from her face at once through the hole that had just opened up in the pit of her stomach.

"I believe you heard me just fine, young lady," answered Missus Hastings coolly, not sounding the least bit sympathetic. "And I don't mind saying that she and I are in complete agreement there."

"But… but…!"

Spluttering nervously, unable to think of anything more articulate to say than that just then as a fresh spike of anxiety gnawed away at her insides, Rhen racked her brain for something to dissuade the older woman from making good on her aunt's request without humiliating herself further by trying to explain just *why* it was she felt she was too old for what was about to happen next.

Only to come up woefully empty.

Oh my god, I seriously can't believe this is happening…

Although she'd definitely been spanked by people other than her bossy boots not-aunt over the course of the last year since she'd started living with her, Dana had never actually delegated the task out to anybody before (well, not counting her Aunt Maureen, that is), and the idea that she might ever do so had never even crossed her mind. Though, in retrospect, it *really* probably should have.

"We prefer to use the word 'bottom' where I come from, dear," replied Missus Hastings evenly, clearly delighting in the sudden change in attitude her announcement had wrought in her sassy houseguest. "But, yes, that is indeed where I intend on chastising you for your reckless behavior in just a moment."

"Of course it is…" grumbled Rhen, snatching up her empty mug from the table beside her and pretending to take another sip from it in a flimsy attempt to hide the rising blush in her cheeks as she continued to grumble sourly into its ceramic confines. "This is freaking *so* not fair."

"Pardon me, young lady?" snapped Missus Hastings, sounding more cross than Rhen had yet heard her as she took a step forward with a stormy glare that instantly had her insides churning with frantic worry. "You're not *arguing* with me now, are you?"

"No ma'am!" she squeaked on reflex.

Missus Hastings definitely wasn't someone that she wanted to be upset with her, *especially* not when she was about to spank her. She actually liked the old woman quite a bit, and not just because she sometimes gave her freshly baked cookies to take home when she was on her way back from classes in the afternoon. Rhen could tell that she was a bit lonely living by herself ever since her husband had passed away a few years earlier, and with most of her grandkids living out of state (or in some cases, out of the country entirely), the young coed suspected that she'd become something of a surrogate grandchild to the retired widow.

And the idea that she'd disappointed her made her feel about two inches tall just then.

"You'd best mind yourself, young lady," huffed the older woman with a sharp cluck of her tongue, once again planting her hands on her hips as she glared down at her, the silver in her brown hair lending her voice an implacable edge of authority. "We'll have none of that sour attitude in my house, thank you very much."

"Yes ma'am…"

Ugh! This is so freaking typical.

Rhen had been hoping that her neighbor might show at least *some* amount of hesitation about putting her across her knee, but clearly that wasn't going to be the case.

And really, she asked herself with an internal put-upon sigh. *Why should it be?*

Missus Hastings had already made it humiliatingly clear that she knew *exactly* how her "aunt" went about dealing with her disobedience.

And she approved!

Whatever. It's probably just because she's from England or something, Rhen tried to tell herself, ignoring for the moment that pretty much *every* adult that she'd had a run in with thus far while in her "Rhenny" persona (and even a few from before she'd moved in with Dana) had tended to treat her in much the same way. *They're all stuck in the Stone Age over there. I mean, come on, they drive on the left side of the road for crying out loud! Of course she's going to think I need a spanking for accidentally crashing into her car just because I was riding around with my eyes closed… Humph.*

"Oh, don't look so glum, you frowny Freda," her neighbor admonished with a thin smile, completely unfazed by her pouting and grumbling as she closed the distance between the two of them and gave her pushed out cheek an affectionate pinch. "It's just a little smacked bottom. I know you're well-used to those by now."

Rhen, at least, had the good grace not to try and deny that

fact. Instead just letting out another harrumph and doing her very best not to crack so much as a half-grin at her neighbor's charming affability.

It didn't work.

"And besides," she continued, letting go of her cheek and gently but *very* firmly guiding her back to her feet with an insistent grip on her upper arm. "I don't think you can truly say that you haven't earned one by now, can you?"

She fixed Rhen in place with an expectant look then, waiting for her to reply, and after putting it off for as long as she could by glaring at the faded wallpaper behind her neighbor's right shoulder, she finally sighed in defeat.

"No ma'am, you're right," she admitted with a roll of her eyes, only managing to sound marginally contrite. "I *guess*."

Quick as a striking snake, Missus Hastings's thumb and forefinger shot out and seized hold of her left ear in a vice-like grip.

"Ack! Hey!" the younger girl yelped, automatically shooting up onto her tiptoes to try and ease some of the pressure being applied to her ear.

"Don't you *dare* roll your eyes at me, young lady!" snapped Missus Hastings, ignoring her protests as she tightened her grip on her ear and gave it a sharp twist that had her dancing around the kitchen in a frantic circle. "I have been exceedingly patient with you thus far on account of your injuries, but I will *not* tolerate any more of your impertinence. Is that understood?"

"Ah! Ah! Ah! Okay, okay!" hissed Rhen through clenched teeth, her eyes starting to tear up at the corners as she was drawn in close enough to be practically touching noses with her incensed neighbor.

"What was that?"

"Eep!" she squeaked, knees going weak as she quickly corrected herself. "I mean, yes ma'am! I'm sorry, ma'am!"

"I should certainly hope so, you naughty thing."

Nodding to herself with the sort of grim determination that Rhen knew from all too much personal experience did *not* bode well for her backside, Missus Hastings drew back her shoulders and began marching her out of the kitchen.

"Now you just come with me to the sitting room," she ordered, not actually giving her a choice in the matter as she dragged her along by the ear. "A thorough dose of Nana Hastings's slipper ought to set some of that attitude of yours to right, I suspect."

"Oh! Owie! I'm coming, I'm coming! Geez!"

The next thing she knew, Rhen found herself being pushed face first over the side of a floral-print couch, grunting in protest a moment later as her hips were hoisted up into place across the top of its elevated, scroll arm; lifting her feet off of the floor entirely in the process. Thankfully, though, with this new position there at least came a blessed release of her throbbing ear. That was of little comfort just then, however, once she felt Missus Hastings pushing down on the small of her back with her left hand, while the fingers of her right took hold of the stretchy, Easy-Pull, elastic waistband of her denim shorts.

"Let's just get a look at those knickers then, shall we?"

"Wait, no, come on!" Rhen whined, squirming like an eel as her neighbor began wrestling her shorts down off of her narrow hips. "Can't we just do it over my shorts, *please*?"

"Don't be ridiculous, child," scoffed Missus Hastings, shaking her head in mild exasperation before at last managing to work her dirt and grass stained shorts to her knees, letting gravity take hold of them from there to pull them the rest of the way down into a crumpled heap on the floor behind her.

SMACK! SMACK!

"And stop all that wriggling nonsense this instant!" she added sharply, delivering two brisk swats to the cartoon dinosaurs printed across the taut seat of the absolutely *adorable* pair of pastel pink panties she'd just exposed.

Like the rest of Rhen's rather childish looking wardrobe, they had been specifically handpicked by her partner because not only did they reinforce her image as a young and bratty teen who thought she was way more grown up than she actually was to anyone who happened to see them (which was proving to be a distressingly high number of people in her experience since moving in with her), but also because they looked even cuter when they were being pulled down for a spanking.

"Ow, hey!" she protested with a petulant huff, back arching and ankles scissoring behind her as twin blossoms of stinging heat suddenly bloomed across the centers of her cheeks. "I'm sorry, okay? Geez!"

"Yes, dear, I'm sure you are," agreed Missus Hastings dryly, not sounding particularly convinced as she took hold of the waistband of her panties and whisked them too down to her knees with the practiced ease of someone who'd spent several decades correcting the bad behavior of bratty adolescents. "Ah, much better."

"Eep!"

Her entire body going as rigid as if she'd just been struck by lightning (it always came as a bit of a shock to her how easily her panties seemed to come down when she was in trouble), Rhen melted back across the arm of her neighbor's couch with a reluctant sigh of defeat.

She'd had a feeling that Missus Hastings wasn't someone who spanked on anything other than a bare bottom, and much to her own annoyance, she'd been right.

Ugh.

And now that she was lying there, ready and waiting to be disciplined, it seemed depressingly likely too that her elderly neighbor was going to prove to be a *very* thorough spanker. Which was a thought that did absolutely nothing to ease the swarm of butterflies roiling around inside her stomach just then.

This sucks.

"Now then, you just stay right there while I go and fetch my slipper," ordered the clearly amused older woman, not sounding out of breath in the slightest after the ordeal of wrestling her shorts and panties down for her. "It's been a while since I've had to put it to use, but I think I still remember where I tucked it last…"

"Fine…" grumbled Rhen sullenly into the couch cushion in front of her, flexing her toes nervously behind her and wishing suddenly that she'd just been taken over the other woman's lap for an immediate hand-spanking instead.

She absolutely *hated* having to wait around for her punishment to begin. Especially like this. The sooner it was over and done with, the better, as far as she was concerned!

"There's a good lass," chirped Missus Hastings with a perfunctory pat across the center of her arched and semi-parted cheeks before adding sternly. "Oh, and don't you dare move a muscle until I've returned or else there *will* be consequences. Is that understood?"

"It's not like I can really go anywhere, you know," the thoroughly embarrassed junior pointed out with a put-upon huff.

"I mean it, girl," Missus Hastings pressed. "If I have to chase you down to get you to take your punishment, you are going to regret it, believe you me."

Though part of her bristled at the implication that she'd be so childish as to try and actually run away from her impending spanking at this point in the process, the steel with which her neighbor delivered that warning still managed to send a nervous shiver coursing through Rhen. Making goosebumps sprout up all across where her cheeks had just been patted.

"Yes ma'am!" she all but yelped, doing her best to try and get more comfortable across her rounded over perch, her cheeks clenching and unclenching behind her as she turned her head to look up pleadingly at her frowning neighbor. "I'll be good, I promise!"

"We'll just see about that, now won't we?" drawled Missus Hastings, cocking one brow as if to say that she very much doubted they would.

A look which earned her a mighty harrumph from Rhen.

"I'll be back in a minute, dear," she repeated with an amused snort, her stern demeanor slipping somewhat as she smiled fondly back at the supposedly thirteen-year-old girl laid out across the arm of her couch, before turning on her heel and moving off down a hallway toward what Rhen could only assume was the house's master bedroom.

Once the old woman's back was safely turned to her, she stuck out her tongue and blew a silent raspberry at her retreating form. Fully embracing her bratty nature now that there was absolutely no chance of her being able to avoid the much-deserved spanking she had coming.

Then again… she mused to herself with a pensive frown, planting her left elbow on the couch cushion in front of her and propping her chin on her palm as she tried once again to wriggle her hips into a position that didn't press so insistently on her bladder without the benefit of actually being able to use her feet to do so. *She did say that she was going to get her "slipper". Hmmm…*

Despite the butterflies swirling around inside her stomach and the embarrassed blush warming her face as cool air pumped in by the house's air conditioning tickled her sit-spots and the crevice between her bare cheeks, Rhen couldn't help but feel a small spark of hope kindling within her chest.

"Like, seriously. How bad could a spanking from some dumb, old, stupid, fuzzy pink bunny slipper actually be, anyway?" she asked aloud to the empty room, squirming anew at the naughty thrill that this act of quiet rebellion sent tingling across her partially-exposed vulva and up to her clit, making it twinge in a decidedly unrepentant way as she tried to imagine how she must look just then. "Besides, heh… She's probably about as old as Grandma is, so I doubt she can even spank all that hard anymore."

Never mind the fact that she'd learned firsthand last Thanksgiving that her grandma was more than capable of making her howl with just a hand spanking when she set her mind to it.

Heck, even if she's doing it on the bare, getting spanked with a smooshy slipper can't possibly hurt that much, right? she reasoned, losing her nerve to continue speaking aloud as she heard her neighbor moving things around in another room. *I'll just put on a good show. Yelp and cry a bit, maybe even squeeze out a tear or two if I can, and then it'll all be over and I'll be back to sipping more of that tasty cocoa!*

Feeling better and better about her current predicament with each passing moment, aside from the fact that she was still lying face down with her bare bottom on full display and about to be spanked, Rhen hummed happily to herself as she idly bobbed her tennis shoe covered feet back and forth behind her in time with her nameless tune.

Aunt Dana is definitely not going to be a picnic later on tonight, but at least this part won't be so bad...

Rhen couldn't help but shiver again as she tried to decide whether she was more likely to receive her comeuppance from her partner with the trusty ebony hairbrush that they kept on the nightstand beside her bed at all times, or the thick leather belt that her grandma had oh so thoughtfully given her as a Christmas present a few months back.

Either way, it was definitely going to suck.

"Right then," announced Missus Hastings a few minutes later, abruptly startling her out of her quiet contemplation of the old woman's antique looking television set and her musings about whether or not she had cable as she strode briskly back into the neatly furnished living room and over to the couch with what appeared to be some sort of dark gray shoe gripped firmly in her right hand. "That's enough dilly-dallying. Let's get down to business, shall we?"

"Right," echoed Rhen with a nod, unsure of what else to say just then but feeling the need to at least say *something* as her neighbor appraised her naked cheeks with a thoughtful expression. "Down to business."

Missus Hastings gave her a slight smile at that, but otherwise didn't acknowledge her reply as she went on to say, "I think we'll have two dozen for your reckless bicycling, and oh, let's see now..."

She paused for a moment then, lightly rapping her slipper against the side of her leg as she mulled the question over in her mind.

"Another dozen for all that cheek you've been giving me. Yes, that ought to be enough to get you to sit up and take notice."

"I guess that's fair," agreed Rhen with a faint blush, doing her best to not let on how relieved she was to hear that she'd only have to deal with thirty-six swats from the old woman's flimsy bedroom slipper.

"Geez, I could do that in my sleep." she snickered to herself under her breath.

"What was that, young lady?" prompted Missus Hastings, demonstrating that she had far better hearing than the petite junior gave her credit for as she stepped in right beside her left hip to loom over her with the menacing air of a grandmother whose patience had just run out.

"Nothing ma'am!" Rhen reassured her quickly, doing a terrible job of sounding contrite just then as she fought down a nervous giggle.

This was almost too easy!

"Hmmm. Yes, I'm sure."

Still sounding less than convinced, Missus Hastings lined up her slipper for her first swat, giving Rhen's bare right cheek a couple of experimental pats with its flexible rubber sole as she got a feel for her aim.

Huh. That feels a bit, uh… heavier than I was imagining it would, she couldn't help but notice, doing her best to try and angle her head to the side without drawing the other woman's attention so that she could steal a glance at the thing in her hand.

"Wait, hold on, what's tha-?" she started to ask.

THWOP! THWOP!

Only to have her words be cut off by a strangled yelp as two back-to-back and shockingly harsh smacks from the sole of the thing gripped in Missus Hastings's right hand exploded across the centers of her upturned buns.

THWOP! THWOP!

Followed by two more against either of her sit-spots.

"Holy- Ack! Crap!"

Squirming in place beneath the old woman's firm grip on her lower back and flailing her legs back and forth behind her as she hissed out several (thankfully unintelligible) curse words through clenched teeth, Rhen threw an accusatory glare over her shoulder and demanded indignantly, "What the heck was that?"

"Why, it was my slipper, of course," answered Missus Hastings, sounding more than a little confused as she hefted the implement in question up high enough for her to get a proper look at.

Narrowing her eyes at the thing in her neighbor's right hand, Rhen scowled.

Whatever it was, it definitely was *not* a fuzzy, pink bunny slipper, that was for sure. For starters, it had laces. Not to mention a thick rubber sole with zigzagging grooves and a canvas body. If anything, it looked more like one of the high-tops she was currently wearing. Albeit about half a dozen sizes bigger than anything that she might conceivably wear.

"But… but…" she spluttered, unsure of how else to articulate her confusion without giving away the fact that she'd been expecting something far less *effective* when her neighbor had said that she was going to fetch her "slipper".

"Oh, I think I see the problem here," laughed Missus Hastings as she continued to splutter and stare, seeming to catch on to what was throwing her off, though hopefully not its exact nature. "I always forget that you Americans call these something else over here. Now what was it again? Trainers? No, that's not it either. Hmmm…"

She flashed Rhen an apologetic smile and waved the shoe in her hand in a lazy arc beside her as she searched for the right word.

"Tennis shoes?" suggested Rhen with a sullen pout, not finding this whole linguistic misunderstanding nearly as amusing as her neighbor was.

THWOP!

"Owie!"

"Ah yes, that's the ticket!" declared Missus Hastings brightly, bringing the well-worn tennis shoe back down against the middle of her cheeks hard enough to make her squeak and toss her frazzled ponytail to and fro behind her as she beat out a staccato rhythm against the cushion in front of her with clenched fists.

"Oh my god, that thing *stings*!" she whined, blowing several strands of loose hair out of her face as the slipper's initial sharp bite gradually gave way to a more generalized burning sensation deeper in her scalded seat.

"Yes, that is rather the point, my dear," agreed Missus Hastings, not sounding the least bit sympathetic as she rubbed first one, and then the other, of her bare, wobbly cheeks, seemingly trying to decide which one she'd swat next. "It wouldn't be much of a punishment otherwise, now would it?"

THWOP! THWOP! THWOP!
THWOP! THWOP! THWOP!

As if to underscore just exactly what she meant, the old woman delivered half a dozen hard and unforgiving swats in just as many seconds, stoking the lingering heat in Rhen's cheeks into a raging inferno as she set her bottom to bouncing and her legs to kicking.

"Urk... Ack!" she grunted, doing her very best to try and ride out the storm of slipper smacks, and just *barely* managing to keep from crying out loud as her neighbor quickly pushed her right up to the edge of what she knew she could comfortably handle in a spanking.

She could already feel tears starting to well again at the corners of her eyes, making the hideously retro floral pattern occupying most of her vision swim and blur, and she had enough firsthand experience with being disciplined by her partner to know that she wouldn't be able to maintain her composure for very much longer now.

"Y... Yes ma'am, I think I see what you mean..."

"Good," crooned Missus Hastings, lightly rapping her slipper against each of her pale thighs as she shifted her aim to just below the undercurves of her cheeks. "I'm pleased to see that we're starting to get somewhere."

"That's one way of putting it-" Rhen began to grumble to herself, sniffling as she furtively wiped away her gathering tears on the back of her hand.

THWOP! THWOP!

"Aieee!"

Only to let out a high-pitched squeal of agony, furiously scissoring her legs back and forth behind her as the backs of her thighs were set ablaze by two more unforgiving smacks.

"I'm sorry, I'm sorry, I'm sorry!" she babbled out all at once, as fresh, hot tears began tracing their way down the sides of her face.

"Yes, I imagine you are," agreed Missus Hastings rather smugly, delivering four more rapid-fire swats to the backs of the panting girl's thighs and *really* putting her back into it this time.

THWOP-THWOP! THWOP-THWOP!

"Oh my god!" howled Rhen, snatching up one of the throw pillows in front of her and burying her face in it to hide her embarrassment.

"Starting to regret your bad behavior now, I take it?" prompted Missus Hastings with an insistent *tap, tap, tap* of her slipper against the center of her still smoldering cheeks, giving her a chance to catch her breath before she continued on with the rest of her punishment.

"Yes ma'am…" the thoroughly miserable younger girl mumbled into her pillow, though still loud enough to be heard despite its muffling.

There was no way in heck she was going to give her a reason to tack on any *more* swats to her punishment!

"Very good," chirped her elderly disciplinarian as she brought her slipper up to her shoulder and took aim once again. "We're just about halfway done, so try and be brave and take the rest of your punishment without too much of a fuss now, alright?"

Rather than wait for her to reply, Missus Hastings instead let fly with another half-dozen savage swats.

THWOP! THWOP! THWOP!

THWOP! THWOP! THWOP!

"Ow, ow, owie! Ack! Owie!"

Which was just as well for Rhen, as she was far too busy yelping and whining to have answered her anyway.

God dang it! she cursed silently, squeezing her pillow for all it was worth as she floundered across the raised arm of her neighbor's couch, sniffling and squealing into its worn threading. *I guess that's the end of Captain Rhen's illustrious combat career. No more space battles for me. As soon as I get out of here, I'm retiring!*

—

If she hadn't known any better, Rhen would have *sworn* that her bottom and thighs were actually smoking by the time Missus Hastings finished delivering the last of her slippering.

For such a lean and seemingly frail old woman, her neighbor sure could swing a slipper like nobody's business!

"Ahhh, there we are," she drawled contentedly, taking a couple steps back to survey her handiwork with a self-satisfied nod. "One well-smacked bottom, and one thoroughly sorry little girl to go along with it. I'd say that's a job well done, wouldn't you?"

"Y-Yeah…" Rhen had to admit, flashing her a wobbly, rueful grimace and laughing just a little, before sniffling again and scrubbing a forearm across her watery eyes. "I think it's pretty safe to say that you made an impression."

About thirty-six of them, to be exact, she added with a silent pout.

Her round cheeks and narrow thighs had swollen considerably under her neighbor's implacable ministrations, and were now painted a striking shade of dark pink with an all-over stippling of darker carmine spots from where the textured grooves etched into the sole of the woman's slipper, or shoe, or whatever the heck it was had bitten into her unprotected hindquarters. It hadn't been the worst spanking she'd ever received, though it certainly must have been somewhere in the top twenty by her estimation, and coming as it was from someone who genuinely thought that she was a naughty thirteen-year-old girl who needed to be disciplined certainly had made it exponentially more embarrassing for her. Regardless, Rhen knew that she'd definitely still be feeling nice and tender by the time she was tucked in for bed that night.

Even without the follow-up butt blistering that she was sure her partner still had in store for her.

"Ugh," she groaned, her grimace giving way to a grudgingly impressed half-grin. "I don't think Aunt Dana could have done much better than that, herself, actually. I'm definitely going to be sleeping on my stomach tonight. Humph!"

Her over-the-top pouting caused one side of Missus Hastings's mouth to quirk up.

"And just like that, the cheek returns!" she snickered, drawing back in beside her and giving her well-roasted buns a couple of motherly pats.

"What can I say?" snickered Rhen right along with her as she reached back tentatively to try and knead away some of the lingering heat still radiating off of them in palpable waves with her good arm. "I bounce back fast."

"Indeed you do," agreed her neighbor, the other side of her mouth joining its fellow to form an amused smile. "You must keep your poor auntie *very* busy."

Feeling a bit loopy after her recent ordeal, and riding high on a wave of endorphins from having just been so thoroughly treated like the naughty little girl people so often mistook her for (loving every second of it in spite of how humiliating it all was), Rhen couldn't help but blush even as she giggled again.

"You have *no* idea."

"Well," her neighbor finally declared after taking a moment or two to shake her head in bemusement at the sassy twenty-year-old turned teenager that she'd just spanked like one of her own grandchildren, helping to ease her off of the elevated arm of her couch and back down onto her own two feet with a firm grip on her upper arms. "I just hope that I've at least managed to give you something to think about the next time you decide you want to ride your bicycle like some sort of loony."

"Oh, you *definitely* have," Rhen quickly reassured her with an animated nod, her left hand still clamped tight over her aching caboose while she did her best to try and keep her hairless groin angled away and out of sight in a rather belated attempt to preserve at least some small shred of her modesty. "In fact, I don't think I'll be in the mood to go riding for a while…"

"I suppose I'll consider this a job well done, then," teased her neighbor, lightly patting the central divide running down the middle of the "this" in question before taking hold of the hem of Rhen's t-shirt. "Alright then, now you just go ahead and raise your arms so that Nana Hastings can get you out of this shirt. Since you're going to be here a while still, I might as well run your dirty clothes through the wash and save your auntie the trouble. They're positively *filthy*, you know."

"Um…" stammered a suddenly far less sassy Rhen with an embarrassed gulp, going almost as red in the face as her bottom as she tried to sidestep out of her neighbor's grip even as her t-shirt was pulled up to her armpits, the humiliating reality that she was perceived by most people as just another bratty teen in need of a healthy dose of mothering reasserting itself with a vengeance and making her stomach twist and somersault. "That's *really* not necessary, ma'am."

"Nonsense, child," clucked Missus Hastings with a shake of her head, following after her and giving the hem of her t-shirt a more insistent upward tug. "Now quit your fussing and do as you're told. I'd rather not have to slipper you again, you know."

"Ugh, *fine*…"

With an exasperated sigh and a truly impressive roll of her eyes that was thankfully obscured by her t-shirt as it was being pulled up over her head, Rhen allowed the old woman to finish stripping her down to just her thin, white camisole.

"But I want extra marshmallows in my next cup of cocoa!"

That managed to draw an amused snort from Missus Hastings as she gathered up the rest of her confiscated bits of clothing, her eyes twinkling with amusement as they noted the totally hairless front of the pouting girl standing in front of her with her arms folded beneath the minimal swell of her breasts.

"I think that can definitely be arranged, my dear. Though, your auntie might be rather cross with you if you spoil your appetite before dinner, you know."

Rhen just smirked at that, looking every inch the well-spanked, though good-natured, brat that she was at heart.

"I'm already in trouble as it is," she pointed out with an over-exaggerated harrumph. "What's she going to do, spank me?"

Laughing now as she turned and began making her way toward the laundry room, her neighbor called back over her shoulder as she went, "That's an excellent point. In that case, you just go ahead and wait for me in the kitchen, and I'll be there in a bit, alright?"

"Deal!"

Chapter 2

Auntie Dana Comes to Collect

After Missus Hastings had finished brewing up a fresh mug of cocoa for Rhen (with the requisite number of extra marshmallows, of course) and another cup of tea for herself, the two of them retired to her living room to wait for the washing machine to finish its work. As it turned out, the petite junior's elderly neighbor did indeed have cable, and for the next couple of hours they sat snuggled up side-by-side on her faded floral couch; watching her equally antique television set as Rhen did her best to ignore the unpleasant sensation of threadbare fibers digging in against the smoldering welts left behind by her run in with the slipper.

The very same slipper which just so happened to still be sitting less than two feet away from her atop the arm of the couch she'd been draped across earlier, mocking her with its silent stare.

Look at it. Sticking its tongue out at me like that, the thoroughly sore twenty-year-old turned teenager thought to herself with a melodramatic huff, glaring daggers at the offending piece of footwear and willing it to burst into flames. *It knows what it did. Humph.*

Thankfully, though, Missus Hastings seemed to be sympathetic to her predicament (even if she'd been the one to cause it) and refrained from chastising her for not sitting still. Although, that said, she still couldn't quite resist poking fun at her at least a little bit during commercial breaks. Offering to let her lie across her lap if sitting was too uncomfortable for her.

Rhen had to admit that that offer *did* sound rather tempting after the second or third break without things cooling off for her any, but putting up with some relatively minor (and totally deserved) pain was well worth it in her opinion if it also meant saving at least a little bit of face. It wasn't much, true, but it was still better than totally giving in to her image as the well-punished little girl having a hard time sitting down after her spanking. And so, shifting her weight onto the side of her hip and leaning in against her neighbor's cradling arm for support so that her cheeks were mostly free of the rasping couch beneath them, the two of them whiled away the rest of their afternoon together absorbed in game shows that she'd assumed had long since been cancelled; having a blast as they played along at home.

—

Fortunately for Rhen, as she had little doubt that Dana would have zero qualms marching her home bare bottomed if given half a chance, her clothes were finished drying by the time her partner arrived to pick her up. And so, it was with a blushing face and a mercifully covered (albeit still somewhat tender) backside that she and her elderly neighbor went to go greet her not-aunt when she at last came to the door.

DING-DONG!

DING-DONG!

DING-DONG!

"Heh. I think someone might just be a bit eager to see you," observed Missus Hastings with a knowing chuckle. "Let's not keep her waiting, shall we?"

"R-Right," agreed Rhen with a much more hesitant nod, feeling a fresh wave of butterflies stirring to life inside of her as she forced herself to close her eyes and take in a deep breath, letting it out just as slowly as she pushed them open once again.

Oh boy, here we go…

True to her prediction, as soon as the old woman had opened her front door, Rhen was all but tackled by Dana.

"Oh my god, Rhen, honey, there you are!" the auburn-haired woman in her mid-forties gushed just as soon as she'd caught sight of her, rushing past their neighbor with only a perfunctory "Hello, Olivia!" as she dropped to her knees in front of her and proceeded to bury her in an avalanche of relieved kisses. "I was *so* worried about you! How could you scare me like that? Riding around without a helmet on? Have you lost your damn mind, little girl? Oh, but forget about all that for now! Are you alright? Show me where it hurts! Do you need to see a doctor? We can go right now if you need to, just say the word!"

"Easy there, love, easy…" soothed Missus Hastings, laying a calming hand on the other woman's shoulder and doing her best to reel her back in before she could completely break down in panic. "She's perfectly alright. Perhaps a bit worse for wear in some areas…"

At that, she pantomimed a spanking gesture and winked, which managed to draw out a shaky laugh from Dana.

"And, of course, there's also the odd bump and scrape here and there, but all in all she's still in one piece and doing just fine. Isn't that right, Rhen?"

Rhen, for her part, fixed her still-smirking neighbor with a pointed huff and made a deliberate show of choosing not to comment on the state of her well-slippered bottom. But, eager to do whatever she could to help ease her partner's frantic worrying, her own stomach twisting and lurching with shame at having made her feel that way in the first place, she quickly nodded her head in agreement.

"Yeah, Aunt Dana, I'm totally fine," she reassured her with an embarrassed wave of her hands, as if she could somehow brush away the last few hours like they'd never happened.

She was honestly just happy to be able to get a word in edge-wise around all of her frantic questions and kisses, and pressed on as nonchalantly as she could, hoping that the quaver in her voice wouldn't shine through.

"Like she said, I've just got some scrapes and a bit of a sore shoulder is all. Really, it's not that big of a deal, I promise."

Even as she was saying it, though, she knew she wasn't being totally honest. And, judging by the stony glares she was getting from her aunt and neighbor, they both knew it too, so she decided not to keep pressing that particular point any further.

Nevertheless, between hers and Missus Hastings's reassurances that she was still all in one piece, Dana at least managed to relax enough to speak without sounding like she was on the brink of a major panic attack.

"Oh, that is *such* a relief to hear," she sighed, squeezing her bashfully grimacing girlfriend one more time and planting a quick kiss on each of her blush-warmed cheeks and her forehead before using her as a support as she climbed back to her feet and turned to face their neighbor with a tired smile. "Seriously, Olivia, I cannot thank you enough for taking care of her like you did today. I don't know what I would've done without you."

Hearing that, Rhen couldn't help but shuffle in place a little bit as she stared shamefacedly down at the tops of her shoelaces, the flush in her face ratcheting up several more degrees all at once as her partner threw a sternly disapproving scowl back over her shoulder.

"It's hard enough keeping track of nearly a dozen hyperactive kids as it is for the daycare without *also* trying to find some way of leaving them alone so I can run down here to pick this one up as well. So, really, thank you."

"Oh, think nothing of it, my dear," waved away Missus Hastings with an easy, grandmotherly smile. "I was more than happy to help. That's what neighbors are for, after all."

"That they are," agreed Dana with another somewhat ragged chuckle, wiping away the last of the tears that had been threatening to spill over with the back of her hand as she flashed the other woman a wry grin, more or less back to her usual calm, collected, and fun-loving self once again. "Though, I have to say, your car might not be feeling quite the same way after what Rhen's bike managed to do to it."

Upon hearing that, the girl in question whose bike it was they were talking about felt her ears perk up and her stomach suddenly sink.

Oh, right... Crap.

She'd been so caught up in the immediate aftermath of her crash and the subsequent spanking that had followed after it (not to mention her gnawing worries over what her partner might have waiting for her when she got her home later that evening), that she hadn't even stopped to consider what her bike might've done to her neighbor's car after she'd been thrown clear of it. Heck, she wasn't even really sure *where* the darn thing was just then.

It's gotta still be in the yard, right?

She doubted very much that anybody would be interested in stealing it if it was in even nearly half as bad of shape as she'd been after her crash.

For a split-second, Rhen found herself smirking as memories of a time when she'd left her bike laying out on its side in the middle of Dana's front yard all day long (and the brisk hand spanking she'd received over the seat of her panties later that evening for it), went flashing through her mind's eye. The lingering twinges of soreness still in her backside just then making her feel almost as if she'd traveled back in time to that moment from nearly a year ago when she'd still been the older woman's assistant at the daycare.

Somehow I doubt she's going to be nearly so forgiving this time around, though, she mused to herself, folding her arms in front of her with another worried grimace.

"Humph."

Deciding to keep on pouting because it was far easier to stay indignant rather than actually face up to the fact that she knew deep down she deserved everything she still had coming (and probably a little bit more, truth be told), Rhen did her best to avoid drawing either of the older women's attention as she sidled over a few inches to her left and eased up onto her tiptoes in an attempt to sneak a peek past them at how bad the damage was for herself. Unfortunately for her, though, her vantage point only offered a view of the hill she'd been flying down seemingly forever ago and not the actual sight of her crash landing itself. And so, she was forced to remain in the dark about how bad it all was while the two "adults" in front of her continued discussing things in a way that made it abundantly clear that her opinions on the matter were most certainly not welcome just then.

"Yes, I daresay my old station wagon is due for a trip to the garage," agreed Missus Hastings with a surprisingly easy-going shrug, not sounding particularly put off by the notion. "Though, thankfully, it seems that most of the damage is just surface scratches and the odd dent here and there. It's nothing too ruinous as far as I can tell."

Her thoughtful expression turned rueful then as she added with a sad shake of her head, "Unfortunately, I don't think the same can quite be said for poor Rhen's bicycle, however. Mind you, I only caught a quick glimpse of it on our way inside, but I'm fairly certain that tire rims are supposed to be round, and that handlebars aren't supposed bend in that direction."

"No kidding," agreed Dana with a wince of her own. "Guess I can't keep putting off getting her a new one anymore. She definitely needs a bike for school."

"Hmmm, yes, I'm sure she does," nodded Missus Hastings crisply.

From the look on her face, Rhen wasn't so sure she wasn't about to launch into a tirade about how back in *her* day, she and her friends walked uphill fifteen miles in the snow both ways to get to school and didn't complain about it.

Smirking slightly herself, apparently seeing the same expression plain as day on the other woman's face as she was, Dana managed to head her off by adding quickly, "And, of course, I'll be more than happy to pay for whatever repair work you need done. Just let me know how mu-"

"You most certainly will *not*!" snapped Missus Hastings, cutting her off mid-sentence with an affronted huff and suddenly sounding much more like she had back when she'd been in the middle of lecturing Rhen for not wearing her helmet.

"But-" Dana tried to argue, momentarily taken aback by the other woman's vehemence.

"This was an *accident*, Dana," their neighbor cut in again with a firm shake of her head, silencing the rest of her protests before she could make them as she planted her hands squarely on her hips in a mirror of the very same no-nonsense pose she so often brought to bear against Rhen. "Albeit one that was entirely avoidable if *someone* had just been riding responsibly."

She turned her disapproving scowl on Rhen then, who let out an involuntary squeak at the fire she saw burning behind her eyes before sighing audibly in relief when she directed her focus back to Dana a moment later.

"And I won't hear any more of this nonsense about you paying for my car's repairs. Especially not when the damage was so minimal."

"Well, alright, if you're sure…" conceded Dana, sounding more bemused than actually cowed in the face of this shorter, elderly woman's wrath. "I still at least think it would be a good idea if Rhen came by on the weekends to do some chores to help make up for it, though."

"Oh, well now *that* I can most certainly accept," Missus Hastings agreed, her stern demeanor melting away all at once as she snickered good-naturedly. "In fact, I think getting to spend some more time with this lovely jubbly…"

At that, she reached over and gave said "jubbly" on the younger girl a couple of fond pats.

"Sounds absolutely lovely."

"Hey! Don't I at least get a say in any of this?" demanded Rhen, feeling as if the conversation had slipped out from under her while she hadn't been paying attention and just barely managing to keep her whining tone in check as she shifted from foot to foot with an indignant huff; resisting the urge to reach back and bat away her neighbor's hand with every fiber of her being as she kept her arms firmly crossed in front of her.

"You do not."

"Afraid not, cutie pie."

Came the replies of the two older women at the same time, each turning a mildly disapproving frown on her before laughing again at the pout they got in return.

"Ugh," she grumbled, rolling her eyes and only managing

to keep herself from smirking right along with them by clenching her cheeks enough to draw a fresh twinge pain from them. "What. Ever."

I guess there are worse ways to kill time on a Saturday... Heh.

—

The atmosphere during the drive back home after Dana and Rhen had finished stowing away the broken remains of her bike in the back of her partner's big red SUV proved to be a rather subdued one. Neither of them had much to say to one another just then, and it was painfully clear to her that her aunt was more than happy with simply allowing her stew to in her own nervousness. Letting her imagination run wild as it conjured up all sorts of horrible possibilities for what might be awaiting her upon their arrival home in just a few short minutes.

Once they stepped inside, however, rather than immediately being hauled across the older woman's lap for a world-class spanking that would surely leave her sobbing into the corner of their front room like a five-year-old with her bright red bottom on display for the whole neighborhood to see, Dana instead just wrapped an affectionate arm around her shoulders and steered her gently, but nevertheless firmly, into their kitchen. There, she pulled out a chair from the table, and just as Missus Hastings had earlier that afternoon, turned it out to face the rest of the room.

"Come here, you," she ordered not unkindly, settling down onto the worn wooden seat with a heavy sigh and tugging her forward to stand between her parted thighs by the stretchy waistband of her shorts. "I want to get a good look at the damage we're dealing with here before we do anything else just yet."

Rhen wasn't quite sure whether or not her partner meant the bumps and bruises she'd taken from her tumble off of her bike, or else the damage that had been done to her backside by their neighbor's slipper (something which she herself was rather eager to see as well, actually), and was just about to ask for clarification when Dana surprised her by leaning in and planting a lingering kiss on her slightly parted lips. At the same time that this was happening, she also gave the waistband of the shorts she still had gripped in her hands a well-practiced yank that sent them sailing down to her ankles in one fell swoop. Once again exposing the dancing dinosaurs printed across her little round backside to anybody and everybody who might be around to see them.

Which, thankfully, was just the two of them.

But still.

It was the principle of the matter, dang it!

"Hey, that's cheating!" protested Rhen, her lips turning down in an adorably indignant pout as she attempted to back out of reach of the seated older woman in front of her, stumbling awkwardly thanks to the shorts tangled up around her ankles, only to then immediately hop forward into an impromptu embrace with a surprised squeak as her cheeks were given a hard, reprimanding squeeze. "Ah! Double cheater!"

"Sorry, hon."

Flashing her an impish smirk, Dana eased her grip after another moment or two more of shameless groping. Relaxing her hands just enough so that her neatly manicured fingernails were no longer digging in against her satisfyingly springy seat.

"But I'm afraid it only counts as cheating if you don't make the rules."

"Yeah, well…" the younger girl grumbled, blowing a few stray strands of hair out of her face with a petulant huff in a blatant attempt to hide just how much she enjoyed being (literally) taken in hand by her coolly commanding auntie. "A little heads up before you decide to pants me would still be nice, you know."

"Oh, would it? I'm sorry," cooed Dana, her lips quirking up in mock-apology. "I just assumed you'd be used to it by now considering how often it seems to happen to you."

Her dark blue eyes twinkled teasingly at her then as she added.

"Maybe I should just confiscate your shorts and skirts for the next few days so that you can get more used to not having them on? What do you think?"

"Humph!" sniffed Rhen, choosing not to dignify that

suggestion with a response as her partner tickled the small amount of bare cheek peeking out from beneath the leg-holes of her panties, making her dance in her grip. "W-Whatever…"

Dana's smirk just widened into a full-on grin at that, though.

"Careful now, missy," she warned with her usual mix of no-nonsense sternness and playful teasing as she released her cheeks, settling her hands firmly on her hips instead and pulling her in just a bit closer with her best "Don't test me, little girl" look. "I'd watch that attitude if I were you."

"Oh yeah?" challenged Rhen, stomach fluttering pleasantly as she took the bait hook, line, and sinker, the furrow between her brows deepening into a truly impressive "make me" scowl. "And why's that, huh?"

"Well, let's see now…" crooned her partner languidly, smiling in a way she reserved just for her as she leaned forward once again for a quick peck before taking hold of the hem of her recently laundered t-shirt, silently ordering her to raise her arms with a slight, upward tilt of her chin. "How about because I'm already planning on washing that fibbing little mouth of yours out until it's absolutely *sparkling* in just a minute here, and I'd be more than happy to do that while you're *also* holding in a punishment enema?"

"Eep!" squeaked Rhen, genuine worry mixing with the fluttering inside her stomach to quicken her pulse as her cheeks clenched reflexively behind her.

Her partner's tone had been relaxed and conversational, but the hard glint she'd seen in her eyes as she'd made that casual threat made it abundantly clear that she was dead serious.

"No thanks, I'll be good!"

"Oh, are you sure? It's really no bother at all if you feel you simply *must* keep giving me sass, you know."

"No, no!" Rhen quickly reassured her, her words coming out all at once in a breathy jumble. "It's fine, I promise!"

"Well, if you're really sure…"

"I am!"

As nervous as she was already, there was no way she about to call the older woman's bluff.

Another night? Absolutely. But not this one.

She was already in enough trouble as it was without provoking her partner into getting *creative.*

"Okay then," she chuckled, letting the idea drop with an amused shake of her auburn tresses that made Rhen's heart skip a beat.

Dana was just so darn mesmerizing when she laughed like that. How she was so lucky to have landed her, she'd never understand.

"No double soap for you tonight, cutie pie."

"Phew!"

Though, now that she'd brought it up, Rhen had to admit she really did rather like the idea of getting cleaned out of both ends at the same time. She'd have to keep that one in mind for the next time she gave her partner a reason to *really* take her to task over.

Maybe she could even carve up a couple of soap sticks and…

"Ahem. Now then," Dana continued a moment later, clearing her throat as she and Rhen both forced themselves to return their thoughts back to the matter at hand. "Why don't you show me how good of a girl you can be by raising your arms for me?"

"Yes ma'am!"

Reveling in the surge of anticipatory dread that was working its way inexorably down beneath the front of her panties and in between her firmly pressed together thighs, Rhen lifted her arms up over her head. Hissing in sharply through clenched teeth as she did so.

Immediately Dana's face went from triumphant to concerned, and she made quick work of tugging her t-shirt off of her entirely, tossing it onto the table behind her without a second glance.

"Are you okay, hon?" she pressed, her voice quickly edging its way back into panic as she maneuvered her around by the hips to get a better look at her right side where it seemed like she was having the most trouble. "What's wrong? Is it your shoulder?"

"Y-Yeah…" confirmed Rhen with a wince, giving the joint in question a couple of wary, experimental rotations, only to be met with another pointed stab of pain. "Ack! It's been like this all afternoon. I… I can move it around just fine for the most part, but if I bring it up too high it really starts to hurt."

"Oh, baby, I am *so* sorry," gushed Dana, reaching up to gently prod and massage both of her shoulders, making her wince again and grit her teeth as she did so, though not enough to actually want to pull away. "Well, it's definitely bruised like crazy, that's for sure. But, on the bright side, it doesn't *feel* like anything is broken or out of socket. I don't think you'd be able to move it at all if it was, and I think you'd *definitely* know if it was broken."

"Yeah… That's kind of what I was thinking too," agreed Rhen, sighing in relief as the pain in her shoulder gradually began to ebb away.

Her partner's magic fingers never failed to make her feel better.

Settling back against her chest, the feel of her warmth against her skin with only a thin layer of camisole between them absolutely intoxicating, she let herself melt under the insistent pressure of her strong fingers as they continued to do their best to knead away the tension and stiffness from her aching joints.

A massage and a spanking, huh? I could get used to this…

"Hmmm… This pain when you raise your arm has me worried," Dana cut in across her hazy thoughts a couple of minutes later, finishing her rubbing and wrapping an arm around her waist so that she could scoop her up onto her right thigh. "I think we'd better take you to see a doctor tomorrow, just to be safe."

"A doctor?" echoed Rhen, not liking the sound of that one bit as she brought her left thumbnail up to her mouth to chew on anxiously.

She'd never been a fan of doctors. Too many pointy needles and embarrassing questions. Not to mention having to get undressed while you were the center of attention for them.

Ugh.

Shivering in disgust, she did her best to ignore the twinge of anxiety underpinning that last qualm in particular.

Noooo thank you.

"Can't we just let it heal on its own? I'm sure it'll be fine in a day or two if I leave it alone."

"No we *cannot*, little girl," shot back Dana almost immediately, squashing that idea before it had a chance to take root with a firm shake of her head. "There is no way on god's green earth that I'm going to just leave this to chance and risk you aggravating an injury that will end up haunting you for the rest of your life. Do you hear me?"

"Ugh, *fine.*"

Conceding the point, Rhen folded her arms in front of her chest with another harrumph. Though, she didn't bother with putting much in the way of actual annoyance behind the gesture this time.

Her position seated on her partner's lap in just her panties and a camisole had done an excellent job of draining away most her remaining sass for the moment.

"Good girl," cooed Dana in that way she so often did when she knew she was just putting up a front because she was embarrassed, her breath deliciously warm against her skin as she pressed a kiss to her forehead before letting her right hand wander down to give her bottom a meaningful squeeze through the thin material of her panties. "It's been way too long since you last had a checkup, anyway, so we might as well take advantage of you being on my insurance and kill two birds with one stone. We can get your shoulder looked at and also get you a full physical and up to date on any vaccinations you might need as well all at the same time while we're at it tomorrow, yeah?"

"I guess that's not a bad idea…"

Despite her dislike of doctors, Rhen was honestly touched by her partner's concern. While she knew that the spankings and rules she'd imposed on her since day one of their relationship were definitely there because she wanted the best for her, and also because she thought she was just too cute *not* to punish, it still always came as a bit of a surprise to her to see just how much she was willing to go above and beyond to make sure that she had everything she needed (and then some).

"I love you, Dana," she sighed, leaning in against her chest and resting her head along the crook of the older woman's neck as she breathed in the familiar, soothing scents of her perfume and laundry detergent with a contented sigh.

She could stay like this forever if given half a chance.

"I love you too, cutie pie," purred her partner in turn, catching her chin between the thumb and forefinger of her free hand (the one that wasn't currently busy fondling a certain bratty bottom) and tipping her head back so that she could kiss her again. "Even when you're naughty."

"How magnanimous of you," deadpanned Rhen, rolling her eyes for all she was worth as she smirked.

"Okay, okay," admitted Dana, the corners of her lips quirking up into a conspiratorial grin of her own. "*Especially* when you're naughty."

God, I love her so much.

"Does that mean I'm off the hook for today then?" the petite junior wheedled hopefully, though she was pretty sure she already knew the answer to that.

"Not. Even. Close," answered Dana, enunciating each word with lighthearted menace while giving her tush a hard squeeze as she shifted her grip from her chin to the back of her head and captured her lips for another, more prolonged, kiss; her tongue winding with hers for a long, blissful moment before they parted.

"Humph," grumbled Rhen, pulling back just enough to level her best pouty glower at her thoroughly amused auntie. "Meanie."

"Brat."

"Bossy boots!"

"Oh, you are *so* going to pay for that one later!"

"Psh. Bring it on."

"Don't you worry, little girl, I intend to."

The two of them continued to cuddle and smooch for a while

longer after that, thoroughly forgetting for the moment that she was still in trouble as they let themselves get lost in the moment. After all, they both knew that there would be time enough for discipline later.

Once they'd finally parted, however, Rhen's face fell again as half-forgotten memories of the last time she'd had the flu and had been stuck waiting in line for nearly four hours to see someone at her college's free clinic came flooding back to her all at once.

"Hey, wait a minute… Did you say you wanted to see a doctor *tomorrow*?"

"I sure did," confirmed Dana, giving the end of her nose an affectionate tap.

"But, like…" the younger girl protested, more so again out of a habit than because she had any actual objections to the idea of seeing a doctor now that her aunt had more or less settled the matter for her whether she liked it or not. "Won't we need to make an appointment ahead of time and have you close the daycare for the day so that we'll have enough time to wait for our turn and stuff? Are you sure that's going to be okay?"

"Oh, don't you worry about any of that," dismissed the other woman breezily, giving her handful of cheek another squeeze as she brushed away her concerns with her free hand. "As it so happens, Auntie Dana already has that all taken care of."

"You do?" asked Rhen, once again surprised by how quick and efficient her partner could be when she put her mind to it.

"You bet your cute little caboose I do!" she laughed. "Do you remember my friend Alana from college? You know, Miss Pierson?"

"Uh, yeah…" nodded Rhen, not quite sure what the woman her partner sometimes went out for drinks with on the weekends (leaving her in the care of her two older "sisters", Abby and Courtney) had to do with anything they were talking about just then.

"Well, *she's* a doctor with her own private practice," continued Dana, her grin broadening with just a hint of mischief behind it now. "And, as luck would have it, she mentioned while we were out a few weeks ago that she would just *love* to give you a little checkup sometime."

"She did?" squeaked Rhen, her voice coming out a full octave higher than she meant for it to as fresh butterflies stirred to life inside her stomach.

"That's right," sing-songed her partner as her grin grew decidedly more teasing. "She actually brought it up the other night when we were out dancing. You remember. That night when you were too busy to come say hello because you were stuck in the corner?"

"Uh, *yeah*," huffed Rhen moodily. "Kinda hard to forget."

She'd been putting off taking out the trash for three days in a row, mostly because she kept forgetting to and totally not at all because she didn't actually feel like doing it, and her aunt had just finished pre-heating her bottom with a wooden spoon for it, when her chatterbox of a friend had burst in through their front door unannounced. She'd gotten one good look at her well-spanked bottom sticking out of its customary corner in the front room, and had then immediately set to teasing her mercilessly about it while she waited for Dana to finish getting ready.

"Ugh. Do we really have to go see *her*?" Rhen whined, her face flushing a hot shade of pink with the memory of how Alana Pierson had managed to coax out every single little detail of her punishment from her while they'd waited for her aunt to finish writing down instructions on a sheet of paper next to a pink plastic bath brush she'd set aside for her babysitters to finish her off with before putting her to bed later that night. "Can't we see someone else instead?"

Seriously. Anyone else would be fine!

That woman was tall, pretty, and *exactly* the kind of bossy that made her knees go weak without even thinking about it.

"Not if we want to get you in for a checkup tomorrow," answered Dana with a matter-of-fact shake of her head, not sounding put off of her plan in the slightest. "Besides, seeing her will be nice since she's already aware of our little *arrangement*."

At that she let the fingers of her right hand slip inside the waistband of her panties, savoring the warmth she found there as she wiggled them beneath her for a better grip.

"Which is helpful, since, despite you looking and acting like you're closer to thirteen than twenty-one, your body actually *is* that of an adult and needs to be looked after as such. So, going to her will provide you with the best possible care while also avoiding any awkward questions that might crop up."

"Oh, uh… Right. That's a good point."

Rhen had gotten so used to automatically being treated like a young teen by everyone she met, that she hadn't even stopped to consider the potential problems with seeing a doctor that might raise. And, upon further reflection, she suddenly found that she was far more willing to put up with whatever teasing Alana might have in store for her if it also meant not having to explain to another doctor just *why* it was that her partner insisted on dressing her like a bratty middle schooler and making her call her "Aunt" Dana.

She'd been lucky with her friends and family so far, who'd all accepted their unique dynamic without much more than an amused smirk (and the collective decision that if that was the way she really wanted to live her life, they'd be more than happy to oblige her as well whenever possible), but that didn't mean she wanted to do it all over again with some random stranger. It had been humiliating enough to come to terms with the fact that she really did benefit from being kept on a short leash and spanked whenever she stepped out of line. She did *not* want to have to try and voice those sorts of things out loud if she could at all avoid it.

"Plus," added Dana, drawing her attention back to the present by digging her fingernails in against her right cheek with a playful wink. "I know that you'll probably be all sorts of pouty and huffy when it's time for her to examine you, so seeing someone who understands, and also believes I might add, that even big girls need discipline from time to time, will help make things go a whole lot easier should your attitude need any… adjusting."

"Humph. If you say so."

"I *do* say so," confirmed Dana, smirking in the face of the adorable, raven-haired girl's pouting. "And, as it so happens, she already said that she'd be more than happy to fit us in after-hours tomorrow evening if we wanted."

"Wait, she did?" demanded Rhen, feeling as if she'd just had the rug yanked out from under her yet again.

It was one thing to agree to go see a doctor.

It was another thing entirely to *actually* be going!

"When?"

"Today," admitted Dana, blushing now just a bit herself. "I *might* have called her immediately after I'd gotten off the phone with Olivia. You know, just to be on the safe side since you'd hurt yourself and all…"

"Awww, that's so sweet of you."

"Well, you *did* have me pretty worried there, you know, cutie pie."

"Oh, uh… Right. Heh. Sorry about that."

"Don't worry, I forgive you."

Dana pinched the cheek she was fondling then, *hard*.

"Mostly."

Then, clearing her throat and reasserting her usual cool control once again, she added with a teasing smirk, "And I can tell you right now that Alana is *very* excited to get her hands on your cute little caboose."

"Oh joy…" droned Rhen, trying to sound annoyed but not quite managing to pull it off as she swallowed her conflicting feelings of dread and excitement.

Rather than help, however, her face instead quickly flushed about ten shades of scarlet and her thighs squirmed together of their own accord as flashes of what might be in store for her at Doctor Pierson's office that following evening flashed unbidden through her mind. And, deciding not to comment further on the matter just then lest she give the woman whose lap she was still seated upon more ammunition to tease her with, she instead let out a nice and grumpy "Humph!" that more or less summed up her feelings on the situation as far as she was concerned.

"And speaking of that cute little caboose of yours…" Dana pressed on past her pouting once she'd given the butterflies inside her stomach ample time to make her squirm. "Let's just take a peek at that and see how well Missus Hastings managed to warm it up for me, shall we?"

Not bothering to wait for a reply, she instead just tipped the younger girl forward across her waiting left thigh, angling her facedown so that she was jackknifed in place over her sturdy leg with her round bottom as the highest point on her body.

"Oof!" grunted Rhen, clinging to her calf for support and blinking several times in quick succession as she attempted to reorient herself to her new upside-down view of the world around her.

"Um… Are you really sure you need to do that?" she asked, stalling for time and not at all liking the direction things were suddenly headed.

"Oh, I *really* think I do," purred her aunt, pouring the kind of emphasis on the word "really" that made Rhen's heart skip a beat as she hooked both of her thumbs into the back of her waistband and began to tug.

"Ugh," the younger girl huffed, scowling as she felt her dinosaurs slip free of her cheeks with hardly a whisper of resistance. "Of course you do."

Grumbling quietly to herself about how totally unfair this all was, she watched through the gaps between the legs of the chair her aunt was sitting on as her panties were quickly pulled down to her knees, before being tugged off of her legs entirely. Leaving her in nothing but her thin white camisole for the second time in a row that day.

"Oooh, now would you take a look at *that*," breathed Dana, letting out a low, appreciative whistle as she rubbed her palm across first one newly exposed cheek and then the other. "She sure did a number on you, didn't she?"

"No fu-"

SMACK!

"Ack! I mean, *freaking*, kidding," agreed Rhen, hastily correcting herself before her tongue could slip and get her into even more trouble than she already was.

No double soap, no double soap, no double soap…

"Yes, well, it's no more than you deserve, little girl," pronounced Dana primly, her lips pursing into a disapproving frown as she gave each cheek a couple of admonishing squeezes. "What'd she use on you anyway? You've got some very interesting welts back here."

"She *said* it was a slipper," Rhen grumbled sourly, choosing to cross her arms in front of her and pout despite the added pressure it put on her lower abdomen and bladder.

At the rate she'd been chugging hot cocoa all afternoon, she knew she'd need to avoid staying like that for too long, or else she might just end up giving her partner even more ideas for ways to embarrass her. Having to go to bed every night wearing a pull-up for no other reason than because she looked too cute in them *not* to do so was bad enough as it was, and there was no way in heck she was going to tempt fate right then and end up having to wear them day in and day out for a week or more just because she had a little accident.

Again.

"A slipper, huh?" prompted Dana, sounding dubious as she traced a fingernail over one of the more prominent welts mottling her niece's backside. "Like one of your bunny slippers upstairs?"

"Humph. I wish," huffed Rhen in response, shaking her head to clear it before any more humiliating ideas related to her nightly attire could take root there. "It was basically just a big tennis shoe. No bunny ears or anything. *Apparently*, that's just what they call them back where she's from."

"Is that right?" her partner crooned, grinning hungrily at the goosebumps she'd managed to raise across her cheeks. "I think I'll have to remember that one for later. It leaves such *pretty* marks."

"Seriously? Don't you think we've got enough implements already?"

"Oh, honey, don't be silly," laughed Dana. "You can *never* have too many implements."

"Ugh. Whatever."

Silently, though, Rhen had to admit that she wasn't entirely opposed to the idea of her aunt getting her hands on a "slipper" of her own either. It *had* been a surprisingly unique and exciting experience to be punished with one, and variety was the spice of life after all, even in spanking. But, on the other hand, she could still very clearly remember how much that stupid shoe had stung, and she wasn't quite so keen to revisit the experience just yet.

"You know, you're still pretty pink back here," Dana pointed out, choosing to ignore the huffy sass being exuded by her. "Though, I suspect that these little pinch marks will be gone by tomorrow morning at the rate you recover."

"That's not super surprising," agreed Rhen, pulling her ponytail free and letting her head dip forward so that her long, dark hair could partially obscure her chagrinned smirk while she repositioned her palms on the cool tile in front of her. "Missus Hastings sure knew how to swing that thing and make it count. Well, make *me* count, but you know what I mean."

"Indeed I do," mused her partner thoughtfully, giving first one cheek, and then the other, a firm squeeze. "I wonder what her secret is?"

"Lots of tea and practice, if I had to take a guess."

"Hah!"

SMACK!

"Maybe I should invite her over later and ask her to give me some pointers."

"Oh my god, don't you *dare!*"

SMACK!

"Ah!"

"Pardon me, young lady?" drawled Dana, keeping her voice stern yet playful as she let her palm rest menacingly against the cheek she'd just swatted.

"Um…" replied Rhen hesitantly. "Don't you dare, uh…

please?”

"That's better."

SMACK! SMACK!

"Now then, I *was* planning on putting you over the edge of your bed and whipping your adorable little butt raw with that belt your granny gave us just as soon as I got you home," continued Dana, her voice taking on a decidedly more lecturing tone to it now. "I cannot believe you would have the *nerve* to ride your bike without your helmet on. And even worse, to *lie* to me about it when I'd asked you if you'd been wearing it just last week!"

SMACK! SMACK!

"Ack! Owie!"

Rhen couldn't help but cringe at the scolding she was getting, to say nothing of the extra-hard swats that had just landed against either of her sit-spots. She could feel her stomach flip-flopping unpleasantly as her partner laid out her bad behavior in such clear and unequivocal terms, and she found herself swallowing hard as her mind raced to try and figure out what horrible new fate might be in store for her that could be even worse than a prolonged belting.

"I'm sorry, Aunt Dana…" she offered weakly, actually meaning it, but knowing that being sorry at this particular stage in the punishment process wasn't likely to do her bottom any good.

"I appreciate that, cutie pie. Really, I do," answered Dana more calmly, giving her cheeks another, more affectionate, squeeze as she breathed out her frustration through her nostrils. "But your behavior was not only sneaky and dishonest, it also put your life and your body in danger, and that is just completely unacceptable."

"I know…"

Doing her best to swallow the lump that had formed in her throat, Rhen let out a shaky sigh.

"I'm really, really, *really* sorry for making you worry like that, and I promise it won't ever, *ever* happen again."

"It had better not, little girl!" growled Dana, her voice

suddenly growing stormy and making Rhen very glad that she couldn't see the hard, unflinching glare that she was sure had just come over her face then. "Because if I find out that you've been riding your bike without a helmet again, I'll be taking it away for at *least* a month."

SMACK!

"*And* wearing your butt out every single night at bedtime with just about anything and everything I can think of."

SMACK!

"You got that?"

"Ack! Yes ma'am, loud and clear!" yelped Rhen, before adding in a fit of self-pity before she could stop herself. "Not that I'll be able to actually *do* any riding with my bike all busted up like it is right now…"

"Now, now, there's no need to pout," admonished her aunt with a firm pat and another long sigh. "Didn't you hear me telling Olivia earlier that I was going to get you a new one before the semester started?"

"Wait, really?"

Now that she mentioned it, Rhen did seem to vaguely recall her saying something to that effect.

"You mean it?"

Even though she was bare bottom up across her lap and facing down all sorts of unpleasant punishments in the very near future, she still couldn't help but perk up with excitement at the prospect of getting her hands on a brand new bike that didn't come seventeenth-hand from a yard sale.

"Of course!" laughed Dana, her girlfriend's sudden change in mood not going unnoticed by her as she tickled the backs of her thighs. "I'll take you to the toy store in a week or two, and we'll find you something that matches that pretty helmet I already bought for you."

She then let her thumb and forefinger pinch a spot along the inside of her left thigh.

"That way you'll always remember to wear it whenever you

see it."

"Oh…" came Rhen's suddenly much less enthusiastic reply, legs shifting and stomach churning as the mental image of her riding to campus on a glittery, pink bike took center stage in her mind's eye.

She already had enough trouble as it was getting her fellow students to not treat her like she was some sort of wonder-child with an attitude problem who'd graduated from high school several years early, and she had a sneaking suspicion that this new "upgrade" to her bike situation wasn't going to be doing her any favors.

"Oh…?" prompted Dana, drumming the tip of her forefinger expectantly against where she'd just pinched.

"Oh, um… Thanks!" Rhen quickly amended, before adding under her breath. "I *guess*."

"You're very welcome, cutie pie," snickered Dana, clearly pleased with the pouty reply she'd managed to wring out of her, before clearing her throat and getting back to the matter at hand. "Now then, as I was saying. In light of the fact that you're all welted up back here, I think what I'm going to do is hold off on taking you to task with the belt until after your bottom has had a chance to fully recover."

"You are?" squeaked Rhen, finding herself dealing with her second shock in just as many minutes.

Talk about lucky!

"That's right," crooned Dana, grinning wickedly as she went on. "I want to work with a clean canvas, and I'm perfectly fine with waiting a bit to make that happen if I need to."

"Oh…"

Scowling again, Rhen let out a disgruntled huff in an attempt to vent some of the butterflies that were suddenly running amok inside her stomach.

"I see."

"Awww, there's no need to sound so disappointed," her aunt cooed, giving her cheeks a couple of comforting pats. "It'll only be a day or two, I promise."

"Oh, that is just *so* reassuring."

Then, feeling like she had nothing left to lose just then, Rhen decided she might as well sass it up a bit more.

"Hey, wait a minute," she said, perking up as if she'd just remembered that she still had a pudding cup in the fridge. "So what you're saying is that I just need to keep getting smaller spankings here and there throughout the day, and then you *won't* be able to use the belt on me?"

SMACK!

"Yeah, just like that!"

"Oh, hah-hah," deadpanned Dana, punctuating her sarcastic laugh with two more hearty swats to the backs of her thighs.

SMACK! SMACK!

"Clever thinking, cutie pie, but I'm afraid you recover way too quickly to make that work for you."

She then glided her right hand up along the inside of her soft thighs, parting them as she went and brushing her fingertips tauntingly over her silky smooth lips. Smirking triumphantly at the moisture she found waiting for her there.

"Ah!" gasped Rhen, legs locking and toes pointing as she felt her partner slip two fingers inside of her at the same time without any warning. "But… but… I-I could… I mean, you could…"

She genuinely tried to continue arguing the merits of her plan, mostly for the sake of being stubborn and putting off having her mouth washed out for a bit longer, but the sensation of Dana casually pumping in and out of her while she lay bare bottom up across her lap made forming coherent sentences surprisingly difficult just then.

"Hmmm… No, that's not going to work, either," her aunt replied with a teasing shake of her head, continuing to speak as if they were actually having a normal conversation while all the while gradually increasing the pace at which she worked her fingers in and out of her. "Besides, I could always surprise you by dragging you out of bed at three in the morning to whip your cute little tush. Then what would you do, hmmm?"

"I… Uh… I would, uh…"

Rhen was way too close to coming to think of anything sufficiently witty to fire back with right at that particular moment, and so instead continued to pant and moan just the way she knew Dana liked. But, just as she was about to tip over the edge into sweet release, her partner abruptly pulled her hand away from between her thighs and delivered two extra-hard swats to either of her sit-spots.

Again.

SMACK! SMACK!

"Ah! Owie! Hey, no fair!"

"Sorry, honey buns, but only good little girls get to come across their auntie's knee," taunted Dana, bringing her fingers up to her lips to sample the fruits of her labor and grinning broadly. "You're just going to have to wait until you've had your punishment, I'm afraid."

"Ugh," grumbled Rhen, knowing that she really should have seen something like this coming as she balled her hands into frustrated fists on the floor in front of her. "Talk about *rude*!"

"Oh?" purred Dana, her voice taking on a decidedly dangerous edge to it. "Rude, am I?"

She shifted in her seat then, leaning her left forearm in firmly against the small of her back and using the fingers of that same hand to spread her lightly pinkened cheeks as wide as they would go, exposing her puckered rosebud to the cool caress of the air-conditioning wafting lazily down from the vent above them.

"Eep!" squeaked Rhen in turn, her smart mouth growing a whole lot less clever as she flushed a boiling shade of stop sign red from her neck all the way up to the roots of her inky black hair while trying (and failing) to clench her buns back together. "N-N-Now hold on just a second…"

Dana was having none of it, though.

"How's *this* for rude, you little sassmouth?"

Chuckling grimly to herself as her not-niece wriggled and

squirmed ineffectually against the forearm pinning her in place, she proceeded to start ruthlessly spanking her directly atop her exposed anus.

SMACK! SMACK! SMACK! SMACK! SMACK!

"Aieee!" squealed Rhen, arms and legs gesticulating wildly as her unprotected back door was mercilessly set upon by a series of lightning-fast swats that all but took her breath away. "Oh my god, Aunt Dana, *please*!"

"Please, what?" taunted Dana, her voice positively dripping with self-satisfied smugness as she continued to turn this extra-sensitive spot on her girlfriend's backside a positively delicious looking shade of crimson, striving to get it to match the blush she could see on her face.

"Ack! Owie! Crap, shoot, dang!" Rhen ground out, unable to form a more coherent response just then as she did her best to try and ride out the pain, hoping against hope that her partner would ease up in another moment or two.

Which, she was quickly coming to realize, was a mistake.

"Go on, now," sing-songed Dana after she'd delivered another dozen or so swats, grinning from ear to ear as she made her naughty girl howl. "Use your words, dear."

SMACK! SMACK! SMACK! SMACK! SMACK!

"You're going to have to make me *want* to stop."

"Oh my god, plcasc, it *hurts*!" Rhen finally managed to get out through clenched teeth, her eyes now leaking a steady stream of hot tears as the hyper-focused bonfire being stoked between her humiliatingly splayed cheeks continued to grow more and more unbearable.

"Yes, I imagine it does," agreed Dana coolly, tutting to herself as if she were being forced to explain something blatantly obvious. "I *am* spanking you right on top of your adorable little tushy hole, you know."

SMACK! SMACK! SMACK! SMACK! SMACK!

"Ow! Oh! Come- Ack! Come on!" Rhen whined, her voice coming out in ragged, panting gasps as each relentlessly punishing swat found its mark, pushing her further and further past the edge of her endurance and not showing any sign of slowing down anytime soon. "I thought you said you weren't going to- Aieee! Going to spank me tonight?"

SMACK! SMACK!

"I said I wasn't going to spank you with the *belt*," Dana corrected, punctuating her reply with two extra-powerful swats made all the more unbearable by a sharp flick of her wrist just before impact. "I never said anything about my hand, though, did I?"

Then, suddenly changing tactics without any warning, she ceased her swatting altogether and instead began to rub two fingers up and down along where she'd just been punishing, savoring the warmth she felt there and occasionally teasing at her girlfriend's scalded opening with the tip of a finger.

"O-Oh…" breathed Rhen, the single word coming out as a sigh that was half acknowledgement and half relieved moan as she melted across her partner's knee, grateful for the unexpected break and savoring the soothing sensation of her strong hand massaging her tingling, aching rosebud.

Unfortunately for her, though, her respite proved to be a brief one, and she soon found herself fighting off a whole new wave of panic as Dana's fingers were suddenly pulled away entirely and her cheeks were allowed to wobble back into place.

"But if you think that you're going to get away with one measly, little spanking for all the crap you pulled today," she went on, her voice coming out in a low, menacing growl as she eased the pressure on her lower back and instead snaked an arm around her waist to pull her in tight against her stomach. "You've got another thing coming, little girl!"

SMACK-SMACK! SMACK-SMACK!

Moving once again without any warning, Dana delivered two hard and fast spanks in a row to each of Rhen's sit-spots, followed by about two dozen more for good measure immediately thereafter.

"But- Ack! But what about the soap?" the bratty

twenty-year-old turned teenager squealed, hardly believing that she was even bringing up such a thing when just the *thought* of those bars of Ivory her aunt kept stashed away underneath their kitchen sink for fibbers and potty mouths was enough to make her gag.

But, hey, any excuse to avoid further spanking just then was looking *very* tempting.

"Didn't you say you were- Ah! Planning on washing my mouth out or something?" she wheedled as best she could while kicking furiously in a useless attempt to throw off some of the heat that had been reignited from her earlier slippering. "Shouldn't- Oh! Shouldn't we just move on to that instead?'

"Oh, don't you worry, hon," Dana reassured her, her righteous, maternal fury having once again been replaced by playful sternness. "There'll be plenty of time for that once I've finished warming you back up, believe you me."

"But- Owie! But isn't it getting kind of late?" Rhen tried again, grasping at straws now as she frantically wriggled her bright red caboose from side to side in time with the flurry of spanks bombarding her thighs. "What about dinner?"

"Hmmm… Now *that*, on the other hand, *is* a good point," allowed Dana, slowing her pace somewhat, but not actually stopping, as she shifted her aim back up to the jiggly centers of her girlfriend's delightfully squirming cheeks. "I suppose I really should just send you straight to bed without any dinner after the way you've been acting…"

"I- Ack! I guess that's fair…" agreed Rhen with a forlorn sigh, not liking that idea one bit, but also knowing that it would be no less than she deserved.

Plus it might end her spanking sooner.

"But that wouldn't be a very fun way to celebrate you finishing another semester of college, now would it?" continued her partner in a far more chipper tone, punctuating the question with a real zinger of a swat directly across the inner center of her sit-spots, not too far off from where she'd just been getting spanked between her cheeks.

SMACK!

"Owie, owie, owie!" yelped Rhen, temporarily forgetting her morose attitude altogether as she busied herself with gritting her teeth and squeezing her aunt's left calf for dear life, doing her best to ride out the sudden surge of white hot fury searing its way into the delicate undercurves of her cheeks. "Not... r-really!"

Smirking to herself at the endearing way her not-niece gasped and moaned across her lap, the material of her thin, white camisole having grown sheer thanks to the sheen of sweat plastering it to her back, Dana at last eased her hold around her waist .With a satisfied sigh, she then settled back against the ladder-back of her wooden chair and took another few moments to quietly admire the view being presented to her, letting Rhen catch her breath as well before resuming her spanking at a much more leisurely pace that still nevertheless managed to make her squeak and yelp from time to time whenever her hard palm found a particularly delicate spot of bottom.

Of which there were a great many.

SMACK. SMACK. SMACK.

"Tell you what," she finally said after another minute more of idle swatting. "I'll order us some pizza after I'm through making sure that you've *completely* learned your lesson, and then we can munch on that and watch something on Netflix. How's that sound?"

"Really? You mean it?"

"I sure do!"

SMACK!

Rhen had to admit that a slice (or six) of pepperoni pizza sounded absolutely perfect right about then, and she felt her stomach growl in agreement. Which was honestly a very odd sensation to experience, given her current position and the way her bottom was stinging as it bounced and jiggled behind her.

"Can we get stuffed crust too?" she asked excitedly, her words bouncing up and down in time with her partner's lazily swatting hand. "Oh, oh, oh! And some of that super yummy garlic bread with spinach and feta!"

"Of course we can, cutie pie," agreed Dana with a fond laugh, letting her slapping palm wander wherever it felt like now as it danced up and down across her cheeks and thighs at random. "Whatever you want is just fine with me."

"Yay!"

Suddenly feeling a whole lot less sorry for herself as she continued to scissor her ankles back and forth behind her, her elation managing to take the edge off of much of the pain in her backside and her gnawing worry (or was that just hunger?) over her impending mouth soaping, Rhen clapped her hands and beamed.

"This is going to be *awesome*!"

Even if she ended up having to sit on a pile of pillows for their impromptu pizza party, it would still all be more than worth it so long as she got to celebrate with the woman she loved.

"Come on, hurry up already! I'm starving!"

Chapter 3

Doctor's Orders

"Oh my *god*, how much longer is she going to make us wait?" demanded Rhen (not for the first time), letting out an exasperated moan and crossing her arms in front of her as she slumped against the padded waiting room chair she'd been sitting in for what felt like forever. "I thought you said she was going to see us after-hours? Why are we *still* having to wait?"

"Patience, Rhen" chided Dana in a soothing voice, keeping her attention mostly focused on the magazine she was reading rather than her pouting girlfriend as she reached over and ruffled her hair affectionately. "I'm sure she's almost done. Just hang in there a little bit longer, alright?"

"But it's already been, like, *twenty minutes*," continued the younger girl, drawing her words out into a prolonged groan and kicking her feet while her partner just rolled her eyes and sighed.

"I know it has, sweetie, but you'll live."

"If you say so."

Had she been less absorbed in her own bored grumbling just then, Rhen probably would've picked up on the tell-tale twitch at the corner of her partner's mouth that all of her complaining was starting to produce. The one that typically meant she was rapidly losing her patience with her despite how much she enjoyed her bratty antics. But, busy as she was glowering at the nondescript drop ceiling tiles above her head, that warning sign went completely unnoticed.

Instead, she continued to grumble through her peevishly puckered lips, "This freaking sucks."

Which proved to be the final straw for her aunt.

"Look."

Laying her magazine facedown across her lap with deliberate care so as to not lose her place, Dana exhaled slowly through her nostrils and turned a level stare on her niece.

"Alana is a busy woman and she's doing us a big favor by squeezing you in at the last minute like this. So, quit your whining and *sit still*. She'll get to us when she gets to us, alright?"

"Okay, okay, fine…" conceded the grumpy junior, blowing half-heartedly at the hair tickling the tip of her wrinkled nose from her adoptive auntie's earlier ruffling, before straightening back up in her seat and switching gears with a fresh harrumph. "You still could have at least mentioned that she was a pediatrician before we got here, though."

"Mmhmm. Yes, dear. I'm sure I could have."

This was the third time since their arrival at Pierson Family Medical that she'd started whining about how her partner had oh so conveniently "forgotten" to mention that her doctor friend from college was someone who specialized in medical care for children under the age of twelve. And, just as before, her pouty indignation was met with long-suffering patience and just the hint of a self-satisfied smirk from Dana. Although, this time around, her tone also bore an unmistakable edge of warning to it that made it abundantly clear her grumbly girlfriend's attitude was tiptoeing very close toward being adjusted for her if she didn't start changing her tune.

"But, like I've already told you, Alana is just as capable of taking care of big girls as she is little ones. Even big girls who can't seem to behave themselves and stop from throwing a fit in her waiting room. So, *please* stop acting like I've somehow tricked you into coming to a veterinarian's office for a checkup, alright?"

"Humph. Whatever," mumbled Rhen under her breath, frowning even harder to tamp down on the sudden twinge of worry the unspoken threat in her aunt's voice produced in her stomach. "At least a vet would've had cute animals to play with or something."

"Rhen…"

"Whaaaat?" snapped the disgruntled twenty-year-old turned teenager, parroting back her partner's warning tone with an equally bratty cadence.

Choosing to ignore her sass, Dana instead gave her left thigh a couple of meaningful pats and a quick squeeze.

"You're really not doing a very good job of convincing me that you don't belong here, you know."

She cocked an eyebrow at her then, her stern demeanor slipping somewhat as she smirked in a way that just *dared* her to keep testing her.

"Now, are you going to behave yourself? Or do I need to go ask that nice lady over there if there's a restroom around here you and I can visit for a little *chat*?"

Taking the hint, Rhen let out another prolonged (albeit less grumpy sounding) sigh and slipped her phone from her front pocket, hoping that she'd be able to stave off any further embarrassing questions by showing that she was at least attempting to behave herself.

Sort of.

It had been a while since her not-aunt had spanked her in such a public place, and the prospect of getting dragged by the ear into a bathroom stall for a quick spanking that would most likely echo out into the main waiting room area for everyone else to hear was enough to make her squirm in her seat while her lower abdomen fluttered pleasantly.

"No ma'am. I'll be good."

"Thank you, honey."

Leaning in for a quick peck to her cheek, Dana picked up her magazine and resumed reading.

"Just sit tight. I'm sure it won't be much longer now."

"Yeah, yeah…"

This is still some baby back bullcrap, though, Rhen added to herself with a sullen harrumph once she was sure her partner's attention was completely absorbed in the article she was reading.

She had *assumed* that they'd be coming to a "regular" doctor's office that evening for her checkup. But, alas, it was not to be.

I mean… I guess this is still technically a regular doctor's office, she tried to tell herself, casting a baleful look around the empty waiting room once again. *If you ignore all the toys and the fluffy cloud wallpaper, it's pretty much just like the clinic on campus, right?*

It wasn't.

And she knew it wasn't.

But she did her best to ignore that fact.

Humph.

It was just too bad that the nice, motherly woman working the reception desk at the far end of the room hadn't batted an eye when she and Dana had shown up for their appointment earlier that evening. After stepping into the cutesy waiting room with its abysmally juvenile decor, Rhen had been hoping that she'd get one good look at her, smile apologetically, and then gently explain that there must have been some sort of mistake and that she and her partner would need to leave.

But noooo.

Instead, she'd been nothing but professional. All but ignoring her as she spoke with her "aunt" without sparing so much as a passing glance in her direction once she'd gotten her name and confirmed that they were on the appointment list. She'd given Dana several forms to fill out, had told them that Dr. Pierson was still with another patient at the moment, and had then asked them to have a seat until she was available to see them. All as if they really *were* just an aunt and her young niece coming in for a routine checkup. Heck, she'd even gone so far as to point out that they had a do-it-yourself coffee bar that Dana was more than welcome to use if she wanted to!

Unfortunately for Rhen and her attitude, though, the woman apparently shared her aunt's opinion that "little girls" weren't supposed to drink coffee (especially not when they were in the middle of fasting for blood work), and she'd had to make do with bottled water instead.

Warm bottled water.

Talk about a double standard, she thought to herself with a petulant glower at the TV mounted in one corner near the ceiling that was currently playing cartoons, wishing very much that it wasn't a rerun she'd seen a million times already. *It's not like one measly little cup of coffee is going to totally ruin my results, right? It's mostly just a blood sugar test, anyway. Coffee doesn't have any sugar in it, does it?*

Smirking in spite of herself, Rhen stifled a snort and pulled up her go-to puzzle game on her phone.

Maybe. But I'm guessing the hazelnut creamer probably does. Plus, there's all those, you know… sugar packets. Okay, fine, fair point. Never mind…

—

Thankfully, she and Dana were only left waiting for another few minutes before the little door next to the reception desk finally swung open. A moment after that, a mother and her pre-teen daughter emerged from the hallway leading off toward the back office and exam rooms, and at last Rhen and her partner were informed that the doctor would see them now.

"About freaking time," she grumbled under her breath.

SMACK!

"Oh!"

Before being propelled forward two steps in an ungainly bunny hop by a solid swat to the seat of her jeans from her aunt.

"Watch it…" she warned darkly, falling into step beside her and escorting her past the receptionist, mother, and child.

All three of them had no doubt caught their little exchange. Given how close they all were it had been pretty much impossible *not* to have. But what they made of it, Rhen had no idea since she deliberately chose to keep her eyes glued straight ahead of her as she sped past them at as dignified a speed-walk as she could manage.

"Okay, okay. I'm going. Geez!"

Moving at a brisk pace down the well-lit hallway, she and her aunt were soon met by a woman with full lips, severe cheekbones, and a broad smile that put the overhead fluorescents to shame.

"Hey there, girl," Alana greeted them, the hem of her crisp white lab coat swishing stylishly behind her as she closed the distance to Dana in three long strides; catching her up in a tight hug before taking half a step back and looking apologetically at the both of them. "Sorry about the wait. It's been *nonstop* all day today."

"Oh, that's totally fine. We're just glad you could fit us in at all," Dana reassured her, slipping an arm around her girlfriend's waist to prevent her from using her as cover as she pulled her in close to be part of the conversation. "Isn't that right, Rhen?"

"Uh-huh. Just *so* happy," agreed the younger girl with a saccharine sweet smile that gradually grew more genuine as she took in the pair of dirty looks her falsely-chipper tone managed to get her.

Not missing a beat, Dana added with a roll of her eyes, "And, as I'm sure you can see, this one needs a good going over in more ways than one."

"It sure does seems that way, doesn't it?" agreed Alana in a tone that straddled the line somewhere between barely-contained laughter and stern disapproval, keeping her sharp eyes fixed directly on Rhen for several long, measuring moments before eventually turning her attention back to her partner with a satisfied smirk. "Well, I'll do my best to make sure she gets everything she needs. But…"

At this, her look suddenly turned apologetic once again.

"I'm afraid I'm going to have to ask you to wait for us out in the lobby, hon."

"Awww," replied Dana, sounding surprisingly petulant to Rhen's ears as she gave the hand on her hip an agitated squeeze. "But I was really looking forward to watching you work! Plus, I'm still worried about her shoulder. Are you *sure* I can't poke my head in for just a little bit?"

"No can do," answered Alana with a resolute shake of her head, laying a conciliatory hand on the other woman's shoulder and looking just as bummed out as she did. "As much fun as that would be, Rhen is still *technically* an adult, and doctor-patient confidentiality requires that I not let you sit in on her examination without her consent.”

Saying that, she turned her gaze back on the younger girl in question, who was currently in the middle of mumbling under her breath about how two years over the age of eighteen (nearly three now!) was far from being “technically” an adult as far as she was concerned, before continuing.

“Then again, if she says she’s fine with it, then that’s a different story altogether.”

Her lips drew back into a taunting smile then as she leaned forward to bring herself down to eye level with her new patient.

“What do you say, kiddo? Would you like your auntie to come hold your hand while we do your checkup? I know those booster shots can be pretty scary for some little girls.”

“Oh my god, no!” huffed Rhen indignantly, her face flushing hot pink as she fought to extricate herself from her partner’s arm before crossing her own beneath the minimal swell of her t-shirt covered breasts and glaring. “I’m perfectly capable of doing all that crap on my own, thank you very much. Humph!”

“My, my,” cooed Alana, her grin not giving an inch as her almond eyes twinkled with mirth. “Such a brave girl!”

“Hah!” snorted Dana in response to that. “More like she’s afraid I’ll decide to tan her bratty little hide the moment I find something to bend her over in the exam room.”

“Uh-oh, has someone been misbehaving?”

“Like you wouldn’t *believe*,” sighed the younger girl’s partner, making a show of dragging a frustrated hand through her auburn hair. “I swear I was *this* close to turning her over my knee right there in the waiting room with all the attitude she was giving me.”

“Aunt *Dana*!” Rhen moaned, rounding on her partner and looking positively mortified.

“Oh hush, cutie pie,” she dismissed with a fond tap to the tip of her nose, just below her furrowed brows. “Alana has seen plenty of spanked seats before. Yours isn’t any different.”

"That's right," agreed the other woman, fixing her in place with a look that was one part warning and three parts teasing challenge. "But I'm sure I won't need to add yours to my list today, will I, Rhen?"

Before smirking again as she added half a heartbeat later.

"Well, I mean… Again."

"No ma'am!" squeaked the younger girl, stomach fluttering as she nodded quickly. "I'll be good!"

"Brave *and* well-behaved. I like it."

Turning back to Dana, she gave her friend another apologetic smile.

"But seriously, Dana, you're going to have to wait out in the lobby. I know it's no fun, but I'll be more than happy to fill you in on everything you need to know about her shoulder once we're done. Assuming, that is, Rhen gives me permission to do so, alright?"

"Fine," conceded the other woman with a put-upon huff, mimicking her naughty niece remarkably well as she added with a good-natured grumble. "Spoil sport."

"Oh, you hush," chided her friend with a mock-stern wag of her forefinger. "You get her all to yourself day in and day out. The least you can do is let me borrow her for an hour."

"Yes, yes, I suppose that's fair."

Planting a quick kiss on her girlfriend's flushed cheek, Dana let her go and began moving off back toward where they'd come from, calling over her shoulder as she went.

"You be on your best behavior now, honey buns, and I'll see you when you're done, alright?"

"I will," waved the younger girl with more energy than she'd been expecting to, only feeling a little bit silly as she watched her partner walk away. "Bye, Aunt Dana."

For as much attitude as she'd been giving the woman, it was honestly *much* easier on her anxious mind to embrace her younger persona for the time being. Which was exactly the reason why she stuck her tongue out and blew a silent raspberry at her retreating form as she disappeared around a corner.

"Ahem. Now then," spoke up Dr. Pierson from out of the blue behind her, laying a firm but friendly hand on her shoulder and making her jump as she began steering her further down the hall and away from the waiting room. "Right this way, sweetheart."

"Yes ma'am," answered Rhen dutifully, her legs moving on autopilot before she even realized what was happening.

Whoa. How the heck did she do that?

"Awww, you're just so polite," cooed the older woman, giving her upper arm a friendly rub. "Dana's definitely done a good job on your manners, hehe. Now, tell me, have you eaten anything since this morning?"

"Ugh. No," snapped the starving junior with a disgruntled harrumph, her stomach growling in solidarity with her over the injustice of it all.

"No… what?" prompted Alana, her voice turning momentarily frosty as she slowed her pace and tightened her grip on Rhen's arm in a way that avoided agitating her shoulder.

"No ma'am!" she quickly amended, swallowing hard as her stomach switched from growling to lurching with fresh nerves.

"There we go! I knew you could do it," the tall doctor replied in turn, her voice warming once again as she pushed open an unmarked door at the end of the hall and ushered her inside a neat and orderly exam room. "And I'm sorry you're so hungry. I know it's hard to miss snack time, but it can't be helped, I'm afraid. We simply can't risk having anything throw off your blood work. On the bright side, though, I'm sure Dana will be more than happy to take you somewhere nice to eat once we're all done here, so just hang in there a little bit longer, alright?"

Now where have I heard that one before? the bratty not-teen thought to herself with a wry grimace.

Still, though, Rhen found herself quickly succumbing to a shy smile as she nodded.

"Yes ma'am."

There was just something about the willowy older woman's

sternly encouraging demeanor that made it hard to stay grumpy with her for long.

Probably has something to do with her spending all day dealing with cranky kids or something, she reasoned, her face flushing slightly as it dawned on her a moment later that *she* had just been deftly handled like one herself.

Not that she really minded all *that* much.

Doctor Alana Pierson was exactly the kind of person who could make Rhen's heart race and knees wobble without much more than a firm look and a pat to her seat. The kind of woman she'd found herself being drawn to ever since she'd started dating Dana. And the kind of woman who had quickly become the driving force behind many of her idle bedtime fantasies.

While it was true that she had a beauty to her, there was nothing soft about it, which only served to make her all the more captivating. Where Dana was all round hips and maternal affection, Alana had a sharp, angular face framed by wavy chestnut hair cropped to just below her ears, and piercing brown eyes that seemed to take in every detail of whatever they looked at with only a glance; making Rhen desperately want to impress her. However, what *really* had the petite junior smitten despite her best attempts to stay petulant in the face of being dragged to a pediatrician for what was sure to be a very humiliating (and thorough) examination, was the even sharper air of authority she naturally carried herself with. With just a few words and a hand on her shoulder, she'd been able to get her doing whatever she said, while at the same time conveying the silent, tantalizing promise that she would be more than happy to deal with her if she wanted to test her patience.

Plus, well, she just looked so darn *cool* in her lab coat and stethoscope!

No wonder she and Dana get along so well…

Shaking her head to clear it before she could dwell any further on the taut curves visible beneath her doctor's very flattering pencil skirt, pantyhose, and maroon blouse as she shut the door behind them, Rhen attempted to busy herself by taking in her surroundings. Standing there awkwardly fidgeting with the hem of her t-shirt, her nervous eyes bounced from the padded exam table and its paper covering that dominated most of the room, what appeared to be a modern workstation computer with a countertop-mounted monitor and keyboard beside it, a backless swivel-stool, and lots and lots of drawers, cabinets, and counter space as she swallowed.

Hard.

Oh boy… I guess I'm really doing this, huh?

"Alright then, kiddo, I want you to start getting undressed for me while I get your paperwork ready," instructed Alana as if in answer to her unspoken question, her brassy alto light and breezy as she brushed past her and over to the back counter where she picked up a plastic clipboard.

"Um… Undressed?"

"Yes, that's right," she confirmed, only half paying attention now as she made a couple of quick notations on a form before directing an expectant look at her over the top of her horn-rimmed glasses. "Down to your birthday suit, please."

Rhen felt her heart leap up into her throat upon hearing that. And, swallowing it, sent it plummeting back down past her suddenly weak knees as she took an involuntary step back, bumping up against the closed door behind her and letting out a surprised squeak.

"Eep!"

This was *exactly* the kind of thing she'd been hoping to avoid when she'd agreed to let her aunt take her to see a doctor.

"W-What for?" she demanded, her indignant tone coming out far more startled than she'd meant for it to as she leaned against the door for support. "Can't you just, like… check my heartbeat or whatever through my shirt?"

She'd even changed into one of her thinner ones and had foregone wearing her usual camisole underneath it just to make the entire process that much easier for her!

"Do I *really* have to get undressed?"

"I'm afraid so," answered Alana, her tone still politely expectant, but her features softening just a bit. "I can't exactly examine your shoulder, or anywhere else for that matter, if you're all covered up, you know."

"I mean…" mumbled Rhen, suddenly finding the tops of her soft pink tennis shoes very interesting as she brought her right thumbnail up to her pursed lips to chew on. "You could try?"

"Young *lady*," her doctor snapped then, forcing her to look back up with a start, her patience clearly having run out as she cut across her flimsy stalling with those two simple words. "Believe it or not, I *have* seen naked twenty-year-olds with mildly underdeveloped bodies before. It's nothing to be ashamed of, I assure you. Now, I understand that this all might be embarrassing for you, but I intend on performing a *full* examination of every adorable inch of you before I turn you back over to your aunt this evening, and you *will* be naked for that. Period. Is that understood?"

She hadn't raised her voice once during the entirety of her reprimand, but the sharpness of her tone coupled with the pointed but empathetic look in her dark eyes still managed to send spasms of fretful excitement rippling through Rhen's stomach and down between her thighs.

"But… but…"

Scrunching her brows together in consternation, she opened her mouth to try and argue some more, but all of her attempts to wriggle her way out from under the other woman's unwavering expectations fell short beneath the force of her withering gaze.

"What if maybe I just, like… Sort of… You know…"

After several long and awkward moments of indecision and unsuccessful attempts to bargain on Rhen's part, Alana finally threw her hands up in the air and let out an exasperated sigh.

"Okay, fine. Have it your way then," she declared, not quite managing to sound all that upset despite the frustrated scowl pulling down at the corners of her mouth. "I had a feeling things might go this way."

Running her free hand across the smooth olive skin of her

forehead and through her neatly trimmed bangs, she shook her head and then turned back toward the counter behind her, setting aside her clipboard with a light *clack*.

"You know, Rhen…" she said, her voice now silky smooth as she pulled open a drawer directly in front of her and extracted something from within that the younger girl couldn't see. "There's a reason why so many parents like to bring their little darlings in to see *me* when it's time for a checkup."

Unable to quite stop herself from giggling, her nervous energy bubbling over, Rhen quipped teasingly.

"What? Is it because of your charming bedside manner?"

"I suppose you could say that," crooned Alana with an easy shrug, her words carrying a playful taunt to them that made the petite junior's toes curl inside her tennis shoes despite the twinge of fear it also sent racing up her spine. "Although, a more accurate assessment would be that it's because I, like your lovely auntie, know a thing or two about handling naughty little boys and girls who can't seem to do what they're told. You wouldn't *believe* how many parents want a physician with a, shall we say, old-fashioned sense of discipline to deal with their little darlings as they enter those *difficult* years. One who isn't shy about swatting a bottom or two should the need arise."

Turning back to face her now, slow-eyed and grinning from ear to ear, she regarded her with a knowing look that did absolutely nothing to ease the churning, contradictory fear and excitement boiling in Rhen's stomach as she hefted what appeared to be a *very* mean looking wooden paddle in both hands.

Tap… Tap… Tap…

Its dark brown surface was mirror smooth and glossy, reflecting the soft glow of the fluorescent lights overhead, and emblazoned across its front in bold white lettering was the phrase "Booster Shot for Bratty Butts".

Swallowing hard, Rhen stared transfixed at the imposing length of polished wood in the other woman's hand for several long moments as her cheeks clenched and unclenched beneath her jeans with memories of the one and only time she'd been paddled by her fuddy-duddy Sunday school teacher, Sister Miller.

Uh-oh…

Then, realizing that she'd been staring for way longer than she'd meant to and seeing that her doctor expected a reply, she opened her suddenly dry mouth to try and say something. To apologize, or maybe to promise to be good, but all that managed to come out were a series of strangled half-sentences.

"I uh… I mean… That is to say… Um…"

Her grin not slipping an inch, Alana gave her left palm a hard slap with her paddle and took a menacing step forward, advancing slowly on the now nervously backpedaling younger girl with an intense look that spelled trouble.

POP!

Only to immediately break the tension in the room when she gave her palm a slightly more overzealous slap than she'd meant to.

"Ah!" she hissed, stopping short and quickly waving the hand she'd just swatted beside her a few times before bringing it up to her lips to blow on it theatrically. "Yikes. I forgot how much of a wallop this thing packs."

Again, Rhen couldn't help but giggle, the icy hand gripping her heart and lungs easing its hold on them enough to allow her to breathe once again.

"Y-You don't say?" she managed to goad with a shaky approximation of her usual sass. "I never would have guessed."

"Heh. Well…" the other woman likewise snickered, apparently pleased to see that her little act had managed to help put her at ease as she stepped back and set her paddle down on the counter-top beside her with a wink. "Let's just say that it's been a while since I've had a chance to be reminded of that firsthand."

Snatching up her clipboard, she once again became all business.

"Granted, I only ever use that particular paddle for certain naughty interns and the occasional big girl like yourself whose mommy or auntie brings her in to see me, but believe me when I say that it's more than capable of getting you to do as you're told and then some."

"Yeah, uh… I'll take your word for it," replied Rhen with a brazen smirk that bent somewhat under the weight of the other woman's stern and steady gaze.

"Will you now?"

Rhen could *feel* the unspoken threat hovering just behind those seemingly innocent words, and wisely chose to keep her mouth shut this time, instead nodding her head once in deference. Then, drawing away from the door she'd been leaning up against for support, she moved on a pair of mostly-steady feet over to the exam table off to her left. Making sure to give her doctor's paddle a wide berth just in case.

After all, she was sassy, not stupid.

"Smart choice," crooned Alana with a tight smirk, clearly well-aware of what the petite junior was trying to pull as she took in her every move with open amusement. "Now then, are you going to be a good little girl for me and get undressed like I asked you to?"

Still smiling, she ran the fingertips of her right hand in a loving caress along the smooth surface of the dark wood resting on the counter beside her.

"Or…?"

She didn't need to finish that sentence, and instead simply left the words hanging in the air between them for several long moments.

Rhen, for her part, found herself seriously considering calling her bluff, if for no other reason than to satisfy her nagging curiosity about what a paddling from a more "reasonably" sized paddle (at least compared to the monstrosity her Sunday school teacher had used on her) might feel like, but that bout of foolhardiness was quickly squashed by her desire to sit comfortably for dinner in an hour or so. Besides, Alana had already gotten a pretty good look at what a "normal" disciplinary spanking from her aunt was like, and had even seen precisely how red it had left her bottom once it was all said and done, so she doubted that the coolly intimidating doctor would take it easy on her if she did decide to give *her* bratty butt a booster shot.

Plus, she still had a date with her grandma's belt at some point in the next day or two, and she *really* didn't feel like dealing with that while also nursing any lingering bruises the paddle might leave behind.

There was always next time, though.

"Alright, alright… You've made your point. I'll be good."

"Awww, I'm so glad to hear that," cooed Alana disingenuously, before sharpening her glare into something that made Rhen's heart skip a beat as she snapped. "Now strip."

"Ugh."

Heaving out a long-suffering sigh to keep from swooning at the way those last two words had made her clit throb, Rhen reluctantly began to undress. Gripping the hem of her t-shirt in clammy palms (even if this game they were playing was exciting, she still didn't like people seeing her undressed any more than she absolutely had to), she quickly stripped it off; turning it inside out as she pulled it up over her head. Then, with her back angled toward the still smirking older woman just a few feet away from her, she took her time turning it back right-side out and folding it neatly before laying it on top of the padded exam table in front of her. This just seemed to amuse Alana, however, who, rather than snap at her to hurry up as her aunt might have when she was stalling for time before a punishment, contented herself with simply watching her every move as she worked.

"You know, Dana talks about you *all* the time when we're out together," she mused while Rhen fiddled with the placement of her t-shirt on the table, drinking in the trim lines of her smooth, bare back and shoulders as she pulled open another drawer beside her and fished out a pair of bright purple rubber gloves without looking.

"She does?"

Rhen couldn't help but smile fondly at hearing that. Even though she and her partner said that they loved each other multiple times a day, it was still nice to hear from someone else that she cared for her.

"Oh yeah," confirmed Alana with a light laugh as she pulled on her gloves, watching as the younger kicked her shoes off into a corner and attempted to do the same with her socks using only her toes. "I'm honestly super jealous that she's managed to snag herself such an adorable little brat to swat and snuggle."

SNAP! SNAP!

"Ah!"

Rhen let out a little surprised squeak and clung to the padded edge of the exam table to avoid losing her footing as the other woman gave each of her gloves a surprisingly loud snap at the wrist while continuing to casually ogle her.

Huh. I always assumed that was just some lame gag they used in movies, she thought to herself with a grimace, willing her racing heart to slow back down to a more reasonable cruising pace as she took in a shaky breath. *Well, live and learn, I guess…*

She knew that she was just trying to distract herself from what had to come next, though. And so, sighing heavily through her nose, she reached down and began to undo the front clasp on her jeans.

Ugh. Here we go…

With one last roll of her eyes and a self-pitying groan for good measure, she pushed the fashionably snug denim hugging her modestly round caboose down past her knees. Revealing at last the extremely embarrassing pair of "panties" her aunt had forced her to put on that morning when she'd picked out her outfit.

"Oh-hoh, and what have we here?" piped up Dr. Pierson right on cue, her amused grin morphing into something far more wolfish as she held up a single, commanding forefinger to prevent her from shucking her bright pink pull-up down to join her jeans around her ankles; the understated, natural authority lurking just beneath her crisp tone causing her to freeze in place half bent over with her hands hovering awkwardly around her hips. "I don't seem to recall you needing to wear anything like this the last time I saw you undressed, Rhen, dear. Don't tell me you've developed a little pants-wetting problem since then? Oh, now that is just *too* precious."

"What? No I haven't!" squawked Rhen, her face flushing tomato red as she rounded on the older woman with her arms crossed self-consciously across her naked breasts.

Straightening up to her full five-foot-one-inch height, looking every inch the bratty and indignant teenager forced to wear a younger sibling's potty training pants after wetting the bed one too many times, she attempted to stomp a foot to *really* drive home her point.

"I'll have you know that I-!"

Only to have her legs get caught up in the jeans tangled around them, knocking her off balance and sending her tumbling toward the exam table behind her.

"Wh-Whoa!"

Windmilling her arms out to either side of her in a vain attempt to right herself, giving her still-grinning doctor an unobstructed view of where Dana had had her face buried before getting her dressed that morning in the process, she quickly lost her footing entirely and was sent sprawling face first across the padded edge of the table with a heavy grunt.

"Oof."

"Careful now. Just because this is a doctor's office, that doesn't mean I want to patch up any extra injuries," admonished Alana, tut-tutting to herself as she glided over to her left side and halted her attempts to push herself back up with a firm hand between her shoulder blades. "Oh, no, no, no, you just stay right where you are, sweetheart. We wouldn't want you to trip and have another *accident*, now would we?"

Choosing not to dignify that particular double entendre with a response, Rhen instead just glowered into the padded surface of the table pressing up against her cheek.

"Humph!"

Thankfully, though, Alana seemed to take her pouting harrumph as a polite acknowledgement rather than a challenge to her authority.

"Attagirl," she cooed, easing the pressure on her back as she casually walked the rubber-gloved fingertips of her right hand down along the valley of her spine, making her shiver.

Eyeing the inch or so of upper cheek peeking out from where she had her bent over, she hummed happily to herself and slipped her fingers into the crinkly waistband of her pretty pink princess pull-up.

"But, as cute as these are, I *did* say that I wanted you in your birthday suit, didn't I? That's right, I did! You're such a clever girl! Now then, let's just get these out of the way, yeah? No, no, don't worry about getting up. I'll do it for you, since you seem to be having such a difficult time with them."

"Oh my god, that's *really* not-" Rhen started to protest, wriggling against the crinkly paper beneath her as she threw a pleading look over her shoulder.

POP! POP! POP!

"Ack! Necessary."

"Now, now," chided Alana, her voice still carrying that odd mixture of encouraging playfulness and deliciously looming threat as she landed three swats in quick succession against the seat of her padded panties, making her bounce up onto the balls of her feet despite the fact that she could barely feel them through the thick material. "There'll be no more arguing from you, young lady. Unless, that is, you've decided that you really *would* like a dose of my paddle, after all?"

"No, no, that's fine!" Rhen quickly assured her, shaking her ponytail in big, sweeping arcs from side to side behind her in a frantic attempt to convey just how okay she was with not getting her bare bottom properly paddled.

"Oh? Are you absolutely, positively, totally and completely sure?" pressed Alana, sounding just as saccharine sweet as she had earlier back in the hall. "It wouldn't take more than two or three minutes, you know. I'm *very* good at dealing with naughty girls bent over my exam table, hehe."

"I'm sure!"

Hearing that, the leering doctor made a disappointed little hum and then sighed.

"Well… Alright then," she huffed, idly palming her cheeks through her pull-up before allowing her voice to grow sharp and frosty once again. "But that's your last warning. You hear?"

"Eep!" squeaked Rhen, swallowing hard and thrusting her hips back against her lightly groping hand on reflex. "Yes ma'am!"

"Awww, I love the way that sounds coming from you."

After giving her backside a couple more friendly pats, Alana eased down onto her heels behind her and began untangling her antsy, dancing calves from their impromptu denim restraints.

"There we go, all better!" she chirped a moment later, popping back up and tossing her inside-out pair of pants, followed half a heartbeat later by her neatly folded t-shirt, onto a nearby chair set against the wall. "Now then, are you going to tell me *why* it is you're wearing a pull-up at your age, or do I need to march you out to your auntie for an explanation instead?"

The heat in Rhen's face all but exploded into an inferno then, scalding her cheeks with its fury as she pictured herself being paraded around the mostly empty waiting room in nothing but her humiliating training panties. Even if it *was* just her partner and Dr. Pierson's motherly receptionist sitting out there now, there was no way in heck she was going to risk letting that happen!

"Okay, okay, I'll tell you!" she blurted out with another panicked squeak, clinging to the far edge of the exam table for dear life just in case the other woman was actually serious about making good on her threat. "Aunt Dana said that I have to wear them for the rest of the week because I was acting like a silly child by not wearing my helmet while I was riding my bike!"

Swallowing hard, she clamped her jaw shut tight around the rest of her explanation before she could keep going and reveal anything about how pull-ups were actually part of her regular bedtime attire, or how her partner liked to put her into them whenever she got the chance. This was definitely a situation where less was more as far as she was concerned. And, even if it *was* more than likely that Dana had already spilled the beans about all of that stuff (and probably more) at some point while she and her friend had been out drinking, she wasn't about to give her anything more to tease her with than she absolutely had to without some more *encouragement.*

After all, where was the fun in that?

"There, are you happy now?" she bit out instead, hoping that a fresh burst of sass might help mitigate some of the roiling embarrassment gripping her lower abdomen, making her heart race and her clit throb.

It didn't.

"Mmmm… Very," purred Alana, patting her knowingly between her parted, quivering thighs and giving that very same throbbing area a firm rub through her pull-up. "I've always liked the way Dana thinks. This look definitely suits you."

Increasing the pressure of her rubbing fingers, making Rhen gnaw at her lower lip as waves of humiliated ecstasy crashed over her, she leaned in close then and murmured directly into her ear.

"And, for the record, little girl, you are very lucky that I wasn't the one picking out your punishment for that little bike stunt you pulled. Because I can assure you that if *I* was your mommy, you would be wearing something *far* more embarrassing than these for the rest of the month, at least."

Saying that, she paused her rubbing and instead squeezed hard enough to make Rhen's hips buck forward against the edge of the padded exam table in front of her with a partially stifled gasp that had her seeing stars.

"They make all *sorts* of adorable diapers in your size, you know."

"Y-Yes ma'am! I mean, no ma'am! Er… I mean, um… I'm sorry, ma'am!" she panted, face flushing even hotter as she tried desperately to come up with a response that would banish the mental image of her lying on her back on the very same table she was currently grinding against with her ankles hoisted up above her in the air as baby powder was applied liberally to her…

"Attagirl," purred her doctor while she continued to struggle with her words and her brain's refusal to stop playing out potential scenarios, licking her lips a as she straightened up and took hold of the waistband of her pull-up once again. "Now then, let's just get these out of the way…"

In one smooth motion, Rhen felt the last of her clothing (such as it was) suddenly be whisked down to her ankles. Leaving her utterly, and completely, exposed in the chilly examination room.

"Well, well, well," crooned Alana in triumph, her breath tickling where she'd just been rubbing as she eased back down onto her heels and slipped her training panties from off of her feet entirely. "For such an indignant little girl who was *just* insisting that she doesn't need pull-ups, you sure did manage to wet this one pretty good."

"Wh-What?" demanded Rhen with an outraged yelp that did nothing to hide her embarrassment, awkwardly shifting her weight from foot to foot in an attempt to vent some of her pent-up energy but staying bent over all the same, painfully aware of just how totally naked she was at that moment (and how tantalizingly close her doctor's strikingly crimson lips were to her own pouting ones) as she continued to snicker behind her.

Rather than answer her question directly, however, Alana instead just leaned in a bit closer and blew a stream of cool air across her damp folds.

"O-Oh!"

The word came out as a high-pitched, gasping squeak coupled with an involuntary shudder, and Rhen suddenly found herself grateful for the support of the table beneath her as she once again rose up onto the balls of her feet and buried her smoldering face in her hands.

"I… I um…"

Swallowing hard, doing her best to remoisten her suddenly dry mouth and get a grip on her rapidly beating heart, she looked up from the dull blue exam table with its top-cover of crinkly paper and stared ahead with unfocused attention at the posters on the wall in front of her.

"I see."

"Yes, I'm sure you do," agreed Alana, falling back into her dry professionalism from earlier as she climbed back to her feet and adjusted her stethoscope. "Incidentally, dear, I'm flattered."

"Oh god," groaned Rhen, her heart skipping several beats all at once in a not entirely unpleasant way as she let out a shaky, little laugh. "Th-Thanks... I guess."

"But," continued her doctor, giving her wobbly backside a couple of friendly pats to help refocus her attention as she sauntered her way over to one corner of the room and dropped her confiscated pair of training panties into a medical waste container. "I'm afraid I'm going to have to dispose of these since they've been... Ahem. Used."

Her lips drew back in a wry smirk then, and she winked.

"Don't worry, though, sweetheart. I've got *plenty* of replacements in the store room down the hall. We'll get you fitted into a fresh one just as soon as we're all done here, okay?"

Then, in response to the worried squeak that little pronouncement managed to produce, she added with a reassuring chuckle.

"And I promise I won't make you wear a diaper since Dana has already decided that she wants you in pull-ups."

"Oh, how so very fortunate for me," deadpanned Rhen, the sarcasm in her voice not quite managing to squash the shy grin on her blushing face. "Yay..."

"Yay indeed," agreed a thoroughly amused Alana. "Now, you just stay put while I get a few things ready, and we'll get started in just a sec, alright?"

"Yes ma'am..." sighed the younger girl, letting herself slump against the exam table beneath her for support once again as she exhaled loudly, doing her best to get her rapidly thudding heart and fiery face back under some semblance of control.

While it definitely wasn't the most dignified of positions to be in, it still at least kept her front (mostly) covered, and she was more than okay with that. Besides, as humiliating as this all was, she had to admit that she *was* rather enjoying herself.

Sort of.

Mostly.

Maybe going to the doctor isn't so bad after all...?

"Good girl."

Idly tugging on the wrists of her gloves, Alana made her way back over to the counter where she'd left her clipboard. There, she began to pull open various drawers and cabinets, laying out several things that Rhen only caught fleeting glimpses of from her position flopped out across the exam table.

Not that she really wanted to see more than that.

Despite Dr. Pierson's rather *unique* bedside manner, she was still more than okay with not dwelling too long on just what all would be involved in her checkup.

Please no needles, please no needles, please no needles...

Her partner had mentioned something about getting her up to date on all of her vaccines the night before, but she was quietly hoping that they wouldn't have enough time for that. It *was* after-hours and all, wasn't it?

Smiling wryly to herself as that cursory thought flitted across her mind, Rhen rolled her eyes and sighed again.

Hey. A girl can dream, can't she?

As she began to grow more accustomed to her total nakedness, and really it wasn't all *that* different from a post-shower spanking from her aunt if truth be told, she propped her elbows up on the table in front of her and rested her chin in her cupped palms; busying herself with reading all about the importance of a balanced and healthy diet on the poster in front of her.

Huh. Wait a minute... Didn't bread used to be at the bottom of the pyramid?

"Hmmm... You know what?" her doctor said smoothly after a minute or two more of clacking about miscellaneous medical materials, pulling her away from her contemplation of proper food group portions as she transferred her tray of tools over to a small metal cart that she wheeled out from around the counter. "You just look so cute all bent over like that, I think I'm going to save checking your weight and height for later so that I can keep you there a little bit longer."

"Works for me," answered Rhen with a mostly nonchalant shrug that only hurt a little bit this time, her idle pouting melting away into a relieved grimace.

She was honestly more than okay with putting off finding out how depressingly short and underweight she was for her age for a little while longer.

"That's what I like to hear," cooed Dr. Pierson, moving her tray over to just behind her and this time taking up a position along her right flank. "Right then, let's just check that temperature, shall we?"

"Sure thing," agreed the younger girl, glancing over and feeling some of the tension in her stomach loosen as she caught sight of the advanced looking thermometer her doctor had just laid out beside her.

Oh thank god...

Her relief was short-lived, however, as she suddenly felt a warm hand take hold of her cheeks, spreading them as wide as they would go without any warning for the second time in as many days.

"Oh come on!"

Despite her earlier promises to be good, Rhen couldn't help but start to squirm again, wriggling her hips from side to side in protest as she tried to get away from Alana's firm grip without crossing the line into actually trying to run away. She could still see the "Booster Shot" paddle just waiting for her on top of the counter off to her right, after all.

SMACK!

"Ah! Can't you-"

SMACK!

"Ack! Just-"

SMACK! SMACK! SMACK!

"Young lady, what did I *just* get finished telling you about arguing with me?" demanded Alana, continuing to keep her

E
F P
T O Z
L P E D
P E C F D
E D F C Z P
Bee Healthy

patient's cheeks spread completely apart as she mercilessly delivered three more very hard swats to her shifting sit-spots.

SMACK! SMACK! SMACK!

"Oh! Oh! Okay, okay!" squealed Rhen, dancing from foot to foot as she hissed in a breath through clenched teeth. "I'm sorry!"

Digging her fingernails in against the far edge of the exam table once again, she forced herself to relax as much as she could, hoping against hope that she hadn't just earned herself a paddling for her sudden burst of brattery.

"Please, I'll be good! I just thought that... You know..."

As quickly as her flash of indignant outrage had come, it had sizzled away to be replaced by petulant resignation. And, unsure of how best to phrase her protests without actually saying anything embarrassing out loud, she instead nodded toward the digital thermometer still resting on the exam table beside her.

"I thought you were going to use *that*."

"Oh, don't you worry, sweetheart," snickered Alana, the menacing air in her voice now dialed back to just a thin undercurrent of warning as she tickled her along where she'd just been swatting. "I'm going to use both."

"But- Eep!" Rhen started to whine again before stopping short and letting out another high-pitched squeak as she felt the press of a *very* cold thermometer tip against her nervously clenched back door. "Wait! Why-? I mean, come on-! Couldn't you just...?"

"Shhh..." soothed her doctor, lightly pushing and twisting the end of the petroleum-jelly-slicked thermometer against where she intended on putting it.

Although Rhen hadn't managed to get a good look at the thing currently working its way inside of her, it sure *felt* like it was way bigger than it had any right to be.

"But... but..."

"It's so rare that I get to use this wonderful rectal thermometer," the other woman continued to explain in a sing-song, all the while ignoring her increasingly feeble protests as she watched her legs go to jelly at the same time as a throaty moan gurgled up from within her. "I know that it's probably a little bigger than what you're used to having back here, but I just couldn't resist. It's been so long since I've had the opportunity to do one of these 'special consultations', you see, and these sorts of thermometers just get the most entertaining results. Wouldn't you agree?"

"That's definitely one way of- Ah! Of putting it," gritted Rhen, the hands she'd moved to bury her face into muffling her sass enough to keep her from getting into any further trouble. "God, this is *so* humiliating."

And she loved it.

"Easy now… Just relax, sweetheart," ordered Dr. Pierson gently, waiting for the brightly blushing junior to comply before pushing her thermometer the rest of the way into place. "Annnnd, there we go. See, that wasn't so bad, was it?"

"I guess not," conceded Rhen with a sullen huff, not quite will-ing to admit out loud that she *might* have been overplaying her complaining just a little bit. "Humph."

Just because last night was way more intense than this, that doesn't mean I can't still complain about it, she told herself with a silent snicker, feeling her reserves of sass starting to rally once again as she let her mind wander back to what she'd gotten up to with her partner later that evening after dinner and three episodes of the show they'd been binging lately. *At least this stupid thing doesn't come with a strap-on harness attached to it.*

Although, if it had, she probably wouldn't have minded too much if the one wearing it happened to be the quietly chuckling older woman behind her. She and Dana would definitely need to have a talk later about scheduling some sort of house call from her doctor friend.

"Attagirl," crooned Alana, fondly patting the small of her back after she'd let her cheeks wobble back into place. "Now, we'll just leave that there for a couple minutes and then see what it has to say, alright?"

"Of course we will…" sighed Rhen, twisting her mouth back into a scowl that didn't quite manage to reach her eyes. "We have to be thorough, don't we?"

"See? Now you're getting it!"

SMACK! SMACK!

Punctuating her praise with two lazy swats, the self-satisfied physician then took a moment to admire the twin handprints she'd just left behind on her still lightly bruised backside.

"Well would you look at that. You totally *do* have a little heart-shaped birthmark on your left cheek. God, that is so *cute*!"

"Huh? I do?"

Doing her best to keep her bare chest still hidden by the exam table, all too aware of how sensitive her erect nipples were just then as they rubbed against the waxy paper beneath her, Rhen craned her head back to try and see what the other woman was talking about. Momentarily taken aback by the sudden change in topic, she found herself wondering how she could have possibly missed something like that after all of the time she'd spent inspecting her spanked butt in the mirror over the last few months.

"Where?"

"Right here!" answered Dr. Pierson.

SMACK!

Pointing out just where she meant with an extra-hard swat to the upper half of her left cheek that had her immediately springing up from the table and dancing from foot to foot with a surprised yelp; inadvertently showing off that she wasn't nearly so upset about the way she was being treated as she was letting on.

"I'll have to- Ack! Have to check that out later. Ah, ah, ah!"

Holy crap, she swats hard! Thank god I didn't take her up on her offer earlier...

"Oh, I'm sure Dana will be more than happy to take a picture for you if you ask her nicely, hon," the *very* amused physician suggested sweetly, drinking in every adorable curve of the glowering girl clutching her caboose in front of her with a broad grin. "Would you like me to call her in?"

"No thanks!" answered Rhen in a hurry as she flopped back down across the exam table with a grunt, her momentary pout giving way to a wry smirk as a fresh frisson of excitement and dread worked its way through her stomach and down to her flexing toes.

Come to think of it, she's probably got one or two pictures of it already floating around in her collection. I'll have to check later…

"Very well then, but in the meantime," continued Alana with a bit more steel in her voice this time, once again pulling her patient away from her daydreaming after she'd finished getting her fill of eying her bare cheeks. "Let's get back to the matter at hand, shall we?"

"Fine…" droned Rhen, doing her best to sound petulant, and not at all like she was enjoying being bent over completely naked with an oversized thermometer protruding from between her (mostly) pale cheeks. "I guess."

"What was that?" prompted the older woman, her tone growing all the more stern as she scooped up her digital thermometer from where she'd left it on the exam table beside her and thumbed it to life. "Don't tell me that was sass I just heard coming from your mouth, *again*, was it?"

"No ma'am!" Rhen quickly replied, her cheeks unconsciously clenching as she did so, making her face flush molten lava hot all over again as she felt the thermometer there give a noticeable bob in time with her own hurried head shaking. "It just sort of slipped out. Sorry, sorry, sorry!"

"Is that right? Well then, I would be *very* careful not to let it happen again if I were you," sing-songed the older woman, the ice in her voice melting away beneath the warmth of her chuckling as she pressed the end of her device against the side of her blazing left temple. "Hmmm, let's see now… Ah, ninety-eight point six. Excellent."

Wow, really? marveled Rhen silently as she brought a hand up to where the thermometer had just been touching, feeling the heat still radiating beneath her skin there as she brushed away a stray lock of hair behind her ear. *I thought it would at least be a little higher than that…*

While she was busy mulling that over, Dr. Pierson glided her way back over to her clipboard. Gathering it up, she made several more notations on the paperwork she had attached to it, before setting her no longer needed instrument aside on the countertop next to her paddle. Then, as if she didn't have a single care in the world, she circled her way back over to Rhen's side and settled her hips against the padded edge of the exam table beside her.

"Just a bit longer now, hon," she crooned, leaning over to lightly flick the tip of the thermometer poking out from her patient with an impish smirk. "Once our little friend here has finished doing its job, we can compare its reading with the one I just took and see if I need to calibrate my more expensive one or not. It's seemed fine all day, but hey, you never know, right?"

"Ugh," harrumphed Rhen, doing her best to feign indifference as a spasm of pleasure and humiliation surged up her spine and jolted between her thighs. "Wh-Whatever…"

"That's the spirit!"

While the two of them waited patiently for the thermometer to finish doing its work, it quickly became apparent to the petite junior that her aunt's friend wouldn't be content to simply wait out the clock in silence. Much as she might have desperately wanted her to.

"Heh. You know what?" she said after only half a minute or so of quiet humming, idly tracing small circles around the dimples at the base of her spine with a fingertip. "Seeing you bent over like this with my thermometer poking out of your cute little caboose brings back a whole lot of memories."

"Um…" ventured Rhen, swallowing hard and trying not to shiver too much at the other woman's touch.

She always had been a sucker for back rubs.

"It does?"

Of all the things to make small talk about, that had not at all been what she'd expected her to say.

"Yep," confirmed the smirking doctor, folding her arms beneath the swell of her lab coat's bosom and fiddling with the end of her stethoscope as she watched her bare backside shift and squirm. "Aside from the hair and your, uh…"

At that, she gave her an apologetic grimace.

"You know… more petite frame, you're the spitting image of your auntie back when she and I were your age and playing doctor in the dorms."

Gazing ahead toward the wall in front of her, apparently lost in memories of times long past, Alana's smirk blossomed into a beaming grin and she sighed.

"Although, *she* at least let me paddle her before I took her temperature. We liked to see if heating her buns up had any effect on my readings or not…"

"Wait, what?" demanded Rhen with a disbelieving snort, thrown even further off balance by this sudden revelation as she struggled to reconcile her mental image of her cool and always in control partner with that of a college coed sporting a well-spanked bottom while her equally vivacious and bossy friend worked a thermometer deep between her ruby red cheeks. "No way! Are you serious? That's hilarious!"

"Oh!" gasped Alana, bringing one hand up to cover her mouth as she giggled. "It seems I let my mouth run away with me for a just bit there. Oopsie…"

The smile on her face hadn't dimmed, but she at least had the good grace to look a *little* embarrassed as she added.

"Some things never change, I guess."

Shrugging then, she ran a hand through her neatly cropped hair, rolling her eyes at herself as her giggles took on a decidedly more nervous edge to them.

"But, uh… Maybe don't mention to Dana that I let that slip just now, yeah? I doubt she'd be all that thrilled to hear I've been gossiping about our old college days like that, and it hasn't been so long since she's had me across *her* knee that I've forgotten how hard she can swing a hairbrush when she's in a mood to."

"Oh, don't worry. I won't tell," Rhen assured her with a giggle of her own, not quite sure yet whether or not she was telling the truth as she let her mind paint a vivid mental picture of her aunt putting this sharp and commanding woman across her lap for a lengthy session with Missus Hairbrush on her toned, bare bottom.

God, what I wouldn't pay to see that.

She was fairly certain that if she *did* bring up what she'd just learned with her partner, she'd find herself flying across her lap far faster than she ever had before, and then probably over Alana's lap as well for good measure not too long after (though, hopefully, that would be *after* she'd finished spanking her silly too). It was a scary thought to be sure, especially considering how thick and heavy that stupid paddle had looked when she'd been menacing her with it earlier, but the prospect of getting even with the woman who was currently *tap, tap, tapping* the end of the thermometer sticking out of her poor bare bottom was a very tempting one indeed.

"Your secret is safe with me. Totally…"

For now, at any rate.

—

After well over half an hour more of poking and prodding, listening to heartbeats and breathing, several not-that-terrible booster shots (even if they *were* administered just below the birthmark on her left cheek), a very large nutrient suppository that made her miss the thermometer almost immediately, drawing blood, and a gentle but meticulous inspection of her still tender shoulder, Rhen was once more allowed to dress (wearing a fresh pull-up from Alana's personal store of supplies), and the two of them made their way back out into the waiting room.

"Alrighty, Dana, babe, she's all yours."

Even though they'd only been separated for a bit over an hour, Rhen's partner still descended upon her for a hug as if she'd been gone for weeks. Nuzzling her against her chest and kissing the top of her head several times in a row before straightening back up and turning her full attention to her friend.

"So, how's she doing?"

"Well," Alana began to answer, directing her gaze toward her patient for a brief moment to confirm that she still had her permission to share everything with her "aunt". "Aside from the cuts and scrapes, which are healing up just fine by the way, good job getting those taken care of so quickly, she's in excellent health. Even if she *is* a bit underweight."

"She says you should let me eat more ice cream," Rhen chimed in then with an impish grin.

"Excuse me, young lady, but I do believe what I suggested was that you try eating a peanut butter and jelly sandwich as a snack a couple of times throughout the day," her physician corrected with a roll of her eyes and a shared smirk with her friend.

"PB and J flavored ice cream, got it."

"Oh, you…" Alana sighed, giving her stethoscope an irritated tug, though all the while still smirking. "I knew I should have brought my paddle with me."

"Yeah, well, you didn't," taunted Rhen, emboldened to full brattiness by being dressed once again, the tantalizing thought of *finally* being able to eat something overriding her sense of back-side preservation as she stuck her tongue out at the tall doctor. "And Aunt Dana already promised that I could have a sundae after dinner if I agreed not to put up a fight about coming here, so hah! Check and mate."

"Careful now, cutie pie," purred her partner then, her hips and chest molding themselves against her lithe frame from behind as she enveloped her in a full-body hug. "You can eat your dessert standing up just as easily as you can sitting down, you know."

Her warm touch coupled with the wolfish grin on Alana's face had Rhen immediately swallowing hard, all of her burgeoning sass shriveling up in the face of the spanking she'd been managing to sidestep her way around all night.

"Yes ma'am!" she squeaked, going scarlet.

Both her aunt and her doctor allowed her stew like that for several more long, embarrassing moments, reveling in her obvious discomfort before Alana finally cleared her throat and spoke up again.

"Ahem. Yes, but as I was saying," she went on, directing her gaze toward Dana while her petite patient strove to get her blushing back under some semblance of control. "Rhen is in excellent health, and even if she is underweight, she's not dangerously so. So, there's nothing to worry about there."

"Heh. I imagine her not subsisting entirely off of a diet of ramen noodles and soda pop helps a lot with that," mused Dana with a satisfied nod. "We try and keep that sort of thing to a minimum at home."

Hearing that, her friend flashed her an approving, professional smile.

"Glad to hear it," she said. "Just keep feeding her *actual* food and make sure she doesn't go skipping meals and she'll be fine. Now, as to her shoulder-"

At that, Rhen felt her partner's grip around her tighten for a brief moment, before just as quickly relaxing as she remembered that she was still tender.

"Is she going to be alright?" she pressed, a pang of worry painfully clear in her voice as she pulled her in closer, as if she could somehow shield her from danger by hugging her more. "Is it sprained? Did she fracture something? Does she need a sling? Do you sell those? Does the drug store? We don't need a prescription for one, do we?"

"Oh no, no, she's fine, she's fine!" Alana quickly reassured her, holding both hands out palm up in front of her in a placating gesture. "She just bruised the hell out of it and maybe pulled a muscle or two is all. She should be completely back to normal in a day or two, and the bruising should be gone by next week."

Hearing this diagnosis repeated aloud for her partner made Rhen want to gloat just a little bit and maybe point out that it really hadn't been all *that* necessary to book her for a full physical after all, but the relief in Dana's voice as she sniffled back a worried sob made that seem entirely too petty all of a sudden.

"Oh thank goodness," she sighed, shifting her in her grip and leaning down to plant a proper, lingering kiss on her lips this time. "You have *no* idea how glad I am to hear that."

"Me too, hon. I'd be so sad if anything happened to little miss cutie-butt here. But, like I said, she's *fine*. So no more fretting about it, you hear? Doctor's orders," her friend chided with a fond half-grin and a lightly admonishing wag of her forefinger.

"Oh, alright," conceded the auburn-haired older woman who, had Rhen been able to see her face just then, would have been very interested to note the bashful look that had come over her for a brief moment with those last two words before being replaced by a playfully teasing grin of her own. "I promise I'll stop bugging you about it and be good."

"Attagirl," praised Alana, the last of her stern doctor persona falling away all at once as her almond eyes sparkled with mischief. "But, if you'd *really* like to help make sure she has a full and speedy recovery, I'd recommend having her take a nice long bath before bed for the next couple of nights. A good soak in some hot water does wonders for sore muscles, you know."

She then dipped her chin down to look Rhen directly in the eye and winked.

"And sore bottoms."

"Humph."

Just as she'd been afraid she would, Rhen's aunt immediately latched onto that idea, and she had to busy herself with counting the clouds on the stretch of wallpaper in front of her to keep from rolling her eyes.

"Oh, that's just perfect! I've been looking for a good excuse to throw her in a bubble bath lately. Thanks!"

"Anytime, hon," snickered the other woman, maintaining eye contact with Rhen all the while in a way that made it abundantly clear that she knew exactly what she'd just done. "I'm always happy to help."

"Ugh," huffed the younger girl in turn, unable to think of anything else to do just then as her face continued to radiate warmth at all the teasing she was being bombarded with. "Can we go already, Aunt Dana?"

"Awww, that's right, you must be starving!" cooed her partner, leaning in to give her another kiss on each of her cheeks and rubbing her upper arms affectionately. "Of course we can, cutie pie. Why don't you go on ahead and get the car started for me, and I'll be there in a minute after I finish saying goodbye and paying our bill. Oh, actually…"

Looking up from her face kisses, Dana cocked an inquisitive eyebrow at her friend.

"Would you like to come with us, Alana? Rhen's in the mood for Mexican and so am I."

"Heck yeah I would, girl!" cheered the willowy doctor without missing a beat. "I've been on my feet all day, and a margarita and some queso sounds like just the thing right about now. I've just gotta lock up real quick, but otherwise count me in!"

"Great!" replied Dana, she and her naughty niece dancing excitedly in place while Rhen echoed her partner's sentiments with an exclamation of "Sweet!"

With the matter now settled, Dana disentangled herself from around her and began steering her toward the door.

"Go on now, honey buns. We won't be long, I promise."

"You got it, bossy boots," nodded Rhen with a renewed sense of vigor, fishing out her aunt's keys from her purse with practiced ease as she made a beeline toward the front door of the little office, all the while being pursued by two matching smirks. "You two take your time. I'll just be on my phone. Thanks for everything Ala- I mean, Doctor Pierson."

"Excuse me, young lady, not so fast!" the physician called after her, her sharp and commanding tone cracking like a whip in the empty waiting room and freezing her in place before she'd made it more than a few steps.

"Um…"

Heart hammering and stomach churning, Rhen reluctantly turned back to face the taller woman, the disapproving scowl on her face filling her with half-formed dread over a public paddling while her knees wobbled and her clit ached.

She'd definitely need to do something about *that* as soon as she got home, that was for sure.

"Y-Yes?"

Gulping hard, she did her best to sound polite.

"Uh, ma'am."

Her grim mask slipping away, Dr. Pierson reached into her lab coat and drew out a piece of candy with a flourish.

"You forgot your lollipop."

Chapter 4

Learning to Set a Good Example

Despite how monumentally embarrassing (and fun) it had been to have her partner strip her naked and all but toss her bottom-first into a bubble bath as soon as they'd walked through the front door later that evening, to say nothing of the *very* thorough scrubbing she received from the rubber ducky washcloth Dana kept squirreled away for just such occasions, Rhen had to admit that her prolonged soak in the foamy water did indeed help. Waking up the next morning, her shoulder barely hurt at all (although it still bore a few faint bruises), and she herself felt well-rested and absolutely wonderful.

Which, of course, just made taking the spanking her aunt decided to spring on her later that afternoon all the more unpleasant since she no longer had any excuse to milk for leniency.

—

"Alright, boys and girls," announced Dana cheerily, clapping her hands to gather everyone's attention around the kitchen table during lunch that afternoon. "Before you all run off to play, there's something we need to take care of."

After lunch announcements weren't an uncommon occurrence at the Johnson Family Daycare. Usually, they were about some fun activity that they were all going to get to do that afternoon, or a special treat they'd earned for being extra well-behaved the day before, and so nobody (including Rhen) thought much about it as they turned away from their idle chit-chatting to hear what Auntie Dana had to say.

Seeing that she had their full attention now, the older woman made a show of clearing her throat and then adopted a very serious expression as she continued.

"So, as some of you might recall, little miss Rhen here had herself a bit of a bicycling accident the other day."

At this, she cast a pointed glance in her girlfriend's direction, and Rhen felt her stomach begin to sink.

Uh-oh…

"As it turns out, she was riding downhill with her eyes closed and ended up crashing into one of our neighbor's cars, putting a pretty big dent into it and just about totaling her bike in the process. Luckily, she herself wasn't hurt beyond a few scrapes and a sore shoulder, but it could have been much, *much* worse since she wasn't wearing her helmet at the time."

Everyone around the table (except for Rhen, who was currently busy trying to make herself invisible) took in suitably shocked gasps upon hearing these horrifying safety revelations, and many of them started making disapproving noises and remarks of their own in the way that young tweens who think they're totally grown up so often do when one of their own gets into major trouble.

"Wow, talk about stupid…"

"Shouldn't she know better?"

"I always wear *my* helmet."

"Oh please," the petite junior muttered under her breath, rolling her eyes at her friends' holier-than-thou attitude. "As if any of you haven't done the exact same freaking thing like a million times before."

She knew for a fact that many of them had, actually, as she'd seen them doing so on her way back home from campus on more than a few occasions. But, she knew too that trying to point fingers right then wouldn't do her any favors maintaining her shaky image as the cool older girl among her little daycare peer group, and more to the point, would just be playing right into her partner's hands. So, instead, she made do with glaring at a knot in the tabletop in front of her while she listened to Dana continue to drone on and on about the importance of wearing proper safety equipment, always playing responsibly, and so on.

Admittedly, she'd actually started tuning her adoptive auntie out almost as soon as she'd gotten going about helmets and bike safety, but that was just because she'd already heard it all before from both her *and* their neighbor. She didn't need a third time around the guilt trip maypole to understand that what she'd been doing was totally stupid. It wasn't like she was *actually* a teenager or anything. She'd just… gotten a little bit sloppy with her bike safety was all. Besides, it was far less humiliating to think about what she still wanted to do that afternoon than it was to be the center of attention just then.

Of course, her partner seemed to pick up on her total lack of focus almost immediately. Forgetting to look appropriately guilty while arranging your carrot sticks by size on your plate was apt to do that. But, thankfully, she didn't call her out on it. Instead, as she wound down in her lecturing, she stepped in close behind her and gave the back of her neck a fond rub, gently drawing her attention back to the present and away from her contemplation of the two stubs of carrot stick that she'd left half-drowned in ranch on her paper plate.

"Now then, since what Rhen did, or in this case *didn't* do, was so serious," she concluded, keeping her voice stern but giving the spot just between her shoulder blades (right where she knew she liked it most) a couple of quick scratches. "I think it's important that you all witness the spanking I'm about to give her for yourselves."

There was another collective gasp around the table at this, and Rhen opened her mouth to argue, but Dana cut her off before she could get a word in edgewise.

"I intend for this to be the one and only time that I have to have this particular discussion with her, and I hope too that it will serve as a helpful reminder the next time any of *you* might think about doing something similar. Am I understood?"

It was a rhetorical question, but everyone still answered it with a bright and cheery, "Yes ma'am!"

"It's only fair," piped up one particularly pleased sounding girl off to Rhen's left, grinning from ear to ear as she nodded sagely. "I would definitely spank her if *I* was the one in charge."

"Yeah," agreed her friend sitting next to her, giving her blonde curls a snootily affected toss that the mortified twenty-year-old turned teenager was sure she'd picked up from watching TV. "She *is* the oldest, after all."

Oh whatever, pipsqueak. Go read another Babysitter's Brigade book, why don't you?

Rhen was suddenly very much regretting using her actual age as an excuse to get her way among her little gaggle of daycare friends so much over the last few months. It had seemed like a good idea at the time, even if doing so hadn't done anything to make the fact that her partner still spanked her like she really *was a* bratty thirteen-year-old any less humiliating. But, as she cast a sour look around the room at all the kids watching her and Dana with expressions of varying degrees of excitement and smug satisfaction, she couldn't help but suspect that at least a few of them were starting to think that maybe it was *her* who should be listening to *them* while they were playing, rather than the other way around.

Ugh. I am so going to tattle on each and every one of you little brats the next chance I get. Just you freaking wait.

Still, as frustrating as her current predicament was, she also had to admit that it wasn't every day that you got to watch someone else get a spanking without your own backside potentially being in the line of fire as well. While Auntie Dana rarely gave spankings in private, she never actually allowed anyone to stand around and gloat while they were happening. (At least not where she could see, at any rate) And so, Rhen couldn't exactly bring herself to be too upset about the air of barely-restrained excitement crackling among her friends just then. Despite how embarrassing this whole situation was for her, she knew that she would have been grinning right along with the rest of them had it not been her butt that was about to get busted.

Of course, that didn't mean she was above trying to weasel her way out of it.

"But… but…" she started to whine, searching for any excuse that might save her seat. "But, Aunt Dana, you can't spank me. It's not even bedtime yet!"

It wasn't a great argument, and it got a lot more giggles from the peanut gallery than she would have preferred, but it was still better than nothing, right?

"I only told you that I was going to tear your cute little butt up, honey buns," answered Dana smoothly, leaning in and planting a quick kiss on her cheek. "I never said anything about *when* I was going to do that."

She gave the spot between her shoulder blades another couple of quick scratches as she added with a triumphant twitch of her lips.

"Or where."

"That's a stupid technicality and you know it," groused Rhen, folding her arms in front of her with a disgruntled huff.

"Yes, well," countered her aunt without missing a beat. "I'm still the one in charge around here, cutie pie. And, unfortunately for you, that means that whatever I say goes, doesn't it?"

"I…"

Swallowing her first reply, Rhen tried to think of some other way to spin things so as to not actually have to cop to the fact that her backside was very much at the mercy of her partner and that there wasn't a thing she could do about it, but a warning squeeze from Dana had her quickly deciding that it was probably better to just cut her losses and move on.

"I guess so."

"See? That's what I thought."

With the matter clearly now settled as far as she was concerned, Dana took hold of either side of her chair and all too easily drew it away from the kitchen table.

"Now then, young lady, I want you to take your chair right out into the front room, and then you and your friends can wait for me there while I go and get the belt, alright?"

Many of the kids who had been watching their exchange

began whispering among themselves as soon as they heard that, their murmuring ticking up several degrees of excitement all at once at the mention of "the belt". Auntie Dana never spanked any of them with anything other than her hand, after all. Rhen must *really* be in trouble!

Dang it, dang it, dang it! the mortified twenty-year-old turned teenager moaned silently, tightening her grip on the hands she had shoved underneath her armpits and blushing even more at all of the excited speculation going on around her. *She couldn't have just waited, like, one more freaking day so that it would just be the two of us?*

Heck, she was supposed to go help Missus Hastings with whatever it was that she'd be doing to make up for denting her car tomorrow afternoon. With a little bit of luck, she probably could have made it all the way to after church on Sunday before they had to deal with any of this!

Heh. Yeah right.

Rhen couldn't help but smirk to herself at her own wishful thinking, before the cold reality of what was about to happen to her settled in along the bottom of her stomach like a lead weight, suddenly making the whole situation much less funny.

"Ugh."

Throwing her hands up into the air and letting out an exasperated sigh, looking every inch the beleaguered teen caught in an unfair system that just didn't understand her, she levered herself up to her feet and turned one last pleading look on her partner.

"Do we *really* have to do this now?"

"Yes, we really do," answered Dana with a thin smile, the telltale wrinkling of laugh lines at the corners of her eyes serving as silent confirmation that she knew *exactly* how embarrassing the next fifteen minutes were going to for her girlfriend and that she couldn't have been more pleased with herself. "As you're so fond of saying, dear, you *are* the oldest one here. And, as such, it's important that you set a good example for everyone else."

Her smile widened just a bit as she said that, and in that moment it took every ounce of Rhen's self-control not to roll her eyes.

"And if you can't do that by following the rules, well…"

Dana gave her a very "what're you gonna do?" kind of shrug, as if she really were lamenting that she was going to have to spank her so soundly.

"Then I'm afraid you'll just have to do so by showing everyone what happens when you decide to break them, won't you?"

Seeing now that she'd been expertly maneuvered into a corner with no possible hope for escape, Rhen planted her hands on her hips and let out one last long-suffering sigh; conceding defeat, but just barely.

"If you say so."

"I *do* say so," confirmed her aunt briskly, spinning her around by her good shoulder and sending along her way with a firm swat.

SMACK!

"Now march."

"Ah! Okay, okay!"

With one hand clamped tight over her freshly smacked right cheek, face twisting into a fretful grimace at the padding she felt there just beneath the soft material of her skirt (she'd completely forgotten she was still wearing a pull-up until that very moment), Rhen beat a hasty retreat out of the room.

"Oh, right!"

Only to skid to a an abrupt halt a moment later and scurry back in to collect the chair she'd just been sitting on, half carrying and half dragging it with her out into the front room while fleeing a chorus of tittering giggles from her friends.

"Ugh. This freaking *sucks*," she whined, just low enough so that nobody else would be able to hear her.

Finding herself suddenly hyperaware of the extra bulk crinkling quietly between her thighs with each and every step she took, Rhen tried to distract herself by muscling the surprisingly solid oak chair into the center of the room, deliberately facing it away from the big bay windows that looked out onto their front lawn so that no random passersby would get the chance to ogle her bare bottom once she was bent over it.

"I mean… I guess they were probably going to find out about these stupid things sooner or later. But still…"

Idly toeing her chair to be more in line with the leather couch behind it as she chewed thoughtfully on her right thumbnail, Rhen found herself seriously trying to decide if she was fast enough to sprint up to her bedroom to change into a regular pair of panties before her aunt started making her way up there to collect the belt.

But, considering the fact that said belt was currently hanging from a hook on the inside of her closet door, she seriously doubted that would end well for her.

"Humph."

Like, I guess pretty much everyone else in my life who matters already knows that I have to wear these sometimes, she conceded with a sour grimace as her daycare friends began trickling into the room behind her, forming a loose half-circle near the back wall and doing their best not to seem *too* excited about the upcoming festivities while Auntie Dana was still within earshot. *So there's really no harm in a few more people knowing, right?*

Truth be told, she could think of more than a few reasons why she didn't want a bunch of tweens that she played with on a regular basis knowing about her childish almost-underwear. Not the least of which being because she knew that any clout that she might have had as one of the "big kids" among them would evaporate the instant they caught sight of the brightly colored padded panties snugged around her hips. It was already bad enough having them see her get spanked by her aunt from time to time without adding *this* to the mix as well.

Crap.

Spankings were one thing, everyone got those (even if she insisted that she was way too old for them), but having to wear pull-ups like you were a freaking three-year-old? Now that was undeniably something only for little girls who couldn't be trusted not to wet their pants, and she knew that her friends knew it too.

Double crap.

Of course, Rhen supposed that she could try explaining to them that her babyish underwear was just a temporary punishment, and that she really did usually wear "big girl" panties (they'd all seen them enough times by now to know that she did, right?), but she doubted that that would really accomplish anything. The bottom line, unfortunately, was that as far as her friends knew, she was a kind of bossy college student whose "aunt" was fond of saying that she was getting too big for her britches. And, in just a moment, they were all going to see that those britches were actually pull-ups.

Triple crap. Crap, crap, crap!

Heaving out a long, frustrated moan, knowing that she had absolutely nobody to blame for the humiliating situation she found herself in now but herself, Rhen crossed her arms in front of her again and forced herself to stand up just a little bit straighter.

Just pretend like they're no big deal, she tried telling herself, sidling around to stand in front of her chair while keeping her back turned to her audience, her heartbeat ramping up all at once as she heard her partner start climbing the stairs up to her room. *Maybe if I play it cool I can convince them that I'm just wearing these as a goof?*

She couldn't help but snicker just a little bit as that idea crossed her mind, the fluttering butterflies inside her stomach making her shift awkwardly from foot to foot with pent-up, nervous energy.

Psh. Fat chance… Nope, I'm just gonna have to put up with extra teasing until everyone gets over this. Thank god it's not a diaper, at least… Dang it, Alana, why did you have to go and mention those yesterday?

Shaking her head to clear it of thoughts of the olive-skinned doctor and her stomach-churningly exciting threats of putting her into something even more embarrassing than a pull-up, Rhen cast her mind about for something else to focus on.

Maybe I should do something to get spanked next week once

I'm back to wearing regular panties again? she mused, pursing her lips and letting out a long breath through her nose. *That would have to work, right? I mean, it wouldn't even have to be like a "real" spanking. It would just need to be something that shows off my panties for a while. I totally bet I could do something just annoying enough to get Aunt Dana to give me a quick attitude adjustment. Hmmm… You know, it has been a while since we've had a nice, rousing chorus of Baby Shark…*

—

Far too soon for Rhen's liking, Dana came sweeping back into their front room clutching the wide black leather belt that her grandma had given them for Christmas in both hands, looking all too ready to dish out some serious discipline.

SNAP-SNAP!

"Alright, kiddo, let's get this over and done with," she announced brightly, giving the doubled-over length of leather a couple of sharp cracks as she strode past her naughty nice and over to the left side of the chair she'd set out for her. "The sooner we start, the sooner you and your friends can go play."

"Oh, really?" chirped Rhen sarcastically, grimacing in comical disgust at the ridiculously thick tool belt that would never fit through a proper pair of belt loops. "Gee, I've never heard *that one* before."

Her brazen bit of sass managed to draw out a few stifled giggles from her gathered audience as they shifted with anticipation behind her. Though, thankfully, no extra swats from her aunt.

"Alright, miss mouthy, that's enough out of you," she said instead with a small twitch of her lips, gesturing toward the chair in front of her with the belt. "Bend over."

Deciding that she really had nothing left to lose just then and feeding off of the reactions she was getting from her friends, Rhen kept her arms folded across the bedazzled front of her shirt and gave a haughty sniff, deliberately refusing to meet the older woman's gaze as she tossed her hair.

"What's the magic word?"

"Oooh…"

Now that one *really* struck a chord among her friends, and Rhen felt her stomach do several flip-flops in a row as she caught sight of the narrow-eyed look of warning her partner was giving her out of the corner of her eye. The annoyed look passed just as quickly as it came, though, and Dana instead just smirked.

"Do I need to go get you a bar of soap to chew on while we're doing this?"

She kept her voice sweet and conversational as she asked the question, but the hard glint just behind her dark blue eyes made it abundantly clear that she wasn't joking.

"I would've thought from the way you were carrying on the other night that you'd have learned your lesson by now. But if you simply *must* continue being sassy, then I'll be more than happy to oblige-"

"No ma'am, that's fine!" Rhen quickly reassured her, sending her dark ponytail whipping from side to side behind her as memories of bitter soapsuds replayed themselves across her taste buds. "I'll be good. I'm sorry!"

"Hmmm…"

Rather than acknowledge her apology right away, Dana instead kept quiet and continued to stare levelly at her. Letting the tension build inside the room as the gathered dozen or so kids watching their little exchange waited with baited breath to see what would happen next.

Surely they weren't about to see a spanking *and* a mouth soaping all at the same time, were they?

After nearly half a minute more of interminable silence, and just as Rhen was about to resign herself to intermittently spitting out mouthfuls of sudsy saliva all afternoon, her aunt at last gestured back toward the waiting chair and winked.

"Whenever you're ready, honey buns."

Oh thank god!

Shoulders sagging with relief, the petite junior flashed her partner a profoundly grateful smile and then took a hesitant step forward. Silently apologizing for the attitude she'd just been giving her and promising to make it up to her later, even as she continued dragging her feet over doing as she'd been told.

"Go on now, stick it out," pressed Dana with a false-impatient cluck of her tongue, one side of her mouth quirking up as she lightly patted the "it" in question with her doubled-over belt. "Show us all that naughty little tush of yours."

"Yeah, yeah…"

Tap.

"Oh! I mean, yes ma'am!"

Letting out one last shaky breath, warmth spreading up her neck to color her cheeks, Rhen at last leaned forward and placed her sweaty palms flat against the well-worn seat in front of her. Bending over to a near perfect ninety-degree angle and thrusting her bottom back just as she'd been ordered to.

"There we go…"

Now that she was in position, Dana wasted little time in stepping in close and flipping up the back of her skirt, casually exposing the red-headed mermaid that had been frolicking just out of sight beneath its pink-trimmed ruffles a moment earlier.

"Well, hello there, Ariel," she cooed, patting the beaming princess affectionately after she'd finished framing the folds of her niece's skirt around her hips, tucking the excess into her waistband so that it wouldn't slip back down prematurely.

Just as Rhen had known it would, the sight of her, the oldest "kid" among Auntie Dana's charges, in an oh so childish pair of training panties proved to be too much to take in without reacting and she heard a chorus of tittering giggles bubble up from behind her as everyone got a good look at her pull-up. Thankfully, though, whatever teasing comments her friends decided to make at her expense were kept low enough so that she wasn't able to hear them above the pounding of her own heartbeat in her ears.

I guess it's kinda hard to be catty when Aunt Dana is literally standing right there in front of you with a belt in hand, she mused to herself, staring down at the swirling wood grain pattern only a few inches away from her face with a wry grimace as a steel band of embarrassment tightened itself around her lower abdomen.

Even so, she was sure she'd still have plenty of opportunities to hear all about what her friends thought of her unexpected and humiliating choice in wardrobe later on.

Freaking, awesome…

"Can we *please* just get this over with?" she hissed at her partner, low enough so that only she would hear.

"In a minute, cutie pie," dismissed Dana with a thin smile, drumming the fingers of her free hand across the inside-out folds of her skirt. "Embarrassment is a part of your punishment, remember?"

"Yeah, yeah…" sighed Rhen, face still boiling despite her attempts to act nonchalant; no match at all for her partner's methods of "enhancing the disciplinary experience".

Which, she supposed, was probably the reason why she so rarely had to punish her for the same thing twice.

Well, usually.

Dana allowed a few more moments pass in tense silence, ensuring that everyone got a good look at her naughty not-niece's bare thighs and pretty pink pull-up before she finally got around to whisking the padded pair of panties down to her ankles, at last exposing the all too familiar sight of her smooth and compact bare bottom to her friends.

"Step out please," she ordered, lightly patting the backs of her calves in case it wasn't clear enough already what she meant. "I don't want you accidentally tearing these up again just because you were kicking around too much."

"Yeah, that would be just *awful,* wouldn't it?" agreed Rhen in a deadpan drawl, slipping first one foot and then the other free of her pull-up, before clamping her thighs together as tightly as she could to avoid showing off anything more than she absolutely had to to her gathered audience. "It's not like they're disposable and we have a whole crapton of them upstairs or anything.”

At least it's not a diaper, she added to herself with a silent sigh of relief, shifting her weight against her clammy palms on the smooth wood in front of her as the memory of Dr. Pierson's breath tickling the side of her ear the evening before ratcheted up the frantic flutter of her heart rate by leaps and bounds. *I uh... I guess things could always be worse, right?*

“Waste not, want not, cutie pie,” chided Dana with a low, playful chuckle, laying her niece's pull-up on the seat in front of her so that she'd forced to look at it and be reminded that she was just a naughty child as far as she was concerned throughout her entire punishment. “Now hang on tight, because these are *definitely* going to sting.”

“No kid-” Rhen started to bite out sarcastically, glaring daggers at the Disney princess smiling up at her.

*SWISH-**CRACK!***

“Aieee!”

Only to have her words be cut short by a high-pitched squeal of pain as she shot back up to her feet, clutching at her scalded seat and the wide band of boiling agony that her aunt had just painted across the centers of both of her cheeks.

“Holy crap, holy crap, holy crap!”

Her impromptu bare bottom boogie managed to draw out a fresh round of giggling from her friends, and it was only after several more hissed in breaths through clenched teeth that it occurred to her just how much of a spectacle she must be making of herself then.

“S-Sorry,” she grit out, hands still gripping her bottom protectively as she cast an apologetic, sidelong glance at her partner and did her best to ignore all of the snickering going on behind her.

“Hurts, doesn't it?” replied Dana with a self-satisfied smirk, arching a single eyebrow in a very “I told you so” kind of way as she shifted her weight to one hip, arms folded.

“Uh... Yeah,” mumbled Rhen, sheepishly kneading her burning bottom and suddenly feeling very silly as she pushed her lips out into a pout. "I guess you could say that."

"Well, good," sniffed her aunt, not sounding the least bit sympathetic. "Like I said earlier, I only plan on having this conversation with you *once*, little girl."

She gestured back at the chair in front of her with the belt then, the motion making its silver buckle clink against itself, and her face grew stonily serious once again.

"Now bend over."

Feeling her stomach lurch and her knees threaten to give way beneath her, Rhen nodded and slowly leaned forward to do as she'd been told, firmly gripping either side of the seat this time in an attempt to hopefully avoid any further extra-embarrassing outbursts.

Tap… Tap…

This time Dana took a moment to line up her aim, lightly rapping the surprisingly heavy length of leather against a spot just above her sit-spots.

Oh god… This sucks.

SWISH-*CRACK!*

Once again the belt bit into her bottom with a snapping report that made everyone inside the room (except for Dana) jump. Painting a broad stripe of vivid pain that flared molten lava hot for several hurried heartbeats before then burrowing deep down to form a pulsing, throbbing ache across where it had just impacted. But this time around, by some small miracle of grip strength and determination, Rhen was able to (mostly) maintain her position. Clinging to her chair for dear life as she stomped her feet and wiggled her hips.

"Oh my god, oh my god," she blurted out all at once, screwing her eyes shut tight against the pain as one foot bobbed up and down behind her in time with her exclamations. "Owie, owie, *owie*!"

"Are we starting to learn our lesson, young lady?" pressed Dana in a stern voice, taking aim once again before her niece had a chance to fully recover from her last swat.

Tap… Tap…

"Y… Yes-"

*SWISH-**CRACK**!*

"Ah! Yes ma'am!"

Sweating now, her breath coming in ragged gasps in between garbled exclamations and promises to be good, Rhen dragged a forearm across her eyes, willing the tears starting to blur her vision to go away. She was already having a hard enough time as it was not looking like a complete baby in front of her friends. She sure as heck didn't need to start sobbing like one too.

"Aunt Dana, please, I'm sorry…"

The words ended up coming out far more plaintive and whiney than she'd meant for them to, but boy oh boy did she ever mean them!

"Yes, I imagine you are, dear," agreed Dana crisply, maintaining her stern matriarch persona to the letter as she lined up her next swat, setting her sights on her girlfriend's quivering, bare thighs this time. "Now, tell me. What are you going to do the next time you want to ride your bike?"

*SWISH-**CRACK**!*

Again, Rhen let out a prolonged squeal as the belt found its mark about an inch or so below her sit-spots.

"Oh god, oh god!"

And, hopping from foot to foot while clutching her chair in a white-knuckled grip, she felt her resolve to maintain her modesty (and what little was left of her dignity) start to crumble around her.

"I'll-"

*SWISH-**CRACK**!*

"Aieee!" she howled as another ruthless lash landed across the backs of her thighs, even lower this time. "Aunt Dana, *please*, I promise I'll never forget to wear my helmet ever, ever, *ever* again!"

*SWISH-**CRACK**! SWISH-**CRACK**!*

"Excuse me, young lady?" Dana barked, her tone hot with maternal outrage as she added two more crimson stripes back-to-back to her girlfriend's dancing thighs, overlapping them across the two she'd just painted. "You didn't 'forget' to wear your helmet. You *chose* not to wear it."

*SWISH-**CRACK!***

"Yeowie! Owie, owie, ah!"

"And then you *lied* to me about it!"

*SWISH-**CRACK!***

"I'm sorry, I'm sorry!"

Sucking in a deep breath that escaped from her half a heartbeat later as a watery sniffle, Rhen risked letting go of her chair for just long enough to bat away her tears before they could dribble down onto Ariel.

"Sorry isn't good enough, little girl!" her aunt snapped as she brought her belt down again full force.

*SWISH-**CRACK!***

"Not when we're talking about your safety!"

She then took a moment to allow Rhen catch her breath, frowning at the angry red welts she'd managed to raise so far before leaning over to roughly brush her fingertips across them, making her niece hiss and squirm as she assessed how well she was making her point.

"I absolutely *refuse* to lose you over something so silly as you not wearing your helmet, Rhen Elizabeth," she growled, her voice a mixture of righteous fury and genuine fear. "You could have been killed if someone had run into you! You'd have gone flying and cracked your head open on the pavement like a god damn egg, and that would've been it!"

Everyone took in a collective, shocked breath at that. Auntie Dana's uncharacteristic cursing hitting them with more force than any silly swat from a belt ever could.

Though, Rhen would argue that it wasn't by much.

*SWISH-**CRACK!***

"Ack! Aunt D-Dana, I…"

Truth be told, she hadn't really thought about any of what her partner was saying, at least not seriously, until just then. Even when she'd been lying sprawled out on her back in Missus Hastings's front yard, or when the woman herself had been tearing into her for her recklessness, she'd only ever *really* imagined the "much worse" way things could have turned out for her as just being a broken arm or something. Not…

All at once the reality of how much danger she'd put herself in and how close she'd come to losing the happy life she'd managed to build with the woman she loved, all just because she didn't feel like wearing some dorky helmet, came crashing down on top of Rhen like a ton of bricks. Up until that point, the danger had never really seemed "real" to her. At least, not until she'd heard the unmistakable terror bubbling just beneath the surface of her partner's scathing rebukes.

Sure, she knew that people sometimes died in bike accidents. She wasn't an idiot. She understood that cars were big, heavy metal boxes that would always win in a fight versus some random squishy person. But that was like… other people.

That was different.

She was different.

Wasn't she?

"I…"

Swallowing hard against the lump in her throat, Rhen tried to answer again, but all that managed to come out of her trembling lips this time was the same word over and over again.

"I… I…"

And then the tears came.

Hard and fast, and completely overpowering.

"Oh god, Dana, I'm so sorry!"

Abandoning her position over the chair, she turned and flung herself at her partner, burying her face against her chest and clinging to her like she was a life preserver on a tumultuous sea as she sobbed into her soft summer blouse.

"Oh honey…"

Tossing her belt onto the chair with a muted *clunk* of metal on wood, Dana encircled her arms around the sobbing girl's heaving shoulders and pulled her in close. Kissing the top of her head and gently rocking her back and forth.

"There, there. It's okay, shhh…"

"I'm sorry! I just… I didn't mean to…"

"I know, honey, I know…" she murmured with a weary, loving sigh, apparently just managing to stave off a torrent of tears herself. "You're safe and that's all that matters, so just let it all out. It's going to be okay. You're safe and I love you…"

The two of them continued to remain wrapped in each other's arms for several more minutes after that, with Dana cuddling the crying girl and murmuring soothing words against the top of her inky black hair, while Rhen let her cathartic sobbing have free reign.

"Deep breaths now, honey buns, deep breaths. It's going to be alright…"

At some point, Dana remembered that they still had an audience. And, while maintaining her hug with one arm, she quietly shooed them away to go play before guiding her niece over to sit on her lap on the couch.

—

When Rhen had at last calmed down enough to speak without having to pause for breath in between hiccups and sniffling, she found herself both exhausted and relieved, but above all else, content.

God, I needed that.

"I'm so sorry, Dana," she murmured against her partner's chest, grimacing bashfully at all the moisture she felt there before pulling back and scrubbing at her red-rimmed eyes with the back of her hand. "Um… Th-Thanks for that, and uh, you know… stuff."

Even after all of their months together, and all the intimate things they'd done on a nearly nightly basis, she still found it impossible to say something like, "Thanks for spanking my bratty butt bright red, I really needed it!" out loud without all but exploding from embarrassment.

Even so, her "Aunt" had proven that she was more than capable of interpreting her bashful brat-talk.

Lord knows she's had more than enough practice by now…

Grimacing at herself, Rhen felt her stomach flutter pleasantly as the older woman's warm thighs shifted beneath her, sending a fresh twinge of not-totally-terrible pain throbbing along her aching welts.

Yeesh. She really wasn't holding back with that thing, was she?

"You are more than welcome, cutie pie," cooed Dana, all traces of her earlier maternal fury gone now as she continued to give her back a reassuring rub. "I'm always happy to help set you back on the straight and narrow whenever you need it."

Smiling softly down at her, she reached up with her free hand and wiped away what remained of the tear tracks on her cheeks with the pad of her thumb.

"Just *please* don't do anything that dangerous ever again, alright?"

"I…"

Blushing all over again, Rhen's brows knitted themselves together in a way that made it look like she might be about to swerve into arguing that she hadn't really been behaving *that* badly some more, before just as quickly letting out a shaky, self-deprecating laugh and melting against her supporting arm.

"God. You're so right. That really was stupid, wasn't it?"

"Just a little bit," agreed Dana, before flashing her a teasing smirk. "Okay, well… Actually, it was *very* stupid, but I didn't want to make you feel bad by saying so just now."

Rhen smirked at her in return then, starting to slowly approach her usual good-natured sass once again.

"Well, I swear it won't ever happen again."

"Good girl," cooed her partner, lightly tapping the end of her nose.

Then, after casting a quick glance around the room to make sure that it was still just the two of them and that they didn't have any spies lurking just around the corner, she leaned in close and captured her lips in a long, happy kiss.

"But," she went on to say once they'd at last drawn apart again, Rhen beaming dreamily up at her while her own lips drew back into an impish, hungry grin. "I do believe that you and I still have something to take care of before I can turn you loose to go play, don't we?"

Following the older woman's gaze back over to the abandoned chair and the belt sitting atop it, Rhen felt her stomach flutter again (far less pleasantly this time) and she tensed.

"Oh god…"

But, just as quickly as the tension had come, it was gone.

"Yes," she sighed, rolling her eyes in exhausted exasperation. "I guess we do, don't we?"

"Awww, don't look so pouty," sing-songed Dana as she tickled her along the inside of her thighs, coaxing another smile out of her as she squirmed around on her lap. "I *did* say that I was going to tear your cute little butt up, remember?"

"Y-Yeah," Rhen managed to get out around a fit of giggles, before scrambling up off of her lap to escape her wriggling fingers before they could close in on the junction between her thighs. "I guess you did, huh?"

Climbing languidly back up after her, Dana gestured toward the chair with its waiting belt and smiling Disney princess pull-up and leveled an expectant look at her girlfriend.

"Then, in that case, I'd suggest you bend over. You and I are *far* from finished here."

—

"Wakey, wakey, sleepyhead," cooed Dana, drawing back the covers on her snoozing girlfriend some hours later. "Awww…"

Smiling down at the bare bottomed cutie she found curled up on her side beneath the blankets, cuddling her stuffed teddy bear and penguin and clearly having decided to make herself more comfortable by stripping down to just her camisole, she leaned forward and brushed her lips ever so gently against her temple.

"Come on now, hon, everyone's gone home for the day. Get up so we can get dinner started."

"Mmmm…" the younger girl mumbled, rolling over onto her other side in an attempt to get away from whatever it was that was so rudely attempting to interrupt her nap. "Gimme five more minutes…"

Between the early summer heat, the emotional turmoil of that afternoon, and what looked to still be a *very* sore bottom and thighs, Dana wasn't at all surprised to find that her not-niece had run out of steam after only an hour or so of playing with her friends in the back yard once she'd been let out of the corner. Heck, if she hadn't had about a hundred little things to take care of, and a dozen or so kids of varying degrees of brattiness to keep an eye on, she would have been snuggled up right there with her!

Still, though, that wasn't to say she couldn't make up for lost time now.

"Five more minutes, huh?" she purred, rolling Rhen all the way over onto her stomach before settling her hands on either side of her narrow hips and drawing her back so that she was kneeling with her perfectly round and adorable little caboose thrust high into the air while she continued to drool into their pillows. "I think I can work with that."

"Mmmm," mumbled the younger girl again, her voice thick with sleep as she shifted her knees a bit further forward to better accommodate wherever her fingers might want to roam. "Better make it ten."

Dana was slightly surprised, and more than a little amused, by her girlfriend's apparent willingness to comply with the extremely revealing position that she'd just been arranged into, but she wasn't about to start complaining. Even after all of their time together, Rhen still blushed scarlet whenever she had her panties pulled down for her before a spanking (and not just when they were out in public as "aunt" and "niece"), but it seemed that for the moment at least, she was content to simply lie sprawled out face-first across the mattress in the room they shared with her rosy rump thrust up high and her soft thighs parted just wide enough to show off all that lay hidden between.

"My goodness. I swear you are just too darn cute sometimes."

Fishing her phone from of her front pocket, Dana set about snapping a handful of pictures of her girlfriend from several different angles. After all, results *that* impressive needed to be preserved for posterity.

And reviewed again and again in greater detail with her magic wand later on that evening after she'd tucked Rhen in for bed.

"Stripes definitely make your butt look fantastic."

Gnawing hungrily at her lower lip, she sidled in nice and close and dragged a single, well-manicured fingernail across a particularly vivid carmine ridge spanning from one cheek to the other in a near perfect horizontal line.

"Oh yes."

Her trailing touch produced a shock of goosebumps as it made its way across the two perfectly round and yielding cheeks being presented to her, and the sight of them in that moment made something deep within her stir with a primal need that took all of her self-control not to act upon right there and then.

They *did* need to get going on dinner, after all.

"I think I like these even better than switch marks."

Rhen snorted into her pillow at that. Apparently awake enough now to appreciate the compliment, but clearly not in any rush to get up as a visible shiver ran through her petite frame.

"Y-You don't say?"

"I do indeed," chuckled Dana, settling down onto the mattress behind her and thumbing open the tube of moisturizer she'd brought with her. "Now then, you just relax and we'll see if I can't work out some of that soreness for you, alright?"

She could tell that Rhen was just about to answer back with something sassy, because of course she was, but her words were cut short by a throaty gasp and then a prolonged and very satisfied sounding moan as the first blessedly cool droplets of soothing cream dribbled down onto each of her inflamed cheeks.

"What was that, dear?" she prompted in a mockingly sweet voice, recapping and setting aside the tube before beginning to massage the pleasantly fragrant lotion into her girlfriend's battered backside, heedless of the little gasps and groans her strong hands wrung out of her as she worked her cheeks like a baker with fresh dough. "Go on now, use your big girl words."

Rather than reply, Rhen instead just buried her face even further into her pillow and arched her back to give her better access to all of her most tender and sensitive areas.

As well as a few others for good measure.

"Mmmm… Such a naughty girl."

Dana was more than happy to accept her kind invitation, and proceeded to take full advantage of her unfettered access to some of her favorite places on her favorite person. Dribbling still more lotion down along her lasciviously parted cheeks and working it in with meticulous care over every inch of her inner divide, around her adorable anus, and then further south still; making sure to give her clit and folds all of the love and attention they deserved.

"Does thinking about the spanking I gave you earlier make you all wet, cutie pie?"

It was a rhetorical question.
Dana could see (and feel) very clearly for herself that it did.

Which was fortunate indeed, because at that particular moment her girlfriend was having a very difficult time forming complete and coherent sentences.

"Refusing to answer the question doesn't make it go away, you know," she teased, lightly rolling her swollen bud between her fingertips. "Do I need to check the sheets to see if you wet the bed while you were napping?"

"Ah!"

"Hmmm…" chuckled Dana in response to that particularly vocal gasp. "You don't say?"

Then, because she considered herself nothing if not thorough, she started to work two tingling fingers deep inside of her panting girlfriend. Lazily pumping them in and out while her free hand continued to work the welts all along her thighs and tender cheeks. This time around, though (unlike two nights ago), she didn't stop when she felt Rhen starting to contract around her fingers, her muffled breathing shooting up an octave or two higher as she drew closer and closer to the edge of release. Instead, she kept right on taking her with her hand, all the while murmuring sweet nothings in a low voice.

"Mmmm… I bet sitting down for dinner tonight is going to be *so* much fun with all these pretty marks to keep you company. Maybe we should bring down a pillow or two for you to sit on so you don't have to eat standing up?"

Dana knew that Rhen definitely had a few key phrases that drove her wild, and she was not at all surprised to find that as she leaned over and purred right into her ear, "I can't believe you were being *such* a little sassmuffin today while I was getting you ready for your spanking. You know, I think I might just have to put you back over my knee again at bedtime since you were acting *so* naughty," that her panting little brat tossed her head back and let out a single, prolonged moan and tightened even more around her fingers.

Then, a moment later, she felt the spasms of one heck of an orgasm overtaking her; sweeping her off into oblivion as she collapsed against the mattress, totally spent.

"My, my," cooed Dana, pulling her fingers free once her girlfriend released her death grip on them.

She took her time sucking them clean, savoring the familiar tastes she found there and watching the younger girl's shoulders rise and fall as her shallow breathing gradually gave way to the slow, deep breaths she took when she was starting to come back to Earth.

"Did you enjoy that, cutie pie?"

"Oh god, yes," groaned Rhen contentedly, not bothering to look away as her cheeks flushed in a way that had nothing at all to do with her heavy breathing.

"Awww, I'm so glad to hear that!" answered Dana in turn

with a bright laugh, lightly slapping the way too inviting set of cheeks stretched out before her like a maroon pair of bongos.

POP! POP!

Honestly, with the faint sheen of lotion covering every inch of them, highlighting their every perfect little curve and dimple, how could she not?

"Oh!"

"Oh indeed," she went on, her lips drawing back into another grin as she took in a deep breath of her own, breathing deep the scents of her girlfriend's arousal mixed with hints tea tree oil and aloe. "Hmmm…"

Planting her hands on her hips, she eyed where she'd just been attending to, licking her lips as she tried to decide whether or not to have her dessert now, or later.

Snorting gently, Dana rolled her eyes.

It wasn't even a contest.

"Get back up on your knees, honey buns," she ordered sternly. "You and I are *far* from finished here."

Chapter 5

A Casual Chat with Auntie Dana

With the last of her discipline for being so irresponsible on her bike finally taken care of and behind them now, things quickly returned back to normal for Rhen and her Auntie Dana. And though most of her Saturday that weekend was spent out in their neighbor's back yard, sweating under the mid-May summer sun as she wrestled with Missus Hastings's frustratingly underpowered lawnmower and criminally heavy weed-whacker, that didn't stop the petite junior from throwing herself into enjoying every single moment of the three week break she'd been allotted before the start of her next round of classes with every ounce of her considerable enthusiasm.

Which, basically just amounted to her sleeping in until her partner came storming in to drag her down for breakfast in the morning, playing with her friends at the daycare for a little while in the early afternoon (something which was more than a little awkward since they all still assumed she was wearing a pull-up underneath her shorts), and lots and lots of lounging around in her bedroom; playing on her computer, chatting with her friends, and just plain old being lazy. No homework. No tests to study for. Just peace and quiet as she whiled away her mini summer vacation without a single care in the world.

It might have been short, but at least it was fun.

And it was about to get a whole lot better!

—

Truth be told, Rhen had been hoping that she'd be able to take the entire summer semester off so that she could *really* let her academic batteries recharge before her classes got underway in the fall and she lost all of her free time. But, when she'd tried floating that idea past Dana a few weeks earlier, she'd shut her down almost immediately.

"There is no way on god's green earth that I'm going to let you put your education on hold just because you don't feel like doing your homework, missy!" she'd declared with an indignant huff, just before yanking her leggings and panties down to her knees and hauling her across her lap at her computer desk. "You've already got nearly a monthlong break before the summer semester starts up, so you'd better just quit your whining right now before I give you something to whine about. You hear me?"

SMACK!

Quitting her whining was proving to be a lot easier said than done for poor Rhen just then, and it took a supreme effort of will on her part not to point out to her partner that she was already giving her plenty to carry on about as she began bouncing her palm off of her bare backside in a rapid-fire staccato that left stinging bright pink handprints wherever it landed.

"Oh my god, Aunt Dan- Ack!" she moaned, her annoyance bubbling up and out of her in the form of several extra syllables to her complaints. "Not so- Oh! Not so hard! I was just asking. Geez!"

"I think you mean you were just *whining*," corrected the older woman, tightening her grip around her waist before she could wriggle free. "*And* starting to throw a tantrum too, I might add."

"It wasn't a tantrum-!" gasped an indignant Rhen.

SMACK! SMACK! SMACK!

"Urk! Owie, owie!"

Only to have her totally well-reasoned arguments dissolve into pained grunts and exaggerated yelps as her partner turned up the heat on her sit-spots.

"So you were just stomping around in the kitchen and slamming cabinet doors because…?"

"Um… Because I, uh… I wanted to, uh…"

Sensing that there was no good answer to that particular

question, Rhen decided to ignore it entirely and return back to the matter at hand. She couldn't let her bossy boots auntie shift the goalpost on her, after all.

"God, this is so unfair!" she harrumphed, pressing her lips together into a puckered scowl as she scissored her ankles back and forth behind her more so out of petulance than actual pain. "It's not like one stupid semester would make that big of a difference, you know."

"Uh-huh," answered Dana dryly, upping the tempo of her swats as she rolled her eyes. "And what exactly happened the *last* time you decided to start slacking off in your studies, little girl? Hmmm? I seem to recall a *very* fretful sophomore on the verge of getting kicked out of her dorm last summer just because she'd been dragging her feet on taking the classes she needed to."

SMACK! SMACK!

She punctuated her remarks with a pair of extra-hard swats to the backs of Rhen's dancing thighs, wringing out two equally whiney yelps from her as she did so.

"To say nothing of how she kept putting off finding a job until it was nearly too late."

"I- Oh! I…" stammered Rhen, her determined pout chipping away under the relentless force of her aunt's pistoning palm as she tried to marshal at least some sort of rebuttal. "I, uh…"

But, try as she might, there was simply no getting around the fact that the older woman kinda, sorta, *maybe*, had a point.

Barely.

Slowing down on her course load and procrastinating over taking the boring core classes that she needed to graduate had definitely been one of the major contributing factors to her near-disaster of a housing crisis the year before. And, as she glared down at the softly bunched carpet fibers just a few inches away from her nose, Rhen had to concede too that the thought of being stuck as a semi-fulltime college student on a perpetual academic treadmill for the next few years was *far* more terrifying than the threat of a visit from Missus Hairbrush at bedtime later that evening if she kept on giving her adoptive auntie attitude.

"Okay, okay. You're right- Ah! You're right!"

"Well now, that was certainly fast," marveled Dana facetiously, continuing to pepper her naughty niece's shifting seat with elbow-powered swats that set her cheeks to wobbling perhaps more enticingly than she would've preferred just then. "I've only had you across my knee for maybe a minute or two, and already you're changing your tune. How wonderful!"

"Oh yeah, it's *totally* changed," agreed Rhen, just as facetiously. "So, uh… Can I get up now?"

As she asked the question, she tried levering herself up off of Dana's lap using the edge of her chair for support, only to be met by a firm hand pushing her back down between the shoulder blades.

"Um… Please?"

"Hmmm…" purred her partner at that, pausing to rub her barely warmed cheeks for a few moments, getting in a good squeeze or two here and there before resuming her swatting in earnest. "No, I don't think so."

SMACK! SMACK! SMACK!

"As lovely as your change in tune is, I think I'm just going to have to keep you here for a little while longer to make absolutely sure your attitude *stays* adjusted."

SMACK!

"Well…"

Dana stopped her swatting to rub again then, humming to herself in open amusement as her palm traced a languid circle around her niece's perfectly poised rear end.

"At least until dinner time."

"Hum-"

SMACK!

"Urk! Humph!"

Still, though, despite the butt blistering she was delivering (along with the sizzling lecture about procrastination that she launched into a moment later), Rhen was still relieved to find that her partner was at least somewhat sympathetic to her point of view. She definitely wasn't going to give her any leeway when it came to slacking off on her studies, but after a minute or two more of uninterrupted bottom burning, she began to slow her pace to only a couple of lazy swats every other second as a conspiratorial grin stole across her face, subverting her exasperated scowl with something far more devious.

"You know, dear…" she cooed, wriggling her fingertips down along and in between the younger girl's thighs, making her gasp. "Just because your break is going to be a short one, that doesn't mean it has to be boring."

Rhen didn't really think that getting to stay home all day and not having to do anything was "boring" per se, but the sly note in her partner's voice had her intrigued nevertheless as she craned her head back to look at her.

"Oh yeah?"

"That's right," sing-songed Dana as she busied herself with shifting her around across her lap, readjusting her position so that she was forced to straddle her left thigh while facing backwards, granting her full access between her splayed legs and inner sit-spots. "In fact, that's actually something I've been meaning to bring up with you for a few days now."

"It-" squeaked Rhen before swallowing hard, face flushing far warmer than her bottom just then as she felt her partner's feather-light touch across the folds of her exposed labia. "It is?"

Rather than answer her directly, however, Dana instead countered her question with one of her own.

"How do you feel about airplanes, cutie pie?"

"There, uh… There fine, I guess. Why?"

"Oh good, I'm so glad to hear you say that," her aunt laughed in relief as she began slapping along the as yet unspanked areas now available to her, taking her time to ensure that she didn't miss a single spot. "I didn't *think* that you had any problems with flying, but you never know until you ask…"

SMACK! SMACK! SMACK!

"Uh… Urk! You- Ah! You were saying?" pressed Rhen a few

moments later when it became apparent that the older woman had lost herself in pinkening her thighs.

"Oh! I'm sorry, sweetie," she laughed, lightly rubbing where she'd just been swatting before resuming her earlier pace. "I guess I got distracted."

"Gee. Wonder freaking why?" mumbled Rhen to herself, just loud enough to be heard over the reports of hard hand impacting soft skin that were filling her bedroom.

SMACK!

"Easy on the sass there, honey buns, you *are* in the middle of getting a spanking you know," chided Dana with an equally as playful tone as she blistered the insides of her girlfriend's thighs with ruthless efficiency. "But, yes, as I was saying. My friend Alana has this trade show thing coming up in a few weeks that she wants me to go with her to."

"S- Oh! So?" Rhen found herself snapping through gritted teeth, unable to quite reel the reaction in despite her aunt's warning, the novelty of her lewd position and the fun back and forth they were having starting to lose much of their charm as the heat continued to build between her legs. "Ow, crap, geez! Come on, that really stings!"

"I know it does," cooed Dana, not doing a very good job of sounding all that broken up about it. "But that *is* kind of the whole point, isn't it?"

SMACK! SMACK! SMACK!

"Wh- Ah! Whatever…"

Desperate for some small amount of relief, Rhen tried squeezing herself around Dana's firm thigh in an attempt to escape the extra-stingy swats that were now assailing her, hoping that the added pressure would somehow dissuade her from going so fast. After all, she hadn't been being *that* bratty in the kitchen before she'd dragged her up to her room, had she?

Unfortunately for her, she really had.

Frustrated about not getting her way, she'd accidentally broken one of their nicer ceramic plates when she'd set (or maybe slammed was a more accurate description?) it down onto the granite countertop next to their sink just a little too aggressively. And, while Dana would never *ever* punish her for something that was an accident (she'd broken dishes in the past when they'd slipped from her fingers while cleaning them without incident), she also had absolutely no problem with blistering her bottom raw if she wanted to throw a tantrum.

Well, her bottom *and* her thighs, apparently.

"Agh! Ack! Okay- Oh! Okay," Rhen finally yelped, trying (and failing) to inject a little contrition into her voice past the rising loss of control over her ability to endure the pain without tearing up. "What does this stupid- Urk! Stupid conference thing have to do with- Ah! With my summer break?"

SMACK-SMACK!

"My, my, aren't we the feisty one tonight?" teased Dana, delivering two lightning-fast swats in a row to the inner chubs just along the base of her naughty niece's backside. "It has a lot to do with your vacation, actually. And if you'd let me get more than one sentence out at a time, you'd know that already, young lady."

Cheeks tensed and teeth clenched, ponytail bobbing back and forth behind her with pent-up frustration and more than a little pain, Rhen let out an exasperated growl and then forced herself to relax. Sagging against her partner's lightly bouncing leg, she allowed herself to get lost in the sensation of her denim jeans bobbing against her clit for a moment as she attempted to recenter herself.

Which, thankfully, her aunt allowed her to do; pausing just long enough to let her catch her breath while she lightly kneaded her tender cheeks.

"Okay, alright, point taken. I'm sorry."

Heaving out a sigh and rolling her eyes, Rhen lifted a hand and made an impatient twirling gesture with it beside her.

"Go on, I'm listening…"

"Uh-huh," deadpanned Dana, gliding her hand further south to dig her fingernails in along where she'd just been swatting.

"Yes, I can clearly see that you're paying just the utmost of attention right now."

"I am, I am!"

"Mmhmm."

She kept her grip nice and tight for several more tense heartbeats after that, deliberately allowing the younger girl's worries over what might happen next to run rampant before finally letting go and returning to slapping her along the insides of her thighs. Albeit not quite as hard as before.

"So then," she continued finally. "This conference Alana's invited me to just so happens to be taking place during the second week of your little vacation. Oh, and just in case you're wondering why she asked me to come with her even though I'm not a doctor, and I'm sure you are…"

SMACK! SMACK!

"Oh yeah, *totally*."

Rhen shook her head with a bemused smirk, tucking a loose strand of slightly sweaty black hair back behind her ear.

"Humph," sniffed Dana, her eyes twinkling with undisguised mirth as she paused to pinch her not-niece a few inches above her left knee. "Well, smarty pants, the reason *why* she asked me to come with her was so that she'd have someone to keep her company while she's mixing and mingling with suppliers and pharmaceutical reps. Apparently, these kinds of things can get pretty darn dull if you're there all by yourself, and she figured that I'd be able to help liven things up."

"Y- Ah! Yeesh," Rhen managed to get out between breathy gasps, trying (and failing) to squirm her way out of her auntie's sharp grip. "Sounds boring."

"Noooo kidding," agreed Dana with an overdramatic sigh of her own, letting go and landing a nice, firm *SLAP!* directly between her girlfriend's pinkened, parted thighs.

"Eep!" she squeaked in return, back arching and legs squeezing together even harder now as fireworks touched off behind her eyes. "H-Hey! No fair!"

"Oh, I know," agreed Dana as she delivered yet another, more forceful, swat to the exact same spot.

SMACK!

"I just don't care."

Before attentively rubbing where she'd just been punishing, grinning from ear to ear at the dampness she found there.

"But hush now, dear. Auntie Dana is trying to tell you something, remember?"

"Yeah- Mmph… Yeah…" Rhen attempted to grumble, though really it came out more as a moan, tipping her head forward so that her dark hair could partially hide her smoldering cheeks and lopsided grin from view. "So, uh… What'd you end up telling her?"

"Ahem."

Clearing her throat, Dana once again returned to swatting at a leisurely pace.

SMACK! SMACK! SMACK!

"Well, as to that… As much as I would just *love* to spend two days straight looking at CPAP machines and downing as much free booze as the show is willing to give me, I would still need to figure out what I'm going to do with *you*, kiddo."

SMACK!

"I'd either have to take you with me, which would be no fun for you since I'd have to abandon you in some boring hotel room during the day while I was gone, or else I'd have to leave you home alone for the weekend all by yourself. And, honestly, I don't think that latter option would be a very good idea. You know how naughty girls and empty houses tend to get along, I'm sure. I would just *hate* to come home and find out that you've been throwing wild parties while I was gone."

"Oh, hah- Owie! Hah," grumbled Rhen with a good-natured roll of her eyes. "Come on, Aunt Dana, you can trust me. I promise it wouldn't be *that* big of a party."

SMACK!

"Ah! Seriously! Twenty people, *maybe* thirty, max."

SMACK!

"Okay, geez! I'm kidding, I'm kidding!"

"You had better be, missy," growled Dana just as teasingly, though she still kept her swats far from playful. "Because if something like that ever did happen while I was away, I can guarantee that you wouldn't be able to sit down for at least a month by the time I was through with you. Do you hear me?"

SMACK! SMACK! SMACK!

"Ow! Okay, yes, got it! It was just a joke," groused Rhen with a put-upon scowl, flexing her toes as she did her best to ride out the pain from those last three swats, finding that her partner's leg was more than up to the task. "But, seriously, Dana, I'm perfectly capable of taking care of myself for a weekend. I'm not *actually* a teenager, you know."

"Oh, I know you aren't, honey buns," replied the auburn-haired older woman with an amused snort, giving said buns a couple of heavy pats to help remind her girlfriend just what position she was in at that moment. "You just act like one."

SMACK!

"A *lot.*"

SMACK!

"Like, a lot, a lot."

SMACK!

"Like, if I didn't know how much you enjoyed being a naughty little brat, I'd be worried, a lot."

SMACK!

"Oh hah-hah…" bit back Rhen, far less sassily this time around as her stomach lurched and her captive hips continued to wriggle of their own accord. "Very funny."

But, unable to quite stop herself from trying to prove her not-childishness, she balled her sweaty palms into huffy fists on the floor in front of her and forced herself to press on.

"No, but really. I promise I won't burn the house down while you're away, and I'd be more than happy to go exploring on my own while you and your friend do your thing if you decide to bring me with you. A trip somewhere for a couple days actually sounds like a lot of fun."

That last sentence managed to get Rhen's stomach flip-flopping even more than her partner's threatening had, but she did her best to ignore it. She'd never been very good at venturing out on her own in strange, new places. She much preferred to stick with the people and things that she already knew, something which gave her partner no small amount of frustration any time she asked her where she wanted to go out to eat, and the prospect of navigating some unknown city all by herself (probably being jostled and bumped around by huge crowds of faceless strangers as she meandered her way through some random downtown street) didn't exactly sound all that appealing. But, she had a point to prove about not being a child (even if she tended to act like one, maybe, sometimes), and she wasn't about to say any of *that* out loud.

Thankfully, though, Dana (as per usual) saw right through her bravado, and was nice enough to save her the embarrassment of fessing up to her anxieties as she returned to busying herself with making sure that her thighs were just as well-warmed as the rest of her backside was.

SMACK! SMACK! SMACK!

"That's very kind of you to offer, cutie pie, but I think I might get some odd looks from the hotel staff if I were to let a presumably thirteen-year-old girl go wandering around all by herself without any adult supervision."

"But... but..."

Rhen set herself to pouting extra hard at this, puffing out her cheeks and glaring at the baseboards ahead of her as she tried to come up with something suitably scathing to fire back with. The only problem was, though, was that her partner had a point. Which made the entire process of arguing with her much more difficult.

"You know, I could maybe just like-" she started to argue, not exactly sure what she was going to say, but unwilling to concede defeat without at least one more attempt at proving that she was a big girl.

Her ID and debit cards *were* just in a drawer inside her aunt's nightstand, after all, and she was free to take them whenever she needed them (something which, depressingly enough, hadn't actually happened in nearly a year now). But, she knew too that trying to point out that she could just show their hotel staff her ID if they gave either of them any trouble wouldn't really fly either.

She'd been turned away from way too many R-rated movies because of her "fake" driver's license to want to go through that embarrassment again.

"Maybe I could…"

Her shaky train of thought was derailed, however, when she felt the pad of Dana's thumb begin to ever so casually circle itself around her puckered rosebud; forcing out a high-pitched squeak of surprise from her in the process.

"Oh!"

"What was that, dear?" the older woman teased, wriggling the first joint of the digit into her with practiced ease while her other fingers set to work rubbing along her damp folds. "Go on now, finish your thought."

"I… I… I, um…" Rhen stammered, unable to string together a proper sentence to save her life just then. "N-Never mind!"

Whatever. It was a stupid idea anyway… Humph!

"Well… Regarding what I plan on *doing* with you," her partner continued to purr, pushing and twisting her thumb around a bit more before pulling it free in preparation for round two. "I just so happened to have an idea that I think would make us both *very* happy. Would you like to hear it?"

"S-Sure!"

"Mmmm… Good girl," Dana crooned, leaning forward to nip at the panting junior's earlobe. "How would you feel about having Courtney and Abby come along with us to keep an eye on you while I'm busy? The conference is taking place somewhere out in LA and is apparently just a twenty minute drive from the beach, so there'd be plenty for the three of you to do while Alana and I are busy rubbing elbows and hobnobbing, or whatever it is you do at these trade show things.”

Straightening back up in her seat with a broad grin on her face, Dana began working two of her well-lubricated fingers into her adorable girlfriend’s even more adorable rear end.

“Ah! Oh… Oh god…”

“See? I thought you might like that.”

Slipping her digits past her perfunctory pouting with relative ease, Dana began working them in and out. Nice and slow.

“Also, I was thinking that maybe I could close the daycare for a few days and we could stay an extra week out there after the conference is over. That way the four of us could have some fun in the sun together, see the sights, and maybe even go to Disneyland for a couple days before heading back. What do you think? I know it wouldn’t really leave you much time to lounge around at home since you’d be starting school again just a week after we get back, but at least we’d get to celebrate your birthday somewhere exciting, right? Doesn’t that sound like fun?”

It did indeed sound *very* fun to Rhen, who immediately let out a squeal of delight at the idea, bouncing with unrestrained glee atop her partner’s lap and inadvertently working the fingers still pumping her from behind in even deeper as a happy bonus.

“Can we go to Star Wars land too?”

“I don’t see why not.”

“Oh my god, Dana, *yes!* That sounds awesome!”

Of course, at first she’d been more than a little miffed at the insinuation that she couldn’t possibly take care of herself (even as she’d gasped and moaned in time with her partner’s pumping), but she’d managed to get over that initial surge of indignation fairly quickly as it occurred to her that she really would have a lot more fun if she had her friends tagging along.

To say nothing of getting to spend her birthday at the happiest place on Earth.

Still, though, it also wasn’t lost on her that she’d basically just agreed with her partner that she needed a chaperone to make sure she behaved herself while they were on vacation. But, instead of facing up to that humiliating admission, she decided to sidestep the issue altogether.

"But, um…" she began hesitantly, her tongue refusing to wrap itself around anything more complicated right then as she did her best to keep her bottom relaxed just like her auntie had taught her to. "I, uh… I d-don't know if Courtney and- Ah! Abby would be able to… to- Ah! To afford to c-come… to come…"

"It definitely sounds to me like *someone* is about to come," snickered Dana as she continued to finger and stretch her girl-friend's back door with deliberate slowness, taking her time to ensure that she would be fully prepared for what she intended on doing to her once she let her up off of her lap while also adding matter-of-factly. "And, yes, dear, I'm sure neither of your friends can afford to pay for something like this out of their own pock-ets. But, luckily for the both of us, Alana said that she'd be more than happy to cover their hotel and travel costs so long as they can take care of everything else on their own. She can just write it all off on her taxes, so it's no big deal if they want to come along. They just have to be okay with being classified as 'support staff'. And, of course, I'll be footing the bill for any fun stuff they take you out to do, or that we all do together, so there're really no worries there either."

"Well…"

Rhen had to admit that if that were the case, then it seemed pretty likely that her two best friends would jump at the opportu-nity to join them for an impromptu vacation. And, sure enough, when she called Abby later that evening (sprawled out on her stomach in bed, the dark purple strap-on that Courtney had helped Dana pick out for Valentine's Day still resting atop the nightstand beside her) she'd said they'd be delighted to.

"You better believe we'll be there, girl!" she'd cheered, before taking a moment to shout across their apartment to her girlfriend to make sure that they actually could come with them.

Courtney had quickly confirmed that they were more than down for the trip, and with that, things had been settled.

"Oh my god, this is going to be so much fun!" Rhen had gushed just as soon as she'd hung up her phone, bobbing her ankles back and forth through the air behind her while Dana sat with her legs crossed at the foot of their bed, watching over her with a broad grin.

"It sure is, cutie pie. It sure is."

—

That had all been nearly a month ago now, and with the spring semester drawn to a close, Rhen was growing more and more excited by the day as the promise of a week of fun in the sun loomed ever closer. But, before any of that could happen, there was one last bit of preparation that needed to be taken care of first.

She needed a swimsuit!

Chapter 6

"Keep it up and see what happens, kiddo."

Despite spending more sunny afternoons than she might care to admit chasing her daycare friends through the sprinklers in her aunt's back yard while giggling up a storm, Rhen wasn't exactly a fan of water-based fun. In fact, it had been so long since she'd actually gone swimming (in public or otherwise) that she didn't even own a swimsuit anymore.

Not that she really minded all that much.

Of course, it wasn't like she *couldn't* swim. She'd actually been pretty good at it back in her early high school days. But, being as lacking in curves as she was, poolside hangouts and trips to the lake had never been something that she'd rushed to be a part of, and whenever she *had* been dragged to one (usually caught up in some sort of group activity that she couldn't easily talk her way out of), she'd always made sure to "forget" to bring her swimsuit with her.

Over the last few months, though, her apprehension and anxieties about the way she looked had diminished significantly. They were still there, of course (and she suspected that they probably always would be to one degree or another), but now the idea of someone seeing her partially or even fully undressed no longer sent her spiraling into a panic attack, and that was something she was *very* grateful for. And something too which she knew was due in large part thanks to her ever-supportive partner's constant encouragement and daily reminders that she was beautiful and that she loved her.

Well, that and her not ever hesitating to yank her across her lap for a royal butt blistering whenever she gave her a good enough reason to. Regardless of who might happen to be around to see them at the time.

There was nothing quite like a healthy dose of exposure therapy every now and then to help inure you to some of your more deep-seated fears, Rhen had discovered. And, while she definitely wasn't ready to go skinny dipping any time soon, she still at least felt reasonably sure that she could put up with being seen in a swimsuit by a bunch of random strangers on a beach without feeling like they were all secretly laughing at her. At least for a little while.

And so, that following Thursday after her ordeal with the heavy leather belt her grandma had given her for Christmas, Rhen, Courtney, and Abby descended upon their local shopping mall to find her the perfect swimsuit, along with a few other things too while they were at it, before they all flew out to California the next morning. Even better, after some begging on Rhen's part, which had mostly just consisted of her pointing out how cute she'd look in her new beachwear and how much fun she was sure the older woman would have stripping it off of her, Dana had caved and given her an extra couple hundred dollars (on top of the fifty that she'd already set aside for the outing) to spend as she saw fit.

So, with cash in hand, she and her friends set out to shop like there was no tomorrow. Intent on enjoying themselves to the absolute fullest before returning to the older girls' apartment for a fun-filled slumber party later that evening. None of them would be getting much sleep that night, they knew, and driving back to Rhen's house in the morning so that they could all carpool to the airport was definitely going to suck, but that was just fine with them.

They could sleep on the plane!

—

"Geez. This place is like a damn ghost town," observed Courtney, looking first one way and then the other as she hugged herself and gave a false shiver.

"Yeah, it's positively *spoooooky*," agreed the darker-skinned girl's bubbly girlfriend from just beside her, tacking on several extra O's as she too mimed a shudder and eased closer for warmth, looking up to her with overly dramatic pleading eyes. "You'll protect me if any zombies start coming up the escalator, won't you, babe?"

"Oh, don't you worry," snickered Courtney, leaning down to nibble playfully at the shorter girl's neck. "I won't let anyone eat you without your express permission."

"Heh. I love a lady who can defend my honor."

"Anytime, hot stuff," she winked, copping a quick feel of caboose while she was close enough to do so. "Always happy to help."

Overhead, inoffensive pop music from nearly a decade earlier was thrumming quietly out of unseen speakers set somewhere along the ceiling, lending the well-lit and largely empty corridors of the two-story building a pleasant (albeit somewhat hollow) feel to them as the three college coeds made their way out of the food court where they'd just been having lunch and into the mall proper.

"Seriously, though, you gotta love that all the schools around here aren't out for summer yet," Abby mused, clasping her hands together in an overhead stretch that arched her back and thrust her impressive bosom forward an extra inch or two as she bounced lightly on the balls of her feet. "With any luck, we'll have this place all to ourselves 'til at least four."

"Oh heck yeah!" exclaimed Rhen, slipping past the two older girls to see just how abandoned the mall was for herself, feeling the smile on her face grow much more genuine as she saw that there were indeed only a few people making their way in and out of a handful of stores in the distance. "It's like our own personal shopping paradise."

Which is something I am more than okay with, thank you very much, she added to herself with a silent sigh of relief. *I sure as heck don't need a bunch of stupid teenyboppers (or anyone else for that matter) eyeballing me while I'm trying to find a swimsuit that doesn't make me look like a freaking twelve-year-old.*

"You sure got that right," agreed Abby, tiptoeing up behind

her and pitching her voice down into a sinister baritone as she slipped her hands beneath the hem of her t-shirt. "Plus, now there's nobody around to hear you scream. Mwahaha!"

"Eep!"

Letting out a surprised yelp that quickly turned into a frantic giggle as Abby's fingers began attacking her sensitive sides, Rhen scrambled forward and rounded on her friend with a scowl; yanking down on where her top had ridden up as she glared.

"Or in your case, squeal, I guess," the blonde amended with a giggle of her own, meeting her glare with a wicked grin.

"Oh, you are *so* dead," growled Rhen in return, advancing on her with menacingly wriggling fingers of her own.

"You think so, bratty buns?" taunted Abby, mirroring her pose as the two of them began circling each other with matching grins.

"I know so!"

Darting forward, Rhen lunged for older girl's midsection, only to have her easily sidestep past her snatching arms, landing a quick swat to the seat of her short-shorts as she did so.

SMACK!

"Ow! Hey, watch it, jerk face!"

"Awww, what's the matter, Rhenny-benny?" she cooed, looking far too pleased with herself for the younger girl's liking. "You sure are talking a lot of shit for someone within easy spanking range, you know. It'd be a real shame if some incredibly good looking girl with just the most radiant smile in the whole wide world made you wet your pants right here in the middle of public when she caught you, now wouldn't it? But, hey, at least there wouldn't be anybody around to see it, right?"

"Sh-Shut up!" stuttered a now red-faced Rhen, faltering for half a step and just barely managing to wriggle out of the way as the other girl made to capture her in a bear hug.

"Oh? Did I hit a nerve?" continued Abby, the impish grin on her face taking away any sting her words might have held as she righted herself from her failed attack and turned to face Rhen with arms wide open. "I'm sorry, kiddo. Here, why don't you come on over and we can hug it out, alright?"

"Yeah right, I'm not falling for that one."

Abby's lips drew further back as Rhen said that, hitting her with a look that warmed her in several embarrassing places all at once as she did so.

"Oh yeah?"

"I… I mean, not again!"

Ever since she'd discovered that her former roommate was nearly as ticklish as she was, the two of them had taken to having these impromptu sparring matches on a fairly regular basis. And, although she almost always lost (even if she *was* only a couple of inches taller than her, Abby was still far stronger than she was), that never stopped Rhen from trying to best her friend. After all, running the risk of maybe wetting her pants if the other girl went a bit too far once she'd caught her was well worth it if it meant returning the favor in kind.

It hadn't happened yet, but a girl could dream.

"Alright, that's enough, you two. Break it up," chided Courtney with a tolerant grin of her own, stepping in smoothly between the two of them and snatching up an ear in either hand.

"Hey! She started it!" protested Rhen, rising up onto her tiptoes to relieve the small amount of pressure being applied by her former TA's thumb and forefinger.

"Yeah right. It's not my fault you can't take a little friendly ribbing," shot back Abby, sticking out her tongue. "You saw it, Court! I was just playing around, and then *she* had to go and start threatening me. I'm innocent, I tell you, innocent!"

"Uh-huh," deadpanned the tallest of the three of them, doing a remarkably good job of maintaining a straight face as she did so. "Well, I'm ending it. So knock it off before I find us a restroom that's big enough to spank you two in at the same time. You hear me?"

"Baaaabe," hissed Abby at that, face flushing even brighter than Rhen's as she danced around in her girlfriend's grip. "Not so loud! Someone might hear you!"

"Awww, what's the matter, hot stuff?" cooed Courtney, mimicking the other girl's tone from earlier as her lips drew back into a crocodile smile. "I thought you said there wasn't anybody around to notice?"

"There's still, like… people working here and stuff, though," mumbled the blushing blonde, pointedly keeping her gaze locked on the scuffed tiles in front of her feet before directing a scowl up at the older girl. "And, besides, we were just messing around. There's no reason to get all, you know… S-wordy about it or anything."

"Yeah," agreed Rhen with as much of a nod as she could manage with her ear still locked in Courtney's grip, all too familiar with how hard she could spank when she put her mind to it and not at all sure if she was entirely joking about finding a spot to tan their hides in or not. "We'll be good, I swear!"

"Mmhmm," drawled Courtney, not sounding all that convinced, but also not looking like she really minded either way. "We'll just see about that."

Then, letting go of the two of them without any further ado, she threaded her fingers in between her girlfriend's and draped her other arm around Rhen's trim shoulders.

"But, in the meantime, we've got some shopping to do!"

Nodding to herself, she began leading them away from the food court.

"What do you say we try Cashman's first? I'm sure they've got all sorts of wonderfully *age-appropriate* options in your size, bratty buns."

With those last two words, Courtney let the hand resting on Rhen's left shoulder glide down along the valley of her spine to give said bratty buns a fond squeeze.

"Ah! Um, well, uh…"

Slipping free of the tall grad student's loose hold on her, Rhen stumbled to an awkward halt, positively glowing with embarrassment as all too vivid memories of Julia (the effervescent saleslady from Cashman's) and the humiliating shopping spree that she and her Aunt Dana had dragged her on nearly a year earlier raced through her mind. It had been bad enough having the two of them picking out an entirely new (and frustratingly fitting for a young teenager) wardrobe for her while she was stuck trailing after them as seemingly little more than a living doll to be dressed and undressed at their whim, and she was in no mood to risk repeating such an outing ever again if at all possible. Besides, Rhen had little doubt that if the panties her aunt and her erstwhile shopping companion had picked out for her were anything to go by, then the ruffly, childish monstrosities that passed for swimsuits in the store's juniors section would fit her like a glove. Which was something that she *definitely* didn't want either of her adoptive older sisters finding out about if at all possible.

Oh god, they probably have Easy-Pull waistbands too... Crap!

Voicing any of that out loud seemed far too much like tempting fate, however, so instead Rhen did her best to affect an air of disinterested nonchalance. Picking at a bit of non-existent lint on her t-shirt and blowing away a stray strand of hair from her face as her friends turned back to see what the holdup was all about.

"I mean, I suppose we *could* go to some rinky-dink department store to look at swimsuits," she sighed, rolling her eyes for added effect. "But, like, uh… Isn't that kind of lame?"

"Heh," chuckled Courtney, arching a single, challenging brow at the shorter girl, who found herself looking away only a moment later after losing their impromptu staring contest. "And where would you suggest we go instead that meets your oh so discerning, and sparkly, fashion sense, *Rhenny*?"

Crap, crap, crap! She can totally read me like a freaking book, can't she? fretted the petite junior with an embarrassed grimace, before forcing herself to straighten up to her full height and once again meet the other girl's stormy eyes.

"How about Blush?"

Then, sensing that she'd need to feed into her friends' desire to tease her just a little bit more if she was going to get her way, she pressed on with a blush of her own.

"I mean, I *am* supposed to be parading around as a

thirteen-year-old, right?" she reasoned, clamping her lips tight around the rest of her words before she could point out that she was actually about to be fourteen, technically speaking. "And what kind of self-respecting teenager would ever be caught dead in something from *Cashman's* of all places at the beach?"

Mentally crossing her fingers, she played her trump card.

"Like, come on. Aren't you guys cooler than that?"

To which both Abby and Courtney let out simultaneous snorts of amusement. Clearly, they both saw right through her flimsy attempts to avoid adding any more childish items of clothing to her wardrobe, but on the bright side, neither of them seemed ready to deny her out of hand.

Which was definitely a start.

"Hmmm…"

Slowly turning to her girlfriend with the same sort of look she usually got whenever she was in the mood to make her favorite raven-haired junior squirm, Courtney and Abby drew in close and began murmuring among themselves, deliberately keeping their voices just low enough so that Rhen was only able to catch the occasional word here and there as she stood straining to pick out what they were saying from a few feet away. Try as she might, though, she knew it wouldn't help. This was a tactic they were both *very* well-practiced in, one they liked to use whenever she was standing in a corner post-spanking, and so she was left with little other recourse than to wait as patiently as she could while shifting from foot to foot and chewing fretfully at her lower lip as they decided what they were going to do with her.

Please say yes, please say yes, please say yes…

After several more excruciatingly long and nerve-wracking moments of deliberation, the two of them at last broke away from their huddle. Then, with an enigmatic grin on her face, Courtney began to unhurriedly close the distance between her and Rhen, Abby trailing just a step or two behind.

"Blush, you say?" she crooned, circling around behind her to lay a hand on either of her shoulders.

"Uh… Yeah?" replied Rhen, shivering despite herself as she gave them a light, massaging squeeze that nearly made her melt.

There was just something about the way the tall, athletic girl carried herself that always made her mouth run dry and her heart jump into overdrive whenever she was close. Which, she suspected, was a skill she'd probably been honing for years.

I bet she spends an hour in front of the mirror every morning working on her smoldering looks, Rhen thought to herself in a shaky attempt to not focus too much on the pleasantly warm body heat radiating just behind her, not to mention the faint hint of spicy perfume that came with it. *Poor Abby must be so flustered nearly twenty-four seven!*

As if sensing what was running through her mind just then, Courtney leaned in close enough for her dark curls to brush against the side of Rhen's ear, and she murmured, "I think that can definitely be arranged, bratty buns. But first…"

Before then winking at Abby, who with Rhen so thoroughly distracted as she was, had little trouble seizing hold of the Easy-Pull waistband of her short-shorts and giving them a sharp, downward yank.

"But first we need to see if that's *really* where you should be shopping," the blonde girl finished for her. "How old are we dressing today, Rhenny-benny?"

"Ack! Hey!" squawked Rhen, scrambling to try and snatch back her shorts as they sailed down to her knees, only to find that Courtney's grip on her shoulders had suddenly grown a whole lot stronger, keeping her locked in place.

"Uh-uh-uh," she sing-songed mockingly, still right beside her ear. "You just stay right where you are, little girl. Your big sisters need to check and see what you've got on first before we decide you're old enough to be shopping at a store like Blush."

"Yeah, we wouldn't want you wearing anything too mature, now would we?"

Pressing her knees together and moaning, Rhen bobbed in place as much as she could, positively mortified.

"Come on, you guys, this is *so* not funny."

Well, at least nobody's around to see any of this right now... I think.

"Looks like you were right, babe," chirped Abby, ignoring her whining protests completely as she took a step back to give her a warm once over that only served to further deepen the color in her cheeks; eying her dark blue panties and their pattern of shooting stars as they shifted from side to side with a broad grin. "She *does* have her big girl undies on today!"

"Of course I do!" snapped the tomato-faced junior, no longer struggling to get her pants back up since that had only worked them further down to her ankles, instead glaring petulantly at her friend while hoping to high heaven that none of the cashiers in the food court behind them were looking their way just then. "What else would I possibly be wearing?"

She chose to forget for the moment that her two best friends had helped her get ready for bed on more than a few occasions since her aunt had started using them as regular babysitters.

"Oh, I think we all know the answer to that one, kiddo," snickered Courtney, releasing her shoulders and squatting down behind her to pull her shorts back up for her. "But since you're dressed the part..."

She gave the area in question a couple of firm pats once she'd finished restoring its snug, denim covering to its proper place around her hips.

"I suppose it's only fair that we take you to Blush."

"Just promise not to blow all your allowance on bath bombs and body spray, alright?" added Abby, waving an admonishing forefinger while all the while still grinning from ear to ear. "Your auntie told you to spend your money *responsibly*, remember?"

Pouting just as hard as she could, Rhen folded her arms across her chest and let out her best harrumph.

"Keep that up, and you won't get to use any of it!"

Then, before either of the older girls could do anything else to embarrass her, she spun on her heel and set off in the direction of

Blush as fast as she could without actually running. Feet stomping and face flushed bright red, but her lips quirked up in a secret smile.

"Meanies."

—

Inside of Blush, surrounded on all sides by tastefully decorated hot pink walls and racks upon racks of trendy clothing, Rhen was immediately drawn to the skimpiest thong bikinis that she could find. Well, in between stopping to admire several different tops and pairs of leggings along the way, that is. Snatching up a few (along with a handful of promising looking pairs of panties that were buy three, get three free) as she began doing the mental math to see how far she'd be able to stretch the cash her partner had given her before she had to start dipping into her allowance. Thankfully, with all the sales going on that afternoon, the answer was: surprisingly far.

Besides, she was pretty sure that she'd be getting a lot of extra spending money from her (actual) aunts and grandma with the birthday cards they'd be sending her next week. Being so thoroughly demoted back to a bratty teen among her extended family members over Thanksgiving break the year before had at least come with a few perks.

Aside from a sore bottom at the deceptively capable hands of her Aunt Maureen, that is.

"Whoa now, not so fast there, kiddo," chided Abby, laying a gently admonishing hand on Rhen's forearm as she reached for a bikini that looked to be little more than the suggestion of a swimsuit. "You and I both know that Dana would absolutely blow her stack if we let you come home with something like that."

"Yeah, bratty buns," agreed Courtney, only half paying attention as she held up two different options from the very same rack to herself without batting an eye, examining her reflection in the mirror provided for the task and frowning thoughtfully. "Aim a bit more toward middle school, would you?"

"Oh please. It's not *that* bad," scoffed Rhen, doing her best to play the warning off for the benefit of anybody who might have overheard them as she shrugged out of Abby's grip and snatched up the swimsuit she'd been eyeing, copying Courtney as she assessed herself in the mirror.

It was definitely a lot closer to PhD than it was to middle school. That was for sure.

"Um… Okay."

She winced, twisting a little bit this way and that, hoping that maybe a different angle might suddenly make it all come together.

It didn't.

"I mean, alright, so it's a *little* on the skimpy side," she conceded as warmth began to crawl its way up her neck to suffuse her cheeks, knowing full well that she didn't have anywhere near the amount of guts required to wear such a daring bikini out in public. "But I could still, like, I don't know… Wear a bathing suit cover with it or something, right?"

To which Abby asked the obvious question with an amused snort.

"And what exactly do you think is going to happen when Dana sees you *without* that cover on?"

"Uh, well…"

"You know she's going to want to see what your swimsuit looks like just as soon as we get out of here, don't you?"

"Okay, yeah, but still…"

Grimacing in consternation and mounting frustration, Rhen blew out her cheeks in a huff.

"Lots of, um, you know… teenagers," she forced herself to push on, the flush in her cheeks only growing warmer as she caught the telltale twitch of her friends' lips at her tacit acknowledgement of her adoptive age. "Lots of… us, wear stuff like this, right? I mean, they wouldn't be selling it here if they- I mean, *we*, didn't, would they?"

"True," agreed Abby, drawing the single word out with a taunting smirk while Courtney chimed in from beside her.

"But those girls tend to be just a bit older than thirteen, you know, hon.”

“Yeah. Give it a few more years and then maybe you can pull something like that off,” finished Abby, completely in sync with her girlfriend as they both shook their heads in bemusement.

“Hey! I’d like to think I’m pretty mature for my age,” grumbled Rhen, opting to pout since she knew she couldn’t press her argument any further without embarrassing herself more.

Though, apparently, that wasn’t an issue for Abby.

“Mature or not, and experience has definitely shown that you fall way more into the ‘not’ side of things,” she crooned as she plucked the rejected swimsuit out of her friend’s only perfunctorily resisting fingers and put it back where she’d found it. “If you, or rather your dear, sweet, *auntie*, think that you’re really mature enough to be wearing something like this, *Rhenny*, then why don’t you just go ahead and tell us how many thongs are in your panty drawer right now, hmmm? Five? Six?”

Her smirk widened just a bit then, and she brought a hand up to the side of her face in mock-surprise.

“Wait. Don’t tell me you’ve had them stashed beneath all those pull-ups this entire time!”

A fresh coil of mortified exhilaration cinched itself tight around Rhen’s stomach at those last few words, squeezing without mercy as she did her best to swallow her leaping heart. In that moment, it was all she could do not to kick Abby right in her stupid shin just to get her to shut up. And, as she eased ever so slightly around to try and see if anybody else had heard her or not, she found herself wishing desperately that she hadn’t tried playing up the whole “I’m a cool teen” angle to get her way.

It didn’t usually work, but on the bright side, at least it was still fun to lose. (Even if it *was* monumentally embarrassing.)

“Okay, fine, I don’t have any thongs!” she admitted in a mortified stage whisper, just loud enough to be heard over the music playing in the store. “But swimsuits aren’t panties, so I don’t see why that should matter in the slightest.”

Then, feeling like she needed to shore up her reasoning just a bit more, she added in a babbling rush.

"Besides, it's not like Dana is actually going to see me in my swimsuit until after we get to California anyway. I'm sure I'll have plenty of time to convince her that whatever I pick is fine by then."

"You know we're flying out *tomorrow morning*, right?" cut in Courtney again, seemingly content to let her girlfriend take the lead on things as she continued checking out different swimsuits against the front of her clothes.

"So?" pushed back Rhen, starting to lose steam, but also feeling like she was too far gone now to just admit defeat. "We've got, like, a four hour flight. That's plenty of time to ease her into the idea of how great I'd look showing off my cute buns, right?"

"I mean, they *are* pretty cute," agreed Courtney, still browsing.

"No arguments here," seconded Abby, before going in for the kill. "But you seem to be forgetting that your auntie told us to send her a picture of you in your swimsuit just as soon we settled on one."

"Okay, yeah," harrumphed Rhen. "But you don't have to actu-ally, like… you know… send her one right away…"

Abby just let out another snort at that.

"Dream on, short-stuff. There's no way in hell I'm risking a trip over Dana's lap just to cover your butt."

And then she giggled.

"Or, I guess in this case, *not* cover your butt."

"Humph."

"Besides," continued Courtney, picking up right where her girl-friend had left off as she returned the swimsuits that she'd been inspecting back to their rack and picked two more at random. "Do you really want to be wearing something that shows off that much skin? What're you going to do when you end up having to go out with a spanked butt?"

"Hey, that's a good point!" exclaimed Abby, her bright green eyes flicking down to where Rhen's backside was doing its best to fill out the bedazzled denim seat of her short-shorts. "You think maybe we ought to find her something red to help it all blend in?”

“I say we go with white,” countered the taller girl, her lightly glossed lips quirking up into a teasing smirk of her own. “If she wants to act like a naughty little brat while we’re out, then she might as well show everyone what happens when-”

“Oh my god, you guys, will you *puh-leez* give it a rest?” interrupted Rhen before her friends could continue exploring that particular train of thought any further, casting another nervous glance behind her through her reflection in the mirror behind the clothes rack. “We’re going on *vacation*, remember? There’s no way Aunt Dana is actually going to spank me unless I really, really, *really* act up.”

“Uh-huh…” deadpanned her babysitters in unison, each flashing the other a knowing look over the top of her dark hair as they rolled their eyes.

“Well then, just to be on the safe side,” Abby pressed on a moment later, her voice thick with unspoken amusement as she reached past Rhen and slid aside several swimsuits before coming away with something that appeared to have some actual substance to it. “How about you go with something like this instead?”

“Oh my god, that is so cute!” exclaimed Courtney, momentarily distracted from her own search for a swimsuit by the sight of the one her girlfriend had just picked out.

It was a white two-piece affair with black trim around the edges and bright red cherries printed all across its stretchy material. The top was clearly made for a girl with a more modest bust like Rhen’s, and its full cups had a bit of extra padding and support stitched into them that would be sure to help whoever wore it fill them out nicely. While the top was fairly modest, the bottom on the other hand was far more brief, having just enough material to cover a respectable portion of the wearer’s cheeks, while still leaving them exposed enough to show off where they (hopefully) weren’t as lacking. It definitely wasn’t a thong, but it was still at least somewhat daring.

“You just *have* to try that on, Rhen.”

"Well…"

As she stared at it, imagining how she might look strutting down a sandy beach with it and maybe a cute, floppy sunhat on, Rhen had to admit that it actually was pretty cute. It wasn't exactly the ultra-sexy thong bikini that she'd been dreaming of all week, but it was still a lot less of a "middle school" swimsuit than she'd feared her friends might pick out for her.

That didn't make it any easier for her to say any of that out loud, though.

Not when it felt like everyone in the store was staring at her right then, quietly laughing at the silly teenage girl whose babysitters had just shot down her attempts to dress more maturely than she actually was.

"I mean, I *guess* it's okay," she grumbled, the words leaving her mouth before she even realized she was saying them as she crossed her arms in front of her. "For a stupid dork."

Arching her brows at that, Abby pursed her lips into a frown.

"Hey now, there's no need to take that kind of tone with us, young lady," she chided, doing her best to imitate the coldly commanding stare that her girlfriend seemed able to summon up whenever she felt like. "It was just a suggestion."

"Yeah, well, maybe next time try and find one that doesn't make me look like a walking, talking fruit stand, would you?" bit back Rhen acerbically. "Or, you know, just let me pick out my own freaking swimsuit."

Truth be told, she actually liked the swimsuit in her friend's hands quite a bit. But, the snickering she'd heard coming from a pair of college-aged girls only a rack or two away from them had suddenly set her on edge to the point where she was saying things without thinking.

"*Excuse* me?" demanded Abby, her eyes flashing with genuine annoyance this time.

Ugh. God dang it. Me and my big stupid mouth!

Part of Rhen wanted to apologize right then and there. To close the distance between her and her friend, squeeze her tight, and mumble that she was sorry for snapping at her like that and that she hadn't meant to hurt her feelings. But, embarrassment and anxiety had her rooted to the spot where she stood, and she soon found herself doubling down despite knowing it was a mistake.

"I *said*, your stupid, freaking swimsuit SUCKS!" she snapped, enunciating each word with exaggerated care and shouting the last one at the top of her lungs, too caught up in not admitting that she'd been wrong to care about keeping her voice down anymore. "Humph!"

Courtney just grinned.

"Uh-oh… Sounds like someone forgot to take her grumpy pills this morning."

"Yeah, no kidding," agreed Abby, letting loose an exasperated sigh and shaking her head.

She then locked eyes with Rhen and flashed her a roguish grin that managed to dull the edge of her stern tone.

"And she's about to get her bratty butt *spanked* if doesn't start apologizing right now."

"Wha-?" Rhen started to demand, before clamping her mouth shut tight and swallowing hard, her cheeks clenching nervously behind her as the girls she'd spotted earlier continued to snicker among themselves a few feet away. "N-Now hold on, let's not get too hasty here. I didn't mean to-"

"Didn't mean to call me a dork?" supplied Abby helpfully, winking at her as she took half a step closer. "Or were you just trying to say that my fashion sense is stupid?"

"Yes! I mean, no! Er… Uh… That is to say," Rhen spluttered, thrown off balance all over again as she tried to spin things in a way that would prevent her from taking an unscheduled trip across Courtney's lap in a nearby restroom. "I wasn't trying to say that your *fashion* sense was dorky or stupid, it's just-"

"It's just that you thought we'd let you get away with wearing a skimpy thong bikini even though you're way too young to be dressing like that?"

"No! I was just hoping-"

Abby's grin grew even wider as she continued to press her attack, keeping her voice loud enough to ensure that everyone around them would be able to hear her clearly.

"Hoping that we'd help you get away with trying to pull one over on your aunt?"

"Of course not!" exclaimed Rhen, trying (and failing) to sound wounded as she took a half-step back in time with the other girl's advance. "I just… You know…"

She looked down at her shoes, guiltily twisting the tip of one pastel pink sneaker into the faux-hardwood floor beneath her as she let her lame non-excuse hang in the air between them.

"Uh-huh," crooned Abby, moving in for the finishing blow with a good approximation of her girlfriend's natural, predatory grace. "I'll tell you what I *do* know, young lady. I know that if your auntie were here right now, you'd be trying that 'dorky' swimsuit on with a bright red bottom. Isn't that right?"

The color in Rhen's face blossomed to about the same shade of red as her hypothetical bottom at that, and it was all she could do in that moment not to stomp a foot in mortified outrage.

"I…"

Truth be told, she was actually super relieved to see that her friend wasn't upset with her over the things she'd said. At least, not if the playful gleam in her bright green eyes was anything to go by. But, ironically enough, that knowledge also made her want to dig in her heels and be even *more* of a brat now. The ebb-and-flow of teasing and sassing with her adoptive older sisters was something that was comfortable and familiar to Rhen, and although she knew that she was courting disaster with each moment that passed without a proper apology from her, she found that she just couldn't resist trying to see how much further she could push things before enough was finally enough.

And so, with a twitch of her lips that she quickly twisted into a grumpy scowl, she once again threw herself headfirst into her role as the bratty teen out on a shopping trip with her cool college coed babysitters.

"Look. I'm sorry, alright?" she snapped, throwing her hands into the air and letting out a frustrated growl for good measure without actually having to try. "I'll try on the freaking swimsuit, so just give it a rest already. Geez!"

Even as she was saying it, she knew that she was probably making a huge mistake. That she was hurtling past the point of no return at Mach speed. But, even so, the matching smirks on her friend's faces as she glared at them with every ounce of petulant indignation that she could summon had the words flying past her scowling lips before good sense could catch them and shove them back down again.

Crap.

Huffing out a laugh, Rhen's former TA went back to her browsing without a second glance.

"Well, you heard her, babe."

"I sure did," nodded Abby, setting the swimsuit she'd picked out back onto its rack with deliberate care before gathering up Rhen's small pile of things to try on from her arms and passing them off to her girlfriend. "You know, I really would have liked to have given her a second chance. But if this is the way she's going to behave, then I guess I don't have much of a choice, now do I?"

"Nope," agreed Courtney, rolling her shoulders in an easy shrug as she arranged the items she'd just been given across one toned mocha forearm. "But, hey, that's alright. We've still got plenty of time for an attitude adjustment before this place starts to get too crowded, so go for it."

She then plucked up the swimsuit that Abby had set aside and laid it across her arm as well.

"And in the meantime I'll just hold onto this until you're done with her. I still want to see what she looks like in it, you know."

"Um… Done with?" squeaked Rhen, attempting to draw back a step only to discover that she'd run out of room to retreat; knowing full well what the darker-skinned girl meant, but hoping that by playing dumb she could maybe put things off for a little bit longer.

At least until they were back at their apartment and away from any potential witnesses to her humiliation.

Her two babysitters just ignored her, however.

"Perfect," chirped Abby, easing up onto the balls of her feet to plant a quick kiss on her girlfriend's grinning lips. "Thanks, hon, you're the best!"

"Anytime," snickered Courtney, sending the bubbly blonde along her way with a firm pat to her seat. "Now you go show that little monster you mean business, yeah?"

Giggling, Abby threw a cheeky salute back over her shoulder. "Yes ma'am!"

"Now, um… Wait just a second," Rhen started to protest as she closed in on her, her brows knitting together into a determined scowl. "There's no need to, um… to you know-"

Abby was having none of it, though.

"Zip it, missy!" she snapped, raising her voice enough to cut across her hemming and hawing as she jabbed an accusatory finger at her chest. "*You* were the one who wanted to act all bratty after Court and I agreed to take you here and help you find a pretty swimsuit for our vacation. And *you* were the one who decided that she'd rather throw a fit than talk things out like a mature adult when she didn't get her way. Well, congratulations, you've just earned yourself one hell of a spanking."

"But… but…"

Batting away her feeble protests with a sharp swipe of her hand through the air in front of her, Abby seized Rhen by the upper arm just like she'd seen Dana and Courtney do seemingly countless times before and began marching her off at a steady pace toward the back of the store.

"The only butt I'd be worried about right now is yours if I were you, little girl," she declared loud enough for the benefit of everyone around them as she gave her arm a firm squeeze. "Now come with me."

"Oh, come on!" Rhen started to whine as she was led away, abandoning all pretense at feigning innocence in favor of dragging her feet as much as she could. "*Please* don't spank me, Abby. I promise I'll be good! Please, please, please just give me another chance!"

Then, seeing that she wasn't getting anywhere with that approach, she tried a different one instead. One that raised the temperature in her burning cheeks by about another thousand degrees.

"Ugh! This is *so* not fair!" she protested. "You can't just spank me like I'm some little kid. I'm way too old for this!"

It was a bald-faced lie, and they both knew it, but desperate times called for desperate measures. After all, who knew? Maybe voluntarily embarrassing herself might manage to convince her usual partner in crime to cut her some slack.

Abby just laughed and shook her head, though.

"Oh come on, Rhen. Has that *ever* worked?"

"No… Not really," sighed the younger girl in grudging defeat.

"Yeah, I thought not," quipped the blonde with a self-satisfied half-smirk, her voice firm and resolute in a very "I told you so" sort of way despite the undercurrent of amusement bubbling just beneath its surface as they continued to make their way further into the store. "Besides, it's not like you didn't see this coming. Courtney and I both gave you *plenty* of chances to get your act together, didn't we?"

"Yeah, but-" Rhen started to answer, before being cut off again.

"So then, I guess you've got nobody to blame for this but yourself, huh, kiddo?"

Again, Rhen opened her mouth to argue, feeling something extra-sassy bubbling just beneath her embarrassed consternation, but the unsuppressed snort of laughter she heard coming from one of the people they passed by along their way had her thinking twice. After all, she didn't need to make any *more* of a spectacle of herself just then.

Abby was already doing a good enough job of that all on her own.

Sensing that she'd won their little exchange for the time being, the buxom junior pulled Rhen in a bit closer as they marched and continued murmuring in a far quieter voice so that only she'd be able to hear.

"This is really for the best, you know," she crooned, letting a quiet giggle slip past her disapproving frown. "I mean, we might as well make sure that whatever swimsuit you end up buying looks just as good around your knees as it does around your hips, right?"

Rhen stumbled and missed a step at that, her stomach lurching with exhilarated embarrassment at the thought of what she might look like with a cute swimsuit hanging around her knees while she stood facing a corner with a well-spanked red bottom on the beach.

Wait a minute… Do they even have corners at the beach? Isn't it just, like, sand and water and stuff?

"Wha-? That's not… C-Come on!"

Thankfully, though, her friend chose to take her garbled mess of a reply as agreement and didn't press the issue any further.

"Good girl," she chirped instead, straightening back up to her full height and pitching her voice once more into something vaguely resembling stern and in control. "Well, not good, exactly. If you'd been being good, then I wouldn't be about to spank you. But I think you get what I mean, right?"

"Yeah, yeah…" Rhen managed to grumble this time, red-faced and rolling her eyes so that she wouldn't have to look at anybody they might be passing by. "Whatever."

"Hah! That's the spirit," snickered Abby. "Now come along, Rhenny-benny. You've got a date with my belt!"

"Huh? Your belt?"

Narrowing her eyes at the polka-dot dress that her friend was wearing, grateful for the momentary distraction, Rhen tried to figure out just what she could possibly mean. Surely she wasn't talking about the pencil-thin bit of decorative leather cinched around her waist, was she?

"Wait, does that thing even come off?"

"It sure does," confirmed Abby, favoring her with a mischievous grin that made it abundantly clear that while she was about to have a blast whipping her best friend's bratty backside, she understood too that they were just playing a game.

Mostly.

"And it packs a *mean* sting to it too. Heh."

"Oh… Well, uh…"

Unsure of how to respond to that, and secretly hoping that the tiny thing would actually prove to be far too insubstantial to make a decent spanking implement despite Abby's claims to the contrary, Rhen decided that it would probably be better if she just returned back to her pouting for the time being.

"Let's just get this over with…"

"Oh, I intend to," sniffed Abby, sounding perhaps a little bit miffed that Rhen wasn't as worried as maybe she'd been hoping she would be.

Which, to be fair, wasn't entirely without reason.

While Abby had given her more than a few bubble baths and had gotten her changed into her pajamas on several different occasions while she and her girlfriend had been babysitting her, she'd never actually *spanked* her before. Aside from the occasional surprise swat to her fully clothed backside, Courtney and her devastatingly strong arms (honed from years of competitive tennis and regular visits to their campus gym) had always handled taking care of any discipline that might have needed dishing out among the three of them. And, in light of that, Rhen was having a difficult time feeling all that intimidated right then.

Not when fun-loving, happy-go-lucky, chat your ear off on the phone for hours on end Abby was the one who would be handling her punishment.

"Smirk all you want, bratty buns," her blonde babysitter grumbled with a rather petulant sounding harrumph. "I can promise that you'll be singing a whole new tune by the time I'm through with you."

"It would kind of defeat the whole point of the exercise if I was only singing half of one, wouldn't it?" quipped Rhen without missing a beat.

"Cute."

"Thanks. I know."

Despite her attempts to remain focused and no-nonsense, Abby couldn't help but crack a smile just a little bit at that.

"I'm going to have to remember to use that one on Courtney later."

"Happy to help."

"Noted. Now hush up. You're supposed to be in trouble, remember?"

"Oh yeah, *totally*."

Shaking her head, Abby let out a prolonged, exasperated sigh.

"Keep it up, little girl. Keep, it, up. It's your butt that's about to get blistered, not mine."

Rhen was just in the process of opening her mouth to answer back, her next sassy remark right on the tip of her tongue and ready to go, when she thought better of it.

"Yes ma'am," she said instead, nodding obediently.

After all, a belt was still a belt (even if it *was* super thin), and a little caution never hurt anyone, right?

Chapter 7

A Nice, Quiet Spanking

As the two of them at last reached the back of the store, Rhen was seriously starting to wonder where exactly her now very determined babysitter planned on taking her. As far as she could tell, there weren't any restrooms hidden away among the displays of bras and body spray that she could be hauled into for a quick attitude adjustment. At least, none that customers were allowed to use at any rate. Which kind of put a major dent in the whole "let's drag Rhen off for a spanking" thing.

Rhen herself wasn't quite sure yet whether or not she was upset about this lack of a private place for a heated "conversation" or not. After all, part of her *was* a little curious to see just how good of a spanker Abby could possibly be. Sure, Courtney often coaxed her into tagging along whenever she went for a workout at their campus gym, but as far as the petite junior could tell, the heaviest thing her friend ever lifted on a day-to-day basis was her laptop.

It wasn't like physics majors were any more prone to working out than computer science majors were.

Rhen was just about to start teasing Abby over her rooky mistake of not planning ahead, when the bubbly blonde surprised her by veering them off in the direction of the cash registers.

Oh crap.

"Wait, hold on-!" she began to protest, fearing that she was about to find herself being bent over the conveniently waist-high countertop that they were suddenly speeding toward.

"You hush your mouth, little girl!"

SMACK!

Before immediately being cut off by Abby's sharp words, and

even sharper swat.

"I am so not in the mood for your crap right now."

The noise drew the attention of the twenty-something clerk working the register ahead of them, and as they drew up level with her on the other side of the counter, she turned her attention to Abby.

"Hello, ladies," she greeted without much enthusiasm, keeping her easy, vaguely bored, saleswoman's smile trained entirely on the taller of the two of them as she spoke. "Is there something I can help you with?"

"There sure is," confirmed Abby with a tight grin of her own. "Would you mind letting us into a changing room?"

"Sure. No problem."

Shrugging, the clerk snatched up a lanyard of jingling keys and began making her way around the counter.

"How many items do you have to try on?"

"Oh, well, um… None actually."

"Huh?"

Seeing the other girl's confusion, Abby's grin turned self-depre-cating and she drew Rhen forward half a step by her grip on her arm.

"You see, my little sister here," she began to explain, throw-ing an exasperated glower in Rhen's direction. "Has been a total freaking brat for me and my girlfriend ever since we got here, and I'm just about at my wits' end with her."

"Oh hey!" exclaimed the clerk, showing some genuine interest now. "Is she the one who was pitching a fit on the other side of the store about swimsuits or whatever?"

"It wasn't a *fit*!" protested Rhen, only to be ignored completely.

"Yep, she sure is," confirmed Abby with just the hint of a sigh. "We're going on vacation tomorrow, and she seems to think that it's somehow appropriate for a girl her age to be strutting around in a thong bikini. Can you believe that?"

"Hah!" scoffed the clerk, sharing in the blonde's amusement.

"What is she, like, twelve?"

"Thirteen, actually," provided Abby helpfully.

"About to be fourteen," grumbled Rhen, arms folded in front of her despite the grip on her bicep.

The two other girls just rolled their eyes and kept on talking, however.

"So… Yeah," continued Abby, attempting to steer the conversation back on track. "I kinda figured that it would be rude to just bend her over in the middle of the store and start wailing away at her bratty backside. Even if she might totally deserve it."

"Would've been entertaining, at least," quipped the clerk with a beleaguered huff that made her silver nasal stud sparkle in the store's track lighting. "You have no idea how much I'd like to do that to some of the little hell spawns that come through here once school is out. Like, Jesus, how hard is it to fold a damn shirt once you're done looking at it?"

"God damn kids," harrumphed Abby, meeting the other girl's gaze and smirking in a way that acknowledged how silly it was for the two of them to be complaining about the "youth" when they themselves were both just barely into their twenties. "I actually worked retail back before my freshmen year, so I totally feel your pain. But, uh… anyway. I was kinda hoping that maybe I could deal with *this* little hell spawn in one of the changing rooms back here? She still needs a swimsuit, you see, and I'd really rather not to have to put up with her giving me and my girlfriend shit for the rest of the afternoon, you know?"

"Oh, yeah no, that's totally fine."

Beaming brightly now, the reinvigorated clerk sashayed her way past Abby and her supposed little sister, moving off in the direction of the clutch of semi-isolated changing rooms tucked away into one corner at the back of the store.

"Right this way, ladies. Nobody's using the big one at the end right now, so I can totally let you have that one if you want. Plenty of room to swing in there. Heh."

"Awww, thanks! That'd be perfect."

"Yeah, *thanks*," grumbled Rhen under her breath, letting herself be steered away toward her doom and suddenly feeling a whole lot less confident about her chances of coming away from this little punishment session with only a lightly smacked bottom.

Abby's grip was surprisingly strong.

"Freaking… awesome."

—

Abby wasted little time in getting down to business just as soon as their eager to please clerk finished scrawling Rhen's name out across the placard attached to the front of their changing room door. Using a bright red dry-erase marker hanging from a string next to it to do so and framing it with a pair of hearts and a smiley face.

"Alright then, kiddo. Let's get to it, yeah?"

Bumping the door shut behind her with a hip, the buxom blonde turned and began advancing on her now cornered best friend with a grin that was just wide enough to show off the whiteness of her teeth.

"Hands on top of your head, if you'd be so kind. I don't want them getting in the way while I'm getting your shorts down."

"Uh… But-" Rhen started to reply, mouth running dry and heart suddenly beating twice as fast with anticipatory dread as she tried backing away, only to discover that a wall seemed to have sprung up behind her while she hadn't been paying attention. "Eep!"

"Come on now, chop-chop," chided Abby, clapping her hands to punctuate her point as she scowled at her. "Don't make me tell you again."

"Alright, okay, *fine*," ground out the shorter girl, doing her best to sound just shy of insubordinate as she moved to do as she'd been told, *slowly*, hoping that an extra dose of sass might help quell the rising tide of conflicting emotions swirling around inside her stomach. "Whatever you say, *Abby*."

"Uh-uh-uh, that's *Miss Jenkins* to you," corrected the

self-satisfied junior with a an admonishing forefinger, making full use of the scant few inches of height she had over her friend as she closed to within looming distance. "Is that understood, *little girl?*"

"Yes, Miss Jenkins," chirped Rhen, saccharine sweet as she rolled her eyes. "Whatever you say, Miss Jenkins. I promise I'll be good, Miss Jenkins. Your hair is looking extra-wavy today, Miss Jenkins."

"Ahhh… Music to my ears," sighed Abby, squatting down in front of her pouting charge and beginning to unfasten the front clasp of her short-shorts with her own deliberate slowness, clearly intent on prolonging her humiliation for as long as possible. "Now put a sock in it and stand still, will you? You don't want me to have to call that nice saleslady back in here to help get you undressed, do you?"

"No ma'am, I'm sorry!" squeaked Rhen, sounding far more contrite and sincere this time around as she straightened up and squeezed her hands together tight on top of her head. "Please, I'll be good!"

"Heh. That's more like it."

Ugh. She sure can play dirty when she feels like it, can't she? the soon to be spanked non-teenager grumbled to herself, suppressing another roll of her eyes as she tried to work some moisture back into her mouth. *I guess Courtney's been rubbing off on her… Greaaat.*

Rhen's new resolve to behave herself lasted for all of five seconds before she inevitably found herself speaking up again. The words bubbling up and out of her in a geyser of sass before she could stop them, rushing to escape the butterflies churning around inside her stomach.

"You know you can just tug those down, right?" she harrumphed, dipping her chin toward her waist while doing her best to ignore the red-faced girl glaring back at her from the floor-to-ceiling mirror just behind her happily humming best friend. "That's the whole reason why it's called an *Easy-Pull* waistband."

Freaking, duh.

"Oh, I'm well aware, bratty buns," crooned the only slightly older girl, drawing down the zipper on her shorts and parting their front to once again reveal the dark blue shooting star panties that she had on underneath. "I've seen Courtney and Dana do this enough times by now to know *exactly* how fast I could be getting these down. But, well…"

Abby looked up at her then, her face splitting into a mischievous grin as she swept the cascading sheath of her long blonde hair back over a shoulder.

"Sometimes it's more fun to do things the old-fashioned way."

She winked.

"Wouldn't you agree?"

"Wh-Whatever," mumbled Rhen, swallowing hard and not doing a very good job of sounding unconcerned as she watched her shorts glide down her silky smooth legs to pool around her ankle socks. "If you want to suck at this and take all day to actually get anything done, then by all means, go ahead. I'm not going to stop you."

"Oooh, it is going to be *so* much fun making your butt burn, you little brat," taunted Abby, rubbing her hands together in triumphant glee. "You know, I'm honestly half tempted to leave the door open just in case anybody wants to come by and take a peek at how red your cute little caboose is gonna get. I bet we could get quite the audience going if we tried. Who knows, maybe there's someone from the university out here shopping right now too? I could have *sworn* we passed by Madison Chambers on our way over here just now…"

"Oh, come on, Abby! That's not-!"

"But," the blonde continued, cutting her off as she softened her features into a reassuring smile. "That's really more Dana's style, isn't it?"

"I…"

"Mmhmm?"

With an annoyed huff through flared nostrils, knowing that she'd tempted fate more than enough for one day, Rhen swallowed the rest of whatever it was that she'd been about to say and instead pasted a mostly-obedient look on her flushed face as a fresh swarm of butterflies took wing inside her stomach; replacing her momentary indignation with something far more embarrassing.

"Yes, Miss Jenkins."

"Heh. That really does sound nice coming from you," mused Abby with a giggle, apparently satisfied. "I'm so glad I finally managed to talk Court into giving me spanking lessons. You have *no* idea how much fun it is being on the other side of the equation for a change."

Her gaze then shifted back down to the junction between Rhen's slim thighs, and her smile took on a decidedly impish edge to it.

"Plus, the view's not half bad either... You naughty thing, you."

"The view?"

Something in the way her friend had said those last few words sent Rhen's dark green eyes trailing after Abby's bright ones, and immediately she felt her stomach lurch and her knees wobble.

"Oh god..."

Burying her now smoldering face in her hands, heedless of the fact that she'd been explicitly ordered to keep them on top of her head, Rhen let out a mortified groan.

Okay, okay, just breathe. This isn't that big of a deal, she tried to tell herself, even as her best friend continued to eye the clearly visible damp spot on the front of her panties with open amusement. *Sure, you just had your pants pulled down for you basically in the middle of a store, and you're definitely wet, but that's alright... Abby has seen you like this before and, uh... People get undressed in changing rooms all the time, right?*

Gritting her teeth, Rhen willed herself to believe her own shaky reasoning.

Of course they do! That's why they're called changing rooms! This is just, uh... This is just slightly more intense is all. It's fine...

It's fine… It's fine.

She almost managed to convince herself too. At least until her panties were sent sailing south after her shorts with only the barest hint of cotton on skin to mark their passing, taking with them any lingering hopes that she might have still held that this was all just some elaborate bluff to scare her into behaving herself.

Dang it, dang it, dang it! This is so beyond not fine. Crap!

Letting out another groan into her cupped hands, Rhen awkwardly shifted her weight from foot to foot, unable to properly vent her feelings on the situation any further than that thanks to the still-warm clothing trapped around her ankles.

"Alrighty, kiddo, it's time to step out of these," sing-songed Abby as she gave the discarded denim's stretchy waistband a slight tug, undiminished in the slightest by her charge's grumpy attitude. "Do you need any help?"

"No. I'm fine," grit out Rhen through clenched teeth, face still covered as she lifted first one foot and then the other, allowing her panties and shorts to be slipped over her shoes and socks without looking. "This is so freaking not fair."

"Oh, I don't know, it sure seems pretty fair to me," countered Abby breezily. "You were being a brat, and now I'm going to spank you for it. Easy!"

Popping back up to her feet with panties in hand, she kicked Rhen's short-shorts underneath the low bench beside her and shrugged.

"Besides, you were the one who decided to keep on acting up after I warned you to knock it off, you know."

She grinned, and her voice took on a slightly more mocking quality to it then.

"But, then again, Dana is always saying that you need a firm hand to help keep you in line. So I guess I shouldn't be *too* surprised that we've ended up here, should I… *honey buns?*"

To which Rhen responded in the only way that she could think of right then. By thrusting her fists down to either side of her hips and giving her now free right foot a nice, petulant stomp.

"Humph!"

"My thoughts exactly."

But, even as all hope seemed lost, one last desperate idea to potentially avert the humiliating disaster that she was about to endure (or at the very least, mitigate it somewhat) occurred to Rhen, and she jumped on it without a moment's hesitation.

It was a long shot, sure, but it was still better than nothing!

Which was literally all that she had covering her bottom just then.

"Wait, Abby, please," she started to whine, doing her best to sound both contrite and obedient without letting any of the very real panic that she was experiencing at that moment slip through. "I know I deserve to be punished. Really, I do. But we're in *public*. People are going to hear if you start spanking me on the bare. Can't you at least let me have my shorts or panties back to help dampen the noise a little bit?"

"Hmmm… Dampen, eh?" snickered the blonde, eying the wet spot on the panties she held stretched out before her in either hand. "I'd say you've already got that part pretty much covered, wouldn't you?"

Rhen chose to ignore that observation as she pressed on, hands clasped together in front of her in supplication.

"No, seriously! Aunt Dana never spanks me bare in public. This isn't fair!"

Her heart skipped a beat as the half-truth came tumbling out of her without her even pausing to think about it, but it was too late to turn back now. While it was *technically* true that her partner had bent her over for a quick panty warming here and there while they'd been out of the house in the past (most recently when she'd been being difficult about buying name brand breakfast cereal while grocery shopping a few weeks earlier), that had never stopped her from baring her backside for a proper spanking whenever the need had presented itself.

Abby didn't have to know that, though.

"Is that right?" pressed her friend, hands on hips and looking both amused and skeptical. "So what about that time back in the dorms then?"

"Oh come on, that wasn't like *public*, public!"

"Suuure it wasn't."

"You weren't even there!"

"I know."

Abby shrugged, and then half turned toward the door to their changing room.

"But Courtney was. Would you like me to go get her and see what *she* thinks I should do with these?" she asked, waggling the younger girl's captured panties at her.

"No, no! That's fine!" Rhen quickly reassured her, waving her hands in front of her in a near panic as she scrambled to block her advance before she could reach for the doorknob. "Look, okay. So *maybe* Aunt Dana has spanked me on the bare in public before, but, like… That doesn't mean you can't cut me a little slack, you know."

"And *you* could have just acted like an adult and not thrown a fit," countered Abby. "But here we are."

"I mean, yeah… But still!"

Pouting at the smug look on her best friend's face, Rhen attempted to steer the conversation (and Abby's attention) away from bringing in Courtney as she sidled back over to where she'd been standing a moment earlier. Deciding that she'd need to make some sort of concession if there was going to be any chance of her getting her way.

"Alright, *fine*, keep the shorts," she huffed. "They're too thick, I get it. But could I at least have my panties back? I swear I'll still feel your belt plenty. It just won't be so loud is all."

"Oh, I really don't think you need to be too worried about that," dismissed Abby with a wave of her free hand, not sounding the least bit concerned as she began folding her captured pair of panties up into a neat, square bundle. "Between how thin my belt is, how loud the music is in here, and how far away we are from everyone else, I seriously doubt that anybody is going to hear anything.”

She smirked then.

“At least, so long as *you* keep your mouth shut and don’t carry on like you usually do, that is.”

“But-” Rhen started to argue, before giving up mid-protest and shifting gears to complain about her friend’s more recent jab. “Hey. I don’t ‘carry on’!”

“Uh-huh,” drawled Abby, her smirk not budging an inch. “Sure you don’t.”

“I don’t!”

“Alright, fine, fine,” conceded the older girl, holding her hands out before her in a placating gesture. “Call it enthusiastic reactions with lots of water works then. I don’t really care. The end result is still the same, you know.”

“Humph.”

“But… I’ll tell you what, kiddo,” she sighed a moment later, shaking her head in sisterly amusement. “I suppose if you simply *must* have your precious panties back for this teeny weeny, itsy bitsy, hardly that big of a deal at all attitude adjustment, then I’d be willing to return them to you.”

She held up a warning forefinger then, and her features suddenly grew serious.

“Provided, that is, you promise to behave yourself and not give me any more guff while I’m punishing you. Deal?”

“Oh thank god!” exclaimed Rhen, actually sagging with relief as tension rolled off of her shoulders in waves. “Deal!”

Ruffling her hair with a fond smile, Abby’s face returned back to its usual lighthearted playfulness.

“Just don’t tell Courtney I went easy on you, alright?”

“Of course,” the younger girl was quick to agree, still shocked that she’d actually managed to get her way for once during a spanking. “My lips are sealed!”

“Well, that’s one way of putting it,” crooned Abby, her own lips drawing back into something wolfish. “Now open up.”

“Huh?”

Confused, but eager to cooperate before her friend could change her mind, Rhen tilted her head to the side a degree or two and opened her mouth.

"Ahhh- *Umph*!"

And then promptly had her shooting star panties shoved right between her lips, filling her mouth with a wadded up ball of cotton that tasted all too familiar.

"There we go," sing-songed Abby, poking her impromptu gag all the way into place while lightly batting away the shorter girl's questing hands before they could reach it. "That ought to keep you nice and quiet while we're taking care of things."

To which Rhen glared, hard.

Oh, you are so dead.

"See? It's working already!" cooed the beaming blonde, seemingly oblivious to the venomous looks being thrown her way as she patted her friend condescendingly on top of her head. "You're welcome, by the way."

Breaking off her stare with a roll of her eyes, Rhen fired back with something sharp and biting that was rendered mostly unintelligible thanks to the panties muffling her words. Which, upon further reflection, was probably a good thing since they most definitely would have gotten her mouth washed out for a week straight had they been any clearer.

"Awww! I love you too, bratty buns."

After catching her up in a brief, sisterly hug, Abby then drew back a step, her playful features growing suddenly serious once again as she planted her hands on her hips.

"But that's enough stalling. It's spanking time! So, why don't you go ahead and bend over with your palms flat against the wall for me," she half suggested and half ordered, her voice brisk and businesslike, though with just a hint of mischief to it still as she jabbed a sparkly-painted fingernail toward the wall beside her. "Go on now, hurry up. We've still got things to do today besides spank your cute butt, you know."

"Yeah, yeah…" grumbled Rhen into her gag, her sour

murmuring emerging once again as a muffled mess that only managed to convey the general outline of what it was that she was trying to say.

Though, apparently, that was still more than enough to make her point.

SMACK!

"And can the backtalk, missy!"

"Humphth."

Stomping her feet instead, Rhen let out a disgruntled harrumph, and with a toss of her ponytail, turned to do as she'd been told.

Well, at least I've got a good excuse to buy those panties I saw earlier, she thought to herself with a wry grimace (or at least the idea of one) as her tongue flexed beneath the soft material pushing down on top of it, adding her own saliva to the moisture already there. *Although, I guess I really ought to put that thong back before either of them notices it with the others…*

Heaving out a put-upon sigh through her nose, Rhen leaned forward and braced her palms against the cool wall opposite the door that she'd been ushered through only a couple minutes earlier. Shuffling back with her legs pressed firmly together until her bare hips were thrust up and out in a sulky surrender.

She'd been spanked by Courtney in this exact same position enough times by now to know precisely how Abby wanted her to stand.

Or in this case, bend.

"Very good," cooed her babysitter, her voice positively dripping with delighted self-satisfaction as she sauntered around to stand beside her, only the slight tremor in her left hand as she laid it along the half-exposed small of her back giving away just how nervous she actually was right then. "Now spread those legs nice and wide for me, please."

She let the fingertips of her free hand wander down along the compact, yet jiggly, curve of Rhen's left cheek as she spoke, slipping them in between her thighs and using them to tickle along their insides to help coax them into a position which left her standing with her feet spaced about a shoulder's width apart, feeling very, *very* exposed.

A feeling which the younger girl was able to confirm was totally justified when she threw a dirty look back over her shoulder and happened to catch a glimpse of her spread-eagle reflection in the mirror behind her.

Yeesh, she winced, sucking on her gag as her brows knit together in consternation at the sight of her own smooth folds. *I guess it's a good thing Dana decided I needed a touch up the other day after all...*

"Awww, there we go. Perfect!" declared Abby, giving each rounded cheek being presented to her an exploratory squeeze. "We wouldn't want you to accidentally lose your balance while I'm busy whooping these adorable buns of yours, now would we?"

"How very altruistic of you," mumbled Rhen sarcastically, the wad of dark blue fabric wedged between her teeth thankfully muffling her words to the point of being unintelligible.

It wasn't like she needed to be giving Abby any *more* excuses to embarrass or discipline her just then.

"Oh, there's no need to thank me," replied the other girl with a tinkling laugh, taking a step back and surveying her target with a crooked grin. "That's what big sisters are for."

"Mmmhumphth."

Rhen snorted, but would have also smiled too had she been capable of doing so just then.

Whatever you say, you big doofus.

The two of them continued to stand there teetering on the precipice of that moment for what felt like a very long time after that. Neither of them sure of what to do next, nor willing to be the one to break the pregnant pause that had risen up between them. Eventually, though, Abby finally seemed to remember that she had a job to do and got to work.

"Ahem."

Clearing her throat in an attempt to mask her growing excitement, she brought her hands up to the pencil-thin belt at her waist and began to undo it. Her nimble fingers making quick work of the narrow silver buckle holding it in place there.

"Now, I *would* say that this is going to hurt me more than it's going to hurt you," she began to explain with a teasing half-grin as she wound the thin strip of leather around her right hand, shortening it to a more manageable length before doubling it over into a twelve inch whippy loop. "But, unfortunately for you, I've been practicing on a couple pillows at home, and I don't catch myself on the backswing anymore."

As if to illustrate just how skilled she'd become with wielding her belt, Abby sent it whizzing through the air just an inch or two away from its intended target, nodding to herself with pride as she did so.

SWISH-SWISH! SWISH-SWISH!

"See?"

Flinching, Rhen curled her toes inside her sneakers as sudden bursts of cool air buffeted her backside. Her as yet unmarked cheeks wobbling as they clenched and unclenched nervously behind her.

"Lucky freaking me…"

Even coming as they were through her panty-gag, the gist of her words was still clear enough to cause Abby's half-grin to blossom into a full-on smile.

"Hey, at least it's not *Courtney's* belt," she said with a shrug. "Now that thing is *scary*."

Shivering theatrically, she hugged herself at the thought of her girlfriend's belt, teeth chattering for good measure.

"Although, to be fair," she continued a moment later, drawing herself back up to her full height while rolling her shoulders in a quick warm up. "Mine isn't that much better either."

Then, without any further ado, she shifted her feet into a wide, stable stance and brought her arm swinging down in a fluid, sweeping arc that sent the coiled over length of shiny black leather in her hand searing across the lower half of Rhen's exposed cheeks at high speed.

*SWISH-**THWIP**! SWISH-**THWIP**! SWISH-**THWIP**!*

"Ahfth!" the petite junior yelped, shooting up onto the balls of her feet and bobbing her hips from side to side in a desperate attempt to shake off some of the sting that had suddenly blossomed there.

It didn't help.

After a moment or two more of fruitless wiggling that did nothing to diminish Abby's aim, she dropped back down onto her heels with a nasally harrumph. Brows knitting themselves together once again in consternation and worry as she glared daggers at the understated wallpaper just a few inches away from her face.

Oh crap…

Gritting her teeth against the surface-deep fire that was quickly kindling into an inferno across what seemed to be the entirety of her bare backside, Rhen's stomach performed several flip-flops in a row in time with Abby's fast-paced swinging.

*SWISH-**THWIP**! SWISH-**THWIP**! SWISH-**THWIP**!*

Yep. She's definitely been practicing.

Unlike the belt her grandma had given her and Dana for Christmas the year before, Abby's left two distinct lines of scalding fury about an inch or so apart each time it struck home. Which, oddly enough, somehow made the entire sensation about twenty times worse. Thankfully, though, *her* stupid belt didn't have nearly as much weight to it as the one her aunt liked to occasionally use on her did. As a result, it impacted with nowhere near the same amount of *oomph* that led to livid welts and bone-deep aches that throbbed for hours on end; reminding you of your punishment each and every time you stood up or sat down (or just so happened to shift your weight around too much without thinking).

Instead, it just stung like crazy!

*SWISH-**THWIP**! SWISH-**THWIP**! SWISH-**THWIP**!*

"Ahfth! Urkfth! Ow, ow, owfth!"

"Oh, quit your whining. It's not *that* bad, you big baby."

Easy for you to say!

Despite being a total novice when it came to spanking, Abby quickly found her rhythm. Swatting seemingly as fast as she could without actually losing any control over her aim or power. In no time at all, she had Rhen dancing from foot to foot (well, as much as she could given her wide stance) while yelping and cursing into her gag. Her words emerging as little more than a garbled mess of "Ahfth!"s and "Urkfth!"s punctuated by sharp exhalations through her nostrils.

But, on the bright side, it was at least quiet.

Even if Abby's lecturing wasn't.

"Are you-"

SWISH-THWIP!

"Starting to-"

SWISH-THWIP!

"Learn your-"

SWISH-THWIP!

"Lesson?" she demanded, marking each couple of words with an extra-sharp snap of her wrist that sent the shorter girl's cheeks to wobbling and bouncing in time with her stomping feet.

Rather than bother with trying to force out some sort of garbled mess of a reply through her saliva-soaked gag, Rhen instead just nodded hurriedly. Hoping to convey just how ready and willing she was to try on anything and everything either of her adoptive older sisters might want to put her in with only the plaintive expression in her rapidly watering eyes.

Again, though, it didn't help.

SWISH-THWIP! SWISH-THWIP! SWISH-THWIP!

"Good girl."

The grin on Abby's face was equal parts self-satisfied amusement and teasing malice as she continued to deliver swat after stinging swat. And, unfortunately for the quietly yelping junior she was directing those swats at, she was showing no signs of slowing down any time soon.

She always *had* been a fan of long aerobic exercise, Rhen seemed to recall.

"Okay then, let's just see if we can't get that lesson to sink in for a little while," declared Abby.

SWISH-THWIP! SWISH-THWIP! SWISH-THWIP!

"We wouldn't want to have to repeat it twice in the same day, now would we?"

Rhen just sighed and rolled her eyes.

Guess I'm sleeping on my stomach tonight…

And, gritting her teeth around her panty-gag, she pushed her bottom out just a little bit further, giving it a defiant waggle.

Oh well.

"Bring itth."

—

What Abby might have lacked in strength and experience when it came to punishing naughty girls, she more than made up for with enthusiasm. The well of seemingly boundless energy that she so often drew upon for gossiping and goofing around with Rhen (something which had gotten *her* into more than a few bits of trouble with her girlfriend over the last few months), now being put to use to power the lightning-fast, bottom-searing swats of her belt with outstanding results.

Soon enough, she'd covered the entirety of Rhen's squirming, sizzling backside in a crisscrossing mesh of thin red welts not all that dissimilar to what the switches her aunt sometimes trimmed from the crepe myrtle in their backyard tended to leave behind whenever she decided to wear one out on her. And, as if that weren't unpleasant enough already all on its own for the shorter girl, when there had at last been no more pale skin left to work with on her cheeks, Abby had simply shifted her aim further south, repeating the entire procedure all over again from the beginning across the backs of her thighs instead.

As humiliating as it might have been to admit to herself, Rhen was definitely glad that she'd been gagged by the time her friend turned her attention to her legs.

She'd absolutely needed it.

"Heh," giggled Abby, starting to sound just a little bit winded now after seemingly an eternity of non-stop swatting (although, in reality, it had only been about three or four minutes, tops). "You sure picked a lousy day to wear short-shorts, kiddo."

"Huh?" Rhen managed to grunt through her gag, blinking away a few stubborn tears clinging to her eyelashes as she turned from her pouty contemplation of the wall in front of her to follow Abby's pointing finger, feeling her stomach drop once again to her antsy feet as she caught sight of her reflection in the mirror behind her. "Oh my godfth!"

"That's right," the older girl sing-songed around another giggle, pulling her wavy golden tresses back into a loose ponytail behind her before redoubling her pace as she shifted her attention back up to the pair of cheeks that she'd been allowing to cool, intent on painting fresh welts on top of the ones that were already there.

*SWISH-**THWIP**! SWISH-**THWIP**! SWISH-**THWIP**!*

"Everyone is going to get to see just how naughty you were today."

*SWISH-**THWIP**! SWISH-**THWIP**! SWISH-**THWIP**!*

"And just how good of a job I did spanking you for it! Isn't that great?"

"Ughfth."

That's certainly one word for it…

Sighing heavily through her nostrils, Rhen let her head flop forward in grudging defeat.

Whatever. Guess I'm buying some leggings too.

She was just about to throw in the towel and admit that Abby was an excellent spanker and that she'd learned her lesson, when her eyes shot open wide and her head flew back in pain and panic as a particularly vicious set of rapid-fire licks found their marks along the extra-sensitive curves of her inner sit-spots.

SWISH-THWIP! SWISH-THWIP! SWISH-THWIP!

"Aieeefth!"

Outraged at this sudden display of spanking prowess, she was just in the process of rounding on her friend with an indignant glare, accusations of not being fair struggling to work their way past her gag, when there came a sudden jiggling of the handle on their changing room door. Followed just a second later by an insistent rapping when it wouldn't budge.

"Who is it?" called Abby, glancing toward the pair of well-worn sneakers visible just on the other side of the partially elevated door.

"It's me, babe," answered Courtney, her voice carrying her broad grin through the thin wooden slats as her feet shifted with unspoken excitement to see how things were going. "Can you get the door for me? It's locked and my arms are kinda full here."

"Oh, right, sure!" exclaimed the bubbly blonde, abandoning her attack on Rhen's hindquarters without a moment's hesitation as she skipped over to where her girlfriend was waiting. "Just a sec, I'm coming!"

Oh thank god, sighed Rhen internally, grateful for the momentary reprieve and all but collapsing under the weight of her own relief as a cool gust of air washed over her sizzling seat when Abby threw the door to their changing room open.

However, her relief was short-lived as it just as quickly occurred to her that her rear end was now on full display to the store at large (or at least the changing room area, at any rate) and that there were probably other people besides Courtney potentially milling about around them at that moment.

"Crapfth!"

And, oh yes, she still had her panties shoved in her mouth.

"Crapfth, crapfth, crapfth!"

And her legs spread a shoulder's width apart to help keep her "stable" for her spanking.

Knees weak and stomach lurching, Rhen hurriedly pushed

BEACH READY
NO SHOPLIFTING
Dressing Rooms under
24 hour surveillance.

herself away from the wall and was just starting to scramble toward an out of the way corner, when Abby threw a warning look back over her shoulder that stopped her dead in her tracks; pinning her in place with a glare that she'd somehow managed to perfect in just the last few minutes.

"You stay right where you are, little girl!" she snapped, though not with much in the way of actual heat, before then stepping aside and gesturing for her girlfriend to join them with a smirk. "Come on in, babe. I'm just finishing up with her."

"So I see," observed Courtney with an approving nod. "I'm glad I didn't manage to miss *all* the fun."

"Nope. We were just getting to the best part!"

"Awesome."

"Humphfth!"

Grinning from ear to ear, Courtney breezed her way into the now slightly snug changing room and deposited the mound of clothes she'd brought with her onto one end of the bench that Rhen had just been in the process of fleeing toward. Then, settling herself down onto it with a sigh, she leaned back and gave her hand a casual wave.

"Alright, hot stuff. Show me what you've got."

"Don't mind if I do," crooned Abby, positively preening as she turned her attention back to their petite and pouting friend. "You heard the lady, bratty buns. Get that butt of yours back to the wall and bend over!"

SWISH-SWISH! SWISH-SWISH!

"I can still see some spots that aren't totally red yet, and I'm not about to let you off thinking that you were able to pull one over on me. Now get moving!"

SWISH-THWIP!

"Ackth!"

Hopping forward, hands clutched tight to where Abby had just caught her with the tip of her belt, Rhen threw a petulant look back over her shoulder. But, other than that little bit of non-verbal sass, she didn't hesitate to take up her position again.

Truth be told, her backside *was* actually starting to lose much of the lingering heat that her friend had been doing her darndest to instill into it now that she'd had a chance to catch her breath. And if the bubbly blonde wanted to show off for her girlfriend a little bit before they got around to trying on the clothes she'd picked out for her, well… that was just fine with her.

She could wait.

Chapter 8

Dishing Out Some Discipline

Some hours later, just as the sun was starting to dip back down toward the horizon, Rhen, Courtney, and Abby stumbled into the older girls' off-campus apartment amid a torrent of gossip and giggling. Thoroughly spent from an afternoon of shopping and shenanigans, they kicked off their shoes and made their way into the tiny apartment's even tinier living room, unceremoniously dropping their new purchases onto the cheap carpet beside the rectangle of wobbly parquet tiles that served as the girls' front entryway as they went.

"Oh, hello there, couch. I've missed you so…" sighed Abby as she flopped down onto the threadbare faux-suede sofa that served as the living room's centerpiece, all but melting into its cushions as she propped her feet up on the scratched and pitted coffee table in front of her.

"Noooo kidding," agreed Rhen with a contented sigh of her own, mirroring the other girl's position (although, she had to slouch quite a bit further forward into the couch's embrace to get her heels up).

"Hey now, come on, you two," chided Courtney in mild exasperation, looking up from where she'd been rearranging their discarded shopping bags against the wall by the front door. "Feet off the table!"

"But baaabe," whined Abby, wiggling her toes in protest at her while Rhen sat statue still and did her best to look innocent. "It's just so comfy, and we've been walking, like, all day. Cut us some slack, will ya?"

"I don't care how comfy it is, it's still rude!" huffed the older girl, swooping in on them like a wrathful hawk and lightly batting their feet back onto the floor before taking a moment to recenter her decorative arrangement of succulents with a disapproving cluck of her tongue. "I swear, it's like you two were raised in a freaking barn or something."

"Sorry," droned Abby, not looking or sounding particularly apologetic as she rolled her eyes at her girlfriend's fussiness.

"Yeah, sorry!" Rhen was quick to chime in as well, sounding much more sincere as she sprang back to her feet on reflex while memories of her own partner's "reminders" about minding her manners briefly flashed through her mind.

She was hardly in the mood for two spankings in one day.

Well, at least not that day at any rate.

That belt of Abby's had stung!

"Heh. It's all good, kiddo," dismissed Courtney, her lips curling into a wry smirk as her keen eyes took note of the way the younger girl's hands drifted back to cup her backside protectively. "Your seat is safe with me so long as your feet stay off the table. It's just a little pet peeve of mine is all."

The warmth in her eyes cooled by a few degrees then as she cast a baleful look in her girlfriend's direction.

"One that someone here ought to know about by now."

"Oh, I'm well aware," smirked Abby, sticking out her tongue. "I just like bugging you."

Prompting Courtney to let out a longsuffering sigh as she shook her head, dragging a hand through her chin-length fringe of dark curls before turning her attention back to Rhen with a look not all that dissimilar to the one on her girlfriend's face just then.

"Look. Why don't you and little miss smartass over there pick out a movie or something for us to watch, and I'll get us some drinks, yeah?"

"Sounds like a plan to me!" declared the bubbly blonde with an incandescent smile just as soon as the words had left the taller girl's mouth, clearly having caught her second wind as she too sprang back to her feet and made a mad dash for the remote sitting on a corner of the ultra-fancy, cinderblock and plywood media center that was propping up their modestly sized flat-screen TV.

"Yeah, alright," shrugged Rhen with a bemused grin of her own, content to let her friend take the lead on finding them something to watch and only feeling a little bit jealous over how much sass she was able to get away with.

Geez. Talk about getting away with murder, she thought to herself with a snort. I'm pretty sure Courtney would have already had me bent over by now if our positions were reversed.

The fading welts on her still slightly sore bottom gave a small twinge of half-remembered pain then as she eyed the coffee table beside her. Picturing just what she might look like with her hands flat on its rough surface while her former TA dragged her shorts down her legs and…

Hmmm… Probably not the safest thing to be thinking about right now, wouldn't you say?

Shaking her head to clear it lest that sudden, embarrassing vision become a reality, Rhen turned her attention back to Courtney and asked with a sheepish grimace, "So, uh… hey. Do you think maybe we could order some pizza or something? I'm starving."

Of course, it was at that moment that her stomach chose to voice its own opinion on the situation with a prolonged growl. Something which amused both of her adoptive older sisters to no end.

"We sure can, kiddo," confirmed the taller girl, ruffling her hair fondly. "I'll take care of that just as soon as we get settled in."

"Yay!" cheered Rhen and Abby together, clapping their hands excitedly.

"Oh, and keep it light, will you, babe?" added Courtney, switching gears from her position beside the couch, her eyebrows knitting together in concern as she caught sight of what her girlfriend was starting to type into the search bar of their video streaming app. "I'm really not in the mood for anything too intense. I just want to relax, alright?"

"Can do, pretty lady," replied Abby, throwing her a sloppy salute over her shoulder with the remote before turning back to what she was doing.

"That means no horror," added Courtney without missing a beat.

"Awww," whined the blonde, fully rounding on her with a pout this time. "What about true crime then? That's, like… historical and stuff."

"Nope, none of that either. I don't need you and Rhen freaking out about people hiding in our linen closet waiting to murder you or whatever."

"Hey, it wasn't a linen closet," huffed Abby, arms folded beneath the ample swell of her heavy breasts, looking affronted. "It was a crawlspace in between the walls, and that totally did happen to someone in New York!"

"Yes, well, be that as it may," smirked Courtney. "I still don't feel like having to make sure the coast is clear every time one of you wants to use the bathroom tonight. So, keep it chill, yeah?"

"Fine…" grumbled Abby, before adding under her breath. "Spoil sport."

Now much more red in the face, she turned back to the TV and began backspacing on her original search phrase, muttering to herself all the while as she went.

"Geez. You ask your girlfriend one freaking time to check if someone's hiding behind the shower curtain for you and suddenly it's like you can't handle a little light murder mystery before bed… Talk about bullshit…"

"What was that?"

"Nothing," chimed Abby, not bothering to look back this time as she said it.

"Heh. That's what I thought, hot stuff."

Grateful for the imposition, but unable to say so out loud without embarrassing herself, Rhen flashed Courtney a thankful look and then moved to go join her friend in front of the TV while the taller girl made her way into the kitchen (which, in reality, was little more than a cramped nook at the far end of the apartment's living room, set apart only by a sudden shift from cheap carpet to cheap linoleum).

However, before Rhen and Abby could find anything promising to watch, they were both sent nearly jumping out of their skin by Courtney's sudden, booming voice yelling at them, or more specifically one of them, from across the apartment.

"Tabitha Marie Jenkins! You get your ass in here right this minute, young lady!"

"Uh-oh… sounds like someone's in trouble," crooned Rhen, not bothering to keep her voice down as a ghoulish sense of glee drew the corners of her mouth up into a taunting grin.

It's about freaking time.

"Psh. I have no idea what you're talking about," sniffed Abby, managing a good approximation of an unconcerned shrug.

Although, she couldn't quite stop herself from casting a wary glance back toward the kitchen as she did so.

"I'm waiting…" called Courtney again, her voice even, but clearly starting to lose patience as her bare foot made a distinct tap, tap, tap against the linoleum floor beneath it. "Don't make me come get you."

"Ah! Okay, I'm coming, I'm coming!" squawked the blonde, vaulting over the rickety coffee table and its artfully arranged succulents in her haste to do as she'd been told, tossing the remote control over her shoulder without looking as she went. "Here, Rhen, pick something good."

"Wha-?" the shorter girl started to reply, before scrambling to catch the remote as it bounced off of her chest and in between her fumbling fingers, only managing to snatch it at the very last moment before it clattered to the floor. "Oh heck no, I'm not missing this!"

Eager to see how whatever trouble was brewing between her two adoptive older sisters was about to play out, she skipped off after Abby just as fast as she could. Not bothering to mask her mounting excitement in the slightest as she tossed the remote carelessly onto the couch as she went. Eager as she was, though, she still made a point of refraining from making any taunting jabs as she skidded to a halt beside her blonde best friend in the kitchen. After all, she didn't want to risk having the already not happy Courtney lumping her into whatever mess her former roommate had managed to make for herself.

She could hold in her teasing until after the intimidating grad student was safely out of earshot.

"What's up, Court?" chirped Abby with a bright, cheery grin, only the fidgeting of her hands giving away her nervousness as she sent a sidelong glare in Rhen's direction.

Courtney was having none of her usual infectious affability, however, and instead jabbed an accusatory finger at the sink beside her.

"Don't you dare try playing all cute and innocent with me, missy!" she snapped, though the small twitch in her cheek gave away the lie to her apparent smoldering anger. "Would you care to explain to me just what the hell is going on here?"

With some reluctance, Abby directed her emerald gaze over toward where her irate girlfriend was pointing, unconsciously nibbling at her lower lip as she did so.

"Oh, um… Weird. It, uh… It kinda looks like a sink full of dirty dishes…"

"See, that's what I was thinking too," nodded Courtney with a faux-sweet smile, as if she'd been worried her eyes might've been playing tricks on her. "And pray tell, oh dear, sweet, beautiful Abby, love of my life. Just whose name is it on the chore wheel for doing the dishes this week, hmmm?"

Blowing out a put-upon huff and rolling her eyes, Abby made a show of turning around and squinting at the colorfully decorated cardboard wheel affixed to the front of their slightly dinged up refrigerator.

"Oh hey, would you look at that. It's, uh… It's me."

"Why, yes, it is you," agreed Courtney, swapping out her smile for a frosty glare. "So then, why do we still have a sink full of dirty dishes when we're supposed to be leaving for our vacation tomorrow morning? I reminded you to do them last night, didn't I?"

"Well, uh… You see…"

"Did you just not happen to notice your name on the chore wheel whenever you went to get a snack from the refrigerator this week? I've picked up more than enough of your empty soda cans to know that you've been in there at least a couple times."

"No, I uh… I saw it," admitted Abby, clearly looking for an avenue of escape that Rhen knew from personal experience just wasn't there.

"So then, why aren't they done?"

Apparently deciding that backpedaling wasn't getting her anywhere, Abby went on the offensive instead.

"Hey. I have been doing them!" she snapped, drawing herself up to her full five-foot-four-inch height and positively bristling with righteous indignation as she glared up at her much taller girlfriend. "They just needed to soak is all."

"For three days?"

All three of the girls in the kitchen took a moment to look back down at the dishes in the sink then, and Rhen was left to wonder if a sauce pan half-filled with murky brown water and floating bits of leftover pasta could really be classified as "soaking".

Undeterred, however, Abby continued to maintain her front of aggrieved innocence. Matching her girlfriend glare for glare and scowl for scowl, even as her hands continued to fidget nervously with her dress.

"Look. Do you want them done properly or not?" she demanded once the flat stares and expectant pauses from Courtney finally became too much for her to handle. "This kind of stuff takes time, you know. I can't just rush through it because you're tired of looking at them!"

"What I want, babe," her girlfriend fired back, carefully metering her tone to avoid actually yelling at the blonde. "Is for the dishes to be done without me having to ask you a million times."

"Well then maybe you ought to pick up a sponge and get scrubbing, huh? Did you ever stop to think about that?"

The silence that followed that last bratty remark was so deafening, that Rhen was pretty sure she could hear the microbial life forms that had made their homes among the piles of dirty dishes in the sink arguing about what was to be done to save their doomed civilization.

Heh. Maybe they can get a single-celled space program up and running by the time Abby gets to them?

Courtney, on the other hand, just closed her eyes, took in a long, deep breath, and then sighed.

"Okay. Fine. Have it your way," she eventually said, pinching the bridge of her nose and muttering something under her breath about being on her last nerve before looking back up again with a coldly determined expression that brooked no further argument.

Although, that sure didn't stop Abby from trying.

"Couch. Now."

"What? Awww, babe, come on! I was just joking! I-"

But the rest of whatever she was going to say was cut short by Courtney reaching out and gently pressing a single, silencing forefinger to her lips, bottling up her litany of excuses and explanations with that understated yet commanding gesture.

"I want you to pick out one of the big wooden spoons for me," she began to say in a cool, even tone, her voice velvety smooth and positively brimming with unspoken threats of dire consequences if she was argued with any further. "Wash it up and make sure you get it nice and wet just the way I like it, and then get that bratty butt of yours out into the living room and over the couch. Am I understood?"

Drawing back her finger with the languid grace of a predator toying with cornered prey, she pinned the blonde in place with a sharp look whose intensity just dared her to try and say something sassy.

"I..."

And, for a moment, it seemed like Abby just might be about to take her up on that challenge.

Lord knew Rhen would have been tempted to had she been the one in her position. In fact, she'd already cooked up a bratty reply on reflex that was just begging to be let loose, and which she very wisely chose to keep to herself.

But, seeming to sense that it was time for her to concede defeat and cut her losses, Abby just nodded.

Albeit rather huffily.

"Fiiiiine."

"Good girl."

With the matter now settled, Courtney allowed her ultra-strict disciplinarian mask to drop away as she leaned in and planted a quick kiss on her girlfriend's pouting lips.

She then stepped past Rhen, ruffling her hair again as she went, and began making her way out of the kitchen, calling over her shoulder in a genially threatening manner, "I'm going to go change into something more comfortable, and when I get back I'd better find you right where you're supposed to be or else I'm not rubbing any lotion in afterward. You hear me, hot stuff?"

"Ugh! God, fine, alright!" spluttered Abby, looking more embarrassed than upset as she shooed the grinning older girl out of the room with frantically flailing arms. "Go on, get! I've got a spoon to prep, remember?"

"Better hurry," chuckled Courtney as she disappeared around the corner that led to their bedroom with a wave. "I won't be long."

"Yeah, yeah…"

Grumbling, Abby nevertheless turned to do as she'd been told with an enthusiasm that belied how nervous she currently looked.

"Sucks to be you," sing-songed Rhen softly, unable to resist getting in at least one good dig at her blushing friend's expense while at the same time making sure to keep her voice low enough to avoid being overheard in case Courtney was eavesdropping from around the corner.

It had happened before, and once was all that it had taken for her to learn that particular lesson.

"Humph. Can I just say that I hate how much of an evil genius your auntie is?" fumed Abby a moment later once she too was sure that her soon to be spanker was out of earshot, the question exploding from her with a mixture of annoyance and giddily grim amusement as she dug out a particularly stout looking wooden spoon from beneath a pile of cereal bowls with milk congealing in their bottoms. "Ever since she taught Court that little trick about getting a spoon wet before using it to spank someone, it's been her favorite go-to whenever I forget to do my chores."

"And how often does that happen, hmmm?" snickered Rhen, grinning slyly.

"Eh, enough times to keep it interesting," conceded Abby with a deepening blush and a shrug, turning her attention fully to the task at hand as she began scrubbing calcified pasta shells from her spoon with a vengeance. "It still sucks, though."

"Hah!" snorted Rhen, unable to quite make herself not feel bad for her friend's predicament, while at the same time also feeling an odd sense of pride at her far greater experience with her partner's "evil genius" creativity. "If you think that's bad, just try getting it over a pair of pre-soaked panties. Now that really stings."

As she spoke, a phantom twinge of punishments long past tingled its way across her seat, making it clench and her swallow hard as she reached back to give both cheeks a firm rub.

"You don't say…?" pressed Abby, a sly grin of her own stealing across her halfheartedly-sullen face as she began rinsing off the bubbly lather that she'd managed to work up on her spoon with all of her scrubbing. "I think I might just have to ask her to give me and Court a little demo of that particular technique the next time we're all over at your house. I'm sure she'd be more than happy to show us how it's done."

Oh crap. She probably would, wouldn't she?

Realizing that she might have just inadvertently dug herself into a very humiliating hole that she'd have a hard time digging herself out of later, Rhen scrambled to steer their conversation back on track. They were talking about Abby and her impending punishment after all, not her own!

"So, uh… If you hate getting it with the wet spoon so much," she began to say, reaffixing her best taunting smirk in place; one that she'd managed to largely perfect thanks to watching her friend's own reactions to her spankings over the last few months. "Then why do you keep forgetting to do your chores?"

"Hmmm…" purred Abby dreamily at that, shutting off the flow of water from the sink and shaking her now pristinely clean wooden spoon dry with a lopsided grin. "Why indeed, I wonder?"

—

When Courtney at last emerged from the bedroom she shared with her girlfriend, now dressed in a comfortable pair of athletic shorts and a gray tank top, it was to find Rhen and Abby once again clustered around the front of the TV. Deep in heated conversation about the merits of one particular version of a movie versus its remake, it seemed as if they were most likely on the verge of another wrestling match if things kept on going the way they were for much longer.

"Look, if you're going to be all stubborn about this, then forget it!" the shorter of the two of them harrumphed suddenly, throwing her hands into the air with a frustration wholly unique to bickering sisters. "Let's just watch more of that British baking show instead."

"Hmmm… Now there's an idea," mused Abby, tapping a thoughtful forefinger against the side of her face as a hungry look stole across her features. "I'm pretty sure that one hotty housewife is still on too. I'd definitely be down to get another look at her muffins if you know what I-"

"Ahem."

"Ack!"

Clearing her throat theatrically, Courtney flashed the two of them her most menacing grin as they let out simultaneous yelps of surprise and rounded on her, looking for all the world like two naughty girls who'd just been caught with their hands in the cookie jar.

"Pardon the interruption, Abby, my dear," she crooned, narrowing her eyes in warning as she planted her hands on her hips. "But I thought I told you I wanted you bent over and ready for your spanking by the time I got back?"

However, while Rhen might have crumbled to pieces under such a stare, the bubbly blonde proved to be far more resilient.

"Oh, right, I knew I was forgetting something!" she exclaimed, lightly rapping her knuckles against her forehead in a self-deprecatingly gesture while at the same time not actually making any moves toward the well-worn couch and the waterlogged wooden spoon she'd left waiting there on one of its cushions. "Sorry, Court. Rhen and I were just so busy trying to figure out what we wanted to watch so we could get around to ordering that pizza you mentioned earlier, and I guess we kinda just lost track of time. But, hey, try not to be too upset with her, alright? The poor girl is starving, you know."

"Yeah, sure, throw me under the bus, why don't you?" grumbled Rhen, tossing a dirty look in her best friend's direction. "It's not my fault you're about to get your butt beat, you big jerk."

"You see what I'm dealing with here?" continued Abby with a strained sigh and a spot-on impersonation of her girlfriend's frustrated glower from earlier as she pinched the bridge of her nose. "She's been like this ever since you went to go change. And, frankly, I'm on my last nerve. So, uh, yeah. Obviously it should come as no surprise that it completely slipped my mind that I was still going to get, uh… you know…"

She made an off-handed twirling gesture with her fingers then, seemingly searching for just the right words as fresh warmth rose up to color her cheeks.

"Spanked… and stuff."

Well. She almost managed to stick the landing.

"Mmhmm. Yes, I'm sure," deadpanned Courtney, rolling her eyes with a tight smirk as she turned and began making her way back into the kitchen, apparently content to put off her errant sweetheart's punishment for just a little bit longer as she pulled open a cabinet above their sink and began rummaging around inside of it for something. "But, even so, shouldn't you be setting a better example for our beloved little sister? I hardly think that Dana would appreciate you teaching her that it's okay to just ignore what she's been told when she's about to get her bratty backside blistered, wouldn't you agree?"

Even with her voice muffled by the cabinet door blocking her profile from view, the teasing note in her tone still rang loud and clear throughout the tiny apartment.

"Yeah, Abby," echoed Rhen smugly, eager to capitalize on the opportunity she'd been presented with. "Set a better example."

To which she got an equally dirty look from her friend in response.

"Oh, bite me, pipsqueak," she stage whispered.

"I know you are, but what am I?" countered Rhen, undeterred in the slightest as she stuck out her tongue.

"Why you little-!"

But, before their brewing scuffle could come to a boil, Courtney spoke up again, cutting across their verbal jabbing like a hot knife through butter.

"Girls…" she drawled in a warning tone, her voice stern and uncompromising without her actually having to raise it past her normal speaking volume. "I can just as easily spank two bottoms as I can one, you know."

"What? But I already got spanked today," whined Rhen, red in the face both from the fact that that was the first thing that had sprung to mind when she'd opened her mouth, and because she'd stomped her foot to emphasize her point while saying it.

Something which managed to produce two simultaneous snorts of laughter from her friends.

"Damn right you did," agreed Abby, looking inordinately pleased with herself despite what they all knew she still had coming.

Which in turn earned her another glare from Rhen.

"Humph. It's not like it hurt that much…" she mumbled petulantly, crossing her arms in front of her with a pout.

"All that sniffling and promising to be good sure seemed to say otherwise," Abby continued to tease, raising her voice to call out to her girlfriend. "Did you hear that, babe? She said my spanking didn't even hurt that much! Can you believe that? Maybe you should spank her too. You know, just to be absolutely sure that she'll behave herself tonight?"

"Oh, come on!" moaned Rhen, an icy hand wrapping itself around her heart and squeezing tight as her fists flew down to her sides in protest. "That is so not fair, you guys!"

"So?" countered Abby, positively beaming now. "It'd still be fun to watch."

"Courtneyyyy!"

Thoroughly frazzled now, Rhen stomped her foot again in protest. No longer caring how childish it made her look or sound so long as it helped save her seat.

"Make her stop. She's being mean!"

"Hmmm… Well, it is tempting," admitted the older girl with a wolfish grin, reappearing at last from behind the cabinet door with a dark green bottle gripped by the neck in one hand and a pair of thin-stemmed wine glasses and a corkscrew in the other. "But I personally think that little Rhenny here would benefit much more from learning by example through you, hot stuff. So I think we'll keep tonight's spanking festivities limited to just your cute caboose as long as she behaves herself. That sound good to you, kiddo?"

"Yes ma'am, I'll be good!" Rhen was quick to reassure her.

"That's what I like to hear."

Oh thank god…

Sighing to herself, Rhen let go of a breath that she hadn't even realized she'd been holding while Abby gave a sour harrumph.

"Yeah, whatever."

"But first," continued the tallest of the three of them, ignoring her lover's sass as she sauntered her way back over to the couch and began laying out her spoils from the kitchen on the coffee table in front of her. "I did say that I was going to get us some drinks earlier, and I'm a woman of my word, so let's do a little pre-spanking pregaming, shall we?"

"Oh hell yeah!" exclaimed Abby, her pouting expression giving way to a brilliant smile as she drew up in front of her girlfriend's makeshift bar, vibrating with barely-restrained excitement as she worked the cork free of its bottle and poured the two of them a little over half a glass each of dark red wine.

"Here you are, my dear," crooned Courtney in her best stuffy sommelier voice. "One glass of our finest vintage pinot noir."

"Why thank you," crooned Abby in return, matching her snooty tone. "It looks absolutely lovely."

Rhen on the other hand, despite having never been a particularly big drinker, still couldn't help but look on with more than a twinge of jealousy as Abby took up her proffered glass and deeply inhaled its aroma.

While it was true that she'd gotten tipsy (and maybe even a little drunk) on a few occasions in the past when she'd been dragged off to parties during high school and college, that had always mostly just been to prove a point to the people she'd been with that she was in fact not a child and could totally handle her liquor (which she most definitely could not). As a result, she'd never really developed a taste for alcohol, or social drinking in general for that matter, like many of her peers had. But, even so, it was still hard not to feel at least a little left out when her two best friends were standing there just a few feet away from her, clinking their glasses together and laughing at some inside joke from the last time they'd gone bar-hopping together.

And so, she did her best to disguise that jealousy by pointedly turning her back to the two of them and locking her attention straight ahead on the TV in front of her instead.

Whatever. Let them have their stupid fun, she grumbled silently to herself, surprised at how much it hurt to be excluded, even from something that she wasn't particularly all that interested in to begin with. This just gives me a chance to pick something to watch without Abby butting in every five seconds to try and convince me that the original version was way better… Humph!

A moment later, though, as if reading her mind, Courtney called out to her and beckoned her over with a warm, sisterly smile.

"Hey now, don't just stand there looking all glum, bratty buns. I've got some for you too, you know."

"Y-You do?" croaked Rhen, blushing at the slight hitch in her voice, and surprised to say the least that that was the case considering how her friends typically treated her age-wise as she turned and tentatively moved to join Abby on the other side of the coffee table from Courtney.

"That's right," sing-songed the athletic older girl with one of her trademark wolfish grins, producing from behind her back a bright pink plastic sippy cup filled near to the brim with the same dark red wine that she and her girlfriend had in their own glasses. "Only thing is. According to what Abby's told me, you're a bit of a lightweight when it comes to booze, and we really can't risk you spilling any of this on our carpet. Soooo…"

"We figured that this would be a good compromise," finished Abby for her. "Security deposits and all that. You know how it is."

She waved away the idea with a very "It can't be helped" sort of gesture as her girlfriend thrust the flowery cup into Rhen's hands and winked.

"Enjoy."

Oh you have got to be freaking kidding me… the twenty-year-old turned teenager grumbled silently to herself, while aloud she spluttered indignantly.

"Where did you even-?" she started to ask, glaring in exasperated disbelief at first the semi-transparent sippy cup in her hands, then back up at her friends again, stopping short as she caught sight of the matching set of hopeful looks on their faces and coming to the sudden realization that this was something they'd been planning for a while now.

It hit her then.

This wasn't a mean prank as she'd at first suspected, but rather a genuine attempt to help her fit in in her own special way. They knew that she wasn't much of a drinker, and had been nice enough to give her an easy out to not participate with them if she didn't want to. And, as embarrassing as the notion of being forced to drink her wine out of a sippy cup might have been, she also was able to recognize that her friends were making a genuine effort to include her in on their fun.

Albeit with a firm reminder that she was still the little sister among their group.

I mean… This is pretty nice of them and all, but still…

"Oh, never mind."

Exhaling loudly in good-natured defeat, she smiled right on back at the two of them and hoisted her kiddy-cup in a half-hearted toast.

"Thanks, I guess."

Grateful as she was, she still couldn't resist getting in at least one good harrumph.

"Humph!"

"Pardon me, young lady?" pressed Courtney, still grinning even as she raised one dark eyebrow at her that carried with it a whole slew of warnings to behave herself.

"Oops! I mean, thank you, ma'am!" Rhen quickly amended, before hiding her jumpiness behind a long, humiliating pull from her sippy cup. "It's um… It's very tasty."

And, to her surprise, it actually was.

"Why you're very welcome, you little cutie patootie," cooed the older girl, all smiles once again as she leaned over the table to kiss her cheek. "I'm so glad to hear you like it!"

"Yeah, this stuff is way better than that cough syrupy crap we used to have during those parties back in the dorms when we were freshmen," chimed in Abby

"Wait, what?" demanded Courtney, rounding on her in disbelief, her pride as a former RA very clearly wounded. "What parties?"

"Oh, don't you worry about any of that," dismissed Rhen, eager to reassert at least some of her dignity as one of the group. "You weren't missing much, I promise."

"Uh-huh," deadpanned the taller girl grimly, before shrugging off her indignation with a shake of her head. "Oh well, not my problem anymore."

"Phew," echoed both Rhen and Abby together before dissolving into a fit of giggles when they each saw the look of relief on the other's face.

"But, uh… yeah. Speaking of illicit parties and people drinking who technically shouldn't be," continued Courtney a moment later, turning to Rhen with a mock-admonishing waggle of her finger as she took a sip from her own, distinctly not a sippy cup, glass. "Don't go telling your auntie on us, yeah? I know it'll be your birthday in just a few more days and all, but somehow Dana strikes me as the kind of lady who takes a dim view to underage drinking."

"You can sure say that again," snorted Rhen, deciding to just roll with this new bit of teasing as she continued to suckle at the hard plastic nub set into the top of her cup, its very nature as a sippy cup forcing her to pace herself and not take any particularly deep swigs of the stuff inside. "One time when we were out to dinner, we both ordered these super tasty strawberry daiquiris, but when I tried swapping out my virgin one for hers while she wasn't looking, she totally caught me and just about wore Missus Hairbru- I mean, she just about wore my hairbrush out on my butt at bedtime that night. So, uh… yeah. My lips are totally sealed, don't you worry."

Much to her own pride and amusement, both Abby and Courtney looked rather impressed with the sheer audacity of her attempted bit of sleight of hand, even as they shuddered visibly at the mental picture she'd managed to paint with her admission of what had happened afterward. Which was something that definitely helped Rhen feel much less embarrassed about her own shiver as her cheeks clenched reflexively beneath her shorts at the memory of it all.

She'd definitely needed a pillow to sit on for breakfast the fol-lowing morning, that was for sure.

"Hmmm, yeah. When you put it like that, it's probably better if we just keep this between the three of us," confirmed Abby with a somewhat shaky giggle, taking a nice, long pull from her glass, seemingly to hide the sudden rosy glow that had suffused her cheeks. "Oh god, babe, this so hits the spot right now."

"Yeah, I figured we might as well bust out the good stuff your parents gave us for a night like tonight," answered Courtney with a low chuckle of her own, taking a far more measured sip from her glass and doing a much better job of hiding her discomfort at the thought of Dana Johnson wearing out an ebony hairbrush on her caramel colored backside. "We never get a chance to have proper slumber parties like this anymore with my schedule being so crazy now, and I missed it!"

"Awww, me too," cooed Rhen around her sippy cup, genuinely touched.

"Definitely the right decision," agreed Abby, taking another, smaller, sip of her drink this time and savoring its taste with a lopsided grin. "But, yeah, like I was saying. Maybe keep this little pre-birthday booze fest on the down low. Okay, Rhenny-benny?"

She giggled then.

"Well, at least for a few more days," she added with a wink. "I'd like to get a good tan going before your auntie decides to take a crack at tanning my hide."

"Don't sweat it, hot stuff. I'll be taking care of that for you in just a second here," snickered Courtney.

"Oh hah-hah, babe," huffed the blushing blonde in return with a roll of her eyes, clearly miffed at having her own silly joke turned against her. "You're just so funny, aren't you?"

"I sure am."

Grinning triumphantly, Courtney plucked the half-drained glass from her girlfriend's grasp and slipped past to set it (and her own) atop their compact kitchen table on the other side of the room.

"Now quit your stalling and get that sweet ass of yours over the couch like the good little bad girl I know you are. Chop-chop!"

"Ugh. You know that's an oxymoron, right?" the blonde said, rolling her eyes.

"Of course I do," replied Courtney, gliding back over to cup her chin in one hand with a wicked grin before pulling her in close for a firm, possessive kiss. "I just don't care."

"But I thought all you grad student types just loved getting nitpicky over stupid stuff like that?" quipped Abby sarcastically, pouting now that she'd run out of wiggle room for putting off the inevitable as she was led around to the back of the couch.

Courtney wasn't about to take any of her bait this time, however.

"Couch. Now," she snapped instead, spinning her around by the shoulder and sending her stumbling in the general direction she wanted her with a hard slap to the seat of her dress.

SMACK!

Which, coming from her, was very hard indeed.

"Ack! Okay, okay, I'm going!" squawked Abby, her right hand flying back to the spot where her girlfriend's iron palm had just sped her along. "Damn! Impatient much? Geez!"

Serves you right, you big baby…

"And what are you smirking at, young lady?" demanded Courtney, rounding on Rhen without so much as a warning then as Abby continued to grumble and move into position.

Rhen, who'd thought she'd been being discreet in her self-satisfied leering, jumped at the sudden question and attempted to mask her amusement behind an unconvincing coughing fit, nearly dropping her sippy cup in the process.

Yikes! That could have been bad, she thought to herself with a sigh of relief, gripping her cup just a little bit tighter as she attempted to rein in her racing heart. I guess it's a good thing they forced this stupid thing on me after all…

"Well?" pressed Courtney, all business now as she yanked her out of her musings with an impatient glare.

"Um, I uh…" stuttered Rhen, swallowing hard.

Holy crap! How the heck does she make her eyes look that scary? It's freaking witchcraft!

"Awww, cut her some slack, babe," snickered Abby, darting over to the table and snatching up her wine glass for a quick sip while the older girl's back was turned to her. "She's probably just not used to not being on the receiving end is all."

"I mean…" conceded Rhen with a shy smile. "It is kind of rare."

Courtney snorted then, her stern demeanor melting away with the noise as she smirked.

"That's certainly one way of putting it."

"Yeah, tell us something we don't know," added Abby with a toss of her hair as she returned to the back of the couch, bending over at last and letting her palms sink nearly up to her wrists against the faded cushions in front of her.

"Okay… How about there's no way in hell I'm going to let you keep your dress down for this spanking just because we have company over?" suggested Courtney helpfully, stepping up behind her girlfriend.

Looping one lean and well-toned arm around her soft waist, she hoisted Abby up and off of the floor entirely without so much as grunt. Hauling her forward across the back of the couch until her bare feet hung suspended nearly a foot above the carpet. Then, grinning from ear to ear, she lifted up the back of her dress with practiced, casual ease and folded it over onto her back.

"And, as great as you look in these," she added with a grim snicker, teasingly snapping the minimal waistband of her girlfriend's daring panties and silently beckoning Rhen to come join her on the other side of the couch with a jerk of her chin. "They're coming down too."

"Awww, come on, babe!" whined Abby, giving her scantily clad, and rather lacy backside an exhorting wiggle. "They barely cover my ass at all!”

SMACK!

“Watch the language, missy!”

“Ack! Fuck! Okay, I’m sorry!” she yelped, making both Rhen and Courtney giggle with her apologetic profanity.

“Apology accepted, but your panties are still coming down,” the taller girl went on to say a moment later, apparently content to let her lover wriggle and squirm as she took her time enjoying their pre-spanking back and forth.

“Humph. Rude.”

“Oh please,” sneered Courtney, her eyes devouring the delectable curves on display before her in their oh so enticing, ribbon-bedecked finery. “As if you haven’t been hoping I’d do this to you all week long, you little tease.”

“Wha-? No! Of course I haven’t-!” Abby started to protest, before letting out a high-pitched squeak and completely losing control of her tongue as her girlfriend slipped two fingers down along the divide between her cheeks, gliding them over the sheer material of her panties until she found exactly what she knew she would.

“Mmhmm,” drawled the taller girl lazily, massaging her dewy folds through the thin fabric in a way that made Rhen’s own tingle with jealousy. “Oh yes, you’re just so upset that I’m about to tear up your bratty little ass, aren’t you?”

“Baaaabe,” moaned the blonde, gnawing at her lower lip as her fists beat out an erratic tattoo against the cushions beneath her. “Y-You’re not supposed to actually say that out loud!”

That one managed to get a snort from both Rhen and Courtney.

“Oh, I think the cat’s already out of the bag and running down the street by now when it comes to how we all feel about spanking, babe.”

“Ugh. Maybe,” conceded Abby with a sheepish grimace.

“Besides,” continued her girlfriend, retrieving her hand without warning and popping her lightly on either cheek. “We’re getting way off track here. Since when has how much skin your panties cover ever been a deciding factor in whether or not I let them stay up for a punishment?"

"Well, I mean…"

Abby had no good answer to that question, though, because she immediately switched tactics.

"Look. It sets a bad example for Rhen, alright?"

"Hah! And how do you figure that?"

"Yeah, Abby," chimed In Rhen, definitely having fun being the one doing the teasing for a change and secretly hoping that her friend would come up with a good line she could use on her aunt later. "How come your panties get to stay up, but mine don't?"

"Oh, you know…" hemmed the other girl, idly scratching at her cheek as she tried to come up with something plausible sounding. "Because, uh… Oh! Because as a mostly responsible adult, I deserve the right to be disciplined with more dignity than a dumb, little teenybopper like Rhen does. You see, she needs to be spanked on her bare bottom, and often I might add, because she's just an immature little brat who-"

SMACK!

"Ack!" yelped Abby again as a sudden, boulder-like impact exploded against the center of her heart-shaped backside, forcing her legs to go rigid as she hissed in a breath through clenched teeth. "Rude."

"Nice try, hot stuff, but that one's not gonna fly with me, I'm afraid," replied Courtney with the same sort of good-natured shake of her head that she so often found herself using during the labs she ran as a TA, her voice (and the swat that had accompanied it) carrying with them a note of finality that meant she wasn't about to change her mind. "As far as I'm concerned, Abby dearest, a naughty bottom is a naughty bottom, regardless of its owner's age, adoptive or otherwise."

She spared a moment to throw a conspiratorial half-grin in Rhen's direction with that last remark before stepping in close and whisking the fretting blonde's frilly, black and white panties down to her ankles in one smooth motion. Then, straightening back up and tossing her captured prize onto the coffee table next to her succulents, she picked up the spoon that had been so patiently waiting for her that entire time and gave each now naked cheek a couple of menacing taps.

"And when I spank a naughty bottom," she continued to lecture, punctuating her remarks this time with two lightning-fast swats to either side of her girlfriend's bottom that set its generous curves to jiggling with each thundering impact.

THWAP-THWAP!

"I spank a naughty bottom."

THWAP-THWAP!

"Not a naughty dress."

THWAP-THWAP!

"Not a naughty pair of panties."

THWAP-THWAP!

"Not even a naughty set of leggings when it's chilly outside."

THWAP-THWAP!

"But a nice-"

THWAP!

"And bare-"

THWAP!

"Naughty, bratty, super cute, and totally adorable bottom!"

THWAP! THWAP! THWAP! THWAP! THWAP!

"Is that clear, young lady?"

"Jesus, fuck, shit, ow!" yelped Abby, cursing up a storm while flailing her feet behind her in an attempt to throw off some of the heat boiling up from her backside, which, unfortunately for her, did very little to throw off the taller girl's aim. "Alright, alright, I get it! I'm sorry, okay?"

"Tsk, tsk," clucked Courtney, shaking her head in mock-disbelief while maintaining her assault on her girlfriend's rapidly reddening backside. "Such language. I am positively appalled that you would continue to speak in such a way in front of our very impressionable little sister!"

THWAP!

"And after we just got through talking about how you should be setting a better example for her too."

THWAP!

"For shame!"

"You know…" piped up Rhen then, sensing an opportunity. "I would've had my mouth washed out with soap if I'd said anything like that while I was getting spanked."

She shrugged as innocently as she could while she spoke, doing her best to look helpful and not at all like she was trying to get her best friend back for her little panty-gag stunt from earlier that afternoon.

"I mean… I'm just sayin'."

"Oh please," growled Abby in turn, a shiver of wry amusement thrumming beneath the strained surface of her words as she grit her teeth through the fury being rained down upon her. "That's just because- Oh! You're just- Ack! A little- Shit! A little brat who- Owie! Who's too- Dammit, Court, I'm trying to say something here! Could you slow your fucking roll for just, like, one second? Shit! Okay, okay- Owie, owie, owie! Never mind- Ack! I'm sorry, I'm sorry!"

"Would you like me to go get you some soap, Courtney?" crooned Rhen with a malicious giggle, her smile sugary sweet as she sidled in just a bit closer for a better look at all of the embarrassing things her best friend was showing off with her squirming. "You wouldn't even have to stop spanking her, you know. She could totally just hold it in her mouth and bite down while you're punishing her. It's a very effective way of doing things, trust me. My grandma used to use that trick on me all the time back when I was in middle school."

"No, no, that's fine," chuckled the older girl, waving away the suggestion with her spoon as she gave her girlfriend's sizzling seat a moment to cool off before starting in on **her** again.

THWAP! THWAP! THWAP! THWAP! THWAP!

"Are you suuuure?" wheedled Rhen, mesmerized by the bouncing ballet of her best friend's bare bottom as it turned redder and redder under her former TA's unrelenting efforts. "I'm pretty sure you guys have a bar in your shower that would be just perfect for this. I could totally go get it for you, if you want. It would just take a second."

"Is that right?" deadpanned Courtney, sparing a measured look in her direction as she continued to piston her tautly-muscled right arm up and down in a steady rhythm that had her girlfriend squealing and promising to never ever forget another chore for as long as she lived. "I'll be sure to keep that in mind the next time you start getting a little too sassy, kiddo. Thanks."

"Wait! I um…"

Blanching, Rhen took a hurried step back and waved her hands in front of her in a frantic attempt to shoo away that idea. Once again finding herself grateful that her drink came with a spill-proof lid as it sloshed back and forth with her movements.

"N-Never mind! Soap is totally stupid and ineffective as a punishment. I have absolutely no idea what I must have been thinking… Heh."

"Are you suuuure?" teased Courtney, mimicking her crooning tone from just a moment earlier.

"Yes ma'am!"

"Hah! Pushover," grunted Abby with a haggard snicker that quickly devolved into another squawk of pain as her thighs bucked and squirmed.

"Oh, she's just being polite is all," chided Courtney with a chuckle of her own, draining away the tension boiling in the pit of Rhen's stomach with a wink as she turned her full attention back to her girlfriend. "But, just remember, Rhenny. Abby might be a total smartass, but she's also right. In this house, only little girls with cute black ponytails, and even cuter undies, get their mouths washed out with soap when they say naughty words. Isn't that right, babe?"

"Damn fucking straight!"

"Humph!" grumbled the shorter girl in response to that, pulling free the scrunchie holding her hair in place and shaking it loose as she folded her arms beneath the petite swell of her breasts and glared daggers at her two adoptive older sisters. "That hardly seems fair."

"Yes, well," conceded Courtney, waving her spoon again as she spoke and not sounding particularly sympathetic to her former student's plight. "Those are still the rules, I'm afraid. And, like it or not, they're here to stay, bratty buns."

The words "Yeah, whatever, like I freaking give a crap" neatly lined themselves up to spring from Rhen's tongue as the darker-skinned girl resumed her swatting, and it took a supreme effort of will on her part to swallow them back down before they could earn her a spot beside Abby on the couch.

"Yes ma'am…" she harrumphed instead a few moments, and about a dozen hard, blistering cracks of the waterlogged wooden spoon, later, sighing heavily.

Talk about rigging the system.

"Good girl. Now let's just see if we can't get this girl to be just as good…"

THWAP! THWAP! THWAP! THWAP! THWAP!

Courtney launched into Abby's spanking in earnest then, and Rhen quickly found herself caught up in a mixture of vindictive satisfaction at seeing her bratty best friend taken down several pegs all at once as she did the well-spanked shuffle right in front of her, and stomach-churning, toe-curling, thigh-squirming, sympathy as her right hand drifted back to cup her own recently spanked seat while her left rose up to her mouth so that she could fretfully nibble on the end of her sippy cup in between suckling at her wine.

Oh god… Please tell me I didn't forget to load the dishwasher before we left for the mall this morning.

Feeling her heart rate suddenly skyrocket into panic mode, Rhen hurriedly began running through the events of earlier that morning in her head.

Okay, *think*. *I woke up, played on my phone for a bit, brushed my teeth, got changed, had breakfast with Dana, and then…*

Her eyes lit up as it all came rushing back to her.

Oh, right!

After she'd finished polishing off her stack of French toast and her second glass of orange juice, she'd found herself going over her plans for the day and what time she and her friends needed to be back to their house by the following morning with her partner (for like, the twelfth time!) while she rinsed off their breakfast dishes and loaded them into the dishwasher for a more thorough going over later.

So she was totally safe on that account.

Unfortunately, though, in her haste to be out the door as soon as possible, it had completely slipped her mind to take out the trash.

Well… crap, she thought to herself with a pouty grimace, feeling her cheeks once again clench beneath the snug denim of her short-shorts as she pictured what would most likely be waiting for her come next week when she and her aunt returned home from their vacation. *Then again, a week is a pretty long time… Maybe she'll have forgotten all about it by the time we're back?*

Shaking her head in mild disbelief, Rhen felt some of her earlier panic resettle itself back down along the bottom of her stomach as a cold lead weight, mixing oddly with the warmth from the wine that had made its home there too.

Or… Maybe not.

Letting out a long, slow breath, the petite junior willed herself not to worry too much about what may or may not be in store for her later.

Whatever. That's future Rhen's problem, not mine.

Besides, there were much more interesting things to focus on just then in the present. Like the world-class butt blistering currently turning her former roommate's ample and impressive backside a positively delightful shade of candy apple red.

Licking her lips as she shifted her weight from one foot to the

other, legs pressed firmly together so that her hands couldn't accidentally wander between them without her noticing, Rhen leaned in a bit closer to get a better look at what lay hidden just between Abby's frantically wriggling thighs.

Hah! Well, on the bright side, at least I'm not the only one who gets more excited than she lets on when she's in trouble.

Staring transfixed at the glistening golden curls shifting from side to side in time with their owner's squirming, carmine hips, Rhen's face split into a wicked grin.

Oh Abby, you naughty thing, you.

—

By the time Courtney was finally finished flambéing her girlfriend's forgetful heinie a few minutes later, the spoon in her hand was looking a whole lot drier than it had been when she'd first started swatting, and the results she'd wrought with it were nothing short of spectacular.

From the tip tops of her round and very swollen cheeks to just below her sizzling sit-spots, Abby's bare bottom was painted a livid shade of hot, throbbing crimson, and sported a great many vaguely horseshoe shaped marks layered seemingly at random all across it in an even darker shade of burgundy. Souvenirs from where the angled edges of the wooden spoon had bitten into her extra ferociously.

Rhen knew from personal experience that marks like that would last for another day or two before they finally started to fade away completely, and in the meantime they would be exceptionally tender to the touch. A fact which Courtney demonstrated right then and there to great effect by ruthlessly poking at them with the handle of her spoon in between none too gently fondling and caressing her handiwork.

"Mmmm… I just love the way you color up back her," she cooed, practically drooling as she settled down on her knees next to the blonde and leaned in close to nibble and peck at some of the more prominent marks she'd managed to raise along her flaming backside.

"Oof. M-Me too," grit out Abby through clenched teeth in equal parts ecstasy and agony, her breath coming in throaty gasps as her girlfriend kneaded her poor, tenderized cheeks with nearly as much force as she'd used to punish them.

Geez. Her poor sisters, Rhen found herself thinking as she remained at a polite enough distance to allow the two coed lovers a moment to kiss and cuddle among themselves before Courtney helped Abby back to her feet. I sure as heck wouldn't want to put any toes out of line if she was the one babysitting me while I was growing up. Not when she apparently has zero problems delivering a butt blistering like that for skipping your chores… Yeesh.

Rhen smirked as the irony of that last thought washed over her, and she shook her head to clear it.

Heh. Whatever.

Thankfully, though, she was saved from having to dwell on it any further by the two older girls at last separating after one more deeply passionate smooch, and the taller of the two of them slipping once again into her role as the stern disciplinarian.

"Okay then, that's enough of a break for now, hon. You get that dress off and I'll take care of hanging it up while you get to work, alright?" she ordered briskly, one hand planted firmly on her hip while she held the other out before her expectantly. "You can finish getting changed once we're done with your second spanking."

"Wait, her second spanking?" blurted Rhen, unable to stop herself as the words flew past her lips in sheer disbelief.

Leaning over, she rubbed her eyes and made a show of double-checking that Abby's bottom was actually as well-spanked as she'd remembered it being just a second earlier. And, sure enough, she once again found herself faced with results that rivaled what her aunt was capable of bringing to bear with Missus Hairbrush only when she was really seeing red.

It was impressive to say the least.

"Oh yeah, I guess you wouldn't know about that part, would you?" sighed Abby with a dramatic scowl that didn't quite manage to reach her smiling eyes.

While she continued to pout, turning away from her girlfriend and pulling her wavy hair aside so that she could draw down the zipper on the back of her dress for her, Courtney supplied Rhen with the details.

"You see, kiddo, when Abby here decides not to do her chores, she gets a spanking."

"Uh-huh…" replied Rhen, nodding along and resisting the urge to tack on something sassy with every fiber of her being.

I mean, that's pretty freaking obvious, you know.

"And once her spanking is over, she then has to finish the chore that she neglected. We can't have it going undone after all, now can we?"

"Definitely not," agreed Rhen, still not sure where this all was headed yet, but content to let the darker-skinned girl spool it out for her at her own pace nevertheless.

"But after that's taken care of, well…"

A malevolent grin blossomed across Courtney's face as Abby continued to half-heartedly grump it up beside her, pulling her dress inside out over her head and tossing it at her girlfriend with a huff and a shake of her hair.

"After that, she gets to take another trip across my lap for however long it took her to get her chores done."

Rhen's stomach did several flip-flops in a row with that last revelation, and she found herself easing up onto her tiptoes and craning her neck to try and get another look at the mountain of dirty dishes still waiting for her friend at the other end of the apartment.

Judging by the crusted on bits of gunk ringing the rims of several of the bowls there, it looked like she was probably going to be there for quite a while.

"Oh…"

"Yeah…" agreed Abby, swapping out her sullen frown for a lopsided grin as she continued on in a resigned yet playful tone, heedless of the fact that she was now standing there in just a bra and a smile. "She likes to say it's to help drive home the lesson and get me to really think about how much easier things would have gone for me if I'd just done my chores in the first place, but…"

She winked then, and Rhen couldn't help but smile back.

"Between you and me, I think she just likes spanking me."

"Eh," shrugged Courtney, looking not the least bit perturbed. "Little of Column A, little of Column B. Either way, you've got a date with a sink full of dirty dishes, my dear, and the sooner you get started on that, the better. Believe it or not, I really would like to do something else tonight besides spank you silly. So get moving, hot stuff!"

SMACK!

"Ack! Right!" yelped Abby, scurrying away with her hands shielding her seat from any further encouragement. "Yes ma'am, I'm on it!"

Yikes. I sure hope I don't look nearly that, uh… enthusiastic, whenever Aunt Dana sends me off with a swat…

Once Abby was situated in front of the sink with the water flowing and a scrub brush in hand, Courtney stepped in beside Rhen and wrapped a friendly arm around her narrow shoulders, pulling her close.

"And while she's busy doing that, you can come with me, Rhenny," she purred, steering her off in the direction of the bedroom she shared with her girlfriend while smelling hypnotically all of sweat and woman. "It's been a long day, and I think we ought to get you into the tub for a quick scrub down of your own before I get you changed into your jammy-jams. Your auntie remembered to pack your pull-ups, right?"

Scowling as her face flushed about the same shade of bright pink as the pull-ups she had stashed away in the bottom of her backpack, Rhen let out an annoyed harrumph.

"Ugh. Yes."

She'd been hoping that Courtney would forget to ask about them so that she could also forget to mention them. But, alas, it was not to be.

"Great," chirped the older girl. "We wouldn't want to risk you wetting the bed, now would we?"

"Awww, and I was totally going to see if that whole putting someone's hand in a glass of warm water while they're sleeping thing actually worked," snickered Abby from her post in front of the sink, one hand still rubbing at her ruby red backside as she worked. "Then again, I guess there's nothing that really says I couldn't still try. I'd just have to figure out if it was an accident accident, or the one I had planned…"

"Humph."

"Tick-tock, babe," called Courtney over her shoulder with a pointed grin as she guided Rhen out of sight. "I'm going to be putting that pizza order in soon, so I'd be double-timing it on those dishes if I were you. That is, of course, unless you want the delivery girl to see your cute little caboose again?"

"Eep! Yes ma'am!" squeaked Abby, yanking her hand away from its rubbing and cranking up the flow of water. "One sink full of not dirty dishes, coming right up!"

"Heh. That's what I thought."

Chapter 9

Even the Best Laid Plans...

"Oh. My. *God*," moaned Rhen as she shuffled forward bleary-eyed on a pair of limp noodle legs, listlessly dragging her roller bag behind her as she went. "Whoever decided it was okay to schedule flights this early in the morning needs to seriously rethink their life."

"N-Noooo- oh… kidding," agreed Abby from just beside her, her words almost completely engulfed by a long yawn that tapered off into a grumpy pout as she flopped against her girl-friend for support, relying on her solid frame to keep her upright as they trudged like zombies toward the security checkpoint at the far end of the bustling concourse. "It ought to be illegal."

Rhen knew that her friend would have loved to harrumph to help underscore her point, but at that particular moment neither of them was awake enough to put forth that much effort. Instead, she made do with glaring at all the perky people speeding by on either side of them with a spring in their step as if it wasn't just past the crack of dawn.

"Fucking morning people…"

"Hey now, come on, you two. It's not that… That, uh… Oh god…" Courtney began to sluggishly chide before giving up half-way through with a piteous groan as the headache she'd woken up with that morning gave another merciless throb behind her eyes. "Yeah, no, forget it. This fucking *sucks*."

Massaging her aching temples with her free hand, the one that wasn't wrapped snugly around Abby's ample waist, she heaved out an exhausted sigh and let her head lull back in a desperate plea to the heavens.

"*Please* tell me there's somewhere to get coffee by our

terminal. I need some caffeine and pumpkin bread, like, yesterday."

"Seriously," droned Rhen and Abby together in a groggy chorus beside her.

Despite Rhen's myriad assurances to her aunt the day before that she and her friends would totally get enough sleep before they flew out to California the following morning, things hadn't exactly gone according to plan.

After a quick bath at the extra-grabby hands of Courtney (complete with a small flotilla of rubber duckies the athletic girl had apparently been saving for a special occasion), and then taking some time to enjoy the *very* entertaining spectacle that was Abby's second spanking of the evening for not doing the dishes. (A spanking that, regrettably, ended a few minutes before their food arrived.) She and her adoptive older sisters had wound up going through another bottle and a half of wine over the course of the next several hours. Scarfing down two extra-large pizzas and a dozen breadsticks in the process, in between several heated games of Mario Party on the battered Nintendo that Abby had recently recused from her parents' house, and marathoning an entire season of the baking show that Rhen had suggested.

It had been *awesome.*

True to Abby's assertion, the housewife that was the blonde girl's favorite did indeed have some marvelous muffins, and they'd ended up carrying her all the way to the finals. But, unfortunately for her and her friends, the prospect of seeing just who was the true master of British baked goods proved to be too much of a temptation to leave unanswered. And, as a result, the three of them had wound up getting to bed only an hour before Courtney's alarm clock had gone off.

What had followed had been a whirlwind of frantically getting changed, brushing teeth, washing faces, and finishing any last minute packing that needed to be done, before rushing out the door and speeding over to Rhen's house to meet Dana and Alana so that they could all drive together to the airport. And while they'd managed to snatch around half an hour's worth of fitful napping on the car ride over, that was still far from enough to recharge the three girls' batteries.

They were all in dire need of a caffeine boost.

Or seven.

"Not to worry, kiddos," piped up Alana, bright and cheery with her hands stuffed into the pockets of her professional looking blazer as she turned and continued walking backwards a few paces ahead of them, her figure no less impressive for lack of its usual lab coat and stethoscope as she and Dana led the way toward security. "I've flown out of this airport enough times by now to know it like the back of my hand. And, as it just so happens, there's a Coffee Kate's right by our terminal. So do your best to hang in there a little bit longer, alright?"

This news was met with a round of weak cheers from Abby and Rhen, and an exhausted groan from Courtney.

"Thank fucking Christ…"

"That's the spirit!"

Still sauntering along at a breezy pace, the sharp-featured doctor favored the three near-comatose coeds with a wry, knowing look, her almond eyes crinkling in amusement at the corners.

"Incidentally, I'd recommend you all grab yourselves a sports drink to go along with that coffee. It'll go a long way toward helping to replenish any electrolytes that might've…"

She cleared her throat and winked.

"Ahem. Shall we say, been *misplaced* during your little sleepover."

Then, with an admonishing, no-nonsense waggle of her forefinger that instantly had the three of them standing up just a little bit straighter, she added, "Also, make sure that you avoid taking any headache medicine with acetaminophen in it. Your livers have already had enough work to do for one day. Just stick to fluids and ibuprofen and you'll be better before you know it. Understood?"

"Yes ma'am…" Rhen, Courtney, and Abby droned in unison, too tired to argue or even look abashed at the older woman's thinly veiled hangover advice.

"Awww, college," sighed Dana wistfully from beside her friend. "Good times."

"Weren't they, though?" agreed Alana with a snicker, turning back and shaking her head. "But, as fun as our own 'slumber parties' were, I'm more than okay with not waking up feeling half-dead anymore."

"You and me both," chuckled the other woman as she drifted back to fall in step with her not-niece, looping her arm through hers as she kissed her cheek. "Waking up with this little cutie is *much* more fun."

—

The line to get through TSA that morning was just as busy as the rest of the airport was. But, despite its sluggish pace, Rhen really didn't mind. Half-dozing on her feet, she was content to simply allow herself to be swept along by the tide of people around her as she leaned back into Dana's arms; head resting against the comfortable pillow of her breasts as she breathed in deep the scent of her perfume and basked in the warmth of their shared body heat.

"You look very pretty today," the older woman murmured into the top of her hair, giving her a quick squeeze as they advanced forward another couple of paces with everyone else ahead of them.

"You really think so?" yawned Rhen, reaching up to rub some of the sleep from her eyes as a shy smile crept its way across her face. "You don't think my outfit looks… I don't know, weird?"

"Absolutely not, honey buns. You look great!"

There'd been very little time to fret about what to wear when Courtney had hauled her out of dreamland earlier that morning, so Rhen had opted to keep things simple.

Sort of.

In an effort to feel less like the only thing she ever wore day-to-day when left to her own devices were slight variations on jeans and a t-shirt, she'd been bugging Abby for fashion advice the last couple months, and as she'd tossed out her (as per usual) bone dry pull-up that morning, she'd decided that today was the day she was finally going to put some of it to the test. So, after stripping off her pajamas and stuffing them into the bottom of her backpack, she'd slipped into a loose-fitting, ruffled skirt that hung halfway down to her knees, and over her usual white camisole she'd decided to throw on a baggy cable knit sweater that she'd bought the day before at the mall, rather than the pink flamingo t-shirt her partner had picked out for her originally.

It wasn't exactly what she'd call high fashion, and it was maybe a little bit on the warm side for the start of summer, but it had looked cute in the moment when she'd put it on and it was cold in the mornings, so she'd stuck with it.

Of course, that didn't mean her confidence had done her the same courtesy. In fact, it had just about completely abandoned her the moment they'd left Abby and Courtney's apartment. So, hearing that her partner thought she looked cute in her first real attempt at a coordinated outfit since that one time back in high school when she'd started really getting into wearing spiked bracelets and fake lip piercings helped to lift a weight from her shoulders that she hadn't even realized she'd been carrying.

"Well…" demurred Rhen, her smile growing brighter by the moment as she picked at a stray bit of nonexistent lint from one of the oversized cuffs swallowing up most of her hands. "I don't know about 'great', but I um… I like it."

Truth be told, she absolutely *loved* her new sweater.

As soon as she'd seen herself in it (after some badgering from Courtney, and Abby threatening to take her belt off again if she didn't try it on), she'd known that she needed it. It's simple yet elegant cut and delicate cream coloring made her look cool and sophisticated, like the self-assured, razor-sharp software engineer that she pictured herself as. And, even if it *did* look a bit on the childish side with the way its baggy sleeves and loose-fitting bust conspired with the ruffles on her skirt to all but swallow up what little curves she had to begin with, she'd still been happy to buy it.

It wasn't like her A cups and narrow hips were doing her that much good to begin with anyway.

She just hoped that her look came off more as "sloppy chic", rather than "comfy clothes for a thirteen-year-old who just rolled out of bed" to everyone else.

Unfortunately (albeit rather predictably), things so far seemed to be leaning much more toward the latter than the former. Her new outfit and its distinct lack of sparkles and graphic tees hadn't stopped Courtney, for instance, from swatting her and Abby out the front door of their apartment when they'd been taking too long to finish getting ready. Although, she'd been pleased to note that her best friend had caught just as many hurried swats to her seat as she had. But, on the bright side, judging by the feel of her partner's body molded against her back and hips and the way she kept twirling a stray lock of her unbound raven hair around her finger as they waited in line, Dana was as big of a fan of her new outfit as she was.

Which, honestly, made it a slam dunk as far as Rhen was concerned.

"Oh yes, I think you look positively *scrumptious*," her partner declared, affectionately kneading her upper arm with her free hand. "I could just eat you up, you're so cute!"

She leaned in closer then, bringing her painted lips right next to Rhen's left ear so that only she would be able to hear her.

"And that's exactly what I'm going to do when I get you alone tonight, cutie pie."

The husky purr in the older woman's voice, combined with the warm breath tickling her ear, sent an involuntary shiver coursing through the petite junior's entire body. Hardening her nipples as it passed them by to settle at the juncture between her thighs with a pleasant thrum that made her knees go to jelly for a brief moment.

"Y-You don't say?" she finally managed to croak after she'd remoistened her dry mouth.

"Absolutely," confirmed Dana with a low, throaty chuckle. "And I'm not going to stop until I've eaten up every… last…

bite."

Before nipping at her earlobe under the guise of kissing her cheek as she straightened back up.

"W-Well then," stammered Rhen, before running out of steam and just grinning crookedly. "Okay… Heh."

"Good girl," chirped Dana, patting her on the shoulder. "Now come along, we're holding up the line."

Ushering her tongue-tied not-niece forward another couple of spots in line, she tucked a few stray tresses of her unbrushed hair back behind the ear she'd just been nibbling on.

"So, did you and your friends have fun at your little sleepover last night?" she asked brightly, shifting conversational gears like a professional stunt driver.

"Wha-? Oh um, yeah. I uh…"

Rhen felt her already flushed cheeks color just a little bit more at the deliberately childish way her partner had chosen to phrase that question. Especially since, as per usual, she hadn't bothered to keep her voice down at all as she'd asked it.

Which only further served to reinforce the image of the two of them as aunt and niece to everyone else around them.

Geez. I thought she might let up on the whole treating me like a teenager out in public thing since she gave me my ID back for our trip, but I guess that was hoping for too much… Humph.

Normally, Rhen would have pouted much more over the way the older woman was able to so effortlessly paint her as a slightly too big for her britches thirteen-year-old to the world at large with only a few simple words and the right gestures, but the compliments she'd just given her about her outfit (and her subsequent promises of some *very* adult activities later on that evening) were enough to keep her from sulking.

If the shoe fits… she thought to herself with a wan smile and a roll of her eyes. *Whatever.*

"Yeah, it was great," she replied instead, feeling herself starting to come back to life under her aunt's embrace as she launched into telling her all about what she and her friends had gotten up to at the mall, along with their night of TV and fun afterward; all the while being careful to omit any mention of the wine they'd gotten sauced on, or the "quiet" spanking she'd received in the fitting room of Blush.

Really, they were just extraneous details anyway, and brevity *was* the soul of wit after all.

But, while she might have been judicious in mentioning anything about her own punishment from the day before, that didn't stop her from recounting in exquisite detail every moment of Abby's own encounter with a sore bottom.

"Oh my god, you should have *seen* her butt by the time Courtney was through with it," she finished her story by saying, taking a page from her partner's book and intentionally keeping her voice at the same excited level that she typically used whenever she was telling her about some new book or game she'd been getting into recently. "It was, like, soooo red! I'm pretty sure you could have fried an egg on top of it if you'd wanted to."

Abby, who was a few spots further back in line from the two them with her girlfriend and Alana, could only huff and glare daggers at Dana's back, for the moment completely incapable of doing anything about the little brat who'd been giving a play-by-play of her dance with the wooden spoon from the night before for all to hear. Wisely, though, she chose to keep her dark thoughts to herself for the time being, lest she inadvertently give away the fact that *she* was the "Abby" the chatty twenty-year-old turned teenager was talking about.

"Mmhmm… Yes, dear, I imagine you probably could," mused Dana with a motherly shake of her head. "I've seen how red Courtney has managed to get *your* tush before, so I'm not at all surprised to hear that she was able to get similar results with your friend."

As she spoke, she let the hand that wasn't busy playing with the shorter girl's bedhead locks glide down along her side, lightly tickling as it went, before eventually settling on the gentle curve of her hip and giving it a fond squeeze.

And it was at that exact moment Rhen knew she'd been

busted.

"Excuse me, little girl," drawled Dana, still keeping her voice light and conversational, though now with an undercurrent of frosty disapproval just beneath the surface as she stopped playing with her hair.

"Y-Yes?" squeaked Rhen, her stomach twisting itself into worried knots as she and her aunt advanced forward another spot in line, suddenly feeling trapped with her back pressed up against her breasts and the way forward and to either side of her blocked off by other passengers.

"Now, correct me if I'm wrong," the older woman continued crisply, shifting her grip to cup her girlfriend's bottom through the layered ruffles of her skirt and giving it a firm squeeze. "But I can't help but notice there seems to be a distinct lack of padding on your caboose right now."

"You, uh… You don't say? That's weird, I must've-" But before Rhen could summon up a believable excuse or explanation, she found herself being forcibly turned to the side by the shoulder and letting out a high-pitched yelp of surprise as her skirt was unceremoniously tugged up in back to reveal the pair of purple and white polka dot panties she had on underneath.

"Eep!"

Two days in a row now! Are you freaking kidding me?

"Well, well, well," crooned Dana, maintaining her hold on the mortified girl's raised skirt as her lips pursed themselves into a disapproving frown. "I thought as much."

Rhen, for her part, just stood there with her panties on full display for several more humiliating moments, spluttering and stammering, completely caught off guard by what was happening, before she was finally able to find her voice again. Snatching her skirt out of her partner's grip, she rounded on her with an indignant glare made all the more adorable by the splash of strawberry coloring her cheeks.

"Oh my god, Aunt Dana!" she moaned, both hands clamped tight over where she'd hastily smoothed down her skirt in back, making doubly sure that it stayed right where it was for the foreseeable future as she stomped a foot. "What're you doing?"

"Don't you 'Aunt Dana' me, young lady," countered the older woman, hands on hips and looking very unimpressed. "Just where on earth is your pull-up?"

"M-My pull-up?" repeated Rhen, trying to sound innocent.

"Yes. Your pull-up."

Geez. Say it a little bit louder why don't you? I don't think everyone at the check-in counter heard you.

No amount of internalized sass would save her, though, and wilting under the pressure of her partner's stern disapproval, Rhen scrambled for an answer.

"Well, um, you see…"

But, coming up empty, she leaned over to the side and flashed her friends a pleading look. One that was met with smug satisfaction from Abby, and general amusement from Courtney and Alana.

Oh thanks a lot, you guys. Suuuuper appreciate the help. Really.

"Don't think your little friends are going to help you talk your way out of this one, Rhen Elizabeth," admonished Dana, her voice still far too loud for her not-niece's liking as she pulled her attention back to the matter at hand by snapping her fingers impatiently. "I asked you a question, and I expect an answer. So tell me, *where* is the pull-up you were supposed to be wearing for our flight today? You know, the one I specifically packed for in case you wet your pants, and that you were *supposed* to have put on as soon as you got up this morning?"

Dang it, Rhen, you just had to try and get sneaky didn't you?

Plastering a shaky smile onto her face, the shorter girl went with the best excuse she had to hand.

"I uh… I forgot it?"

"Mmhmm."

Dana wasn't about to let her off the hook so easily, though, especially not with so many people watching their little kerfuffle now.

"Did I, or did I not, pack *two* pull-ups for your sleepover last night?"

"You sure did," piped up Courtney then, choosing that moment to be helpful as she raised her voice loud enough to be heard from her spot further back in line. "She told me the second one was for in case she wet the bed."

"No I didn't!" blurted Rhen with a high-pitched squeak, going red in the face all over again as she tried frantically to shoo away the taller girl's words. "I only said that *you* said it was there in case I needed it."

"And I suppose you just *happened* to neglect to mention that the 'in case you needed it' I was referring to was for our trip today?" finished Dana for her, arching a brow.

"I mean… Sort of?" answered Rhen after an incredibly long half-second, finding herself once again impressed with how easily her aunt could ferret out the lie in a half-truth.

"So you thought you'd try pulling a fast one on me and your babysitters then, did you?" she pressed, refusing give her even an inch of wiggle room. "Did you seriously not think I was going to check if you were wearing them at some point today, young lady?"

That was, in fact, exactly what Rhen had been counting on.

"What? No, of course not! I um… I was just…"

Crap.

Mortified beyond belief that they were having this conversation where everyone in the concourse could hear them, she quickly decided that her best bet for the time being was to change the subject altogether.

"Look. I'm sorry, alright? But do we *really* have to talk about this now?" she half whined and half begged, glancing furtively from side to side at the milling press of people watching them from their spots in line as they waited for their turn to go through security.

She could already feel them starting to turn against her, overhearing some of the comments they were making to their friends and neighbors as they watched on with looks ranging from polite bemusement to stern disapproval not all that far off from her aunt's.

"Oh dear… Sounds like someone's in for it when she gets home…"

"Poor kid, but she really ought to know better."

"No kidding. It might be embarrassing, but if she's got a weak bladder, then she really *should* be wearing some sort of protection, shouldn't she?"

"Oh, of course. Just imagine if she had an accident while up in the air. They'd probably have to turn the plane around! You know, my cousin Doris told me about someone who…"

"What a sneaky brat!"

"I mean… She's definitely too old to be wearing pull-ups. But, hey, precautions are precautions, and if you've got a history of wetting your pants, well…"

Looks like sloppy chic is totally out the window now, fumed Rhen silently. *Freaking, awesome.*

Unfortunately for her too, she wasn't the only one picking up on what was being said around them. Dana was able to hear just as well as she was, and the general buzz of adult disapproval aimed at her not-niece was doing nothing to diminish her righteous indignation.

"Oh no, you're not getting off that easily," she rumbled, advancing on the younger girl and forcing her to back up another step as the line moved ahead. "You know exactly how I feel about fibbers, don't you, little girl?"

"Ugh. *Yes,*" harrumphed the sullen junior, already tasting soap suds on her tongue. "But I-!"

"Uh-uh," interrupted Dana, holding up a hand to silence her, her philosophy of embarrassment being an integral part of the punishment process coming into full bloom now as she refused to let her naughty niece try and sweep her bad behavior under the rug. "*You* were the one who decided that she wasn't going to do as she was told and just hope I wouldn't notice. And little girls who tell fibs and try to sneak around behind their auntie's back get their bottoms spanked and their mouths washed out, don't they?"

"Yes ma'am…" mumbled Rhen with a sour nod before rallying herself for another attempt at saving her seat, far less concerned now about how she might look to the people around her than she was about her prospects of sitting comfortably for their vacation. "But, look, it's not like I was *trying* to lie to you! It's just, um…"

Looking away as she nibbled at her lower lip, she heaved out a beleaguered sigh through her nose.

"I just didn't think that I needed to wear, um… To wear one of those *things* for our flight is all."

"Is that right?"

"Um… Yes?"

The twitch of the older woman's dark red lips at that was more than enough to communicate she knew her girlfriend was doing her best to sell her a bill of goods. But, as always, she was content to continue their dance for as long as it took to tire her out.

They both knew how this would all end. Now it was just a matter of when, not if.

And if the petite twenty-year-old turned teenager wanted to sass herself into even *more* trouble than she was already in, well… That was her choice, now wasn't it?

"Okay then, Rhen, tell me. Do you remember what happened the last time we took a long trip together and you weren't wearing one of those 'things'? Because I sure do."

"Of course I remember!" snapped the shorter girl, going absolutely crimson.

You weren't likely to forget wetting your pants in the middle of a busy rest stop parking lot after downing five extra-tall glasses of soda with lunch and not being able to get to a restroom for nearly an hour.

"That's good to hear," sing-songed Dana, her voice going silky smooth as they advanced yet another step. "So then, do you really want to risk having *another* accident just because you're embarrassed about having to wear some childish undies for one little flight? Undies that people aren't even going to see, mind you."

She smiled with purpose then.

"Well, so long as you behave yourself, that is."

"I… I…" spluttered Rhen, scrabbling desperately for any excuse that might save her at least a little bit of face. "Come on… That's not… It's not… It's not like I'm going to do… To do *that* again! I haven't even had anything to drink today, or to eat for that matter."

"Oh, so now you're not properly hydrating either?" interjected Alana, leaning around from behind Dana with a reprimanding look of her own that mostly hid the upward tilt at the corners of her mouth. "Proper nutrition is important for a girl your age, young lady, and dehydration is no laughing matter either."

Seemingly about to lose it and start cracking up, she covered her momentary smirk with a prolonged sigh and a roll of her eyes as she dragged a hand through her chestnut waves.

"I cannot believe you would be so irresponsible, Rhen. Didn't we *just* have a conversation about you eating well and taking care of yourself last week when you came to see me for your checkup?"

"That's definitely one way of putting it…" grumbled the raven-haired girl, more than a little annoyed at having yet another adult berating her for her bad behavior.

"Care to repeat that?" demanded Alana with a good deal more steel in her voice this time. "You're not too big for me to spank, you know, so I'd watch that mouth if I were you."

"Sorry ma'am!" squeaked Rhen on reflex, the combined force of both her aunt's and her doctor's stares making her suddenly wish that she'd worn her pull-up that morning after all.

Breathing out heavily through her nose, Dana shook her head.

"You know… I've got half a mind find some nice, quiet spot to tan your hide in just as soon as we're through security, if for no other reason than to put a lid on some of that sass for the next few hours."

"Oh! I've got a pass to the sky lounge," volunteered Alana. "Take her there. The girls and I can get some coffee and breakfast going, and you can deal with little miss mouthy in comfort and style while someone cooks you a tasty omelet."

"Hmmm… I have to admit that *does* sound rather nice…"

"Doesn't it, though?"

"It sure does," agreed Rhen, nice and blasé as several things dawned on her all at once and she found herself experiencing a sudden resurgence of bratty confidence. "But I'm afraid you're going to have to take a rain check on that spanking, Aunt Dana."

Holy crap, I think I just might be able to get away with this… Probably.

"Oh?" her partner pressed, looking skeptical but apparently willing to humor her for the time being. "And why is that?"

Resisting the urge to gloat, Rhen did her best to keep her voice (mostly) neutral.

"Well, besides the fact that it would be totally unfair of you to spank me over just wearing my panties like a normal girl my age," she began, riding high on a wave of adrenaline and near-panic at how much fun she was having talking back to her not-aunt while the older woman's eyebrows continued to climb ever higher in bemused consternation.

"Mmhmm…" answered Dana in a very "You'd better be going somewhere with this" kind of way. "That's certainly *one* way of looking at the situation."

Keep it together, Rhen. You've got this!

"Well, uh… yeah. Besides that," continued the shorter girl, slightly less smug this time as she squirmed under the expectant weight of her partner's dark blue eyes, marveling for the seemingly millionth time at how pretty they always looked when they were narrowed at her like that. "I'm pretty sure the TSA wouldn't appreciate it if you just started spanking me in the middle of public, or even in a bathroom for that matter. They aren't exactly known for being the biggest fans of loud noises and yelling in crowded airports, now are they?"

"Humph. Yes, I suppose you *do* have a point there," conceded Dana, furrowing her brows and looking vexed. "I'd rather not have us wind up on the no fly list just because your bottom needed warming."

"Exactly," crooned Rhen, covering her triumphant grin with a yawn and a stretch as she added. "Also, like, come on. It's *way* too early for a spanking. Let's just get some breakfast and talk this over later once we're all rested and not feeling so crabby, yeah?"

Only there's not going to be a later, she added silently, giddy with the thrill of managing to pull one over on her aunt for a change. *You and Alana have to leave as soon as we get checked into the hotel, and you aren't going to be back until way late tonight, so I doubt you'll be up for any rigorous bottom smacking by then. And, even if you tell Courtney to do it for you, she's hardly in any condition to deliver anything up to her usual standards. She's one strong breeze away from tipping over and puking her guts out. So check and mate, bossy boots. This cutie pie is flying pale-cheeked and pull-up free. Hah!*

"Hmmm…" came Dana's slow reply after taking a few moments to mull things over, rubbing her chin thoughtfully before finally flashing her girlfriend a toothy, wolfish grin as she conceded defeat for the time being. "I guess we'll just have to deal with this tomorrow then, won't we?"

Oh… right. Tomorrow.

Rhen had honestly forgotten that that was an option.

"Uh…"

"Yes, that'll work just fine," nodded Dana to herself, back on balance again as her features smoothed themselves once more into their usual configuration of no-nonsense sternness and wry amusement. "I'm sure hotel soap will get the job done more or less. And, if not, we can always pick up some Ivory when we're in town. Oh this is perfect! Now you won't have to worry about any of this hanging over your head and we can all just enjoy our vacation in peace. Isn't that wonderful?"

Crap.

"Suuuuper," deadpanned Rhen, snatching up the handle on her roller bag and spinning around to face forward again with a harrumph. "I'm just *so* lucky."

But, stuck as she was in the middle of a crowded line, she couldn't exactly stomp off anywhere, and she didn't put up any resistance when her partner gathered her back into her arms and pulled her in snug against her chest.

"Nice try, cutie pie," Dana purred, giving her a quick squeeze and a peck on the cheek.

Her smile was hidden behind her back, but Rhen could still hear it in her voice.

"Hey, it was worth a shot," she mumbled back, her stomach thrilling with the promise of things to come as she and the older woman advanced forward another spot in line.

"I'll give you an A for effort, at least," snickered Dana, before adding just quiet enough for Rhen to hear. "And a week's worth of sore bottoms if you sass me like that in public ever again, little missy."

Swallowing hard, Rhen burrowed herself a little bit deeper into her partner's embrace to hide her blush.

"Oh, come on, you can't be mad at me for that. I was just playing my part as the bratty teen."

"Mmhmm," chuckled Dana, surreptitiously wriggling her fingers underneath the girl's moodily crossed arms to tickle her sides. "Well, as always, you did a wonderful job 'pretending' to be a spoiled little brat. And you're going to *keep* playing that part when you take a nice, and very long, trip over my knee tomorrow morning."

"I, uh…"

Of course, that was *also* the moment Abby chose to stage whisper to her, "Don't sweat it, bratty buns. I'm sure she'll have forgotten all about it by the time we're through security."

"I wouldn't count on it, Abby, dear," Dana called back over

her shoulder as both Courtney and Alana snorted with laughter. "You know me a little bit better than that by now, don't you?"

"Good point," acknowledged the blonde, nice and chipper as she shrugged. "Sorry, Rhen, I tried."

"Yeah, thanks a lot. Suuuuper helpful, Abby. Really."

—

"Next in line, step forward, please," called a crisply commanding voice from a few feet in front of Rhen, going completely ignored and prompting its owner to growl in irritation.

"That means *you*, short stuff."

"Huh?"

Glancing up from her phone after a tap on the shoulder from her aunt, the raven-haired girl being glared at was shocked to discover that they'd somehow reached the front of the line without her even realizing it.

"Oh shoot, my bad!" Rhen apologized with a start, developing a sudden case of butterfingers as she scrambled forward while juggling her phone and her suitcase, tripping over the latter in her haste to get going and nearly sending the former flying out of her hands in the process. "Coming! I'm com- Crap!"

"Whoa now, careful there, hon," laughed Dana, deftly plucking the phone from her not-niece's fumbling fingers as she stepped past the her and ushered her along with a firm hand on her waist. "You don't want to go cracking your screen so soon after we just got it fixed, do you?"

"Hey! Come on, that's not fair!" whined Rhen as her phone disappeared into her partner's purse, back on balance now as the two of them closed the distance to the podium where a dour looking woman in her mid-forties with salt and pepper hair pulled back into a no-nonsense bun was waiting for them. "I was using that, you know."

"And you can have it back once we're through security and you've had your breakfast," the older woman promised, as patient as ever as she fished out her boarding pass and ID from her purse. "If you can behave yourself for that long, that is."

"Of course I can!" insisted Rhen, cheeks puffing out in an indignant pout, but unwilling to risk arguing the point any further lest she end up losing her phone for the duration of their flight.

"Good. Then why don't you show me how well you can behave yourself by getting your papers ready for the nice lady?"

"Yeah, yeah…" she mumbled, simmering in childish resentment over the high score she'd just lost as she dug her own ID and crumpled boarding pass from one of the small pockets sewn into her skirt. "Killjoy."

"Good morning," greeted Dana pleasantly, ignoring her girlfriend's grumbling as she deposited her credentials into the waiting TSA woman's outstretched palm.

"Morning," she echoed back as she absently scanned the barcode on the redhead's boarding pass and ran her ID under a small black light before returning them to her with a companionable half-grin. "Sun's barely up and you're already neck deep in backtalk, huh?"

"You can sure say that again," agreed Dana with an easygoing laugh, taking back her papers and tucking them away in her purse with a shake of her head. "Sorry about all the hubbub earlier, by the way. She can be *such* a handful sometimes."

"Nah, don't worry about it," replied the other woman with a chuckle of her own, waving away her apologies as she just as absently took Rhen's proffered boarding pass and ID. "Happens all the time, believe it or not. There's just something about flying that gets kids cranky, I guess."

She spared a moment to skewer the younger girl standing beside her "aunt" with a pointed look then as she added flatly, "Even the ones who you'd think would know better by now."

Oh bite me, lady, thought Rhen to herself, not actually daring to say so out loud.

"Well that's a relief to hear," breathed Dana with a self-deprecating sigh. "Still, she's definitely going to be running around with a sunburnt seat by the time I'm through with her, that's for sure."

"A woman who likes to get straight to the bottom of things," nodded the TSA officer approvingly, her half-grin broadening into a proper smile. "I like it."

"Oh yes," crooned Dana, dragging her fingernails in lazy circles between her girlfriend's shoulder blades as she matched the other woman's amused look. "My little Rhenny here is very well-acquainted with my lap. Aren't you, honey buns?"

"Whatever…" mumbled Rhen in response to that, not meeting either woman's eye as she stared fixedly at a point just past the TSA officer's left elbow.

"I swear… All of this fuss over a little extra precaution in case she has an accident on the plane," sighed Dana shaking her head in exasperation. "Some girls, I tell you…"

"They just love to see how far they can push their boundaries, don't they?"

"And then some!"

"It was still worth it," piped up Rhen, rallying her reserves of petulance as she came to the conclusion that since she was already in trouble as it was, there really wasn't much point in fretting over adding a little bit more to her tab for being sassy. "I'd much rather take a spanking than have to wear one of *those* stupid things."

At least in public at any rate…

"That mouth soaping is totally going to suck. But, hey, it's whatever."

Flashing the two older women her best unrepentant grin, she shrugged.

"You win some, you lose some, right?"

"Oh, Rhen…" sighed Dana, pinching the bridge of her nose in an effort to mask the note of amusement in her voice. "What on earth am I going to do with you?"

"Buy me breakfast?" supplied the backtalk-happy junior without missing a beat.

"Cute."

"I know I am. You already told me you liked my outfit today, remember?"

"Oh you are just *begging* for it, missy…"

Rhen couldn't help but stick her tongue out at that, her heart racing a mile a minute with the thrill of being so brazenly bratty.

"Too bad you've got to wait until tomorrow, huh?"

"*Excuse* me?"

"Heh. Well it certainly seems like you've got your work cut out for you," interjected the TSA officer before the two of them could continue their verbal jousting, her own face a mixture of amusement and mild disapproval as she took in the exchange going on in front of her.

"You'd think so, wouldn't you?" snorted the auburn-haired older woman, rolling her eyes at her self-satisfied niece as the corners of her mouth drifted up into a sly grin. "But she'll start singing a different tune just as soon as her panties come down tomorrow morning. It's amazing how quickly Rhen is able to find her manners once her little tush is bared for a spanking. Why, just the other day, she was trying to tell me that she didn't need to go to bed on time because-"

"Oh my god!" moaned Rhen in a desperate attempt to shut her partner up before she could continue recounting her disastrous attempt at renegotiating her bedtime, her devil-may-care façade crumbling away all at once to be replaced by a look of utter humiliation as she mumbled sourly. "You don't have to tell her *that* much, you know."

To which both women just laughed.

"Awww, there's no need to be embarrassed, darling," soothed the TSA officer with a patronizing pat on her head. "Yours are hardly the first set of sassy buns to come waltzing through this checkpoint anglin' for a spankin'."

Folding her sweater-mitten arms in front of her as the tips of her ears bloomed with fresh heat, Rhen let out her best harrumph.

"Could you maybe hurry it up? We're kind of in a hurry here."

Ignoring her grumbling entirely, the salt and pepper security officer turned her attention back to smoothing out the crumpled up boarding pass she'd been given.

"You know, you really shouldn't ball these things up," she scolded instead, frowning in mild annoyance as she dragged the bent and creased piece of paper back and forth along the edge of her podium in an attempt to smooth it out enough to get its barcode to scan properly.

"Uh… Sorry," mumbled Rhen, looking genuinely abashed this time. "I didn't think it'd make a difference."

"Just don't let it happen again, alright?" dismissed the officer, getting a fervent nod in return as she set the now slightly curled pass aside and picked up the twenty-year-old turned teenager's ID from where she'd set it earlier. "It makes the wait for the people behind you that much longer. And we wouldn't want to do that, now would we?"

"I guess not…"

As she had with Dana's ID before, the TSA officer held Rhen's underneath the small black light mounted to the front of her podium to verify that it was authentic. Seemingly satisfied, she was just about to pass it and her boarding pass back to her, when something caught her eye and she drew them back.

"Hmmm…"

Pressing her lips together, she let out a low, contemplative hum as her hard eyes flicked down to the ID in her hand, up to the girl standing before her with her hand still awkwardly outstretched, and then back again.

"You know, ma'am…" she began to say a moment later, speaking with deliberate care as she drummed her rubber-gloved fingertips against the faux-wood top of her podium and let her gaze wander the length of Rhen with a newfound attention to detail. "It's a bit out of the ordinary from how we typically handle parents traveling with cranky kids, but if you'd rather not wait until you reach your destination, I'd be more than happy to escort you two somewhere private where you could finish that discussion you were having in line earlier with your…"

She cleared her throat meaningfully then and arched a brow.

"Daughter?"

"Niece," corrected Dana with a pleasant smile, apparently catching on to where the other woman was headed.

"Oh, right. Your *niece*, of course…" the officer amended with wink. "If you would prefer, you can request a private security screening for the two of you, instead of going through the regular process out here with everyone else."

Wait a minute, she can't be about to suggest what I think she is…

"The rooms we perform those in are nice and quiet, and above all else, far enough away from anyone who might be caught off guard by any… Ahem. 'Percussive racket' that might arise as a result of an extra-vigorous pat-down a parent or guardian might choose to provide their charges in addition to our standard screening procedures."

Oh my god, she is! Crap, crap, crap, crap, crap!

"A private screening, eh?" replied Dana smoothly, glancing down to where Rhen was staring wide-eyed at the two of them in mounting horror, mouth agape. "Now there's an idea."

Grinning from ear to ear, she reached over and closed her not-niece's jaw for her, ruffling her tousled hair affectionately as she did so.

"I really *would* prefer to wipe the slate clean with her as soon as possible. I don't like making her wait once she's earned a spanking."

"Swift and decisive is definitely the way to handle these sorts of things," agreed the other woman with a firm nod.

"Whoa, hold on! W-Wait just a second," Rhen started to protest, ice cold butterflies dive-bombing around inside her stomach as her heart rate skyrocketed. "You can't be serious-"

But before she could really get going, her partner was speaking over her again, silencing her with a look and a quick squeeze of her shoulder.

"I think that sounds like a wonderful idea, Officer…?"

"Taylor," the other woman finished for her, gesturing to the laminated ID badge hanging from a retractable lanyard clipped to her right lapel. "But you can just call me Nicole. Everyone else does."

"Well, it's very nice to meet you, Nicole. I'm Dana Johnson, but I suppose you already know that," replied Rhen's partner in turn, shaking the woman's hand with a wry grin.

Rhen, on the other hand, was still far from happy about the sudden turn that things seemed to have taken.

I was supposed to be safe from spanks for the day, darn it!

Drawing herself up to her full height and doing her best to look every inch the adult the TSA woman *knew* that she was, she stepped in between the two women making plans for her bottom and held her hand out, palm up, wiggling her fingers expectantly.

"Look. It's nice of you to offer and all, but that really won't be necessary. Now if you could give me back my boarding pass and ID, a regular screening will be just fine. Thanks, Nicol-"

"That's *Officer* Taylor to you," interrupted the woman behind the podium, all of her pleasantness from a moment earlier freezing over in an instant as she stared her down with every ounce of authority her position granted her. "And if I were you, *young lady*, I'd zip those lips and wait patiently until the adults are finished talking. Is that clear?"

"Yes ma'am!" squeaked Rhen, jumping back a step as if she'd just been shocked. "I'm sorry!"

So much for the adult route. Humph.

"Hmmm… You will be soon enough, I think, cutie pie," spoke up Dana after letting her not-niece stew in her own embarrassment for a few more moments under the TSA woman's disapproving stare. "But, yes, as *I* was saying, we would be more than happy take you up on your offer of a private screening, Nicole. Thank you."

"Great," replied Officer Taylor, all business now as she gestured for a man in a royal blue TSA uniform shirt to come take her place behind the podium. "Right this way then, ladies."

Taking up a now very nervous Rhen's hand in hers, Dana

turned back toward where Alana, Courtney, and Abby were still waiting to approach the podium with their boarding passes.

"You guys go on ahead and we'll catch up with you later," she said. "This shouldn't take too long, I'm sure."

"Oh no, not long at all," agreed the TSA officer, gesturing them toward an unmarked door set into the wall next to the scanning equipment as she assessed Dana's purse and Rhen's roller bag with a keen professional eye. "I should be able to have both of you done in just about ten minutes give or take."

"Great," beamed Dana. "We'll meet you at our gate in twenty then."

"But... but...!"

"Oh yes, dear, you're right," the older woman nodded facetiously as she led her brat of a girlfriend away, her grin going wolfish. "Let's make that twenty-five, just to be safe."

You have got to be freaking kidding me...

"Have fun," called Abby, blowing the two of them a kiss as Courtney and Alana looked on with amusement (and a jealous pout in the case of the latter).

"This is such bullcrap," muttered Rhen under her breath, stomach flip-flopping with anticipatory dread at what she knew awaited her at the end of their trek.

Oh well... At least I won't have to worry about getting it later, right?

While that might have been the case, she still found that it was very little comfort to her soon to be spanked backside.

Humph.

Chapter 10

TSA Trouble

Moving at a brisk, clipped pace, Officer Taylor escorted Rhen and Dana through a series of drab and dreary hallways lit by buzzing fluorescent lights overhead, leading them deeper and deeper into the bowels of the airport's administrative wing before at last stopping in front of a nondescript wooden door with a plastic sign set into the wall beside it that simply read, "Screening Room 2".

"Alright, ladies, here we are," she announced brightly, unlocking the door with a key hooked to her lanyard and waving the two of them inside. "Come on in and make yourselves at home."

"Don't mind if I do," sing-songed Dana as she pulled her reluctant girlfriend after her into the sparsely furnished interior. "Thanks again for doing this, by the way, Nicole. I know things are really busy this morning, and I appreciate you making the time for us like you are. It means a lot."

"Think nothing of it, ma'am," waved away the officer, the hard soles of her flats clacking out a staccato rhythm on the shiny floor beneath her as she followed them inside, letting the door slam shut behind her with a heavy *THUD!* as she went. "I always enjoy helping out people in relationships like yours."

She then favored the petite girl pouting moodily beside her aunt with a snide grin.

"Plus, I'd be lying if I said I didn't love watching spoiled little cuties like Rhen here get their just desserts."

Yeah, I just freaking bet you do, said cutie thought to herself with a silent huff, glaring daggers at the woman, but wisely choosing to keep her mouth shut for the time being.

It was just the three of them now in what she was fairly

certain was a soundproof room, and she wasn't about to run the risk of finding out if the TSA officer was just as spank-happy as her partner was. Not when there were so many armless metal chairs arranged neatly along the far side of one wall that looked like they'd be perfect for taking someone across your knee while sitting on.

"Oh yes," agreed Dana, turning a glacial look on her not-niece. "After the way she's been carrying on this morning, I'd say she's earned herself a double serving of red derriere flambé, along with a full three-course meal and a box of leftovers to boot."

At the mention of food, Rhen's stomach gave an audible rumble.

"Ugh! Can we just get this over with already?" she found herself snapping as her aunt and the salt and pepper security officer both snickered, her grumpiness from her lack of sleep and skipping out on breakfast rearing its ugly head as she gave her disheveled hair an irritated toss and redoubled her glowering. "Like, you *saw* my ID, NIc- I mean, Officer Taylor, so I know you know how old I really am. And, quite frankly, I'd appreciate it if you could just cut the crap and do your freaking job without treating me like I'm some sort of tween with an attitude problem."

Even as the words were leaving her mouth, Rhen knew that they were a mistake. And not just because the worry, frustration, and embarrassment churning around inside the pit of her stomach right then made them come out sounding far more like a whiney series of demands from a petulant child not getting her way than the rebuke of a highly educated young woman who was meant to be taken seriously.

The hard looks on her Aunt Dana's and Officer Taylor's faces as she finished her tiny tirade were also a pretty good indicator that she'd royally screwed up as well.

Uh-oh…

"Er… Uh, I, uh… That came out wrong-" she started to back-pedal, before being cut off by a very irate Officer Taylor.

"Alright, now you listen to me and you listen good, *little girl*," she growled, putting enough tight-jawed maternal fury behind those last two words to make it abundantly clear just where Rhen stood as far as she was concerned as she closed the distance between the two of them. "The only thing *I* saw out there was a disobedient brat pitching a fit in the middle of my line because she'd been caught in a lie by her auntie."

Standing so close now that shorter girl's vision was dominated entirely by a view of a full chest pushing out from beneath a surprisingly well-cut royal blue button up, she glared imperiously down her nose at the impudent twenty-year-old turned teenager.

"Or did I mishear something when Miss Dana said that you were supposed to be wearing a pull-up today?"

"No... I mean... That's not...!" spluttered Rhen, rooted to the spot by a sudden burst of knee-knocking, thigh-squirming panic as she frantically searched for something to focus on that wasn't the implacable stare avalanching down on top of her.

Huh. It just says 'officer' on her badge. I thought for sure there'd be a number or something there...

"Well?"

Nostrils flaring, Office Taylor's right hand shot out to take hold of Rhen by the base of her delicate chin, turning her head up and forcing her to make eye contact with her.

"I asked you a question."

Heart racing, the shorter girl swallowed hard, fighting the urge to cross her arms as her fingers fiddled with the cuffs of her sweater.

"I uh... I guess she did say that, um... Y-Yes ma'am..."

"That's what I thought," harrumphed the older woman, refusing to let her mind wander far as she gave her chin a firm (but not actually hard) squeeze to keep her focus locked straight ahead. "And *are* you wearing a pull-up right now?"

"No..." mumbled Rhen, rolling her eyes and attempting to vent some of her pent-up nervousness with a pout that was made extra-cute thanks to the rubber-gloved hand squeezing her blushing cheeks together.

"Excuse me?" pressed Officer Taylor, turning her head to

the side and leaning in close. "What was that? Speak up now. Or would you rather I just check what you decided to wear this morning for myself?"

"No ma'am!" repeated the shorter girl with a frightened squeak, standing up ramrod straight and clapping both hands to the seat of her skirt. "I uh… I'm sorry, ma'am. I'm not wearing a pull-up, no."

"Awww, there we go," cooed the TSA officer, all smiles now as she let her go and affectionately patted her on top of her head, mussing her dark hair. "I knew there was a polite young lady hiding somewhere beneath all that attitude."

"Yes ma'am," nodded Rhen again, not trusting herself to say anything else right then as she nibbled on the end of her left thumbnail, her other hand still clamped tight against her backside.

"I see you've had some practice with this sort of thing," chimed in Dana then, rescuing her girlfriend from being the center of attention as she flashed the other woman an amused grin.

"Oh, well… Heh. I guess you could say I know a thing or two about making sassy girls call me Mommy," acknowledged Officer Taylor with a tight smirk. "In fact, just the other day I had to get on my own girl's case after I found out she hadn't been doing her reading assignments for her art history class."

"You don't say?" crooned Rhen's partner at that, casting a baleful look in her direction as she added. "This one's a bit of procrastinator as well."

"I'm *shocked*."

"Right? Whoever said that growing up had anything to do with how old you actually are never took a tour of a college dorm."

"That's for sure," snorted Officer Taylor, shaking her head before glancing down at her watch and frowning. "Oh! But speaking of procrastinating, I think we'd best get down to business if you two want to have enough time to grab some breakfast before your flight."

"Works for me," harrumphed Rhen, finally giving in to her urge to cross her arms as she did her best to think about what she wanted to eat after they were free of this stupid screening room rather than her looming trip over her auntie's knee. "The sooner we're done here, the better."

"I couldn't have put it better myself, cutie pie," laughed Dana, leaning in to kiss her pouting lips before turning back to the TSA woman. "Alright, Nicole, what's first?"

—

A few minutes later, after making short work of waving a metal detector wand over the two of them, a quick pat-down (which confirmed for Officer Taylor that Rhen was indeed not wearing a pull-up underneath her skirt), and a cursory search through her partner's purse, it was the twenty-year-old turned teenager's turn to have her carryon luggage inspected. Collapsing its handle, the TSA woman picked it up and laid it out on its side on the squat metal table that she'd used earlier to inspect Dana's belongings.

"Okeydokey then, let's just see what we've got going on in here, shall we?" she said, unzipping the small suitcase and throwing open its lid.

"Hmmm… By the looks of things, I'd say what we have is a *mess*," observed Dana dryly, her eyes narrowing in disapproval as she ran them over the smooshed together mess of balled up clothes and charging cables that was her girlfriend's attempt at packing a suitcase.

"She does have an interesting approach to organization, doesn't she?" mused the other woman with a bemused shake of her head.

"I'd say 'naughty' is a much more apt descriptor…"

As she spoke, Dana leveled a *very* unimpressed look at her niece.

"And honestly, I'm a little surprised that she'd think this was at all acceptable considering that the last time her bedroom started developing such a 'creative' look to it, she found herself tidying it up with a bright red bottom full of soapy water."

"Oh really now?" pressed Officer Taylor, turning to regard the woman beside her with a newfound curiosity. "You spanked her *and* gave her an enema?"

"Two whole quarts with a healthy dose of Ivory to make sure she paid attention," confirmed Dana with a wicked grin. "She's used to them enough by now that I could have easily gone with four if I'd really wanted to make a point, but I figured that two and a sore seat would be enough to get her to sit up and take notice."

"And did it?"

Rhen, for her part, remained uncharacteristically quiet on the matter. Nibbling at her lower lip and doing her best to blend in with her surroundings as her face all but burst into flames.

I knew I should've just checked this stupid thing...

"Well, she's been keeping her room as close to spotless as a girl her age is liable to get, so I'd say so," crooned Dana, reaching out and pinching one rosy cheek. "What do you think, honey buns?"

I think you wildly overestimate how much soapy water my backside can accommodate, the younger girl grumbled to herself, while aloud she demurred.

"Yes ma'am... Once was definitely more than enough for me to learn my lesson."

At least for a couple more months, anyway.

Officer Taylor let out a low, impressed whistle at that.

"Sounds to me like I need to invest in an enema bag as soon as possible," she chuckled.

"Oh you should!" insisted Dana, patting her arm excitedly. "They're super easy to use, and have such an entertaining effect on naughty little girls. *Especially* the mouthy ones."

She spared a moment to drink in the miffed look that had developed on her not-niece's face at that last bit.

"You'd be amazed how quickly this one's attitude dries up once Auntie Dana starts pushing our old friend The Nozzle inside her tush."

"Hey! I'm not like, *that* mouthy, you know…" insisted Rhen, her cheeks clenching together on reflex beneath her skirt.

"Of course you aren't, sweetie," agreed her aunt with an insincere smile. "That's why I only had to give you three quarts after church that one time when you-!"

"Okay, okay, we get your point!" interrupted Rhen before her partner could finish embarrassing her further.

"Heh. Well then…" drawled Officer Taylor, ignoring the shorter girl's pouting altogether as she gave Dana an appreciative nod. "I think I'll be ordering one tonight, thanks."

The grin on her face flattened out, though, as soon as she turned her attention back to the petite junior fuming silently beside her.

"But getting back to the matter at hand, I'm afraid I'm going to have to dump out little miss messy's entire suitcase and go through it piece by piece," she sighed, rubbing at one of her temples. "Selective screening regulations require that I verify she isn't attempting to smuggle anything illegal inside her luggage, and that's kind of impossible when everything's all crammed together in there like this."

"Oh, that's totally fine," Dana reassured her with an apologetic wave. "We both understand that you've got to do your job, Nicole."

"Wait, you mean I'm *not* supposed to bring my cocaine and AK-47 in my carryon?" piped up Rhen over her aunt's apologies, rolling her eyes at all the tongue-clucking going on over her ultra space efficient packing techniques. "Well gee, I wish someone would have told me that sooner. I *knew* I should have checked those!"

While the gasp of surprise that left the shorter girl's mouth as she lightly bounced the heel of her palm against her forehead might have been fake, the one that escaped her partner was entirely genuine.

"Rhen Elizabeth Mathews! What on earth has gotten into you,

young lady?"

Totally aghast at her not-niece's flippant attitude, Dana rounded on her and quick as a striking viper snatched up one of her ears between her thumb and forefinger, twisting it sharply and forcing her down over the metal table in front of them as she did so.

"We do-"

SMACK!

"*Not!*"

SMACK!

"Make those-"

SMACK!

"Kinds of-"

SMACK!

"Jokes-"

SMACK!

"At. The. *Airport*!"

SMACK! SMACK! SMACK!

"Ack! Okay, *okay*!" squawked Rhen all at once, bottom smarting despite the layers of ruffles dampening the impact of her partner's palm and practically climbing up onto the low table digging into her thighs in an attempt to ease some of the pressure being applied to her ear. "It was a dumb joke and I shouldn't have made it! I'm sorry, I'm sorry!"

"You're damn right it was a dumb joke," growled Dana.

SMACK! SMACK! SMACK!

Getting in three more heavy-handed slaps to the underside of her niece's skirt before dragging her back to her feet and spinning her around by the ear to face the woman she'd just been sassing.

"That kind of attitude is completely unacceptable, little girl. Now apologize to Officer Taylor."

"I'm- Ah! I'm sorry for my- Oh! For my behavior Officer Taylor!" the thoroughly cowed younger girl half hissed and half moaned through gritted teeth, dancing on her tiptoes beside her aunt. "I swear it won't happen again!"

"You'd better make doubly sure that it doesn't," admonished the older woman, wagging a bright blue rubber-gloved forefinger at her. "Because joking or not, comments like that can very easily land you on the no fly list if you're not careful."

"T-They can?" squeaked Rhen, going suddenly pale as her knees wobbled beneath her.

"That's right."

Nodding gravely, the TSA officer pursed her lips into a thin line and watched with barely-restrained amusement as the shorter girl wilted under the weight of her mounting worries and dread.

"But…"

Then, beaming brightly, she reached out and playfully tapped the tip of her nose with the very same forefinger she'd just been wagging.

"Luckily for you, sweetheart, the penalty for juvenile offenders is typically just a slap on the wrist."

And snickered.

"Or in your case, the bottom."

"Oh thank god!"

Sagging with relief as Dana released her grip on her, Rhen rubbed gingerly at her throbbing ear with one hand while the other drifted back on instinct to cup her tingling backside.

"I guess that's better than the alternative…"

Only to realize after the fact that she'd effectively just admitted that she *was* a "juvenile" offender, rather than an adult like she'd been arguing she was up until that point.

Oh well, what else is new? she sighed to herself with a rueful grimace. *It wasn't like I was doing that great of a job showing off how mature I am to begin with anyway. I guess I can put up with being Rhenny the bratty teen for a little while longer…*

That thought sent a shiver down her spine, pulsing directly between her legs and making them threaten to give out from under her for the second time in less than a minute.

Not that I really have much of a choice.

Pouting as the sobering reality that she was going to get spanked by her aunt in front of this no-nonsense TSA woman in just a few short minutes whether she liked it or not settled in along the bottom of her stomach, Rhen watched on with a quiet huff as Dana moved back to stand beside the preening officer.

"Do you mind if I fold and repack while you go through things, Nicole?"

"Not at all," answered Officer Taylor with a friendly shake of her head, tipping the contents of Rhen's little suitcase out onto the table in front of her and sliding the pile of clothing and cables over so that the other woman could reach them more easily. "In fact, why don't you just go ahead and help me sort through this whole mess so we're not here all day?"

"That sounds like an excellent idea!" declared Dana, making a show of rolling up her sleeves. "Two sets of hands makes for half the work, as they say. And based on what I'm seeing here, you could definitely use all the help you can get."

"Oh please, it's not *that* bad," groused Rhen, shuffling awkwardly beside her partner as she watched the two women begin rifling through her belongings.

"Not that bad?" echoed Dana incredulously, shaking out and holding up a pale yellow sundress that she'd found buried underneath three different hardback novels (Rhen hadn't been sure which one she wanted to read, so she'd brought all three of them with her just to be safe). "Rhen, honey, all of your pretty clothes are going to be a wrinkled mess by the time we get to California!"

Clucking her tongue and mumbling to herself, she folded the dress back up as neatly as she could and laid it down inside the empty suitcase.

"You really need to be more careful, dear."

"Look. It's not my fault, alright?" huffed the blushing girl, unable to keep her excuses bottled up for more than a moment. "Abby and Courtney wanted me to do a fashion show for them last night, and there wasn't enough time to refold everything this morning when I was putting it into my carryon before we left."

"And you couldn't have just done that last night *after* you were finished playing dress up with your friends?”

“Well, I uh…”

Digging the toe of one sneaker into the tile floor beneath her, Rhen did her best to meet the older woman’s stormy expression with a sheepish grin.

“I was kinda hoping that maybe you would do it for me?”

“Mmhmm.”

Dana was not amused.

“Corner. Now,” she ordered, turning back to what she was doing without a second glance and pointing to the wall beside her, snapping her fingers to get her moving. “Hands on top of your head and nose touching the wall just like we do at home. And if I hear another peep out of you before it’s time for you to go across my knee, you can do it with your skirt and panties off. Am I understood, young lady?”

“Yes ma’am!”

Eager not to give her partner any reason to change her mind about what she should be wearing while she was doing it (and only belatedly realizing that her acknowledgement could be mis-construed as a “peep” if she was in a bad mood), Rhen scrambled over to the corner she’d been ordered to and assumed her usual timeout position.

Well, at least there’s nobody here to see me like this, she thought to herself in a bleak attempt to find a silver lining among the storm clouds of her current predicament, wrinkling her nose as she worked to get as comfortable as she could in these unfa-miliar surroundings. *Not to mention I’m still coming out of this whole thing without a pull-up… Even if I do have to pay for it with my butt.*

Smiling to herself as nervous butterflies stirred to life inside her stomach and her thighs shifted together of their own accord, Rhen let out a barely audible snicker.

It could always be worse, right?

Somehow, though, she doubted that she’d still be feeling like she’d come out on top by the time her aunt was finally through with her. It being early in the morning apparently hadn't done anything to diminish her arm's swatting power, because those spur of the moment swats from earlier had *hurt*!

Oh well…

—

Despite her partner and the TSA officer's moaning and groaning about her packing job, the two women still managed to sort through and properly refold every embarrassing little item in Rhen's carryon in just a few short minutes. In no small part due to the fact that it was mostly just made up of her purchases from the day before, her pajamas, a few books, and a couple of chargers for her phone and tablet.

Probably would've been done a whole lot sooner if they hadn't stopped every two freaking seconds to comment on how cute my panties were or how nice I'd look in one thing or another, harrumphed the raven-haired not-teen to herself from her spot facing the corner, her lower back and shoulders just starting to ache from holding the uncomfortable position.

"Alright, honey buns, are you ready for your spanking?" called Dana, drawing her out of her self-pitying contemplation of the wall in front of her as she picked up one of the armless chairs from the back of the room and moved it to its center.

"Ugh. I guess so," harrumphed the girl, nose still pressed tight to the dusty intersection of bricks in an attempt to hide her nervousness.

"That's what I like to hear. Now taxi that tush on over so I can get you ready for takeoff," invited the older woman with a soft giggle, settling herself gracefully down onto her chair and patting her lap. "Hurry up now, time's-a-wastin'."

"Yeah, yeah…"

Sighing with resignation only partially exaggerated, Rhen pushed away from her corner and slowly turned to face her doom, dragging her feet as much as she dared to as she crossed the all too short distance over to her patiently waiting partner.

"Now, now, let's not have any more of that sulking," she chided gently, reaching out to take hold of her by the wrist as she came within range and pulling her around to stand in front of her. "You earned this punishment fair and square by trying to be sneaky, not to mention all of that attitude you piled up on top of everything, and now you're going to take it like a big girl. Is that understood?"

"Yes ma'am. You're right, I'm sorry," Rhen mumbled dutifully, just barely managing to keep in another put-upon sigh as she jerked her head back behind her with a pleading look. "But does *she* really have to be here for this?"

"Afraid so, kiddo," answered Officer Taylor before Dana could, a small smirk tugging up on one side of her mouth as she stood leaning against the wall beside the door to the room. "TSA regulations require that I remain with you both until you've been cleared to fly, and you're not getting the thumbs up from me until I've seen *you* go bottoms up over your auntie's knee."

"But, like… Couldn't you just wait outside? It's not like there's anywhere for us to sneak off to, and Aunt Dana could come get you once she's finished… You know…"

Rhen made a vague, twirling gesture with her hand, unable to bring herself to say the word "spanking" out loud despite being about to go across her partner's lap.

"Taking care of things."

"Well, yes, I suppose I *could* do that," conceded the salt and pepper security officer with a shrug, her smile widening by a couple of teeth. "But then I'd be missing out on all the fun, now wouldn't I?"

"You sure would," sing-songed Dana in agreement, cracks starting to form in her stern demeanor as she locked eyes with the other woman and winked, before turning a teasing grin back on her niece. "Besides, when have I ever not given you a spanking just because there was someone there to see it?"

"Um…" hesitated the shorter girl, her tongue pressing itself to the roof of her mouth as she struggled to find a way to answer that question without actually answering it. "Sometimes?"

"Rhen…" came her aunt's reply, low and dangerous. "Now is definitely not the time to be testing my patience, little girl."

"Okay, okay, never mind. I was just asking. Geez!"

'Is that right?" purred Dana, her tone going sugary sweet once again as she leveled a gimlet stare at her niece, one filled to the brim with silent promises of all sorts of extra-humiliating punishments should she try questioning her authority so brazenly a second time. "Just remember, young lady. If you want to behave like a brat in public, then you can just as easily get spanked like one too. Is that understood?"

Rhen had to bite the inside of her cheek to avoid giving voice to her honest opinions on that particular maxim of her partner's.

"What-freaking-ever," she harrumphed instead, rolling her eyes and balling her hands into frustrated fists at her sides. "Can we just get this over with?"

"We sure can!" chirped Dana brightly, her newfound sunny disposition not dimmed in the slightest by her not-niece's stormy glower. "Now, why don't you show Officer Taylor how good of a little helper you can be for me by getting that skirt up nice and high so I can bare your cute little caboose?"

She phrased it as a question, but the shorter girl could tell by the hard gleam in her partner's dark eyes that it was very much an order, and one that she ignored at her own peril.

Oh crap. She's totally switched into full on daycare mode, hasn't she? she realized with a sudden surge of giddy terror in her lower abdomen. *I must've ticked her off more than I thought…*

"Yes ma'am!"

Blushing scarlet, Rhen seized a fistful of ruffled skirt in either hand, and with one last pouting glare over her shoulder at her uninvited witness, began hoisting the layered material up past her waist; gripping it for dear life and not stopping until she'd once again fully exposed the panties she'd decided to wear that morning.

"Whoo lordy, those are cute, aren't they?" piped up Officer Taylor with an appreciative wolf whistle, her eyes glued to the rounded seat of the pale purple and white polka dot panties in front of her. "I can see now why she wanted to wear them so badly."

"Oh yes, they're absolutely adorable," agreed Dana, clearly in no rush now as she too appraised her girlfriend's choice in panties. "Are these new, Rhen?"

"Uh-huh," she nodded in reply, face flushed tomato red at having her underwear be on display for all to see as she smiled shyly at her partner. "I bought them yesterday when we were at the mall. Do you, um… Do you like them?"

"I sure do," confirmed the older woman with a broad grin, leaning in and turning her hips one way and then the other to see what she looked like from different angles. "They're maybe a little bit sheer in the back for a girl your age, but that's alright. It'll just make your cheeks look all the cuter once they're bright red and shining through."

Huh. I wonder what color purple and pink makes when you mix them together…

"But," continued Dana, holding up a single disapproving forefinger and tapping it against the furrow of trepidation that had formed between her girlfriend's brows. "Whether or not they're cute, or how much I like them, is neither here nor there, because these panties are *not* what you were supposed to be wearing this morning. Are they, Rhen?"

"No ma'am…"

"That's right," nodded her partner firmly, her voice as cutting as it was calm as she leaned forward and took hold of the pink-trimmed waistband on either side of her hips and began rolling it down, turning her brand new panties inside out as she eased them down to hang stretched taut between her knees. "And you had better just thank your lucky stars that I didn't think to pack Missus Hairbrush with me, because I can promise you she'd have *quite* a bit to say about your choice in undies this morning, little girl. Believe you me."

Shivering from the frigid air now caressing its invisible fingers along her silky smooth folds and exposed cheeks, Rhen's shy smile quirked up into something a bit cheekier as she let out a nervous giggle.

"Noooo kidding."

A thorough hairbrushing this early in the morning and on a bottom as chilly as hers was just then would have been absolutely *horrendous*.

Thank goodness for tiny miracles, I guess.

"You know..." cut in Officer Taylor then, her voice charming enough to peel the paint off the walls as she dragged her gaze away from Rhen's wobbly cheeks to meet her partner's eye. "I think I might just be able to help you out with that if you'd like, Dana."

"You can?" replied Rhen and her partner together at the same time, the former horrified and the latter intrigued.

"Yep," confirmed the TSA woman with another broad grin. "You two don't mind waiting a couple more minutes to get started, do you?"

"Yes-" Rhen began to harrumph, only to be overruled by her aunt with a discreet pinch to her inner thigh. "Ah!"

"We don't mind waiting," she answered serenely, maintaining her grip on her disobedient girlfriend as she smiled pleasantly. "Isn't that right, cutie pie?"

"Y-Yes ma'am!" squeaked Rhen, squirming and dancing in place as much as she could without dislodging her panties from around her knees or dropping her skirt.

"Mmmm... There's my good girl," cooed Dana, releasing her hold on her and patting the smarting patch of skin she'd just been pinching as she turned her attention back to the TSA officer standing beside the door. "So, what did you have in mind, Nicole?"

"Oh, nothing much," the woman replied with an easy shrug, reaching for the radio clipped to her belt. "Let me just get in touch with someone real quick and we'll see what I can rustle up."

"Take your time, we can wait."

Settling back in her chair and crossing one leg over the other, Dana continued to drink in the sight of her girlfriend's delightful nudity.

"And *you* can stay right where you are until I tell you otherwise, missy."

"Yes ma'am…" mumbled Rhen, face going scarlet as she gnawed fretfully at her lower lip.

I knew getting away with just a hand spanking was too good to be true… Dang it!

While she continued to pout silently, the TSA woman behind her thumbed her walkie-talkie to life, letting her eyes wander back to the younger girl's naked cheeks as she brought it up to her grinning lips.

"This is Officer Taylor. Do we have anyone near impound right now?"

"Yeah?" came a mildly irritated sounding voice amid a burst of static a few seconds later. "What's up?"

"Ah, hey there, Mandy. We've got ourselves a Code Penmark here in Screening Room Two that I could really use some help with if you've got a sec."

"Is that right?" snickered the other woman, sounding far less irritated this time.

"Oh yeah, and she's a *real* sassmouth too, girl. She's been giving me and her poor auntie lip like you wouldn't believe!"

"Well now, we can't be havin' that."

"Nope, we sure can't," agreed Officer Taylor, her smile growing all the more taunting as Rhen threw another dirty look over her shoulder at her. "Do you think you could pull something from impound that'll make an impression on a grumpy middle schooler?"

"Middle schooler?" huffed the younger girl under her breath, turning her glare back to a patch of wall just above her equally as amused aunt's head while shifting her weight from one foot to the other. "I know I'm short and all, lady, but you could have at least said freshman…"

Then again, she supposed that having this whole fiasco start over her not wearing a pull-up for their trip, combined with the fact that she barely topped five feet on her tip-toes and was completely devoid of even a single pubic hair between her narrow, splayed thighs probably wasn't doing her any favors when it came to presenting as more mature.

Actually, maybe being a middle schooler right now is better? she tried reasoning to herself, wishing very much that she'd had a chance to go to the bathroom before she'd been called to stand before her aunt. *At least if I'm in middle school getting spanked is a little less out of the ordinary and humiliating, right?*

It wasn't much of a silver lining, she knew, but it was still better than nothing.

While Rhen was lost amid a swirl of her own grumblings and attempts to downplay her smoldering embarrassment, Mandy came back with a reply on the radio.

"Hmmm… A *middle schooler*, eh?" she drawled, her voice tinged with wry amusement. "Yep, I think we've got just the thing in the cage. Give me a few minutes to sign it out and then I'll be right there."

"Thanks, hon. You're a lifesaver. See you soon."

"Ciao."

"And that's that taken care of."

Returning the walkie-talkie to her belt, Officer Taylor made a show of dusting off her hands and hooking her thumbs into her pants, looking very pleased with herself.

"Now we just have to wait for Mandy to get here and then you can tan little Rhenny's hide to your heart's content."

"Works for me."

Sighing contentedly, Dana pushed a stray lock of her auburn hair back behind an ear and matched the other woman's amused expression with one of her own.

"I'm more than alright with not wearing out my palm on her if I can avoid it. Plus, truth be told, I could sit and ogle my cutie pie all day. So, take your time."

"She's definitely ogleable, that's for sure," agreed Officer Taylor. "I can see why she keeps you so busy."

"Raising an obedient young lady is a fulltime commitment, I'm afraid," replied Dana piously.

"Don't I know it, sister."

Giving her salt and pepper bun an amused shake, the TSA officer settled back against the wall to wait.

"So… How long have you two been seeing each other?"

—

Rhen continued to remain at uneasy attention with her bare bottom on full display and covered in goosebumps for what she could only assume was an eternity, wishing with every fiber of her being that she'd just worn her stupid pull-up that morning like she was supposed to as the two older women made small talk around her. Neither of them deigned to include her in their conversation, even as they discussed her relationship with Dana (as well as Officer Taylor's own recently blossomed romance), but they nevertheless managed to keep her pinned in place both front and back with their watchful stares. Ensuring that she had no other choice but to stay right where she was, holding up her skirt and showing off every delicate charm that usually lay hidden beneath her adorable outfits.

Well, at least on those days when Dana hadn't decided her naughty niece could do with an extra dose of humility in the form of having her pants and panties privileges rescinded.

"You know, Nicole, if you're looking for something to *really* get your girl's attention, there's this wonderful little shop at the mall here in town that sells these fantastic hairbrushes," she was in the middle of saying, when at last there came a knock at the door. "Oh! Never mind, it looks like we're out of time. I can text you the details later, though, if you'd like."

"That would be great, hon, thanks," nodded the other woman, reaching over from her spot beside the door and pulling it open as she called out into the hallway beyond. "Come on in, Mandy."

Oh boy, here we go… Rhen groaned to herself as another pair of hard-soled shoes click-clacked their way into the screening room.

"Well now would you look at that. Not even ten yet, and already in trouble," came a snide drawl from a few feet behind her, its owner apparently unruffled in the slightest by the sight of a supposedly thirteen-year-old girl standing with her panties around her knees awaiting a trip across a knee. "What's the matter, darlin'? Your momma get sick of you kicking up a fuss while y'all were waiting to go through security?"

"Something like that," mumbled the mortified not-teen, her lips compressing in annoyance for a brief moment as she glared daggers at the sly look on her partner's face.

"Would you believe she actually told me I couldn't spank her because we were in public and it'd cause a scene?" laughed Dana as she waved hello to the newcomer.

"As if she hadn't been doing that all by herself already," scoffed Officer Taylor, rolling her eyes in solidarity. "Kids these days, I tell you…"

"Bet she's regrettin' actin' the fool now, ain't she?" sneered Mandy as the door clicked shut behind her.

Trapping Rhen with three women who were all dead set on seeing her seat sizzled for her sass.

"I should hope so," sniffed Dana, turning a hard look on her girlfriend that managed to strangle whatever protest had just been on the tip of her tongue. "How about it, little girl? Are you starting to think that maybe you should have just done what you were supposed to in the first place instead of trying to get sneaky?"

Flushing as bright a shade of red as she knew her bottom would be soon enough, Rhen fumbled her way through several indignant (and largely unintelligible) attempts at a snappy comeback before eventually giving up with a disgruntled huff and falling back on what she knew everyone in the room wanted to hear from her just then.

"Ugh. Yes ma'am…"

Then, in an effort to distract herself from the humiliating wetness that she could feel starting to build between her legs from being interrogated with her panties around her knees in front of two other adults, she threw a petulant look over her shoulder at the newly arrived TSA officer.

"Not that it's any of *your* busin- Uh..."

She'd been intending on bringing the full brunt of her bratty consternation to bear on the woman, but as she caught sight of what she held in her hands, she felt her stomach drop like a stone.

Along with her jaw.

"Is that a *paddle*?" she demanded with a horrified squeak instead, mounting dread and morbid curiosity mixing together in the pit of her sunken stomach to send a thrill of terror tingling along her exposed labia. "What the heck? You can't be serious!"

Who on earth packs a paddle in their freaking carryon? she added to herself, wincing internally as it occurred to her half a heartbeat later that her aunt might be just such a person.

"Pardon?" replied Mandy, looking down at what had the adoptive adolescent so spooked and blinking in confusion before letting out a deep and melodious laugh as understanding clicked into place on her dusky features. "Oh no, darlin', this ain't a paddle. Though, I can definitely see how you might make that mistake at first glance. Most people tend to."

"Sure looks like a paddle to me," mumbled the shorter girl skeptically, twisting the hem of her skirt in a white-knuckled grip and wishing very much that she could chew on her thumbnail instead as she scrutinized the exotic implement.

She'd been expecting someone's forgotten hairbrush, or maybe a belt or something. Not whatever horrible monstrosity it was that the olive-skinned woman was menacingly tapping against her open palm!

From her spot craning her head back over her shoulder (because there was absolutely no way in heck she was going to *further* cement her image as a disobedient middle schooler in the eyes of the smirking TSA officers behind her by giving them a clear view of her pristinely bare slit), she could see that it was made out of some sort of highly polished caramel colored wood with intricate patterns of crashing waves engraved into its broad surface. And while it was hard to tell for sure just by looking at it out of the corner of her eye, judging by the way the other woman was holding it, it looked to be long enough to cover one of her cheeks (and then some!) with a single swat. It was also *way* too thick for her liking, and beyond being both long and heavy, it was also easily twice as wide as both of her hands were put together side-by-side; rounded on one end before tapering gracefully down into a comfortable looking handle at its other. One that had some sort of wrist strap made from coarsely woven fibers threaded through a hole at its base.

In Rhen's opinion, it looked very much like a paddle. Or maybe a miniature boat oar? Or perhaps some sort of comically oversized hairbrush? But, as the broadly beaming TSA woman continued to explain, it was apparently none of those things.

"This here, little lady, is what's known as a patu," she said, enunciating the last word with two syllables and a soft "a" sound.

"Which is…?" deadpanned the twenty-year-old turned teen-ager, the butterflies inside her stomach overriding her natural inclination to be polite in the face of authority.

Especially when she had her panties around her knees.

"Heh. I think I see what you mean now about her havin' a mouth, Nicole," snorted the woman with the exotic implement, ignoring Rhen's scowl entirely as she turned a wry look on her friend. "Here she is standin' bare assed and about to get spanked somethin' fierce, and she's actin' like I just pulled the plug in the middle of her after school cartoons. What a little sass-brat!"

"Oh, if only you knew…" sighed Dana, the grin on her lips doing a poor job of making her exasperation sound all that convincing. "She's usually a lot more respectful than this, actually. She just tends to get a bit snippy whenever she has to be reminded that she's not too old to take a trip over my knee. Isn't that right, cutie pie?"

"Whatever," grumbled Rhen, refusing to meet anyone's eye just then as her cheeks heated up even further. "I'm just expressing myself. It's not *my* fault if you've all got a stick up your butts."

"Oh-hoh, is that so?" countered the auburn-haired older woman smoothly, completely unfazed by the waves of sullen petulance radiating off of her girlfriend.

It was pretty difficult to pull off an aura of disdainful nonchalance when you were naked below the waist and looked every inch the grumpy teenager trying (and failing spectacularly) to hide how nervous you really were, and Rhen was no exception.

"Would you care to rephrase that, *little girl?*"

"Um…"

Swallowing hard, Rhen shifted her weight from one foot to the other and back again for several seconds before finally working up the nerve to speak.

"Maybe I misspoke just a bit there… I'm uh… I'm sorry, um, ma'am."

"See?" chuckled Dana, uncrossing her legs and sitting up straight in her chair. "She likes to think she's got what it takes to really give me attitude, but she's far too sweet to keep it up for long."

Leaning in a little, she gave the side of her naughty niece's hip a condescending pat.

"Pout all you like, but deep down you're just Auntie Dana's sassy little cinnamon bun, aren't you, Rhen?"

Rhen, for her part, just shifted her gaze down from the wall behind her partner, to a spot just in front of her shoes with a sheepish nod, content to keep quiet for the time being.

Or so she thought.

"But, speaking of cartoons, you two should have *seen* the meltdown she had a couple months back when I told her she was grounded for a week. She actually *begged* me to give her another punishment so that she wouldn't miss what happened next on her shows."

"Wha- That's not- I didn't *beg*-!"

"Is that right?" crooned Mandy over the shorter girl's spluttered attempts at salvaging her dignity. "So what'd you end up doin'?"

"Well, I'll tell you at first I was *this* close to sending her out to cut me a switch or three and then grounding her for *two* weeks on sheer principle alone," admitted Dana, holding up her thumb and forefinger about an inch or so apart. "But, well… She's just too hard to say no to. So, in the end, we compromised. I told her that I'd knock a day off of her being grounded for every morning she decided to take a spanking with her breakfast instead."

"Hah! That's diabolical!"

"And did she go for it?" asked Officer Taylor, sounding genuinely intrigued. "That's a pretty steep trade just to avoid losing your TV time."

"Heh."

Chuckling, Dana spread her hands theatrically and favored the two other women with a wink.

"Let's just say that by day seven, poor Auntie Dana's arm was about ready to fall off."

"Could've fooled me," harrumphed Rhen, her pale cheeks clenching with the memories of spankings past as the TSA officers behind her burst into a fit of laughter.

In truth, it had actually been a spanking at breakfast (with the wooden spoon!) *and* having to sit on her punishment mat whenever she wanted to watch one of her shows or use her laptop for anything other than homework. But she wasn't about to share that extra tidbit of humiliating information if she could avoid it.

"You're kidding me!"

"Oh lord, that's precious."

"Yes, my little Rhenny takes her cartoons very seriously."

"Oh my god, they aren't *cartoons*, Aunt Dana!" snapped the girl in question with an affronted sigh of disgust that only served to produce even more peals of laughter from everyone around her. "I've told you before, it's called *anime*. It's from Japan, and it's a legitimate art form that's totally different from stupid American cartoons. So can you *please* try and get it right?"

"Yes, yes. You're right, dear. I'm sorry," soothed her partner with a mollifying gesture, rolling her eyes good-naturedly as she turned her attention back to the two women cracking up at the sight of the indignant little bare bottomed girl lecturing her aunt about the finer points of foreign entertainment. "But getting back to the matter at hand, I have to admit that I'm also rather curious about what you've brought for us, Officer…?"

"Oh you can just call me Mandy," waved away the other woman, moving further into the room to stand beside Rhen. "And I'd be happy to elaborate. You see, while this thing here might *look* like a paddle, it's actually a traditional club used by the Maori people of New Zealand. I'd never heard of one before either, but apparently they were used back in the day to wallop the ever-loving daylights out of enemy warriors using these hard edges here. But, as I'm sure you can tell just by lookin' at it, with a little creative adjustment to what part you strike with…"

She demonstrated just what she meant by lightly slapping the smoothly textured and surprisingly heavy width of the patu against the center of Rhen's bare backside.

POP!

"Oh!" gasped the girl, more caught off guard by the sensation of cold wood on her even colder seat than anything else as she shot up onto the balls of her feet with a squeak.

"Sorry, darlin', didn't mean to startle you."

"I wasn't *startled*," lied Rhen around another pout as she dropped back down onto her heels, glowering at the twitch in her aunt's cheek.

"Of course you weren't."

Grinning triumphantly at the reaction she'd managed to get out of her, Mandy transferred the patu to her other hand and reached up to ruffle the back of her hair as she continued addressing her partner.

"As you can see, with just a little tweak in how you use it, a patu can be quite the effective little tail blazer. Ain't that right, sugar?"

"Yeah, I guess so…" mumbled Rhen darkly.

"You guess?" prompted the woman beside her, her voice edged with warning as she directed a look at her out of the corner of her eye.

"I guess so, *ma'am*," the shorter girl repeated sweetly, still smarting from the undignified squeak that had been wrung out of her a moment earlier.

"New Zealand, huh?" echoed Dana before her not-niece could dig herself into an even deeper hole, raising an eyebrow in polite interest as if she and the TSA woman were making small talk about the weather, and not deliberately drawing out the humiliation of the girl next to them. "And how on earth did something like that end up getting confiscated by the TSA in *Iowa* of all places?"

"Your guess is as good as mine on that one," laughed Mandy. "But someone apparently decided that it would be a good idea to pack this thing in their carryon a few months back. And, well, we couldn't exactly just let them bring a wooden club onto a flight, now could we?"

She shrugged then, and passed the souvenir bludgeon over.

"We told 'em they could have it back when they got home, but they never came to collect, and it's been sitting in our contraband cage ever since."

"Some people…" sighed Officer Taylor with an agitated shake of her head.

"Oh this is just *perfect*," marveled Dana, grinning from ear to ear as she hefted the improvised implement in her hands and gave her right thigh a couple of experimental slaps.

POP! POP!

Only to wince and rub at the top of her sensible slacks with a surprised laugh.

"Goodness me! Yep, that'll definitely get her attention."

"Ain't that the truth," agreed Mandy with a devious grin. "It's become one of our go-to picks whenever we have an extra-mouthy boy or girl flying with us who needs something special to get them actin' right."

"I know my Ellie just *hates* it," snickered the salt and pepper security officer from her spot beside the door.

"Oh please," Mandy countered. "That girl would cry her doey little eyes out over a lickin' with a feather duster if she thought it'd get her out of trouble sooner."

That managed to get a snort of amusement from Officer Taylor.

"You're not wrong there," she conceded with a wink. "It's just too bad for her then that she sounds so cute when she's sniffling."

Then, leaning over slightly to catch Dana's eye, she made a show of tapping her wristwatch.

"But enough about me and my girl. Miss Dana and her niece here have a flight to catch, so we'd better get down to business if they don't want to keep their friends waiting any longer than they have to."

"Yes, that would be best, I think," agreed the woman in question with a grateful nod. "And let me just say that it's nice to know that I'll be able to take care of this attitude adjustment with such a lovely implement. You both have been so kind to go above and beyond for us like you have, and we really appreciate it."

Leaning forward again and laying a warm hand on her naughty niece's clammy hip, she began guiding her around to stand next to her right side.

"Isn't that right, cutie pie?"

Refusing to dignify that question with a response, Rhen instead just blew a stray bit of hair out of her face with a huff. Only to have it fall right back into place in front of her eyes a moment later.

"Humph."

Luckily for her, though, that seemed to be an acceptable enough answer for Dana. Who, after tucking her borrowed patu under her arm, took hold of her left wrist and hauled her forward, guiding her across her lap with a hand on her lower back for support.

"Oof!"

Toppling forward into the all too familiar position with a grunt, grateful for the added bit of modesty it provided her front (even though she knew it wouldn't last long once her buns started broiling), Rhen did her best to get comfortable as her partner dragged her further across her thighs with an arm around her waist. Soon enough, her toes were no longer touching the tile floor at all and she was forced to grip her partner's calf for support as she lay jackknifed over her lap. Her pale cheeks now the highest point on her body and naturally parting slightly to reveal just a hint of what lay between thanks to the angle she was laying at.

At least it's only two people watching me and not a whole crowd of strangers at our departure gate, she tried telling herself, her stomach flip-flopping as she struggled to remoisten her suddenly dry mouth. *It could always be worse, right?*

"Alright, honey buns, are you ready?" cooed her aunt as she *tap, tap, tapped* the patu against her bouncy bare backside, getting a feel for her aim.

"No..."

"Excuse me?"

Tap... Tap... Tap...

"Ugh!" growled Rhen, letting her head flop forward in reluctant acceptance as humiliation and dread warred for supremacy inside of her. "Yes ma'am..."

"Good girl."

WHOOSH-SMACK! WHOOSH-SMACK! WHOOSH-SMACK!

Only to have it shoot right back up again as three separate and deliberately paced explosions of hard wood on soft skin detonated against her backside; left, right, and center. Oval shaped bursts of molten lava heat blossomed almost immediately in their wake all across her naked nates then, sizzling up from where she'd just been swatted to emerge from her mouth as three equally as distinct yelps of surprise and pain.

"Ack! Ah! Owie!"

Followed by another.

WHOOSH-SMACK!

"Oh!"

And another.

WHOOSH-SMACK!

"Owie!"

And *another*!

WHOOSH-SMACK!

"Holy crap, that thing is so freaking mean!" she gasped, relaxing all at once across her aunt's lap as soon as she'd paused long enough to let her to catch her breath.

"I told you so," laughed Dana, giving her throbbing buns a couple of gentle pats and gliding the velvety smooth wood in slow circles across them, each etched line on its polished surface tickling her already toasty caboose. "Not feeling so sassy now, are we?"

"No ma'am!" Rhen reassured her, eager to please and hoping that her belatedly obedient adjustment to her attitude might earn her a reprieve from further punishment.

Knowing all the while that it wouldn't.

"Good," chirped her partner, confirming her suspicions for her as she began none too gently rapping the patu against her cheeks once again. "Now hang on tight, sweetie, because I'm about to give you a double dose of *exactly* what you've been begging for all morning."

"Oh god…" moaned the shorter girl, squirming ineffectually under the arm pinning her in place in an attempt to vent some of her rapidly building panic.

Tap. Tap. Tap.

It didn't help.

"Aunt Dana, I'm *sorry*!"

WHOOSH-SMACK!

"That's nice, dear."

WHOOSH-SMACK!

"But that doesn't change the fact-"

*WHOOSH-**SMACK**!*

"That you were being *very* naughty-"

*WHOOSH-**SMACK**!*

"And now you have to pay-"

*WHOOSH-**SMACK**!*

"For your bad behavior."

*WHOOSH-**SMACK**! WHOOSH-**SMACK**! WHOOSH-**SMACK**!*

"Does it, missy?"

All the while as she lectured, Dana kept her voice as calm and as measured as each of the bottom-searingly powerful swats she delivered to punctuate her rebukes, making it abundantly clear that she was *not* messing around. And, soon enough, Rhen was sobbing like the disobedient child that so many people so often mistook her for (and that she herself knew she was deep down inside). The extra-heavy weight of the patu's teeth-rattling impacts shattering her brittle resolve to put up a brave front for her two witnesses as fat, hot tears rushed in to cloud her vision and dribble down her cheeks.

"Aunt Dana, *please*. I'm sorry, I'm sorry!"

*WHOOSH-**SMACK**! WHOOSH-**SMACK**! WHOOSH-**SMACK**!*

But, as they both knew.

*WHOOSH-**SMACK**!*

She would be a *lot* sorrier by the time her aunt was finally through with her.

*WHOOSH-**SMACK**!*

Which was going to be a while.

*WHOOSH-**SMACK**!*

Because they were just getting started.

Ashley OTK

Chapter 11

Birds of a Feather

In the end, it wasn't the longest or the hardest spanking that Rhen had ever received, but by the time it was finally, mercifully, over, the raven-haired girl's cheeks were hot to the touch and suffused with a bone-deep ache that throbbed and pulsed in time with her heaving breaths as she sobbed across her partner's lap.

"There, there, sweetie. Shhh…" the older woman soothed, slipping a hand beneath her baggy sweater and gliding it up and down along the valley of her spine as she passed the patu back to Mandy with a nod of thanks. "You took your spanking very well and I'm proud of you… That's it… Let it all out. It's over now…"

It was a familiar litany, as familiar as the frantic apologies and promises to be good that Rhen had been blubbering just a few moments earlier as her spanking reached its rapid-fire crescendo, but it was nevertheless comforting for the exhausted girl to hear as she strove to get herself back under some semblance of control.

"I'm s-sorry," she found herself sniffling again as she lay spent across the broad expanse of her auntie's thighs, the feather light touch of her right hand along her sizzling seat combined the fingernails scratching her back in all the right places gradually buoying her up out of her haze of pain and abandoned dignity to float in the jelly-limbed endorphin rush that always followed a particularly thorough going over.

"I know you are, honey buns," cooed Dana, sounding far more winded than she usually was after such a short spanking.

That patu had apparently taken quite a toll on the both of them!

"And I hope too that you'll remember this little chat next week when we're getting ready to fly home," she added with a smirk, giving the center of her girlfriend's well-cooked caboose a couple of lightly reprimanding pats.

"Yeah, no worries there," groaned Rhen, tentatively reaching back to verify that her backside was actually still attached to her as she rolled her eyes. "You definitely made your point. Trust me."

"Good."

Batting away her questing hand, her partner gave her bottom a couple more much firmer pats as a silent reminder of just who was the one in charge of it.

"Because if we have to deal with this again, I'm not going to be nearly so nice about it."

"Wait, that was you being nice?" demanded Rhen, some of her old sassy energy starting to return as she tossed her hair and heaved out a melodramatic huff. "Could've fooled me…"

"Oh please, you were over my lap for *maybe* three minutes, you big baby," chided Dana with a laugh, giving each of her girl's cheeks one more *very* mean squeeze for good measure.

And being rewarded with two delightful yelps back-to-back in return.

"Ow-! Hey-! Come on, that's not fair!"

"I keep telling you that I'm the one making the rules here, dear, not you," tutted the older woman as she rolled her girlfriend over and gathered her lithe body up to sit on her lap, leaving her stop sign red rump hanging partway on and partway off of her left thigh as she clung to her and hid her smoldering face against her chest.

Then, leaning in close so that only Rhen would be able to hear, she added in a husky, taunting murmur, "And you should know by now that I'm not above playing dirty if it means making you squeal, you adorable little sassmuffin."

Suiting actions to words, she let her left hand drift down to pinch the fullest part of the shorter girl's sensitive seat.

"Eep!"

"Yes, just like that," she nodded, unable to quite suppress her chuckle as she patted the spot she'd just pinched. "You have such a lovely voice. *Especially* when you're hitting those high notes."

"Wh-Whatever," stammered Rhen into her breasts, steam practically billowing out of her ears with how hot both sets of cheeks felt just then. "Meanie."

"The meaniest."

Kissing her cheek, her partner straightened up in her seat and resumed rubbing her back.

"Now you just catch your breath and then you can get dressed, alright?"

"Okay…"

After another minute or so more of being gently rocked back and forth in the older woman's encircling arms as she reeled in her frayed nerves, and not at all being surprised to find a pair of erect nipples lurking just beneath the thin material of the bra she had on underneath her blouse, Rhen had calmed down enough to the point where she was now much more chagrinned over having had to be taken across Dana's lap in the first place than she was overwhelmed with how much her backside hurt.

I can't believe I actually thought she wouldn't check if I was wearing it or not… Talk about being wildly overoptimistic. Geez.

That wasn't to say her bottom didn't still hurt, however. In fact, it was positively *aching*, and any overly ambitious shifting of her weight against it produced a sharp twinge of pain. One that sent a faint echo of the patu's previous impacts reverberating through her cheeks to pound mercilessly between her thighs, making her want to wince and grin all at the same time as she squirmed involuntarily, kicking the entire process off all over again.

She could tell already that it was going to be a very long flight.

Hopefully we won't hit too much turbulence…

"Bet you wish you had some padding for your bottom now. Don't you, cutie pie?" Dana snickered into the top of her hair, reading her body language like a book as per usual.

"Ugh. Maybe…" admitted Rhen, pulling back from her enough to drag a forearm across her tear-stained face. "That freaking patu thing is almost as bad as The Board!"

"Awww, you poor baby," teased Dana, leaning in to plant a quick kiss just above her niece's frustratedly furrowed brows, falling in love with her all over again in that moment as she glared petulantly back up at her with the barest hint of a smirk tugging up on one corner of her mouth. "I knew I should have packed an extra pull-up in my purse just in case."

"Yeah, sure, because that'd *totally* make me feel better," snarked Rhen, crossing her sweater-mittened arms in front of her chest with a melodramatic sigh. "It's not embarrassing enough already to be spanked at my age. You might as well put me in a freaking pair of training panties too while you're at it for good measure."

"Hey now, it's not my fault you look so cute in them," countered Dana, playfully tapping the tip of the sulking girl's nose. "And you know perfectly well by now that if you don't want your bottom warmed, all you have to do is behave yourself, missy. So stow the attitude."

"Hey, I do behave myself!" insisted the not-teen, swapping out her pout for a saucy grin. "It's not my fault you're so bossy."

"Bossy, huh?"

"Yeah, that's right. Bossy!" she repeated, sticking out her tongue. "You're the bossiest boss to have ever bossed, you big pair of bossy boots, you!"

"Careful now, cutie pie…" warned her aunt pleasantly, bouncing her atop her left thigh in a subtle reminder of just what she wasn't wearing at that particular moment. "We're not so pressed for time that you can't take a second trip across my knee before we get out of here, you know."

"Yeah, yeah… Alright," huffed Rhen, her grin bending out of shape somewhat as her tender tush tensed beneath her, a fresh surge of dread sizzling a hole in the pit of her stomach. "Point taken. I'm sorry."

"I thought you might see things my way."

"You know…" spoke up Officer Taylor then, her voice sugary

sweet from her position next to Mandy beside the door.

Rhen groaned.

Oh god. What is it now?

"I might just be able to help you with your little pull-up pre-dicament, Dana."

"You don't say?" replied the auburn-haired older woman just as coyly, letting her left hand glide back down to cup her girl-friend's seat as a gentle reminder to watch her mouth. "I had no idea the TSA carried pull-ups."

"Oh, we don't," laughed the officer, shaking her head as she and her friend smiled knowingly. "But as luck would have it, my girl's hips aren't that much bigger than Rhen's are, and I just so happen to have some… Well, let's just call them 'adoles-cent-minded incontinence aids' in my locker that I'm *sure* would get the job done. If you're interested, that is."

"Adolescent what nows?" interjected Rhen, not quite sure where the other woman was headed, but not at all liking the conspiratorial twinkle in her eye. "I really don't think that's necess- Ah!"

Only to be silenced by a sharp squeeze to her left cheek from a set of well-manicured fingernails.

"She means diapers, cutie pie," Dana clarified for her, her smile growing wider by the moment as she turned her attention back to the other woman. "And after the way she's been acting today, I think that sounds like an *excellent* idea, Nicole. An extra dose of embarrassment is just the thing she needs to keep her on the straight and narrow and remembering who's in charge around here. Thank you so much."

"Think nothing of it. I'm just happy to help," preened the TSA officer with just the hint of a malicious grin. "Now you just give me a minute to find someone to bring them in, and then you two can be on your way, alright? This shouldn't take more than a few more minutes, I promise."

"But… but… That's not… You… You can't be serious!"

"Sounds like a plan to me," replied the horrified girl's partner brightly, all the while still serenely smiling as she leaned over and slipped her purple panties off from around where her feet were dangling a few inches above the floor between her parted thighs, tucking them into her pants pocket without a second glance as she nudged her slack-jawed not-niece with her shoulder. "Isn't there something you would also like to say to Officer Taylor, young lady?"

She kept her grip on said girl's seat nice and tight as she asked the question, and sensing that there was no way out of what was to come that didn't involve her bending back over again for another spanking, Rhen grudgingly nodded her head.

"Th-Thank you, ma'am…"

"For…?" prompted Dana, clearly intent on extracting every last ounce of humiliation she could from this unexpected turn of events.

Swallowing down several choice words and all too adolescent sounding complaints and protests, Rhen kept her eyes locked on her bare knees as she mumbled, "For um… For giving us, um… a diaper to use… and stuff…"

You big jerk.

"Oh, it's no trouble at all, sweetheart. Like I told your auntie earlier, I know a thing or two about dealing with bratty little girls," the older woman waved away as she brought her walkie-talkie up from her belt and thumbed it to life again. "Elizabeth, come in, please."

Another moment or two passed in mortified silence in the chilly room as Rhen tried desperately to wrap her head around how she'd managed to wind up in such a compromising predicament, before the radio crackled with a fresh burst of static, followed by a young woman's voice.

"Yes ma'am, I'm here!"

She sounded just breathless enough to give the impression that she'd been hurriedly scrambling for her walkie-talkie as soon as she'd heard her name being paged.

Prompting Mandy to let out a quiet snort as she shook her

head in amusement.

"Hey there, hon," replied Officer Taylor, her voice carrying the broad grin spreading across her features as she shared a look with the woman standing next to her. "Could you please do me a favor and bring that purple shoulder bag sitting on the top shelf of my locker to Screening Room Two?"

"The uh…" came the younger woman, Elizabeth's, reply a second later, sounding decidedly less enthusiastic this time. "You mean the one with the, um…?"

"Yes, dear," nodded her superior with a throaty chuckle. "*That* bag. Get someone to cover for you, and then go grab it from my locker, alright? The combo is nine-fifteen-seven."

"R… Right…"

There was an audible swallowing sound on the other end of the walkie-talkie then.

"Um, if this is about-"

"Not to worry," interrupted Officer Taylor, cutting the younger girl off before she could get going with whatever excuse she was about to give. "It's for a mouthy passenger whose aunt thinks she could use some extra help keeping her bladder in check during their flight."

Well, at least she didn't call me a middle schooler this time, Rhen found herself thinking with a grimace. *For whatever that's worth…*

"Oh, um… Right, of course," came a much more confident sounding reply from the radio, along with a sigh of relief. "In that case, I'll be right there!"

"That's my good little helper," cooed Officer Taylor as her hazelnut eyes sparkled with mirth. "Also, we're in a bit of a hurry here, so no dragging your feet or stopping off to say hi to anyone along the way. You got that?"

"Yes ma'am, you can count on me!"

"I should hope so, young lady," nodded the TSA woman, all business once again as she turned her wrist over to check the time on her watch. "You've got three minutes. Starting… now!"

—

Exactly two minutes and forty-seven seconds later, there came a hurried knocking at the screening room door, and Officer Taylor pulled it open to reveal a girl in her early twenties. She had a round face and bunches of bouncy red hair, and was huffing and puffing after having apparently sprinted the entire way there from wherever it was that she'd been stationed earlier.

"H… Here's your bag, ma'am…" she wheezed, shrugging the dark purple satchel off of her shoulder and clearly hoping not to have to touch it any more than she absolutely had to as she held it out in front of her by the very end of its woven canvas strap.

"Well done on being so speedy, Ellie, dear," praised the salt and pepper security officer with a pleasant smile, making no effort to relieve the girl of her burden as she gestured her inside and pointed her toward where Dana stood with a scarlet-faced Rhen beside the inspection table they'd used earlier to go through her luggage. "But she's the one you should be bringing that to, not me."

"Oh, right, of course."

Blushing at her minor misstep, Ellie double-timed it over to where Dana stood and once again thrust her bag out by the shoulder strap.

"Here you are, ma'am. Thank you for waiting!"

"And thank *you* for being so on top of things," sing-songed the older woman, ignoring the proffered bag as well and instead stepping in close to pick a stray bit of lint off of the girl's uniform shirt before tipping up the laminated badge clipped to her lapel. "Officer… Oh, excuse me, *Trainee* Evans."

"It was my pleasure, ma'am!" Ellie practically yelped, doing her best to look the very picture of consummate professionalism as her arms started to tremble from the strain of keeping the bag held straight out in front of her.

"Mmhmm. Yes, I'm sure it was, dear," chuckled Dana as she ruffled the panting girl's fiery curls and at last took the diaper bag from her. "Now run along. I can take it from here."

"Oh thank god…"

Sagging with relief, the TSA trainee flashed Rhen a look that was equal parts sympathy and snide amusement.

"Good luck, shrimp," she mouthed with just the hint of a snicker, before performing a crisp about face and snapping off a textbook salute to the two women watching her like a pair of highly amused hawks. "Will that be all, Officer Taylor, ma'am? Officer Washington, ma'am?"

"Yes, I believe it will," replied the woman who had summoned her, giving her a nod of approval and hooking a thumb toward the door beside her. "Why don't you go help Miguel with the scanners for a bit?"

"Scanners. Right. I'm on it!"

Ellie immediately set off at a brisk pace toward where she'd just come from then, the rubber soles of her all black high-tops squeaking on the polished floor beneath her as she sped along it. But, as she was reaching for the doorknob, she was stopped dead in her tracks by a firm hand on her shoulder.

"Actually…" drawled Officer Taylor, her voice a low, teasing purr that caused Rhen to break out in sympathetic goosebumps under her skirt. "Now that you mention it, there is one more thing I'd like to check."

"Th-There is?" squeaked the younger girl, looking back at her, face innocent and body guilty.

Instead of answering her question directly, however, her superior officer instead stepped in nice and close behind her and took hold of the waistband of the perfectly pressed (and borderline skintight) black slacks she was wearing.

"Let's just get a quick peek at what's going on back here, shall we?"

Keeping her movements just as relaxed and fluid as her voice, Office Taylor wriggled and tugged on the younger girl's pants until she'd managed to work them down in back enough to reveal several inches of bright pink crinkly material with a white flower pattern stamped across it.

"Ah, excellent, just what I was hoping to see!" she laughed, stepping aside to give Rhen and her partner a clearer view of the redhead's rump. "I'm so happy we aren't having a repeat of our obstinate behavior from last Friday, Elizabeth."

"No ma'am," agreed Ellie, the tips of her ears flushing nearly as pink as the diaper she had on underneath her uniform. "I've kept it on all shift, just like you told me to."

"That's what I like to hear, little one. And have you been drinking your water too? And I mean *actual* water. Soda pop doesn't count, remember?"

"I'm almost finished with my second bottle!" she declared, her voice a mixture of pride and embarrassment as she smiled shyly at the woman who'd taken her under her wing.

And over her lap.

"Awww, that's my good girl."

Readjusting the waistband of her trainee's pants for her, Officer Taylor gave her padded posterior a couple of fond pats.

"Now you just radio me or Miss Mandy when you're ready for a change. Alright, sugarplum?"

"Understood ma'am!" nodded Ellie, face flushing even brighter now as she reached for the doorknob in front of her once again.

She'd just managed to twist it and was in the process of pulling it open, when her superior stopped her for a second time.

"Oh, and before I forget," she said, her tone growing noticeably more frosty as her eyes hardened to match. "Have you finished filling out those ten-forty-fives yet?"

"Um… mostly?" replied the shorter girl, not betraying the guilty look on her face by turning back this time.

"Mostly, huh?" repeated the salt and pepper security officer evenly. "Well, in that case, you can show me *exactly* what 'mostly' means later on tonight, and then I'll decide how 'mostly' red that little tush of yours is going to be by the time I'm through with it."

That managed to pull a frustrated moan out of the shorter girl, her carefully cultivated mask of professionalism slipping away entirely now as she bunched up her free hand into a frustrated fist that she bounced ineffectually against the side of her hip.

"What? No! Come on! Do we *really* have to do that?" she whined. "I promise I'll get them done before my shift is over if you just give me a second cha-"

"Uh-uh," interrupted Officer Taylor. "That's what you told me yesterday, and it's not going to fly. You hear me?"

"I guess..." conceded Ellie with a harrumph.

"Elizabeth..."

"Eep! Er, uh... I *guess* I'd better get those reports done as soon as possible? Heh... heh..."

"Mmhmm. You just go on and scoot before I decide you need a little warm up to put you back on track," ordered Officer Taylor only half-seriously, nodding toward where Mandy stood a few feet away, still holding her patu. "I'll be by to check on you in an hour or so, alright?"

"Yes Mommy- I mean, ma'am!"

"Good girl."

Propelled along by a quick kiss to her smoldering cheek and a sharp swat to her seat, Officer-Trainee Elizabeth Evans scurried out of sight just as fast as her squeaky shoes could carry her.

"Oh my goodness, what an adorable little go-getter!" gushed Dana as soon as the girl's fiery locks had disappeared from sight around the doorframe.

"Isn't she a peach?" agreed the TSA woman, turning back to her with a broad, self-satisfied smile. "Tastes like one too."

She winked.

"Well, maybe fried peach cobbler, but I think you get what I mean."

"Loud and clear," snickered Rhen's partner, rubbing her own girl's back affectionately as her eyes traced over the curves of the bare cheeks hidden just beneath the folds of her skirt. "That one's a favorite around our house too."

"Huh? It is? But we usually have apple cobbler..." piped up the shorter girl, only half paying attention as she continued to struggle with processing what she'd just witnessed.

I knew there was something weird about the way her hips looked in those pants! she mused to herself, casting a weary, sidelong glance at the deceptively innocent looking purple bag that her aunt had set on the metal table beside her. *Guess I know why… Yikes.*

Then, as if reading her mind once again, her partner turned her lazy grin back on her.

"Alright, cutie pie, it's your turn," she declared, sliding the bag aside and patting the table expectantly. "Go ahead and hop on up so I can get you changed, and then we'll go grab some breakfast."

"W-W-Wait, h… hold on!"

Flushing scarlet from her neck all the way to the roots of her inky black hair, Rhen tried (and failed) to formulate some sort of means of talking her way out of things as the sudden realization of what was about to happen to her crashed down on top of her like a ton of bricks. However, before she could think of anything to say that might save her from her impending humiliation, Dana had taken half a step toward her and she'd found herself backing up and tripping over the low table behind her.

"Wha-? Oh!"

Letting out a yelp of surprise, she flung her arms out to either side of her and windmilled them about in an attempt to regain her balance. But Dana wasn't about to let her get away so easily, and taking another step forward, lightly tapped the center of her forehead, sending her toppling back onto her tender tush with a solid.

THUMP!

"Crap! Ah! Owie, owie, owie!"

Immediately taking advantage of her momentary distraction, her aunt then pushed her the rest of the way down by the shoulders until she was lying on her back on the icy, metal surface beneath her.

"There we go, just like that."

Wriggling like a well-spanked eel as her ankles were taken hold of by a pair of strong hands and shifted up onto the table with the rest of her body, Rhen tried one last time to change her partner's mind.

"Wait, Aunt Dana, *please*! You can't be seriou-!"

"Shhh…"

Only to be silenced by a firm fingertip pressed to her lips.

"Just relax, honey buns," Dana half ordered and half soothed. "We'll be done before you know it, I promise."

"But… but…"

"Young lady," she then chided, lending a touch of steel to her voice this time to cut across the rest of the whining being thrown at her. "You and I both know that you've had issues controlling your bladder on long trips in the past, and it would be inexcusably irresponsible of me to knowingly let you get onto this flight without at least some sort of protection for in case you have an accident."

Turning away from her (for the moment) cowed girlfriend, Dana unzipped the purple bag at her fretfully shifting feet and began rifling through it.

"Now that *could* have been a pull-up," she continued to lecture as she laid out an identical diaper to the one Ellie had been wearing, along with a bottle of baby powder beside the bag. "But since you decided you wanted to be sneaky about it, *this* is what you're going to wear instead. And if I were you, I'd start reeling in all that backtalk unless you'd like to *keep* wearing them for the rest of our vacation. Is that understood?"

"Oh god…"

Swallowing hard, her stomach flip-flopping seemingly nonstop, Rhen decided to drop the rest of her arguments before they could get her into any further trouble.

"Y-Yes ma'am."

"There's my good girl."

All smiles once again, Dana took hold of the mortified junior's ankles and lifted them (along with her hips) up off of the shiny table.

"Like I said, just relax and this'll all be over before you know it. Alright?'

Again, it wasn't really a question, and Rhen was left with little choice other than to bob her head in acceptance.

"Fine…"

And it was at that exact moment, as her aunt slipped the bright pink diaper beneath her dark red hips and then lowered her onto it, forcing her knees apart so that she could begin powdering her all over her front, that she swore she would never *ever* try weaseling her way out of wearing a pull-up ever again.

For, as humiliating as those were, she understood now that there were far worse things in the world than a little extra padding and a Disney princess around her hips.

At least *those* didn't crinkle.

—

"So, uh… Are we even on the whole pull-up thing?" Rhen asked sheepishly some ten minutes later as she and her partner left Mandy and Officer Taylor behind and began making their way through the concourse toward their departure gate.

"Hmmm… Yes, I'd say we're just about square," mused Dana as she leaned over and gave the ruffled seat of her skirt a hefty smack.

POMF!

"Ah!"

"Oh yes," she laughed as her girlfriend scampered forward and rounded on her with a mortified glare that didn't quite manage to reach her eyes. "We're definitely even."

Closing the distance on her, she captured her lips in a quick kiss with just a hint of tongue on teeth, before threading her arm through hers and once again steering them off in the direction of their waiting friends and some much-needed coffee.

"My goodness, Alana is just going to *love* hearing about this."

"Ugh. Tell me about it…"

"You know, maybe we ought to plan a trip to New Zealand for Christmas this year. What do you say, cutie pie? I hear it's nice

Absolutely
Not Allowed

and warm out there in December."

"What, is eBay not good enough to find your own patu?" snickered Rhen.

"Oh, I'm sure it would be just fine," shrugged Dana, giving her arm a quick squeeze. "But there *are* other things besides exotic spanking implements to see out there. Weren't you the one saying just the other day that you'd love to go see where they filmed Lord of the Rings?"

"Huh. Well when you put it like that…"

Trudging along while doing her best to ignore the faint twinges of pain still radiating from her sore bottom as she and her partner chatted amiably among themselves, Rhen had to admit that there were certainly more auspicious ways to start a vacation. But, as she cuddled up with the love of her life and let her take the lead on navigating their way through the press of people waiting for their flights (the thick diaper hidden just out of sight beneath the layers of her skirt crinkling audibly with each and every step she took), she found that she really didn't mind all that much.

Sure her spanking had hurt, and sure it was beyond humiliating to be walking around wearing something that was somehow even *more* childish than a pull-up. But, on the bright side, her partner loved her and she wasn't in trouble anymore.

And for a brat like her, that was enough.

She'd just have to make sure she and her friends did something else besides go to the beach that afternoon.

You know, now that I think about it, today really does feel more like a museum and movies day. Plus I've always wanted to see the walk of fame…

Chapter 12

Burning Buns in the Summer Sun

Despite its rocky start at the airport, Rhen's vacation with her partner and friends turned out to be even more fun than she could have possibly imagined. Over the last four days since they'd arrived, time seemed to have taken on a whirlwind pace all its own. Between stuffing themselves at fancy restaurants on Dana's dime, trips to multiple museums and art galleries to get out of the afternoon heat (and because Courtney was adamant that they come away from their trip with something else besides just a great tan), and taking in the sights around LA, it seemed like they were constantly on the move without a moment to spare.

Heck, it was already Tuesday and they hadn't even had a chance to visit Disneyland yet!

Rhen wasn't too worried about that last bit, though, since her partner had already promised that they'd be spending all of Wednesday and Thursday there celebrating her birthday before flying home the following afternoon on Friday.

Even better than her impending trip to the happiest place on earth, however, was the fact that in all of their running around since landing, Rhen had managed to avoid taking even a single trip over her aunt's knee. Or anyone else's for that matter! Granted, she had a sneaking suspicion that that was probably due more to the fact that Courtney and Abby were *far* more lenient with her than Dana was, but she wasn't about to start complaining about it. Not when she'd managed to spend all of her time in California so far without having her panties taken down for her even once.

Well, sort of.

She'd had to beg Courtney to let her ditch the stupid, crinkly diaper that she'd been forced into wearing once they were finally alone in her and Dana's hotel room that first afternoon, which hadn't exactly been (that much) fun. Even with all of her whining and increasingly frantic arguments that there was absolutely no chance of her losing control of her bladder now that they were back on the ground, along with her pouty accusations that the two of them were just trying to torment her (which neither of them made any effort to deny), her adoptive older sister had only given in after she'd promised to let her "change" her into a fresh pair of panties of her choosing. Something which she and Abby had spent an inordinate amount of time debating as she lay there with her skirt rucked up past her hips, worrying at her lower lip.

As far as Rhen was concerned, though, a few short, humiliating minutes on her back while her two best friends had their fun playing dress up with her was a small price to pay to restore her dignity.

Even with all the pictures Abby insisted on taking.

"Dana told us to get lots and lots of pictures while she's not around, remember?" she'd wheedled, tauntingly patting the padding between her thighs with a wicked grin. "And do you *really* want to run the risk of her putting you into another one of these just because she didn't get any good shots of you wearing it?"

"Seems like a no-brainer to me," Courtney had chimed in as well, settling at last on a pair of panties that went with the t-shirt she and her girlfriend had insisted on changing her into. "You know she'd totally do it too."

"Well…"

In the end, Rhen had to admit that the two of them probably had a point. And after a prolonged impromptu photo shoot with her in a multitude of different embarrassing positions, she'd finally been returned back to her usual wardrobe and they'd been able to start having fun.

—

During those times when she and her friends (or starting later that Monday, she and her friends and her partner) hadn't been busy zipping around the city seeing the sights and extracting every last ounce of fun that they could before their summer semester started up, Rhen had insisted that they go play at the beach. Which was something that she hadn't had the chance to do since she actually *was* thirteen.

At first, she'd been more than a little hesitant about being seen in public wearing her new swimsuit, despite Abby and Courtney having managed to find her an absolutely killer one that she loved to death. Even with the extra bit of padding that the colorful two-piece gave her up top and the flattering cut of its bottoms, to say nothing of all the positive feedback her friends had lavished upon her the moment she'd tried it on, it had still taken a supreme effort of will on Rhen's part to muster up the courage to shrug out of her cover up and go play that first afternoon they'd walked down to the beach from their hotel. But, once she had, she'd been overjoyed to find that things were far less terrifying and humiliating than she'd at first feared they'd be.

For starters, it helped a ton that as a random tourist among many at a fairly busy beach, she was just one more face in a sea of strangers whose members were constantly changing day-to-day. As such, nobody paid her any special attention or cared that at the age of twenty she looked far closer to thirteen. To the people around her, she was just another kid in the crowd. And, although she blended in far better with the teenagers reveling in the start of their summer vacation than she would have liked to admit, she was honestly having too much fun to really care.

For the first time in what *also* felt like nearly a decade, she was finally able to walk around in a swimsuit in public without worrying about the image she presented to the people around her. She didn't have to pretend that she was someone she wasn't by chugging cheap booze that she could barely stand the taste of, or doing her best to make everyone she was with see her as some sort of legendary party girl in order to assert herself as one of the group. Nobody gave her any mocking looks for the way she failed to fill out her swimsuit, and Courtney, Abby, and Dana all treated her just the same as they always had.

To the casual observer she might have been written off as

just another teen among many, but that was just fine with her. Nobody gave a teenager having fun at the beach with her aunt or her coed babysitters more than a passing glance. And with that implicit anonymity, she was finally free to cut loose and enjoy herself without also trying to make sure that everyone around her understood that she was *actually* a junior in college and a proper adult.

She could just be herself.

And it was positively liberating!

Unfortunately, though, this newfound sense of freedom came with one major (albeit rather familiar) drawback. Namely, that blending in as she did with the rest of the younger crowd swarming the sand every afternoon, the eagle-eyed twenty-something that acted as the lifeguard for the beach she and her friends kept visiting had zero problems treating her like one as well.

Which, inevitably, came back to bite her right on the rump.

Just like it always did.

—

"Ah! Oh! Ah!" hissed Rhen as she raced across the beach as fast as she could, nearly tumbling head over heels across a pair of sprawled out sunbathers in her haste to avoid having the soles of her bare feet touch the hot sand any more than they absolutely had to.

The water is right freaking there! How the heck is this stuff so hot? Stupid global warming!

"Sorry!" she called back to the two startled sunbathers with only a cursory wave, not actually bothering to look back as she left them in her literal and proverbial dust.

"Slow down, you little-!"

Rhen didn't bother listening to the rest of whatever the grumpy lady she'd nearly planted a foot into had to say about her navigation skills, and instead kept on running. So tantalizingly close to the lapping waves now, she made it a grand total of three more steps before a new voice boomed out from far too close behind her.

"Hey!" it barked. "Hey you, stop!"

Oh god, not again.

It was the unmistakable, commanding shout of none other than Jill, the rules-obsessed (and frustratingly attractive) lifeguard that was in charge of this particular stretch of beach.

Please let her be talking to someone else, please let her be talking to someone else, please let her be talking to someone else…

Crossing her fingers with a wince, Rhen continued to sprint across the sand, dodging and weaving between people and hoping against hope that if she could just put enough distance between her and the angry voice chasing after her that its owner would lose interest and leave her alone. That particular tactic hadn't actually worked for her the day before. Nor had it the day before that. And, unsurprisingly, it didn't work that afternoon either.

"I'm talking to *you*, polka dots!" shouted the irate lifeguard once again, this time with an accompanying shrill blast from the whistle she kept around her stupid, swanlike neck. "Don't make me tell you again!"

"Dang it…"

Mortified beyond belief at being singled out for breaking the rules (again), Rhen's steps began to falter and hesitate, before finally coming to a reluctant stop only a few yards short of the shoreline.

"I have a name, you know!" she snapped before she could stop herself, her stomach thrilling with a giddy mixture of frustration and adrenaline as she whirled around to face the lifeguard in a huff.

"Yeah?" demanded the taller girl, stomping over to her in four determined strides of her long legs. "And what is it?"

"It's Rhen. Rhen Mathews," sniffed the petite junior.

Only to realize after the fact that she'd just elevated herself from anonymous annoyance to named nuisance.

Crap!

"Well then, Rhen," continued Jill, articulating each word with palpable annoyance as she towered over her by a good head and a half. "It's nice to know that your *ears* work at least. Now then, let's give those eyes a shot."

Without pulling her simmering glare away from her for even a moment, the sun-kissed blonde jabbed an accusatory finger off to her right, pointing back at the squat lifeguard tower she'd just chased her down from. Or, more specifically, the three foot tall wooden sign affixed to the base of its railing.

"What does it say on that sign?"

Even without leaning over to see past the imposing older girl's impressively muscled torso, Rhen knew perfectly well what the sign said. She'd been ignoring it for three days in a row now after all. She also knew too that there was no way out of answering her question. Not unless she wanted to try running for it again. Which, considering the fact that the lifeguard's long, graceful legs could easily match her one stride for every three of her own, seemed like a pretty bad idea.

"Well?" demanded Jill, her startlingly cerulean eyes narrowing in impatience as Rhen fought to drag herself out of their depths.

"Uh…"

Swallowing hard, she made a show of peeking out from around where the lifeguard stood with her hands planted imperiously on the hips of her red one-piece swimsuit, squinting as if she'd just now noticed the sign in question.

"Oh hey, would you look at that. Um… 'No Running'. And it's even in big, bold letters too… Huh."

"That's right, *no running*," repeated the taller girl, Rhen's attempts at lightening the mood fizzling out against three days' worth of growing irritation. "And, correct me if I'm wrong, but haven't I already had to tell you to knock it off, like, two days in a row now?"

Hesitating again, Rhen flashed her her most charming smile. "Um… Maybe?"

"That was a rhetorical question," sighed Jill, pinching the

bridge of her nose. "I've seen your polka-dotted butt running around here all week when you thought I wasn't looking, so cut the crap, alright? The innocent act isn't going to work on me."

"Okay. Fine. You got me," admitted Rhen with a begrudging harrumph, wishing very much that she'd bought a more forgettable swimsuit just then as she wriggled her toes deeper into the blessedly cool sand beneath her feet. "But, look, it's really not my fault this time, alright? We couldn't find a closer spot to put our stuff down on, so I *had* to run."

"Had to, huh?"

"Well, *yeah*. Duh. How the heck else was I supposed to make it to the water without burning my feet off? It's not like I can control how hot the freaking sun is, you know."

As she stood there listening to her flimsy explanation, Jill's pale eyebrows had continued to creep higher and higher up her forehead. What little patience she'd had to begin with clearly starting to wear thin.

"Ever heard of sandals?"

Oh…

At her remark, Rhen felt her face warm up enough to match the soles of her feet from a few moments earlier.

"I uh… Oh yeah," she nodded slowly, suddenly feeling significantly more self-conscious. "I guess I could have worn those, couldn't I?"

Her admission did nothing to lessen the lifeguard's exasperation, however, and instead only drew out another heavy sigh from her.

"Uh-huh. That's about what I thought," she said, rolling her eyes as she reached forward to take hold of her by the wrist. "Alright, kiddo, come with me."

"What? Why?" squawked Rhen, scrambling back out of reach and stumbling over someone's abandoned bucket in the process as a surge of panic welled up in the pit of her stomach.

"Oh please. You know perfectly well why," scoffed Jill as she closed in after her. "I told you *exactly* what was going to happen yesterday if I caught you running on my beach again."

"Uh…" Rhen tried to stall, scrubbing back through her recollection of the day before and mostly just coming up with memories of feeding stingrays at the aquarium and an exceptionally delicious sushi dinner later that evening.

"I *said*," the taller girl interrupted, filling in the blanks for her as she successfully snatched up her wrist this time. "That if I caught you breaking the rules here just one more time, that I was going to spank you silly. So come on. You and I are going to have a little chat back at the tower."

Of course, it was at *that* moment that Rhen's memory decided to kick in again. Playing back that embarrassing encounter from the day before with perfect clarity and drawing up a fresh blush to warm her cheeks.

"Wait, what? That's not- You can't-!" she spluttered in protest as Jill turned and began marching back toward where she'd come from, towing her along behind her by the wrist.

"My beach, my rules," she countered with an unconcerned shrug that did some very flattering things with the muscles all up and down along the sinuous line of her mostly exposed back. "Now you can either come along quietly and then go back to playing with your friends once we're done. Or…"

Jill gave her captured wrist a firm squeeze then.

"You can pack up your stuff and never come back. *After* I've finished blistering your butt, that is, of course. Your choice."

The indignity of being kicked out of this beach that she'd come to love so much, all because she couldn't follow some (stupid!) safety rules, was honestly a lot more embarrassing for Rhen than the actual threat of a spanking from this very determined girl dragging her across the sand was. But that wasn't going to stop her from complaining about it.

"But… but… This isn't fair!" she whined, all of the other half-formed (and definitely super eloquent) arguments that she'd been preparing in the back of her mind evaporating in an instant as it occurred to her with an unpleasant lurch that being spanked by the well-toned lifeguard wasn't something she really wanted to have happen either.

Maybe once they'd gotten to know each other a little bit better and there weren't so many people around to see them. But certainly not right now!

Oh god, please don't let anyone I know see us...

"Look. Come on. I was, like, *barely* even jogging," she lied through her teeth, switching to damage control mode in the blink of an eye. "You can't spank me for that! That's... that's..."

She wanted to say that it wasn't fair again, but she was pretty sure repeating herself like that wasn't going to do her any favors just then.

"Can't you give me one last, final, 'this for sure had better not ever happen again' chance? I swear I won't even so much as speed walk from now on! *Please?*"

Jill wasn't about to be dissuaded, however, it seemed.

"Wow, a rule breaker who doesn't want to take her spanking? I've never seen that one before," she marveled facetiously, coming to an abrupt halt and letting Rhen go as she rounded on her with a grim expression that was softened only somewhat by the small twitch at the corners of her glossy lips. "What ever shall I do?"

"Be cool and let me go?" suggested the shorter girl with an optimistic smile, only to be silenced by a frigid glare that sent an actual shiver down her spine despite the heat of the sun beating down on top of her.

"Heh. Not a chance on your life, kiddo," snorted the lifeguard with some genuine mirth this time. "You were warned. And once I decide someone's getting a spanking, they're *getting* a spanking. No ifs, ands, or buts about it."

At that, her severe mask cracked entirely and a tiny giggle escaped from her upturned lips.

"Well, there is *one* butt, I suppose," she allowed, patting her own for emphasis. "But I think you know what I mean. Now come on before you end up sassing yourself into getting double."

"But... but..." protested Rhen again, gesticulating wildly as a familiar sensation of anticipatory dread rushed in to fill her from head to toe, making her knees grow weak.

Jill just sighed and shook her head, however, her grin fading away to a tired not-quite-smile. "Look. I'm trying to be nice here and not just kick you out, but you're really starting to try my patience, and that's super not a smart idea when you're about to get spanked. Believe me."

Pressing her lips together into a thin, defiant line, Rhen let out a petulant growl and sent a small shower of sand flying everywhere as she kicked her foot in frustration.

"Oh my god, how is this even allowed?" she demanded, her hands bunched up into sulky little fists at her sides.

"My beach, my rules," the taller girl shot back again with another shrug, completely unfazed by her brewing tantrum. "And they've been in place for quite a while now, so I wouldn't waste my breath hoping that they're suddenly going to change just because you don't want to take your punishment. Now, are you going to start behaving yourself and come along quietly, or am I going to have to carry you?"

"*C-Carry* me?" squeaked Rhen, blanching at the very notion.

"You wouldn't be the first," countered Jill with a playful wink.

The way she said it made it sound like she was probably just joking, but the thought of this devastatingly cool and in control girl tossing her over one broad shoulder and carrying her off back to her lifeguard tower for a spanking wasn't exactly doing anything to help Rhen's sudden case of jelly legs. Especially since she knew from far too much personal experience that a determined disciplinarian would have very little difficulty sweeping her up off her feet and toting her along like a disobedient sack of potatoes to wherever they wanted. (Or just tucking her under their arm and whaling away at her trapped backside until they'd decided she'd learned her lesson.) Fortunately for her, though, she was saved from having to come up with a witty rejoinder to the lifeguard's challenge by another voice calling out to them from out of the blue.

"Excuse me, is there a problem here?"

"Aunt Dana!" Rhen found herself crying out in relief, mentally kicking herself as soon as the words had left her mouth for including the "Aunt" part as she whipped around to see her partner approaching them at an easy pace.

Smooth, Rhen, real smooth. Way to make yourself totally sound like you're too old to be spanked. You're nailing it. Really.

"Nope, no problem at all," answered Jill with an unsinkable smile as she too turned to face the auburn-haired older woman, hooking a thumb over her shoulder as she continued to explain. "I just happened to catch this little speed demon here running around my beach for the *third* day in a row now, and she and I were about to go have a nice long chat about following the rules back at the lifeguard tower."

"Oh really now?" asked Dana, not sounding nearly as outraged at the other girl as Rhen had been hoping she would as she turned a decidedly unhappy look on her. "Is this true, young lady?"

"I uh…"

Squirming under the weight of her partner's stern gaze, the round sunglasses she was wearing doing very little to diminish her disapproval, Rhen tried to come up with a clever way of telling the truth that didn't actually involve her admitting to any wrongdoing.

"Maybe?"

Out of habit, she reached back to tug at the seat of her bikini bottoms, attempting to coax as much coverage from them as she possibly could. Which, given her current predicament, seemed like a good idea.

"Maybe?" pressed her partner, the air between them going thick with unspoken promises of sleeping on her stomach that night should she keep trying to beat around the bush. "It either is true, or it isn't. So, which is it?"

"Alright, *fine*," harrumphed the shorter girl with a toss of her ponytail, folding her arms beneath the modest swell of her breasts and doing her best to pout through the small surge of excitement that the feel of the additional material rounding out the top half of her bikini produced in her. "It's true… I guess."

Not one to go down without a fight, however, she rallied for one last attempt at saving face and jabbed a finger at Jill.

"But she was running too, you know!"

"I'm a lifeguard," replied the other girl easily. "I have to."

"Yes she does," agreed Dana with a pointed nod at her not-niece. "And the fact that *you've* been caught doing this three days in a row now certainly makes things much more serious, little girl. I cannot *believe* that you would be so disrespectful to… to um…"

She broke away from her glowering for a brief moment to quirk one quizzical brow at the lifeguard.

"What was your name again, dear?"

"Jill," supplied the now smirking girl helpfully.

"Right, Jill," repeated Dana with a half-grin of her own before reaffixing her earlier scowl. "I cannot believe that you would be so disrespectful to Jill like that. What on earth were you thinking?"

"I um… I dunno…" mumbled Rhen, twisting a toe into the sand at her feet as she bounced her gaze between her partner's unimpressed glower and the lifeguard's perfectly chiseled collarbones. "The sand was just, like, really hot and stuff, and I wanted to get to the water faster. I didn't think it was going to be that big of a deal…"

"Oh my god, are you kidding me?" cut in Jill then, some of her earlier professional outrage resurfacing as she threw her hands into the air in frustration. "You've nearly stomped on *so* many sunbathers! Not to mention the fact that you've ruined at least two sandcastles as far as I've seen. And, even if you *hadn't* been bothering anyone, that still wouldn't have made the way you've been acting okay. People leave crap in the sand all the time, you know. You could have easily tripped or cut your foot open on something."

"That's *right*," agreed Dana, this time with an accompanying finger wag, feeding off the taller girl's indignation. "The rules are there for a reason, whether you like them or not, Rhen."

She then lifted one of her feet off the ground and gave her green flip-flop a little wiggle.

"And if the sand is too hot for you to walk on, then you should wear your sandals like everyone else."

"That's what I said!" exclaimed Jill, obviously grateful to have another adult who understood where she was coming from and could share in her annoyance.

At that, Dana's stern demeanor melted away entirely, and she turned an apologetic smile on the lifeguard.

"I am so sorry she's been such a handful for you, dear," she sighed. "She's usually a lot better behaved than this, but she's just been so excited to play at the beach that I think she's been forgetting that the rules still apply to her, even if we're on vacation."

"Hey, don't sweat it," waved away the effervescent blonde. "This actually happens a lot more often than you might think. Usually a warning is enough to get most kids her age to knock it off, but well…"

She gave an easy shrug then.

"For those who don't want to listen, a quick trip back to the lifeguard tower for a little chat and some time facing the wall usually does the trick."

"Mmhmm, I just bet it does," mused Dana with a knowing chuckle, eyeing the taller girl's solid and well-defined forearms and biceps appreciatively. "But, just so that we're both clear on what's about to happen here and I can go back to reading my book in peace, this 'little chat' you're planning on having with my girlfriend is one that involves her bending over and getting spanked, right?"

"Oh god…" moaned Rhen, burying her burning face in her hands. "This seriously can't be happening right now."

This time, though, it was the lifeguard's turn to fumble with her words.

"Wait, wait, wait. Hold up. Your uh… Your girlfriend?" she repeated, whipping her blonde head back and forth between Rhen and her partner in bewilderment. "But didn't she just call you her-”

“Her aunt?” supplied Dana with a crocodile smile, her sunglasses crooking down her nose as she inclined her head in amusement at the flustered girl.

“Uh, yeah…”

“She sure did,” the older woman confirmed, her smile not budging an inch. “You could say we have a bit of a *unique* dynamic to our romantic relationship. But don’t let her adorable looks fool you, Rhen is more than old enough to know better than to act like a naughty child.”

She winked then.

“Not that that’s ever stopped her before.”

And her smile broadened into something conspiratorial.

“Or saved her cute little tush from a taking a trip over ‘Auntie Dana’s’ lap whenever she’s been caught misbehaving.”

“So then you two are actually…?”

“That’s right,” sing-songed Dana, unwavering in her amusement as she gave the taller girl some time to process this new information. “We’ve been together for about a year now.”

“Oh. I uh…”

Jill’s round face burst into a blush nearly as red as her swimsuit as sudden understanding dawned on her delicate features.

“Okay, *wow*. Gotcha. Didn’t really see that one coming, but now that you mention it, I guess it makes sense.”

She gave the back of her neck an embarrassed rub then and let out another giggle, running her eyes up and down Rhen with a newfound interest; reassessing every inch of her.

“God. I’m glad you mentioned something. I could have *sworn* she was-”

“Yes, yes, I know, dear. It happens all the time,” soothed Dana with a sympathetic nod, still grinning from ear to ear. “Now then, if I’m not mistaken, you were just about to explain to me how you planned on disciplining my disobedient ‘niece’ for her rule breaking?”

“R… Right, I was! Ahem.”

Still blushing, but also grinning from ear to ear now too, Jill paused long enough to give her head a quick shake and clear her throat, slipping back (more or less) into her earlier professional enthusiasm, but with a much more excited undertone to it this time.

"You pretty much hit the nail right on the head, ma'am. I'm definitely planning on spanking her. Although, to be fair, what I have in mind isn't really anything *too* wild," the lifeguard reassured the shorter girl's partner. "I usually handle repeat offenders like her with just a couple dozen swats over the seat of their swimsuit with my hand, and then have them stand facing the wall for about ten minutes to make sure they've learned their lesson and to give them a chance to catch their breath."

"Oh come now, that hardly seems like enough of a punishment after all the trouble she's been giving you," tutted Dana as she gave her finger another wag, though this time it wasn't particularly chiding. "I've always believed that if you're going to give a girl a spanking, you need to give her a *spanking*. After all, she's never going to learn her lesson if all you have to take her to task with are flimsy half-measures. You need to be much firmer with her than that."

"Yes, well…" conceded Jill, looking abashed. "She's not really a local, so this is usually about all I can safely get away with without riling up a bunch of snooty tourists."

"Is that so?" purred Dana, her smile turning predatory. "And what if she *was* a local?"

"Heh. Well if that were the case," answered the lifeguard, her own mouth drawing back into a similar smile as she refound her footing. "She and I would be having a much longer chat on her bare bottom."

A tiny giggle managed to escape her then as she leered hungrily down at Rhen.

"And a much louder one."

"I see… Now that's more like it," nodded Dana approvingly. "Well, in that case, why don't you just go ahead and give her the full local treatment then? I promise I won't be mad at you for giving her an actual spanking instead of playing patty-cake with her polka dots."

"Um… Are you really sure about that ma'am?" pressed the lifeguard, her face a mixture of budding excitement and sudden worry. "It's not going to be something she'll be forgetting anytime soon if I do."

Grinning, she made a show of flexing one tanned and *very* toned bicep for the two of them.

"Not to brag or anything, but I've been told I've got kind of an arm if you know what I mean, and I wouldn't be letting her up for a while once we got started. Like you said, she's been giving me a *lot* of trouble."

That managed to draw a huffy scowl from Rhen, and a tinkling laugh from her partner.

"Oh honey," she grinned, waving away the other girl's concerns without a second thought. "She's more than used to it, trust me. You just go ahead and spank her until you think she's learned her lesson, and then give her a little bit more for good measure, alright?"

"Right," nodded Jill firmly, not bothering to hide her enthusiasm this time. "I can do that. One sizzled seat coming right up!"

"What?" demanded Rhen, incredulous and red-faced as her heart leapt into her throat, propelled upward by a fresh surge of panic and more than a little excitement. "You can't just do that! I'm not a local. You can't treat me like one!"

"Eh, you've been here three days in a row now," countered the lifeguard. "That's close enough."

"But… but…!"

"Young lady, you will do as you are told and take your spanking like a big girl," admonished Dana, leaning in close enough for her girlfriend to see the storm brewing behind her dark blue eyes, even through her tinted lenses. "And if I hear you've given Jill any trouble, and I do mean *any* trouble, you and I will be repeating this discussion later on tonight back at the hotel. Am I understood?"

Undone by her partner's menacing tone, her legs threatening to give out from under her once again as her stomach flip-flopped with a nervous thrill, Rhen nodded quickly.

"Yes ma'am!"

"Nice," commented Jill, her smile positively luminous now.

"Oh, don't let all her huffing and pouting fool you," laughed Dana, her forbidding demeanor blowing away like a cloud on a summer breeze as she straightened up again. "She's a total push-over when it comes to getting her bottom swatted. All you need is a stern tone and a firm hand, and she's putty in your hands."

"Awww, that's adorable!" cooed Jill, clapping to herself with excitement. "What a sweetheart!"

"Isn't she, though?"

Ruffling her scowling not-niece's hair affectionately and looking extremely pleased with herself, Dana leaned in for a quick kiss and then turned and began walking away back toward where she'd been sunbathing earlier at an easy, unconcerned pace. Calling over her shoulder as she went.

"You two have fun now."

"Will do!" waved Jill, arm high in the air as she and the red-faced shorter girl watched the auburn-haired older woman's cheery swimsuit cover disappear back into the crowd.

"Ugh! This is such *bullcrap*," moaned Rhen as soon as she was sure her aunt was safely out of earshot.

SMACK! SMACK!

Only to be rewarded for her efforts by a pair of offhanded and perfectly executed swats right where the back of her bikini bottoms left two crescents of bare skin exposed behind her.

"Yeow!" she yelped, stomach leaping right along with her feet as she hopped in place at the unexpected impacts.

Holy crap, she's got a mean swing!

"Unless you're in the mood to make the rest of the walk back to my tower without your bikini bottoms on, I'd knock it off with all the sass, 'kiddo'," advised Jill, not sounding particularly annoyed anymore, but looking *very* determined nevertheless.

"Oh my god, you wouldn't!" gasped the shorter girl, all of the indignant color draining from her face in an instant. "You can't!"

"Try me."

"But… but…"

Swallowing hard, Rhen felt all of the blood that had just drained out of her cheeks rush back with a vengeance.

"But this isn't a nude beach!" she found herself blurting out in a desperate attempt to distract herself from the mental images the lifeguard's threat was conjuring within her. "You can't just *do* that! It's… it's… it's not allowed!"

She swallowed nervously.

"Um… Right?"

"Technically speaking, no, it isn't," agreed Jill with a playful grin, her eyes alight with unabashed mischief. "But the tide yanks people's swimsuits off all the time. You'd hardly be the first person to go scrambling for cover after the ocean decided to pants you."

"Wha-? But we're not-!"

Eyeing the shoreline that was some fifteen yards away from them at that moment, Rhen had some serious doubts as to whether or not that explanation would really hold up to scrutiny or not, but she wasn't about to risk finding out for herself.

"Humph. Fine," she harrumphed instead, folding her slender arms in front of her and shifting her weight onto one sassy hip as she struggled to get her embarrassment and pounding heart back under control.

That evidently didn't count as straightening out her attitude in Jill's eyes, though.

"Okeydokey, have it your way then."

Rolling her eyes, but still smirking, the towering lifeguard stepped around behind Rhen, and without a single moment of hesitation, began tugging down on the back of her polka dot bikini bottoms, causing her to bunny hop forward a good three feet with both hands clamped to her seat.

"Okay, okay, you've made your point!" she blurted, rounding

on her as she hurriedly restored her swimsuit to its proper place around her hips, inadvertently giving herself a wedgie in the process. "I'll be good. *Geez*!"

"Uh-huh," replied Jill, pinning her in place with a look not all that dissimilar to one she'd seen Dana wearing only a few moments earlier. "We'll just see about that, now won't we?" "Yes ma'am!" answered Rhen in a hurry, putting as much obedient energy as she could behind those two words as she straightened up to her full height on reflex. "I swear I'll be good!"

"Hehe, now that's more like it."

Nodding to herself in blatantly amused self-satisfaction, Jill strode forward once again and this time took up Rhen's hand in her own as if she were a small child, and not just someone she was about to spank like one.

"Right this way," she ordered in a sing-song voice, pulling her along as she began leading the way once again toward the open-sided, elevated wooden platform and observation hut that was her lifeguard tower. "Oh this is going to be so much fun!"

"Yeah, yeah…" grumbled Rhen, too mortified to do anything else besides roll her eyes as she allowed herself to be led away.

Scowling at the other girl's enthusiasm and feeling a spot tingling just between her shoulder blades where she was sure her aunt's stare was boring into her as she watched them walk away, she let out another harrumph.

"Shouldn't you be, like, a little less excited about all this?"

She knew it was a silly question to ask, especially given the people that she was friends with, but she just couldn't help herself. Not when the bubbly lifeguard was actually *humming* to herself now.

"Huh? Why wouldn't I be excited?" asked Jill as she wove the two of them between several people lounging on beach towels beneath umbrellas. "I just got the green light to spank your adorable little butt until its cherry red and sizzling. Of course I'm excited. That's awesome!"

"Oh. Well, um, uh…"

Rhen had honestly not been prepared for such a straightforward and oddly flattering response.

"Thanks?"

"You're welcome," giggled Jill. "Although, I don't think you'll be in much of a mood to thank me in just a minute, hehe."

Yeah… Somehow I think you might just be right about that one.

Deciding then that she was probably better off keeping her big mouth shut for the time being, Rhen pressed her lips together into a fretful grimace and tried not to think too hard about what was about to happen to her.

Ugh. I knew we should have just gone shopping today.

—

Half a minute (and far too many people waving hello to Jill) later, they reached the base of the cheerily painted lifeguard tower, and the horrifying reality that there was no more putting off what was about to happen to her went cascading down Rhen's spine like a bucket of ice water.

Oh god…

"Humph. How is this thing even close to being a tower?" she found herself demanding, the butterflies that had been building up inside her stomach finally breaking free and forcing her to speak after what felt like an eternity of holding everything in. "It's, like, *barely* even off the ground."

In truth, the structure actually overlooked the beach by a good six feet or more, and even standing on her tiptoes she was unable to see anything happening at the top of it. But, as far as she was concerned, a proper tower was something that had crenulations and was home to a wizard. Not some rinky-dink beach shack with a boogie board hanging from its roof.

At least its rainbow flag paint job was fun.

"Oooh, I don't know. It's high enough for me to see everything that's going on around here," dismissed Jill breezily, tugging her up along the wooden ramp that led onto the observation platform at the top of the tower. "And, unfortunately for you, kiddo, it's also more than high enough for everyone else to see *your* bratty little butt getting spanked without any problems either."

"Wait, what? Hold on!" squawked Rhen at that, her head swiveling frantically from side to side and discovering to her horror that the view from her elevated position was indeed quite spectacular. "Oh my god, Jill, you can't seriously be planning on-"

"Yep," confirmed the other girl, just as easy and carefree as before as she let go of her hand and started stretching her arms and shoulders, seemingly limbering up for what was to be a pro-longed bout of aerobic exercise.

"But, like, can't we do this inside?" begged the twenty-year-old turned teenager, flailing one panicky arm at the small hut next to them atop the tiny tower.

It was surrounded on all sides by tall windows, and she doubted very much that it would do anything to stop her cries of pain or the reports of Jill's hard palm from carrying to anyone who might be close enough to hear them, but at least if they were in there she'd be able to hide her naked butt from the general public.

"Come on, please?"

"Hmmm…"

Jill seemed to consider her request for one long, nerve-wracking moment, tapping thoughtfully at her cheek as she stared off into space, before at last giving her broad shoulders an uncon-cerned shrug and smirking.

"Nah."

"But… but… but why not?" demanded Rhen with a strangled, frustrated moan, stomping one foot in protest and making the entire structure beneath their feet tremble.

SMACK!

"Hey now, watch it, kiddo. This isn't a jungle gym, you know," reprimanded the lifeguard with another lazy (and feet lifting) swat to the seat of the younger girl's swimsuit that had her teeth clenching together as hard as they could to keep her high-pitched squeal of surprise from escaping. "And not that I really need to explain myself to a naughty little rule breaker like you, but, well…"

At that, she turned a diabolical grin on Rhen that sent an electrifying tingle directly between her legs.

"You and I are going to be having a *very* long talk about what is and isn't appropriate beach behavior. And while that's certainly important, and *way* overdue if you ask me, I can't just abandon my post simply because you don't want anyone to see your cutie patootie getting its much-deserved comeuppance."

She made a broad, sweeping gesture with her hand then, taking in everyone splashing, swimming, and lounging all around them on the sand below. From their elevated position, there suddenly seemed to be a great deal more of them than there had been back at ground level just a few moments earlier.

"People are still having fun out there, and I need to make sure I keep an eye on them, just in case. So, no, we are not going to do this inside, sorry."

"Ugh. I guess that makes sense…" conceded Rhen with a harrumph, hating to admit that the other girl might have a point even as part of her thrilled with the knowledge that she was about to receive her most public spanking ever.

"I'm *so* glad to hear it meets with your approval," sniffed Jill, some of her earlier annoyance bubbling up past her exuberance as she sent her stumbling along with another casual swat.

SMACK!

"Now bend that butt of yours over the railing, you little sassmuffin," she ordered with a snicker, pointing toward a section of wooden railing that looked out over the ocean and which would provide the lifeguard with the best possible vantage point for watching the beach (and everyone else the best possible view of Rhen's face as her backside was being reddened). "It's high time you and I got down to business."

Rhen found herself biting down hard on the inside of her cheek to avoid voicing her own thoughts on how much time they had to kill. As much as she might have wanted to, those perfunctory swats were starting to add up alarmingly fast, and even more distressing, they were easily as explosive (if not more so) than what Courtney usually brought to bear whenever she was in the mood to *really* make a point.

I guess all those muscles aren't just for show, she thought to herself with a wince, even as her eyes wandered appreciatively up and down over the taut curves visible beneath the other girl's swimsuit. *Oh well, at least it's just going to be her hand. I can handle that... I think.*

Heaving out her best put-upon sigh, one that mostly succeeded in masking her nervous giggling, Rhen stalked over to the spot that the taller girl had indicated, rolled her eyes, and bent over.

Or at least, she tried to.

Unfortunately for her, the top crossbar of the wooden rail that ran around the perimeter of the tower came up nearly to her chest. Which made bending over it a rather difficult proposition.

"Oh, right. My bad."

Noticing her predicament, Jill hurriedly ducked inside the observation hut and grabbed a small stepstool.

"Here we go," she sing-songed, plopping it down in front of Rhen and patting it fondly. "Stand on this, please."

"Oh, uh…"

Face coloring all over again (there was something undeniably juvenile about having to stand on top of a pastel pink stepstool in order to take her spanking) Rhen let out another, much more genuine, sigh of embarrassment and moved to do as she'd been told.

"R-Right."

"There we go…" cooed Jill, eyes glued to the seat of her swimsuit as she watched her take up her position leaning over the railing, stepping in right behind her once she was in place and gently coaxing her feet about a shoulder's width apart. "Yes, just like that. Nice and stable. Perfect."

"If you say so," mumbled Rhen darkly, swallowing hard as she felt the other girl's nimble fingers slip into the back of her swimsuit.

"I *do* say so," she answered sweetly, her grip tightening noticeably around the stretchy material as her voice took on a hard edge to it. "Is that going to be a problem, young lady?"

"No ma'am!" the shorter girl was quick to reassure her, giving her head a vigorous shake that sent her dark ponytail flopping back and forth behind her.

"Heh. Now that's more like it," crooned the lifeguard as she began peeling down Rhen's polka dot bikini bottoms, only stopping when she had them stretched snugly between her parted knees. "Awww! Oh my god, look at you! You're just *adorable*. Now I really wish I *had* made you walk back here bottomless. That would've been so much fun!"

Clearly intent on taking her time and enjoying herself to the fullest despite insisting just a moment earlier that they needed to get moving, Jill gave the two pristinely pale and delightfully jiggly cheeks she'd just uncovered an exploratory squeeze.

Or six.

"Mmph…"

Gnawing at her lower lip as her legs went to jelly beneath her, Rhen had to fight hard to regain her focus.

"H… Hey, come on… Are you sure you should be doing that out here?" she managed to ask without sounding too breathless, hoping that she might be able to wheedle her way into a private(ish) spanking after all.

"Oh, don't sweat it," dismissed Jill with a laugh. "We're high enough that people can only see the broad strokes of what's going on up here. As far as they're concerned, you're just getting a couple of pre-spanking rubs while I lecture you."

"I uh… I see."

Works for me.

"Mmmm… I bet your 'aunt' must have *so* much fun with you when you two are out in public," crooned the lifeguard, turning her full attention back to the naked girl at her mercy. "From a distance, and heck, let's be real, even up close, you totally pull off the whole bratty teen thing insanely well. I seriously never would've been able to guess that you were out of high school if she hadn't filled me in."

At least she didn't say middle school… Rhen thought to herself with a wry grimace and just the barest hint of a self-satisfied smirk. *That's got to count for something, right?*

"Also, you being totally shaved back here, like, totally ties your whole look together super well," the taller girl added, seemingly as an afterthought as she began squeezing a bit harder. "Whose idea was that anyway? It's *such* a great touch."

"N-No comment," stammered the petite junior in as dignified a manner as she could manage, her heart leaping into her throat with the knowledge that she was so completely on display for the lifeguard.

"Oooh, that's fine," snickered Jill, lightly dragging a fingertip along the middle of her exposed lips and grinning wolfishly at the glistening residue it came away coated in. "You're already saying *more* than enough back here already."

"Eep!"

A horrible dark red heat rushed up Rhen's neck and into her cheeks at the unexpected touch, not the least of which because her hips had thrust themselves up and back in an attempt to follow after the trailing finger as it had pulled away.

"Hey!" she protested, her tongue moving faster than her brain as she scrambled for some way of salvaging at least part of her dignity. "I was swimming, alright?"

"Uh-huh," replied the lifeguard in an amused deadpan, her mouth quirking to the side as she gave each round, vulnerable cheek in front of her another hearty grope. "You know, you're usually wet in a more general sense of the word if you've just been in the water."

"Well, um, I uh… You see-"

"I guess we're just going to have to add fibbing to your list of infractions as well," interrupted Jill with a mock-disappointed sigh and a conciliatory pat. "Tsk, tsk. You really are a naughty one, aren't you?"

"No comment," repeated Rhen with a pouty harrumph this time, refusing to dignify that question with a response as the taller girl began giving her bottom a series of firmer and firmer pats; either getting a better feel for her aim, or just enjoying the bounce her touch was producing.

"That's alright," she replied cheerily, perking up as her patting came to a sudden and ominous halt. "I don't mind keeping you here longer."

SMACK! SMACK!

Before delivering two explosive swats in quick succession that had Rhen up on her tiptoes again, yelping in surprise and pain as twin supernovas bloomed atop the centers of both her cheeks.

"Ack! Holy- Ah! Crap!"

"After all, it *is* my duty as a lifeguard to ensure that you come away from our little discussion today fully committed to obeying *all* the rules," continued Jill just as conversationally as she brought her hand up past her shoulder again. "Regardless of how long that might take."

SMACK! SMACK!

"And watch the potty talk! We're still in public, you know."

SMACK! SMACK!

"S- Ow! Sorry!"

"No worries. Just don't let it happen again, alright?"

Jill started spanking in earnest then, raining down burning swats in a high-speed back and forth pattern with all the fluid grace of someone who had done this many, many times before. And it was right about then that Rhen realized she'd definitely bitten off way more than she could chew.

"Ack! Oh! Please-!" she yelped, trapped in place over the railing and unable to do anything more than shake her head and flail her arms uselessly in front of her as the athletic and very much in charge lifeguard beat out an unrelenting tattoo of miniature explosions against her bare backside. "I'm sorry, I'm sorry, I'm sorry!"

"Oh really? That's great news!" cheered Jill, sounding

genuinely pleased with herself.

SMACK! SMACK! SMACK!

And punctuating her enthusiasm with three increasingly hard swats to the center of Rhen's clenching and unclenching seat.

"Now hang on tight, because we've still got a *long* way to go."

SMACK!

"Aieee! Yes ma'am!"

Oh crap, oh crap, oh crap!

Rhen was no stranger when it came to being taken to task by strong and experienced spankers, but Jill was in a league all her own when it came to dishing out discipline. Her hand felt like it was several times heavier than it had any right to be, and she was seamlessly alternating between swatting with just the heel of her palm (which didn't particularly sting, but felt like a tiny boulder pummeling against the deep tissue of her backside like a pissed off jackhammer), and slapping with her fingers and palm together (which just stung like crazy).

SMACK! SMACK! SMACK! SMACK! SMACK!

And while Jill's hands weren't exactly big in proportion to their owner, she still had to be well over six feet tall. Which, unfortunately for Rhen, meant that the lifeguard's relatively dainty palm didn't have to wander far to get full coverage of both her buns.

Or the delicate thighs beneath!

"Look. I know you've already heard this all before," she started to lecture once she settled into a steady spanking rhythm, not exactly sounding angry, but definitely not in the mood to be argued with either. "But the rules are there for your safety and everyone else's, and you *will* obey them."

In less than half a minute she'd already managed to paint the shorter girl's gyrating bottom and upper thighs a uniform shade of bright pink that was quickly making its way toward fire engine red, and had shifted her stance to wrap her free arm around her trim waist. Locking her in place against the side of her hip as she continued to piston her palm up and down without mercy.

"And just because you don't feel like following those rules does *not* mean that they don't still apply to you."

SMACK! SMACK! SMACK! SMACK! SMACK!

"Or that they don't have consequences if you choose to ignore them. Am I making myself clear?"

"Ack! Okay, okay! I get it- Oh! I get it!" erupted Rhen, abandoning any naïve hopes that she might've still had of taking her punishment in stride as her feet left the stepstool entirely and began flailing in the air behind her, leaving her supported only by the railing beneath her stomach and the lifeguard's steel band of an arm around her waist.

Teeth gritted against a particularly ruthless series of rapid-fire swats to the extra-sensitive inner curves of her sit-spots, she found herself throwing a dirty look over her shoulder to make sure that the other girl hadn't secretly swapped over to using a barbed wire hairbrush or something while she hadn't been looking.

"Ow! Crap! Geez! You've made your freaking point, alright?" she bit out, stubbornly refusing to fully break down into the tearful gasps and squeals that she so desperately wanted to. "Can't you- Ow! Ease the heck up already?"

"Smart mouth? Really?" snorted Jill, not slowing her smooth, measured pace in the slightest as her perfectly plucked eyebrows climbed up her forehead in amused disbelief. "Do you *really* think it's a good idea to be sassing me right now?"

SMACK! SMACK! SMACK! SMACK! SMACK!

"It's not, *sass*!" Rhen fired back around another series of barely-stifled grunts and pained exhalations through gritted teeth. "I'm just- Oh! I'm just saying- Urk! That you don't have to- Owie! Have to spank- Ah! So *hard*!"

The corners of Jill's mouth twitched up even higher at that.

"Hmmm… Maybe," she conceded with a small head tilt and a pair of matching red handprints to an as yet unspanked area of the shorter girl's thighs.

SMACK-SMACK!

"But this way is a lot more fun, wouldn't you agree?"

"Ugh!" groused Rhen, not quite willing to argue that point as her bikini bottoms went sailing off her feet to land against the wall of the observation hut somewhere behind her. "That's not- Ack! Not the freaking *point*!"

Her indignation only served to further widen the other girl's grin, however.

"Alrighty then, little girl, have it your way," Jill laughed, planting her left foot onto the stepstool beside her and propping Rhen's backside up even higher atop one bare, rock solid thigh placed strategically just beneath her groin. "I can keep this up all day, you know."

SMACK! SMACK! SMACK! SMACK! SMACK!

Yeah. That's what I'm freaking afraid of!

—

Whether or not Jill was actually capable of spanking her all day would forever remain a mystery to Rhen (although she had a worrying hunch that she probably wasn't bluffing), as after only a minute or two more of bucking and grinding against the taller girl's tanned leg, they were interrupted by someone calling up to them from the base of the lifeguard tower.

"Hello up there! Mind if I pop by for a second?"

"Oh hey, Karen. What's up?" greeted Jill brightly, coming to an abrupt halt mid-swing and waving the newcomer up before transitioning into palming Rhen's sizzling seat once again (ostensibly checking how warm she'd managed to get it so far and not at all just because she enjoyed the feel of it).

"Wha-? Who's that?" demanded the shorter girl with a startled squeak, caught between bone-deep relief that her bottom was no longer being blistered, and a fresh surge of heart-hammering, thigh-squirming panic as she heard a pair of sandals begin ascending the ramp off to her left. "Wait, no! Don't come up here! G-Go away! Can't you see we're-"

SMACK!

"Easy there. It's just Karen, you silly goose," soothed Jill, pausing her kneading just long enough to deliver an open-palmed swat to the center of the compact caboose still propped up by her elevated thigh. "She's here all the time with her kids. There's no need to freak out."

"But-!" Rhen tried to argue again, more so out of habit than anything else as her thighs clamped themselves together in an effort to hide any evidence that she might've recently been *swimming*.

Jill was having none of it, though.

"She's also seen me spank plenty of bratty butts before."

SMACK!

"So just relax, alright?"

"Ack! Okay, okay! *Fine*."

"My, oh my. It sure seems like you've managed to land yourself a lively one this afternoon," commented the woman as she stepped onto the observation platform, her voice carrying the same broad, unapologetically amused smile that so many adults tended to share with one another when discussing discipline as she took in the sight of the bright red, supposedly adolescent tush on full display just a foot or two in front of her.

"You can say that again," snickered Jill, making a show of blowing on her partially pinkened palm and shaking it out with a grimace. "She's a lot tougher than she looks, actually. She's seriously starting to wear out my poor hand."

"Oh cry me a river, you big baby," harrumphed Rhen with just a twinkle of satisfaction, crossing her arms in front of her and glaring at all the people having fun on the beach below.

Some of whom actually had the nerve to wave back at her!

God, this is humiliating…

"Well, that'd certainly explain all the sass," mused the newcomer with an easy laugh. "It's amazing what girls who think they're too big for a spanking believe they can get away with, isn't it?"

"Noooo kidding," agreed Jill, giving the naked seat tucked under her arm a friendly pat. "But I think this one's starting to learn her lesson. Aren't you, Rhen?"

"Pretty sure I learned it about a million freaking swats ago…"

SMACK!

"Ow! Hey!"

"The key word here being *starting*," continued the lifeguard, rolling her eyes good-naturedly as Rhen mumbled something unintelligible under her breath. "We're definitely going to still be at this for a while, I think."

"Oh, I wouldn't worry too much, dear. Give it another minute or two, and I'm sure she'll be promising you the sun and stars," encouraged the older woman with a motherly shake of her head. "But, speaking of… That's actually why I came over here in the first place. I mean, I hate to interrupt while you're busy and all, but…"

"Hey now, don't even worry about it," dismissed Jill. "We were just barely getting into her warm up anyway. What's up?"

"Oh, well, as it so happens, I was thinking that maybe I might be able to do something for *you*, actually," replied Karen, sounding just a bit bashful, as if she'd had to run over from next door to borrow a cup of sugar. "I happened to catch most of your initial confrontation with little miss speedy feet here, and after the way she nearly trampled over me and Gerald, I thought I'd bring you something special to help straighten her out. Assuming that is, of course, that you don't mind the imposition."

"What?" demanded Rhen, her squirming kicking into overdrive at this very unwelcome bit of neighborly concern.

SMACK!

"Quiet, kiddo, the adults are talking," chided Jill with another friendly (albeit rather heavy-handed) pat while she and the other woman shared a look. "And I'd be absolutely delighted to use whatever you've brought for me, Karen. Thanks!"

"Oh really? That's wonderful," sighed the older woman, hand to her chest in relief as her tone shifted from hesitant to sly and playful. "You do such an important job around here, and we wouldn't want to risk you throwing out your shoulder over something so silly as spanking a stubborn little sassmouth, now would we?"

"Awww, that's so sweet," blushed Jill, her smile going radiant as she tucked some of her platinum hair behind an ear.

Rhen was far less moved, however.

"Oh my god, she's already doing just fine as it is!" she insisted, attempting to stomp a foot without thinking and only succeeding in flailing adorably. "Seriously, lady. Like, this *super* isn't necessary."

Her objections went completely ignored by the two women, though, and she was left to watch on over her shoulder with a scowl as they continued their conversation.

"So," bubbled Jill, bouncing the leg beneath Rhen excitedly as she angled to see what the other woman was hiding behind her back. "What'd you bring me? It's not a pool noodle, is it?"

"No, no," Karen reassured her, producing with a flourish what appeared to be an elongated table tennis racket. "It's *this*!"

Oh crap.

"Huh. You brought a paddle to the beach?" replied Jill, sounding more than a little confused, but not so much so that she wasn't going to use it.

"Oh, don't be silly!"

Laughing to herself, the other woman mimed an underhand tennis swing with the apparent not-paddle.

"Well… Maybe," she admitted a moment later, smiling sheepishly at the dirty look she got from Rhen. "It's actually a paddle-ball *racket*. But, yes, I suppose if you take away the ball part, it's just a paddle. Either way, you can trust me when I say it's more than capable of getting the job done without you having to strain yourself too hard."

She winked then.

"There's definitely a reason why it stays in our car all the time."

"Well shoot, when you put it like that…"

Reaching out a hand, Jill accepted the definitely-a-paddle with a nod of thanks, wrapping her fingers around its rubber grip and grinning from ear to ear.

It looked big enough to cover the width of an entire cheek in a single swat, but thankfully was much thinner than the patu had been. Still, Rhen wasn't looking forward to finding out how it felt.

Unfortunately for her, Jill didn't seem to share those reservations.

"Hmmm…" she mused to herself with an excited giggle, giving the paddle a couple of test swings through the air beside her and making Rhen squirm as the breeze they produced whispered across her bare skin, raising goosebumps . "Oh yeah, this'll *totally* work. Thank you so much, Karen. You're a life saver!"

"Of course, of course, think nothing of it, dear," demurred the other woman, sparing a moment to shoot Rhen a smugly satisfied look before turning to go. "I'll just leave you to it then. Oh, and feel free to hang onto that after you're done. I'll be by to grab it later."

"Sounds great," nodded Jill, using her new paddle to wave her off as she began descending the ramp. "Thanks again!"

"Yeah, *thanks*. You're suuuuch a help, *Karen*," Rhen mumbled darkly as well, her face a mixture of worry and anticipation that she was grateful was mostly hidden from Jill's view.

She already knew there would be no dissuading the taller girl from paddling her raw. Not when she was humming happily to herself as she worked her hand through the wrist strap of the stupid thing. But she wasn't about to let her know how much that thought excited her.

Or stop her from complaining.

"You know, I really think you were doing just fine with your hand," she grumbled with a pout.

"Oh yeah?" prompted Jill, still sounding far too cheery for her liking as she pressed the smooth surface of the paddle against the center of her cheeks. "If that's the case, then this ought to be even better!"

"But… but…" spluttered Rhen, her bottom clenching on reflex behind her as fresh butterflies took wing inside her stomach. "But, um… But isn't that cheating?"

"Cheating?" echoed the lifeguard, sounding genuinely bemused as she began rubbing her implement in slow, lazy circles around her target area.

"Yeah, cheating!" insisted the petite junior, knowing that she was grasping at straws now, but not caring so long as it helped put off the inevitable for just a little bit longer. "That thing is a performance enhancing device and should be illegal! If you use a paddle, can you really say that *you* were the one who spanked me?"

That managed to at least get a snort of laughter from Jill.

And absolutely zero sympathy.

"Hmmm… You might have a point there," she allowed, almost sounding as if she really believed her. "Thankfully, though, I'm the one in charge, and I say it's fine."

"Oh come on!"

"Awww, there's no need to be so nervous. This thing is just some light plywood. It's not that scary, I promise."

Jill demonstrated just what she meant then by giving each of Rhen's wobbly cheeks a couple of mild pats.

"See?"

Rhen could indeed feel that the paddle was pretty light, though not nearly as light as she'd been hoping it would be. It felt like it had about the same amount of heft to it as one of her aunt's wooden spoons. Just with a whole lot more surface area.

Which meant it was *definitely* going to make an impression.

"Yeah, okay. I guess that's not *so* bad."

With a reluctant sigh, she relaxed herself back across the other girl's thigh and supporting arm, surrendering herself just as she knew she would have to eventually.

"Let's just hurry up and get this over with, alright? I've still got stuff I want to do today, you know. Humph."

"Sure thing, miss grumpy pantsless," chirped Jill, bringing the paddle up past her shoulder with a broad, excited grin. "Now hold on tight, because this is gonna *sting*."

"Yeah, whatev-"

THWAP-THWAP-THWAP-THWAP-THWAP!

"Oh my god! Holy crap! Ow, ow, owie, AH!"

The lack of weight to the paddle did absolutely nothing to make it any easier to take, and in many ways actually made things a whole lot worse. While it didn't pack the same teeth-rattling, hip-jarring, heavyweight punch that the patu had, that was of little consolation considering it stung about billion times more than the lifeguard's hand had.

And allowed her to swing it nearly as fast.

At least with the patu her aunt had been forced to pace herself!

"Soooo, what do you think? How's that feeling?"

THWAP-THWAP-THWAP-THWAP-THWAP!

Jill seemed to be approaching Mach speed with her newfound implement, having quickly shifted to only bringing it up past her elbow before bringing it back down again. Sacrificing her wind up for a faster pace that left no room for Rhen to catch her breath. By the time one swat had registered for her, two more had found their marks, and they were all burning like crazy!

"Am I starting to make an impression?"

"Oh my freaking god, *yes*!" the thoroughly unhappy twenty-year-old turned teenager managed to get out as she gasped and yelped, wriggled and squirmed, not bothering to try and hold anything in anymore as her bottom and thighs were peppered with a series of seemingly nonstop swats that totally eclipsed the patty-cake session that had been her earlier warm up. "Please, please, please! Ow! Oh my god, I'm sorry, I'm sorry, I'm sorry! I *swear* I won't break any more rules!"

She didn't care that everyone could hear her squealing and begging now. If she was going to get paddled like a little brat, then she might as well fully embrace the experience, right?

Not that she really had much of a choice.

"Wow, that's quite the turnaround," teased Jill playfully, taking her time as she worked her way down Rhen's thighs and back up again, making sure not to leave any spot unspanked. "Not talking back too much now, are we?"

"No ma'am!" howled the junior, feet flailing behind her in an out of water parody of swimming that probably would've been pretty entertaining to watch had she not been the one doing it. "I'll never, ever, *ever* run on the beach ever again, I *promise*! From now it's just- Oh! Just slow walks by- Urk! Moonlight, and maybe some light skipping!"

"Awww, that's so great to hear!"

Tightening her grip around her bucking waist, Jill shifted her knee directly between Rhen's thighs and kicked her paddling into overdrive.

THWAP-THWAP-THWAP-THWAP-THWAP!

"But, just to be safe on the safe side, I think I'd better still give you something to remember me by the next time you start thinking maybe the rules don't apply to you. Okay?"

"Ugh. What- Urk! Whatever!"

"Whatever…?"

THWAP-THWAP-THWAP-THWAP-THWAP!

"Ah! Whatever, *ma'am*."

"That's the spirit!"

Well, at least the ocean is right there, Rhen tried to tell herself, grinning in spite of the fury raining (or more accurately, hailing) down on her backside as she ground against deliciously firm lifeguard leg, swimming in a sea of blistering heat and toe-curling pleasure. *With any luck, I should be able to cool off pretty quick once this is all over… Whenever the heck that'll be!*

Jill definitely wasn't showing any signs of slowing down anytime soon, which boded very ill for her prospects of sitting comfortably at dinner that evening.

Or on any rides tomorrow.

But, that was just fine with her.

As far as souvenirs went, this was pretty great.

God, I love the beach…

Chapter 13

Birthday Surprise (And a Spanking)

"Birthday dinner, birthday dinner, gonna go eat my birthday dinner!" Rhen sang aloud to herself, twirling and dancing her way through the parking lot of the Lonesome Dove Bistro while her partner and friends finished stepping out of the hired car that had driven them there that evening.

"Hey now, don't go running off without us, cutie pie," Dana called after her, taking a moment to smooth out her cocktail dress and adjust her elegantly piled hair before trailing after her at an unhurried pace along with Courtney and Abby.

"Yeah, yeah."

Undeterred in the slightest, the younger girl continued to hopscotch her way up to the front of the restaurant before turning around with a cheeky grin.

"Hurry up already, would you? I'm starving!"

Two days of back-to-back trips to Disneyland had done very little to diminish her energy levels, and instead had only served to further wind her up to the point where she was all but vibrating with excitement. The happiest place on earth had more than lived up to its name, and she'd had an absolute blast and a half exploring it with her partner and two best friends by her side. The rides had been *so* much fun, especially with Abby coordinating everything for them with their fast passes to avoid having to stand in line all day. They'd taken more photos than she could count, many of which featured her posing with the various walk-around characters at Dana's insistence. And, best of all, she'd even managed to sweet talk her "auntie" into buying her a ton of different souvenirs that she hadn't realized she'd needed in her life until she'd seen them.

Who would've ever guessed that they sold such cute clothes right there in the middle of the park?

One thing was for sure, Rhen was definitely going to have to take her time packing tomorrow morning if she wanted to get everything to fit inside her suitcase for their flight. But, that was just fine with her. She and her partner had had way too much fun playing dress up *not* to buy the outfits that they had, and she couldn't wait to get in trouble wearing some of them.

Which had very nearly been that very afternoon when she and Abby had ran off to Splash Mountain without letting either of their partners know where they were going.

So far, her twenty-first birthday had proven to be the best she'd ever had. And now, to top it all off, they were about to sit down to what was sure to be (at least if all the reviews she'd read the night before were anything to go by) an absolutely outstanding meal. Dana had even booked a small private room for them to celebrate in!

In anticipation of their dinner plans that evening, Rhen had decided to eat a smaller than normal lunch that afternoon (and not *too* many snacks around the park), and was now practically drooling all over herself as the tantalizing scents of roasting meat and fresh baked bread drifted out to greet her from the restaurant. Which, combined with the knowledge that there was also going to be delicious cake and presents to open after they were all finished eating, was enough to have her practically bouncing off the walls.

Well... Almost.

As excited as she was, she still made it a point to keep herself reined in just enough to avoid having her aunt decide to do so for her. Dana had gone so far above and beyond for her birthday party and their vacation as a whole, and she wasn't about to spoil the mood by being an (actual) brat. Plus, the absolute *last* thing she needed just then was to have the many-layered skirt of her brand new party dress lifted up for her before she'd had a chance to get changed. Luckily, avoiding an attitude adjustment wasn't proving to be too difficult a task for her since Abby was just as hyped for their fancy dinner as she was, which left their partners with little choice other than to keep up or be left behind entirely.

"My, my," teased Dana, her crimson-painted lips quirking up into a loving smile as she and her friends joined her outside the antique wood and glass double doors of the tastefully understated restaurant. "If I didn't know any better, I'd swear someone was maybe just a little bit eager to start eating."

"She's not the only one," piped up Abby, clutching her stomach and grimacing as if she were wasting away. "I'm about ready to keel over here."

"Awww, poor baby," cooed her girlfriend, the setting sun making the smattering of freckles on her face stand out as she laid a strong hand on either side of Abby's broad hips and pulled her in tight for a kiss. "I offered you some of my granola bar earlier. Why didn't you take it?"

"Uh… Maybe because those things are gross and I wanted to save room for some *actual* food?" sassed the shorter girl, before jumping in surprise as Courtney's right hand drifted down from her waist to pinch her plump cheeks through the thin material of her dress. "Oh!"

In retaliation, she bumped the taller girl off balance with her hips. Or, at least attempted to. Courtney's solidly built core and natural prowess as a lifelong athlete kept her from going anywhere, though, and instead her girlfriend earned herself a swat to go along with the pinch.

SMACK!

"Oh my god, baaaabe!" whined Abby, hand clasped protectively to her scalded left cheek. "*Rude.*"

"Sorry, hot stuff," smirked Courtney, looking anything but as she pulled her in close once more and dipped her head down for another kiss. "Thought I saw a fly on your butt."

"Uh-huh," huffed the blonde, her pout tickling the darker-skinned girl's grin that much wider. "Sure."

"Oh goodness, you two are just so cute," sighed Dana, snapping a picture of the play-quarreling lovers with her phone while they continued to lock eyes and glower at one another in each other's arms.

"Yeah, no kidding," smirked Rhen, before looking from her partner to the entrance of the restaurant and back again as it occurred to her that they didn't seem to be heading that way anymore. "Uh… Aren't we going inside? You said we had a reservation for seven, right?"

"We sure do," the older woman reassured her with an enigmatic smile, leaning in to tap the tip of her nose. "We're just waiting on one more person is all."

"Another person?"

That was certainly news to Rhen. Alana had already flown home at the start of the week, so unless her partner had made better friends with their Lyft driver than she'd realized, she was at a total loss as to who it could possibly be.

"You'll see…"

"Oh, come on! Can't I at least get a hint?"

"Nope, it's a surprise."

"Ugh! Meanie."

Seeing that she wasn't going to get anywhere with her aunt, Rhen was just about to start pestering her friends for any information they might have, when she heard a familiar voice calling out to them from the parking lot behind her.

"Hey there! Hope I didn't keep you guys waiting."

"Oh no, not at all, dear," reassured Dana, waving in greeting to the girl click-clacking her way along the pavement behind Rhen on a pair of heels. "We just got here ourselves, actually."

"Phew! I thought for sure I was going to be late with how bad the traffic was."

"Wha-?"

Whirling around, the layered ruffles of her cream colored party dress swishing adorably about her hips with the movement, Rhen broke into a shocked and delighted grin.

"Jill!"

"Heyo, kiddo," waved the off-duty lifeguard, resplendent in an impressively well-cut pink and gold dress that showed off an even more impressive amount of sun-kissed thigh. "Been keeping out of trouble?"

Blushing bright at the question, and the chorus of snickering it got from the three women behind her, Rhen decided to pretend that she hadn't heard it as she submitted to a hug and a hair ruffle.

"This is so crazy. What're you doing here?"

"I invited her, silly," supplied Dana, wrapping her arms around her from behind and resting her chin atop her head with a grin just as bright as her girlfriend's. "You two seemed to really be *hitting* it off the other day, so I invited her to come celebrate with us tonight. Plus, I figured buying her dinner would be a nice way of making up for all the trouble you were giving her earlier this week."

"Pretty sure we're more than even on that account," grumbled Rhen, still smiling as she snaked her arms back behind her between her and her partner to give her bottom a rueful rub. "I'm still glad you could make it, though, Jill."

"Of course!" beamed the lifeguard, not looking the least bit sorry for the truly legendary paddling she'd delivered just two days earlier as she tucked some of her platinum hair behind an ear and adjusted the pink bow holding the rest of it in place. "How come you never mentioned that today was your birthday, anyhow? You'd think that would've come up at some point with how long we had to chat while you were cooling off…"

"Well, uh…" hesitated Rhen, blushing all over again.

Truth be told, she'd actually just assumed that she wouldn't ever see the girl again after she'd been turned loose upon finishing her corner time standing next to the beach's "No Running" sign with her bikini bottoms around her ankles. But, looking back on things now, she supposed that might've been a bit naïve on her part. They'd had a surprisingly nice talk about their lives, their majors, and just about everything in between while her sizzling seat had gradually cooled off in the shade of the lifeguard tower, and after she'd been allowed to redress and had scampered off to go build a sandcastle, Dana had swooped in to pick up their conversation right where she'd left off.

I hope she got her number. It'd be nice to stay in touch…

"My bad. I guess it kinda just, uh… slipped my mind or something."

"Well, you *were* a bit distracted," conceded Jill with a knowing look that did nothing to lessen the petite junior's blushing as she thrust a small gift bag stuffed with bright pink tissue paper out in front of her. "Either way, happy birthday!"

"Wha-? Oh! Um, uh, th-thank you," replied Rhen, suddenly feeling incredibly bashful under the other girl's undivided attention as she accepted the sparkly bag. "You know you really didn't have to bring anything. I'm sorry if-"

"Hey now, don't even worry about it," dismissed Jill with a wave and another dazzling smile. "It's nothing too crazy, but I figured I might as well bring *something* to your party."

"Well, um… Thank you!"

"I hope you don't mind that I invited her, hon," prompted Dana then, swooping in to save her flagging girlfriend as she gave her shoulders a gentle squeeze.

"Of course not, the more the merrier!"

Shrugging off her embarrassment (and her partner's hold on her) as her earlier excitement and hunger returned in full, Rhen spun on her heel and began leading the charge into the delicious smelling restaurant.

"Okay, now let's eat!"

—

Judging by the warm, flaky rolls and fluffy butter set out as an appetizer at their table, dinner was already proving to be just as good as Rhen had been dreaming it would all that afternoon. Even better, now that she was officially twenty-one (and she wasn't out in her usual teenage persona), she was actually able to order as many fun boozy drinks as she wanted to without fear of sleeping on her stomach for it later that night.

Which was something she took full advantage of almost immediately, if for no other reason than to show off that she could.

"Wait, you're twenty-one?" marveled Jill after she'd finished placing her own order for the most whipped cream covered strawberry daiquiri they had on the menu. "Huh. I totally called nineteen, *maybe* twenty, tops."

"You did?" pressed Abby, sounding just as surprised.

"Not fourteen?" continued Courtney with a teasing grin.

"Well…"

Succumbing to a shy smile, the lifeguard cast an apologetic look in the birthday girl's direction. One that was met with only a half-hearted pout.

"I might've been leaning a bit more toward high school freshman at first…" she admitted, before adding in a rush. "But that was before Dana cleared things up for me!"

"Don't sweat it," sighed Rhen, her own frown cocking partway up into a self-deprecating smirk. "I'm just glad you didn't say middle schooler."

"Yeah," snickered her former TA, propping an elbow on the table in front of her and resting her chin in her cupped palm. "Besides, if you think she looks young now, you should see her in a pull-up. Now *that's* some next level cuteness."

"Courtney!"

"Oh my god, really?"

Jill's face had colored nearly as bright a shade of pink as Rhen's had upon hearing this bit of news, but she didn't look particularly put off by it. If anything, her smile had grown even wider.

"Yeeeep," confirmed the two coed lovers sitting across from her at the same time.

"She wears them as part of her PJs every night," the taller of them elaborated, while her girlfriend added with a giggle. "We 'babysit' her from time to time whenever she or Dana wants a night off, and we always make sure to help her get ready for bed. After all, we wouldn't want her having any accidents."

"Awww, that's just adorable!"

"Yes, my little Rhenny always looks extra cute come bedtime," agreed Dana, laying a comforting hand between her girlfriend's bare shoulders as she leaned in to kiss her broiling cheek. "Don't you, honey buns?"

Rhen *wanted* to sulk at all the teasing being heaped on top of her, but it occurred to her as she glared at no one in particular that all four of the women sitting at the tastefully decorated table around her had already seen her spanked before (and had done so themselves at various points in the past). And, as such, she really didn't have anything to be embarrassed about with them anymore. Outside of the fact that they all thought she needed to be kept in line that way in the first place, that is. So, since she no longer had any secrets left to keep about the nature of her relationship with her "aunt" or how she chose to deal with her day-to-day, she decided that there was no point in trying to deny it.

Plus, she'd be lying if she said she didn't look good in her juvenile sleepwear.

And so, rolling her eyes, she grinned right along with everyone else.

"You'd better freaking believe I do!" she declared as proudly as she could without collapsing into a fit of nervous giggles. "I rock a pair of pull-ups like nobody's business."

"They look especially good when they're around her knees," added Abby.

"Oh, I dunno," mused her girlfriend, tracing a fingertip around the rim of her glass of ice water with an impish chuckle. "Off entirely isn't too bad either, if you ask me."

Well, she *almost* had nothing to be embarrassed about.

"Humph. Rude."

"What?" teased the blonde, looking affronted as she batted her eyelashes at her. "It's true!"

"Yeah, so?" grumbled Rhen, skin prickling with exhilarated embarrassment. "You still don't have to say that part out loud, you know. It's not like I go around talking about *your-*"

"Would you like to see some pictures, Jill, dear?" prompted Dana before Rhen could finish getting even with her friend, reigniting the flames in her girlfriend's cheeks (and stopping her mid-tirade with a squeak) as she fished her phone from her purse. "I've got just the cutest little shot of her in her jammy top and a Sleeping Beauty one that I took last night. She even fell asleep with her Mickey Mouse ears still on. It's just precious."

"Yes, yes, yes!" clapped Jill eagerly, bouncing in her chair. "Show me, show me, show me!"

"Ugh."

Sighing in resignation, Rhen gave her hair a toss that made the sparkly earrings she had on glitter in the candlelight.

"If you're going to start playing show and tell, then at least start with the ones we took last Christmas. Geez."

"Why, that sounds like an excellent idea, cutie pie. Good thinking!"

—

After their plates had been cleared and the waitstaff had brought in a truly magnificent looking birthday cake to compliment the small pile of presents at the far end of their table, Rhen was just about fit to burst with excitement. (Slowed only slightly by her stomach full of chicken marsala and half a dozen dinner rolls.) The candles were then lit, Happy Birthday was sung, and while one of the servers stood off to the side recording on Dana's phone for her, she blew them out in one long breath to a round of applause and cheers from everyone in the room.

"Thank you, thank you," preened Rhen, popping up from her seat to take a bow and blow kisses to her admiring audience, before moving to pounce on her still smoking birthday cake. "Alright, now who wants a slice?"

"Uh-uh-uh."

THWOP!

Only to stop short with a startled yelp, whirling around to glare at her partner, pink-faced and pouting after she gave her perfectly positioned posterior a firm swat.

"Not so fast there, cutie pie."

"Awww, come on!" whined the shorter girl, allowing herself to be guided by the elbow back down into a seated position on the older woman's lap, face burning and avoiding eye contact with any of the smirking servers on their way out the door as she wriggled her hips atop her stocking-covered thighs in an attempt to get more comfortable. "I ate all my vegetables, didn't I? I'd say that more than qualifies me to eat my bodyweight in chocolate cake. Humph."

"Now, now, there's no need to pout. I know you're excited," soothed Dana with a smile that lit up her dark blue eyes, their midnight depths made all the more alluring by the smokey eye-shadow curling around them as she walked her fingers up her birthday girl's bare left arm. "But, before we get to cake and presents, there are two *very* important bits of business that we need to take care of first."

Cocking her head to one side, Rhen blinked up at the older woman in confusion.

"There are?"

Let's see… We had dinner, sang the song, I blew out the candles…

"That's right," sing-songed her partner, pressing a kiss to her soft pink lips before nodding at Courtney. "Do you have it, dear?"

"Sure do!" declared the athletic TA, springing to her feet and hurrying over to Dana's side with something she'd just pulled from her purse. "Here you go."

"Thanks for keeping it safe for me. You're a peach."

"No prob. I was happy to help!"

Stepping away, she winked at the pair of them and then drifted back over to her girlfriend's side as Dana pulled open the lid of the ring box she'd just been given.

"Wha-?"

Breath catching in her throat, Rhen felt her heart race into overdrive and her stomach give the biggest flip-flop of her entire life as her eyes fell on the twisted white gold band inside. Its inlaid diamonds sparkling spectacularly in the gentle glow provided by the small LED built into the top of the box.

"You've made me so very, very happy since we met, Rhen, honey," beamed Dana, her voice thick with emotion as she forced herself to pause and take a deep breath before pressing on. "And I would love nothing more than if we could continue being happy together for the rest of our lives."

"Dana, are you-?"

"I love you so much," she continued as the girl on her lap's eyes began to well with tears, matching her own already misty ones. "Will you marry me?"

"I..."

Suddenly unable to make her tongue work, Rhen swallowed. *Hard.*

Then, her voice quavering with shock, delight, excitement, and no small amount of nervous butterflies, she threw her arms around her partner's neck and captured her lips in as passionate a kiss as she could muster for as long as she could before the pesky need to breathe finally got in the way and she was forced to pull back.

"I love you too, Dana," she said with a smile so big it made her face hurt. "Of course I'll marry you!"

As the two teary-eyed lovebirds continued to grin dreamily at one another, neither of them quite yet willing to believe that this was all really happening, their dinner guests erupted into another round of tumultuous cheers and ecstatic applause.

"Heck yeah!"

"That's great!"

"Awww, I'm so happy for you two! Congratulations!"

It was truly the greatest birthday present that Rhen could have possibly hoped to receive.

"Thank you all so much for being here for this," Dana finally managed to sniffle around a thoroughly contented sigh, dabbing carefully at the corners of her eyes with her napkin once she'd been able to at least somewhat catch her breath. "It means a lot. Really."

"You bet," nodded Courtney, flashing the older woman an encouraging thumbs up as she wrapped an arm around her own girlfriend, pulling her close. "We wouldn't miss this for the world!"

"No kidding," agreed Abby, snuggling up against the taller girl, still beaming. "You two make *such* a cute couple. I'm so glad you're finally locking it down!"

"Mmhmm…"

Nuzzling her bride-to-be, Dana's face broke into a wicked grin and she nipped playfully at her ear.

"There's no way I'd ever let this one get away without a fight. Not when she fits so perfectly across my lap."

"Heh. No arguments here," snickered Rhen, straightening up on the older woman's lap and wiping away her own tears on the back of her hand, extremely grateful that she'd decided to forego wearing eyeshadow that evening. "Although, now that you mention it, I can't help but feel like this is going to make church a little bit awkward moving forward."

While the congregation she and Dana attended every Sunday was remarkably progressive when it came to their views on LGBT issues (subscribing to an extremely modern flavor of Christianity that very lightly picked and choosed from the front half of the New Testament and tended to ignore just about everything else piled up around it in favor of a fairly loose "live and let live" philosophy for most everything else that didn't involve childrearing and discipline), the fact that she'd placed her "niece" in a Sunday school class with a bunch of *actual* teenagers did seem like something that would need some sorting out sooner rather than later.

"Yes, well… About that," Dana started to say, huffing out an embarrassed laugh as she took the sparkling engagement ring from its velvet box and slipped it onto the shorter girl's left hand for her, kissing her knuckles after she'd spent a moment admiring it in the candlelight. "Janice and Father Jacob actually knew about us from the start. So I wouldn't be too worried there."

"Wait, they *did*?" gasped Rhen, looking equal parts shocked and horrified to learn that her no-nonsense Sunday school teacher had had so little problem paddling her panties in front of her entire class despite knowing exactly how old she really was. "Oh, you have *got* to be kidding me!"

"Afraid so, honey buns. I explained our whole situation to them both that first week, and we all agreed that we might as well start you off somewhere a bit more… *age appropriate*, since it'd been a while since you'd been to church and we were just starting to get you used to all of your new rules and punishments."

"But-! But the Board?"

"Yes, yes, I know."

Kissing her fingers again, her partner smirked at her in a way that wasn't the least bit apologetic.

"That one's entirely on you, though, I'm afraid. She gave you every chance to avoid it, and you just kept on acting up, didn't you?"

"Well, I mean… I guess that's fair."

Rhen was still way too elated to summon the sass to truly sound annoyed.

"She still could've at least done it out in the hallway or something…"

"And *you* could have just done as you were told," countered Dana with a playful tap to the tip of her nose. "Besides, did you seriously want every single parent in the congregation drifting over to watch you take your licks just so your little friends wouldn't see your cute panties?"

"Humph. No comment."

"Awww, don't pout," the older woman cooed, coaxing a fresh grin out of her naughty not-niece by tickling her sensitive sides. "I know this might be a bit of a shock for some of our friends who still actually think you're my disobedient niece, rather than just my bratty girlfriend… Heh, or I guess now you're my sassy *fiancé*, huh?"

She paused for a moment as a happy giggle escaped her lips,

one that was echoed by everyone at the table (especially Rhen).

"But, that's alright. We can figure that part out as we go."

"Yeah, I guess that's true…" sighed the shorter girl, still beaming despite the blush on her face.

"Besides," broke in Courtney then with a wolfish grin. "It's probably still better that most people mistake you for her niece. I mean, it's a lot less embarrassing to get your cute little bratty buns spanked for being a sassy *teen* than it is as an 'adult', riiiight?"

That managed to get a scoff from Rhen, who was doing her best to affect an air of indifference as she admired her new ring, feet kicking happily back and forth in front of her.

"Okay. You might have a point there."

Then, hoping to steer their conversation away from her backside and who knew about it getting spanked (or how old she really was while it was happening), she wriggled around to sit facing forward on her partner's lap and reached for her cake once again.

"Alright, *now* who wants some cake?"

Only to have her hand be gently batted away for a second time.

"Patience, cutie pie," admonished Dana. "I did say that we had *two* bits of important business to take care of first before we could get to cake and presents, didn't I?"

"What?" sassed the shorter girl with a smirk, shaking her unbound hair in her partner's face for added annoyance as she settled back against her breasts with her arms crossed. "Don't tell me you've got a second ring hidden on you somewhere?"

"Hmmm… No, not quite," the older woman purred, using her feet to push her chair further back from the table before gently guiding her bratty bride-to-be back to her feet with her hands on her waist, turning her around to face her as she did so. "Although, now that you mention it, I *was* thinking you and I could go pick out one for me sometime this next week."

"Oh yeah, totally!" agreed Rhen with an eager nod, her earlier giddy exuberance returning with a vengeance as she wiggled her left hand in front of her, making her engagement ring sparkle in the private room's subdued lighting. "We should also get them engraved too while we're at it."

"That sounds like an outstanding idea," answered Dana with a warm smile, wrapping her hands atop the shorter girl's own in an attempt to draw her attention back to her. "But, first things first. Before we do anything else, we need to take care of your birthday spanking."

"B-Birthday spanking?"

Rhen tried to bite back on the question, but it had already escaped her lips by the time she realized she was asking it.

"That's right, little girl," her partner crooned, giving her captured hand a gentle squeeze. "It's tradition."

"Heck yeah it is!" cheered Abby along with Courtney and Jill.

"Well, uh…" gulped the twenty-one-year-old *still* turned teenager, going red in the face all over again as everyone in the room erupted into excited clapping and chanting.

"Birthday spanking, birthday spanking, birthday spanking!"

"Wait, wait, hold on!" squeaked Rhen, jerking in place as if she'd just been shocked by the electric atmosphere in the room. "Come on! Aren't I too old to spank now?"

She knew it was a flimsy defense, and clearly Dana did too, judging by the way she arched her brows at her.

"Really?" she drawled, angling her head to the side to share an amused look with their audience before squeezing her hand again and pinning her in place with her best "Now you listen to me, little girl!" stare. "Is that *seriously* what you think?"

"Maybe?" continued Rhen, putting on her most dazzling smile. "Like, just a teensy, tiny bit?"

Dana simply continued to stare her down, though, saying nothing. Until, finally, the pressure became too much for her to handle and she caved.

"Okay, fine, I guess I'm not," she conceded with a stomp and a huff as the tips of her ears went bright pink. "But, um… We don't really have to do this, like, right now, do we? Can't we at least wait until we're back at the hotel?"

"Hmmm... No," shot down her aunt, her smile growing wolf-ish enough to rival Courtney's own as she watched her squirm. "I think we need to take care of this right here and right now."

"Oh yeah, *totally*," agreed Abby with a mischievous grin.

"Seconded," nodded her girlfriend, her stormy eyes crackling with barely-restrained mirth.

"Thirded!" sang Jill, not even bothering to pretend to hide her excitement as she clapped and bounced in her chair with glee. "Spank her silly, Dana!"

"Well now, it looks like it's unanimous," declared the older woman with obvious satisfaction, releasing her grip on the shorter girl's hand and leaning back in her chair to gloat. "Sorry, Rhen, but the party has spoken. My hands are tied, I'm afraid."

"Humph. Traitors."

"So how do you want to do this?" pressed Abby, ignoring the blushing birthday girl's grumbling entirely as she too pushed back from the table and jumped to her feet for a better view of the upcoming festivities. "Courtney has a hairbrush in her purse if you'd like to borrow that."

"Hey, wait a minute!" Rhen started to argue, feeling her stom-ach dropping to her ankles as the situation started to spiral even further out of her control. "It's *my* birthday spanking. Don't I at least get a say in any of this?"

"Nope," all four older women said at the same time, each bearing a teasingly triumphant grin.

"Ugh!" she erupted, throwing her hands into the air in defeat. "You guys suck."

"Love you too, kiddo."

Well, at least the doors to our room are shut...

Casting a baleful glance over her shoulder (and attempting to knock her own smirk down into something at least resembling a scowl), Rhen couldn't help but notice with a small twinge of worry that said doors also happened to have some rather lovely floor-to-ceiling windows set into each of them. Ones that would allow anyone looking in from the right angle to see her across her aunt's lap without any problem.

For all the good that'll do me.

That wasn't a huge concern for her, though, since she knew from personal experience (and watching her partner celebrate a handful of birthdays at the daycare) that such spankings were all in good fun and (thankfully) given over clothes. Even with her being older than the usual birthday brats to take a trip over Auntie Dana's knee, her spanking would be done in less than a minute.

And, even if it wasn't, she still had her secret weapon.

"Alright then, cutie pie, let's get down to business, shall we?"

Taking hold of her left wrist, Dana started tugging her around to stand next to her right thigh, laying an affectionate arm around her pearl-studded waist and giving it a squeeze.

"Ready?"

"Yeah, yeah…" grumbled Rhen with a melodramatic sigh, still smiling as she allowed herself to be tipped over her fiancé's lap and positioned so that her bottom was now the highest point on her body. "Hurry up, would you? We don't have all day- er, I mean *night*, you know. I want my cake!"

This drew a round of amused tuts and "Ooohs" from her audience, just as she'd been hoping it would.

"Well now," grinned Dana, smoothing out the layered skirts of her dress with a low chuckle. "Someone sure is feeling confident all of a sudden, isn't she?"

More than you know, bossy boots. Hehe.

"Sounds to me like she wants you to spank her *really* hard," drawled Courtney, supported by a chorus of agreements from Abby and Jill.

"Yeah!"

"Make her squirm, Dana! She has such a cute little yelp!"

Spurred on by her friend's teasing (and confidence in her own choice of clothing to absorb the majority of any hard swatting),

Rhen gave her bottom a taunting wiggle.

"Yeah, come on. Do your worst, noodle arms!"

"Noodle arms?" gasped Dana in faux-outrage. "Young *lady*!"

THWOP!

Delivering a reprimanding, full-armed swat for good measure.

"We do *not-*"

THWOP!

"Talk-"

THWOP!

"Like-"

THWOP!

"That!"

THWOP! THWOP! THWOP!

"Oh, no, please," deadpanned Rhen, giving her virtually untouched hips another wiggle as her self-satisfied smirk blossomed into a full on smug smile. "I'm soooo sorry."

Not to be outdone by her sassy niece, Dana allowed her head to lull back in exasperation as she let out a long, frustrated groan.

"You really are incorrigible. You know that?"

Heh. I'll show you incorrigible.

"See? What'd I tell you?" Rhen continued to taunt, giggling at her own raw audacity. "I really *am* getting too old to spank!"

"Yeah right," mumbled Courtney out of the corner of her mouth as she took a pull from her wine glass, her voice carrying an audible eye roll with it that had everyone in the room giggling.

Especially Rhen.

"Alright then, birthday girl, I'll tell you what," countered the auburn-haired older woman after she'd managed to get her serious persona back in place, patting the petite junior's petite bottom with another chuckle. "If you're really so mature, then why don't you tell me how many swats you think I should give you? Your actual age, or your *actual* age?"

"Hmmm... How about zero?"

THWOP!

“Cute.”

“Thanks, I know.”

“Fourteen it is then, you little brat.”

“Hey, you said I could choose!”

“Yes, well, I believe you just did with all that sass.”

“Yeah… I guess I did, huh?”

While Rhen could certainly appreciate spending a third less time across her partner’s knee in public (even with her dress down and the doors to their private room firmly shut), she still couldn’t help but blush as the older woman made it abundantly clear that even though they were getting married, she was still very much her naughty niece.

And would be spanked accordingly, whenever and wherever she felt was necessary.

“Is that going to be a problem?” pressed Dana, gliding her hand down along the layers of her ruffled dress to her bare right thigh.

“No ma’am!” Rhen was quick to reassure her, going rigid across her lap as she willed her dress to stay right where it was.

A fun spanking was still a spanking, after all, and she wasn’t about to give the waitstaff any more reasons to smirk at her by letting them see her get one over her underwear.

“I’ll be good!”

“Uh-huh.”

Dana didn’t exactly sound convinced, but she did at least leave her dress where it was as she returned to patting her bottom menacingly.

“Now that’s more like it.”

Then, raising her arm up high, her face split into a massive grin.

“Ready everyone?”

“No,” grumbled Rhen.

Only to be drowned out by everyone else’s shouts of “Yes!”

“Alright then, here… we… go!”

THWOP!

"One!" they chorused in unison.

THWOP!

"Two!"

THWOP!

"Three!"

THWOP!

"Four!"

Just as she'd predicted, Rhen's birthday spanking was entirely tolerable and lots of fun, not even hurting a little bit. Even better, the many layers of her evening wear helped to mute the report of her partner's palm as it impacted with her seat. However, rather than bring her hand down again for swat number five, Dana instead paused mid-swing as a suspicious look stole across her features.

"Hmmm…"

Uh-oh.

Worrying fretfully at her lower lip, Rhen did her best to play it cool even as she felt the wheels starting to come off of her clever plan.

"Um… Is something wrong? You didn't lose count, did you?"

"No…"

Keeping her voice silky smooth, her fiancé (god, even when she was nervous it still felt so amazing to think of her that way!), gave her bottom a thoughtful squeeze and a firm rub.

"Not quite."

Then, without any warning, she seized hold of the hem of her dress and yanked it up well past her hips, giving everyone in the room an unobstructed view of her panties.

All six pairs of them.

"Eep!"

"Aha! I *knew* something didn't feel right!" exclaimed Dana, giving the tightly wrapped cheeks on her lap a hard slap which produced only a muted jiggle and another dull *THWOP!* for her efforts.

"Oh my god, that's hilarious!"

"I think you mean naughty."

"Awww, I think it's cute…"

"W-Wait, I can explain!" squeaked Rhen, her face erupting into a hot blush that had nothing to do with the pleasant buzz she had from all the fruity cocktails she'd been enjoying with her dinner.

"Oh, I'm sure you can," purred Dana, fingering one of the many pairs of panties wrapped snugly around her naughty niece's birthday bottom. "And while I certainly appreciate your ingenuity, cutie pie, that still doesn't negate the fact that this is not how you should be dressed, now is it?"

"Well…" hemmed the shorter girl, scratching at her cheek with a nervous laugh. "I mean, *technically* no, but I-"

"And correct me if I'm wrong," continued Dana, not interested in letting her get going with a fresh round of excuse making. "But when I laid out your outfit this morning, I did not include…"

She paused in her scolding to give Rhen's seat an expectant pat then.

"Ugh. Six," the raven-haired girl provided with a dutiful huff.

"Ah, right, *six* pairs of panties to go along with it," nodded her partner, delivering three swats to the back of each bare thigh to underscore her point.

SMACK! SMACK! SMACK!

SMACK! SMACK! SMACK!

"Did I, little girl?"

"No ma'am!" squealed Rhen, legs kicking animatedly behind her as her flats slipped free of her feet to clatter to the floor. "It was just a prank! I'm sorry!"

"Suuuure you are," teased Dana, lightly gliding her palm up and down along the pink patches she'd just painted.

"Okay, not really," admitted the younger girl, letting herself go limp across her partner's lap with a pouty harrumph, her confession drawing out another round of amused snickering from her audience. "But being ten percent sorry is still being sorry, you know."

"Uh-huh," snorted Dana as she started casually bouncing her palm off of first one cheek and then the other. "That was very-"

TWHOP.

"Very-"

THWOP.

"Naughty of you."

THWOP... THWOP... THWOP...

"Wasn't it, Rhen?"

Again, Rhen hesitated, nibbling nervously at her lower lip as she tried to think of a way to spin things in her favor.

"Sort of?"

"Sort of?" echoed her partner, letting her hand wander back down to her thighs. "I believe we've already had this discussion once this week, little girl. It either was, or it wasn't. So, which is it?"

"Well, okay, fine. I guess technically speaking, it was naughty," huffed Rhen again, blushing even harder now as she rallied her reserves of sass. "But it wasn't my fault!"

"Oh? And how do you figure that?"

Shivering as Dana began dragging her fingernails up and down along her bare thighs. Making elongated horseshoe patterns as she moved from the back of one knee to the other, pausing only when she reached her seat to glide her fingers between her legs for a firm rub before continuing on. Rhen grit her teeth and jabbed an accusatory finger at Jill.

"I was still sore because she spanked me too hard!"

All eyes turned to Jill then, but rather than be embarrassed by the accusation, she instead just met the younger girl's dirty look with a dazzling smile and a little wave.

"I'm not surprised," she admitted, giving her tied back hair a little flip. "It *was* a pretty good paddling if I do say so myself."

"Hell yeah it was," agreed Abby with a fist-bump for the

lifeguard. "You do great work."

"Thanks!"

"See? See? She admits it!" gesticulated Rhen wildly.

"The only thing I admit is that you got exactly what you deserved, kiddo."

Ignoring that, Rhen continued to persist with her paper-thin argument.

"I *had* to wear extra panties today, Aunt Dana."

Only to run out of steam almost as soon as she'd started.

"Just in case you, uh… you know…"

"In case I decided to spank you?" suggested her partner with a helpful pat.

"Uh, yeah… Basically."

"Yes, well, be that as it may," she continued, clearing her throat pointedly and bringing her hand up high. "Regardless of how sore you might be."

THWOP!

"That is still no excuse-"

THWOP!

"For dressing-"

THWOP!

"Like a mummy lingerie model!"

THWOP!

"Am I understood?"

"Humph."

"Oh? Do I need to borrow that hairbrush from Courtney, after all?"

Dana kept her voice light and breezy as she asked the question, but the way her fingernails drummed against Rhen's unprotected thighs made it abundantly clear to the younger girl just where that hairbrush would be put to use if she did.

"Oh! Um, nope! You're right, I'm sorry!"

"That's *better*," harrumphed her aunt with a quick pinch to her inner thigh and a low laugh at the squawk it produced. "The only time your bottom should be *this* padded, missy, is when you're wearing your pull-ups."

"Or…" cut in Courtney then, not needing to actually finish the sentence as she and her girlfriend shared a wicked grin.

"Or?" asked Jill, looking confused.

Rather than answer her question directly, Abby instead pulled up one of the (many) photos she and the other girl had taken back in Dana and Rhen's hotel room last Friday.

"Awww! Is that?"

"It sure is!"

"Oh my god, that's so cute!"

"I know, right? It's totally fits her perfectly too, doesn't it?"

"Absolutely!"

"Humph. It's not *that* cute…" grumbled Rhen, unable to actually see Abby's phone with her hair hanging down in front of her eyes, but still able to hazard a guess as to what was being shown.

"Uh-uh-uh. No sulking now, birthday girl," Dana chided with another pat.

"But she's-!"

"She's just showing off how cute you look in that diaper Officer Taylor gave us. And you *do* look cute in it, so there's no need to throw a fit."

"But… but…"

Heaving out a long sigh of defeat that was only partially exaggerated, Rhen decided to just concede the point.

"Yes ma'am."

"Good girl. Now, what do you say we get a look at how sore you really are back here, hmmm?" she cooed, not actually waiting for a response before she began peeling away the top layer of tautly stretched panties from her naughty niece's extra-rounded rump. "I didn't notice anything this morning when you were getting out of the shower, but if you've spontaneously developed any bruises since then, I really ought to make sure you're alright…"

"Safety first," agreed Jill, clearly enjoying herself as she and the other two witnesses to Rhen's humiliation broke down into another fit of giggles.

"Exactly!"

Biting back on the urge to say something sassy, Rhen instead hid her smoldering face in her hands as one by one, each pair of panties she had on was pulled down past her hips, along her smooth legs, and then off of her frilly ankle-sock covered feet entirely. A task which took considerably longer than it had putting them on in the first place since her aunt insisted on stopping to let everyone admire each pair as they were revealed in turn before adding them to the growing pile on the table in front of her.

In the end, when at last the final pair of panties (a black and white striped affair with hot pink skulls and crossbones printed all over it) was finally removed and passed off to Jill (who had taken it upon herself, along with Courtney and Abby, to fold and sort each pair by color and cuteness), it was to reveal a pristinely pale and completely unblemished backside.

"Well, well, well, would you look at that," marveled Dana facetiously, gliding her fingertips along the bare chubs now on full display across her lap. "Not a single mark to be seen. Color me *shocked.*"

"More like color her red, am I right?" interjected Abby, receiving a high-five from her girlfriend.

"Hah! Nice, babe."

"Um… Okay, so," Rhen began to backpedal, breaking out into goosebumps under her fiancé's feather-light caress. "It's *possible* that I *might* have *maybe* over-exaggerated things just a little bit…"

"Oh really now?" wondered Dana aloud, leaning in against the small of her back and taking hold of one bare cheek in either hand with a hard squeeze. "I think we'd better just double-check that to be sure…"

"Wha-? Wait, hold on!" squeaked Rhen, only catching on to what the older woman had in mind a moment before it happened. "Eep!"

"Hmmm… Well, what do you know? Nothing here either," announced Dana with a vicious grin, holding her captive cutie's cheeks apart as wide as they would go as she adjusted her position on her chair to give their audience a better view. "How about you, ladies? See anything interesting?"

"Yep!" snickered Courtney, licking her lips as she watched on with a hungry stare. "No bruises, though."

"Ditto," echoed Abby with a giggle, cuddling up next to her girlfriend as her thighs squirmed together beneath her dress under the table.

"It looks like someone is having fun, though, at least," offered Jill helpfully.

"No kidding. You think maybe *that's* why she had on all those extra layers?"

"She should've just worn a pull-up in that case."

"Oh my god, you guys suck," groaned Rhen, red in the face, but still smirking in spite of everything.

She *was* having fun, after all.

"Now, now, it's important to get a second opinion on these sorts of things, honey buns," admonished Dana, her voice the very model of motherly patience and concern as she allowed said buns to wobble back into place. "And we wouldn't have had to be so thorough in the first place had *you* not been telling us fibs."

She gave the center of her bride-to-be's bare backside a couple of very menacing pats then to emphasize her point.

"Would we?"

"Well, I mean…" hesitated Rhen, trying once more to think of some way of spinning things that would save her seat (and now probably her mouth as well) from further punishment.

"Yes?" prompted Dana, tickling her fingers down along her cheeks to settle in between her thighs as she waited for a response.

"I'm sorry?" the petite junior offered with a breathy gasp, wriggling and blushing even harder now as she fought not to let on how close she was to release already.

Keep it together, Rhen. Keep… it… to- O-Oh god, how is she so good at that?

"Awww, I forgive you," cooed her partner, allowing her fingers to caress and toy with where she would be returning to later that evening for an extended after-party snack. "And, luckily for you, birthday girl, I'm even willing to forget all about your fibbing and not wash your mouth out."

"Oh thank god!" sighed Rhen, melting across her knees again as Abby, Courtney, and Jill all groaned in disappointment.

"Yes, yes, I know, girls," commiserated Dana, pulling her fingers away from their teasing and giving the jelly-limbed brat's bottom another series of fond pats as she winked at their audience. "But I think we can *all* put that sassy tongue of hers to *much* better use once we're back at the hotel… Assuming, of course, she's up for it, that is…"

At that, she paused long enough to allow Rhen to voice her consent to what she was proposing, patiently drumming her fingernails along the central divide between her cheeks.

"Heh," the petite junior snickered after taking a moment to catch her breath, blushing crimson at the mental images her mind was already painting for her. "I don't see why the fun has to stop after dessert."

"Damn right," agreed Abby, while Courtney and Jill just nodded excitedly.

"My thoughts exactly," continued Dana, sounding just as excited. "I think it's safe to say that someone here is going to be up *well* past her bedtime tonight. But for now…"

SMACK!

"Oh!"

"We have a birthday spanking to get to."

SMACK!

"Don't we?"

Despite the high-pitched yelp that had just escaped her lips, Rhen did her best to try and play off her surprise and pain with her best haughty pout.

"Humph. Whatever."

Which only succeeded in earning her another swat.

SMACK!

"Ah!"

Followed by three more in quick succession further down.

SMACK! SMACK! SMACK!

"Ow! Oh! Owie!"

"You know you're all supposed be counting, right?" teased Dana then, grinning at their audience as she kneaded the light pink handprints now adorning the younger girl's backside.

SMACK!

"Or not."

SMACK-SMACK!

"I don't mind warming her up a bit more if you'd like to wait."

"Yeah, well-" Rhen started to grumble, before being cut off by another.

SMACK!

"Ack! I sure-"

SMACK!

"Oh! Do!"

Gritting her teeth and whipping her head around to glare at her friends, she growled at them.

"Get to freaking work, you-"

SMACK!

"Ah! Slackers!"

"Language, birthday girl," chided Dana with a bemused shake of her head and another swat to balance out the one she'd just delivered to her not-niece's left sit-spot.

SMACK!

"Just because I'm not washing out that adorable little mouth of yours, doesn't mean that I can't find somewhere *else* to stick some soap."

"Yes ma'am!" yelped Rhen with some genuine worry this time, cheeks clenching behind her in momentary panic. "I'll be good!"

"Of course you will, sweetie," purred Dana, pausing once again to massage her bottom back to a more relaxed state before working the pad of her middle finger down along where she thought a soap stick or two might fit nicely.

"Uh…" spoke up Courtney then with a crooked grin, looking to the others for help. "Does anyone remember what number we were on?"

"Nope," chirped her partner.

"Sorry," offered Jill with a shake of her platinum hair.

"Oh my god," groaned Rhen in genuine exasperation this time. "It was like three hundred or something!"

SMACK!

"Now what did I *just* get through telling you about fibbing, young lady?" chided Dana with a laugh.

"That I probably shouldn't do it?"

SMACK!

"Exactly."

SMACK!

"And, since nobody here can seem to remember where we were, I suppose the only fair thing to do is start over from the beginning."

"Oh come on!"

SMACK!

"I wasn't asking you, little girl. I was asking your party guests. Now, ladies, does that sound like a plan to you?"

Getting three eager nods in return, Dana's face split into an even broader grin and she gave one of her smoky eyes a broad wink.

"Alright then, from the top now…"

SMACK!

"Yeow!"

"One!"

SMACK!

"Oh!"

"Two!"

SMACK!

"Geez, alright. I'm sorry!"

"Three!"

"That's nice, dear."

SMACK!

"Ah!"

"Four!"

"Now take your birthday spanking like a big girl and start counting along with everyone else."

"Fine-"

SMACK!

"Urk! I mean five!"

"Five!" echoed everyone after her.

SMACK!

"Six!"

This time Rhen lent her voice to the count along with everyone else, laughing despite herself even as her cheeks wobbled and stung.

"Ahhh, there we go. *Much* better."

Slipping her fingers back down between her thighs, Dana leant over and kissed her birthday girl's temple, drinking in the heady scents of her perfume and strawberry shampoo as she murmured against her flushed skin.

"Happy birthday, Rhen. I love you."

"I love you too, Dana," the petite junior sighed contentedly, feeling herself starting to drift away on by another wave of teary-eyed happiness, even with her bare behind up in the air behind her. "Thanks for making tonight so special."

"Anytime, sweetheart."

Then, with another kiss, her fiancé straightened back up in her seat and gave her lightly pinkened caboose a brisk couple of pats.

"Alright then, let's wrap things up so you can get across Courtney's lap. I'm sure she's just dying to get her hands on your birthday buns."

"Wait, *what*?"

"You'd better believe it," confirmed the athletic TA with a rich laugh, draining the last of her wine before pushing her chair back from their table and smoothing out the dark material of her dress. "Abby and I've been drooling over them ever since we saw her in those Little Mermaid short-shorts this afternoon."

"I know! Weren't they just *precious*?"

"Oh, come on!" squawked Rhen, her heart rate skyrocketing into the stratosphere for the second time that evening. "What about my cake?"

"Don't you worry, cutie pie," her partner reassured her with a slightly firmer series of pats this time. "You can have a slice after you and I are finished."

"But-"

SMACK!

"Oh!"

"And you can open a present after Courtney's done with you."

SMACK!

"And another after Abby."

SMACK!

"And then the last one after Jill!"

"See? it's nice and fair," preened Abby, licking her lips excitedly.

"Oh my god, you guys totally planned this, didn't you?" Rhen attempted to harrumph, though it came out sounding much more like a giggle.

"Maaaaybe," her partner teased, circling her palm around her cheeks before giving each a firm squeeze.

"It only seemed fair to let us all have a chance to share in wishing you a happy birthday and making sure you remember to behave yourself this year," Courtney added.

"If it makes you feel any better, *I* didn't know until the last minute when Dana texted me," offered Jill, not looking the least bit apologetic as she beamed at her. "But I have to say, I like the way she thinks!"

"Humph. You guys suck," snorted Rhen, smiling right along with everyone else and not even pretending to pout this time. "But, I guess it can't be helped. Birthday spankings *are* a tradition, after all."

And, truth be told, she wouldn't have had it any other way.

Chapter 14

Splish, Splash, and Lots of Sass

Things quickly returned back to business as usual for Rhen and Dana upon arriving home that following evening. And, as cheesy as it might've sounded, they were both genuinely grateful to have a vacation from their vacation. California had been a ton of fun, but being able to just sit back and veg out at home was not without its charms.

Plus, the internet was a whole lot better than their crappy hotel Wi-Fi had been.

However, as much as Rhen might've wanted to while away the remainder of her summer vacation hiding out in her bedroom playing on her computer, it was sadly not to be. Between being booted out the door first thing Saturday morning to go do chores for Missus Hastings, spending most of her Sunday at church (which, thankfully, proved to be far less awkward than she'd feared it would be), and keeping up with making sure all of her daycare friends knew exactly who was the best at freeze tag and Mario Kart, time seemed to be slipping by faster and faster.

Before she even realized it was happening, it was already Wednesday night!

The last week of her summer vacation was more than halfway over, and she could practically *feel* her free time starting to slip through her fingers. Granted, she and Dana had managed to put together a class schedule for her upcoming semester that wasn't exactly grueling per se, but having to go to school four days a week and stay on top of homework every night was all time that she didn't get to spend playing games and watching YouTube.

Or, reading books.

Ever since she'd been strong-armed (across Dana's lap) into

going to bed at a reasonable hour "for a girl her age", and had learned that her partner was deadly serious about not letting her play on her phone after lights out, Rhen had rediscovered her fondness for reading actual, physical books. While browsing the internet and watching videos on a bright screen propped up on a pile of blankets only a few inches away from her face wasn't considered good sleep hygiene by her aunt, she'd eventually caved after a fair bit of whining on her part and agreed to let her to read in bed (but only for half an hour!) in order to help herself relax and get sleepy.

Soon, what had mostly just started as an excuse to have something to do other than stare at her ceiling fan while she waited for her body to get tired at nine-thirty in the evening (operating on vampire time for so long had really done a number on her ability to fall asleep before the sun had risen), had quickly become her favorite part of her nightly routine. After a nice, long, and delightfully hot shower, she'd change into her pajamas, kiss her partner goodnight, and then crawl under the covers and dive back into whatever book she was in the middle of reading at that moment. Getting lost in far off lands and planets beyond the stars was way more fun than she'd remembered it being back in high school, and in seemingly no time at all the little bookshelf Dana had bought for her had begun to fill up with thick fantasy novels, sci-fi space operas, and detective thrillers as she tore her way through series after series.

Thank goodness there was such a fantastic used book store just off campus!

Unfortunately, though, like many of the things she was passionate about, Rhen had a tendency to let herself get a bit too carried away and lose track of time while she was reading. In fact, it wasn't uncommon at all for her to wind up staying up an extra hour or two past her normal bedtime just because she hadn't been paying attention to the alarm clock beside her.

That, or she'd just gotten to a really good part and knew she could hear Dana coming up the stairs far enough in advance to successfully avoid getting busted.

The light from her bedside lamp didn't leak under her door enough to give her away when it was shut. And, the fact that on most school nights she still slept in her own room (she and Dana liked having their own space, and her partner didn't have to worry about accidentally waking her up that way), meant that she could usually get away with sidestepping her bedtime so long as she was careful about it.

Usually.

That Wednesday, though, was not one of those nights.

—

"Well now," remarked Dana cheerily, hands on hips and looking down on Rhen with a mixture of amusement and disapproval from the foot of her bed. "I was wondering why you hadn't come to say goodnight yet."

"Ah!"

Letting out a high-pitched yelp of surprise (she'd been so engrossed in her book that she hadn't even heard her door opening or her aunt stepping inside over the hum of the air conditioning), Rhen jumped hard enough to send her copy of *The Destruction of Emperors* flying right out of her hands.

"Whoa now, easy there, honey buns," laughed the older woman, scooping up the fallen hardback and making her way around to the side of her bed. "There's no need to start throwing things. It's just me."

"Holy cow, you scared the crap out of me!" breathed Rhen with a shaky laugh of her own, hand to her chest as she fought to get her racing heart back under control. "Maybe try knocking next time, would you? I'm way too young to be having a heart attack!"

"Sorry about that," smirked her partner. "I just figured you'd hear the squeaky third step and know I was on my way up."

"Third step? But I didn't hear-" the shorter girl started to reply, before realizing what she was about to admit to and stopping herself mid-sentence with a pout. "Humph. You stepped over it, didn't you?"

"Maybe…"

Her smirk growing impish now, Dana passed the book back to her and gestured for her to mark her place with the lacquered, wooden bookmark she'd given her for her birthday.

"So. Do you want to explain to me why you're still up and not in your jammies even though it's nearly midnight, or should I just bend you over and start spanking?"

"Midnight?" gasped Rhen, all wide-eyed innocence as her stomach churned in a not unpleasant manner at the casual way her fiancé had just phrased her plans to blister her backside. "You don't mean, like, *midnight*, midnight, do you?"

"Mmhmm. That is exactly the one I'm referring to, young lady."

"No way, that can't possibly be right!"

Doing her best to continue looking dumbfounded, the petite junior sat up a bit straighter in bed and made a show of looking over to the alarm clock on the nightstand beside her that she'd been so studiously ignoring for the last two hours.

"Oh crap, it totally is! Well, shoot…"

She let out an exasperated, self-deprecating sigh then, as if the very notion of staying up past her bedtime was something that she'd never imagined happening to her.

"Sorry about that, Aunt Dana. Time must've gotten away from me while I wasn't paying attention or something. I had no idea it had gotten so late."

"Really?" pressed her partner skeptically, though the small twitch at the corners of her lips didn't go unnoticed. "You seriously had *no* idea what time it was at all?"

"Nope," shrugged Rhen, favoring her with her most innocent look. "This book is really just that good, I'm afraid."

"Uh-huh."

Dana rolled her eyes at the obvious lie, but then smiled sweetly once again as she passed her naughty niece a shovel to help dig herself into even deeper trouble with.

"That still doesn't explain why you haven't gotten changed, you know. Have you even showered yet, young lady?"

She was still smiling as she asked the question, but there was an undeniable air of menace lurking just beneath the surface of her words now.

"Well…"

Looking sheepishly down at her denim shorts as butterflies began to stir around inside her stomach, Rhen seized upon the first excuse that came to mind.

"I was *going to* in, like, five more minutes, but uh…"

She gestured lamely back at her jerk of an alarm clock then with its damming time on full display for all to see before surreptitiously tugging down on the suddenly much too high for her liking cuffs of her shorts.

"I must've, you know…"

Making a twirling motion with her hand, she hoped that that would somehow be enough to save her seat as she ran out of steam.

But, of course, it wasn't.

"Thought that I wouldn't be by to check on you?" suggested her fiancé for her, the corners of her mouth quirking up even higher at the way her question made her squirm. "And that you'd be able to just ignore your bedtime so long as you heard me coming enough in advance to make it look like you were already asleep?"

"Well… I mean…"

Dana arched a brow in silent warning not to lie to her again, and Rhen puffed out her cheeks in another pout.

"Okay, fine. So maybe I was," she admitted, heaving out a dramatic sigh as she rallied for a counterattack. "But, come on! It's not that big of a deal, is it? I'm in bed, aren't I?"

"No…" answered Dana patiently, hands returning to her hips as she settled fully into lecture mode now. "You're *sitting* on your bed, wearing your clothes from today and reading a book. You're not *in* bed at all. You're not even *ready* for bed for that matter."

"But-!"

Rhen opened her mouth to argue the finer philosophical points of just what "ready" meant, prepared to contend that she could sleep just as well in a pair of shorts and a t-shirt as she could her actual pajamas, when her partner cut her off.

"Have you brushed your teeth?"

"No…"

"Washed your face?"

"Not really…"

"Gone potty, taken a shower, put on your pull-up?"

With each embarrassingly juvenile and damning question, Rhen felt her cheeks growing warmer and warmer, and the butterflies inside her stomach more and more agitated. Until, finally, it all became too much for her to bear.

"Alright, alright, I get it!" she harrumphed, throwing her hands up in defeat before crossing her arms in front of her with an impudent glower at the opposite wall ahead of her. "But can't you cut me some freaking slack here? It's still summer break, you know."

"You'd better just watch that attitude, little girl," Dana snapped, her tone turning frosty enough to send a shiver down Rhen's spine as her brows knit themselves together in annoyance.

"Sorry ma'am!" squeaked the shorter girl, now markedly more polite than she had been just a moment earlier.

Dana just ignored her, though, instead tossing her hair with a put-upon sigh of her own as she continued, "I'm well aware that you don't have school right now. That's why your bedtime is eleven."

Her frown deepened then, as she went on with a determined glare and an admonishing finger wag.

"Or rather, that's why it *was* eleven. That's now been rolled back to nine-thirty until further notice since you seem to think that you can just ignore the rules so long as you're sneaky about it."

"What, nine-thirty?" whined Rhen, pounding her hands and

feet against her comforter in protest. "Oh, come on, that is so not fair!"

She hadn't had a bedtime that early since she'd moved in with her partner last summer!

"Can't it just be ten-thirty instead? That's still plenty early, right?"

Dana wasn't having any of her pleading, however.

"Keep it up, missy, and it's going to be *eight*-thirty with a visit from Missus Hairbrush to help tuck you in every night as well," she replied sweetly, hands returning to her hips as she cocked her head to the side with a challenging smirk. "Would you like that?"

"Nine-thirty is fine!" folded Rhen in a hurry, cheeks clenching and thighs squirming as her eyes darted fretfully to the seemingly innocuous oval-shaped ebony hairbrush on the nightstand beside her.

"I thought you might say that," crooned her partner with a nod of satisfaction. "I know you're a total night owl, Rhen, but getting enough sleep is important, alright? Especially when you've got things to do in the morning, like we do."

"Uh… We do? Oh, right, *tomorrow*. Crap…"

Rhen had honestly forgotten all about the meeting she had scheduled with her academic adviser for that following morning. Which was probably why Doctor Holloway had decided to invite Dana as well.

"But, like, come on," she continued with a fresh huff, determined to at least save some amount of face and not feel like a *total* middle schooler. "That's not until ten!"

"True," conceded her partner with a shrug. "But you still need enough time to have breakfast, get changed, and do your chores, don't you? You weren't seriously expecting to just roll out of bed and head straight on over, were you?"

"I guess not…" sighed the twenty-one-year-old turned teenager, pouting hard before noticing the all-too-familiar predatory grin that had blossomed on the older woman's face with those last few words.

Oh crap.

"Well, uh… I guess I'd better get to sleep as soon as possible then, huh?" she pressed on quickly, scrambling to get her legs underneath the covers as her stomach twisted itself into worried and excited knots.

"Oh no, not so fast there, cutie pie," her aunt cut in with a low chuckle, settling down onto the edge of the bed beside her and effectively pinning her in place as she leaned in to kiss her cheek. "You know darn well that in *this* house, little girls wear their jammies to bed."

Gliding her fingertips up along her arm until they reached the back of her neck, her smile grew even wider.

"Don't they?"

"Yes ma'am…" grumbled Rhen with a half-grimace, half-smirk.

"That's right," sing-songed Dana, threading her fingers through the back of her hair and yanking her close without warning as she growled. "And little girls who refuse go to bed on time get punished. *Hard.*"

She then crushed her lips against her bride-to-be's own, capturing them in a savage, hungry kiss that made it abundantly clear who was the one in charge just then as she shoved her tongue deep inside her mouth, making her moan and melt into her reprimanding grip before pulling back with another growl and hauling her to her feet.

"Now come with me, you little brat," she ordered, dragging her by the hair (though not actually hard enough to be more than uncomfortable) out of her room and into the hall. "If you can't handle getting ready for bed on your own, then Auntie Dana is just going to have to do it for you!"

—

As soon as the lights came on inside their master bathroom, Rhen found herself being shoved face first over the edge of the counter between her and her aunt's sinks with orders to stay right where she was as the older woman set about preparing a bath for the two of them. And so, not wanting to run the risk of Dana remembering that there was an enema bag in the cabinet under the sink just to her left (along with a dozen diapers Alana had included with the birthday present she'd brought over last weekend), Rhen made sure to do exactly as she was told.

Albeit with maybe just a *bit* more sass than was strictly necessary.

Blowing away a few stray, tickling strands of hair from her nose with a huff, she watched through the reflection in the mirror situated only a few inches away from her face as her mildly miffed partner set about filling their oversized garden tub with hot, steamy water; dumping in half a bag of oatmeal and chamomile soaking salt, along with a liberal splash of bubble bath, as she did so.

"I thought you said I needed to get to bed?" Rhen teased with an accompanying waggle of her hips, sticking her tongue out at her partner's back. "Wouldn't it be faster if I just hopped in the shower for a quick rinse?"

"Hmmm… Maybe. But then where would be the fun in that?" countered Dana smoothly, turning to regard her with a mischievous grin. "Although, now that you mention it, we really *should* be making more efficient use of our time, shouldn't we? After all, there's no sense in just standing around watching the water rise when I could be killing two birds with one stone here."

"Uh…"

Rhen was just about to ask what she meant by that, already pretty sure that she wasn't going to like the answer, when her aunt picked up the long-handled, pink plastic bath brush that Courtney and Abby had given them for Christmas from the far edge of the tub and began advancing on her with a determined glint in her eye.

"Eep!"

"That's right, little girl," she crooned, sauntering up behind her while menacingly tapping the hard, bumpy, circular head of the brush against her open left palm. "It's your favorite bath time buddy.”

“More like, least favorite,” grumbled the shorter girl, grimacing as Dana laid the length of viciously stingy scrub brush onto the countertop beside her.

“Awww, now don’t say that. I think you two just need to get to know each other better is all.”

“Uh, yeah. No thanks,” harrumphed Rhen, cheeks clenching beneath her shorts and panties as she felt the older woman’s clever fingers slip their way into them. “I’ll, um…”

She swallowed nervously then, face warming at what she knew came next even as her stomach lurched with excitement.

“I’ll pass.”

Unfortunately for her, though, that wasn’t in the cards for that evening, and she was left to pout as her bottom was bared. Her Easy-Pull waistband fully living up to its name as it, along with her panties, slipped free of her hips and sailed down to her ankles with barely a whisper of resistance to mark their passing.

“God, you’re cute,” sighed Dana, stepping in close and grinding her fully clothed hips against her naked cheeks as she leaned down to kiss her.

“Cute enough to not get spanked?” asked Rhen hopefully, fluttering her eyelashes and doing her best to look adorable.

“Now, now…”

Her partner nipped playfully at her ear then, grinning wickedly at the squeak it drew from her before catching her lips in another, rougher kiss.

“You know that’s not how this works.”

“Can’t blame a girl for trying,” Rhen huffed, pushing her lips back out into a pout as they parted.

“No… But I *can* tan her hide for it. So, why don’t you go ahead and step out of those shorts and panties for me, honey buns?” directed Dana, straightening back up with bath brush in hand and lightly bouncing it off of her bride-to-be’s springy seat as she waited for her to comply. “You and I are going to see just how many swats I can give you before the tub is finished filling, and I want to make sure you're able to kick and squirm as much as you like."

"How very generous of you," sassed the shorter girl, rolling her eyes as she did as she was told, sending her clothes flopping away somewhere behind her with a flick of her foot.

CRACK! CRACK!

And being rewarded for it with a pair of back-to-back swats to either side of her bare bottom.

"Ah! Ack!"

"I *am* pretty nice, aren't I?" preened Dana as she settled in beside her and pressed down firmly on the small of her back with her free hand, pinning her snugly in place as she lined the brush up to begin her barrage. "Now, hang on tight, cutie pie. This is going to hurt you a *lot* more than it's going to hurt me."

CRACK!

—

"And. I. Think. That. Will. Just. About. Do. That!" announced Dana several agonizingly long minutes later, emphasizing each word with an extra-hard *CRACK!* of smooth plastic against soft skin, before finally releasing her hold on Rhen's sweat-soaked back and moving off to stop the flow of water into the tub.

"About… freaking… time…" panted the shorter girl, pushing herself back up onto a pair of wobbly legs and turning to survey the damage in the slightly foggy mirror behind her, letting out a fresh hiss of pain as she did so. "Yeesh."

"Right?" laughed her partner with a self-satisfied shake of her head. "Not too shabby for a rush job, now is it?"

"Noooo kidding," agreed Rhen, reaching back to rub furiously at her stinging seat and letting out a long, contented moan at the fresh ache doing so produced. "I'm *definitely* sleeping on my stomach tonight."

It had by no means been the longest or hardest spanking she'd ever received, but she was still beyond grateful that her aunt's rapid-fire assault on her bottom and thighs had come to an end.

Dana hadn't been holding back in the slightest as she'd been swatting, and while she'd definitely been going for quantity over quality with the spanks she'd been giving, that had done very little to hinder her from turning her tail a vivid shade of strawberry red that, had she not been looking at her own teary-eyed reflection just then, Rhen would have sworn was actually smoking.

It might not have been her worst spanking ever, but it was still definitely somewhere in the top twenty, that was for sure.

And, as a happy bonus, she also now had a pretty great vantage point to watch as her partner began stripping down in front of her. Taking her sweet time as she did so and smirking all the while at her handiwork being reflected back at her by the bathroom mirror.

"Yes, well, you have no one to blame for that but yourself, sweetie. If you'd just gone to bed on time like you were *supposed* to, you would've been sleeping soundly on a set of perfectly pale and pristine cheeks right about now, wouldn't you?"

"Yeah, yeah…" huffed Rhen, flushing pink enough to rival said cheeks as she looked away from the older woman's captivating curves with a bashful grimace. "There's no need to start busting out the alliteration. I get your point."

"Oh you do, do you?" pressed Dana, slipping off her bra and reaching for a bar of soap sitting in a dish perched along the edge of the tub beside her. "Because it sounds to me a lot like you and I need to start off bath time by scrubbing out that sassy mouth of yours, young lady."

"Yes ma'am-! I mean, no ma'am! Er, uh, I'm sorry ma'am!" replied Rhen in a jumbled hurry, batting away that horrifying idea with frantically waving hands as she backed up a step, bumping her bare backside against the hard, only slightly rounded edge of the countertop behind her and letting out a yelp of surprise and pain that had Dana grinning from ear to ear.

"Ah, there we go. Music to my ears."

"Humph. Meanie."

Her partner just continued to smile at her, knowing she'd completely won already.

"You know… As much fun as it is to watch you stand there pouting in just a shirt and a scowl, you're going to have to finish getting undressed sooner or later, cutie pie," she pointed out, kicking off her lacy panties and gesturing toward the bright green top still clinging to the younger girl's torso.

"Oh! Uh… R-Right!"

Scrambling to finish getting undressed if for no other reason than to distract herself from the older woman's bold nakedness and ravishing stare, Rhen made short work of pulling her shirt (along with the bralette that Dana had given her for her birthday since she was starting to get "older") up and off entirely. Tossing them both onto the pile with the rest of her other clothes without a second glance and making a beeline toward the tub.

"Heh. I'm glad to see I've managed to light a fire under your seat after all," her partner snickered as she made her way back over to where she'd just been standing and gathered up her abandoned bath brush, giving her palm another firm slap as she turned to face her.

"Oh my god, are you serious?" protested Rhen, angling her seat out of reach with both hands behind her back for added protection, leaving her pert breasts with their erect nipples and her arousal slicked vulva completely exposed for her highly amused fiancé. "I thought you said we were done?"

"Now, now," purred Dana, advancing on her like a predator cornering its prey. "Believe it or not, these things are actually pretty useful *during* a bath as well as out of one."

"Er… Uh… Yeah, I guess that's true…" conceded Rhen, looking away with a grumpy huff to mask her embarrassment and leaving herself completely open to a kiss on the cheek.

As well as a firm pat between her legs with the bristly head of the bath brush.

"Oh!"

"Indeed," chuckled her partner with another pat and a broad grin. "Now why don't you go ahead and get those adorable little cheeks into the tub and we'll get things started?"

—

"Ahhhh…"

As Rhen sank down beneath the delightfully warm and bubbly water, letting out a contented sigh as it rose up to her shoulders, Dana knelt on a low stool beside the edge of the tub and picked up a squat glass sitting next to the shampoo and conditioner.

"Eyes closed, please," she ordered gently, dipping it into the water and pouring its contents over the younger girl's head as soon as she'd complied.

She did this a few more times, getting her hair sopping wet and dripping, before setting it aside and pumping out a generous amount of shampoo into her palm from the top of the bottle beside her.

"Oh god, that feels so nice," groaned Rhen, sinking just a bit lower into the tub as her partner began massaging the tingly tea tree shampoo into her scalp, working up a thick lather in her dark hair and turning her limbs to jelly beneath her firm but soothing ministrations.

"See? I'm not *that* big of a meanie," teased Dana, making the younger girl splutter and snort out a laugh as she tickled her fingers along her collarbones. "Most of the time, anyway."

"Yeah, yeah…"

Smirking, Rhen conceded the point with a splash to her fiancé's face, earning herself a tweaked ear in the process.

"Alright, now sit up for me, honey buns. It's time to rinse."

"You got it, bossy boots."

Wriggling herself back up out of her slump, grimacing as her movements ground her still tender tush against the hard surface of the tub beneath her, Rhen righted herself and leaned forward so that Dana could rinse the shampoo out of her hair.

Five cupfuls of water (and a bit more spluttering on her part as it trickled down past her lips) later, her hair was free of suds and ready for round two. Which Dana set to with a delightfully floral smelling conditioner, working it into her scalp just as she had with the shampoo earlier and once again reducing her bride-to-be to a jelly-limbed mess under her expert touch.

"Mmmm… You're going to smell absolutely delicious by the time I'm through with you," she murmured against the younger girl's ear, breathing in the fresh scent of her and sighing it out as she brushed aside her conditioner-laden locks and pressed her lips to the side of her neck in a long, tender kiss.

"You think so?" Rhen half giggled and half squeaked, heart beating faster and faster inside her chest as she felt the older woman's teeth bite down possessively against her slick skin while at the same time her hands slipped beneath the waterline to fondle her breasts. "Good enough to eat?"

"Oh, I think that can *definitely* be arranged," Dana replied with a throaty laugh, licking the marks left behind on the petite junior's neck before leaning further in to kiss her properly.

As her tongue quested for hers, she set to work playing with her rock hard nipples beneath the bubbles. Tracing her fingertips in firm, tight circles around her areolas and giving them the occasional flick. Then, after another minute or so more of casual fondling, she sent her right hand gliding further south along Rhen's taut belly to in between her parted thighs, dragging her middle and ring fingers over her smooth lips and humming in supreme satisfaction at the noises it produced in her bride-to-be.

Arching her back as her partner's nimble fingers found her swollen bud, Rhen let out a breathy moan and abandoned herself entirely to the moment. As skilled as she was as a spanker, Dana was no slouch when it came to putting her hands to other, more delicate, tasks either, and she soon found herself adrift on a sea of pleasure; gnawing at her lower lip and gasping and groaning in ecstasy as her fiancé massaged her breasts. Occasionally pinching and twisting her nipples to hear her squeal as she continued to stoke the fires between her legs, the water in the bathtub doing absolutely nothing to cool either of them down as Dana brought her along toward a climax.

"You like that, naughty girl?" she purred into her ear, her hungry grin widening even further as she increased the pressure against her clit, familiar enough with her natural rhythms by now to know that she was on the brink of one fantastic orgasm.

"Y-Yes ma'am," panted Rhen, knowing just as well exactly what her partner wanted to hear from her right then as she ground her hips against her hand, doing everything they could to help her finish the job.

"Well, good," chirped Dana with a kiss to her cheek, pulling her hands away without warning and shaking them off as she straightened back up beside her. "But, I'm afraid bad girls like you don't get to come quite so easily."

"Oh my god, what the heck?" demanded Rhen with a petulant groan, splashing her hands down in front of her in frustration and plunging them beneath the surface to finish what her partner had started there. "That is so not fair!"

"Uh-uh-uh," tutted Dana, leaning in once again and pinching her nipples.

Hard.

"Noooo touching, young lady."

"Ah!" gasped Rhen in reply, hands flying out of the water with an eruption of bubbles as she flailed them about in an attempt to make it abundantly clear that they were nowhere near her clit. "But... but, Aunt Dana! I'm, like, *soooo* close! Come onnnn!"

"Shhh…" was the older woman's only reply, pressing another kiss to her cheek as she gave her nipples another sharp tweak and continued on in a taunting sing-song. "If you want to come… You're. Going. To. Have. To. Earn. It."

"Okay, okay, okay, *fine*," Rhen hurriedly agreed, toes curling and uncurling as she wriggled and squirmed, before finally letting out a long sigh of relief as Dana eased her grip and returned to gently massaging her breasts.

"See? Now was that so hard?"

"Humph," she grumbled in reply, reaching up to flick bubbles at her fiancé with a huff and a smirk. "Pretty sure I earned at least two or three orgasms with that bath brushing you gave me earlier, you meanie."

"Oh please," snorted Dana, giving her breasts a slightly firmer

squeeze in retaliation for her bubbly bombardment. "You and I both know you totally had that coming. Now quit your whining, or I'm going to have you edging for the rest of the week, you little sassmouth."

"Whining? Who's whining?" Rhen hurriedly corrected herself, trying to hold back another smile as her clit ached with a need so powerful it made her want to weep. "No whining here, no siree!"

"Uh-huh…"

Releasing her breasts after one final squeeze, Dana reached over and picked up the bath brush that had been waiting oh so patiently off to the side that entire time and swept its bristles playfully across her naughty niece's shoulders.

"Alrighty then, young lady. Since you're in such an obedient mood, why don't you go ahead and hop up onto your knees for me? I think it's about time we got to work getting that sassy seat of yours squeaky clean."

"Fiiiine."

Despite the teasing sing-song in her partner's tone, Rhen soon discovered that she was completely serious about making sure her backside (along with just about every other part of her body) came away from her bath squeaky clean and velvety soft.

Pumping out a healthy dollop of body wash onto her palms (rather than using the stupid bar of Ivory she kept around just in case her mouth needed washing during bath time as well), Dana leaned forward and began working the vanilla scented soap up and down along her back. Gliding her palms in smooth circles around her cheeks and up her sides, before tracing her fingernails back down along the valley of her spine as she hummed to herself. Upon reaching her shoulders, she paused for a few blissful moments to knead away any tension that might've still been lingering there, before pulling back to get more body wash and setting to work lathering up her front as well. After making doubly (and triply) sure that the modest swell of her breasts had been covered in a sufficient number of suds, she began working her way lazily back down to the junction between her thighs; never actually letting her fingertips stray too close to where Rhen wanted them to venture most, but drawing tantalizingly close enough to make her moan on far too many occasions to be an accident.

"Humph," she grumbled, flicking away a bit of bubble from her shoulder with an exaggerated pout as her partner pulled away once again to get more soap. "You know it's rude to tease people, right?"

"True…" agreed Dana, turning her attention to her arms with an unconcerned chuckle. "It *is* pretty fun, though."

Rhen was *very* tempted to respond to that bit of shameless self-incrimination by suggesting that maybe she wasn't the only one who deserved to get a spanking that evening, but memories of the far too thorough switching she'd received the last time she'd said something like that to her auntie kept the words locked up tight inside her head where they couldn't get her in trouble. Dana had *not* appreciated her blatant disrespect of her role as the authority figure in their relationship the last time her sass had gotten the better of her, and she'd made sure that that was abundantly clear by ensuring she actually *did* sleep on her stomach that night.

And the night after that.

And… the night after that.

Squirming on her knees as butterflies began to stir to life inside her stomach, fretting that her partner could somehow read what was going through her mind just then, Rhen fired back with something that she knew was safe to fill the air between them.

"Meanie."

"Cutie."

Phew.

Eventually, after Dana had finished going over her ankles and toes (with her sitting on the edge of the tub and leaning against her for support), she reached for the bath brush once again and this time turned her attention to the task of exfoliating her sudsy skin with its moderately stiff bristles. Scrubbing vigorously, she soon had her skin feeling extra clean and silky smooth, forcing

Rhen to admit that the length of flexible plastic and bristles was indeed a very effective bath time accessory (on top of being a ruthless spanking implement) just as her partner had said it was.

The only problem was, though, was that it was a little *too* effective in some areas.

"Up," Dana ordered, tapping her between the shoulders after she'd finished going over them, gesturing for her to stand. "I want you to bend over so I can get at those cheeks, understand?"

Too relaxed to even pretend to sass, Rhen reluctantly hauled herself back to her feet in the middle of the tub, dribbling water all down her front in a myriad of tiny waterfalls as she leaned forward and rested her wet elbows on the windowsill in front of her.

"Ah!"

And then immediately found herself shooting right back up again in surprise and more than a little discomfort as the bristles of the bath brush came into contact with her buns.

"Oh no, you just stay right where you are, young lady," admonished Dana, forcing her back down with a triumphant grin and redoubling her attack on her cheeks. "I said I was going to get this bottom squeaky clean, and I *meant* it."

"But... but...!"

For as soft and relaxing as those bristles had felt only a few moments earlier as they'd been scrubbing their way up and down along her back and arms, they seemed to have suddenly grown significantly more stiff and pointy as her partner put them to work scouring her seat with a vigor that reignited the flames from her earlier spanking and then some.

"You really- Urk! Don't have to- Ack! Do it so- Ah! R-Rough, you know!"

"Oh, but I do. I really, *really* do," insisted Dana, putting a little more elbow grease behind her scrubbing motions as she tackled her naughty niece's sit-spots next. "We need to get these cheeks looking extra clean for our meeting with your academic adviser tomorrow, after all."

"No we- Oh! Freaking don't!" whined Rhen through gritted

teeth, stomping a foot to emphasize her point and sending a small tidal wave of foamy water splashing over the edge of the tub in the process. "She's not even going to *see* my butt!"

CRACK! CRACK!

"Keep giving me attitude like that, little girl, and she most definitely will be seeing your bratty backside, believe you me."

"Ack! Okay, okay, okay!" Rhen hurriedly backpedalled, doing her best to rein in her protests as she shifted her weight from foot to foot in a futile attempt to shake off some of the heat from the twin swats to her sit-spots. "I'll be good. Geez."

"Mmhmm. Yes, dear, I'm sure you will," nodded Dana dryly, giving her bratty bride-to-be a friendly pat with the bristles of her brush. "But, even so, it never hurts to be prepared."

"Speak for yourself. Humph!"

CRACK!

"Watch it…"

"Yes ma'am!"

While Dana might not have been totally convinced by Rhen's sudden, heartfelt commitment to behaving herself, she did at least spin the head of the bath brush back around and return to scrubbing her seat with its bristles. Which the shorter girl did her best to endure with as much grace (and the minimum amount of gasping and grimacing) as possible.

After all, an energetic scrubbing was *far* more preferable to an energetic spanking.

And, truth be told, the sensation wasn't really all that terrible once she got used to it. For as much as she was complaining about it stinging, it wasn't nearly so awful as being forced to sit on the coarse, scratchy fibers and stiff rubber bristles of the welcome mat that her aunt had repurposed to be her "punishment mat". Having to perch her bare bottom on top of that stupid thing after a prolonged session across Dana's knee felt like she was being bombarded by a non-stop barrage of mildly stingy spanks that were scouring her rump raw. And, when viewed in that light, the rasping movements of the bath brush's bristles against her still tender tush were far more bearable. Pleasant, even.

At least, up until the point when she was ordered spread her cheeks.

"We might as well make sure we get you nice and clean *every-where*," Dana reasoned with an impish grin, using the non-bristly side of the bath brush to help encourage her legs further apart before proceeding to give her poor, defenseless anus and vulva an extremely thorough going over that left them feeling both raw and tingly.

And which did absolutely nothing to diminish her knee-trembling need for release.

Well… I guess I'll at least be prepared for if worst comes to worst tomorrow. That's got to count for something, right?

Even if it did, Rhen had to admit that she would be just fine if she never found out for sure.

Humph.

—

After Dana had finished scrubbing Rhen all over until her skin was glowing in more ways than just the red in her cheeks, she'd joined her in the tub. And, though it had been a bit of a snug fit, Rhen had still had a wonderful time simply soaking with her fiancé amid the bubbles. Lounging against her breasts as she sat on her lap cuddling, talking, smooching, and generally just enjoying each other's company in the soothing quiet of their master bathroom. It had been *exactly* what she'd needed to wind down after a long day and an even longer spanking. And now, as she finished drying off her disheveled, conditioner-soft raven locks, she was just about ready to keel over and pass out.

However, judging by the look on her partner's face as she watched her fold her bath sheet and return it to its spot on the towel rack (there was no way Rhen was going to run the risk of *another* bath brushing so soon after her last one just because she wasn't paying attention and left it on the floor like she usually did), she could already tell that it was probably going to be a while still before the two of them curled up under the covers together.

Which, if she was being totally honest with herself, was just fine with her.

"Alright, young lady, come with me," Dana ordered with a mischievous grin, taking her by the hand and leading her back into their bedroom with long, purposeful strides that would've had the younger girl worried had she not already been disciplined earlier. "I think it's about time you showed me just how much you feel like coming tonight."

"Heh. Well…"

Stomach fluttering with anticipation and a strong desire to be put to work as her eyes stayed locked on her partner's swaying, naked hips, Rhen's stride developed a pronounced spring to it.

"If you insist."

"There's my good girl."

Upon reaching Dana's side of their bed, the older woman settled gracefully down onto the edge of it. Pulling her around to stand in front of her, before yanking her in close for a deep and lingering kiss.

"I love you so much, Rhen," she murmured in a husky voice against the side of her mouth as their lips parted. "Always."

"I love you too, Dana," echoed the petite junior with a soft sigh, drawing back enough to stick out her tongue as she added. "Even if you *are* a big meanie pants."

"And don't you forget it!"

Laughing, Dana pushed back a stray lock of damp hair from her face and eyed the naked brat standing before her with an expression that made Rhen suddenly feel like she'd just been lured into a trap by a hungry predator.

"Now then, honey buns…"

Looking for all the world like a queen sitting atop her throne, she eased back on her hands against the mattress and spread her legs wide.

"Since you seem to be in such a cheeky mood, *still*, how about you put that pretty little sassmouth of yours to good use?" she teased, a crocodile smile blooming out of those last few words as she quirked an expectant brow at her bride-to-be. "Do a good enough job and I might just let you come before I tuck you in tonight."

"Awww, do you need a bedtime story?" cooed Rhen right on cue, doing a very poor job of not sounding sassy as she planted her hands on her hips in a spot-on imitation of her partner and leaned forward with a smirk. "Boy, I sure would love to help you out, Aunt Dana, but *someone* got real spank-happy the last time I was up past my bedtime reading. Then again… Maybe if I had a later bedtime things would be different? Say… eleven-thirty, perhaps?"

"Uh-huh."

Her joking at least managed to get a small chuckle from her aunt.

"Very cute."

As well as a sustained and very hard pinch to her left nipple.

"On your knees, little girl," she ordered in a saccharine sweet voice, dark eyes going flinty as she gave her pinching fingers a firm twist and a downward tug. "*Now*."

"Ah! R-Right away!"

Between Dana giving her "the look" at full force, her bottom still being tender from her recent spanking, her clit positively aching from being teased and denied for so long, and now the sharp, exhilarating pain being applied to her breast, it was enough to completely knock Rhen's legs right out from under her.

"Mmmm… Much better," purred Dana, releasing her grip on her bride-to-be as she fell to her knees and instead cupping her delicate chin for another kiss. "Now get to work."

"Yes ma'am!"

Blushing scarlet, but eager to please despite her sass, Rhen shuffled in close between the auburn-haired older woman's splayed thighs, bringing her face only a scant few inches away from her slick vulva; its neatly trimmed patch of rust colored pubic hair standing out in sharp contrast to her own silky smooth and totally bare slit. Rhen was pleased to see that she wasn't the only one who'd been enjoying herself during their bath time together, and with a self-satisfied grin, she leaned forward and pressed her lips to Dana's own in a prolonged, tender kiss.

"Mmmm…" she groaned, long, low, and deeply satisfied as Rhen began dragging her tongue along the length of her folds and around her hood with firm, steady movements of her tongue just like she'd taught her to. "Yes, just like that, cutie pie- Ah! Oh god… G-Good girl…"

Settling in to rock her partner's world, the petite junior began tracing out the letters of the alphabet with her tongue, taking special care not to wander too far from her clitoris as she did so. She had no idea if the whole alphabet thing actually made a tangible difference or not when it came to eating out the older woman, but that was fine with her. It gave her a game plan to follow, and Dana always seemed to enjoy herself when she used it. Which, in the end, was all that really mattered.

"Oh my god, oh my god, d-don't stop," her bossy boots auntie panted, one hand fondling her full breasts while the other rested atop Rhen's head, keeping her exactly where she wanted her as she began to plunge her tongue in and out of her opening. "*Y-Yes!* Right there… Oh god… Mmph!"

Chuckling to herself at how breathless she was making her fiancé (the vibrations of which had her arching her back on the bed and letting out a sharp cry of delight), Rhen swapped out her tongue for the middle two fingers of her right hand, working them in and out of her with practiced ease as she redoubled her attack on her swollen bud. She could tell that Dana was already on the brink of release as it was, so she decided not to hold anything back and instead deployed her secret weapon right there and then to bring things to an explosive finale. Humming out one long, unrelenting note, she mercilessly lashed her tongue against where she knew her partner was the most sensitive. And, sure enough, only a minute or so later she was seizing a fistful of her dark hair and shoving her bobbing face in tight against her groin.

"Oh my god, oh my god! Don't you *dare* stop, Rhen Elizabeth!"

Riding her face for all she was worth, Dana's thighs clamped themselves around her head, squeezing hard until, finally, she arched up once again and let out a prolonged, high-pitched cry of ecstasy. Being swept away by the waves of pleasure pounding through her body just then, she convulsed around the fingers still inside of her. Squeezing tight and panting heavily for several blissfully dazed moments, before eventually collapsing back down against the mattress, chest heaving and totally spent.

"Heh."

Snickering, Rhen allowed herself to flop back onto the carpet behind her once her partner released her death grip around her hand and head. The small burst of pain that accompanied her cheeks hitting the floor only serving to further add to her heady sense of self-satisfaction as she sat there licking her lips and savoring the taste of a job well done while she waited patiently for Dana to finish riding out the aftershocks of her orgasm.

"Not too shabby for a sassmouth, huh?"

"Mmmm… Yes, that was *very* good," purred the older woman once she'd more or less caught her breath, sitting back up and regarding her with a twinkle of amusement in her dark eyes as she adopted a more admonishing tone. "But I don't seem to recall giving you permission to stop, young lady."

"Eh, what can I say?" shrugged Rhen, flashing her an unrepentant smirk. "You seemed like you were down for the count. So I figured I'd take a little break."

Dana just scoffed at that, rolling her eyes and matching her smirk.

"Oh please. I think you know me a little bit better than that by now. Get over here, you little brat!"

Without missing a beat, she stooped forward and pinched her bride-to-be's ear between her thumb and forefinger, giving it a sharp twist and yanking her up and over her left thigh in one smooth motion; wedging it directly between her splayed legs and bouncing it tauntingly as she did so.

"Oof!" grunted Rhen, caught off guard by the sudden change of position, but not at all surprised by it either as she ground herself against her partner's leg, ostensibly trying to get more comfortable as she settled in for her impromptu attitude adjustment. "Oh, come on! You- Ah! You came, didn't you?"

SMACK!

"That is entirely beside the point," dismissed Dana with a sharp slap to her left cheek.

SMACK!

Followed by one to her right.

They weren't particularly hard swats. Just enough to impart a little heat to wherever they landed and make their recipient squirm. But, that was still more than enough to push Rhen right back up to the edge of release once again.

"I will not tolerate you being lazy, young lady."

SMACK!

"Hey! I wasn't being *lazy*-" Rhen began to squawk in protest.

SMACK!

Before being cut off once again by another wrist-flick powered swat from her partner.

"*Aieee!*"

One that exploded directly atop her exposed and pouting lips, delivering a sharp bite and toe-curling tingle along the length of their folds that coursed straight into her clit as it ground against the thigh beneath it, taking her breath away.

"Oh?" crooned Dana, gently rubbing where she'd just swatted and grinning from ear to ear. "Are we starting to think that maybe talking back isn't such a bright idea right about now?"

"Yes ma-" Rhen began to answer.

SMACK!

Before abandoning her attempt at a proper reply altogether as her hips bucked and ground atop the older woman's leg once again, feet flailing animatedly back and forth behind her as her mind went blank.

"Oh my god! Owie, owie, owie!"

"Quiet, little girl!" her partner snapped in response, punctuating her order with a flurry of stingy swats to the exact same spot over and over and over again.

SMACK-SMACK-SMACK-SMACK-SMACK!

"Do you *want* the neighbors to hear how naughty you are?"

"Y-Yes ma'am!" gasped the petite junior hurriedly, positively drenching her fiancé's thigh as she writhed atop it, only to realize her mistake half a heartbeat later and scramble to amend her answer before it could be used against her. "I mean, no ma'am!"

The last thing she needed was *another* public spanking. Not when the memories of her time at the beach were still so humiliatingly fresh in her mind.

And probably always would be.

Dana had printed out the picture she'd taken of her standing bare bottomed next to the beach's "No Running" sign after her paddling from Jill, getting it framed and putting it on her nightstand next to the engagement photo they'd taken on her birthday. It was definitely beyond cute, Rhen had to agree, but that still didn't make it any less embarrassing.

Especially since her partner had included a copy of it along with the engagement photo they'd mailed to her grandma.

"I see..." Dana purred, returning to her rubbing with no small amount of amusement in her voice as she slowly began to work two fingers into the younger girl's opening.

Which did absolutely nothing to ease her wriggling or whining in the slightest.

"Ah! Oh god! Please, I'm gonna-!"

"Tsk, tsk... Didn't I *just* get finished telling you to keep it down?" she tutted, idly pumping away while she bounced her thigh between her legs to help coax her along toward her first climax of the evening. "I know you have a difficult time doing what you're told, but you could at least *try* and behave yourself, you know."

Rhen, for her part, wasn't even pretending to pay attention now. She was far too busy floating along in her own little world to care, grinding against her partner's leg as she took her from behind.

"Oh, who am I kidding? We both know that's not going to happen," the older woman continued with a mock-resigned sigh, speeding up her hand movements and increasing the pressure against her clit. "But that's okay. I like keeping you in line. You just go ahead and come for me, and then we'll find something to keep that naughty mouth of yours busy, alright?"

Rather than answer, Rhen instead abandoned herself entirely to her partner's sweet caress. And, soon enough, she too was caught up in a wave of ecstasy. Moaning and gasping as she convulsed around Dana's fingers, she finally reached the orgasm that had been eluding her for so very, very long.

"Mmmm… Yes. That's my good girl," the older woman preened, pulling her fingers free and patting her pink cheeks fondly before gently maneuvering her onto her belly against the mattress. "Now you just stay right there and catch your breath while Auntie Dana gets ready for round two, alright?"

"Y… Yeah, sure…" panted Rhen, eyes closed and smiling dreamily as she drooled into their comforter. "Whatever you say…"

She continued to lie like that, just drifting along in a post-climax haze as she listened to Dana rummaging around inside her dresser, searching for something before eventually finding it.

"Ah, here we go!"

Cracking one eye open and rolling over onto her side to see what she was up to, Rhen felt her heart rate instantly accelerate back to Mach speed once again as she finally noticed that her partner was in the middle of slipping into the leather harness for their strap-on.

Noticing her stare, Dana grinned triumphantly.

"I *said* I was going to put that sassmouth of yours to work, and I meant it, cutie pie," she teased with a wink as she pulled the various straps around her hips nice and snug. "Now quit your pouting and get over here. This thing is going right up your adorable little ass in just a minute, so I'd start lubing it up if I were you."

"Oh my god, are you serious?" whined Rhen, rolling off the bed in a huff and stomping her way over to where the older woman stood with hands on hips.

"I sure am," crooned Dana without even a hint of sympathy, her grin growing ever wider as she jabbed an expectant finger at the spot of carpet just in front of her feet. "And don't even pretend like you don't love this, you little brat."

"Humph," grumbled the shorter girl as she dropped to her knees and eyed the length of dark purple silicone with an indignant scowl that didn't quite reach her eyes. "That's, like, *hardly* the point and you know it."

In an effort to cover the blush now creeping its way up her cheeks as her partner smirked down at her knowingly, she glanced over to the alarm clock sitting on her bedside table and snickered.

"Somehow I'm starting to get the feeling that we're both going to be pretty tired come tomorrow morning. Or, I guess… today morning?"

"Heh."

That managed to get another snort from Dana, who leaned forward and tipped her head back for a kiss by the back of her hair.

"Don't worry about it. We can just sleep in and grab some coffee on our way to campus."

"Oh, Aunt Dana, that's so very *naughty* of you," teased Rhen in reply, running her tongue along her lips in anticipation as tingles coursed down her body from where her aunt had her gripped. "What happened to all that talk about me needing to eat breakfast and do my chores and all that other stuff, hmmm?"

"I keep telling you I'm the one who makes the rules around

here, cutie pie," countered the older woman, tightening her hold on the back of her hair and silencing her sass by yanking her mouth down onto their strap on, stuffing it between her lips exactly how she planned on stuffing it between her hips before too long. "Now get to work."

Chapter 15

Traditional Solutions to Modern Problems

Though the timing was a bit tight with the two of them sleeping in that following morning, Dana still managed to have them up and out the door early enough in advance to swing by the Coffee Kate's near Rhen's campus for a quick macchiato and a slice or two of pumpkin bread before their meeting with her academic adviser. She still wasn't a big fan of her not-niece substituting caffeine and snacks for actual food, but since they planned on having a proper lunch before they went shopping for a new bike that afternoon, she decided to make an exception to her usual rule of starting the day off with a healthy breakfast.

However, while they might have been doing well on time as they entered the science and technology building where Rhen's program was housed, they soon found themselves facing an all new problem. Namely, actually finding the room where their meeting was supposed to take place.

Rhen could have *sworn* that she'd passed by Doctor Holloway's office at least half a dozen times on her way to and from her machine learning class last semester. But now, as she and her aunt meandered from floor to floor of Buckley Hall without actually coming across the stupid thing, she was seriously starting to wonder whether or not it had somehow disappeared off the face of the earth entirely.

"Are you *sure* we're in the right building, hon?" prompted Dana after they'd poked their heads into yet another empty classroom. "She said she wanted you to meet her here, specifically?"

"Yeah, no, this is definitely the right place," insisted the petite junior, feeling her face flush and her stomach churn with quietly mounting worry as they grew later and later for their appointment. "At least… I think it is… Maybe."

Truth be told, Rhen had actually only ever spoken to her academic adviser a handful of times, and even then she'd always tried to keep those conversations short and surface level lest she start asking uncomfortable questions. Like, for instance, why she hadn't been taking the rest of the general education classes she needed to graduate. But, from what little she *did* remember of their brief introductory meeting that first day after she'd officially declared her major, she wasn't a woman you wanted to keep waiting. Oh, she was nice enough once you actually got her going on a topic, insightful and eager to help the students she'd been assigned by the Computer Science department do well in whatever way she could, but she'd also heard from way too many of the others in her program who'd taken some of her classes that she was a total perfectionist and real stickler for punctuality.

Crap, crap, crap! Where the heck is that stupid office?

"Do you think maybe we should try asking for her at the student center instead?" her partner suggested after another minute of increasingly agitated speed walking and fruitless searching. "They might have a directory you could look her up in, you know."

"Oh. My. *God.* No, I don't think we should walk all the way over to the freaking student center. We're already super late as it is, and that would just end up eating even *more* time that we don't have!" exploded Rhen, feeling her hopes of making a good impression seriously starting to dwindle as she leaned around a corner and saw yet another long, empty hallway full of nondescript doors with only numbers on plaques beside them to indicate what they were for.

Ugh. This is such bullcrap.

Doubling down on venting her frustration as a fresh spike of caffeine-fueled adrenaline coursed its way through her nervously fidgeting body, she rounded back on her aunt and snapped, "Could you just, like, be quiet for one second and let me think? It's around here somewhere. I'm sure of it!"

"*Excuse* me?"

Dana narrowed her eyes in warning at her niece as her nostrils flared.

"Look. I know you're feeling anxious right now, Rhen, but if you take that tone with me just *one more time* I am going to turn you over my knee right here and now in one of these conference rooms," she scolded sharply, her voice rising with her irritation and making it abundantly clear that she was giving her first and only warning to knock it off. "I don't care if we're running late. You do *not* talk to me like that. Am I understood, little girl?"

Hands flying back to the seat of her skirt on reflex, Rhen nodded vehemently and cast a fretful look back down the hallway they'd just come from in an attempt to see whether or not anybody had overheard her partner's humiliatingly loud threat to adjust her attitude for her if she didn't shape up. And immediately let out a panicked squeak as she locked eyes with a pair of smirking grad students who just so happened to be heading their way right then.

One of whom she recognized as her old web design TA.

Crap!

"Okay, okay, you're right," she hurriedly acknowledged, stomach coiling tight with a mixture of embarrassment and genuine remorse for biting off her partner's head like she had. "That was totally out of line. I shouldn't have snapped at you like that."

Then, deciding that it was far better to be perceived as a bratty teen, rather than simply an immature adult who still needed to be *treated* like one, she sent a petulant glower back at the two girls who'd stopped a few feet away from them to watch the unfolding drama, and then refocused her attention on her still frowning fiancé.

"I'm really, *really* sorry, Aunt Dana. *Please* don't spank me," she pleaded in as respectful a tone as she could manage, all too aware of the highly amused tittering her words were eliciting from their audience. "I promise it won't happen again."

"You promise, huh?"

Dana still sounded dangerously unconvinced, but Rhen could tell that she'd at least managed to make a dent in her partner's resolve to punish her.

"Yes ma'am!"

"Awww. Okay then, honey buns, I forgive you," she cooed, keeping her back turned to the other girls as she flashed her bride-to-be a knowing smirk, apparently satisfied that she'd made her point for the time being as she reached out to ruffle her hair. "Just don't let it happen again, alright?"

"R-Right!"

Spinning on her heel, grateful to have managed to avoid a (completely deserved) spanking and eager to put as much distance as she could between her and the two now disappointed grad students as soon as possible, Rhen sped off toward the nearest stairwell she could see at top speed, calling over her shoulder as she went.

"Come on, follow me! I'm pretty sure we just need to head up another floor is all."

It has to be on the fifth floor, right? I mean, I know I've definitely seen signs for her office hours posted around there somewhere... I think.

However, Doctor Holloway's office continued to elude them.

"Okay, fine. I give up!" the flustered twenty-one-year-old turned teenager eventually declared upon finishing a second (totally fruitless) circuit of the fifth floor and its classrooms, loosing an elaborate sigh as she threw her hands up into the air and rounded on her aunt. "Let's just find someone and ask them for directions."

"Why, that sounds like an *excellent* idea," marveled Dana with just a hint of strained, motherly patience, turning her niece back around by the shoulders and sending her along her way with a forceful pat to her seat. "Lead the way, cutie pie. I'm right behind you."

—

Despite Rhen's newfound change of heart, there were, unfortunately, very few people actually wandering around Buckley Hall that morning who could help them out. Since the university was still technically between semesters, campus itself was a total ghost town with only a handful of staff and a few grad students quietly going about their business to be seen. But, with little choice other than to persevere, she and her partner continued to press on back the way they'd come, keeping their eyes peeled for anyone who might look like they knew what they were doing.

And, ideally, who hadn't overheard her aunt threatening to spank her a few minutes earlier.

As they worked their way down through the building floor by floor, passing by the same empty lecture halls and conference rooms as before, Rhen was seriously starting to regret not having just cut her losses sooner and hustling over to the student center to see if they had a staff directory or something. But, just as they reached the first floor and it seemed like she wasn't going to have a choice in the matter, she and Dana finally managed to run into someone who was able to point them in the right direction. And so, after a hurried jog to the nearest elevator and a blessedly short ride up to the *ninth* floor of the building, they at last found themselves outside of the personal office of the Computer Science department's data management and analytical analysis professor.

Albeit nearly twenty minutes late.

Oh god... She's going to freaking kill me, isn't she?

"Go on, then," prompted Dana, gently shepherding her forward with a hand on her lower back as her steps began to slow and falter. "We'd better not keep her waiting any more than we already have."

"R... Right."

Swallowing as much of her nervousness as she could, Rhen squared her shoulders and drew herself up to her full, diminutive height. Then, approaching the slightly ajar office door, she knocked.

"Uh, hello? Doctor Holloway? Are you in there?"

The force of her rapping knuckles supplied the answer to her question for her as the well-oiled door swung open to reveal a dark-haired woman of about Dana's age, seated behind a broad, wooden desk and sucking idly on the cap of a ballpoint pen as she stared intently at something on the screen of an open laptop in front of her.

"Ah, there you are!" she announced brightly, setting aside her pen and swiveling in her chair to take in the two tardy newcomers with an easy smile tempered only slightly by a hint of annoyance. "I was starting to worry you'd forgotten about me, Miss Mathews."

Rising from her seat and smoothing down the front of her blouse, she circled around the sizable stack of file folders next to her laptop, making her way past the large plate glass window that overlooked the campus quad below and over to where the two of them now stood, clearly intent on welcoming them properly.

"Please, come on in and make yourselves at home."

"Right! Sure! Yeah, totally!" blurted Rhen in a hurry as she double-timed it into the slightly cramped office, stepping around a stack of papers on the floor and pressing her back against a shelf laden with thick technical and reference manuals, making room for Dana as she followed in after her at a much more leisurely pace.

"I hope you'll forgive us for being so late, Doctor Holloway," she said by way of greeting as she shut the door behind her. "We wound up getting ourselves a little bit turned around while looking for your office, I'm afraid."

"Oh no, really?" replied the adviser, her carmine lips bowing into a concerned frown as she looked from Rhen, to her partner, and back again. "That's odd… I'm fairly certain I included my room number and contact information in that email I sent you, young lady."

"Uh…"

Rhen felt her stomach suddenly tighten at the way the other woman so effortlessly shifted from addressing her as "Miss" to "young lady".

"You, um… You did?"

"Yes. I did."

She nodded with much more confidence this time, her frown

deepening as she continued regard her coolly.

"I always make sure to include that information at the end of any email I send my students to schedule a meeting."

She arched a brow at her then, hands making their way to her hips in a gesture very reminiscent of one that Dana had been directing her way not too long ago.

"You *did* read it all the way through, didn't you?"

"Well, uh… You see…" stammered the shorter girl, forehead growing hot as she struggled to recall as much as she could of the lengthy summons she'd received earlier that week. "I was kinda busy when you sent it, so I only had a chance to skim through it."

"Skimmed it, huh?" pressed Doctor Holloway, sounding skeptical but not particularly surprised. "You mean to tell me you didn't have a *single* moment to spare between Monday morning and now to read it properly?"

Seeing now that that was very much a mistake, Rhen flashed her unimpressed adviser her best sheepish grin while her stomach continued to churn with embarrassment and remorse for the second time in less than an hour that morning.

"Um… Yeah… I sorta figured that since we were going to be meeting anyway, that maybe we could, um… You know…"

She threw a pleading look in her partner's direction then. One that was met with a very "You're on your own, little girl" kind of smirk.

"I see," was her adviser's only reply after allowing her to squirm under her exacting gaze for several more excruciatingly embarrassing seconds, eventually dismissing her with a roll of her eyes as she turned her attention to Dana instead and held out a hand to her with a cordial smile devoid of any of her earlier frustration. "And you must be her aunt. It's a pleasure to meet you. I'm Doctor Holloway, but you can just call me Jane."

Accepting the woman's outstretched hand, Dana matched her pleasant smile with one of her own as she gave it a firm shake.

"It's nice to meet you too, Jane. I'm Dana Johnson."

She then shot a sidelong glare back toward her bride-to-be,

one that wordlessly conveyed that they would most definitely be discussing this little lapse in communication later, before continuing on as if she really *were* the younger girl's aunt.

"Thank you so much for taking the time to meet with us. I'm sure you're busy preparing for the next semester right now, so it means a lot. And, yes, like I'm sure my niece *meant* to say, we are both very sorry for keeping you waiting."

Then, more sharply.

"Aren't we, *Rhen*?"

"Yes ma'am!"

"Oh, no, please don't worry about it. It's fine, I assure you," dismissed the professor with a negligent wave of her hand, sounding significantly less annoyed than she had just a moment earlier while she'd been addressing her student directly. "You two just gave me a chance to catch up on some emails and office work I'd been neglecting is all. And, really, now that I think about it, this is partially my fault anyway. I should've gotten your contact information from Rhen earlier in the year so that I could CC you on our meeting info directly, rather than trusting that she'd forward it along for me like I'd asked."

"Come on. I gave her the freaking gist, didn't I?" grumbled the raven-haired girl under her breath, feeling more and more like an irresponsible teenager at a parent-teacher conference with each passing moment as she clamped down on the urge to cross her arms and pout.

Her sass earned her another warning glare from Dana, and an odd look of satisfaction from her adviser before she turned and gestured toward the two straight back chairs arranged before her desk.

"Well, you two are here now and that's all that really matters, I suppose. So, please, come have a seat and we'll get started."

"Of course," nodded Dana, gliding her way over to the desk while Rhen stiffened and answered hurriedly.

"Right!"

Eager to salvage her reputation in her adviser's eyes, she

scrambled for her own seat with as much get-up-and-go energy as she could muster, receiving a small nod of approval from the dark-haired older woman as she settled back behind her desk.

"Ahem. Now then," Doctor Holloway continued, clasping her hands in front of her as she cleared her throat. "Since Miss Mathews has failed to inform you as to why we are all meeting this morning, Dana."

At that, she directed another disapproving frown in Rhen's direction.

"Or seems to even be aware of that reason herself."

Before pointedly turning her attention back to the only other adult in the room as far as she was concerned.

"Allow me to elucidate the matter in her stead."

"By all means, please do," replied Dana easily, sharing a commiserating look with the annoyed adviser. "Whatever you have in mind to help Rhen, I'm all ears."

"Me too," interjected the girl in question earnestly, doing her best not to give away just how embarrassed she felt right then as she squirmed uncomfortably in her minimally padded seat.

She was painfully aware of how the bottoms of the Mary Janes her aunt had insisted that she wear that morning just *barely* managed to graze the floor beneath them. Which was doing absolutely nothing to help her feel less like she'd been summoned to the principal's office for a serious dressing down.

"Well, as Rhen's academic adviser, it's my duty to ensure that she has all of the support she needs to succeed in her studies. Which, for most students, usually amounts to keeping an eye on their grades and being there to help them find study groups or rearrange their schedules as the need arises. I like to allow my students as much autonomy and room to grow as possible. However, I must admit that I feel like I've been dropping the ball where Rhen is concerned by sticking to my usual 'my door is always open if you need anything' policy. In all the time since she was accepted into our program, she hasn't once taken the initiative to reach out to me for help, and I've been letting that slide since she hasn't actually failed any of her classes. Although, she *has* come dangerously close on more than a few occasions."

Blushing once again, Rhen struggled to think of some way of spinning that succinct and rather unflattering description of their relationship so far in her favor. But, trying to assert that she was fully capable of handling her course work on her own when both of the women in the room with her knew for a fact that she wasn't, seemed like a counterproductive idea to say the least. So, instead, she just kept her mouth shut and schooled her features into an intently focused (and above all else, polite) mask as Doctor Holloway continued.

"Now, as it so happens, a couple of weeks ago I was in the process of reviewing her grades from last semester. And, upon putting them alongside her individual course results from the start of her freshman year to present, I was able to spot a rather interesting trend that prompted me to start reevaluating my approach with her."

Tapping out a short sequence of keystrokes on her laptop, the now smiling adviser spun it around to face Rhen and Dana, and then leaned forward in her chair to point out the top section of a *very* detailed spreadsheet.

"If you would be so kind as to direct your attention here, this graph depicts Rhen's overall grades for each of the classes she's taken since she began her studies with us," she said with no small amount of professional enthusiasm, tracing a fingertip along a multicolored bar graph. "As you can see, at the start of her freshman year she was doing quite well. Mostly A's and one or two B+'s as indicated by the color shift from green to yellow here. But, as we begin moving our way through semester to semester, things quickly dip down into C, and even D, territory."

"Hmmm… Yes, I definitely see what you mean," nodded Dana, pursing her lips thoughtfully as she scooted in closer and ran her eyes over the neatly organized data in front of her, the very visible shift from mostly green and a little yellow to predominantly orange with splashes of bright red painting a very clear (and damming) picture of her niece's academic performance. "But what's this spot near the end of the graph here? That's quite the spike, isn't it?"

"Ah, I see you've also managed to spot the same thing I did," replied Doctor Holloway with a satisfied nod. "Rhen had more or less flat-lined out into earning C's and the odd D near the end of her freshman year, and she managed to keep that streak going for quite a while, but then some time during the latter half of summer semester last year something clearly changed. Because, like you say, she was suddenly back to predominantly earning all A's in each of her classes."

"Heh. Is that so?"

Oh god. Please don't say what I think you're about to…

"Indeed," chuckled the adviser with a knowing twinkle in her eye. "And, as I'm sure you've already guessed, our Rhen's miraculous grade spike just so happens to coincide directly with her moving out of the dorms and into your home."

Her face split into a conspiratorial grin then.

"Now, I'll be the first to admit I was rather skeptical that a simple change of scenery could elicit such a substantial shift in academic performance all at once. But, after speaking with her professors and TAs from last fall, particularly one Miss Courtney Summers, it all snapped into focus."

"Oh, I'm sure it did," mused Dana, matching the other woman's grin as she shifted her seat a bit closer and wrapped an affectionate arm around her not-niece's shoulders. "Rhen's granny and I talked it over, and we both agreed that it would be best if she came to stay with me instead of moving into an apartment on her own once she was phased out of the dorms. She's a *very* smart girl as I'm sure you're well aware, but she also has a tendency to procrastinate and not apply herself if left to her own devices. And, well… Let's just say that Auntie Dana knows a thing or two about keeping young ladies like her focused on what needs doing."

Giving the younger girl's shoulders a reassuring rub, she leaned over and kissed her cheek.

"Even if they might think they're too old for it."

"Geez. Just go ahead and spell it all out for her, why don't you?" pouted Rhen, no longer caring how immature she might seem now that the cat was more or less out of the bag.

"Now, now, there's no need to embarrassed, Rhen," her adviser soothed. "I know it's perhaps a little, uh… *unorthodox* for a girl your age to still be getting spanked when she acts up at home, but…"

She shrugged then and gestured back at her spreadsheet.

"The data doesn't lie, now does it?"

To which Rhen had to give a begrudging nod.

"No ma'am…"

She *did* have a point, after all.

Even if she didn't like it.

"Humph."

"It's actually a lot more common than you might think," put in Dana then while her niece continued to glower petulantly. "As strange as it might seem, some girls simply need a firm hand to help keep them on track and doing what they're supposed to, regardless of how old they might actually be. Like you said, the data very clearly shows what happens when Rhen is left to manage herself alone, and if a hot bottom every now and then gets her to straighten up and fly right, then there's absolutely nothing wrong with that in my book."

"Nor mine," agreed Doctor Holloway, beaming. "I actually used to teach math and programming at a private school that held very similar beliefs back before I got around to finishing my PhD. So I've seen firsthand just how much direct and immediate consequences and corporal punishment can impact a student's academic performance for the better. In fact, that's exactly the reason why I wanted to have this meeting today in the first place."

"Oh? It is?"

"It is?" echoed Rhen with a squeak, sounding far more concerned than her partner did just then.

"That's right," nodded her adviser, turning her warm smile entirely on her now as a note of steely determination crept its way into her firm but supportive tone. "As I've already explained, it's my job to ensure that you live up to your full potential as a student while a member of this program, Rhen. And after analyzing the data surrounding your grades and conferring with the people who know you best, it has become painfully obvious that you, my dear, are in desperate need of a uniquely more 'hands on' approach from me than what I've been providing you so far."

"I am?" the shorter girl squeaked again, not at all liking the direction things were suddenly headed, nor the determined nod that she got in return from her adviser.

"I believe what we need to do is establish a series of academic goals and standards for you to adhere to, along with a system of disciplinary measures to fall back on when you fail to do so. Something along the lines of the arrangement you had with Miss Summers last fall, only expanded further to encompass all of your studies."

Rhen's jaw actually fell open at that, silently working itself up and down as her brain struggled to find the words to express how this horrifyingly embarrassing turn of events made her feel.

"W-Wait a minute! Are you saying you want to *spank* me?" she finally blurted out, deciding that confronting the question head on (as much as that sucked) was her only real option.

"Well, that's a bit of an oversimplification of what I'm saying," admonished her adviser, her pleasant, motherly smile cooling by a few degrees in the face of her burgeoning tantrum. "But, in essence, yes. I am proposing that from here on out, should you fail to apply yourself to the best of your ability, that *I* will be applying some very firm discipline directly to your seat of learning."

"Oh my goodness, that sounds like an excellent idea!" exclaimed Dana, her face brightening with genuine delight as she scooted forward in her seat excitedly. "I can't believe something like that never occurred to me before. You're a genius, Jane!"

"Why thank you," demurred the other woman with just a hint of bashfulness. "It's certainly an out of the ordinary approach for most college juniors, I'll admit, but I genuinely believe that it's the best course of action for Rhen."

"Hey, if it works at home, then there's no reason why it can't also work for her at school, right?"

"Precisely. Nothing focuses a bright and rambunctious girl's attention more than the promise of a sore bottom if she doesn't get her act together."

"Hah! Don't I know it."

"But… but…! You can't just, like, *do* that, can you?" Rhen finally managed to get out, face ablaze as her adviser and aunt energetically discussed the merits of treating her like a disobedient child. "Isn't it against the rules or whatever for a professor to spank a student?"

"Well, as a matter of fact, yes, it is," conceded Doctor Holloway, holding up a hand to forestall any further interruptions when she saw the hopeful look blossom on the younger girl's face. "But after conferring with the dean, I've been assured that so long as I obtain your consent, as well as your guardian's, any and all 'non-standard corrective measures' we might devise for you will be considered above board."

"But-!" Rhen tried to argue further, mortified beyond belief that the dean of students (along with god only knew how many other people) was apparently fine with what was being proposed for her, before being cut off by a sharp glare from the woman sitting across the desk from her.

"*You*, young lady," she scolded, jabbing a finger in her direction for added emphasis. "Have not been doing nearly as well as you could have been these last few semesters, and I will *not* tolerate you slacking off any longer."

"Oh, come on! Two A minuses and a few B's are still pretty good, you know," countered Rhen with an indignant glower, earning herself a tweaked ear from Dana in the process.

"Watch it, little girl," she warned, tightening her grip as she did so. "I believe I've already had to tell you once today to it knock off with all the attitude. If I have to do it again, you are *not* going to like what happens next. Do you hear me?"

"Ow! Oh! Ack! Oh my god, Aunt Dana, please!" yelped Rhen, half rising out of her chair to keep her ear from coming off. "I'm sorry, I'm sorry! I'll be good, I promise."

"You had better be, missy," harrumphed her fiancé, releasing her grip and shaking her head in exasperation. "Now apologize to Doctor Holloway."

"Yes ma'am…" mumbled the now thoroughly chastened twenty-one-year-old turned teenager, one hand still cupped gingerly around her throbbing left ear as she turned back to her adviser with a sullen pout. "I'm sorry, Doctor Holloway. I was being rude just now. It won't happen again."

"That's alright, dear, you were just proving my point for me," replied the dark-haired professor evenly, an expression of profound self-satisfaction settling onto her stern features as she picked up where she'd left off. "Now, as I was saying, I've been keeping tabs on your performance since you started with us, and it's obvious to me that you have an innate understanding of the material we cover in our program. Moreover, when you actually make an effort to apply yourself, instead of just coasting along on that innate understanding, you consistently produce some truly outstanding results."

"Um… R-Really?" stammered Rhen, totally caught off guard by such frank and honest praise coming on the tail end of being scolded.

She knew she had a natural talent for software development, but she was genuinely surprised to hear how highly her adviser thought of her.

"Really," nodded Doctor Holloway, a fresh smile lighting up her face. "In fact, I think you might even be PhD material if you can just manage to get yourself into gear."

"Whoa, PhD material?" echoed the petite junior, sitting up a little bit straighter in her seat now as her stomach thrilled with the idea.

"Mmhmm, that's right. But, like I said, you're going to need to really step it up if that's something you'd like to pursue. I know your GPA won't make a difference when you're looking for a job after graduation, but grad schools definitely care about that sort of thing when you're applying to them, especially ours. Plus, if you want to do well on the GRE, you're going to *really* need to make sure you have good study habits in place. Putting in the bare minimum amount of work won't do you any favors, trust me."

"Oh, yeah. No, for sure. Totally," nodded Rhen absently, disregarding all but the first part of that last statement as her mind raced with possibilities, all of her earlier indignation and embarrassment completely forgotten about now.

Up until then, college had just been the thing she was doing because it was what you were supposed to do after you finished high school. She'd picked computer science as her major because she liked programming and the classes seemed like they'd be interesting and not a total pain, but she'd never truly been passionate about her education before.

That is, until now.

"Hmmm… *Doctor* Rhen does have a pretty nice ring to it, doesn't it?"

"I sure think so," encouraged Dana, ruffling her hair.

Grinning goofily, Rhen pictured herself giving a lecture before a crowd of eager students, or strutting her way through a massive data center while a crisp white lab coat just like Alana's billowed dramatically behind her.

Wait a minute, would I even wear a lab coat if I were a doctor of computer science? I mean, I suppose there's nothing that says I couldn't wear one, but still… Eh, whatever. If I want to wear a lab coat, I'll wear a lab coat! I'm the one with the PhD, aren't I? Hmmm, I wonder if Doctor Holloway has one? I don't think I've ever seen her in one before, but maybe that's just because I haven't taken her classes yet? Oh! Maybe she'd let me try it on if I asked her nicely. That would be awesome! Then again… It'd probably be way too big…

"Ahem."

Clearing her throat loudly enough to draw her out of her reverie, her adviser directed her attention back to the matter at hand.

"I'm pleased to see that you're excited, Rhen," she said, a bit more firmly this time. "But for now let's focus on your more immediate future. Starting with the three of us putting together a list of specific rules and academic standards that you will be beholden to from this point forward, alright?"

"Sure, sounds great," the petite junior nodded.

"Excellent."

Doctor Holloway's eyes hardened then.

"Oh, and just so that we're both crystal clear, I want you to understand that you *will* be getting spanked this semester."

Grimacing, Rhen opened her mouth to try and argue, but once again found herself silenced by a raised hand.

"Look. I know you'll be leaving here today fully convinced that you'll never actually wind up in my office for correction because you're all fired up and ready to prove yourself to me, but take my word for it. You are going to be here a lot more than you might think. As I mentioned, I used to teach at a private school, so I know a thing or two about dealing with bright and gifted students. And, as much as you might hate to admit it, a girl like you needs to know that there are boundaries you aren't allowed to cross and that your actions have consequences."

Again, Rhen wanted to deny it, but the events of the last year or so since she'd moved in with Dana more than confirmed that her professor's read on her was an accurate one. And, judging by the look on her partner's face, they both knew it too.

"Oh, don't get me wrong," smirked Doctor Holloway, her earlier dour mood evaporating in an instant. "I'm sure you'll probably stick to your new plan like glue for the first week or two of next semester, but sooner or later you're going to start getting complacent. It'll probably start with something small like putting off your homework for an extra hour because you're sure you can finish it quickly, or maybe you'll start zoning out in class because you feel like you understand the material well enough to not bother taking notes. Whatever the case may be, at some point you *are* going to slip up. Which is totally natural and not something you need to feel bad about. But, when you inevitably do, just know that we *will* be dealing with it. Understand?"

Well, at least she's honest.

Unable to truly bring herself to be upset about this new development in her school life despite how humiliating it was sure to be, Rhen instead just let out a resigned sigh, matching her adviser smirk for smirk.

"Do I have a choice?"

"Not really," she replied cheerily. "But something tells me you're than used to that by now."

That managed to get an amused snort out of Dana.

"Don't worry," she snickered, kissing her not-niece's cheek while she scowled grumpily. "She is."

"Humph."

"Well, great," declared Doctor Holloway, rubbing her hands together eagerly before turning her laptop back around to face her. "Now that we've gotten that preliminary discussion out of the way, shall we move on to fleshing out the actual details of this new arrangement? I have some ideas for what it should look like already, but I would love to hear any input you two might have as well."

She deigned to nod briefly in her pouting student's direction then.

"Especially you, Rhen. After all, it's your caboose that's going to be on the line here. So I want to make sure you feel like we're being fair with what rules and goals we set for you."

"Yeah, yeah, whatever..."

Tossing her hair dismissively, Rhen did her best to give off the impression that she couldn't have cared less what they ended up deciding now, even though they were about to start putting together a list of things her adviser would be allowed to spank her for whenever she wanted to. Now that she was back on the familiar ground of doing what she was told by an authority figure who regarded her as someone who needed a firm hand to keep her in line (Dana hadn't been exaggerating when she'd said that she was used to not having a choice when it came to rules and discipline), she could feel herself quickly starting to slip back into the comfortable role of being a smart but sassy teenager. And with that new shift in attitude came the desire to simply let the "adults" in the room take the lead on things while she begrudgingly accepted whatever they decided on. She trusted the two of them to do what was best for her, and if she was being totally honest with herself, having concrete boundaries and consequences really did help to put her at ease and feel safe.

Not that she'd ever admit *that* out loud.

"Let's just get this over with, alright?"

Judging by the bemused look on her academic adviser's face, it seemed pretty clear that she wasn't buying her unconcerned affectation even a little bit. But, thankfully, she chose not to call her out on it.

"Alright then," she continued with a pleasant, albeit expectant, look. "I think a good place to start is with your grades. Specifically, I propose that we keep things nice and simple by setting a target grade that you will be expected to maintain in all of your classes."

"Sounds easy enough," shrugged Rhen. "What're you thinking? Minimum B+ on everything?"

"Oh please," scoffed an incredulous Dana. "We all know that you're fully capable of maintaining an A average if you put your mind to it, cutie pie."

"I agree," nodded Doctor Holloway firmly. "However, in the interest of precision, I propose that we set her minimum grade requirement to a score of ninety-four percent, rather than simply just saying 'Get an A on everything'. Based on the data in that spreadsheet I showed you two earlier, that number is right in the sweet spot of what Rhen is capable of achieving without also putting any undue amount of stress on her in the process. My goal here is to help her live up to her potential and stay motivated, not burn her out under a mountain of perfectionist stress."

"Hmmm…"

Pursing her lips, Dana hummed thoughtfully for a moment or two as she studied her niece, and then nodded.

"Yes, I think that seems pretty reasonable."

On reflex, Rhen found herself wanting to argue that that was way too high of an average for her to maintain. But, as she mulled it over further herself, she had to admit that her adviser was probably right. As she'd said, she *did* have an innate understanding of the subject matter of her major, and with a little extra effort on her part, maintaining a ninety-four in all of her classes was entirely doable. Though, the handful of general education classes she was still in the process of working her way through were definitely going to suck a whole lot more as a result. Computer science stuff she could handle all day, no problem. But English Lit and Economics? Now *that* would be a pain in the butt for sure.

Oh well… If I just do my best, then they shouldn't be literal pains in my butt, at least.

Something in her expression must have stood out to Doctor Holloway, because raising an eyebrow, she added in a warning tone, "Just to be clear, young lady, that ninety-four percent standard doesn't just apply to your overall grade for a class each semester. I fully expect you to do at least that well on every test, every quiz, every homework assignment, and any miscellaneous group activities that might crop up during class as well. Am I understood?"

"Uh…"

Now *that* was slightly more daunting. But, again, aside from her general education classes, she was fairly confident that she could handle it without too much trouble. She'd just have less wiggle room than she'd originally thought, was all.

Oh god, she was right! I'm already planning on slacking off. Geez. Get it together, Rhen!

"Yeah, no, I can definitely handle that!" she assured her in a hurry. "Ninety-fours on everything from here on out. Got it!"

"And should she need it, there *are* study groups and tutors that she can use too, right?" pressed her aunt with an encouraging pat on the back.

"Of course," nodded her adviser, picking up her pen and

scribbling something on a piece of paper next to her laptop. "In fact, I'll go ahead and compile a list of groups for the classes she'll be taking this semester and send that info over to both of you this evening so that you'll have it handy in case she needs it."

That managed to loosen the tense knot that had been forming in Rhen's chest, and she let out a breath that she hadn't even realized she'd been holding. She was reasonably sure that she'd be able to keep her grades up where they were supposed to be if she just paid attention in class and did all of her required reading. But having actual other people to compare notes with and work out stuff that didn't make sense would also be pretty useful too if all of the (non-spanking) extracurricular tutoring Courtney had given her in physical science was anything to go by.

"Thanks, Doctor Holloway."

"You're very welcome, dear," replied the older woman, setting aside her pen and quickly typing out what they'd settled on so far into the text document she'd prepared ahead of time for their meeting. "Now, moving on, I think we can go ahead and skip making any rules regarding when and how long you should be studying for. I'm not here to micromanage your life, and you know yourself better than anyone else, so I'll leave all of that up to you and your aunt."

"As it so happens, we actually already have some rules in place for homework and study time," supplied Dana helpfully. "That was one of the big things we had to deal with a lot when Rhen first moved in with me, but after a few sessions with the wooden spoon she's more or less gotten procrastinating on her homework out of her system. Haven't you, cutie pie?"

Blushing furiously, Rhen just mumbled something that vaguely sounded like "Yes ma'am", but otherwise didn't comment.

At least she didn't mention the punishment mat…

"Well, that's just excellent," beamed Doctor Holloway. "Establishing good study habits at home is the cornerstone of doing well at school. But remember, Rhen, if you ever need any additional help, all you have to do is ask, alright?"

"Right!" she squeaked in response, stomach still aflutter from her aunt's casual explanation of how she'd helped her stop putting off her homework.

"Good girl- Oh!"

Covering her mouth, it was her adviser's turn to blush this time.

"Pardon me, dear. That was rather unprofessional of me. I shouldn't speak to you like you're a child."

"Eh, don't sweat it," shrugged Rhen with a wry grin. "I mean, you've already told me that you're going to be spanking me sooner or later, so I don't think you need to be too worried about stuff like that at this point."

"Plus she *is* a good girl," added Dana with a wink. "Most of the time, anyway."

"Heh."

Composing herself once more, Doctor Holloway brought her hands back to her keyboard.

"Shall we move on to classroom conduct then?"

"Works for me," nodded Rhen, starting to feel more like an actual college junior again instead of an unruly middle schooler with an attitude problem. "What'd you have in mind?"

"Nothing too draconian, I assure you," her adviser promised. "Aside from the obvious things that we don't actually need to write down, like not cheating or skipping class, I have just two rules I'd like for you to follow."

Raising a forefinger, she continued.

"First of all, be on time to all of your classes. And I do mean *actually* on time. I will not be accepting tardies, young lady. Unless you have a very good excuse, there is absolutely no reason why your caboose shouldn't be in class and at your seat five minutes before the bell rings."

"I uh…"

Rhen felt her cheeks heat up once again as she remembered just how late she and her fiancé had been to this very meeting.

"I can definitely do that."

"Wonderful," praised the woman sitting across from her,

smiling sweetly as she raised another finger. "Now, my second rule is also a simple one. When you're in class, there will be no horsing around or goofing off. You're here to learn, and I expect you to be paying attention and participating. Not talking with your friends or playing around on your phone or laptop. Am I understood?"

Feeling much more confident in her reply this time around since she actually liked her classes, Rhen nodded quickly.

"Yes ma'am!"

Doctor Holloway winked.

"Good girl. You get to class nice and early and find yourself a seat at the front of the room, alright?"

Rhen couldn't help but snicker at that.

"Guess I'm a nerd now, huh?"

"Honey, you're a computer science major," pointed out Dana with a teasing grin. "I think that ship sailed a long time ago."

"Humph. Rude."

Sharing a laugh with the ostensible aunt and niece, the dark-haired professor set about quickly typing in the two rules that had just been agreed upon before turning her attention back to them with an easy grin.

"Alright then, before we move on to discussing the particulars of how discipline will be administered, there is one last thing I'd like to establish, if I may. It isn't really a rule, per se, but I still think it's important."

Swallowing audibly at the offhanded way her adviser had just mentioned spanking her, still trying to wrap her head around the fact that she apparently had no qualms about doing so, Rhen did her best to focus on what she was saying and look attentive.

"Um, what did you have in mind?"

Noting her unease, Doctor Holloway gave her a comforting smile.

"Oh, it's nothing to worry about, dear. I'd just like for us to meet every week to review how your classes are going. I've taken the liberty of checking your schedule for the upcoming semester, and I think that Friday at noon would be ideal. Will that work for you?"

Well, there goes my day off, the petite junior thought to herself with an internal huff. *Oh well...*

"Yeah, that should be fine," she said aloud, pulling her phone from her pocket and adding a weekly recurring event to her calendar so that she wouldn't forget.

Or be late.

"I'll be there."

"Very good," replied her adviser, nodding in approval at the way she was planning ahead. "I know it's annoying to have to come to campus when you don't have any labs or classes, but I promise these meetings won't take too long. I just want you to always have a dedicated time where you can voice any concerns or worries you might have so that we can address them quickly before they turn into serious issues further down the road."

"Yeah, no, totally," agreed the petite junior, starting to warm to the idea as she favored the woman with a chagrinned smirk. "That would honestly be super helpful, thanks."

"It's my pleasure," preened Doctor Holloway, clearly pleased to see her student's attitude shifting from sullen to attentive so quickly as she continued. "Plus, us meeting at the end of every week will also give *me* a chance to take care of any outstanding behavioral issues I might've noticed cropping up lately that either went unnoticed by your professors, or just weren't serious enough for you to receive a discipline referral for."

"Humph. Yeah, I guess that's true too," conceded Rhen with a halfhearted pout, hoping to hurry the conversation along past the topic of discipline as quickly as she could.

Only to stop dead in her verbal tracks as a ball of ice formed in the pit of her stomach.

"Um... Did you just say 'discipline referral'?"

"Mmhmm, that's right," nodded her adviser, sliding open a drawer beside her and retrieving from within a distressingly thick stack of pre-printed half sheets of paper that she laid out on top of her desk. "These are basically the same ones we used back at my old private school, only I've gone ahead and pre-filled in your name on all of them since they're obviously just for you."

"Oh, now that is just *precious*," cooed Dana, plucking up a pair of sheets from the pile in front of her and passing one to her niece for a closer look. "Do you mind if I hold onto this, Jane? I just *have* to share it with her granny."

"Not at all, go right ahead. I've got plenty."

Now there's an understatement.

"Precious" wasn't exactly the word that Rhen would have used to describe the form in her hands, but she had to admit that there was a certain stomach-fluttering thrill to be found in the inherent "officialness" of it all. None of the schools she'd ever attended while growing up had practiced corporal punishment (at least not in the last couple of decades anyway), and part of her had always been curious about what it would be like any time she happened to see a scene of a principal paddling a student in a movie or on TV.

Be careful what you wish for, I guess... she thought to herself with a shiver, running her eyes along the way too official looking piece of paper to distract herself from the nagging worry that these things were most likely going to be seeing a *lot* of use.

As her adviser had said, her name was already printed at the top next to where it said "Student", and below that were lines for the date, the name of the person filling out the referral, what subject they were teaching, and then an area below that to explain why it was being written. Embarrassingly enough, rather than just having a blank line like the other fields, Doctor Hollo-way had seen fit to pre-prepare a list of common offenses that she clearly thought would be coming up on a regular basis judging by how many sheets she'd printed out. Along with a checkbox for "Other", there were also ones for "Tardiness", "Unprepared", "Not Participating", "Incomplete Work", "Failure to turn in Assignment", "Poor Attitude", "Talking Back", and most humili-ating of all, one that simply read "Needs Motivation".

CORPORAL PUNISHMENT DISCIPLINE REFERRAL

Student: _______Rhen Mathews_______   Teacher: _______________________

Date of Incident: _______________   Subject: _______________________

REASON(S) FOR DISCIPLINE:

- ☐ Tardiness
- ☐ Unprepared
- ☐ Not Participating
- ☐ Incomplete Work
- ☐ Other

- ☐ Failure to turn in Assignment
- ☐ Poor Attitude
- ☐ Talking Back
- ☐ Needs Motivation

____

____

____

Comments:

____

____

____

____

____

____

"Um… Are you sure these things are *really* necessary?" Rhen found herself asking, hoping against hope that if she just phrased the question nicely enough, the dark-haired older woman sitting across from her would change her mind about handing them out. "Can't I just, like, tell you if I do something wrong in class? Or, you know, maybe my professors could email you or something?"

"I'm afraid not, dear," replied Doctor Holloway gently but firmly. "After we're finished here, I'm going to be sending out a copy of your academic standards and disciplinary procedures policy to all of your professors and their respective TAs, along with a couple dozen of these forms for them to use as they see fit. I know that will probably be embarrassing for you, but they need to be aware of your unique circumstances if they are to help you do your best. Just because I'm the one who will actually be handling your discipline, that doesn't mean your teachers shouldn't be involved as well, you know."

Unsurprisingly, Rhen found that she had a very strong differing opinion on that particular idea, but she wasn't about to share it just then and risk getting a live demonstration of what someone filling out a discipline referral for her looked like.

"I guess so…"

"You guess so?"

Recognizing the warning tone in the other woman's voice, she quickly looked up from her pouting contemplation of the form in her hands and straightened in her seat.

"I mean, yes ma'am!"

"That's better," nodded her adviser approvingly as she slid aside her stack of referrals. "Now then, if one of your professors or TAs feels that I need to address something with you, all they have to do is fill out one of these forms. From there you can either come see me directly after your class or lab is finished, assuming that I'm available, that is, or you can just hold onto it and we'll deal with it during our weekly meeting on Friday."

The idea of having to actually come and *ask* for a spanking definitely made Rhen's insides twist with an all too familiar sense of anticipatory dread as she nodded and squeaked out another, "Yes ma'am!"

She'd been hoping that her shiny new engagement ring would maybe help add some years to her appearance and stop people from automatically dismissing her out of hand as a bratty teen that upcoming semester, but clearly that had just been wishful thinking.

Oh well. I'll just have to really be on my best behavior for a while, I guess. I'm sure if I can just put a couple weeks together without giving anybody a reason to write me up, that they'll totally forget all about those stupid forms… Hopefully.

"Hmmm… Speaking of spanking," interjected her partner into her fretful musing, causing her to jerk away from her thoughts with a blush as her cheeks clenched on reflex beneath her at the mention of the S-word. "I think we really ought to discuss that part next, don't you?"

"Absolutely," agreed Doctor Holloway, dragging a fingertip across her laptop's trackpad to dismiss its screensaver before she resumed typing. "I actually have a system in mind for that already. Just like the referral sheets, it's the same one we used back at my old school. It was always very effective back then, but I'd still like to double-check everything with you, Dana, before we set anything in stone."

"Of course, of course. What did you have in mind?"

"Glad to see I get a vote in this part too," the twenty-one-year-old turned teenager among them grumbled under her breath, going completely ignored by her aunt and adviser as they continued on with their discussion as if she hadn't said anything.

"Well, for more minor offenses we would usually give a student an over-the-knee hand spanking. Not anything too severe, mind you. Just enough to get their attention and give them something warm to sit on for the rest of the day."

"That seems pretty reasonable to me. I do the same thing with her at home, actually," replied Dana with an easy smile, before dropping a bombshell that increased the blush in her bride-to-be's cheeks tenfold. "I presume such a spanking would be given bare bottom?"

"That's right," confirmed the adviser, smiling just as easily. "Though, admittedly, that's mostly just because such spankings were typically reserved for younger students who a firm talking to and a quick trip over a knee still made an impression on. By the time a girl reached high school age, we switched over to using a paddle over panties instead to deal with misbehavior."

Dana nodded sagely at that.

"More responsibility requires more severe consequences, right?"

"Precisely!" agreed Doctor Holloway, clearly happy to see that they were both on the same page regarding spanking philosophy. "However, as effective as the paddle might be, I personally don't see any reason why we shouldn't leave both options on the table for Rhen. In my experience, big girls can be made to cry just as easily as little ones once they find themselves over a knee."

She looked back to her nervously fidgeting student then, regarding her levelly.

"Plus, if I'm being totally honest, I'd really rather not have to paddle her raw every single time we need to address some minor bit of misbehavior."

"No arguments here," piped up Rhen right on cue with an insolent smirk, earning herself a pair of amused chuckles from the two older women this time.

"Nor here," agreed her partner. "If she wants to act like a disobedient middle schooler, then you just go ahead and treat her like one, Jane."

"Oh, I will. Don't you worry."

That managed to knock Rhen's smirk back down into a pout.

"Um… You guys know that I'm not *actually* a little kid, right?"

"Well then, you shouldn't have any problems keeping your panties up all semester, huh, cutie pie?"

"Humph. Exactly!"

"Yes, well, as to that," continued Doctor Holloway with a tolerant grin, sliding open another drawer in her desk and this time pulling from it a sizable length of tan colored wood. "This is what we will be using to address any more serious breaches of conduct, Miss Mathews."

"Oh my, now that's quite the paddle," marveled Dana, accepting it as it was passed to her and hefting it appreciatively before handing it over to her niece for inspection.

Rhen could tell immediately that it was long enough to cover both of her cheeks in a single swing, and heavy enough to make sure that she wouldn't be forgetting what it felt like any time soon. It had two neat rows of six holes each drilled into its smooth, glossy surface. Each of them was about the size of a quarter, and as she gave it a couple of test swings, she could hear an uncomfortable amount of air hissing through them evilly.

"Uh… What's up with the holes?" she found herself asking, not sure if she really wanted to know the answer or not.

"What you're holding there, young lady, is what is known as a Spencer Paddle," explained the analytics professor, sounding as if she were in the midst of delivering a lecture to one of her classes instead of enumerating the finer points of a spanking implement. "It was invented by a schoolteacher in the 1930s, and is the type of paddle that we used with all of our high schoolers back at my old school. The holes in the surface of its striking area help to reduce wind resistance by up to sixty percent while it's being swung through the air, thereby allowing each swat to impact with far more kinetic energy than a more traditional paddle might impart."

"Great…" deadpanned Rhen.

Yep. Definitely shouldn't have asked.

"Where the heck did you even get this thing, anyway?"

"Yes, do tell," encouraged Dana, taking the paddle back from her niece and giving her thigh a couple of experimental pats. "I'm seriously tempted to get us one for back home."

"Don't you freaking dare, Aunt Dana," Rhen growled good-naturedly, before seeing the sharp look in her partner's eyes and adding in a rush. "I mean, um… *Please* don't you dare?"

"Heh. We'll see, cutie pie."

"I can certainly put in a request for one if you'd like me to, Dana," Doctor Holloway offered helpfully. "There are some very talented young men and women in the university's mechanical engineering department who have a real knack for woodworking. After explaining what I needed to them, they were able to whip that up for me in just a single afternoon."

"How very productive," grumbled the petite junior sitting across from her, glaring daggers at the stupid paddle and doing her best not to think too much about who else on campus might know about this little "arrangement" between her and her academic adviser. "Bunch of freaking nerds…"

"Now, now, don't pout, Rhen," her adviser admonished gently, as Dana set the paddle back down on top of her desk. "If it's any consolation, you at least won't have to take any paddle swats on your bare bottom. As I said, we always delivered those over a student's panties back at my school."

Then, pursing her lips in thought, she added pensively.

"Although, now that I think about it, I suppose there's no real reason why we *couldn't* do your paddlings on the bare as well. After all, it would just be the two of us… But, on the other hand, I do rather enjoy having a firm delineation between serious and non-serious offenses to help drive home the gravity of one's misbehavior. Hmmm… No, I think we'll keep things as they are for now, unless bare bottom paddlings prove to be necessary in the future."

Phew.

"I wouldn't worry too much about it, Jane," chimed in Dana then with a casual wave of her hand as she settled back in her seat, crossing one leg over the other and winking. "Either way, she'll be going over my lap for a second dose at bedtime whenever you have to punish her, and Auntie Dana *always* spanks bare."

Dang it. I was really hoping she'd forget about that whole "punished at school, punished at home" thing.

"Oh Dana, you're a woman after my own heart!"

Sharing another laugh with the auburn-haired older woman, Rhen's adviser made short work of putting the finishing touches on her Academic Action Plan and then printed out a hard copy for them both to sign.

"You two just go ahead and jot down your names and the date here where it says 'Guardian' and 'Student' and then this will all be official, alright?"

"Sounds great!"

"Yes ma'am…"

Putting pen to paper suddenly made everything feel much more real for Rhen (even more so than handling that stupid paddle had), but like her adviser had already said.

She didn't really have a choice in the matter.

"Excellent," chirped Doctor Holloway, setting the paper aside to scan in later after she too had affixed her signature to the bottom of it. "And now that that's been taken care of, all we have left to do now is deal with your one outstanding discipline referral, Rhen. After that you and your aunt can be on your way. I'm sure you're both ready to get something to eat by now. I know I sure am."

"Tell me about it- Wait, *what*?" demanded Rhen, completely aghast. "The semester hasn't even started yet! How the heck do I already have a referral?"

"Well, you *were* over twenty minutes late to our meeting this morning, you know," pointed out her professor patiently, gesturing back at the clock on the wall behind her before retrieving a now familiar form from the drawer where the paddle had come from. "I took the liberty of filling this out for you while I waited."

Of course you did.

"Ahhh, good thinking, Jane," Rhen's aunt nodded in approval, settling back in her seat once again to enjoy the upcoming show. "The sooner she gets used to these new rules, the better, I say."

"Exactly! Consistency is key when it comes to discipline."

That's easy to say when you're not the one getting disciplined... Humph.

Stomach roiling with anticipatory dread and no small amount of embarrassment, Rhen tried to think of something to say that would save her seat from being scorched. But, after a moment or two more of indignant spluttering and failed attempts to rouse a defense, she knew it was time to throw in the towel.

"Ugh! Okay *fine*," she harrumphed, exhaling forcefully as she rose to her feet with what little dignity she still had left. "How do we do this?"

The pleasant smile on her face growing slightly more strained, Doctor Holloway rose from her seat as well and gestured to the corner of her desk directly in front of where Rhen now stood.

"Bend over right there, please," she ordered, picking up her paddle and circling around to her student's left flank as she flopped down onto her elbows with a truly impressive roll of her eyes, positioning her body at a near perfect ninety-degree angle for punishment.

Seeing that her form still bore a considerable amount of sass to it, however, Doctor Holloway gave the center of her hips an admonishing pat with her paddle.

"Legs straight, knees together, and palms flat on the desk in front of you, young lady."

Realizing then that it was probably a very bad idea to continue antagonizing her soon to be spanker, Rhen quickly adjusted her stance.

And her attitude.

"Sorry ma'am!" she squeaked, ponytail bobbing animatedly with her apology.

"Much better," her adviser crooned, setting her paddle aside after one more pat and taking hold of the hem of her pleated skirt. "Now we'll just get this out of the way…"

Of course, it was at that exact moment, as her professor's fingers were tightening around the material in her hand, that Rhen remembered just what her partner had picked out for her to wear that morning.

Oh god, here we go…

Suiting actions to words, Doctor Holloway lifted the back of her skirt up past her hips and folded it over onto the small of her back. Revealing a pair of truly adorable pink and white striped cotton panties with portraits of Disney princesses, hearts, and flowers printed in an explosive array of pastel pinks and baby blues all across their taut surface.

"Oh my. Now these are certainly… Ahem. *Cute*," she observed diplomatically, very clearly doing her best to hold in a laugh as she paused to admire the unexpectedly juvenile pair of panties while Rhen's face flushed hot enough to light the desk beneath her on fire.

"Aren't they, though?" mused Dana, drawing out the words as she too enjoyed the darling display, every curve of her not-niece's round, chubby cheeks standing out in stark relief beneath the snug cotton. "She *really* needed a new wardrobe when she first moved in with me. So many of her old clothes were ratty and falling apart, and if I'm being totally honest, were also a bit on the skimpy side for a girl her age. So we decided to just toss it all out and start fresh from the beginning. And, well…"

A crocodile grin spread across her face then, one that was mirrored a moment later by the very amused adviser.

"I just couldn't resist buying her underwear that was a bit more, shall we say, in line with her behavior. Honestly, they fit her way too well *not* to get them. Plus, I figured that if she was going to be taking regular trips across my lap anyway, she might as well look extra cute while doing it."

"Hmmm… That seems like pretty sound reasoning to me," agreed the dark-haired professor, letting loose with a low, throaty chuckle this time. "I must say, I wasn't expecting to be hit with such a heavy dose of déjà vu today. If I didn't know any better, I'd swear I was looking at the caboose of one of my old middle schoolers right about now."

"You don't say?" snickered Dana. "Maybe you ought to just put her over your knee then?"

"I'm sorely tempted to, believe you me."

"Oh, hardy-har-har," grumbled Rhen, doing a poor job of actually sounding all that upset by the comparison even as she gave her hair an irritated flip. "Do you think you two could stop staring at my butt already? I know it's cute and all, but some of us still have things they'd like to do today."

"Yes, I suppose we really ought to get a move on," sighed Doctor Holloway wistfully, picking up her paddle once again and lining it up with the centers of her student's princess-patterned peaches, giving them a couple of firm taps as she got a feel for her aim. "Though, now that you mention it, we really should decide how many swats constitute a 'normal' paddling for you, Miss Mathews."

"Um… How about, like, three?" Rhen suggested hopefully, earning herself an extra-firm pat in the process.

"I appreciate the vote of confidence, my dear, but I'm afraid I can't swing quite *that* hard," chided her adviser lightheartedly.

"And, even if I could, we're aiming for tender cheeks, not shattered coccyx. So, we're going to need a higher number than that."

"Okay, fine," sassed Rhen in reply, unable to stop herself. "Four."

"Heh. I knew there was a reason why I kept 'talking back' as one of the options on your referrals."

The reminder of those forms, only a few inches away from her nose now, was enough to stifle any more witty comebacks that might've been brewing inside of Rhen.

"How many swats did you usually give back at your old school?" asked Dana then before she could get herself into any more trouble. "If it helps, our church uses a child's age to determine how many swats they should receive."

"You know, that's not a bad idea," mused the other woman with a contemplative frown. "Although, then we'd have the opposite issue of too many swats."

At that she gave Rhen's cheeks a couple of light pops.

POP. POP.

Pops that had her exhaling sharply in surprise with how much they stung even through her panties.

"Twenty-one swats for being late is a little much given that it's only her first offense. Even if she *was* extremely late."

"Yes, I suppose that's true," nodded Dana, now also frowning as she rubbed her chin.

"You might be on to something with your earlier suggestion, though," the adviser continued, brightening once again. "For our high school students, we used their grade to determine how many swats they would receive. That way, the older they got, and ostensibly the more they should know not to act up in the first place, the more appropriately severe their punishment would be."

"Makes sense."

"I'm glad you see it my way," she chuckled. "Now, even though Rhen doesn't technically have a proper grade number anymore, if we simply extrapolate out from twelfth grade by adding one for her freshman, sophomore, and junior years, we get fifteen.

Which sounds like just the right amount of swats to me."

"Are you *sure* we can't just do twelve?" the shorter girl pressed, heart fluttering anxiously inside her chest as she shifted her weight from one foot to the other in a vain attempt to get more comfortable.

POP.

"Oh!"

"Nope, I'm afraid not, dear," replied her adviser sweetly. "But I'd be more than happy to tack on a few additional swats for sass if you'd like."

"No thanks! Fifteen is fine!"

"Hmmm… I like the positive attitude," the other woman crooned, still easy and conversational as she pressed the hard, unyielding length of polished wood against her intended target. "But I think we'll still include an extra swat just to be on the safe side."

"Humph. Whatev-" the bent over twenty-one-year-old turned teenager began to huff out in reply.

WHOOSH-SMACK!

Only be cut off mid-harrumph as the pressure against her backside suddenly vanished. Being replaced half a heartbeat later by a jarring, high-speed meteor strike of an impact that forced her up onto the balls of her feet as a rectangular bar of molten fury exploded across the centers of both her cheeks at the exact same time.

"Urk! Oh my god, *owww*," she moaned, hissing in air through clenched teeth and slapping her palms against the desktop beneath her as she fought down the urge to reach back and rub her still boiling backside. "You could have mentioned you were about to start, you know!"

"I believe the response you're looking for, young lady, is 'One. Thank you, ma'am'," supplied her adviser evenly, punctuating her reply with another firm pat from her paddle.

Oh crap…

Rhen could already tell that Doctor Holloway hadn't been

bluffing about her skills as a disciplinarian. And, what was worse, she wasn't holding back in the slightest either! Even with her panties still (mercifully) up around her hips to absorb the initial biting sting of the paddle's impact, their thin material had done absolutely nothing to negate the sheer amount of force that it had brought with it.

Or the lingering, smoldering heat now settling in across her cheeks.

"One. Thank you, ma'am!"

"Much better."

WHOOSH-SMACK!

"Owie, owie, owie!"

Her adviser also hadn't been exaggerating about those darn holes increasing the effectiveness of her swats either. Apparently, cutting down on wind resistance really did have a serious *impact* on paddle performance.

"T-Two. Thank you, ma'am!"

Part of Rhen's brain immediately latched onto that idea in an effort to not dwell on the fact that her bottom was already throbbing after only two swats. But, unfortunately for her, the burning in her backside was a lot more pressing than her halfhearted attempts to estimate angular momentum and drag coefficients in her head.

"My goodness, you are a wriggly one, aren't you, dear?"

WHOOSH-SMACK!

Once again bringing her paddle crashing down in a smooth, fluid arc, pivoting her hips as she did so and following through like a pro, Doctor Holloway managed to get her first proper howl out of her student as she layered her third swat atop the full centers of both her cheeks.

"Th-Three... Thank you, ma'am..."

"*Breathe*," she admonished gently, noticing the way Rhen was tensing up as she did her best to ride out the pain from this latest impact. "Trying to tough things out will only make it worse."

"Yes ma'am..." sighed the younger girl, her taut muscles

gradually loosening themselves as she did as her professor had ordered, feeling more than a little silly at having to be told to do so in the first place.

It wasn't like this was her first paddling after all!

Tossing her hair with another heavy sigh, she readjusted her stance until she was the very model of obedient submission.

"Awww, I knew you could be a good girl for me," praised Doctor Holloway, taking aim a few inches further south now as she prepared for her next swat. "Now, hang on tight. We've still got a long way to go, I'm afraid."

WHOOSH-SMACK!

—

Although her adviser continued to not show even the slightest amount of mercy as she meted out the rest of her punishment, cracking her paddle against the back of her panties like a hammer on an anvil every ten to fifteen seconds, Rhen was able to take it (mostly) in stride. With each impact she rose up onto the balls of her feet, squealed out a yelp of pain, sounded off whatever number they were on with the appropriate amount of gratitude, and then eased back down onto her heels with a haggard sigh as she began mentally preparing herself for the next one.

It was beyond unpleasant, and totally humiliating to say the least (somehow, getting it over her extremely childish panties made it even worse than if she'd just been bare bottomed), but she knew for a fact that it could always be worse.

Doctor Holloway was absolutely relentless in her paddling, but the actual paddle itself wasn't nearly so heavy as The Board was, which in turn made it infinitely more bearable. Sure, it still stung like crazy. Especially with those stupid holes to help speed up its descent. But, since it was relatively light and thin (not so much as that awful paddleball racket Jill had used on her had been, but close enough for it to make a difference), it instead only seared her skin, rather than penetrating down into the deep tissue of her cheeks in a way that would leave them sore well into the following day.

Instead, her bottom was just going to be tender to the touch all afternoon.

By the time the sixteenth, and final, swat had found its home against the back of her panties, blending in with the rest of the all-encompassing sea of flames that was her swollen, steaming bottom just then, Rhen was panting heavily and fully determined to go over every single email she received from that point on with a fine-tooth comb.

"S… Sixteen. Thank you, ma'am…"

"Think that's going to be enough to help you get to class on time from here on out, young lady?" pressed Doctor Holloway not unkindly, eying the splash of bright red peeking out from under where her panties had ridden up between her cheeks during the course of her punishment.

"Oh my god, yes ma'am! For *sure*!"

"Great!" she chirped, setting her paddle back down onto the desk beside her and holding out her arms, not a single trace of sternness to be found in her demeanor now. "In that case, we're done. Now get on up and give me a hug, kiddo."

Not bothering to adjust her skirt as she pushed herself away from the now slightly sweaty desk, leaving her panties completely exposed in back to hopefully cool off a bit more, Rhen turned and threw herself into her adviser's arms, hugging her tight while she did the same. As awkward as such an idea might have seemed to her just an hour earlier, Rhen had long since found that getting spanked silly by someone who cared for her had a tendency to endear them to her rather a lot.

"You took that very well," Doctor Holloway praised, patting her back reassuringly as she clung to the front of her blouse, clearly used to such reactions from her recently rehabilitated students.

"You sure did," agreed Dana, sounding just as proud as she stood to join them, enveloping her not-niece in a hug from behind as well.

Rhen let out a small hiss at the sudden press of warm, firm thighs against her smarting cheeks, but trapped as she was between the two older women, she had no other choice but to do her best to ignore it. An act which was easier said than done, considering that her bottom was still sensitive enough that any amount of even grazing contact with it was enough to set off a fresh wave of soreness.

Sitting down for lunch (let alone actually driving to the restaurant they'd picked out earlier) was *not* going to be fun.

"Ah! Um, th-thanks, you guys…"

After a couple seconds more cuddling, Dana and her adviser disentangled themselves from around her frame, and while her aunt busied herself with readjusting her skirt (taking advantage of the opportunity to pull her panties down in back for a quick inspection of the state of her rosy cheeks as she did so), Doctor Holloway retrieved a three ring binder from yet another drawer inside her desk. One with the words "PUNISHMENT LOG" printed in bold black letters on a sheet of printer paper that had been affixed to its front.

"Now then, if you would be so kind as to sign here where it says 'Student'," she said, her tone breezy and efficient as she laid the binder out where Rhen had just been bending over, flipping it open to the first page where she'd already copied over all of the pertinent details from her discipline referral. "You two can be on your way."

Grimacing, her stomach fluttering with fresh butterflies as she took in the meticulously laid out ledger before her, Rhen found her sassy side rearing its head once again.

"Ugh. Do we seriously need to keep a record of every single time I get spanked?" she demanded, pushing her lips out into a pout even as her cheeks gave a warning throb beneath her skirt.

That paddle was still sitting on top of her adviser's desk, after all.

"Having clear and comprehensive analytical data to draw conclusions from is important, young lady," Doctor Holloway replied simply, holding out a pen to her. "*Especially* when it comes to disciplinary action. Having each incident documented like this will allow me to catalogue and analyze what areas you might be struggling with so that I can more effectively help you in the future."

"Oh, um… Huh. I guess that makes sense," the younger girl found herself conceding, the computer scientist inside of her also very interested to see what kinds of insights into her behavior her punishment log would yield as time went on. "Just promise not to show this to anyone, alright?"

"Of course, dear," nodded her adviser sweetly. "This stays between you, me, and your aunt."

As she said that, though, her brows furrowed introspectively.

"Then again… Now that I think about it, I'm sure there are probably quite a few grad students doing dissertations on childhood and adolescent development who would be *very* interested in what we end up documenting here…"

Hearing that made Rhen's cheeks clench on reflex beneath her skirt, which in turn made her squeak as they gave another angry twinge in protest.

"That, uh…"

Swallowing hard and doing her best to will the flush in her cheeks to go away, she briefly considered demanding once again that her disciplinary history be kept confidential. But, catching sight of the paddle lying on top the desk only a half a foot or so from her log had her deciding that it wasn't worth the hassle. Even before this whole Academic Action Plan thing had taken shape, she'd already had a reputation as some sort of early high school grad with an attitude problem among her fellow students. A reputation that had only been further exacerbated by Courtney's frequent (and less than subtle) promises to tan her hide if she didn't behave herself back when she'd been her TA. To say nothing of the *very* public bare bottom spanking that Dana had given her the night she'd moved out of the dorms.

It was already an open secret on campus that she was a brat who had her sassy seat warmed for her whenever she needed it, so at this point she figured she might as well share her data with those who could make good use of it.

Hey, maybe I'll even get some credit in their papers? That could definitely help with grad school applications, right?

"Okay, fine, whatever," she harrumphed with a good-natured smirk, bending over and taking her time signing her name in order to give her hands something to do besides massage her bottom while she ignored the knowing looks from the two older women standing beside her. "If you think it'll help, go ahead and let them have access to it, I guess."

"Sure thing, kiddo," replied Doctor Holloway, giving her tush a fond pat as she stepped past her on her way to return her paddle back to its home inside her desk.

"Eep!"

Shooting back up to a standing position with her hands clamped protectively to the back of her skirt, an action which only served to further remind her how sore her bottom was as she danced in place, Rhen directed her most powerful pout at her adviser, resisting the urge to return her smile with every fiber of her being.

"Have a wonderful rest of your day, Miss Mathews. I look forward to seeing you next Friday," she said smoothly, dismissing her with a nod as she shared a grin with her aunt. "Oh, and don't be late."

Chapter 16

A Double Dose of English Discipline

That weekend found Rhen back at Missus Hastings's house a couple hours after breakfast Saturday morning. Upon arriving and giving the old woman a hug, submitting to a forehead kiss, and downing a cup of hot cocoa while she enjoyed her mid-morning tea (as was their tradition now), she'd been turned loose outside with a firm pat to the seat of her short-shorts and orders to mow the grass, whack the weeds, and water the plants in the back garden.

"Hop along now, child. No dilly-dallying!"

"Sure thing!"

"Oh, and Rhen?"

"Uh… Yes ma'am?"

"Do try and make a proper job of it this time. I don't want to see any sloppy lines out there once you're finished."

"R-Right!"

By now, Rhen was pretty familiar with the lay of the land in her neighbor's front and back yards, and though her lawnmower and weed-whacker were both positively ancient and heavier than any piece of gardening equipment had any right to be, she still was able to knock out two of the three tasks she'd been given in only a couple of hours. Though, by the time she was finished clearing out the last of the seemingly perpetual horde of weeds that were constantly encroaching their way into the gardens in the back yard (and had dragged the overstuffed bag of grass clippings out to the curb for the garbage man to collect on Monday), her poor arms felt like they were about ready to fall off and her palms were positively throbbing from constantly being rattled around by motor vibrations.

But, on the bright side, Missus Hastings's lawn looked absolutely pristine.

You know, if college doesn't work out, I might just have a career in landscaping...

"Phew!"

Flopping out on her back beneath the sprawling shade of a tall oak, breathing in deep the earthy scents of freshly cut grass and her own sweat, Rhen spent several long, blissful minutes just lying there catching her breath. Drifting along amid a melody of birdsong, the occasional low rumble of a car passing by her neighbor's house, and the distant din of children playing in the park up the street as she watched the bright blue sky through the gently shifting leafy canopy overhead.

"God, I'm beat..."

It wasn't quite noon yet, and already the summer sun and thick humidity were taking their toll. Making her sweat like she'd just finished running a marathon and wish desperately that the breeze would pick up already as she plucked languidly at her half-soaked tank top. Despite all that, though, she didn't really mind. Her grandma had always said that hard work built character, and truth be told, she really rather enjoyed these weekly opportunities to simply zone out and sweat. They were an excellent workout and always helped to clear her head.

Plus, Missus Hastings (or rather, *Nana* Hastings as she insisted she call her) was really nice and always baked some truly out of this world desserts for her every time she came to visit.

Living as far away as she did, Rhen only ever got to see her actual grandmother around Thanksgiving or Christmas these days, and she missed her dearly. Oh, they still talked on the phone about once every other week or so, and she'd recently had success teaching her how to video conference, but that just wasn't the same as actually getting to spend time with her in person. So she was more than happy to indulge her neighbor by filling in as her surrogate grandchild on the weekends. Even if she *was* a bit of a strict taskmaster who enjoyed prodding her along with a friendly swat or two where needed.

Or just when she wasn't looking.

"Heh. Speaking of…"

Rolling over onto her stomach and pushing herself back to her feet on a pair of tired (though, thankfully, no longer leaden) legs, Rhen slowly began trudging off toward the coiled length of dark green garden hose her neighbor kept near the back porch of her house.

"Okay, Rhen, get it together! Just one more thing, and then you're done for the day," she told herself, doing her best to psyche some energy back into her sun-drained body as she gave her face a couple light slaps. "Let's do this!"

With her stomach already rumbling in anticipation of lunch and whatever freshly baked treat she'd be helping her neighbor prepare that afternoon, she eased down onto her heels before the hose spigot and gave its handle a firm, counterclockwise twist.

And was immediately hit in the face by a pressurized burst of water!

"Ack! Blech!"

Stumbling back with a surprised laugh, Rhen belatedly brought her arms up to shield her already soaking face. And, as the flow of water from the spigot started to level out, she found herself caught up in a strong wave of nostalgia for summers long past back at her grandma's house in the country.

Which gave her an absolutely fantastic idea.

"Hmmm… I mean, I *am* already sweaty and kinda soaked," she reasoned aloud. "So I might as well, right?"

Nodding to herself, answering her own rhetorical question with a lopsided grin (after all, there was no way she *wasn't* going to do it now that she'd thought of it), Rhen snatched up the business end of the burbling hose from off the ground where it was soaking her sneakers and began drifting off in the general direction of the dark swathes of rich brown dirt that comprised Missus Hastings's modest flower beds and vegetable patch. As she walked, uncoiling the hose by dragging it behind her through the neatly cut grass without paying the slightest bit of attention as to whether or not it snagged on anything, she pointed the nozzle in her hand up toward the sky and placed her thumb over the top of it, creating her own impromptu summer shower as a steady geyser of pressurized water shot up into the air above her head.

"Ah!" she gasped with another giggle as the first pitter-pattering droplets of hose-warmed rain exploded against her forehead and sweat-soaked locks, sending a delighted shiver down her spine.

Oh yeah, this was definitely the right call.

Soon enough, her hair was totally drenched and plastered to her face and neck, and the brief and breezy outfit that Dana had picked out for her that morning was completely soaked through to her skin, showing off the cute pink bralette she had on underneath her white tank top. But, again, she didn't mind. The lukewarm water fountaining forth from the hose was a blessed relief in the face of the incessant heat of the noontime sun beating down on top of her, filling her with fresh energy as she caught her second wind.

As she began meandering her way back and forth between the rows of flowers and leafy green vegetable stalks, soaking them and herself in turn as she whistled *I'm Singing in the Rain* (she knew it was a bit cliché, but she just couldn't help herself), Rhen made sure to take plenty of breaks to splash around in the mud puddles she was creating. After all, playing in the rain was fun! And before too long, she was digging her toes deep into the wet dirt and kicking as hard as she could to see how high and far she could get the mud to fly, in between skidding along the slick earth on just one foot while pretending to be a figure skater.

It was an absolute blast, and Rhen found herself seriously starting to wonder why it was that she hadn't played in the *actual* rain in so long.

"Oomph!"

That is, at least up until the point when her feet slipped out from under her and she wound up plopping face first into the muddy garden.

Okay. Maybe it's time to reel it in just a little bit...

Clawing her way back to her feet, spluttering and spitting out dirt and leaves from her mouth as she wiped away great big globs of mud from her face and front (feeling suddenly very grateful for her neighbor's rule about leaving her phone in the kitchen while she was doing chores so that she wouldn't get distracted), Rhen picked up the hose from where it had landed after her tumble, puffed out her cheeks as she took in a deep breath through her nose, shut her eyes tight, and sprayed herself point-blank right in the face.

"Whargabarble- Blech!"

It wasn't exactly a pleasant sensation, but it at least got all of the grit and grime off of her forehead and cheeks. And, after letting out the breath she'd been holding with an embarrassed laugh, she slowly began working her way down her front, arms, and legs.

Only to have the flow of water abruptly be cut off just as she was reaching the tops of her thighs.

Uh-oh. That can't possibly be good.

"Good gracious, child! What on earth are you doing out here?"

Yep. Definitely not good.

"Oh, uh… Hey, Nana Hastings," Rhen answered with a sheepish grin, dropping the useless hose at her feet and slowly turning to face the older woman as she stalked toward her, still wearing her apron and looking more than a little miffed. "I was just, you know… finishing up watering the plants and I, uh… kinda slipped."

"Slipped, is it?" replied her neighbor, her voice holding a mixture of amusement and patent disbelief as she ran a critical eye over her drenched and dripping form. "I dare say you did a good deal more than just 'slip', my dear. Why, just look at the state of you. You're positively *filthy*!"

"Oh, come on, it's not that, uh… bad," Rhen started to argue, before trailing off as she glanced down at her outfit again and saw that it was still stained a nearly uniform shade of brown all across its front despite her best efforts to wash it clean with the hose. "Er… Uh, yeah… Okay, I think I see what you mean."

"I should certainly hope so, you naughty thing. It looks as if you've been having a bloomin' mud bath out here with a sty full of pigs!"

"Well, I mean…"

Rhen paused for several seconds then as she struggled to find her words, acutely aware of the trail of sweat trickling its way down the small of her back as she continued to wilt beneath her neighbor's expectant gaze. The bright, noontime sun picking out the strands of silver in her hair and making them sparkle.

"I guess I was kinda, sorta, *maybe* playing just a little bit, but-"

"More than a little, I'd say," countered her adoptive grand-mother sharply, her frown deepening as she gestured at the water-logged garden behind her. "Not only are you a mess, but you've also managed to just about drown my poor petunias in the pro-cess. And would you look at that fence!"

"Fence?"

Feeling her stomach starting to sink from "this is bad" to "oh crap, oh crap this is *really* bad!", Rhen reluctantly dragged her attention away from the front pocket of her neighbor's lace apron and over toward where she was pointing.

"Oh."

Missus Hastings's formerly pristine privacy fence seemed to have developed a rather avant-garde splatter pattern to it.

"Okay, hold on. I can explain!"

"Can you now?" the older woman pressed, the creases around her eyes crinkling in wry amusement.

"Yeah, no, you see, the thing is-"

"You do realize that I have a window that looks directly out onto the back garden from my kitchen, don't you?"

"I um…"

Rhen swallowed.

"I did not."

Crap.

"More's the pity for you then, I suppose."

With her face flushing hot enough to make the water still clinging to her brow surely start to steam at any moment, Rhen tried to think of something to say that would explain away the huge mess she'd made. But, considering that her neighbor had most likely been watching her that entire time, she decided that it was probably a much safer bet to just fess up and face the music. She wasn't sure how Nana Hastings handled fibbing in her house, but she had a feeling she probably wouldn't enjoy finding out if she tried to be too selective with the truth just then.

"I'm in trouble, aren't I?"

"Yes, indeed you are, my girl," nodded her neighbor, before her face broke out in a sly, playful grin. "Fortunately for you, though, I have something right here in the garden that ought to smarten you up in a hurry."

"Oh boy, here we go…"

Already resigned to her fate (but unwilling to fully submit to it without at least *some* grumbling), the petite junior let out a sigh and cast her gaze about for a likely looking bush or tree.

"Let me guess. Is it a switch?"

"Switch?"

Frowning in puzzlement, Missus Hastings started looking left and then right just as Rhen was doing, before stopping herself a moment later with a laugh.

"Oh no, dear, I was thinking of something else entirely. But, now that you mention it…"

Stepping past the befuddled (and still highly embarrassed) twenty-one-year-old turned teenager, she moved over to the vegetable patch that she'd recently face-planted into and plucked from the ground a long, thin bamboo rod that looked like it had once been part of a tomato trellis. Giving it a sharp flick and sending a dirt clod or two flying toward the fence as she did so.

"I suppose a stiff dose of the cane wouldn't go awry right about now either."

"Wait a minute, a cane?" squeaked Rhen, feeling equal parts confused and nervous as the whippy rod in her neighbor's hand swished menacingly back and forth through the air beside her. "Where are we going? And, um… Isn't that thing kinda thin for you to be leaning on?"

Her tentative questions prompted Missus Hastings to let out another laugh, long and hard this time as she clutched her sides and trembled with mirth, before eventually wiping away a tear from her eye and flashing the shorter girl another one of her trademark motherly smiles.

"I believe what you are thinking of, dear, is a walking stick."

She then flexed the long length of bamboo between her hands, bending it into an upside down letter U.

"*This* is a cane. And, judging by the feel of it, it's one that ought to be able to paint some right proper tram lines across that soggy bottom of yours."

"Great…" deadpanned Rhen, not quite sure what trains had to do with anything they were talking about just then, but willing to bet that it was probably something unpleasant.

Haven't any of you people ever heard of, like, a hairbrush or a belt before? Geez.

Shifting her weight from one foot to the other with a wet squelch, she crossed her arms over her muddy front and stuck out her tongue.

"Or would you prefer I say it's 'jolly good'?"

"Pip pip! Cheerio! Two and a quarter pence," teased Missus Hastings with a benevolent smirk. "You Americans do rather enjoy your Mary Poppins caricatures, don't you?"

"Maybe," harrumphed Rhen, hiding her embarrassment behind a pout. "I'd definitely prefer a spoonful of sugar to whatever the heck that stupid thing is, at least. Humph."

"Oh, I'm well aware," snorted her neighbor. "I've seen how many marshmallows you add to your cocoa."

That managed to bring a grudging half-grin to the shorter girl's lips despite her attempts to stay sullen and grouchy. Even when she was in trouble with her, there was just something about the silver-haired old woman standing before her with her improvised implement of disciple in hand that never failed to make her smile.

"Yeah, yeah…"

Rolling her eyes, Rhen uncrossed her arms and planted her hands on her hips, heaving out her best aggrieved sigh and playing her role as the bratty granddaughter to the best of her ability. After all, if she was going to be punished like one (which, truth be told, she probably deserved), then she was going to embrace the moment come what may, attitude and all.

"So, uh… What do I do? Bend over?"

"For starters you can take those hands off of your hips," sniffed Missus Hastings. "You're not a teapot, are you, girl?"

"Well, I *am* short," smartmouthed the petite junior without missing a beat. "But I don't think you can really call me stout."

"Young lady…"

"Sorry, sorry!"

Sensing that she was about to topple head over heels across that razor-thin line dividing her current upcoming punishment from a much, *much* worse one, Rhen quickly pulled her hands away from her hips. Clasping them respectfully behind her back instead as she did her best to look sweet and innocent.

"I was just joking, ma'am."

"Yes, I'm sure you were," replied Missus Hastings dryly, pinning her in place with an admonishing stare that only held the barest amount of actual annoyance before offering the mud-clumped end of the garden cane to her. "Now, you just hold onto this for me. There's still something I need to collect before we begin."

"There is?" replied Rhen with another squeak, leaning away from the ridged rod as if it were some sort of poisonous serpent.

"Of course," nodded her neighbor as if that were already obvious. "Caning your impertinent backside wasn't actually what I had in mind for your punishment. But, since you brought it up,

I don't see the harm in taking this opportunity to acquaint you with yet another fine English tradition while we're in the process of correcting your bad behavior."

Her lips turned up into a teasing smirk then.

"Plenty of schoolgirls back in my day got the cane when they chose to be naughty. And if it worked then, it'll certainly work now."

Ugh. Me and my big freaking mouth.

"I guess you might have a point there," conceded Rhen with a grimace, suddenly finding something at her feet terribly interesting as her cheeks flared with fresh warmth. "But, um… Are you sure they used it on *college* schoolgirls?"

She knew that appealing to her actual age with Missus Hastings was a long shot, and could backfire on her spectacularly if she wasn't careful, but she just couldn't help herself. Apparently, her fiancé had revealed a lot more than the old woman had originally let on during that initial phone call all those weeks ago when she'd crashed her bike into her car, because after she'd returned from their vacation last weekend, she'd immediately spotted her engagement ring and had congratulated her on her upcoming marriage without batting an eye.

And had then promptly turned her over her knee right there in the kitchen for "skipping" her chores the week before.

"A schoolgirl is still a schoolgirl, regardless of what form she's in, young lady," Missus Hastings said with a brisk air of finality, putting an end to her fleeting hopes with a wink. "But if you'd like a smacked bottom before you go home this afternoon as well, I'd be more than happy to oblige."

"No, no, that's fine!" Rhen quickly reassured her, hands flying out from behind her back to wave away the idea.

"Well, if you're sure…"

"I *definitely* am. Trust me."

"Very well then," crooned her neighbor, still with a mischievous twinkle in her eye as she wiggled the cane before her once again. "In that case, be a dear and take this, would you? As much as I might enjoy it, we really can't spend all day dealing with your naughtiness. I still need to prepare lunch, you know."

"Oh! Um, right!"

Moving on autopilot, Rhen did as she was told, feeling her stomach explode into a cloud of butterflies as she wrapped her fingers around the thick wood of the cane.

Oh god, I swear it wasn't this big just a second ago...

It was only about the width of her thumb, but as she surreptitiously flexed it in between her hands, she had a sneaking suspicion that that was probably going to be more than enough to draw train tracks across her butt or whatever it was that her neighbor had said she was going to do to her.

"There's a good lass," crooned the elderly woman, tapping the tip of her nose playfully. "Now you just run along and wash that off. I'd rather not get your bum all dirty."

Her smirk returned to her then, and she raised a teasing brow.

"Well, dirtier."

Dismissing her with a wave, she finished by saying.

"While you're attending to that, I'll prepare the ginger."

Now *that* managed to catch Rhen's attention.

"G-Ginger?" she demanded with a start, already knowing where the other woman was most likely headed and feeling her damp cheeks clench beneath her clinging shorts as a result. "You don't mean..?"

"Oh? Have you been figged before, then?" asked Missus Hastings, sounding surprised.

At Rhen's continued, comically horror-stricken look, she nodded to herself with a highly amused chuckle.

"Well now, that *is* a surprise. I didn't think anyone still used ginger as a punishment these days. Certainly not over here, at any rate."

"Yeah, well," Rhen finally managed to huff out in response, not needing to pretend to sound petulant this time as her face went crimson with memories of her Thanksgiving break the year before. "My grandma is, uh..."

She realized only then as she was speaking that she was coming dangerously close to divulging some truly humiliating details about what had happened when she'd tried to pretend that she was too sick to go look at Christmas lights with her family last November. And, with a fresh pout, cut herself off.

"She, uh… Yeah. She's definitely more old fashioned than most people, I'd say."

"Is that right?" drawled her neighbor, her grin growing wider and wider by the moment. "Well then, this ought to be old hat for you, my dear."

Laughing to herself, she turned and began moving off in the direction of her vegetable patch.

"Go on now. Off you pop," she admonished breezily. "Clean up that cane and then park yourself in front of the wall next to the back door. I'll be around to deal with you once I've finished preparing the rest of what we'll need for your punishment."

"Ugh. Yes, Nana Hastings…"

—

Not at all eager to take up her position in time out, Rhen spent as long as she felt she safely could preparing the garden cane for its impending date with her backside. Using her hands to work away as much of the clumped on dirt clinging to its smooth-grained surface as she could, she gave it (and herself where she was still muddy) a thorough going over with the hose, rinsing it repeatedly until it looked and felt practically brand new. Unfortunately for her, though, her attention to detail also brought with it an unsettlingly intimate familiarity with every stupid inch of the whippy stick. Which ensured that by the time she finally set it on top of her neighbor's patio table and moved to face the wall with her hands on her head, she was a mess of conflicting emotions and thigh-squirming, cheek-clenching, knee-wobbling dread.

Those ridges definitely looked like they were going to *hurt*.

But, even so, she also couldn't deny that she was more than a little curious to see what her bottom would look like once her neighbor was through thrashing it. If the cane was anything like a switch, then it was sure to leave some very pretty (and exceptionally tender) marks for Dana to kiss better when she tucked her into bed later that evening. Assuming, that is, she didn't decide to reignite them with a pre-bedtime blistering of her own.

Either way, she knew for certain that she'd be sleeping on her stomach with her pull-up holding in whatever heat was still left smoldering in her seat when all was said and done that night.

Oof. Sitting for services tomorrow is going to suck.

Luckily, Rhen wasn't left to stew in her worries and mounting excitement for very long. For seemingly no sooner had she settled in to wait beside the slightly ajar back door, than it swung open once again and Missus Hastings stepped out onto the concrete patio holding a paper plate with a freshly carved ginger root set atop it.

Oh crap...

Though she had only ever been subjected to this particular punishment the one time (which was still way more than enough as far as she was concerned!), as the fretful twenty-one-year-old turned teenager stared balefully over her shoulder, watching as her neighbor sauntered over to the wicker patio table and set her paper plate down next to where she'd left the garden cane waiting for her, she could already tell that Missus Hastings knew *exactly* what she was doing when it came to figging. And, even worse, that she wasn't planning on going easy on her in the slightest.

The piece of ginger that she'd selected to drive home her disappointment with her landscaping decorum had been expertly pared into a tapered plug that flared out to nearly twice the width of her pinky near its middle, before curving back down again into a ringed divot near its rounded base that would prevent it from slipping free or sliding too deep inside of her once it was in place. Granted, it wasn't anywhere near as large as what she was used to taking from Dana.

But still.

She knew that what the deceptively innocent looking length of glistening, oil-saturated ginger might lack in size, it would more than make up for in raw, unadulterated, burning fury.

"Now don't you go pulling faces with me, child," her neighbor scolded while wagging an admonishing forefinger in her direction, clearly trying to look serious even as traces of a thin, satisfied smile tugged up on the corners of her mouth. "You have only yourself to blame for what's about to happen, and you know it."

Part of Rhen was incredibly tempted to fire back with something sassy as she turned away from her vigil facing the wall, remembering only at the last second to stop her hands from wandering too close to her hips as she did so and instead dragging one through her dark hair while rolling her eyes. Being witty and seeing how far she could push things before getting into even more trouble was always fun, but considering that she was already facing what was likely to be a pretty severe punishment as is, she opted instead to heave out a long sigh and nod her head with the bare minimum amount of expected obedience.

"Yes ma'am, you're totally right. It's completely unbecoming of a proper young lady and all that jazz."

Well, she *had* said "ma'am", hadn't she?

That counted as being obedient, didn't it?

"I couldn't have put it better myself," replied Missus Hastings with an affected, haughty sniff that managed to partially cover her snort of amusement. "To think that at your age you would *still* need to be dealt with in such a manner. Why, it's no wonder you keep your poor aunt as busy as you do. Running around like a little rapscallion. I tell you, it's absolutely inexcusable!"

Despite her best efforts to at least (sort of) appear contrite, that still managed to get an unrepentant smirk out of Rhen.

Now who's the one channeling their inner Mary Poppins?

"Oh? Is there something you find amusing about being naughty, girl?"

"Of course not, ma'am," she replied lazily, stifling her snicker behind a hand while using the other to gesture for her to continue. "I uh… Something was just tickling my nose is all."

"Was it now?"

"Yep, totally. Go on, I'm listening. You were saying something about how I shouldn't make faces? Or was it that I shouldn't be running with onions?"

Missus Hastings's perfunctory frown deepened significantly then, and Rhen thought that she might've maybe pushed things just a bit too far with her attitude. Until, that is, the old woman let out an exasperated sigh of her own and shook her head, muttering under her breath about needing strength from above before fixing her in place with another pleasant, motherly smile.

Then she *knew* she'd stepped into it.

Big time.

"Right then, you little madam. If that's the way you wish to act, then so be it."

She jabbed a finger at a spot just in front of Rhen's tennis shoes then, and her tone grew suddenly steely.

"Strip."

"Strip?" squeaked shorter girl, that one, single word sending a cascade of tingles down her spine and between her legs.

"I am not in the habit of repeating myself, Rhen Elizabeth," her neighbor replied coolly, crossing her arms in front of her apron and tapping a foot impatiently as she waited for her to comply.

"But… but…" stammered a now profoundly flustered Rhen, her gaze darting toward the second story windows of the surrounding houses that all had a clear view into her neighbor's back yard. "But someone might see!"

That managed to at least put a crack in the old woman's stern facade. Unfortunately, it only revealed amusement, rather than sympathy.

"Yes, well, that's just too bad for you, now isn't it?"

"Oh, come on-!"

Leaning forward so that the two of them were at eye level, Missus Hastings placed a fingertip to Rhen's lips, silencing any further arguments from her with that one simple gesture.

"Modesty is reserved for those girls who can behave

themselves," she explained in a lilting, nursery rhyme sing-song, her coffee dark eyes sparkling with mirth as she pulled away a moment later and winked. "But I wouldn't worry too much about it. Your reputation precedes you, my dear. Should anyone happen to notice what's going on, they'll simply see a naughty girl getting exactly what she deserves, and nothing more."

"Humph. I guess you've got a point there," conceded Rhen with a pout, her fingers reaching hesitantly for the waistband of her shorts as she did her best not to think too much about how many other people may or may not have seen her standing in the corner post-spanking through the big bay windows that looked out onto the front lawn of her and Dana's house. "But, um, do I really need to take *everything* off? Wouldn't just my shorts and panties be enough for… for, um, you know…?"

She made another face then, grimacing.

"Everything."

"Pardon me, young lady," countered Missus Hastings, not yielding an inch. "But did I *say* I wanted you to take off just your shorts and knickers?"

"Well, no. But I-"

"Then I suppose you'd best get to disrobing completely then, now shouldn't you?"

Geez. That accent really makes it hard to argue.

"Ugh, fine, whatever!" Rhen finally harrumphed after losing their silent battle of wills, fumbling with the button clasp on her short-shorts instead of just yanking them down in a futile attempt to prolong the inevitable as she continued to grumble under her breath. "This is freaking so not fair…"

"My idea of fair is the only one that you need concern yourself with right now, young lady," chided Missus Hastings with another sniff. "And if I don't see a very contrite little miss standing before me in nothing but her birthday suit within the next sixty seconds, you can look forward to a damn good slippering before your bath as well. Is that understood?"

"Bath?"

With a surprised jerk and a tangled half-step back, Rhen sent her shorts and panties sailing down to her ankles as she shot back up with both hands covering her exposed groin.

"Wh-What bath?"

"Oh, don't be silly, child," dismissed her neighbor with a negligent wave of her hand. "You can't seriously expect me to send you home to your aunt looking as if you've been rolling around in a pigsty all day, now can you?"

At the mention of her fiancé, Rhen felt her stomach lurch again (and her clit give a not unpleasant throb beneath her palms).

"Um…"

Looking forlornly down at the dirt-stained shorts and panties pooled around her equally dirty ankles, she winced.

"Do you think you could maybe get these looking clean again before I leave?"

At that, Missus Hastings chuckled. Her stern mask slipping away entirely in the face of her worry as she gave her a reassuring pat on the shoulder.

"I'll do what I can, but I wouldn't get my hopes up. I'm afraid that vest of yours is most likely already ruined. Getting dirt and grass stains out of white clothes is difficult even at the best of times, and you've managed to do quite a number on it."

"Ugh. No kidding," grunted the shorter girl, plucking sourly at her soiled shirt with one hand while keeping the other clamped firmly in place over her bare slit. "Maybe I should just go roll around in the mud some more. At least then it would all be even."

"That's certainly one option," quipped her neighbor with a light chuckle. "Though, I sincerely doubt Dana would appreciate the deception."

"Yeah, probably not…"

Sighing to herself, Rhen kicked off her shoes and pulled her tank top and bralette up and over her head, leaving her in just a pair of mud-crusted socks and a pout.

"I'd really rather not have to suck on any soap tonight if I can avoid it.”

“That certainly seems like a wise decision to me,” concurred her neighbor, unashamedly admiring the tan lines accenting her understated curves as she gathered up her discarded clothes, holding out the pile for her to deposit her socks on top of before setting it all on the patio table behind her and turning back with an impish grin. “My goodness, you do cut quite the scrummy figure, don’t you?”

“Um… You really think so?” asked a suddenly bashful Rhen.

“I do indeed! It’s no wonder Dana enjoys playing dress up with you so much. I’d be doing much the same were I in her position.”

“Heh. Well, um, thanks!”

Blushing profusely, but unable to quite stop herself from smiling shyly at the compliment, Rhen moved her hands away from where they were covering her breasts and between her legs and gave the old woman a playful twirl and a saucy shake of her hips for good measure.

“Careful now, young lady,” she warned, grinning broadly. “You keep looking that cute and you might just find yourself walking home in a pretty new dress one of these days.”

That mock-threat prompted Rhen to stick out her tongue again as she settled her hands deliberately on her hips, which in turn had Missus Hastings letting out another long-suffering sigh while shaking her head.

“Dearie me, you are just *incorrigible*, aren’t you?”

Rhen smirked.

“Well… Maybe just a little.”

“More than a little, I’d say,” her adoptive grandmother chuckled, stepping aside and gesturing back toward the table beside her. “No matter, though. Nana Hastings knows just how to deal with cheeky little girls like you. Now then, be a dear and bend over, would you?”

Deflating somewhat as the humiliating reality of what was about to happen to her abruptly reasserted itself, Rhen’s face fell back into a pout.

"Yes ma'am…"

With a toss of her hair to mask her nervousness, she crossed the short distance over to where the other woman stood patiently waiting for her and dipped her naked frame forward across the tightly-woven wicker table, propping herself up on her elbows and forearms.

"*All* the way down, if you would," insisted her neighbor, pushing gently between her shoulder blades until her petite breasts were pressed flat against the textured surface beneath her, forcing her up onto the balls of her feet and slightly parting her cheeks in the process. "Ah, there we are. That's better."

Pat. Pat.

"*Much* better."

"That's certainly one way of putting it…"

"Pardon me?"

Pat.

"Um…"

"Did I ask for your opinion, girl?"

SMACK!

"No ma'am!"

"Then I suggest you mind that tongue of yours before it winds up tasting soap!"

SMACK!

"Yes ma'am! Sorry ma'am! It won't happen again, ma'am!"

"See that it doesn't."

SMACK!

"Now then, back to the matter at hand."

Settling in alongside the shorter girl's left hip, Missus Hastings glided her fingertips down along the grooved valley of her spine, making her squirm and giggle as she tickled her sensitive skin. In due course, she reached the center of her cheeks, whereupon she slipped her fingers into their central divide and spread them as wide as they would go, exposing her tightly clenched rosebud to the gentle kiss of the summer sun.

"Eep!"

"No, no, you just keep that nice and relaxed for me," she admonished primly, giving the "that" in question a sharp pop with the fingers of her free hand.

SLAP!

"Ah!"

Breathing out a slow, ragged breath, her face positively boiling from embarrassment now as her toes curled and uncurled against the warm concrete beneath her feet, Rhen gave her head an obedient bob.

"Y-Yes ma'am."

"There's a good lass," cooed Missus Hastings, patting her fondly between the cheeks once again before reaching back behind her and plucking up her ginger root from its paper plate. "Right then, let's just get our friend here tucked into its new home and then we can move along to your caning."

"Oh joy-"

Rhen's attempt at a sour grumble was immediately cut short, though, as the cool, wet, almost slimy tip of the bulbous root butted up against her back opening.

"Ah!"

It was pretty difficult to maintain a sassy front when you were about to be so thoroughly humbled, after all.

"That's right. Here it comes…"

Gnawing at her lower lip and stifling a moan, Rhen screwed her eyes shut tight and did her best to keep her bottom as relaxed as possible as her neighbor began to work the ginger plug inside of her. Huffing and puffing through her nostrils as, millimeter by painstaking millimeter, she slowly pushed its naturally lubricated length in past her opening. Each irregular facet on its firm surface making itself painfully known as it was twisted left and then right on its way through, ensuring that the exterior of her rosebud got an equal amount of oil worked into it as the rest of her did.

"Easy now, dear, we're almost halfway there. Just stay relaxed.

You're doing wonderfully…"

Huh. Halfway already?

Despite how humiliating it was to have her surrogate grandmother pushing a homemade punishment plug inside of her compact caboose, Rhen had to admit that aside from its less than ergonomic shape, it really wasn't all *that* bad. The sensation of its moist, fibrous girth inside of her wasn't exactly pleasant, but it didn't particularly hurt or sting either.

Maybe I was just overreacting the last time this happened or something?

She was just about to breathe out a sigh of relief, grateful to have dodged a bullet, when the heat from the root suddenly began to build.

"Urk!"

And build.

"Ack!"

And *build*.

"Oooh!"

Gritting her teeth, Rhen did her best to ride out the waves of heat radiating off of the ginger root. Hoping against hope that it was all just a momentary hurdle she would acclimate to in another moment or two. But, rather than get any easier, things just kept on getting worse. At first it had only been a mild tingling sensation (which had actually felt kind of nice), but then that tingling had blossomed into an insistent warmth, which had in turn leapfrogged to a scalding boil without any warning!

Nope. She definitely hadn't been overreacting last time.

"Oh my god, oh my god!"

Ginger freaking *burned*!

"Not very pleasant, is it?"

"No ma'am!" she moaned as the remainder of the root slid home inside of her all at once, causing her to cinch down tight around its fluted base with a pained gasp as her eyes burst open wide in panic. "Please! I'm sorry, I'm sorry, I'm sorry!"

"My, my, it's only been in there for a second or two, and

already you're so much more polite," marveled Missus Hastings with a chuckle. "Color me impressed."

"Yeah, well," Rhen managed to grouse through clenched teeth, huffing out an exasperated laugh of her own in spite of herself as a sheen of sweat began to form on her brow. "It's kind of hard *not* to be at this point, you know!"

By some small miracle, the heat from the ginger seemed to have finally reached its crescendo. But that, unfortunately, just meant that it was now holding steady at a near intolerable boil, making the offhanded slap her neighbor had delivered to her sensitive back door just a few moments earlier seem like a gentle caress by comparison.

"Crap, crap, owie, crap!"

"Goodness! Had I known that a little figging was all it would take to curb your cheeky streak, I'd have done it sooner," snickered the other woman, gliding her hand in smooth, comforting circles up and down along the small of her back. "Perhaps I ought to send some home with you for your aunt to enjoy as well?"

"Eep!"

The thought of her partner having access to a steady supply of diabolically potent ginger was enough to make Rhen's legs turn to jelly.

And her clit positively *ache*.

"Um… You really don't have to do that, ma'am!"

"Now, now, there's no need to be shy on my account," teased Missus Hastings, feigning innocence as she continued to watch her squirm. "It's really no bother at all, I assure you. I have more than enough to spare."

"Ugh! That is, like, so not the point!" harrumphed Rhen, stomping one foot as she threw a dirty look over her shoulder at her smirking neighbor. "Dana seriously doesn't need any extra help keeping me in line. Trust me."

"Is that right? Hmmm…"

Drumming her fingertips against her bare skin, Missus Hastings pretended to give the matter some serious thought for a few moments.

"Alright then, I'll tell you what," she finally said after she'd allowed the tension inside the shorter girl to reach its peak. "If you can manage to behave yourself for the remainder of our time together this afternoon, I'll keep our little friend here just between the two of us."

At that, her face split into another impish grin and she gave the center of Rhen's cheeks a firm pat.

"Or rather, between your cheeks."

"Yeah, no, totally! You got it!" she hurriedly agreed, not even pausing to roll her eyes at that lame joke in her haste to reassure the older woman. "I'll be an absolute angel, I *swear*!"

"An angel, you say?"

That managed to draw out an amused snort from Missus Hastings.

"Well, you certainly have the cheeks of a cherub, I'll grant you that," she laughed, giving said chubs an affectionate pinch. "Alright then, love, you have yourself a deal."

Pop.

"Now, up you get."

"Yes ma'am!" squeaked Rhen, going ramrod straight in record time and immediately regretting it when doing so caused her to accidentally clench up around the ginger root once again, touching off a fresh wave of scalding hot pain rippling out from deep between her cheeks. "Ack! Crap! Shoot! Owie, owie, owie!"

"Ah, I see you've stumbled upon what happens when you don't keep yourself completely relaxed."

"Uh... It freaking sucks?" she groused, hands hovering awkwardly behind her back as she debated with herself as to whether or not pawing at her burning bottom would make things better or worse.

"Precisely," confirmed her neighbor with a playful tap to the tip of her sulkily wrinkled nose, still grinning from ear to ear. "Figging is such a wonderful addition to a caning. It really helps a disobedient young lady focus on her punishment, rather than simply trying to muscle her way through it."

"Oh yeah, because we definitely wouldn't want things to hurt *less*, that's for sure."

Ignoring her sass, Missus Hastings picked her cane up from off the table and gave it a couple of vigorous swishes through the air beside her.

SWISH-SWISH! SWISH-SWISH!

Which had the petite junior's snug seat tightening on reflex all over again.

"Ugh. *Ow*. Do you have to do that?"

"Not really," admitted the old woman with an easy shrug. "But you have to admit it is rather entertaining, though."

"Humph. Maybe."

This is so not fair…

"Right then," she continued, apparently satisfied with the whippiness of her cane as she slashed it through the air one final time. "Come along to the garden, my little lamb. It's high time that naughty botty of yours collected some stripes."

"Uh… Garden?" echoed Rhen, waddling awkwardly after her neighbor's retreating form as she stepped off the patio, her hands drifting back to shield her hairless front once again just in case anyone in the surrounding houses happened to be walking by an upstairs window at that moment.

It wouldn't do much to spare her dignity if they were, but at that point she was willing to take whatever she could get.

"Of course," nodded Missus Hastings as she led them along the slate steppingstone path winding its way through her back yard and over to a clear patch of ground only a few feet away from the tree the petite junior had been lounging beneath earlier. "I need room to properly swing if this punishment is to be effective. Plus, it's such a lovely day. We really ought not to squander it by staying cooped up inside."

"Heh. I guess that's true," conceded Rhen.

Even if she'd really rather not spend it being figged and caned (well, maybe just figged), she had to admit that her neighbor had a point. It really was the perfect summer afternoon. There wasn't a cloud in the sky to be seen, and as she basked in the direct warmth of the sun beaming down on her clammy, still slightly damp skin, wriggling her bare toes between the freshly cut blades of grass at her feet while a faint breeze whispered its way through the leaves in the trees above her head, she supposed that there were worse ways to spend a Saturday.

That wasn't going to stop her from pouting as much as possible, though.

"So, uh…"

Abandoning her attempts to seem even a little bit mature, she crossed both arms in front of her modest chest and shifted her weight onto one impudent hip, only mildly regretting it this time as the ginger flared in protest.

"Can we get this over with already?"

"Why, yes, I believe we can."

Smiling faintly, evidently not bothered in the slightest by her sudden surge of attitude, Missus Hastings tapped her lightly on the seat with her cane and pointed at the ground in front of her.

"Go on and grab your knees for me."

Swallowing hard as a whirlwind of butterflies stirred to life inside her stomach, all of her earlier brashness blowing away with a semi-shaky exhalation, Rhen reluctantly moved to do as she was told. Bending over slowly so as to avoid jarring her ginger, she slid her sweaty palms down along the front of her smooth, suntanned thighs until she reached a comfortable feeling spot just above her shins.

"Like this?"

"Come now, we both know you can do better than that," her neighbor chided her mildly once she was in position, rapping the cane against her sit-spots for added emphasis. "You've got quite a small bottom, my dear. Push it out so that I can actually get at it, would you?"

"Oh god, this is so humiliating."

"That is rather the point, you know."

Sighing, Rhen surreptitiously rolled her eyes.

"Yeah, yeah…"

Please just let that stupid cane thing be as quiet as a switch is.

Adopting the position expected of her required Rhen to spread her legs far more than she'd been hoping she'd have to. Drawing the skin of her hips and thighs taut in a way that she knew would make things hurt even more than they were already going to since she wouldn't have as much of the jiggle from her cheeks to help absorb any of the upcoming impacts.

On the bright side, though, her new partially spread-eagle stance at least made it a whole lot easier to avoid clenching her bottom by accident.

SWISH-SWISH! SWISH-SWISH!

That all quickly became the least of her worries a moment later, however, when Missus Hastings began swishing the cane back and forth behind her once again. Tickling her bare and pouting lips with an impromptu air current that sent an electrifying tingle up her spine.

"Now then, it's usually 'six of the best' for errant schoolgirls such as yourself," the old woman explained matter-of-factly. "But, considering your penchant for naughtiness, I do believe a double dose of discipline is in order."

"Ugh. Of course you do…"

"What was that?"

SWISH-SWISH! SWISH-SWISH!

"Did I just hear you say you'd prefer eighteen instead?"

"No ma'am!" squeaked Rhen in a hurry, hands tightening around the sides of her knees as she bobbed her buns nervously in place. "Twelve is fine!"

Tap. Tap. Tap.

"Well, if you're certain…"

"Oh yeah, I *definitely* am."

"Very well then," sniffed Missus Hastings. "In that case, you'd best prepare yourself, young lady. These are not going to be pleasant, I can assure you."

Tap… Tap…

When at last the first stroke of the cane finally came, it was faster and with far less fanfare than Rhen had been expecting. One moment the flexible rod in her neighbor's hand was *tap, tap, tapping* away against her naked cheeks, building up the tension inside her stomach as the ginger continued to sizzle away, and then the next-

SWISH-THWACK!

"Aieee!"

Shooting back up to her feet, both hands clamped tight to her boiling bottom, Rhen began to dance in place. Hopping frantically from foot to foot, yelping and hissing and generally making a spectacle of herself as that one razor-thin line of pure, explosive agony left behind by the cane's high-speed collision with the center of her caboose continued to burn and burn and *burn*; swelling beneath her touch into a raised, puffy ridge that spanned uninterrupted from one cheek to the other.

"Oh my god, oh my god. Owie, owie, *owie*!"

Fortunately for her, Missus Hastings was kind enough to allow her her momentary freak out. Patiently standing off to the side with one hand on her hip and the other holding the cane angled down toward her feet as she took in the entertaining display of her naked form wriggling and bobbing, gyrating and squirming, with a self-satisfied smile.

"Are you quite finished, dear?" she eventually asked once Rhen had managed to more or less tire herself out.

"Y… Yes ma'am," she panted, gently kneading her welted backside.

It was still broiling, and massaging it really didn't make things hurt any less, but there was a deeply satisfying ache to be found in the act. One that she knew she'd be replaying in her head over and over again after she'd been tucked into bed later that evening.

"Back down into position then, if you would."

With a grudging nod, Rhen stiffly moved to do as she was told, groaning all the while to herself as she did so.

One down, eleven to go…

"There's a good lass," her neighbor cooed, once again *tap, tap, tapping* out an ominous rhythm against her partially parted cheeks. "Now, do try and hold still this time, would you? If I have to tell you again, we shall start over from the beginning."

"I will!"

Squeezing her slightly trembling legs for dear life, which made the ginger inside her bottom burn all the brighter, Rhen readied herself as best she could for the next stroke of the cane.

Which, again, she didn't have to wait long for.

Tap… Tap… SWISH-THWACK!

"Ah! Oh! Yeowie!"

Breathing out sharp, pained exhalations through her nostrils, Rhen vented her tightly controlled reactions by bobbing in place as a second sharply focused line of blazing heat was scored across both of her cheeks just an inch or so below the first.

"Oh gosh, oh crap…"

She could feel both of them pulsing and throbbing in time with her racing heartbeat, the fury of their initial impacts relentlessly burrowing its way deeper and deeper into her tender backside with each passing moment until they blended together into an all-encompassing heat fanned ever hotter by the ginger.

But, hey, at least she managed to stay in position this time.

Somehow.

"I take it you felt that one?" Missus Hastings inquired conversationally.

"Uh, yeah," bit out Rhen with an exasperated, half-strangled laugh. "It was kinda hard not to."

For as much as the cane had taken her breath away, though, once she'd had a chance to actually process the sensations that she was being bombarded by, she had to admit that it *was* pretty exhilarating. Plus, the highly compartmentalized lines of throbbing heat left behind in its wake were actually kind of nice in a weird way.

They also hurt like crazy!

"You know, we can totally stop now if you want. I've definitely learned my lesson. I promise."

"Hmmm... Perhaps you're right."

Tap... Tap... SWISH-THWACK!

While the cane might've been fairly quiet as it flew through the air, Rhen certainly wasn't.

"Ack! Owww!"

"Then again, it's far better to be safe than sorry."

Tap... Tap...

"Now, straighten up those legs, girl. We've still got a long way to go."

"Ugh."

Heaving out a watery sigh and the beginnings of a sniffle, Rhen eased her bottom back up into position and mentally prepared herself for stroke number four.

"Yes ma'am."

—

Over the course of the next six or seven minutes (though it felt more like six or seven *hours* to Rhen), Missus Hastings laid on nine more neat, horizontal stripes across her increasingly wriggly bottom.

With each stroke of the cane, she paused just long enough to allow the younger girl time to hiss in a sharp breath and groan her way through the initial biting sting from the ridged bamboo. Watching with immense satisfaction as it gradually burrowed its way deeper and deeper into her tender cheeks, transforming into a lingering, throbbing ache that would have her sitting uncomfortably for the rest of the weekend. And, all the while as this was happening, the ginger nestled snugly between Rhen's buns continued to sizzle and burn, adding an additional dimension of discomfort and pain to her punishment that, true to her neighbor's prediction, made it impossible for her mind wander far.

And made any time she tensed her bottom on accident an absolute nightmare!

All in all, it wasn't the most severe spanking that Rhen had ever received (it *was* only twelve swats in total, after all), but it was certainly one of the most memorable. And one that left her bottom (and thankfully only her bottom) covered in a series of twelve partially-overlapping weals, each about the width of a pencil and stained a vivid shade of strawberry red with traces of violet near their puffy, swollen edges that continued to pulse and throb long after her ordeal was finally over.

It had also left her a complete and total sobbing wreck. But, as she stood there nestled into the crook of her surrogate grandmother's arm, being held close as she rocked her back and forth while patting her back reassuringly, she couldn't say that she hadn't enjoyed the experience (at least after the fact). This latest foray into UK flavored discipline had been fun! Although, she definitely wasn't in any hurry to repeat it any time soon.

Perhaps in a month. But certainly not next week.

Well… Maybe.

It would all depend on how her first meeting with her adviser went next Friday.

Eventually, though, after her weeping had subsided and she was no longer sniffling with every other breath, Missus Hastings held her out at arm's length by the shoulders and beamed fondly down at her.

"Do you think you've learned your lesson, love?"

Drawing a forearm across her red-rimmed eyes with one final sniff and a shake of her head to clear it, Rhen returned the older woman's smile with a sassy smirk.

"Heh. Something like that."

"Goodness me, it would seem that someone has managed to bounce back rather quickly," the old woman chuckled, giving her shoulders a light squeeze. "Tell me then, oh cheeky one, what pearls of wisdom have you come away from this discipline session with?"

"If I'm going to play in the mud, don't make a mess or drown the flowers?"

"Hmmm… Yes, I suppose that'll do," replied Missus Hastings mock-seriously, wagging a forefinger at her. "And don't you forget it!"

"Yes ma'am!" replied Rhen with a sloppy salute, before surrendering to another grimace as her now extremely tender rosebud flexed in protest around the ginger root still lodged inside of her. "Um…"

Glowing a bright shade of red from her neck all the way to the roots of her dark, frazzled halo of hair, she gestured self-consciously back behind her.

"Do you think maybe I could take this thing out now?"

"In due time," dismissed her neighbor with another easy laugh, gesturing toward the garden where this whole mess had begun. "We'll get you sorted out just as soon as you've finished tidying up the mess you made."

"Oh, come *on*!" demanded the shorter girl, hands bunching into frustrated fists at her sides as she stomped a foot. "This is, like, so not fair! I already got punished. You can't make me keep it in now!"

Her huffy protests didn't budge the older woman in her resolve, however.

"Keep up the hysterics, and you can expect to keep that fig in until bath time, young lady," was her only reply, an all too familiar note of warning edging its way back into her tone as her eyes hardened momentarily.

"Oh! Um… N-Never mind! I can hold it in until everything's cleaned up, don't worry!"

"Can you now?"

Missus Hastings held Rhen in place with her cool stare for several more long, tense moments, before eventually smiling once again and ruffling her hair.

"Right then. Now that that's settled, I'm off to go ring up your aunt and inform her that you will be late in returning home this evening. And, while I'm doing that, *you* can get to work."

"Okay," nodded Rhen, casting a hopeful glance back toward

the patio and her pile of dirty clothes still on the table there. "Um… Can I at least put on a shirt or something first?"

"Oh heavens no, don't be silly, dear!" laughed her neighbor. "That's all going right into the wash."

"But… but… But someone might *see*!"

"Then I suppose you'd best be quick in clearing away all those mud splatters, shouldn't you?"

Moaning to herself, Rhen's hands once again drifted back to cover her front. Now that her punishment was over, and the overall heat from the ginger had died down to a more manageable low simmer, she was growing much more aware of her current complete exposure. Cleaning up the mess she'd made wearing nothing but a dozen welts and an unwanted gardening accessory was definitely not how she'd been hoping things would go after her caning was finished.

But, she had to admit it *did* feel pretty appropriate given the circumstances.

"Humph. Yes ma'am…"

"Very good."

With a parting pat on the head, Missus Hastings turned and began moving back toward her house, idly swishing her cane back and forth beside her as she went.

"By the way, does turkey on whole wheat sound good to you for lunch?"

At her question, Rhen's stomach gave an audible rumble, and she smirked.

"Oh yeah, that sounds awesome!"

"Wonderful," laughed Missus Hastings. "And after we're finished with your bath, you can help me make ginger snaps."

Feeling slightly less enthusiastic about that last part, but still optimistic about them tasting great nevertheless, Rhen flashed her surrogate grandmother a thumbs up.

"You got it, Nana Hastings!"

Chapter 17

A Refresher Course in Self-Control

Over the course of the next three weeks, Rhen settled back into the rhythm of life as a busy college student. Every morning she rolled out of bed at eight(ish), enjoyed a quiet breakfast with her fiancé, hurried her way through whatever chores she might have to do that day, and then sped off to campus on her brand new bike.

Which, while a mortifying shade of bright, sparkly pink, at least didn't have any tassels clipped to the ends of its handlebars. (Although, it *did* still have a rather fetching wicker basket attached to its front.)

"Hey, you can't beat the classics," Dana had reasoned when she'd started to whine about it looking too childish while they'd been out shopping after their meeting with her academic adviser. "And besides, this way you'll always have somewhere to put your books and things while you're riding it."

Rhen had tried to argue that that was what a backpack was for, but when she'd voiced that particular opinion, her partner had just leaned in nice and close and whispered into her ear.

"Little girls with bright red bottoms who wear pretty princess panties ride bikes with baskets on the front of them."

Before then snaking her hands around her hips to take hold of the hem of her skirt in back, starting to lift it up past her thighs right there in the middle of the store.

"But if you'd like to keep making a scene, I'd be more than happy to show you what kinds of bikes little girls with freshly spanked *bare* bottoms ride as well. Spoiler alert, they're the same bike."

"No thanks!" Rhen had squeaked, her still sore cheeks

clenching beneath the thin material of her partially exposed pant-ies, the memories of her all too recent encounter with the Spencer Paddle still fresh in her mind. "Uh… Actually, now that I think about it, a basket is just fine."

"See? I thought you might see things my way."

With the matter settled, Dana had then smoothed down the back of her skirt, patted her fondly, and they'd made their pur-chase without any further fuss. And, after giving it a couple of test rides around the neighborhood, Rhen found herself having to admit that it actually *was* pretty nice still having a basket on her bike.

Especially when she was riding back home after her classes were done for the day.

By then she was totally over having to lug her heavy backpack around anymore, and being able to simply toss the stupid thing onto the front of her bike was a total godsend for her poor, ach-ing back as she pedaled her way back home in the late afternoon.

Typically, she was able to time things so that she arrived back at her and Dana's house just as the last of the daycare kids were being picked up by their parents or older siblings, which usually spared her the indignity of having to say hi to any of them or put up with them asking if she'd been behaving herself lately.

After parking her bike in its proper place behind the fence next to their garage, she'd come inside, kiss her partner hello, and then speed up to her bedroom to take care of her homework as soon as possible (in between watching maybe one or two YouTube videos, just to keep her mind sharp and focused). From there, she and Dana would eat dinner together either at home or at a local restaurant to give her fiancé a chance to get out of the house for a while, and then they'd usually spend the rest of the time before she had to get ready for bed either cuddling on the couch watch-ing TV or simply enjoying each other's company in the same room while they busied themselves with stuff on their laptops.

So far it had been a pretty good semester for Rhen. She really enjoyed all of her classes (even English lit), and best of all, she'd managed to avoid getting into any serious trouble with her adviser.

Or at home for that matter.

Oh, she still found herself being pulled across Dana's lap here and there for a brisk spanking from time to time, but those were all relatively minor affairs usually stemming from her getting just a bit too mouthy for the older woman's liking or neglecting to do a chore. In the grand scheme of things, they were hardly more than prolonged attitude adjustments, really. And, as far as Rhen was concerned, she'd been behaving herself pretty gosh darn well these last few weeks.

But, of course, it wouldn't last.

—

"So, what're your plans for after your meeting today?" Dana asked over the rim of her cup of coffee during breakfast that Friday morning.

"Oh, nothing much," answered Rhen, pausing in her response to chew and swallow another mouthful of ketchup covered scrambled eggs before continuing. "I was thinking about maybe swinging by the book store for a bit and then seeing if Abby wanted to hang out."

"That sounds like fun," mused her partner with a fond smile. "Is your homework all finished?"

"Yep! And before you ask, *no*, Doctor Holloway doesn't have anything to 'address' with me today either."

I think.

"Well now, look at you!"

Dana sounded genuinely pleased to hear that despite it meaning that she wouldn't get the chance to soak up all the gory details of her bratty bride-to-be's encounter with another dose of school discipline over dinner that evening.

"You've been doing really great this semester, Rhen. I'm so proud of you."

"Awww, well, uh…"

Demurring under her partner's praise, the petite junior looked down at her plate and pushed around some of her eggs as her stomach fluttered pleasantly.

"Thanks. Heh. Though, I mean, I guess I owe a lot of that to you."

Looking up from her breakfast again, still blushing, she smirked at the older woman.

"You definitely know how to keep me motivated."

"Oh, come now, the power to succeed was in you all along," teased Dana with a wink. "I just had to coax it out was all… Repeatedly."

That managed to get a snort from Rhen.

"Seriously, though, cutie pie," she continued, setting down her fork. "I'm proud of you."

Half-rising from her seat, Dana leaned across the table, wordlessly inviting the shorter girl to kiss her. An invitation which Rhen readily accepted without a moment's hesitation. Rising up onto her tiptoes and locking lips with her partner, she tasted the faint hints of premium dark roast and maple syrup on the older woman's tongue as it rolled across her own before parting.

"I love you, Dana."

"I love you too," beamed her fiancé, settling back onto her seat with a contented sigh. "And I think that since you've been doing so well this semester, you deserve a little treat."

"Can I start going to bed at ten-thirty again?"

"Hah! You wish," she laughed, producing a tight-lipped huff from the shorter girl as she flopped down onto her own seat. "But I *will* kick in an extra twenty dollars for your trip to the book store today. How's that sound?"

"Oh heck yeah! Screw staying up late!"

Being between her regular weekly allowances, Rhen only had ten dollars to her name at the moment, and the prospect of suddenly having triple the money to spend on books that afternoon was enough to make her bounce in her seat. Though, at the audible crinkling from her pull-up this produced, she opted instead to channel her enthusiasm into an extra-large mouthful of eggs.

"Thankth Aunth Danath."

"You're very welcome, dear," replied the auburn-haired older woman with a bemused shake of her head. "Also, please try not to talk with your mouth full. I'd hate to have to revisit our discussion on table manners from Sunday."

"Oh yeath…"

Swallowing her oversized bite of food by washing it down with a healthy swig of orange juice, Rhen flashed her partner a shameless smirk.

"Sorry, my bad."

"Mmhmm," she answered in turn, pressing her lips together in a mock-frown.

To which Rhen just stuck out her tongue.

"Speaking of money, though," Dana continued a few moments later, dabbing at the corners of her mouth with a napkin before laying it on her plate and pushing it and her utensils off to the side. "There's something I've been meaning to ask you about."

"Um…"

Sensing that she might've just inadvertently wandered onto thin ice, Rhen straightened up in her seat and set her fork down with deliberate care as well.

"There is?" she asked, already starting to feel the first tell-tale stirrings of butterflies inside her stomach as she quietly ran through all the misbehavior she might've been trying to keep under wraps lately. "What's up?"

Rather than answer her directly, Dana instead slipped her phone from the front pocket of her robe and thumbed it to life.

"Let's see now…"

Pulling up her mobile banking app, she logged in and then looked up from her screen with a fresh frown.

"Do you know anything about a three hundred dollar charge from something called Undersight LLC?"

Oh crap.

Feeling the blood drain from her face all at once, Rhen swallowed.

Hard.

"Uh… Undersight?"

"Yes, that's right," nodded Dana, her brows coming together in suspicion. "That's one of those games you like to play, isn't it?"

"I mean…"

She fixed the shorter girl in place with a long, hard stare then. Waiting patiently for her to stop avoiding the issue until, finally, the tension became too much for her to handle, and what little of a façade of innocence Rhen had managed to throw up on such short notice came crumbling away.

"Okay. Well, um, you see… The thing is…" she began to explain in fits and starts, feeling her heart rate accelerate along with her embarrassment as heat rushed in to refill her pale cheeks. "I um… I kinda bought some in-game currency the other day."

"You did, huh?" pressed Dana, keeping her voice even and patient as she stared her down. "Three hundred dollars definitely seems like it's a bit more than just 'some', wouldn't you say?"

"I mean, *yeah*," agreed Rhen quickly, her words starting to tumble out faster and faster as she squirmed nervously in her seat, no longer caring that they could both hear her pull-up crinkling beneath her as she did so. "But, like, the thing is, they were having this start of summer event thing and I really wanted this limited edition skin for my character. Only, they wouldn't let you just, like, you know, buy it. You had to get it through loot boxes, which you could only get with in-game currency, which you could only get with actual money. And, like, even then, it was still totally random what you'd actually get and the stupid thing was a triple-rare so it was, like, extra hard to get. And it just wasn't showing up, and they kept on offering these bundle deals where if you spent twenty dollars or more they'd give you an extra ten percent bonus in credits, and I thought it wouldn't take that much to get it, but it kept on not showing up, so I kept on buying more, and um, I guess I spent way more than I thought I had and I-"

"Whoa now! Easy there, cutie pie," Dana cut her off, holding up a hand to stem the tide of her ever increasingly frantic explanations. "I think I get the picture. You wanted something in your game, but it was a random chance if you'd get it or not, and you ended up losing track of how much you were spending. Is that about right?"

Licking her suddenly dry lips, feeling equal parts nervous and embarrassed, Rhen nodded as she stared forlornly down at the few bits of scrambled egg still remaining on her plate.

"Yes ma'am…"

Smiling tenderly at the red-faced younger girl, Dana reached across the table and laid a hand atop her own, rubbing her knuckles with the pad of her thumb in a soothing gesture.

"I think we both know you messed up big time here," she said with just the hint of a laugh. "And also that maybe it would be better if we didn't take any trips to Vegas any time soon."

"Yeah, no kidding," snorted Rhen, batting at the beginnings of frustrated tears with her free hand.

Blowing through twice her monthly entertainment budget in a single night definitely qualified as "messing up big time" in her book. Especially when she didn't even have anything to show for it except a bunch of worthless commons and duplicates of skins she already owned.

"I'm sorry, Dana."

"I know you are, kiddo," her partner replied, wordlessly signaling that they were finished with the "adult" portion of their conversation and were now back to their roles as strict aunt and naughty niece. "And I forgive you."

Sniffling, Rhen looked up with a pair of watery green eyes. Even though her stomach was now a dive-bombing swarm of butterflies, she was still profoundly relieved to hear that.

"Th-Thanks, Aunt Dana."

"Of course, cutie pie."

Giving her hand a firm squeeze, the older woman then added.

"And before you ask, no, I'm not mad at you. But I am disappointed."

"That's fair," conceded Rhen with a miserable grimace.

"I *also* think," her partner continued, her face settling into a grim mask of determination that shattered any hopes the younger girl might've still been harboring of escaping this incident with only a stern talking to. "That in light of this recent slip-up, you, young lady, need a refresher course in self-control."

Hearing that immediately sent Rhen's stomach plummeting to her ankles, and she found herself blushing all over again. It had been a couple of months since she'd been forced to endure a punishment enema, and she'd really been hoping that she'd be able to keep that streak alive at least until the end of the semester. But, alas, it was not to be.

"Um… Are you sure we *have* to do that?" she asked, already knowing the answer to her question, but holding out hope nevertheless that today might be the day she got lucky.

Narrowing her dark eyes in warning at her, Dana's voice grew suddenly firm and implacable.

"What do you think?"

"Yes?"

"Rhen…"

For one fleeting moment, Rhen was sorely tempted to try and argue her case further (or at the very least attempt to bargain for an extra-severe spanking or something instead of an enema). But, recognizing that she was already in enough trouble as it was, she knew that that would just make things way worse. Plus, if she was being totally honest with herself, she wholeheartedly agreed that she deserved to be properly punished for what she'd done.

That didn't make it suck any less, though.

Breathing in deep through her nose, she pursed her lips and let out a long, frustrated harrumph that ended in a pout.

"Okay, *fine*," she groused, pointedly looking away from her frowning partner as she caved to the inevitable with all the good grace of an actual teenager. "I don't really see the point since I already said I was sorry, but if it'll make you feel better, then whatever, I guess…"

"Mmhmm," deadpanned Dana, her chair scraping across the tile floor behind her as she pushed back from the table and rose to her feet, bringing to bear every inch of height she had over the petite junior as she glared down at her. "Keep up the attitude and see where it gets you, little girl. You're already getting a spanking after we're done here, but that can just as easily be a hairbrushing if you don't knock it off."

"Yes ma'am! Sorry ma'am!" squeaked Rhen, scrambling to her feet in a flash and immediately starting to gather up their plates and utensils in an attempt to look busy and obedient.

"No, no, you just leave those there. I'll take care of them later," her aunt admonished, lightly plucking the fork out of her hand before hooking a thumb over her shoulder toward the other end of the kitchen. "Right now I want to see that disobedient little butt of yours bent over the counter."

"But-!" the red-faced twenty-one-year-old turned teenager started to whine, thoroughly in the grip of pre-punishment panic now as she hovered awkwardly over their dishes.

"I'd hurry if I were you," Dana cut her off again, the barest hint of a grin tracing its way across her lips. "Unless, that is, you'd *like* for all your little friends to see you getting your enema."

Now *that* managed to energize Rhen.

"No thanks!" she yelped, all but sprinting toward her customary spot next to the kitchen sink as her fiancé trailed after her at a leisurely pace, the corners of her lips abandoning their attempt at looking serious as they twitched up in amusement.

"There's my good girl."

Snapping her head around to glare grumpily over her shoulder at the sugary sweet praise, sticking out her tongue for good measure, Rhen rolled her eyes and then fell across the countertop with a dramatic huff.

"Yeah, whatever."

Which just made Dana smirk all the more.

"Rhen, Rhen, Rhen… What, oh what, am I ever going to do with you?" she sighed as she sauntered up behind her, taking hold of the waistband of her pajama bottoms on either side of her hips and dragging them (along with her pull-up) down to her ankles in one smooth, practiced motion.

"I'm sure you'll think of something," sassed the shorter girl, nibbling on the end of her left thumbnail as the cool air of the kitchen wafted across her now naked bottom and legs, raising goosebumps all across their smooth, pale surface.

"Well," chuckled Dana, lightly tickling the backs of her knees in a silent command to step out of her clothes. "You're certainly not wrong there."

"Humph!"

With a quick peck to the shorter girl's bare left cheek, she gathered up her discarded pajama bottoms and pull-up, laying the former on the countertop next to her blushing bride-to-be, before moving off toward the trash can to toss out the latter.

As she returned back to her side, retrieving the silicone rubber enema bag and its accompanying plastic tubing (along with a fresh bar of soap) from underneath the sink, Rhen kept her gaze locked firmly on the white tile backsplash ahead of her. She knew from way too much personal experience that watching her partner prepare her supplies would just make the butterflies fluttering around inside her stomach that much worse (which was the entire point), so she did her best to think about *anything* other than how in just a few short minutes Dana would be spreading her cheeks and staring hungrily down at her-

Focus!

Shaking her head to clear it, deliberately shifting her legs further apart to avoid her thighs rubbing themselves together of their own accord, Rhen redoubled her efforts to count all the tiles in front of her nose.

Ten, eleven, twelve…

Unfortunately, though, no matter how hard she stared, that couldn't stop her ears from hearing everything that was going on right beside her.

Fidgeting in place against the chilly granite, she listened with mounting horror (and more than a little embarrassing excitement)

as her aunt started up the flow of water in the sink and began working up a lather across the bar of soap in her hands, humming happily to herself as she waited patiently for the water to reach an appropriate temperature for her purpose. Soon enough, the flow was reduced to little more than a trickle, and holding the head of the bright blue bag open beneath the faucet, Dana began slowly filling it up with warm water that grew significantly soapier as it cascaded down over the bubbly bar of Ivory she held just above its opening.

Oh god… Rhen moaned silently to herself, stealing a look over to her right and immediately regretting it. *I always forget just how much that stupid thing can hold.*

When at last the walls of the enema bag had swollen to their full two quart size, Dana cut off the flow of water from the sink and then hung it up by a white plastic hook from one of the cabinet knobs directly above her naughty niece's head. She then proceeded to uncoil the length of clear plastic tubing attached to its base, coaxing out any air bubbles that might still be lingering inside by lightly flicking its walls periodically as she worked her way down its length before eventually reaching the narrow, plastic nozzle at the other end.

"Let's see now…"

Releasing the small clamp at the base of the nozzle, she let out a short spritz of water to confirm that everything was flowing properly, before then closing it off again and nodding to herself in satisfaction.

"Perfect."

"Oh god…" groaned Rhen, aloud this time, swallowing hard.

"Please," scoffed her aunt in response.

SMACK!

Giving her bare, wobbly cheeks a firm swat before turning her attention back to the enema nozzle in her hand.

"We both know you're more than used to this by now, you naughty thing."

"That doesn't mean it still doesn't suck, you know,"

harrumphed the shorter girl, watching sourly as her partner began working the bar of sudsy soap up and down along the length of the nozzle to lubricate it.

"Yes, yes, I know, dear…" soothed Dana, repeating the process around the perimeter of her bride-to-be's nervously twitching back door with a soapy fingertip, working it in and out of her a handful of times before pulling it free with a wet *POP!* "But it has to be done."

Wiping her hand off on the front of her robe, she then stepped around to Rhen's other side, and using her free hand, parted her cheeks with a long-suffering shake of her head.

"Now just relax, and this will all be over before you know it."

"Humph. Fi- Eep!"

Despite her attempts to at least *seem* defiant, Rhen found herself being cut off mid-sulk by the sudden press of the narrow enema nozzle against her defenseless rosebud. Its soap-slicked tip slipping inside of her with humiliating ease, wringing an involuntary squeak out of her in the process.

"Ah! Oh god!"

"That's right, just like that…" cooed Dana, working the four inch length of plastic in and out with undisguised amusement, twisting it this way and that, before finally sliding it all the way home and allowing her cheeks to ease back into place around it. "Now you hold onto that for me, alright?"

"Y-Yes ma'am!"

"Good girl."

The older woman's tone grew frosty then.

"I can promise that if that comes out before I say it can, you're definitely not going to like what happens next."

With that ominous warning, she released her hold on the base of the nozzle, forcing Rhen to clench down tight around it lest it accidentally slip free, ratcheting up the irritation from the soap by several notches all at once.

"Urk!"

In actuality, she knew (or at least hoped) that Dana was

keeping a close eye on things and would be sure to catch it before it popped free. But, the tactic was still nevertheless an effective one at ensuring her attention was focused wholly on the matter at hand.

Which *sucked.*

"Ready?" she asked a moment later, once Rhen's strained panting had more or less subsided to only a slightly labored huffing and puffing.

"I… I guess so…"

"Alright then, here we go," announced Dana, thumbing the clamp on the nozzle open.

"Mmph! Oooh!"

Groaning, Rhen bit down on her lower lip as her back arched, the sensation of warm, soapy water flooding into her enough to make her immediately start dancing from foot to foot in fretful discomfort. Despite how many times this had happened to her in the past, there was just no getting used to the feeling of being so thoroughly filled from behind. Which meant that she was left with no other choice but to grit her teeth, clench her cheeks, and bear with it for however long it took.

"Are we starting to regret our actions, little girl?" inquired Dana, standing somewhere behind her with her arms crossed below her breasts, watching on with a mixture of amusement and steely resolve.

"Yes ma'am! I'm sorry ma'am!"

"I should certainly hope so," she sniffed unsympathetically. "You really need to pay closer attention to how much money you're spending on things, Rhen. I know it might not seem like a lot when it's just little purchases here and there, but as I'm sure you're noticing now, a little can suddenly add up to a whole lot more than you were expecting if you're not careful."

"Yeah, no freaking kidding," growled the shorter girl through gritted teeth, breaking out in a sweat as she struggled to keep her grip on the nozzle while her insides continued to swell.

The sensation honestly wasn't *that* unpleasant, but the

addition of the soap to the warm water was enough to make her insides cramp in a distressing way that made her wish very much that she could run to the bathroom right then.

"God, please tell me it's almost empty," she moaned, letting her head plonk down onto her crossed forearms as she continued to squirm her weight from foot to foot in a futile attempt to vent some of her nervous, panicky energy.

"Oh… I'd say we're just about halfway through now," Dana answered after stepping in and easing up onto the balls of her feet to double-check the water level in the gradually shrinking silicone bag. "Give it another couple minutes and it'll be done, cutie pie."

"Ugh. Okay, I can do that…" panted Rhen, her voice coming in deep, ragged breaths now as she willed herself to not start begging.

"Well," added Dana with a roguish smirk. "I should say that we're about halfway through with *this* bag."

She gave her naughty niece's shifting seat a couple of firm pats then, eliciting a startled gasp from her.

"We're going to do two this time."

"*Two*" squawked Rhen in horror, her legs nearly giving out from under her at the very thought.

"That's right," confirmed her aunt in a firm, but gentle, voice. "You've gotten pretty used to these since we started using them last year. So if I want to make an impression on you, it's going to take more than just a measly two quarts, I'm afraid."

"Oh come on!" the petite junior whined, bobbing in place in frustration and immediately regretting it when doing so sloshed the water inside of her around with a very undignified gurgle.

Glowing scarlet now, Rhen buried her smoldering face in her hands.

"I've learned my lesson, I promise."

"Mmhmm. I'm sure you have, dear," replied Dana, her tone unyielding. "But that doesn't mean you get to skip out on your punishment, now does it?"

With no choice other than to accept that (unless she felt like

earning an additional punishment for her trouble), Rhen stomped a foot (again, immediately regretting it) and let out another harrumph.

"Ugh!"

Looking up once again, she blew out an exasperated breath, dislodging several locks of hair that had gotten into her mouth, and returned to glaring at the tiles in front of her.

"Meanie."

"Just the meaniest," agreed Dana, leaning down and kissing her sweaty cheek. "Hang in there, cutie pie. We'll be done soon, I promise."

"Humph. Yes ma'am…"

—

When at last she'd taken every last drop of her full four quart enema (which, as frustrating as it was to admit to herself, wasn't nearly as impossible as she'd feared it would be), Rhen felt like she was ready to burst at any moment. But, true to her aunt's prediction, she'd been able to hold it all in.

Barely.

"Okeydokey, honey buns," Dana announced cheerily, laying one hand on the small of her back while gripping the base of the enema nozzle with the other. "I'm going to pull this out. Are you ready?"

"Ready" was a pretty subjective term in Rhen's opinion just then, but considering that every moment she delayed taking up her position in the corner was another moment she would be forced to endure the irritating pressure and humiliating sloshiness of the soapy water inside of her, she nodded and mumbled through gritted teeth.

"Yeah… I guess so."

"Are you *sure*?" pressed her partner, her voice tinged with just a hint of mischief as she lightly drummed her fingers against the base of the nozzle, making her nearly wet herself in the process. "I can always go get you a diaper if you're worried you might not be up to it. Alana did say they were perfect for times like these, you know."

Ugh. She freaking would, wouldn't she?

"No thanks!"

"Well…"

Her teasing smirk widening into a full on wicked grin, Dana wrapped her fingers around the thin plastic base of the protruding enema nozzle one by one, savoring the mounting tension in the room as her bratty bride-to-be wriggled restlessly against the countertop.

"If you're positive you won't need it."

"Oh my god, I freaking am!"

Shaking loose the dark hair plastered to her sweaty forehead, Rhen blew out an exasperated breath and threw a dirty look over her shoulder.

"Can we *please* just get this over with?"

"Of course!"

With no other warning than those two cheery words, Dana plucked the nozzle free from between her quivering cheeks in one smooth motion.

"Ah! What the heck?"

Letting out a startled yelp, Rhen shoved herself up off of the by now warm countertop and rolled over to face her partner with an accusatory glower while her hands flew back to lend her bottom all the help they could.

"Yes?" asked Dana, her face the very picture of innocence as she waggled her newly claimed prize back and forth beside her.

"You know what you did!" huffed the shorter girl, pushing out her cheeks in the most annoyed pout she could muster while resisting the urge to stomp her foot.

That would just be a recipe for disaster.

Unfortunately for her, though, her attempts at looking affronted were largely undercut by the involuntarily dance she was still performing as she struggled not to totally humiliate herself.

"Oh my god, oh my god. Holy crap," she whined, as a series of short gasps and moans escaped from her fretful lips. "This is, like, *so* much worse than that first time!"

"Oh, is it?" quipped her partner, still playing innocent.

"Of course it is!" she snapped, still trying to sound upset even as a spontaneous bout of near-hysterical laughs welled up within her.

She always got a bit giggly when she was feeling overwhelmed, and that morning was proving to be no exception.

"Well then, that's just perfect," declared Dana in sternly triumphant satisfaction, mercifully cutting off the shorter girl's need to think of a witty rejoinder by taking hold of her upper arm and turning to drag her out of the kitchen. "Now come with me, young lady. You're going to think about how irresponsible you've been while you stand in the corner holding that enema in for ten minutes. Is that understood?"

"Okay, okay, okayyyy," moaned the distraught twenty-one-year-old turned exceptionally remorseful teenager, ready to agree to just about anything right then as she allowed herself to be escorted into their front room, both hands still hovering awkwardly behind her in a futile attempt to somehow help preserve her dignity.

It didn't help.

"Ten minutes, little girl," her aunt repeated as they reached her usual corner, guiding her into place and maneuvering her hands up on top of her head.

Sniffling to herself as she flexed her fingers against her slightly damp hair, Rhen nodded into the spot where the two walls in front of her met.

"Yes ma'am…"

"Good girl."

With a parting kiss to her cheek, and a sadistic pat to her shifting seat that made her gasp, Dana swept out of the room and back into the kitchen to take care of their breakfast dishes.

"I'll come get you when the timer goes off. You don't move a toe out of position until then, you hear me?"

"Oh my god! I won't, I won't!"

Just freaking go already, would you?

"Alrighty then, have fun."

Now alone in their front room with only her labored panting and the relentless *tick, tick, tick* of the old grandfather clock behind her for company, Rhen settled in for what was sure to be one of the longest stretches of ten minutes in her entire young life. Despite her distress, however, she still genuinely felt bad for her overspending. And, though it was humiliating, she fully agreed that she deserved every moment of her punishment.

Even if it totally sucked.

On the bright side, though, as she surreptitiously checked the time over her shoulder (there was always a chance Dana might poke her head back in to check on her), she still had at least half an hour to go before the first of the daycare kids would be arriving. With any luck, she'd be out of the corner, free of her enema, and hopefully finished with her spanking by the time any of them started to show up.

It wasn't ideal. They'd almost certainly see her sniffling in timeout with a bright red bottom as they trickled in. But, it was still better than nothing.

"Ugh."

Sort of.

—

When at last Rhen was freed from her seemingly perpetual purgatory staring at the bumpy drywall pattern directly in front of her frowning face while she danced from foot to foot with her hands on top of her head (Dana had mercifully allowed her not to have to shove her nose all the way *into* the actual corner like she usually did), she immediately fled toward the nearest first-floor bathroom at Mach speed. Where, at last, she was finally able to relieve herself.

It wasn't a particularly dignified escape, especially not with her partner cackling as she watched her run away, but at least her punishment was finally over.

Well, the worst part at any rate.

Humph. For as much as they suck, you definitely can't say an enema doesn't get results… she grumbled to herself, feeling a good twenty pounds lighter as she eventually shuffled her way shamefacedly out of the bathroom after washing her hands.

Even having not yet been spanked, Rhen was already fully determined to never let her spending get out of hand ever again. She was going to install a finance tracker app on her phone just as soon as she could. And that alone was enough to make her blush nearly as red as her soon to be sizzled bottom as she padded her way across the sun-warmed hallway floor and back into the front room where she'd been standing vigil.

There, she found Dana waiting for her, now fully dressed for the day to come and holding her pajama bottoms draped across one arm.

"Come here, you," she ordered with a fond smile, beckoning her over with her free hand.

Rhen, who didn't need to be told twice just then to obey, immediately crossed the remaining distance over to where her fiancé stood in three quick strides, burying her face against her front as she clung to her.

"I'm so sorry, Dana," she murmured against her chest, squeezing tight as she fought back a sudden surge of remorseful tears. "I know I already said it was an accident, but I still feel really, *really* bad about everything and I… I…"

"Shhh… There, there, it's alright, honey buns, I've got you," soothed her partner, resting her chin atop her frazzled hair and rubbing her back with one hand while the other fondled her pristinely pale bottom. "You don't need to feel bad. I forgive you."

Those three simple words were enough to drain all the coiled tension inside the younger girl out in one long, ragged exhalation.

And a rather undignified sniffle.

"Th-Thanks…"

"You're very welcome," cooed Dana, kissing the top of her head. "And I hope you know too that no matter what, I'll always love you."

She let the hand gripping her bottom give it a firm squeeze then.

"Even when I have to punish you."

"Heh."

Grimacing, but still feeling significantly more relaxed now that she knew for sure her partner wasn't mad at her, Rhen pulled back enough to look up into her smiling eyes.

"Don't worry. I'm pretty used to your particular brand of tough love by now."

"I should certainly hope so," snorted Dana, letting the hand that had been rubbing her back drift down to join its fellow at her cheeks, giving them a much firmer squeeze this time.

"Ah!"

"Speaking of which, you little brat…"

Digging in her nails, eliciting a fresh yelp from Rhen as she bunny hopped in place, her voice took on a low, dangerous purr.

"I hope you haven't forgotten that you still have a spanking coming your way."

"Ugh," harrumphed the shorter girl, bonking her forehead playfully against her breasts in retaliation as soon as she'd eased her grip. "Do we have to?"

"Sorry sweetie, I'm afraid so. A promise is a promise, and Auntie Dana *always* keeps her word."

"Humph. Tell me about it…"

Untangling herself from around her bride-to-be with a snicker, Dana took a step back and playfully tapped the tip of her nose.

"Now you go get changed and then park yourself right back in the corner where you belong, missy. I expect to see you there within the next ten minutes, understand?"

Her grin took on a predatory edge to it then that made Rhen's insides squirm excitedly.

"You do *not* want me to have to come find you."

"Oh come on! Can't we do this n-?" she started to argue, only to be cut off mid-sass by a forceful kiss to her pouting lips before they could voice the rest of her protests.

"I've still got things to take care of before everyone starts showing up, so you're just going to have to wait," Dana said once she'd pulled away, leaving no room for argument as she pressed her pajama bottoms into her arms. "But don't you worry, cutie pie. You'll still be biking to campus on a sore seat, I promise."

"Great," deadpanned Rhen, rolling her eyes.

"Isn't it though?" teased her partner, stepping aside and gently swatting her on her bare bottom, reminding her once again that she was still completely naked below the waist and that people would be showing up to their house before too long. "Now get going, unless you'd like for all your little friends to see you standing in the corner like this instead."

"No thanks!"

Sufficiently motivated now, Rhen sped out of the room as fast as she could, clutching her pajama bottoms to her chest as she barreled her way through their front entryway and upstairs to her bedroom.

And, although she'd be the first to admit that an enema and a spanking certainly weren't the most ideal way to start her morning, she also couldn't bring herself to be all that upset about it, either. Dana loved her and cared enough to discipline her whenever she messed up, and that was something she wouldn't trade for anything in the world.

Even if it meant having to swallow a double dose of humiliation before it was even lunch time.

"I love you, Dana!" she called back down the stairs as she reached the door to her room.

"Love you too, cutie pie."

Oh yes. It was definitely going to be a good day.

Chapter 18

Many Hands Make Light Work

Returning to her corner, now fully dressed and with time to spare, Rhen soon found herself caught between the all too familiar sensations of mind-numbing boredom and stomach-churning anxiety that always seemed to accompany a pre-punishment timeout. But, doing her best not to think too much about how before too long she'd be feeling a burst of cool air as her skirt was flipped up in back and the waistband of her panties was dragged down across her smooth cheeks on its way to her knees, she settled in to wait for the inevitable order to come lie across her aunt's lap.

Only, it never came.

Instead, she was left standing there, nose pressed to the wall and hands on top of her head, waiting. Listening on as Dana busied herself around the house, straightening things up and squeezing in a quick phone call with one of her design clients before the day got going in earnest. And, with each sluggishly passing minute, and eventually each new kid who was dropped off by their parents, she found herself growing more and more nervous. The butterflies inside her stomach stirring up into a tornado of worry and mortified dread with no outlet other than for her to dance awkwardly in place, her cheeks clenching and unclenching beneath the taut confines of her panties as they awaited their appointment with her auntie.

Of course, the little passing quips from the parents who saw her standing there as they accompanied their kids inside to say hello to her partner didn't exactly help things either.

"Uh-oh! In trouble already, Rhen?"

"Let me guess. Did you forget to clean your room last night?"

"Looks like Dana's about to get her morning workout in. You're just so helpful, aren't you, dear?"

"You might want to spank her sooner, rather than later, Dana. She looks like she's about ready to wet her pants with the way she keeps squirming around."

Oh, hah-hah. Yuck it up, Sharon. Everyone's a freaking comedian, I swear...

Wrapping herself in a cloak of chilly dignity, refusing to sass back at any of the patronizing comments being lobbed her way (largely because she knew doing so would most likely just prompt her partner to invite the people she'd be snapping at to stick around and watch her upcoming punishment), Rhen instead satisfied herself with glaring indignantly at nothing in particular as she carried on imaginary conversations in her head that she won handily.

And, as the clock behind her continued to tick away, marking the passage of first ten minutes, then fifteen, twenty, and finally a full half hour without her being summoned out of timeout, she resigned herself to the fact that she was going to be given a public spanking. She doubted very much that Dana planned on using her as an object lesson again like she had back when she'd been caught riding her bike without a helmet on. But, even so, it still seemed pretty likely that she'd have at least a handful of witnesses watching from just out of sight around the corner as her bottom was warmed for her that morning. Which, while definitely humiliating, at least wasn't totally out of the ordinary for her fiancé's daycare either.

As far as the tweens she looked after were concerned, Rhen was just like the rest of them when it came to getting in trouble. (Even if she technically was way older than all of them.) Which meant that if Auntie Dana decided you were getting a spanking, then you were *getting* a spanking.

Period.

Oh well

On the bright side, though, she was at least able to take solace in the fact that it was only going to be a hand spanking this time.

Of course, she'd still probably cry. Dana always did her best to bring her to tears whenever she was administering a capital P punishment, after all. But, that was still better than trying to fall asleep on her stomach later that night just because Missus Hairbrush decided she wanted to have a word with her about her spending habits.

Albeit just barely.

"Hah! Now why am I not surprised to find you here?" drawled an amused young woman's voice from a couple of feet behind her, startling Rhen from her zoned-out mulling over of where she wanted to eat lunch that afternoon.

"Wha-?" she started to ask, half turning from where she had her nosed pressed to the corner.

Only to be stopped by a pair of firm hands on her shoulders.

"Uh-uh-uh," tutted the voice in a condescending sing-song, steering her back into position. "You know that's not allowed, Rhen."

"But-!"

"No buts, missy. Rules are rules."

"I…"

"Yes?"

"Ugh. Never mind."

Giving up on rounding on her friend with a glower, mostly because she knew she was right and she didn't need to heap any more trouble onto her plate just then, Rhen instead settled for stomping a foot as she let out an annoyed harrumph.

"What the heck are you even doing here, Anna?" she grumbled into her corner, doing her best to sound as annoyed as possible. "Shouldn't you be in class or something?"

"I'm taking the semester off," answered the younger girl with a nonchalant shrug, fingers fiddling with the black stone choker around her neck as she added with a sinister snicker. "And is that *really* how you should be talking to your 'auntie's' new assistant, young lady?"

"Assistant?" Rhen squeaked, her heart leaping into her throat with the word.

"Yep!" confirmed Anna, her voice positively brimming with excitement now. "Didn't she tell you I was starting today?"

As a matter of fact, Rhen's partner had neglected to mention anything to her about hiring the recent high school grad from their church as her new daycare assistant (the very same job that she herself had bombed out of so spectacularly the day they'd first met), but it didn't exactly take a genius to figure out why.

She'd wanted to spring it on her just like this!

Oh my god, Dana, you are so dead, Rhen thought to herself with a rueful smirk.

While aloud she simply said, "I guess it must've slipped her mind," doing her best to keep her tone breezy and conversational despite it being muffled by the walls hemming her in on either side of her face.

It was surprisingly difficult to come across as a social equal when you were stuck standing in the corner like a naughty child.

"But, uh, yeah. Congrats, Anna!" she went on, pushing through her surprise and embarrassment to summon some genuine enthusiasm. "I'm totally stoked to hear you're going to be giving her- I mean us, some help around here. That's awesome."

And, despite the fresh splash of bright red warming her (thankfully) hidden face, she actually meant it.

Even though she'd had a bit of a rocky start with the willowy younger girl now simultaneously gloating and making casual conversation behind her, Rhen really did like Anna. True, she did have a bit of a bossy streak to her when it came to exercising the meager amount of authority her mother granted her in their Sunday school class, but with the exception of her occasional friendly pats to the seat of her church dress when no else one was looking, she really wasn't all *that* bad. In fact, she'd found that Anna was downright nice once she'd actually gotten to know her. They'd ran into each other on campus by complete accident a few months back, and after bonding over some cheap burgers and fries in the student union, they'd become fast friends.

Which just made her wish all the more that she hadn't started the girl's first day on the job in such an embarrassing position.

Whatever. It was bound to happen sooner or later, I'm sure, Rhen sighed to herself, feeling the tension drain from her shoulders now that her initial shock at being "caught" standing in the corner had passed.

"Well now, I'm glad to see you two are hitting it off so well," spoke up Dana then from out of the blue, making her jump about a foot in the air with another high-pitched squeak.

She hated out how easy it was to sneak up on her while she was in timeout.

I swear. It's like she's deliberately trying to startle me sometimes. Humph!

"We sure are," answered Anna for her, her voice taking on a wickedly amused edge to it. "Sorry if she's not supposed to be talking to anyone, Missus Johnson. I just couldn't resist the chance to tease my favorite brat while she's stuck in the corner, you know?"

Her frank response managed to draw out an indulgent chuckle from Dana.

"That's fine, dear. I completely understand," she replied, before adding with a mild hint of menace. "Just be careful you don't do that with any of the other children, alright? As I'm sure you've noticed by now, there are *two* corners in this room, and I have it on good authority from your mother that you're no stranger to standing in one yourself."

"Heh. Yes ma'am," came the willowy brunette's dutiful reply, sounding at least somewhat chastened. "I promise I'll keep my friendly ribbing confined to Rhen and only Rhen."

"Good girl."

"Thanks!"

"Goody-goody," snorted Rhen, keeping her voice pitched just low enough so that only Anna would be able to hear her.

Or, so she'd thought.

"Excuse me, little girl?" her partner demanded, her tone

caught somewhere between steely disapproval and warm amusement as she swept in past her new assistant and seized hold of her by the ear.

"Ack! Nothing ma'am!" she squawked as she was spun around to face the two of them, dancing on the balls of her feet.

"It sure didn't sound like nothing to me," piped up Anna, dimples forming in her cheeks as her lips drew back in a taunting smirk.

"No, it really didn't," agreed Dana, her tone still walking that fine line between laughter and exasperation as she shook her head. "In fact, it sounded a *lot* like someone was saying she's ready for her spanking."

"Oh yeah. I definitely heard 'spank me, spank me'."

"No you didn't!" insisted Rhen, suddenly developing a case of cold feet despite wanting to get everything over with just a moment earlier.

Neither of the "adults" in the room seemed to care, however.

"Anna, dear," her aunt went on as if the two of them were discussing the weather and not her impending bottom blistering. "I've still got about a million and a half things I need to get done around here before lunch time. Would you do me a favor and take care of her for me?"

"Wha-?"

Stiffening in her partner's steely grip, Rhen felt the bottom drop out of her stomach and plummet like a boulder to the floor.

Oh come on… No way…

Anna seemed to be just as caught off guard as she was. Though, nowhere near as embarrassed.

"You mean…?" she started to ask, reaching up to tuck back a lock of hair that had come loose from the messy bun she'd piled on top of her head as her gaze shifted from her new boss, to Rhen, and back again.

"Yes, that's right," nodded Dana with an encouraging smile. "I'd like you to spank her for me."

"Aunt Dana, no!" moaned a horrified Rhen at that, stomping a foot and being rewarded for her efforts with a sharp twist to her ear. "You- Ow! You can't be serious!"

"I don't recall asking for your opinion, little girl," snapped her partner, tugging her up even higher onto her tiptoes. "So unless you'd like a second trip over my knee before dinner tonight, I'd zip it, lock it, and put it in your pocket. You hear me?"

"Ow! Ack! Okay, okay, fine!"

Rolling her eyes, Rhen nevertheless wisely chose to keep her lips clamped shut tight around the rest of the complaints straining to escape from her just then.

Now was definitely not the time to be pressing her luck.

"Now then, Anna," her partner continued sweetly, as if they hadn't just been rudely interrupted by a bratty child. "Do you think you can handle blistering this one's backside for me?"

"Uh…"

Seeming to decide that this wasn't some sort of elaborate practical joke and that she hadn't been hearing things, Anna shook her head to clear it (dislodging the strand she'd just tucked away in the process) and drew herself up to her full height.

"Yes ma'am! You can count on me."

"Thank you, dear, you're a total lifesaver," replied Dana with a sigh of relief, releasing her hold on her bride-to-be and sending her stumbling forward toward the younger girl with a firm pat to the seat of her skirt. "Ahhh, it's going to be so nice having someone I can actually delegate things to around here for a change!"

"Yeah, Anna, you're *such* a help," deadpanned Rhen, coming to a stop just in front of her friend and crossing her arms over the minimal swell of her chest with a petulant huff.

Much as she hated to admit it, though, her partner did have a point. While she always tried her best to help out around the daycare whenever she could, no matter what she did, none of the tweens Dana looked after actually thought of her as an authority figure.

Especially not when so many of them were already taller than she was.

"Happy to help, ma'am," preened Anna, practically glowing from the praise, her new charge's annoyance only further fueling her bubbly disposition.

"Oh, and one more thing before I forget," added Dana while Rhen continued to sulk, stepping in close and murmuring something into her new assistant's ear.

She kept her voice low enough that her petite not-niece was unable to parse out exactly what was being said, but whatever it was had Anna's eyes widening to the size of dinner plates as her face lit up with surprised excitement.

"Oh, wow. Are you sure?" she asked a moment later, swallowing hard.

"Mmhmm," nodded Dana, stepping back with a wink. "I have complete faith in you, hon. It's much easier than you might think, and I'll be just downstairs if you need any help, alright?"

Swelling with pride, Anna flashed her boss two thumbs up

"Right!"

Rhen, for her part, was far less excited about this new mystery directive her partner had just given, but her sour glare was met only with further unflappable motherly warmth as she reached out and ruffled her hair.

"Okay then, I'll leave you to it," she crooned as she sauntered her way out of the room and back toward the kitchen. "Be sure to come check in with me once you're done, Anna. I'm sure I'll have plenty more for you to do by then."

"Yes ma'am!" chirped the brunette. "She'll be nice and sorry by the time I'm through with her, don't you worry!"

"I'm sure she will," called Dana with a chuckle, before adding more firmly as she threw a hard glare over her shoulder. "*Behave*, Rhen."

"Yeah… yeah…"

And just like that, it was all suddenly over and her fate was sealed.

Now standing alone in the room, just the two of them, Anna turned to her with a look that was equal parts sympathetic and smug.

"So," she started to say, stepping in close and dropping her voice down to a conspiratorial murmur. "Would you rather we take care of this here, or up in your room?"

Recognizing the question for the olive branch it was, Rhen immediately seized upon it, changing her grumpy tune to one of grudging acceptance in a heartbeat.

"Upstairs, please."

"Somehow I thought you might say that," snickered Anna, grinning.

"Your powers of deduction never cease to amaze," the shorter girl shot right on back, matching her knowing look with a tolerant pout.

"I am a woman of many talents, aren't I?"

"Uh-huh. Whatever you say, Anna."

"Whatever I say, huh?"

At that, her aunt's assistant's grin turned wicked.

"How's this then? It's time for your spanking, little girl!"

"Wait, like, *now*?"

Somehow Rhen had imagined things taking longer to get going.

"Yes now!"

Taking hold of her upper arm in a firm grip, Anna began frog-marching her out of the front room while all the while continuing to excitedly chew her ear off.

"Come on, hurry up! Stop dragging your feet," she ordered, escorting her past a trio of suspiciously loitering twelve-year-olds who scattered at their approach. "I'm so excited to see your room!"

"Alright, alright, I'm coming," laughed Rhen, scurrying to keep up with her friend's longer strides as she was pulled along toward the foot of the stairs.

And, despite the butterflies swirling around inside her stomach, the humiliating thrum reverberating between her legs with each hurried step she took, and the sobering knowledge that the younger girl dragging her toward her doom was going to do her darndest to make her cry like a little girl (and would almost certainly succeed), Rhen found that she just couldn't stop herself from smiling.

Sure, it totally sucked that she was about to get spanked by yet another one of her friends. And, sure, she knew the balance of power between the two of them would never quite be the same once this was all over. But, she also knew too that she was in good (if slightly overeager) hands.

And that made all the difference.

—

Unfortunately for Rhen, her newfound sense of cautious optimism evaporated the instant her bedroom door swung open.

Oh god, here we go. No turning back now, I guess…

"Oooh, your room is way cleaner than mine is," marveled Anna with an appreciative whistle as Rhen led her through an abbreviated tour, drawing particular attention to some of her favorite posters, the 3D printer she'd gotten for her birthday, and the handful of PVC figurines arranged in exciting poses on top of her bookshelf. "You and Dana did such a great job decorating in here. I swear, it's like I'm back in my old room from middle school. I especially love these little guys."

Striding over to her neatly made bed, Anna gathered up the stuffed teddy bear and penguin that had pride of place atop the center of her mattress, giving each an experimental hug before nodding in satisfaction.

"Oh yeah. *Very* cuddly."

"Aren't they, though?" agreed Rhen, brightening somewhat as she accepted the bear back from her friend and gave it a quick nuzzle herself.

"This one's Kuma," she explained, setting him back down next to her pillow with reverent care before doing the same with her penguin. "And this guy's Tux. Dana bought them for me the day after I moved in, actually."

"Awww, I love that. You two are just *so* precious!"

"Yeah, we do make a pretty good couple, don't we?" demurred the shorter girl.

"For. *Sure.*"

A small smile stole across Rhen's face with that, and she busied herself with making sure that both of her nighttime snuggle buddies were arranged just so against her pillows in an attempt to hide her blushing cheeks while Anna eased herself down onto the edge of her bed.

"Well, uh… Alright then," she ventured tentatively, clearing her throat and dusting off the tops of her blue-jean covered thighs. "I guess it's time to, you know…"

Meeting her anxious gaze, also unsure of how best to proceed, Rhen just grimaced and nodded.

"Yeah…"

A faint trace of pink swept in to color Anna's cheeks then, and she took a moment to nervously lick her lips before seeming to find her confidence once again.

"Okay, yeah."

Nodding to herself, she sat up straight and fixed her in place with her best "I'm the boss and you'll do what I say" look.

Which, to her credit, *did* make Rhen's insides squirm just a little bit.

"It's time for your spanking, young lady."

But, faced now with this sternly demanding version of her friend, the flustered twenty-one-year-old turned teenager suddenly found her petulant side rocketing into overdrive. And, rather than acquiesce like she knew she should, she instead heaved out her best aggrieved harrumph and stomped a foot.

If Anna wanted to boss her around, then she was going to have to work for it!

"Oh my god, this is, like, so not fair."

Rather than be intimidated by her sudden surge of brattiness, however, her whining only seemed to further cement Anna's confidence. Confidence which she brought to bear with devastating effectiveness as she leaned back against the mattress and regarded her coolly.

"And how do you figure that, short stuff?" she asked, buffing her nails on the front of her shirt.

Short stuff? Rhen fumed silently. *Why you...*

Up until that point, she'd always found the younger girl's teasing nickname for her to be fairly endearing, at least when it was just the two of them hanging out on campus. But now, poised as she was to be taken across her lap, it instead only served to further increase her impudent agitation and drive home just how massive the gulf between their levels of authority had suddenly become.

Plus, it also really didn't help that they were both staring at each other at eye level right then with Anna sitting and her standing.

"It's super unfair, *because*," the petite junior began to explain, pouring all of her affronted indignation into that one, single word as she rolled her eyes.

Only to then run out of steam as Anna continued to simply stare her down with a patiently condescending look.

"Yeah?"

"Uh..."

Grinning now, she made a twirling motion with her hand.

"Go on, I'm listening. You were saying it's super unfair that I, your aunt's assistant who she specifically *told* to spank you and who therefore by all accounts has every right to, you know, spank you, is being unfair because..."

"Well, um, you know... Because, like..."

"Mmhmm?"

But when Rhen only continued to mouth ineffectually at her, searching for a reply that didn't make her sound like a frustrated middle schooler not getting her way, she decided to press her advantage.

"Correct me if I'm wrong, *Rhenny*," she interrupted sweetly, sitting up straight once again. "But you're the one who messed up here and earned yourself a spanking, aren't you?"

"I mean…" mumbled a now red-faced Rhen, twisting a toe into the plush carpet at her feet as she plucked an imaginary bit of lint from the front of her t-shirt. "Maybe."

"Excuse me, young lady, but maybes are babies," chided Anna, doing a remarkably good job of maintaining a straight face as she did so. "Can you please use your big girl words and answer my question?"

Her entire demeanor was positively radiating smug triumph now, and Rhen's dirty looks were only further adding to her amusement.

"Okay, *fine*. Yes, I did mess up," she finally admitted once it became clear that Anna was going to let her stew in her own embarrassed silence for as long as it took for her to give her the answer she was looking for.

"See? It's totally fair then," gloated the younger girl, before seeming to take some small amount of pity on her and adding. "And, besides, you were already going to get it anyway. So it's not really *that* big of a deal if I'm the one doing it, is it? The end result is still the same, right?"

Rhen was honestly hard pressed to argue with her there, so she didn't even bother, instead switching to an entirely different tactic.

"But I'm older than you!"

Again, though, Anna remained completely unflappable in the face of her impotent whining.

"Yeah, so?"

"So! So, uh… You know…"

"Believe it or not, knowing how old you really are actually makes this whole thing way easier for me."

"It does?" squeaked Rhen, taking half a step back as her stomach flip-flopped in a not totally unpleasant way.

"I mean, *yeah*," laughed Anna with a shake of her head. "If you were an actual teenager I'd totally feel bad that you were about to get your butt busted. But, since you're old enough to know better, I can pretty much tan your hide as much as I want with a clear conscience."

She snorted softly then, gesturing to indicate the adolescent styled room they were currently in, Rhen's equally adolescent outfit, and her general demeanor all at once.

"Not that you've made it all that hard for me to forget you're not *actually* a kid. Heh."

Grimacing now, Rhen felt a sudden surge of embarrassed apprehension and self-doubt well its way up from deep within her.

"Um, I guess that's fair," she conceded. "But, like, are you sure you don't think this whole thing is kinda…"

Flushing scarlet all over again, she felt her gaze being drawn inexorably back down toward the tops of her socks as she finished in an embarrassed mumble.

"You know… Weird?"

"What?" demanded Anna, sounding genuinely surprised. "Of course not!"

"Really?" pressed Rhen, forcing herself to meet the younger girl's amber eyes. "But-"

"Look."

Anna's face took on a bemused but kind expression to it then as she brushed aside the rest of whatever it was she'd been about to say.

"There're plenty of girls our age that still get spanked, so there's seriously no reason to feel like you're the only one who has to put up with it, alright?"

Feeling the tense knot inside her stomach beginning to loosen somewhat, Rhen's lips made a valiant attempt at an upward twitch. She knew that the willowy brunette still caught the business end of her mother's paddle from time to time, but she hadn't really thought there were others still taking trips across parental laps after they'd finished high school. Much less ones in their twenties.

"Really?"

"Oh yeah," laughed Anna. "You know Rebecca Stewart?"

"Uh-huh…"

Rebecca was a girl in her mid-twenties who'd been studying abroad for the last year and a half and had only recently returned home to live with her parents while she finished her dissertation. She seemed nice enough, but Rhen hadn't really had a chance to get to know her yet since she was still stuck in "remedial Sunday school" as her aunt and Sister Miller liked to call it.

"Well," continued Anna in a conspiratorial tone, her eyes alighting with mischief as she leaned in close. "I happen to know, because I overheard my mom talking to her mom about it on the phone last week, that little miss world traveler got her ass absolutely *roasted* after she came home at five in the morning without returning any of her parents' calls."

"No way!" gasped Rhen, momentarily forgetting that she was in for a very similar treatment before too long.

"I'm serious! Apparently she was pretty buzzed too and decided to drive home instead of leaving her car at her friend's house, and her mom just about hit the roof when she found out. *And*, get this. She totally wants my dad to make her a paddle now."

"Oh my god, her poor butt!" giggled the raven-haired twenty-one-year-old turned teenager.

She knew all too well just what kind of paddle Anna's mom preferred to use, and it definitely made an impression. (For about a day and a half at the very least!)

"Yeah, no kidding," agreed Anna with a sympathetic wince before easing back against the mattress once again. "So, like, if *she's* still getting spanked, then you have nothing to be embarrassed about."

"I guess so…"

"Besides," she went on, her mischievous grin returning even wider now. "I actually think it's really cute that you and Dana have this whole aunt and niece thing going on. It might not be, uh… the total norm or whatever, but hey…"

She shrugged.

"If it works for you, then who cares?"

Hearing that, Rhen let go of a breath she hadn't realized she'd been holding until just then and nodded gratefully.

"Thanks, Anna. That means a lot. Seriously."

"No prob," waved away the younger girl, before rubbing her hands together excitedly. "Plus… If I'm being totally real with you here, I've been *dying* for a chance to get my hands on that cute little butt of yours again ever since that time Mom gave you The Board back during Sunday school."

"R-Really?" squeaked Rhen, going red all over again, but not particularly hating the twinge of excitement Anna's words had sent rippling through her stomach.

"Mmhmm," she replied, nibbling on her lower lip as she ran her eyes up and down along her compact frame. "And you'd best believe I'm going to be watching you like a freaking hawk from now on. I fully intend on taking advantage of every chance I can to help your 'aunt' keep you in line."

She winked at her then as the two of them shared a giggle.

"Cutie pie."

Rhen couldn't help but stick her tongue out at that, though.

"Oh bite me, you big bully."

"What was that?" challenged Anna, a note of saccharine sweet menace creeping its way into her voice as she turned her attention toward the nightstand just a couple feet off to her right. "You know, I can't help but notice that there's a pretty mean looking hairbrush just sitting there. Maybe I ought to save myself some trouble and use that instead?"

Her bravado blowing away like dust in the wind, Rhen immediately folded.

"Wait, no please! I'm sorry!"

"Oh, are you?" asked Anna, teasing out the question as she started leaning toward the nightstand, stretching out her arm and wriggling her fingers with exaggerated slowness. "Are you *sure* I'm not going to need this?"

"You won't, I promise! I'll do whatever you say."

"See, now was that so hard?" she laughed as she sat back up.

"I guess not," huffed Rhen sourly.

Her pouting only continued to feed into Anna's control of the situation, however.

"Grump it up all you want, kiddo. Either way, your butt is mine from here on out, so I'd get used to it if I were you."

Huffing and puffing in exasperated indignation, but unable to really do anything about it (even if she'd wanted to), Rhen had no choice but to agree with a begrudging, "Yes ma'am."

"Great!"

With the matter clearly now settled as far as she was concerned, Anna gave the tops of her thighs an eager couple of pats.

"Now come here. It's time to get you ready."

"Ready?" echoed Rhen, even as her legs began to move on autopilot, drawing her inexorably forward until she was standing just an inch or two away from the younger girl's knees.

"Well, yeah," she scoffed, rolling her eyes. "You didn't seriously think I wasn't going to spank you on the bare, did you?"

"I mean…" mumbled the shorter girl. "I'd kind of hoped so."

"Sorry, kiddo," chirped Anna, leaning forward and turning her hips to the side so that she could gain access to her skirt's button clasp and zipper. "But Miss Anna believes in punishing a naughty girl's *bottom*, not her panties."

A nervous little giggle escaped from her lips then, putting a slight dent in her firmly in control persona. One which Rhen couldn't help but share in as well.

"Cute."

"Like that one?" she asked with a coy smirk. "I've been working on it all week."

Rhen was just about to fire back with something sassy to tease her friend, when the button clasp she'd been fiddling with suddenly came free, allowing gravity to snatch her skirt away from her hips and send it plummeting down to pool in a crumpled heap around her ankles.

"Well, well, well… Bumblebees, huh?" drawled Anna, clearly pleased with her discovery as she shifted her back around to face her. "That seems appropriate."

Grinning wickedly, she reached around and gave her bottom a sharp pinch.

"Ah!"

"See?"

Her face now ablaze as her hands twitched at her sides, desperately resisting the urge to betray how embarrassed she felt just then by trying to hide her panties with the hem of her shirt, Rhen kept her attention focused squarely on the poster pinned to the wall ahead of her.

"Y-Yeah… I guess so."

She hadn't *meant* to do that with her choice in underwear that morning, she'd just grabbed the first pair she'd seen, but it seemed she had a natural talent for irony.

"Anyway," continued her soon to be spanker, idly tracing one of the swirling dotted lines that trailed after the happily flying bees with a fingertip. "These panties weren't the ones who were being naughty, now were they?"

Realizing that she was actually expecting an answer to that question, Rhen nodded just enough to not seem like she was being uncooperative.

"No."

"No… what?"

Blowing out an exasperated huff through her nostrils, she glowered at her friend.

"No, *ma'am*."

"Very good," cooed Anna, before plucking at her waistband with a frown. "Which means, cute as these are, they're still going to have to go, I'm afraid."

"Oh yeah, you sound real torn up about it," grumbled Rhen under her breath, shuffling awkwardly in place.

"Mmhmm…"

Anna was only half listening to her now as she leaned forward and began rolling her panties down for her. Turning them inside out over and over again as she gradually worked them down off of her hips, unveiling her pale cheeks and smooth mound one interminably slow inch at a time.

The entire process ended up taking a lot longer than what Rhen was used to in these kinds of situations. Normally, when her bottom was being bared for a spanking, it was all over in just a couple of seconds. One moment her panties were right where they were supposed to be, and then the next they were suddenly around her knees or ankles with very little time to actually think about how they'd gotten there. But, with Anna's prolonged approach, she was forced to be painfully aware of each and every little shift of the stretchy material against her skin as it was peeled away.

As her panties reached the lower half of her cheeks, for instance, she felt the cotton wedged between them stubbornly refuse to come free. Instead, it continued to stretch more and more taut with each turn before finally slipping out all at once as her waistband rasped its way down past her sit-spots, the gusset between her legs following shortly thereafter with distressingly similar results.

And, worst of all, with each new rotation, her panties grew more and more snug. Slowly transforming from an adorable pair of childish undies into an impromptu pair of cotton shackles cinched snugly around her legs.

"This is the way Mom likes to do it," Anna explained when she noticed the look of confusion on her face, giving her bright yellow underwear one final twist before wriggling them the rest of the way down into position just above her knees. "It stops you from being able to kick as much."

"Great…"

"Yep, it totally sucks," she agreed with a commiserating wince, before letting out an excited gasp and covering her mouth to hold in a laugh as she got her first good look at the bare slit she'd just uncovered. "Oh my god! She totally keeps you shaved, doesn't she? I *knew* it!"

Flushing hot tomato red from her neck all the way to the roots of her raven dark hair, clutching her naked bottom behind her for dear life with both hands in order to stop herself from covering her front, Rhen nodded sheepishly.

"Uh… Yeah," she admitted, squeezing just a bit harder as she did so. "She says that, um, you know… That my looks should match my behavior, or whatever."

"Heh. I just bet she does," snickered Anna, dragging a pair of fingertips along the smooth stretch of skin just above her folds. "Oh wow, you have some really soft skin. Like, damn, girl."

Swallowing hard, her heart pounding out a rhythm of exhilarated embarrassment inside her chest, Rhen shivered.

"Th-Thanks. I've actually been using a scrub brush in the shower for a few weeks now and it's really made a difference, I think."

"Mmmm, yeah. Totally," nodded Anna, looking just a little bit jealous. "Dana is definitely one lucky lady, that's for sure."

"No arguments here," snorted the petite junior, her heightened state of nervousness and humiliation drawing out a burst of giggles from her as she gave her bare cheeks another hard squeeze in an attempt to burn off some of her mounting anxiety.

It didn't help.

Thankfully, though, Anna seemed to remember then that she was supposed to be disciplining her, rather than just chit-chatting while she admired her snug curves. And so, with a quick cough and an overly loud clearing of her throat, she drew herself back up to her full height and planted her hands on her hips, pinning her in place with her best disapproving scowl.

"Alright, you, that's enough goofing around. Being cute isn't going to stop me from spanking you, so don't even try!"

Rhen couldn't help but roll her eyes at that, matching the other girl's stern look with her best apathetic teen sneer.

"Whatever you say," she droned with a dismissive toss of her hair. "Just make it quick, would you? I have a meeting on campus that I need to get to."

Anna's mask of bossy, self-assured determination slipped then. Her smirk bending out of shape into a fretful frown as she cast a quick glance toward the alarm clock on the nightstand beside her.

"Oh crap, you do?" she asked in a hurry. "When?"

Oops.

"Sorry, sorry, I was just teasing, Anna," Rhen quickly back-pedalled, touched by the concern in her friend's voice (and feeling more than a little guilty for making her worry in the first place). "It's actually not until noon, so don't sweat it. We've still got plenty of time for, for uh…"

Suddenly not quite able to meet her gaze anymore, she instead directed a pout at the stuffed teddy bear and penguin ogling her from the head of her bed and gestured ineffectually behind her.

"You know… All this."

"Phew!"

Letting out a relived breath that quickly transformed into a laugh, Anna once more took up her mantle as the no-nonsense daycare disciplinarian, now looking genuinely annoyed and more determined than ever to roast her buns.

"Geez! Don't scare me like that, you little brat. You nearly gave me a heart attack!"

"Sor-ry," harrumphed Rhen, drawing out the word with an insolent scowl. "But it's not my fault you're bad at time manage-ment, is it?"

Taking the bait hook, line, and sinker, Anna rolled her eyes and shook her head.

"Oh yeah, just go ahead and keep piling on the attitude, kiddo. You're just giving me all the excuses I need to *really* have some fun with you."

"Oh my god! You're not supposed to say that part out loud, you dingus."

"Oops, sorry," she giggled. "Guess I need more practice at this."

"Yeah, no kid-" the petite junior standing in front of her began to reply, only to be cut off by a yelp of surprise as she was seized by the wrist and yanked forward.

"Come here, you!"

Growling playfully, Anna sent her tottering around to her left side, the panties locked around her knees forcing her to take awkward, shuffling, baby steps, before upending her across her lap.

"I've had just about enough lip from you for one day."

Again, Rhen tried to protest.

"Wait, hold on-!"

SMACK! SMACK!

Only to have her pleas be overridden by a pair of surprisingly sharp slaps to the centers of either of her bare cheeks.

"Oh! Owie!"

It had all happened in the blink of an eye, and now her vision was dominated entirely by an up close view of thick carpet fibers and the legs of her study chair and desk. Funnily enough, though, in that moment, rather than be concerned about how she was about to be punished severely, Rhen instead found herself mostly just struck by how odd everything looked from this vantage point. Since Anna was left-handed, she was being presented with an entirely different view of her room than the one she was used to seeing when Dana had her over her knee at bedtime.

Huh. How'd all those candy wrappers get under there? I should really take care of that before-

SMACK!

"Yeowie!"

"Not-"

SMACK!

"Feeling-"

SMACK!

"So-"

SMACK!

"Mouthy-"

SMACK!

"Now-"

SMACK!

"Are we?"

SMACK! SMACK! SMACK!

Demanded Anna, punctuating her scolding with a high-speed volley of hard, merciless swats that had Rhen hissing in a breath through clenched teeth.

"Yes-! I mean no-! I mean *yes*!" the shorter girl yelped, scissoring her ankles back and forth behind her as much as she could while she tried (and failed) not to let on just how much the younger girl's palm had stung.

Thankfully, she was given a brief respite to catch her breath as Anna paused to assess the faint series of overlapping pink handprints she'd managed to paint across her cheeks so far.

"So," she asked conversationally, setting aside her lecturing tone for the moment as she rolled her shoulders, limbering up before resuming swatting at a much more leisurely pace. "What'd you do, anyway? Dana didn't seem too happy with you when I got here."

"Ugh," grumbled the shorter girl, a fresh surge of guilt and embarrassment roiling around inside her stomach as her body jerked forward with each slap. "That's none- Ow! Of your- Oh! Business."

"Uh-huh," snorted Anna, her voice punctuated by the sharp reports of hard palm against soft skin.

SMACK! SMACK! SMACK!

"Sure it isn't."

"It isn't!"

"Are you *sure* about that?"

"Yes I freaking am!"

"Okay, fine, have it your way. Guess we're doing this the hard way..."

SMACK! SMACK! SMACK!

Despite her best efforts to keep a lid on things, Rhen was only able to hold out for about another minute or two more before her aunt's new assistant's continued assault on her sit-spots finally eroded her will to stay silent.

"Okay, okay, okay!" she squealed. "I'll tell you, I'll tell you!"

"See?" crooned Anna, abruptly stopping her swatting and switching to massaging the shorter girl's steaming sit-spots instead. "Now was that so hard?"

"No ma'am…"

"Great."

SMACK!

"So fill me in already, you goof."

Letting loose with a heavy sigh, Rhen did just that. Recounting every mortifying detail of her overspending spree to her friend over the course of the next couple minutes as she gently kneaded her bottom for her.

Omitting the punishment enema part, of course.

"Okay. Wow. *Yeah*," clucked Anna, drumming her fingertips against her springy left cheek as she shook her head in amazement. "You definitely deserve to get your ass blistered for that one."

"But… but…!" Rhen started to protest, searching desperately for any way out of what she'd earned. "Anna, please! I promise I've learned my lesson already. You seriously don't have to keep spanking me. I'll be good!"

But, heartfelt as her whining might have been, Anna just laughed.

"Oh please, don't be such a baby," she scoffed, rolling her eyes. "A hand spanking is nothing. If my mom had caught me blowing through that kind of money, she'd make sure I couldn't sit down for a month!"

SMACK!

"Ack!"

"Maybe even two!"

SMACK!

"Owie!"

Rhen didn't at all doubt that. From the one time she'd been

on the receiving end of Sister Miller's ire, she'd learned all too quickly that she was not a woman to be trifled with when it came to delivering a spanking.

"This still sucks, though. Humph!"

"Yeah…" sighed Anna in agreement, tucking that same pesky lock of hair back behind her ear before shifting her friend a bit further forward across her lap, pushing her buns up even higher. "I can't really argue with you there. A spanking is still a spanking."

"See? See? So you should totally cut me some slack!"

"Hmmm… Maybe."

Anna continued to drum her fingertips against her bottom for a couple moments more, seeming to be mulling her demands over before finally speaking again.

"Alright, here," she finally said, leaning over and snatching up the stuffed bear on the bed beside her and offering it to Rhen. "If this is going to be so hard for you, then you might as well have a friend to help you out along the way."

Accepting the bear, mortification and appearances be dammed, Rhen nodded gratefully and held him tight to her chest, preparing herself as best she could for Anna to start again. It wasn't quite the break she'd been hoping for, but it was still better than nothing.

"Thanks," she mumbled into the top of the fuzzy head beneath her chin.

"Of course!"

SMACK!

"Now, where were we?"

—

After cutting loose with a nonstop explosion of energetic, open-palmed smacks for a solid three minutes straight, Anna was eventually forced to come to a stop once again. Though, this time, it wasn't because of any complaining on Rhen's part.

Not that she hadn't been doing her darndest to convince her

that she'd done enough as well, mind.

"Geez, holy cow!" the younger girl gasped, shaking out her palm in an exaggerated attempt to cool it down. "This is a lot harder than Mom makes it look. No wonder she likes to use a paddle. My poor hand is killing me!"

"My heart weeps for you, truly," deadpanned Rhen through gritted teeth, flexing her toes behind her as she forced herself to take long, deep breaths in an attempt to stave off the tears that were already starting to cloud the corners of her vision.

Despite her complaining to the contrary, Anna had actually been doing an absolutely outstanding job so far making her friend regret her actions. She was very clearly a natural when it came to dishing out discipline, and had she been there to see it, her mother would've been beyond proud of her daughter's prowess for making naughty girls howl. After only a minute or two of somewhat shaky pacing and swats of varying intensity as she got a feel for the way she should move her arm and how to compensate for the petite junior's increasingly animated struggling, she'd managed to hit her stride. Settling into a speedy rhythm that left very little room for Rhen to catch her breath during the near perpetual torrent of hard, sharp swats she'd been pelting her with. As a result, her poor bottom was already hot to the touch and more than a little tender. Though, thankfully, nowhere near as much so as she knew it could've been had she decided to actually make good on her threat to use her hairbrush.

However, if the pace that the younger girl had managed to set for herself so far was anything to go by, she wasn't going to be sitting comfortably at all for most of that afternoon by the time she was finally through with her.

Which seemed to be a depressingly long amount of time still. *Ugh*.

"Are we about done here?" Rhen grumbled, trying to distract herself from the pulsing heat in her seat as she shifted around on her friend's lap in an attempt to somehow angle her hips toward a cooling breeze that just wasn't there. "I think you've definitely made your point by now."

"Quiet you!" snapped Anna playfully.

SMACK!

"Owie!"

Punctuating her command with another speedy swat.

"Hasn't anyone ever taught you that you're not supposed to talk back to your elders?"

SMACK!

"We'll be done when I *say* we're done."

"But I'm older than you!" moaned Rhen, sounding anything but as she squeezed her bear tight and furiously bobbed her ankles back and forth behind her.

"Yeah, so? I'm bigger," countered Anna with a snort. "*And* I've got permission to spank you, so I'd say that makes me the older one here for all intents and purposes."

SMACK!

"Wouldn't you agree?"

At that, Rhen opened her mouth to argue further, her jaw working without any actual words coming out. However, rather than give in to prudence and admit what they both knew to be true, she instead worked herself back up into a moody huff as she shot back.

"Oh my god, what-freaking-ever. Just hurry up and finish spanking me, you stupid nerd!"

It hadn't been a smart thing to say, and she immediately felt bad for doing so. Unfortunately, though, that didn't exactly make things any better.

"Okay then, have it your way," sighed Anna, only sounding somewhat annoyed that she had to keep punishing her. "I was actually going to start winding things down, but since you want to keep being difficult, I guess we'll just keep going."

SMACK! SMACK! SMACK! SMACK! SMACK!

"I know I was just complaining about my hand hurting and all, but I can definitely tell that this is hurting you a lot more than it's hurting me."

"You can-" Rhen gasped.

SMACK!

"Ow! Say that-"

SMACK!

"Oh! Again."

"Okay!" Anna giggled. "I can definitely tell that this is hurting you a lot more than it's hurting me."

SMACK! SMACK! SMACK!

"Har-"

SMACK!

"Yeowie! Har."

"Like that one?" she teased, punctuating her question with a flurry of swats to one cheek.

SMACK-SMACK-SMACK!

And then the other.

SMACK-SMACK-SMACK!

"Because Mom sure didn't last week."

That managed to wring a genuine snicker of amusement from Rhen. (Though it was quickly subsumed by more yelps as Anna continued to pour more and more power into her attack on her bouncy bottom.)

"In fact, she didn't like it *so* much, she started spanking me… here!"

SMACK! SMACK! SMACK! SMACK! SMACK!

"Aieee!"

A howl of pure agony erupted from Rhen then as the younger girl turned her attention exclusively to her as yet untouched thighs. Ruthlessly working her way all the way down to where her panties pinned her legs together just above her knees and back up again, over and over.

And over.

The joking had obviously come to an end now as Anna wrapped one surprisingly strong arm around her trim waist, drawing her in tight against the warmth of her belly as she increased the tempo of her swats from a heavy downpour to a furious typhoon.

"Oh! Ack! Noooo!" squealed Rhen, unable to properly kick her legs in time with the stinging swats thanks to the panties restricting her movements but doing her best to anyway. "Anna- Owie! Please- Ouch! I'm sorry!"

"Suuuure you are," drawled the younger girl, her small hand continuing to strike hard and fast.

Oh my god! How is her hand so freaking stingy?

For someone who hadn't ever given a proper spanking before that morning, Anna had certainly caught on quick. And, even worse for Rhen, her compact palm and rigid fingers were like a miniature hairbrush in their own right!

SMACK! SMACK! SMACK! SMACK! SMACK!

"I am!" she moaned again and again, burying her now tear-streaked face into her teddy bear's fluff as her buns continued to bounce and burn. "I am, I am, I am, I *am*!"

Her increasingly childish squeals and whining went completely unheeded, however, as Anna continued to pepper her backside with momentary bursts of stinging pain. Each one exploding like a firecracker against her naked cheeks, compressing them beneath the force of their impact before springing back once again for more as the initial biting sting faded into the greater tapestry of heat suffusing her entire frantically wriggling bottom and thighs.

While Anna's swats weren't anywhere near as hard or heavy as Courtney's or Jill's were, her persistent pace and unrelenting speed gave the uselessly struggling twenty-one-year-old turned teenager absolutely zero time to catch her breath or get a grip on the furious, raging bonfire in her cheeks that she was continually piling fuel onto. And, after only two or three minutes more of enthusiastic spanking, she'd successfully reduced her to a sniveling, sobbing mess. By then, Rhen had long since abandoned any further attempts to try and beg or plead her way out of her punishment, and instead had resigned herself to the reality that all she could do just then was yelp and howl, whimper and cry, as she soaked her teddy bear with her tears.

In that moment she was nothing more than a disobedient, bratty little girl getting exactly what she deserved. And she'd stay right where she was until her aunt's assistant decided that she'd finally learned her lesson.

Which was just as it should be.

—

Eventually, after what felt like two or three eternities worth of implacably energetic bottom blistering (though in reality it had only been about six or seven minutes judging by the alarm clock on Rhen's nightstand), Anna's pace began to slow and lighten, before finally coming to a stop altogether.

This time for good.

"Alrighty, short stuff, we're done," she declared, breathing heavily and gently rubbing away some of the heat radiating from Rhen's bright red bottom and thighs as she continued to quietly sob across her lap.

"I'm sorry… I'm sorry…"

"Shhh… It's okay. I forgive you," the other girl soothed. "You just take your time and let it all out, alright?"

"Y-Yes ma'am…"

Even though Anna had only been using her hand to punish her, Rhen had always known that she would end up crying long before her spanking was finally over. Her nerves had been frayed all that morning, and past experience had taught her over and over again that that was a recipe for waterworks when it came time for her panties to come down. She just hadn't been expecting to cry quite so hard is all. (Especially not across her friend's lap!) But, between disappointing her partner with her reckless overspending, the humiliating enema she'd been forced to endure after breakfast, and the fact that her punishment had come at the hands of a girl nearly three years her junior, she'd completely lost control about halfway through her spanking and hadn't been able to rein herself in the slightest.

Which, honestly, had been just what she'd needed.

Completely spent, but feeling about a million times better now (and about a million times more sore), she continued lie draped across Anna's lap like a limp noodle, sobbing out all of her remaining sorrow, embarrassment, and guilt. Letting it all drain from her body for the next couple of minutes until her breathing began to ease and she no longer felt like her chest was locked between the jaws of a steel vice.

Or that her buns were being held against a hot iron.

"I'm sorry, Miss Anna…" she repeated again, unable to think of anything else to say just then to fill the deafening silence that had rushed in to replace the echoing reports of palm striking flesh and her repentant sobs.

Even though she hadn't done anything personally to upset the younger girl (aside from a healthy bit of sassing, that is), it still felt like the right thing to say.

Although, she hadn't actually meant to tack on the "Miss" part.

Dang it. She's going to be completely insufferable now, isn't she?

"Awww, don't sweat it, kiddo," Anna crooned, immediately proving her right as she gave her left cheek a friendly squeeze. "I forgive you."

After making sure her right one got a similar treatment, she gave the center of her smoldering seat a couple firm pats.

"Ready to get up?"

"God, yes," groaned Rhen, sliding back across the younger girl's lap until she was kneeling on the carpet next to her.

Oof. My poor butt.

Hissing to herself, she began kneading her tender tush, carefully massaging away as much of the lingering ache as she could. Riding to campus later definitely wasn't going to be fun. That was for sure.

You know… It's a nice day out. Maybe I should just walk?

"You alright?" prompted Anna, drawing her out of her self-pitying reverie as she smiled fondly down at her and began straightening out her messy hair.

With feather light caresses, she brushed aside the dark strands still clinging to her tear-stained cheeks and runny nose, tucking them behind her ears.

"Yeah…"

Sniffling around a wan smile, Rhen pulled away once her hair was more or less back in order and scrubbed a forearm across her red-rimmed, watery eyes.

"Geez. You don't hold back, do you?"

"Nope," laughed the other girl, not sounding the least bit guilty. "But, in my defense, you *were* giving me a ton of attitude."

"Humph. Fair enough," conceded the thoroughly chastened not-teen, using her aunt's new assistant's legs to lever herself back up to her feet. "I'll just have to be more careful around you from now on, I guess."

"At least if you ever want to sit down again," agreed Anna with a smirk, before clucking sharply at her as she began reaching for the tangled panties around her knees. "Hold it right there, little girl. Did I say you could pull those back up?"

Batting aside her reaching hands, she gave the bright yellow panties a sharp tug, sending them plummeting the rest of the way down to Rhen's ankles (along with any hopes she might've had that the last of her humiliation was finally behind her). The sudden loss of her panties, even if they hadn't actually been covering anything, was enough to make her feel about ten times more exposed now, and her hands immediately clapped themselves over her hairless front.

"Anna!" she whined, venting her frustration and embarrassment by shifting her weight from foot to foot in a classic post-spanking dance.

"Don't you 'Anna' me!" snapped the younger girl, her hands returning to her hips as she glared at her indignantly. "Just because we're friends doesn't mean that you get to do whatever you want when I'm in charge!"

"Oh come on!"

"I'm serious, Rhen," she continued, bristling at this blatant challenge to her authority. "I didn't give you permission to pull your panties back up, and you getting all huffy about it isn't going to make me change my mind."

"But-!" spluttered Rhen, completely undone by her stern tone, only to be cut off once again.

"Shush!"

When she'd complied (albeit with a sullen huff), she went on.

"As it so happens, your aunt specifically told me *not* to let you have your panties back after I was through spanking you. So there."

"She *what*?"

Rhen had no doubt that the willowy brunette was telling the truth, so she didn't bother wasting her breath demanding to know if she was serious or arguing that she was being unfair. (Which she totally was!)

"You already spanked me, though!" she moaned instead, stomping a foot for good measure and nearly falling over in the process thanks to the tightly wound panties still caught up around her ankles. "Why can't I- Ah!"

Thankfully, though, Anna was there to catch her before she could actually tip over. But, unfortunately for her, she also wasn't at all impressed by her tantrum.

"Young lady!"

Holding her steady on her feet with her right arm wrapped firmly around the front of her waist, the recent high school grad pistoned her palm up and down against Rhen's scarlet seat half a dozen more times in half as many seconds.

SMACK-SMACK-SMACK!

SMACK-SMACK-SMACK!

"Do you *want* to go back over my knee?"

SMACK!

"Ack!"

"Huh?"

SMACK!

"Owie!"

"Do you?"

Unable to get away, Rhen was forced to make do instead with bobbing up and down on the balls of her feet as the younger girl let loose with three of her hardest swats yet.

SMACK! SMACK! SMACK!

"Oh my god, Anna, I'm sorry, I'm sorry!" she yelped, arms flapping out to either side of her as if she could somehow fly away from the fury being rained down on her already sore cheeks.

"That's *Miss* Anna to you-"

SMACK! SMACK! SMACK!

"Little-"

SMACK!

"Girl."

SMACK!

"Alright, alright! I'm sorry, Miss Anna! I'm sorry!"

"That's-"

SMACK!

"Better!"

Snapped the irate brunette, easing her grip around her waist and giving her stinging palm a vigorous shake as Rhen did her best to get her frantic huffing and puffing back under control before she started crying again.

"Now then," continued Anna a moment later after they'd both managed to compose themselves, sounding slightly out of breath once again. "As I was saying before you decided to throw your little fit."

At that, Rhen winced and a fresh tinge of pink rose up to color her face.

"Uh, yeah... Sorry about that."

"Don't sweat it, short stuff. It's water under the bridge," the younger girl reassured her, patting her bottom affectionately as a sly smile stole over her. "But, yeah. The reason why you're not allowed to have your panties back is because your aunt specifically told me to put you into a pull-up once I was done spanking you."

"Eep!"

A huge wave of red rushed in to darken Rhen's face even further then. Up until that point she'd managed to keep her night-time sleepwear and occasional punishment panties a secret from the younger girl.

Or, at least, she'd thought she had.

"Ugh," she moaned, tossing her hands into the air in surrender. "Of course she did."

"Now, now, there's no need to pout," soothed Anna, still smiling, but at least sounding somewhat sympathetic. "I think it's pretty safe to say that you and I are well past the point of needing to feel embarrassed about your childish side."

To underscore her point, she gave Rhen's right cheek a firm squeeze and directed a meaningful gaze toward her bare folds.

"Or am I wrong in saying that I just spanked a *very* bratty teenager?"

Well, at least she didn't say little girl.

"Humph. I guess not…"

"See? Isn't everything so much easier when you're not constantly giving me attitude?"

Rather than dignify that teasing question with a response, Rhen instead continued to glare for as long as she could before the amusement twinkling in the other girl's amber eyes finally got the better of her.

"Yeah, yeah…" she sighed, surrendering herself to a sheepish grin. "I guess you have a point there. Although, you know, technically speaking, you're the only one of us who's actually a teenager."

"Mmmm, maybe," conceded the nineteen-year-old with another squeeze. "But I'm not the one with a bright red butt who's about to get put into a pull-up, now am I?"

"Fair enough," squeaked Rhen, before grumbling under her breath. "You big jerk."

Ignoring her pouting, Anna bounced back to her feet and gestured for Rhen to slip off her panty-shackles as she cast a searching look around her room.

"Alright, so uh… Where *are* those pull-ups, anyway? Dana didn't actually say."

"Oh! Yeah, they're, uh…" Rhen began to answer in a half-distracted voice, hopping on one foot before losing her balance altogether and toppling onto her bed. "Oof!"

Rolling over and sitting up, she was just about to point the younger girl toward the top drawer of her dresser. But, as she finally got her feet free from her bumblebees and looked from them, to the still smirking Anna, and back again, she hesitated.

"Uh-huh?" she prompted, looking out from beneath a pair of quizzically quirked brows.

Starting to panic just a little bit now, and desperate to salvage at least *part* of her dignity, Rhen racked her brain for some way of avoiding having her friend see the neat stack of pull-ups inside her dresser drawer next to her panties.

"Um…" she hesitated, before brightening a moment later as a solution suddenly presented itself. "Oh, uh, right! They're in our master bathroom."

"Your, um… Your master bathroom?"

"Yep, that's right," nodded Rhen, waving toward her closed bedroom door. "It's the second door down the hall and to the left. They're in the cabinet beneath my- I mean, the left, sink. You can't miss 'em."

This time it was Anna's turn to hesitate, but just barely.

"Are you sure it's okay for me to go rummaging around inside your guys' room like that? I mean, it might be better if you went and got them instead, don't you think?"

Rhen was honestly tempted to take her up on that offer, if for no other reason than to avoid having her see just how many different childish pull-up patterns her fiancé had managed to find for her over the last few months. But, the prospect of one of the other daycare kids catching a glimpse of her scampering down the hall with only a pair of socks on below the waist was enough to have her ditching that idea in a hurry.

"No, no, it's totally fine," she said instead, attempting to hide her embarrassment behind unrolling her panties and folding them properly.

She was going to have to toss them into her laundry hamper after this was all done, but a little extra tidiness never hurt anyone, right?

"Well, I guess if you're sure it's alright…" answered Anna, nibbling on her lower lip as she stared off into space thinking for a moment before seeming to find her resolve once again and continuing on more firmly. "Right. Okay. In that case, get up, missy!"

Not actually waiting for her to comply, she tugged Rhen back to her feet by her upper arm and ushered her over to stand in the corner next to her closet door. Then, grabbing her hands, she maneuvered them up on top of her head just like she'd seen them downstairs, and with a self-satisfied nod, pressed her face forward until the tip of her nose butted up against the intersection of the two walls ahead of her.

"There we go, perfect."

"If you say so," mumbled the shorter girl, all too aware of how far her ruby red rump stuck out in this position.

SMACK!

Apparently Anna had noticed too, because she couldn't resist giving it a quick swat as she turned to leave.

"You just stay put, alright?" she called, not looking back as she stepped out into the hallway.

Leaving the door to her bedroom wide open.

"Humph. Yeah, whatever."

Rolling her eyes, knowing that trying to sneak over and shut her door would just be asking for trouble, Rhen let loose with an elaborate sigh and settled in to wait. Quietly hoping that nobody would decide they suddenly needed to use the upstairs guest bathroom while Anna was on the hunt for pull-ups.

You are the wall… Become the wall… she told herself instead, straining to hear the din of running and playing kids on the floor below, listening in particular for the sounds of feet on stairs. *Blend into the wall… Nobody can see you. You're just a… I don't know, a coat rack… With a bright red butt… Ugh.*

A derisive snort escaped from Rhen then, and with a mortified groan she switched back to debating with herself if she was more in the mood for a hamburger or a burrito for lunch that afternoon.

This sucks.

—

After what seemed like a *very* long time for someone just popping down the hall to grab something from underneath a sink, Rhen eventually heard the confident *thump, thump, thump* of Anna's socks on the hardwood floor outside her bedroom. Followed half a heartbeat later by effervescent humming as she sashayed her way back inside.

"Okeydokey, kiddo," she sing-songed, bumping the door shut behind her with a hip. "I think that's enough corner time for one day. Why don't you go ahead and turn around for me, please?"

"Please, huh?" Rhen began to tease, unthreading her fingers from atop her head and moving to push herself away from the corner. "You know you're still the one in charge here, right? You don't have to be so-"

Only to stop short with a high-pitched squeak as she turned and got her first good look at what the broadly beaming younger girl held in her hands.

"Eep!"

"Surprise!"

"Oh my god!" Rhen gasped, jerking back against the wall and just about having a heart attack right there and then as her bottom flared in protest at being treated so roughly. "Wh-Where did you get that?"

BAND
POPULAR WITH
ZOOMERS
The Wa
Ashley OTK
Leila Hann

"Under the sink, just like you said," answered Anna, all but dancing in place as she beamed down at the colorfully printed diaper she held in both hands.

Crap! I knew I should've hidden those under something!

Mentally kicking herself for the oversight, but unable to voice any of her frustrations out loud without further humiliating herself, Rhen opted instead to stare in abject horror at the crinkly monstrosity her friend had brought back with her as she spluttered.

"But... but... But that's not a pull-up!"

"Well, yeah," agreed Anna with a dismissive roll of her eyes. "I mean, I was *going* to bring back one of those. But after I saw these sitting there next to them, I just couldn't resist."

Grinning with purpose now, she held the diaper out before her and gave the frolicking bunny rabbits printed across its absorbent surface a couple of hops to help underscore just how cute she thought they were.

"Like, *come on.* They're adorable! How could I not?"

Compressing her lips in annoyance, Rhen let out an exasperated growl. But, much as she hated to admit it, she was actually having a pretty difficult time disagreeing with her friend just then. The diapers Alana had bought for her were definitely cute, and she'd be lying if she said she hadn't been curious to see what she might look like wearing one of them. But, that didn't mean she was anywhere close to being okay with letting Anna of all people put her into one. It was bad enough that this willowy girl just barely out of high school had already spanked her to tears, but to be *diapered* by her too?

That was beyond humiliating.

"Oh my god, this isn't fair!" the red-faced twenty-one-year-old turned red-bottomed teenager moaned, completely at a loss for what to say next as her traitorous brain started trying to figure out if the skirt still pooled in a ring beside her bed would be long enough to totally hide the extra padding she'd have around her hips soon, or if she'd need to change into a longer dress. "You're supposed to put me in a *pull-up,* not a freaking diaper, Anna!"

She knew it wasn't a particularly solid defense, and all the whining and foot stomping that came with it certainly weren't doing her any favors, either. But, flimsy as it was, it still managed to strike a chord with her aunt's assistant.

"Hmmm… That's a good point," she admitted, frowning thoughtfully at the bunnies before looking back up at her again with a distinct note of apprehension this time. "Do you think I should maybe go double-check with Dana just to be sure she doesn't mind?"

"Yes!" yelped Rhen, before realizing what she was saying and adding just as quickly. "I mean no!"

Her abrupt about-face seemed to transform Anna's lingering trepidation into smug amusement. And, as the worried tension visibly drained from her face, she fixed her in place with a rakish grin.

"Are you absolutely sure?" she pressed, making as if to move toward the door again. "There were only a few of these in there, you know."

"Yeah, no, totally!" repeated Rhen, scurrying around to cut her off. "I mean, a diaper is *basically* a pull-up, right? They're just a little thicker and stuff is all."

She was in full damage control mode now, and her filters were completely gone as justifications and excuses started tumbling out of her one after the other amid a flurry of arm flailing.

"Besides, they're actually mine, technically speaking. A friend of ours gave them to us for my birthday a few weeks ago, so it's totally fine if you want to use one. In fact, you'd be silly *not* to now that I think about it. Dana thinks I look mega cute in them, so if anything, she'd probably, you know, praise you and stuff for your, uh… your go-getterness or whatever…"

"Well now, when you put it like that… I guess I don't have much of a choice, now do I?" giggled Anna. "Okay, fine. If it really means that much to you, I'll be more than happy to change your diaper for you, Rhenny."

"Gee, thanks a lot, Anna. You're a real pal."

"That's *Miss* Anna," corrected the younger girl, her amusement turning devious as she stuck out her tongue. "And I expect to hear you ask me properly using the magic word, little girl."

"Of course you do."

"I'm waiting."

"Ugh, fine. Please…"

"Please, Miss Anna…" interjected her friend.

Scowling, but unable to claw her way out of the hole she'd managed to dig herself into, Rhen surrendered to the inevitable.

"Please, Miss Anna, will you…"

She swallowed then, her face very nearly catching on fire as she forced herself to push on.

"Will you please diaper me?"

"Why, of course I will, sweetie," agreed the other girl easily, favoring her with her best attempt at a benevolent, motherly smile.

Which, to her credit, was more than passable. She *was* a fast learner, after all.

"Uh, thanks," huffed a very bashful Rhen, staring down at the tops of her sock-covered toes with a pout as she struggled to center herself once again.

I can make this work. I can make this work. I can make this work, she kept telling herself over and over again, willing the gnawing ache in her clit to go away. *All I have to do is let her put that stupid thing on me for now and then switch into a pull-up before bedtime later. No one will ever have to know about this, especially not Dana. It'll be fine. It'll be fine. It'll be fine…*

Almost certainly able to read what was going through her mind just then, Anna ruffled her hair and gestured toward the bed beside her.

"Okay, short stuff. Lie down on your back for me and we'll get started," she instructed in a sugary sweet voice. "I didn't see any wipes or baby powder underneath the sink when I went looking, but I'm sure we'll still be able to get you properly changed without them."

"Uh-huh."

Mumbling darkly to herself and blushing hot enough to rival her still sore seat, Rhen slowly dragged her feet toward her bed. Climbing up onto it, she shot one last obstinate glare at the diaper in her friend's hands and then flopped out onto her back just as Anna had asked, dragging the front of her t-shirt down to shield her naked groin as she pressed her knees firmly together.

"You know, I've always wanted a little sister to play dress up with," admitted the brunette with a self-deprecating smile, one that Rhen couldn't help but return as she watched her circle around to kneel before her at the foot of the bed.

"I'm *so* glad I can help you out then," she replied, mostly meaning it even as she rolled her eyes. "Maybe next time, though, we can stick to regular clothes?"

Anna giggled.

"We'll just have to wait and see, won't we?"

Wrapping her fingers around her calves, she gave them a firm tug.

"Scoot down some for me," she directed, pulling her closer. "There we go, just like that. Alright, now hips up."

With a firm grip around Rhen's ankles, she guided her thin legs up into the air, scooting in closer as she did so and easing her back until her stop sign red cheeks left the comforter altogether and she had enough room to slip the back half of the diaper beneath her.

"And down we go," she cooed a moment after that, lowering her back into place with a rustling of plastic and padding that immediately had the petite junior covering her face to hide her shame. "Perfect!"

"Oh god…"

"Hehe. You are *such* a cutie," mused Anna, her grin turning impish as she coaxed her knees apart and got her first proper look between them since before the start of her spanking. "And judging by the looks of things here, I'd say we're getting this on you just in the nick of time. We can't have our little Rhenny running around with wet panties, now can we?"

"Humph."

"I'll take that as a 'yes'," she crooned triumphantly, folding the front of the diaper over between her spread legs and holding it in place with her right hand while she used her left to pull the tapes on the back part pinned beneath her bottom around and over, securing the bunny rabbits in place around her waist with a contented nod. "Hey now, that doesn't look half bad if I do say so myself."

Uncovering her face, but still blushing, Rhen's gaze flitted down to inspect the other girl's handiwork.

"Yeah," she agreed reluctantly, shifting her crinkly hips from side to side in an attempt to get used to the odd sensation of thick padding preventing her from being able to fully bring her thighs together as she pushed herself back up into a sitting position. "I've, um… I've only been 'dressed' like this a couple times before, but I'd say you did a pretty good job."

"Why thank you!" preened Anna, settling back onto her heels on top of the mattress in front of her. "Mmm-mwah!"

Bringing her thumb and forefinger to her lips in an exaggerated chef's kiss, she winked.

"You look like a total snack right now, you know that?"

"I…"

Too tired to try and sass any longer, Rhen just laughed and shook her head.

"Okay, yeah," she conceded, glancing at her reflection in the full-length mirror beside her closet door. "No arguments here. I'm cute as heck."

"It's just too bad you guys don't have a pacifier…" sighed the brunette, giving her cheek a thoughtful tap as she ran her eyes up and down her entire frame before stirring with fresh excitement. "Wait a minute, *do* you have a pacifier?"

"Oh my god, *no*!" exclaimed Rhen, going rigid.

"No… You don't have a pacifier? Or just, no, you don't want me to go get it?"

"Both!" she squawked, arms flailing to either side of her to emphasize her point.

"Okay, okay," soothed Anna, holding her hands out before her in a gesture of surrender. "I was just asking. No need to get cranky."

Crossing her arms in front of her, Rhen pushed her lips out into a pout.

"I am so going to get you back for this someday."

"Awww, that's sweet of you," cooed the other girl, slipping her feet out from under her hips and climbing off the bed. "But I really don't need any thank you notes or anything. I'm just doing my job, after all."

"Uh-huh," replied Rhen flatly, following after her and grimacing as her tender backside shifted beneath her.

As she straightened out her shirt, attempting to coax an extra inch or two of coverage from it while continuing to grumble to herself (though, now more so to keep up appearances than anything else), Anna stepped in close and wrapped her in a firm embrace, squeezing tight.

"This was so much fun! Thanks for being such a good sport about everything. I know that couldn't have been easy."

"Heh."

Unable to bring herself to stay upset with her friend, Rhen returned her hug just as tightly, snickering into her shoulder.

"You're welcome."

Before kicking her playfully in the shin.

"You big jerk."

"Oh, you are just the biggest brat I've ever seen," laughed Anna, hopping back and snatching up her wrist before she could get away. "Alright then, little girl, have it your way. I was going to be nice and let you get dressed first, but since you want to act up, you can just come straight with me to apologize to your Auntie Dana."

"But-!"

"No buts! Unless, that is, you'd like *yours* to get another spanking.”

Weighting her options, either getting spanked again and most likely being marched downstairs without a skirt on anyway, or just giving in and hoping that nobody saw her or that if they did they'd assume she was just wearing a pull-up (a really thick pull-up), Rhen heaved out an aggrieved sigh and nodded.

“Yes, Miss Anna…”

Chapter 19

Pushing the Reset Button

"Alright now, just attach the invoice… do a quick spell check… and… send!"

Falling back into the cushy leather of her office chair with a contented sigh, Dana Johnson smiled to herself as she swiveled idly from side to side, basking in the warm afterglow of a job well done. She'd just wrapped up putting the finishing touches on a major project for a client who was rebranding their business and needed an all new set of logos and an overhaul of their website to go with them, and all that was left to do now was sit back and wait for her payment to arrive. Which, given the amount of hours she'd poured into getting everything ready for them as quickly as she had, was going to be pretty darn substantial.

An extra zero on the end of the final total, substantial.

Hmmm… Rhen said she wanted one of those new Nintendo things the other day… Maybe I'll surprise her while we're out tonight?

Opening her eyes once again, she wriggled her way back up from her slouch and turned her wrist over to check the watch her bride-to-be had given her for her birthday a few months ago, letting out a self-satisfied snort as she saw just where the hands on its ornate face were pointing to.

"Not even noon, huh?"

Ever since she'd hired Anna Miller a few weeks back to help out with the daycare, Dana had been delighted to discover that she no longer had to scramble to catch up on things with her other job during the weekend. Summer was always an extra-busy time for her since everyone was out of school for their break while their parents still needed to go to work, which usually meant that she was completely swamped Monday through Friday and wasn't able to get any of her freelance work done until after dinner in the evenings. But, with the reliable brunette keeping an eye on everyone while they played after lunch, she was actually able to pop into her home office and tackle whatever design work she had on her plate for an hour or two at a time!

While still keeping an ear out for any major hiccups that might require her immediate attention, of course.

Thankfully, though, Anna had proven herself to be quite adept at maintaining order among the dozen or so kids she looked after during the week, and she hadn't yet had to swoop in to rescue her from a pack of unruly tweens who'd gotten too big for their britches. The girl was a total sweetheart, and all the kids thought she was just the coolest thing ever with her willingness to help chase down the ice cream truck and the streaks of bright purple she'd recently dyed into her hair (luckily, none of them had noticed the ginger way she'd been sitting the day after she'd gotten those), which in turn meant that whatever Miss Anna said was treated as gospel from the get go and received very little pushback.

Of course, it also didn't hurt that everyone had gotten a *very* good look at what had happened to Rhen during her first day on the job either. Seeing the oldest among them (adult or otherwise) being paraded about with a ruby red backside and thighs peeking out from underneath a diaper of all things had swiftly granted her new assistant a reputation as someone *not* to be trifled with. As a result, she'd so far been able to quell any potential disobedience with just a firm warning and the occasional hands-on-hips glare.

Heh. It'll be interesting to see how much longer that lasts for. I give it another two weeks, tops.

Dana was just in the midst of admiring her new engagement ring and trying to decide who among her adorable horde would be the one to finally work up the nerve to call Anna's bluff (after all, no self-respecting twelve-year-old could resist the siren song of poking the bear for long), when her phone's text message alert went off; cutting its way through her idle musings as it rumbled against the desk in front of her. Wondering if it might be Rhen finally letting her know what movie she wanted to see after they were done shopping at the mall that evening, she leaned forward and scooped up the device. But, when she got a good look at the name on her screen, she was surprised to find that the message was actually from none other than Courtney Summers.

[Hey Dana, is Rhen home?]

Huh. Now that's sort of an odd question…

Granted, it wasn't at all out of the ordinary for the athletic TA to be texting her. They occasionally met up for coffee during the week when she didn't have kids to take care of, and they both liked to go on double dates at least once or twice a month, but it *was* a bit strange that she would be asking her that question considering she had her bride-to-he's phone number as well. Still, Dana supposed that Rhen could have just as easily let her phone die by accident or something (she did have a bad habit of forgetting to plug it in when she went to bed that they were still working on, after all), so she didn't pay it any more mind than that as she quickly tapped out her reply.

[She's down the street at our neighbor's helping with some chores]

[What's up?]

This time the typing indicator on her text messaging app appeared and disappeared several times in a row for about a minute straight before the girl finally replied.

[I…]

[Sorry]

[It's kinda hard to this put into a text]

Definitely curious now after receiving such a surprisingly short message when very clearly there was more she wanted to say, Dana frowned and shot back.

[Is everything alright?]

Courtney's reply was far faster in coming this time around, though was no less puzzling.

[Yeah]

And then a second or two later.

[Actually, um…]

[I know it's super short notice and all, but would you mind if I came over so we can talk in person?]

[Of course not!]

[You know you're always welcome here]

Again, the typing indicator on her screen flashed on and off several more times before Courtney at last replied.

[Thanks]

Followed half a heartbeat later by a follow-up message.

[Um… Please don't be weirded out, but I'm actually already in your driveway]

"Oh really now?"

Rising from her chair, Dana tugged up on her office window blinds. And, sure enough, there she saw the younger girl's Jeep idling in front of her house.

"Uh-oh… This must be more serious than I thought."

Feeling her stomach twisting with worry on the TA's behalf now, she hurriedly typed out two short messages.

[That's totally fine, dear]

[I'll meet you at the door]

Then, closing her laptop, she turned and began making her way downstairs, fully determined to get to the bottom of whatever it was that had the usually unflappable Courtney Summers so wound up and flustered.

"Just hang in there a little longer, kiddo," she murmured to herself. "Auntie Dana will get you straightened out in no time. Don't you worry."

—

After sharing a brief hug hello and waiting for the taller girl to kick off her tennis shoes, Dana led the way into the kitchen; knowing that whatever Courtney had to say, it would probably be easier to do it sitting down.

"Coffee?" she asked, picking up a pair of mugs from the rack next to the sink and turning to face her guest with her most disarming motherly smile. "You look like you could use a pick-me-up."

Or three.

"Um, yeah, sure," mumbled Courtney noncommittally, fiddling with the floppy tail-end of her belt before seeming to remember her manners and adding quickly. "If you don't mind, that is!"

"Of course not, honey. Just give me a minute to get things going, alright?"

Turning back to the counter behind her, Dana set her mugs aside and switched on the coffee maker, keeping up a steady stream of casual conversation all the while as she went. But, try as she might, all she got for her trouble were short, often mumbled, monosyllabic replies.

Oh dear. That's definitely not a good sign…

Courtney wasn't exactly the biggest chatterbox in the world, true, but she was still usually far more engaged than this.

"Why don't you have a seat and make yourself more comfortable?" she eventually suggested after a minute or two more of unsuccessful attempts at idle chit-chat, nodding over her shoulder toward the table as the water inside her Keurig came to a boil.

"Oh! Uh, yeah, sure! Totally! Sounds great!" the jittery TA agreed in a hurry, springing away from where she'd been leaning against the edge of the island fidgeting.

Hmmm… On second thought, better make that a decaf, Dana mused to herself, holding back a smile as she watched her scrabble toward the nearest seat she could find, practically diving into it. *I think she might just explode if I don't.*

—

"Thanks…" mumbled Courtney a short while later, accepting a steaming mug from Dana once the requisite amount of cream and sugar had been added to it.

"You're welcome, dear. Drink up, now."

Settling down into the chair beside hers and resisting the urge to wrap an arm around her shoulders for the time being, the auburn-haired older woman instead contented herself with quietly sipping her coffee as she waited for the younger girl to gather her thoughts. But, after several awkward minutes of watching Courtney cycle through wrapping her hands around the sides of her mug, squeezing tight and then immediately letting go when it became too hot for her, picking it up to blow on it and taking a perfunctory sip to cover her movements, before setting it back down again only to repeat the entire process a few seconds later, she decided that a more direct approach was in order.

"So," she ventured conversationally, resting her chin in her hand, arm propped up on the table beside her as she leisurely circled a fingertip around the rim of her mug. "What's on your mind?"

"Um, well, uh…"

Fumbling with her words, Courtney's agitated mug-fiddling increased tenfold.

"I um… It's just that I uh-"

"Courtney," Dana said more firmly this time, interrupting her hemming and hawing as she laid a calming hand on her shoulder and gave it a quick squeeze.

"Y-Yes?" the younger girl all but shouted, jerking to attention as if she'd just been shocked and sending a splash of hot brown liquid cascading over the rim of her mug and onto her hand. "Ack! Fuck! Shit! Oh my god, I'm so sorry, Dana. Let me just-"

"*Breathe*," the older woman cut her off again, refusing to let her rise from her seat as she tightened her grip on her shoulder. "You look like you're about to have a panic attack, honey."

That, at least, managed to draw a small (albeit shaky) laugh from the younger girl as she released her death grip on her mug, brushing the back of her wet hand off on the front of her jeans.

"Sorry…"

"Hey now, there's no need to apologize. Accidents happen. Now just *breathe*," repeated Dana, slowly exhaling herself in an attempt to get her to follow suit.

"I… I think I can handle that."

With a self-deprecating wince, Courtney did her best to do as she was told. Taking in a long, deep breath through her nostrils, holding it for a five-count, and then slowly exhaling it in a pencil-thin stream through pursed lips over and over again until her pounding heart had settled back down.

All the while as she was doing that, Dana made sure to keep her hand perched reassuringly on her shoulder, massaging it gently until she felt the last of the remaining tension still coiled in the firm muscles there begin to relax.

"There we go. Isn't that so much better?" she prompted with an encouraging smile.

"Yeah…" sighed Courtney, her full lips making a valiant attempt at taking up their usual confident half-grin. "Thanks for that."

"Anytime, sweetheart."

Letting her shoulder go with one more quick squeeze, Dana returned to her coffee.

"Now then, you just take as much time as you need, alright? Rhen won't be home for at least a couple more hours, so there's no need to rush."

"Okay…"

After taking a couple more long pulls from her own mug to steady her nerves, Courtney set it back down with deliberate care and did her best to meet her gaze.

"This all feels kind of stupid now that I have to say it out loud," she admitted, channeling much of her lingering anxiety into rubbing her fingertips up and down along the grain of the tabletop in front of her.

"Hey now," interrupted Dana before she could lose her confidence again. "Your feelings are *not* stupid, and I promise you won't get any judgment from me. So, let's hear it."

Taking heart from her encouragement, the smile on Courtney's face grew significantly more genuine as she took in another deep breath.

"Well, um, lately I've been under a lot of stress. Like a *lot*, a lot. For starters, my adviser has been breathing down my neck about my thesis all semester. I've got my defense in only a couple more months and I *still* need to make a bunch of revisions to it before that happens so I can submit the updated version for the panel to consider. Only, the thing is, between class and work, I haven't had any time to sit down and, you know, actually *do* any of that."

"Oh dear, that's definitely not good."

"Don't I know it," snorted Courtney. "And on top of all *that*, I've also been running myself ragged and skipping lunch a bunch just to keep on top of everything for this stupid class I TA for because the professor who supposedly 'teaches' it is a total ass-hole who makes me do all the fucking work for him and- Oops!"

Covering her mouth as she stumbled to a sudden stop, a faint blush blossomed across the TA's high cheekbones.

"Uh… Sorry about that," she mumbled sheepishly.

"Heh. Don't sweat it, sweetheart," snickered Dana, waving away her embarrassment with a wink. "*Adults* in this house can swear all they like."

"Phew!" the other girl laughed, a hint of genuine relief ringing in her voice. "Well, uh… like I was saying, things have just been mondo stressful for me lately between my thesis, my classes, doing research for my adviser, and doing pretty much *everything* for the class I TA for, and, like… it's seriously starting to take a toll. When I get home, I'm just *so* drained and I can't seem to bring myself to do any of the stuff that I know I need to get done, let alone anything actually fun. I just end up flopping out on the couch and trying to destress by watching stuff on my phone until it's time for bed or Abby bullies me into eating dinner."

"You're skipping lunch *and* dinner?" interjected Dana before she could stop herself.

She'd meant to let the younger girl finish unburdening herself before she said anything else, but the notion of her skipping meals had her motherly instincts kicking into overdrive.

"Uh-huh," Courtney nodded miserably before going on the defensive when she saw the disapproving frown starting to pull down on the corners of her mouth. "And, look, before you say anything, let me just say that I *know* that's bad, okay? Like, really, I do. In fact, I'd be willing to bet that's probably a big reason why I've been feeling so shitty in general lately. But, either I just can't find the time to eat during the day, or I just don't have an appetite when I get home, so I really don't know what to tell you. Again, I know that's not good and whatever, but it is what it is."

"You should still at least try to eat *something*, you know…" tutted Dana in concerned counterpoint, quietly tamping down on the urge to reach out and tweak the TA's ear for her.

She really wasn't used to putting up with so much sass these days.

"Even if it's just a granola bar or a cheese stick or something," she went on. "It doesn't have to be a big fancy meal every time. Your body just needs to have something to work with, is all."

"I know, I know…" groaned Courtney. "I've been *meaning* to do that, but it's just so hard with how busy I've been. And by the time I remember to try and find a snack, I can't seem to summon the motivation to actually go get one, you know?"

Sighing long and hard, she rolled her head around her shoulders, popping her neck as she tried to collect her thoughts once again.

"And while we're on the subject of shitty feelings. I've *also* been snapping a lot at Abby too, which sucks total ass. Hell, even when I'm not doing that, I still end up feeling like I'm not really 'there' with her when we're at home together because I'm just so tired and stressed. And, like, we've talked about it and whatever, and she says she gets it, but I can still tell it hurts her feelings and I just wish I didn't feel like this all the time, and… and… uh, yeah…"

Here, Courtney's confidence seemed to finally fail her. Though, thankfully, she didn't start hyperventilating this time.

Instead, she just looked like she was about to start crying.

Or maybe punching something.

Or both.

Dana knew full well that it could easily be both.

"Well now, that's quite a lot to be stressed about if I do say so myself," she spoke up with an easy laugh, filling the silence left behind in the wake of the younger girl's increasingly frustrated explanation before things could become awkward. "But you have nothing to feel embarrassed about, hon, I promise. I know first-hand just how much grad school can grind you down. I've been there myself, and it's definitely not a fun experience sometimes. *Especially* if you're someone who's hyper-competent and used to being the one that others rely on like you are. When things start piling up around you like that then, it's very easy to start feeling like you're just treading water and about to get pulled under, isn't it?"

Courtney couldn't help but nod her head at that, looking exhausted and forlorn.

"Tell me about it."

"That's alright, though," Dana went on, reaching out to pat her on the back. "You're not even through your mid-twenties yet. You're allowed to be a stressed out student. Heck, once you graduate, you're allowed to be a stressed out regular adult too! I know I've had plenty of nights in my twenties and thirties when all I wanted to do was curl up in a ball and let the ground swallow me whole. It comes with the territory, I'm afraid."

Seeing the look of beleaguered recognition lighting up the other girl's face now, Dana felt like she was starting to get a better idea of what had her so frazzled (aside from the obvious, that is) and why she'd chosen to come see her when it would be just the two of them alone in the house. And so, deciding to take a shot in the dark, she summoned up her most reassuring motherly smile and pressed on.

"And I also happen to know from way too much personal experience that when you get caught in cycles like these where you feel like you're just spinning out of control and can't seem to get a grip on anything, what you *really* need is a hard reset."

Before adding with a wink.

"Isn't that right?"

Again, Courtney nodded. This time looking away with the faintest hint of a blush as her lips twitched.

"Maybe…"

"Maybe, huh?"

Dana could more than empathize with the younger girl's plight. Feeling like you had to be even-headed and in control all the time could be monumentally draining at the best of times, and piling on the need to ask someone else for help only made things that much worse. But, as tempted as she was to just hug it out with her until she felt better, she understood that what she needed from her right then was some tough love.

Which, fortunately for her, she had in abundance.

"Now, I think I might already know the answer to this next question, but I'd still like to hear it from you anyway, young lady," she said evenly, lacing her words with a generous helping of no-nonsense steel. "What would have happened if you were living at home right now and you'd been acting the way you've been describing?"

"Um…"

Rather than answer her right away, the TA kept her eyes locked on the half-drained mug in front of her, twisting it this way and that as a proper flush crept its way up to darken her cheeks this time.

Bingo.

"Well?" Dana prompted after it became clear that she was going to need some extra encouragement if they were ever going to get to the bottom of things.

"I… I… Um…"

At last, Courtney opened her mouth to speak, but all that managed to escape her lips were indistinguishable mumbles and the odd harrumph.

"Excuse me?"

Refusing to give the younger girl even an inch right then, Dana's hand shot out and seized hold of her chin in a tight grip, tipping her head back and to the side, forcing her to look at her.

"Wha-? Dana, I-!"

"When I ask you a question, I expect a clear and respectful answer. *Not mumbling*," she reprimanded sharply, leaning in until they were practically nose-to-nose. "Am I understood?"

For half a heartbeat, Dana was seriously concerned that she might've overplayed her bossy mommy hand just a little bit, but when the athletic girl at last met her gaze (her stormy eyes now misty as she fidgeted in her seat), she knew that she'd hit the mark dead on.

"Yes ma'am, I'm sorry!"

"Awww… I know you are, sweetheart," she replied sweetly this time, all of her earlier fiery outrage completely snuffed out as she pressed a kiss to her forehead and let go of her chin. "And I forgive you. Just try and do better next time, alright?"

"R-Right!"

Breathing out a sigh of relief as she straightened up in her seat, the blush on Courtney's face grew a several shades hotter and she let out a nervous laugh.

"Oof. Did you know you're *really* good at doing that?"

"I did, actually," admitted the auburn-haired older woman with a wink as she grew serious once again. "Now stop trying to change the subject and answer my question."

"Yes ma'am…"

Looking chagrinned, but somehow more relaxed than she had since arriving, Courtney forced herself to press on.

"Um… Well, uh… Yeah," she ventured, rubbing at the back of her neck as she picked her words carefully. "I guess if I'd been acting like this at home… I um… I guess my mom would've probably blistered my butt like nobody's business."

"Mmhmm. I thought as much," purred Dana, her dark eyes twinkling with amusement now as she turned her attention back to her coffee.

Pausing to take a sip, she collected her own thoughts before settling on a plan of action and setting her mug back down on the table in front of her with an air of finality.

"Just when was the last time you had your panties taken down for you, anyway, young lady?"

"Uh…" Courtney stalled again, taking a distracted pull from her mug as she visibly strived to think of some way of not actually having to answer that question out loud. "I think it might've maybe been back during Christmas break when Abby and I were baking with Rhen?"

"You *think* so, huh?" snorted the older woman. "Seems to me like the kind of thing you'd be able to remember pretty easily. You're not *that* well-behaved, are you?"

"Um… Maybe?"

Rolling her eyes theatrically, Dana loosed a prolonged, long-suffering sigh.

"Well, regardless. I'd still say it sounds like you're long overdue for an attitude adjustment."

Blushing positively scarlet now, Courtney nevertheless conceded the point.

"Yeah… I guess you're right…"

"I guess you're right, *ma'am*," Dana corrected, again layering steel on top of her now very stern demeanor.

"Yes ma'am! Sorry ma'am!"

Hah. That never gets old.

"So, um…" Courtney continued a few moments later after marshaling her resolve once again. "Will you, um… Would you mind, you know…"

"Will I spank you?" Dana finished for her with a laugh.

Wincing at hearing it said out loud so causally, the younger girl still managed to nod.

"Uh, yeah…" she agreed, before remembering her earlier admonition and adding quickly. "Um, ma'am."

To which Dana smiled in approval.

"I'd be more than happy to, dear," she replied easily, holding up a hand to forestall her next reply. "But first I need to know something very important. Have you discussed *any* of this with Abby yet?”

“Um…”

Directing her attention back down to her mug, Courtney spent several long seconds swirling around its contents before mumbling sheepishly.

“I was kind of hoping that maybe we could just keep this between the two of us?”

“Uh-uh,” answered Dana flatly, shaking her head. “Sorry, hon, but that’s not how this works. Abby is your *partner*, and while you definitely owe her more than one apology by the sounds of things, that doesn’t mean she’s still not there to support and love you. Moreover, by trying to go behind her back and deal with all this by yourself, you’re robbing her of the opportunity to be there for you when you need her the most. You two need to learn to rely on each another when things get hard, not just when they’re fun and easy. That’s what being in a healthy relationship is all about.”

Just as she’d hoped it would, her scolding managed to strike a nerve with the athletic girl. As she’d spoken, her face had fallen further and further, until she looked as if she might burst into tears at any moment.

“Oh god, you’re so right…” she groaned, plonking her elbows down onto the table in front of her and burying her head in her hands. “Ugh. I feel like such a fucking jerk.”

“Now, now, don’t be so hard on yourself,” soothed Dana. “You two are both still young and figuring all this stuff out. It takes time, and there’s nothing wrong with needing someone to point out when you’re making a mistake.”

“I guess you have a point there,” grumbled Courtney into her hands, her cupped palms muffling her response.

“You’re darn right I do.”

Snickering, Dana patted her on the shoulder.

“Trust me, kiddo. I’ve made plenty of relationship mistakes in my time.”

She paused then to let out a wistful exhalation.

"I just wish I'd had such a wise and absolutely gorgeous older woman to help me avoid some of the bigger ones back when I was your age."

That managed to draw out a snort of amusement from the other girl, the tension in her shoulders draining away all at once as she flopped back in her chair, totally spent from the emotional rollercoaster she'd been stuck on for the last few minutes.

"Gee, thanks," she deadpanned, rolling her head over to look at her with a playful smirk. "I had no idea I was so lucky."

"Just the luckiest," grinned Dana, before settling back into stern mom mode once again and adding with an admonishing finger wag. "Now I want you to call Abby and explain to her how you've been feeling again, apologize, make up, and then tell her *exactly* what's about to happen."

"Wha-?" Courtney started to demand, before being cut off by a firm poke.

"No arguing. You're in enough trouble as it is already."

It took every ounce of self-control Dana possessed not to burst into a fit of laughter right there and then as she watched the range of naked emotions play themselves out across the other girl's face with that last statement. Somehow, though, she managed to hold it together and continue to look totally stoic as defiance, followed by incredulous disbelief, then embarrassment, a clear desire to argue, and then finally grudging acceptance all had their moment in the sun.

"Alright, alright… ma'am," Courtney at last huffed, the pout on her face making her look about a decade younger than she really was as she straightened up in her seat and fished out her phone from her purse, looking to her hopefully. "Um… Do you mind if I step outside real quick?"

"Uh-uh," denied Dana out of hand once again. "You can make your call right where you're sitting, little girl. And I'd better hear you explaining *everything* to her. I'm going to be right here next to you listening the entire time, and I can promise you now that you do not want me to have to do it for you."

Shivering, her mouth twisting into a petulant grimace, the athletic grad student nevertheless nodded her head of short-cropped hair obediently.

"Yes ma'am."

Then, thumbing her phone to life with only a slightly shaky hand, she tapped her girlfriend's name on her speed dial and brought the device up to her ear.

"Uh… Hey, babe. It's me…"

—

Several minutes, and one initially stilted but eventually cathartic conversation later, Courtney hung up her phone and turned back to face her soon to be spanker with a drained (but happy) smile.

"Feeling better?" Dana prompted, reaching out to rub her back.

"Uh-huh," she sighed, her shaky exhalation transforming partway through into a relieved laugh. "She was, uh… kinda surprised."

"I heard," snorted the older woman. "You still did the right thing, though."

"Yeah, yeah. I know…"

At her annoyed huff, Dana couldn't help but smirk.

"Having to admit you need your bottom spanked definitely isn't easy, is it?"

"Tell me about it," groaned Courtney, the faint smile on her face dipping somewhat. "But, yeah. She says she totally gets where I'm coming from and that she forgives me… So long as you give it to me good."

"Oh, don't you worry," Dana chuckled, dragging her nails between her shoulder blades in the same way Rhen liked. "I promise you'll be one extremely sorry little girl by the time I'm through with you today."

"Gee thanks," grumbled the TA, arching her back as the older woman's fingers found just the right spot. "I don't know if you heard or not, but we're, um… we're actually going out for a little make-up dinner later on tonight."

She swallowed then, wincing.

"Guess I'm gonna be sitting sore for that."

"You bet your sweet little cutie patootie you will be," teased Dana, drawing her hand back and tapping her playfully on the tip of her wrinkled nose. "Still, though, I think that sounds like an excellent idea."

Then, brightening as an idea struck her, she added.

"Oh! I know! I've got a gift card for Raurie's Steakhouse kicking around inside a drawer up in my office. Why don't you two go there?"

"Oh man, are you serious? Isn't that place, like, crazy expensive?"

"Hmmm… Maybe just a *little* bit," conceded the older woman, holding her thumb and forefinger about an inch or so apart as she winked. "But I don't mind. I literally forgot I even had the silly thing until just now, so it's all yours if you'd like it. Just don't go overboard on the boozy drinks, and you two should be able to eat like queens."

Throwing her arms around her suddenly, Courtney pulled her into a bone-crushingly tight hug.

"Oh my god, thank you so much, Dana! Abby will love that!"

"Happy to- Urk! Happy to help, kiddo," she wheezed, giving her a quick squeeze in return before they parted. "So, did she say anything else?"

"Not really…"

"Not really? That sounds a lot more like *some* really to me," chided Dana. "Out with it, missy."

Deflating somewhat now, Courtney gave her sagging shoulders a brief shrug.

"It's nothing really," she mumbled. "She just wished me luck, is all."

"Hah!"

Shaking her head, Dana allowed a healthy dose of wicked

amusement to creep its way into her voice this time.

"Well now, that was sweet of her. Lord knows, you're definitely going to need it."

Just as she'd known they would, her words immediately had the younger girl shifting nervously in her seat, nibbling at her lower lip as her eyes were drawn inexorably down toward her lap.

"O-Oh yeah?"

"What do you think?"

"I um… Well…"

With that one simple question she'd managed to put Courtney at a total loss for words once again. And, as she continued to shift awkwardly in her seat, Dana decided to let her stew in her dread for a while longer. Watching on with a firm scowl for several more long, increasingly worrisome moments as she slipped deeper and deeper into the proper headspace for what was to come next.

"Why don't you go and grab Rhen's hairbrush for me?" she eventually suggested, allowing the corners of her mouth to drift back up into a thin smile.

Though she'd phrased it as a request, they both knew it was anything but.

"Um… Her brush?" echoed Courtney, not quite able to meet her eye as she said it.

"That's right," she confirmed in a menacing sing-song. "You remember where it is, don't you? I do believe you've used it on her enough times by now to not need me to give you directions."

"I uh…" hesitated the TA again.

Dana wasn't about to give her any breathing room, though.

"That's not going to be a problem, is it?"

"No ma'am! I just wasn't expecting-"

"Wasn't expecting me to actually tan your hide for real?" she suggested before she could finish forming her excuse.

Grimacing once again, Courtney gave her a reluctant nod.

"I guess so…"

"Well, guess again, kiddo," she shot back with a brusque air of finality. "You said your mother would've blistered your butt after the way you've been behaving, and that's *exactly* what I'm planning on doing as well."

Looking equal parts chagrinned and nervous now, Courtney abandoned the arguments that were surely brewing within her and instead chose to surrender.

"Yes ma'am…"

"Good girl."

With the matter now settled, Dana pushed herself back from the table and began gathering up their mugs.

"Now you just go ahead and grab that brush," she said by way of dismissal, sashaying her way off toward the sink to rinse them out. "You can meet me in the front room whenever you're ready, alright?"

Rising up after her on a pair of much shakier legs, the soon to be very sorry TA exhaled slowly, visibly willing herself not to panic.

"Um… Okay. I'll uh… I'll be there soon, uh… ma'am."

"That's what I like to hear," cooed Dana, pausing in her cursory scrubbing to peer back over her shoulder. "Oh, and Courtney?"

"Yes ma'am?" the other girl all but yelped, stopping dead in her tracks on her way toward the front of the house.

"You'd better not keep me waiting."

"Right!"

Sufficiently motivated now, she sped from the kitchen like a bat out of hell, demonstrating just why she'd been a varsity athlete for most of her life as Dana chuckled to herself and turned back to their dishes.

Oh lordy. The bossy ones are always so much fun to startle.

—

Dana chose to take longer than she strictly needed to drying off their mugs and returning them to their spots on the rack beside the sink (allowing Courtney enough time to fully come to grips with what was about to happen to her and stop off for a quick trip to the bathroom if she needed to), before making her way at a leisurely pace into her front room. There, she found a very skittish TA waiting for her; worriedly shifting from foot to foot before the couch with hairbrush in hand, looking like she'd rather be anywhere else just then.

"Bring back any memories?" she asked by way of greeting, gesturing at the brush.

Pulling a face, Courtney gave a minimal nod.

"Kinda."

"Kinda?" prompted Dana as she breezed past her to settle down in the middle of the couch. "Why just kinda?"

"Momma- Uh, er- *Mom*, usually used a belt when she was really ticked off with us."

That managed to get a laugh from the older woman.

"It's hard to go wrong with the classics."

"If you say so…" mumbled the other girl with an exaggerated pout, one hand drifting back to glide along the denim clinging to her hips as what must've been many memories of punishments past resurfaced.

Holding in a smirk, Dana turned up her palm and wriggled her fingers expectantly, nodding wordlessly toward the brush. Which Courtney wasted little time in passing along with obvious relief.

"Well, I'll give you this," she said as she gripped its polished, ebony handle, giving her free hand a couple of firm test swats.

POP! POP!

"You're *much* speedier than Rhen is."

"Oh… Oh yeah?" asked the TA around an audible gulp.

The way she'd shaken out her palm after that pair of pops hadn't gone unnoticed, it seemed.

"Mmhmm," purred Dana, drinking in every inch of her lean, toned figure and elegant curves as she shuffled nervously in front of her. "I swear, that girl hems and haws over a spanking like nobody's business. You'd think she'd never gotten one before."

"Tell me about it," snorted Courtney, rolling her eyes in a transparent attempt to distract herself from her own desires to prolong the inevitable. "She's worse than Abby."

"Yes, well."

Sensing an easy opportunity to put the other girl in her place, Dana leveled a sugary sweet smile up at her.

"You aren't going to give me any trouble, are you, honey?"

Narrowing her eyes at that, recognizing that she'd been expertly maneuvered into a corner, Courtney shook her head.

Albeit grudgingly.

"No ma'am…"

"Great!"

Tucking the brush under her hip for safe keeping, Dana beckoned her closer, keeping her tone mockingly saccharine all the while as she did so.

"Now then, you just bring that cute little caboose on over here and Auntie Dana will get it ready for its spanking."

"Yeah, yeah… What-fucking-ever.." sighed Courtney, scrubbing a hand through her hair as she stepped in close enough to for her legs butt up against the front of the older woman's knees.

"Excuse me?" drawled Dana, allowing more than a little motherly menace to work its way into her voice this time. "Would you care to repeat that, *little girl*?"

Just as before, it only took a firm couple of words and a hard stare to get the TA to come apart at the seams.

"I'm sorry, ma'am!" she squeaked, jerking to attention. "That came out by accident, I swear!"

"Mmhmm…"

Dana held her in place with an icy stare for another moment or two more before warming once again.

"Let's just do our best not to have any more 'accidents' like that from now on, alright? I'm sure you'd hate to find out what it's like to be spanked with a bar of soap in your mouth, after all."

Shivering at the thought of such a horrible fate, Courtney

nodded quickly.

"Yes ma'am! It won't happen again."

"See that it doesn't, missy," scolded Dana with an exaggerated finger waggle before winking as she pressed on. "Alright now, hands on your head, please."

Looking as if she'd rather do anything but, the tall grad student nevertheless complied. The bracelets on her wrist jangling softly as she moved to thread her fingers together atop her head just as she'd seen Rhen do seemingly a million times before.

"Very good… Now that's what I like to see."

Leaning forward with just the hint of a smug smile tugging up on one corner of her lips, Dana began unfastening the hot pink belt fastened around the younger girl's waist.

"Bad little girls need to learn to do as they're told if they don't want to keep getting their naughty bottoms spanked."

"Uh-huh… Er, I mean, yes ma'am."

Heh. What a cutie pie.

It was always so much fun making the girls who were used to being the ones in charge squirm for a change.

With her belt now out of the way, Dana next turned her attention to the four shiny silver buttons holding together Courtney's stylish (and snug) jeans in front. With deft, practiced movements, she made short work of them. Undoing the top button and then pulling the two halves of denim apart, popping the three remaining clasps free all at the same time to reveal a triangular wedge of lime green panties beneath.

"My, oh my, how *pretty*! I had no idea you were wearing such cute panties today, Courtney," she teased. "Don't tell me you picked these out just for little old me?"

"Oh god…" moaned the soon to be bared girl miserably, shifting her weight from one foot to the other and inadvertently revealing even more of her dayglo underwear in the process.

"Yes?" prompted Dana as she hooked her thumbs into the waistbands of both her jeans and panties on either side of her hips. "Was there something you wanted to say, young lady?"

She kept her hands right where they were for several moments more as Courtney tried (and failed) to master her embarrassment.

"N-Nothing ma'am..." she finally managed to mumble, closing her eyes and tipping her head back as she exhaled in defeat.

"Not quite feeling like a big girl anymore, now are we?" prompted the older woman, knowing that she needed to push hard if she were ever going to get anywhere with her.

Again Courtney shifted sullenly in her grasp, but this time her reply was far faster in coming.

"That's one way of putting it..."

"One way, huh?" echoed Dana archly, not at all liking the note of sass she was still detecting in her voice. "How's this, then?"

Deciding to squash this seed of defiance before it could take root and spoil the mood she was going for, she gave the jeans and panties in her hands a firm yank, dragging them both down to her knees in a series of determined tugging motions.

Geez. Where's an Easy-Pull waistband when you need it?

"Ah! No, please! Not my panties too!" begged Courtney, knees bouncing in place of letting go of her head to pull her clothes back up.

"Mmhmm, that's about what I thought," mused Dana aloud, deciding to really hammer home just who was the one in charge right then as she continued to work the younger girl's pants and underwear the rest of the way down to her ankles for her.

In so doing, she also happened to get an eyeful of just what had lain hidden out of sight beneath her brightly colored panties up until that point.

"Well now, this is new..." she crooned, drawing a fingertip up and down along the smooth folds of the other girl's labia to clarify just what she meant in case it wasn't already painfully obvious. "Did someone decide she wanted to try copying our favorite bratty teen, perhaps?"

Glowing positively neon herself now, Courtney's contrite misery overflowed in the form of another prolonged moan as faint goosebumps broke out all across her newly exposed skin.

Perfect.

"Oh? Am I wrong?" teased Dana, pressing her advantage as she lazily swirled a fingertip around her hood, making her gasp and quiver. "Did your razor 'slip' then, maybe? You wouldn't be the first young lady I've come across who'd developed a sudden case of butterfingers in the shower, you know."

"N-No- Oh! I was just, y-you know… Trying something different," the flustered TA tried to explain, doing a very poor job of looking like anything other than a little girl who'd been caught with her hand in the cookie jar as she added in a petulant mumble. "Abby likes it…"

"I'll just bet she does."

Still snickering, Dana settled back against the cushions behind her and gave her broad lap an inviting pat.

"Alright, hon, that's enough goofing around. Climb aboard and let's get started."

"R… Right!"

That was one order Courtney didn't need to be given twice. Moving her hands from atop her head, she began shuffling her way over to her right side, tugging down on the hem of her shirt in a futile attempt to hide her hairless front from view (which only further exposed her pert bottom) as she did so.

"That's it. Just like that," the auburn-haired older woman encouraged as she dipped forward and settled her surprisingly substantial weight across her thighs with all the natural grace of a lifelong athlete who was well-versed in the act of bending over for a spanking. "Good girl. Now let's just get these up here…"

Giving her firm cheeks an encouraging couple of pats, Dana wriggled herself further back into the couch and then leaned over to wrap an arm around the taller girl's knees, dragging them up onto the couch beside her so that both her legs and torso were now supported by its steady frame.

"You're just a *bit* bigger than the naughty girls I'm used to having across my lap," she explained. "So I think this'll make things much more comfortable for the both of us."

"Gee, thanks."

Despite the worried tension coiled tight in the younger girl's seat, the two of them couldn't help but share a smirk at that.

"Well… Relatively comfortable," Dana amended, gliding her palm up and down along her full bottom a handful of times, getting a feel for her target area.

And because the girl who it belonged to had the most captivating combination of firm, yet bouncy, cheeks she'd ever come across.

Oh my goodness, yes. Just look at that jiggle! This is definitely going to be a delight to spank.

As she did, Courtney reached out and grabbed one of the throw pillows in front of her, tucking it under her chest along with her arms.

Hmmm… I wonder if she's a reacher? Dana mused to herself, giving her sit-spots a couple of extra-firm squeezes before reaching behind her for the hairbrush. *Guess we'll find out soon enough.*

"Ready?" she asked aloud, lightly bouncing the oval head of the heavy ebony brush against one cheek and then the other.

Groaning into her pillow, Courtney nodded, the couch muffling the majority of her response.

"I guess so, ma'am."

"Alright then, sweetheart, hang on tight," Dana cautioned, deciding to head off any potential escape attempts by wrapping her left arm around her waist from the start, pulling her in tight against her stomach.

Geez. I really need to hit the gym again…

Shaking her head to clear it of any extraneous thoughts of washboard abs that might distract her from the task at hand, she gave each cheek one final pat and then brought the oval head of the brush up past her shoulder. Then, with one last exhalation, she sent it crashing back down at full force, kicking off the athletic TA's spanking with a blazing flurry of swats to the meatiest parts of her sizable seat.

CRACK! CRACK! CRACK! CRACK! CRACK!

"Ack! Oh! Urk!" Courtney grunted as the brush found its mark over and over again, its ebony surface (polished by Rhen's own bare bottom over the course of many, many, *many* spankings) mercilessly biting into her unprotected cheeks with relentless fury. "Geez- Ow!"

With each swat that landed, her cheeks compressed for a brief moment before springing back again with a rippling jiggle, all but begging for more as the head of the brush left a pale oval in its wake that rapidly filled with red as the next two or three swats set her bottom to bouncing anew.

"Do I have your attention now?" Dana demanded over her half-suppressed yelps, continuing to beat out a scorching tattoo from the tops of her shifting cheeks to just above her thighs.

"Y- Oh! Yes ma'am!" gasped Courtney, her messy bob tossing to and fro as she struggled to hold in her cries.

"Good. Now let's start with something simple," the older woman pressed on, turning her attention exclusively to her sit-spots. "Are you going to keep snapping at your girlfriend?"

CRACK! CRACK! CRACK! CRACK! CRACK!

"No! No! No!" came the expected reply in turn, punctuated by the taller girl's sock-covered feet furiously kicking against the couch behind her, working the legs of her jeans loose and causing them to flail behind her like twin flags of surrender. "I won't, I won't!"

"And what about skipping lunch?" Dana demanded a moment later, pouring even more force into her movements.

CRACK! CRACK! CRACK! CRACK! CRACK!

"I-" Courtney started to reply, before stopping short. "I'll try!"

"*Try*? Oh no, no, no, little girl," Dana growled, letting some genuine irritation seep its way into her voice as she vented her disapproval against the backs of her dancing thighs. "We do *not* skip lunch. Period. Eating is important! Your body needs fuel to function, and without it you're just going to get cranky and tired. Then how are you ever going to get your work done, hmmm?"

"But- Ack! But...!" protested the TA, starting to sound genuinely miserable now. "But my professor- Oh! Won't let me!"

"Won't *let* you?" exploded Dana.

CRACK-CRACK!

Underscoring her outrage with two truly breathtaking swats just below Courtney's ample cheeks that she knew for sure would leave some very tender marks.

"That's ridiculous!"

"I tried to- Ow! To tell him- Oh! That I was supposed to have a break!" moaned the younger girl into her cushion. "But he wouldn't listen!"

Positively fuming now, Dana shifted her aim back up toward the meatier parts of her bottom as she continued to pummel it ruthlessly.

"We'll just see about that!" she huffed. "The next time he decides to give you shit for eating *lunch*, you tell him to call *me*. I'll set him straight, don't you worry."

CRACK! CRACK! CRACK! CRACK! CRACK!

"That is completely ridiculous. I swear, the nerve of that man! Where the hell does he get off acting like that? It's ridiculous is what it is!"

"But- Urk! But- Owie!"

"No buts!"

CRACK! CRACK! CRACK! CRACK! CRACK!

"You're going to tell your adviser about this as soon as we're done here. And if they won't do anything about it, then I'll get in contact with the dean and see what *she* has to say about it. Making you skip meals is completely unacceptable, young lady!"

"Okay, okay!" howled Courtney, nodding furiously. "I'll do whatever you want, I promise!"

"Good girl."

Forcing herself to breathe out the remainder of her righteous indignation (after all, it wasn't *her* fault that her boss was a total idiot), Dana eased her iron grip around the younger girl's waist and dialed back the force of her swats to something more sustainable as she continued peppering her bottom with punishing blows.

CRACK! CRACK! CRACK! CRACK! CRACK!

One thing was for sure, though. Courtney definitely wasn't going to be forgetting this trip across her lap any time soon.

And, *she* was going to be sending some very irate emails later that evening.

I just cannot believe that man. Taking advantage of a poor college student like that. It's completely ridiculous! Well, we'll just see what the employment center has to say about that after I'm through giving them a piece of my mind. Humph!

—

Keeping one eye trained on the antique grandfather clock off to her left (it was way too easy to lose track of time while spanking a genuine cutie like Courtney, and much as she would've loved to play with her all afternoon she understood that what she needed from her right then was a strictly regimented punishment), Dana continued to mete out one merciless swat after another to her bouncy bare bottom and firm thighs. Pelting them at a steady, measured pace of about one *CRACK!* of the ebony brush per second for several interminably long, unrelenting minutes as she gradually darkened the skin there to a dusky maroon with a faint dusting of white near the centers of her cheeks where they were the most swollen; eventually beginning to coax up a fine layer of bruising to compliment the blazing redness there, deepening it to something that truly hurt just to look at.

CRACK! CRACK! CRACK! CRACK! CRACK!

And yet, despite having so far endured what was by any measure a *very* severe spanking (one that would have no doubt left her petite not-niece sobbing hysterically and promising to move heaven and earth for her), the stubborn TA hadn't yet so much as shed a single tear. Let alone shown any genuine signs of remorse. Instead, she'd kept her hands balled into obstinate fists beneath the pillow wedged under her chest and her teeth clenched tight as she struggled to endure her punishment with the minimum amount of fuss possible.

"Ack! Urk! Owie! Ouch! *Shit*!"

Goodness me. This girl is one tough nut to crack…

Dana doubted very much that she was actually capable of raising blisters on Courtney's seat even if she'd wanted to, but one way or another, she still fully intended on leaving her bride-to-be's surrogate older sister with a bottom that was tender to the touch well into next week.

She just wished she'd stop fighting her so much over it.

CRACK! CRACK! CRACK! **CRACK! CRACK!**

"I bet your bottom is feeling pretty gosh darn sore right about now, isn't it, little girl?" she chided sharply, snapping her wrist with her last couple of swats to help encourage the proper response from her.

"Yes- Ohhh! Yes ma'am!"

"Well, good," sniffed Dana, tossing her hair as she tightened her grip around her wriggling waist in preparation for a fresh go at her sit-spots. "You deserve every single swat of this spanking, and I can guarantee you'll be remembering it every time you sit down for the next week!"

CRACK! CRACK!

"At least!"

"Yeah, no- Ack! Kidding!" grunted the other girl, breathing rapidly in and out through her mouth like she'd just eaten a dozen jalapenos and was in desperate need of a glass of water.

Still, though, while it was painfully obvious that she was in no small amount of discomfort, she continued to refuse to give in to the tears that Dana could sense were lurking just beneath the surface of her resilient façade.

Ugh. This is seriously starting to get ridiculous.

Rolling her eyes as she huffed and puffed, trying to surreptitiously catch her breath without letting on that she was starting to run out of steam, the auburn-haired older woman paused in her swatting just long enough to draw her forearm across her sweaty brow before continuing to piston her arm up and down once again.

Spanking Courtney was proving to be quite the workout!

CRACK! CRACK! CRACK! CRACK! CRACK!

Despite the fact that they both knew she needed a proper release, the athletic TA was still used to being the one in charge. Which, combined with her naturally high pain tolerance, was making the entire process of getting her to break down and let go of control for a little while an absolute nightmare.

Unfortunately (or fortunately, depending on your point of view on the situation) for her, though, Dana knew just how to deal with willful, overgrown little girls like her.

"Alright then, missy. Have it your way."

Coming to an abrupt, mid-swing halt in her assault on Courtney's sizzling seat, she tucked the hairbrush back beneath her hip and leaned over to her right where she began tugging her already partially discarded jeans and colorful panties the rest of the way off her legs for her; tossing them over the arm of the couch beside her without a second glance. Now, with only a pair of sporty black ankle socks to preserve her modesty below the waist, she dragged her further forward across her knees and then pushed her right leg off of her lap entirely, parting her thighs.

"Wha-?" the startled grad student began to gasp as she felt the first caress of cool air across her suddenly exposed labia, only to immediately have her half-formed question answered for her as Dana hooked a leg over the back of her knee, locking it in place as she began to lay into the ultra-sensitive insides of her splayed thighs with the head of her hairbrush.

CRACK-CRACK-CRACK!

CRACK-CRACK-CRACK!

This time around, Courtney's reactions were *far* more in line with what she was looking for.

"Aieee!" she howled in shock and agony, her cries ratcheting up several octaves all at once as her delicate skin was set ablaze at a breakneck pace that completely annihilated her will to tough out her punishment. "Oh my god, Dana- Yeowie, owie, owie!

No- Ack! Please- Ah! I'll be- Oh! I'll be good! I'll be goooood!"

"Now we're getting somewhere," declared the older woman with immense self-satisfaction, continuing to mercilessly flambé the poor TA's tender thighs with rapid-fire, wrist-powered swats of the ebony brush.

CRACK-CRACK-CRACK!

CRACK-CRACK-CRACK!

"Little girls getting their bottoms spanked need to cry. Not act like they're putting up with a minor inconvenience because they got caught being naughty."

"But- Ow! But...!"

"No buts!"

CRACK-CRACK-CRACK!

CRACK-CRACK-CRACK!

"I want *tears*."

Right on cue, she then began to hear the first telltale sounds of remorseful sniffling coming from somewhere off to her left among the pillows where Courtney's face was hidden. Followed half a minute later by a prolonged wail that quickly broke down into racking, heartfelt sobs.

Geez. It's about damn time.

"That's it, sweetheart," she cooed, not slowing her swatting in the slightest as she started branching out to the rest of her thighs once again; working her way up from just above the backs of her knees to the tops of her cheeks and back down again, before turning her attention to the vulnerable insides of her legs for another round. "You were being a very naughty girl, and now Auntie Dana is giving you the spanking you deserve. So you just go ahead and let it all out, alright?"

Howling and yelping up a storm now, Courtney did just that. Soaking the throw pillow beneath her face in a mortifying mixture of tears, snot, and saliva.

"Aunt Dana, please! I'm *sorry*!" she moaned, tacking on the title seemingly without even thinking about it as she reached back to try and somehow shield her red-hot seat from further punishment.

Dana was ready for her, though.

"Oh no you don't," she admonished, intercepting her wrist and pinning it against the side of her hip as she continued to broil her buns for her, pouring a bit more power into her next batch of brush swats.

CRACK-CRACK-CRACK!

CRACK-CRACK-CRACK!

"There will be none of that, young lady."

"Ah! Owie! Ack! But it- Ow, ow, ow! It *hurts*!"

"Oh, does it?" asked Dana facetiously, unable to resist the urge to break down the usually so in control grad student's walls just a bit further.

"Yessss!" she howled in response, just as she'd been hoping she would, pounding her one free foot against the couch behind her for all she was worth as her other scrabbled ineffectually against the hardwood beneath it, her sock preventing her from gaining purchase there.

"Well great," her spanker laughed easily, slowing her pace now that she'd successfully brought her bottom to a boil, only needing to keep it simmering now as she continued to drive her lesson home.

CRACK! CRACK! CRACK! CRACK! CRACK!

"That *is* kind of the whole point to all this, you know, silly goose."

Preoccupied as she was with sobbing, Courtney really didn't have the presence of mind to fire back with anything approaching her usual wit. Instead, she continued to squeal and squawk as her trapped hand strained toward her seat. Which, given her well-toned physique, was actually proving to be a difficult battle for Dana to contend with.

She was just about to order her to tuck her hand back under her chest, when a devilish idea struck her.

We're getting close to being done anyway, she reasoned to herself, a wicked grin stealing across her face. *I might as well make it a memorable finale for her, right?*

"Alright, honey," she cooed innocently, coming to another stop in her swatting and releasing her vice grip around the girl's wrist. "If you want to reach back so badly, then you just go right ahead."

Courtney, who was far too grateful for the reprieve to question why she was suddenly being allowed to do so, immediately did as she was told. Arching her back and seizing hold of a great handful of throbbing cheek with her right hand.

"Ah!" she hissed, eyes screwed shut tight as she kneaded her scalded flesh.

"Does that feel good?" prompted the auburn-haired older woman after allowing her to catch her breath for half a minute or so.

"A little bit…" mumbled the TA into the couch, the tips of her ears going pink as she refused to look back at her.

"Great."

Chuckling, Dana gave her other cheek a friendly pat, before allowing her voice to grow steely once again.

"Now I want you to give that a good hard squeeze and pull it away from the other one for me."

"*What?*" squawked Courtney, going rigid with disbelief.

"You heard me!" snapped the older woman with a pair of hard hand spanks to punctuate her rebuke.

SMACK! SMACK!

"I plan on roasting all these sweet spots back here in the hard to reach places, and you're going to help me do it."

Suiting actions to words, she drew her other cheek back for her and poked pitilessly at the inner cleft near the base of her shamefully shaved vulva.

"Now spread 'em," she ordered, digging in her nails just enough to curb any further arguments. "I am not going to tell you again, little girl."

Shivering, Courtney nevertheless did as she was told, sniffling in self-pity all the while as she did so.

"Oh my god, you are such a… a…"

"A meanie?" suggested Dana with a smirk.

"*Yes*!"

"And you're a brat," she replied with an affectionate jiggle of the bun in her hand. "Now get a good grip. I'd better not see you letting go before I'm finished."

"But-!"

CRACK! CRACK! CRACK!

"Owie, owie, ack!"

"I do believe I already made myself abundantly clear about how there will be no buts," tutted Dana, all business once again as she continued to methodically redden the inner slopes of the other girl's cheeks, ensuring that each step she took for the next day or two would bring with it a keen reminder of their time together that afternoon.

"But it hurts!" whined Courtney, her tears returning with a vengeance as she clung desperately to her right cheek.

"You think so, huh?" smirked the older woman. "Trust me, hon. You're getting off light. There are *much* worse places I could be swatting right now."

Deciding to illustrate just what she meant, she adjusted her grip on the brush and angled a trio of lightning-fast swats directly against her puckered back door.

CRACK-CRACK-CRACK!

Followed by one to her pouting lips.

CRACK!

"Aieee!"

"See?" she pressed on sweetly, turning her attention back to her comparatively less sensitive inner sit-spots.

"I do, I do, I doooo!" Courtney wailed miserably.

Awww, you poor dear, Dana sighed to herself, her face twisting into a sympathetic grimace. *I hate having to be so hard on you, but you were the one making that choice in the end, you know.*

Aloud, though, she kept her attitude brisk and businesslike, showing not a single ounce of mercy.

"Very good," she chirped, pressing down against the small of the thrashing TA's back with her elbow to hold her steady as she worked to get both sides of her inner cleft to match in intensity. "Now you just hang on for a little while longer. We're almost done, I promise."

—

In the end, it only took another minute or two more of high-precision punishment before Dana finally decided that the now totally spent girl sobbing across her lap had had enough. Truth be told, she'd actually been reducing the amount of force she was putting behind each of her swats after that initial flurry to the insides of her cheeks. Mostly just letting the weight of the brush itself and the soreness of her already throbbing bottom do the work for her as her punishment coasted to a stop to all on its own.

Not that Courtney was in much of a state of mind to actually notice.

By the time they were finished, she was far, *far* too busy sobbing herself hoarse as she lay sprawled out jelly-limbed, half-on and half-off of her thighs to care.

"That's it… Let it all out, sweetheart," the auburn-haired older woman soothed, setting aside her hairbrush as she glided her left hand in gentle, reassuring circles along the small of her back. "You did such a good job taking your spanking. I know that must've been very hard, but you did it anyway and I'm proud of you."

As she'd known they would, her words only served to further wring tears from the distraught younger girl, but that was alright. What she needed right then was a good hard cry, and one way or another, that was exactly what she was going to get.

"I'm s-sorry, D-Dana…" she eventually managed to croak, punctuating her apology with a long sniffle before burying her face in her couch cushion once again.

"Shhh… I know you are, sweetheart. Shhh…"

Continuing to rub her back, occasionally throwing in the odd scratch here and there for good measure, Dana kept on cooing reassuring nothings at her. Until, little by little, Courtney was able to at last rein in her sobs and sniffles. Returning more or less back to her usual self, save for the puffy red circles around her eyes, and the even puffier and redder cheeks and thighs still splayed out behind her.

"Feeling better?"

At her answering nod and the watery smile over her shoulder, Dana grinned right on back at her.

"I'm so glad to hear that," she sang, patting her scalded bottom in celebration and being rewarded with a sharp intake of breath through gritted teeth.

"Yeesh! Careful back there, would you?" winced the athletic TA, her momentary discomfort giving way to an exhausted laugh at the unrepentant expression on the older woman's face.

"Sorry, hon," she chirped, doing a very poor job of sounding even a little bit remorseful as she gave her seat another friendly *POP*.

"Humph! Yeah. *Sure* you are, you big meanie."

"Hah. Now you're starting to sound like someone else I know," teased Dana, gesturing off to her side with an amused shake of her head. "You'd better be careful with all that pouting, though. Missus Hairbrush is still just right over here if we need her, you know."

"Uh-huh."

Despite her attempts to at least *seem* unconcerned, Courtney's deadpan response was largely robbed of its oomph thanks to the glistening tear tracks still visible on her flushed cheeks.

"Can I get up now?"

"In a minute," dismissed Dana, pulling her right leg back up onto the couch for her. "First thing's first, though. You and I need to have a chat."

"W-We do?" squeaked Courtney, suddenly sounding more

than a little panicked as she squirmed in discomfort; the tender insides of her thighs being pressed so roughly together touching off fresh fires between them. "I thought you said we were done!"

"Easy there, honey. It's *just* a talk this time," the older woman reassured her with a chuckle, rolling her over on her lap and helping her up into a seated position so that she was perched atop her left thigh with her sock-covered feet resting on the hardwood floor between her legs.

Even though she was quite a bit taller than Rhen was, she still more or less fit, and the position had the desired effect of giving her easy access to her sulking face and runny nose as she struggled not to let on just how uncomfortable having to rest her full weight on her freshly spanked bottom was for her right then.

Choosing not to comment on the rather adorable looks that she was giving her as she tried to surreptitiously readjust herself into a position that didn't hurt, Dana fished a handful of tissues from her pocket. She'd grabbed them on her way out of the kitchen, knowing that she'd need them eventually, and now that moment had come.

"Alright, sweetheart, be a big girl and blow into this for me," she prompted in a sugary sweet voice, bringing one of the tissues up to the darker-skinned girl's red-tipped nose and pinching gently.

With little choice other than to do as she was told or run the risk of being turned back over her knee, Courtney blew into the tissue, looking every inch the well-spanked five-year-old she surely must have felt like in that moment.

"There we go," cooed Dana, drawing away the tissue with an affectionate smile. "Isn't that so much better?"

"I guess so…" huffed Courtney, before letting out a yelp of surprise as the thigh she was sitting on gave a sudden hard bounce, jarring her bruised bottom enough to elicit a fresh burst of pain. "Ah! I mean, yes ma'am!"

"See?" purred Dana, her dark eyes twinkling with undisguised mirth. "That's what I thought you said."

"Uh-huh. Yeah. Er… ma'am."

Still grinning, savoring the look of sullen indignation on the other girl's face, she then set about drying the tears still clinging to her cheeks with her remaining tissues.

"Now then," she went on once she'd more or less restored her pretty face back to an approximation of its usual self.

She'd still need to splash some water on it and give it a good scrub in the bathroom later after she'd finished sufficiently marveling at the damage to her bottom in the mirror, but for now it was close enough.

"I think you and I both know that as nice as a hot bottom might be for helping to reset things, a single spanking alone isn't going to be enough to keep this from needing to happen again, now is it?"

Heaving out a long, shaky sigh, Courtney rubbed at her eyes with the back of one hand and nodded.

"Yeah… You're definitely not wrong there."

"I rarely am," snickered Dana. "But, yes. While I know you can't control everything in your life, there are at least *some* things you can do to help manage your more major stress factors."

Again, Courtney nodded.

"Like making sure I actually eat lunch and dinner?" she suggested with a wry smirk.

"That's an excellent start," agreed the older woman, matching her smirk with one of her own. "But I think we can do a bit better than just that. What about if you…"

—

For the better part of the next half hour, the two of them went back and forth picking apart Courtney's daily routine and the weekly tasks that she needed to get done, looking for ways she could make things easier for herself and avoid collapsing under the weight of her own responsibilities like she very nearly had. It was a long and draining talk to be sure, but in the end they both came away from it feeling reasonably confident that she wouldn't be needing a second trip across Dana's lap to destress any time in the near future.

Maybe for something a bit more on the lighter side, judging by the pair of *very* visible headlights poking out from beneath the front of her snug top, but not for any serious punishments.

"Thanks again for everything, Dana," the athletic TA sighed, now back to her usual wry, confident self as she slipped off her knee and back onto her feet, reaching back and gingerly prodding at her still swollen backside. "As much as it sucked, I really needed this."

"Think nothing of it, dear. I'm always happy to help," the auburn-haired older woman reassured her, climbing up after her and enveloping her in a warm embrace. "If you ever need anything like this again, or just want to talk, I'll always be here for you. Remember that."

"I'll be sure to bring an ice pack next time," snickered Courtney, rolling her eyes good-naturedly as the two of them parted and she began reaching for where her pants and panties still lay intertwined across the arm of the couch.

However, she didn't get very far before her hand was intercepted by Dana's own, darting out like a striking viper to snatch up her wrist in a steely, maternal grip.

"Excuse me, young lady. I don't recall giving you permission to get dressed."

"But-!" a dumbstruck Courtney tried to protest, tugging down on the front of her shirt with her free hand as she looked desperately to her clothes, the huge bay windows behind the couch with their curtains fully drawn back, and back to her again. "But someone might see!"

"So?" prompted Dana, looking not the least bit concerned.

"So… So it's not *fair*!" she whined. "I'm not like… like..!"

They both knew that what she wanted to say was "I'm not like Rhen!", but she wisely chose to keep that particular argument to herself.

Not that it would have helped her in any case.

Refusing to budge even a little bit, Dana shook her head.

"Little girls who get spanked in *this* house stand in the corner with their bare bottoms on display for everyone to see."

"I… I…"

The tall TA continued to mouth at her like a mortified fish out of water for several long, disbelieving moments before finally seeming to come to terms with the fact that there really was only one response she could possibly give right then.

At least, if she ever wanted to be able to sit down again.

"Yes ma'am…" she groaned, her face flushing hot enough to match Rhen on even her best days as she continued to remain pinned in place by a disapproving scowl.

"That's better."

Suppressing a satisfied smirk, Dana spun her firmly toward the corner that was the most visible to the front yard (and anybody who might happen to be passing by).

"You can do the walk of shame just like everyone else. Now scoot!"

SMACK!

Actually jumping forward with the hard impact of the older woman's palm against her left cheek, Courtney went scrambling toward the corner just as fast as her long legs would carry her, both hands clamped tight to her sizzling bare bottom as her socks slipped and slid on the hardwood floor beneath them.

"Yes ma'am! Sorry ma'am! Right away, ma'am!"

Chuckling to herself, feeling an immense sense of satisfaction at a job well done, Dana trailed after her at a much more leisurely pace; eager to see just how cute she'd look once she had her hands on top of her head and her nose pressed all the way against the wall in the time-honored position.

Something told her that she was very much going to enjoy the view.

Chapter 20

Bubble, Bubble, Brats in Trouble

Perhaps not all that surprisingly, Rhen continued to collect her fair share of hot bottoms and displaced panties as June gradually gave way to July and her summer semester drew to a close. But, through a combination of good behavior (and even better luck), she nevertheless managed to avoid any *serious* disciplinary action that might've left her sleeping on her stomach and sitting sore the following day.

Not that that did much to save her seat from the more routine punishments she found herself on the receiving end of every few days or so.

Missus Hastings, for instance, always seemed to be able to find some reason or another to put her over the arm of her floral living room couch for a brisk dose of her slipper or six of the best from her garden cane whenever she came to see her on Saturdays. It usually came down to something relatively minor. Like being a few minutes late to her house in the morning (despite not actually having a set time that she was supposed to be there by), being "slapdash" with how she did the chores assigned to her, or demonstrating some "truly dreadful" manners in the form of resting her elbows on the kitchen table while they ate lunch. Even so, Rhen really didn't mind these weekly doses of English discipline all that much. In fact, she'd found that trying to outfox her ostensibly strict and exacting older neighbor was a lot of fun! Plus, the delicious baked goods she plied her with after she was through toasting her buns always made the hard kitchen chair she insisted she sit on to eat them *much* more bearable.

Even if she refused to play fair sometimes and spanked her anyway despite being a perfect angel all afternoon.

"Sure, you were minding your p's and q's today, love," she'd reason as she tugged down her panties in back for a mild hand spanking while they waited for their cookies to finish baking. "But that doesn't mean you weren't *thinking* of all sorts of wickedness you could get up to while my back was turned, now does it?"

Thankfully, though (despite what she was sure were more than a few close calls), Rhen had so far managed to avoid any repeat encounters with her neighbor's back yard supply of ginger. And, even better, the dress she'd bought for her a couple weeks back was actually really cute.

She'd even gotten it custom tailored to fit her perfectly!

Unfortunately, Rhen had had a *very* visibly red bottom shining through the snug material of her white cotton panties (courtesy of her academic adviser's Spencer paddle) that Friday afternoon her neighbor taken her in to get fitted. A fact which she and the seamstress taking her measurements had found no small amount of delight in teasing her about. Especially after they'd managed to coax the entire story out of her and had decided that they really ought to have her take her underwear off entirely so that they could get the most "accurate" results possible. Which, for better or worse, had left her with two sets of rosy red cheeks and a dress that fit her like a glove.

Even when its skirt was rucked up past her hips in back.

For as embarrassing as that all might've been, however, Rhen felt that she could at least take solace in the fact that she hadn't been on the receiving end of the teeth-clenchingly mean *WHOOSH-SMACK!* of Doctor Holloway's paddle all *that* often. Though, that wasn't to say she hadn't become intimately familiar with the faded pattern on the cheap carpet inside her adviser's office over the course of the last semester.

True to her prediction, she'd lasted all of about two weeks before she'd finally slipped up and failed to turn in one of her homework assignments on time. Which, apparently, had been just the signal her professors and TAs had been waiting for to declare open season on her butt. After they'd realized that Doctor Holloway was totally serious about enforcing her new academic excellence standards as described in the memo she'd included with the stack of discipline referrals she'd sent them, it seemed like hardly a week went by without her coming away from at least one of her lectures or labs with a freshly filled out write-up for some minor bit of misbehavior or another.

But, while it was definitely annoying to have her discipline log growing far faster than she would've preferred, she had to admit that this new arrangement at school really wasn't all that bad. True, it was definitely humiliating to be turned over her adviser's knee for a prolonged bare bottom spanking with a heaping helping of scolding to go with it like she was some sort of unruly twelve-year-old. But, on the bright side, she and the older woman had finally developed the kind of close relationship and rapport that they'd been lacking up until then, and had even ended up having some really good conversations during their weekly check-ins. What was more, her grades were higher than they'd ever been (even more so than when Courtney had been her TA that first semester after moving in with Dana). Which, combined with her newfound goal of attending grad school after she'd finished her bachelor's, had kindled a zest for her studies within her that she'd never experienced before.

College was actually fun!

She just wished that Anna would stop trying to make her bike rides to campus so freaking uncomfortable.

After that initial double-whammy of a spanking *and* a diapering her first day on the job, she'd (thankfully) managed to avoid giving the younger girl another excuse to bare her buns for her. At least for a little while, at any rate. As it turned out, however, deliberately refusing to call her "Miss Anna" in front of a handful of daycare kids and then telling her to "bite me" when she insisted that she be more respectful had apparently not been a very bright idea. Especially since the recent high school grad hadn't even afforded her the courtesy of retreating up to her bedroom to deal with her that time, and had instead simply tucked her under one arm and spanked her right there in the middle of the living room while all of her friends watched on in glee;

waiting patiently for her to finish so that they could resume their game of Mario Party.

Which she still managed to win! (Even if she had to do so while standing up.)

All in all, Rhen was extremely happy with how her life had been going so far that summer. She had a loving fiancé (who also never failed to find a reason to pull her across her lap from time to time), good friends (who, likewise, weren't averse to the occasional bottom warming while they were hanging out), and she was doing better in school than she ever had before. And, while it was true that she found her panties being pulled down for her perhaps more than she would've perhaps liked, she'd still managed to avoid getting herself into any *serious* trouble since that morning when Dana had brought her unintentional spending spree to light.

Of course, everyone's luck eventually runs out. And for Rhen, that time just so happened to be the Thursday afternoon right before the start of finals week.

—

Waving goodbye to Anna as she sped off in her mother's old sedan, Rhen couldn't help but smile to herself. So far it had been an awesome day, and with no homework assignments hanging over her head or discipline referrals to deal with during her weekly review that following afternoon, she was feeling pretty darn good as she parked her bike just out of sight behind the garage. True, she'd need to spend all of her free time Saturday and Sunday powering through her notes in preparation for her finals next week (especially English Lit), but that was a problem for Weekend Rhen to worry about. For the next day and a half, provided her aunt didn't start asking any inconvenient questions about her study schedule, she was free and clear to do whatever the heck she felt like.

Which, most likely, would just be lounging around in her pajamas playing with the new Nintendo Switch Dana had bought for her a few weeks back.

"Hey, I'm home!" she called out into the blessedly empty front entryway of their house, kicking off her shoes and socks and haphazardly toeing the entire mess into its usual spot against the wall beside the door.

"Welcome home, cutie pie," came her partner's reply from somewhere deeper inside the house. "How was school?"

"Oh, you know… Not too bad," Rhen replied lazily, drifting off toward the kitchen where she'd heard the older woman's voice coming from, intent on snagging a quick kiss and a soda before heading up to her room for some pre-dinner time fun on her laptop. "It was just a review day, so it was all pretty chill."

"Well now, that's good to hear."

Setting aside the rag she'd been using to wipe down the countertops, Dana moved to meet her halfway on her trip to the fridge. Wrapping her up in a tight embrace and planting a lingering kiss on her lips as she caught her.

"Mmmm… You taste extra delicious today," she purred as they parted, licking her lips and leering hungrily down at her. "I love getting hold of you right after you've had something sweet."

"Happy to oblige," smirked Rhen, rising up onto the balls of her feet for another smooch. "Cupcakes were half off at the student union and I couldn't resist."

"I don't blame you," her fiancé snickered, going in for another taste. "From what I can tell, they were pretty tasty."

"The tastiest," agreed the shorter girl, her smirk growing playful as she added. "Promise you won't be mad I spoiled my appetite?"

Truth be told, Rhen wasn't actually worried about getting in trouble for her little pre-dinner snacking stunt. If Dana decided to spank her for it, it wouldn't be a particularly long or hard punishment, and being sent to her room with a freshly warmed pair of honey buns would be well worth the four dollars she'd saved on snacks that afternoon. Plus, the chance to get away with something was always way too tempting of an opportunity to pass up.

"Hmmm…" her fiancé mused for a moment or two as she

stared deep into her dark green eyes, her lips pursed as if she were really giving the matter some serious thought while in reality she was just counting the flecks of gold in her irises.

"Hmmm?" echoed Rhen goadingly, unable to stop herself as she molded her body against the older woman's own in a transparent attempt to sway her decision. "Is that a yes?"

Ignoring her sass, Dana smirked.

"Alright, alright, I suppose I can let this particular bit of naughtiness slide this *one* time," she allowed, pulling her further up onto her tiptoes with a firm, two-handed squeeze to her seat. "Just don't let it happen again. You hear me, missy?"

"Oh!" squeaked the shorter girl in reply, letting out a surprised giggle as her stomach gave a pleasant flip-flop. "Yes ma'am!"

"Good girl."

Letting her go after one more kiss, a smug half-grin then stole across Dana's face.

"So, did you and Abby have a good time getting coffee today?"

"Uh…"

Feeling a sudden frisson of nervous energy surge its way down through her heart, past her lurching stomach, and in between her wobbly legs, Rhen willed her voice to stay as calm and nonchalant as possible as she took an involuntary step back and swallowed.

Hard.

"C-Coffee?"

Smooth, Rhen. Real smooth.

"Oh, you know…" her aunt elaborated, planting one hand on her hip as she regarded her coolly. "Coffee Kate's? Specifically, that one right by your campus? The one that just so happens to send *me* an email every time you use their app to buy something because it pulls money from my account?"

"Uh…"

"Not ringing any bells?" she teased, her grin returning in full as she refused to let her wiggle her way out of answering. "That's alright. Maybe this will help jog your memory? It's the one that you and Abby went to today at oh, let's see…"

She slipped her phone out of her front pocket and thumbed it to life. Taking her sweet time pulling up her email as her naughty niece continued to wilt in front of her.

"Ah, here we are. At three-forty-two this afternoon."

Allowing a look of over-exaggerated shock to replace her wry grin, Dana's brows shot up toward her auburn hair and she gasped.

"Well now, wait a minute! Isn't that also the same time that you were supposed to be in your English Lit class?"

Oh god… Yep. Busted.

Still, though, never one to go down without a fight, Rhen rallied her defenses as best she could. Which, for better or worse (and she knew it was definitely worse), amounted to little more than her doubling down on playing dumb.

"Um, are you sure that was me?" she asked as innocently as she could, furrowing her brows in theatric befuddlement. "When was the last time you changed your password? Maybe someone hacked your account or something?"

"Hmmm… I don't think so," mused Dana, her tone taking on that dangerously amused edge to it that usually preceded a *very* hard spanking as she turned her phone around to show off the damning evidence on display in her inbox. "Somehow I just don't see some nefarious Russian hacker going to the exact same location that you do on your way back home. Or, for that matter, ordering a venti iced caramel macchiato with three extra shots of blonde espresso."

Her lips turned down slightly with that last bit.

"Incidentally, I thought you and I agreed you wouldn't keep pumping your drinks so full of espresso? Caffeine is fine in moderation, but one shot is more than enough for you, hon. You're not pulling a double shift in the sass mines, you know."

Opening her mouth to argue that a little extra espresso here and there really wasn't that big of a deal in the grand scheme of things, Rhen just barely managed to stop herself. Now was definitely not the time to be getting into that kind of argument. Especially not when she was still harboring some small amount of (rapidly dwindling) hope that she'd still be able to talk her way out of all this.

Seeming to sense what was going through her mind just then, though, Dana decided to cut straight to the chase.

"I really would suggest you not keep trying to lie to me, little girl," she warned, allowing just the hint of a low growl to edge its way into her voice as she held up a hand to cut off whatever it was that her bride-to-be had been about to say next. "I've already talked with Courtney, and she and I both know all about your little hooky stunt this afternoon."

"Wait, what? How?" demanded Rhen, following her partner's advice with a disbelieving pout.

"Oh come on," snorted Dana in turn, rolling her eyes. "It doesn't exactly take Jessica Fletcher to figure out that if you were going to cut class it would probably be with a friend. So I decided to give Courtney a call after I got that email I showed you. And, sure enough, she was able to get the whole story out of your little partner in crime almost immediately."

"Oh my god, that is so not fair!" protested the now thoroughly embarrassed twenty-one-year-old turned teenager, stomping a foot for good measure as she contented herself with complaining about *how* she'd been caught now that she could no longer deny it any further. "Using Courtney like that is totally cheating. You know Abby can't keep a secret!"

That, at least, managed to draw out a grimly amused chuckle from her fiancé.

"Yes, you're certainly not wrong there," she agreed, her stony façade cracking under the weight of her amusement. "That girl is an even worse liar than you are."

"Ugh. Tell me about it," huffed Rhen, heaving out an aggrieved exhalation before putting on her most innocent expression. "Okay, look. I know I messed up here, but I swear it's not my fault."

"Not your fault, huh?" questioned Dana, disbelief tugging at the corners of her mouth as she cocked a brow. "And how exactly do you figure that?"

"Well, uh…"

Rhen honestly hadn't been expecting her to humor her like she had. And, as a result, she suddenly found herself at a complete loss for what to say next.

"I mean…"

"Mmhmm? Yes, go on. I'm listening," drawled the older woman, her dark eyes sparkling with unabashed mirth as she made a twirling gesture with her hand. "The reason why *you* aren't responsible for skipping *your* class to go spend time with your friend this afternoon, even though you both are more than old enough to know better, is because…?"

"Is because…"

Chewing on her thumbnail, Rhen racked her brain for something good. But, try as she might, no miraculous defenses sprang to mind. And so, seeing that she was totally busted and that there was nothing she could do to save her backside from what was sure to be an extremely thorough spanking in just a few short minutes, she pushed her cheeks out into a pout and decided that if she was going down, she might as well take her best friend with her.

"Okay, finc!" she harrumphed, crossing her arms in front of her chest, the pair of shortalls she was wearing just then doing absolutely nothing to make her look any less like a sulking child as she glared at a spot on the floor just to her aunt's left. "I shouldn't have done it, yeah, but it was all Abby's idea. She *made* me do it!"

"Oh yes, I'm sure you had absolutely no choice in the matter whatsoever," deadpanned Dana, not looking the least bit convinced.

"I didn't!" insisted Rhen, having a very difficult time maintaining her attempt at affronted innocence as her voice rose up several octaves all at once with her whining.

"Uh-huh."

Cutting loose with an aggrieved sigh of her own, her partner pinched the bridge of her nose and shook her head.

"As it so happens, little girl, I really don't care whose idea it was. You were *both* being naughty, and now you're *both* going to get it good."

"Oh come on, that's not fair!"

Sighing again, Dana locked eyes with her in a way that made it abundantly clear that she was on her very last nerve.

"You keep saying that, but you and I both know it absolutely is," she admonished evenly. "You did the crime, and now you're going to do the time. Simple as that."

Then, as if on cue, their doorbell rang. Putting an abrupt end to their one-sided argument with a loud, chiming *DING-DONG!*

"Ah, and speak of the devil," crooned Dana, some of the annoyance draining out of her as she favored her peeved and pouting not-niece with a wicked grin and turned to go answer the door. "That must be them now."

"Wait, what?" squeaked Rhen, stomach lurching as she scrambled to follow after her as she strode with purpose out of the room. "Them? Them who?"

"Why, Courtney and Abby, of course," replied her aunt smoothly, sashaying her way into the front entryway of their house seemingly without a care in the world as she elaborated further. "After talking it over, she and I decided we might as well deal with you two together once you got home."

Before adding with a snicker.

"That girl is nothing if not punctual, I'll give her that."

Rhen, for her part, was in no mood to appreciate her former TA's time management skills just then. Not with the thigh-squirming specter of a double spanking suddenly looming over her, pretty much guaranteeing that she would be sleeping on her stomach that night.

And probably the night after for that matter.

Her fiancé and Courtney had a tendency to feed off of one

another when it came to dishing out discipline together, which never boded well for her backside.

"Oh my god, Dana, you can't be serious?" she demanded, the question coming out far whinier than she'd meant for it to as her heart rate shot into overdrive, heating up her face by several degrees.

"As a heart attack, cutie pie," came her aunt's reply as she wrapped her fingers around the doorknob.

"But... but-!"

However, whatever Rhen might've had in mind to say next, she never got a chance to. For no sooner had she come to grips with the fact that she and her best friend were in for a very thorough comeuppance for their class ditching, than Dana was throwing their front door wide open.

"Well, hello there, you two," she sing-songed, waving at the two coeds on the porch in front of her. "You're right on time."

"Heyo," came Courtney's reply, sounding just as jovial as she waved back.

Followed a moment later by a much more sour sounding, "Yeah... Uh, hey." from the blonde at her side after a firm nudge in the ribs from her elbow.

"Well now, I see someone's in a good mood," snorted Dana as she stepped aside and gestured for the two of them to come in. "Don't tell me you started the fun without me?"

"Nope, not yet," the tall TA reassured her as she and her girlfriend stepped over the threshold and began slipping off their socks and shoes. "Although, she definitely wasn't doing herself any favors, I'll tell you that."

Laughing to herself as Abby's face flushed a bright shade of pink, Courtney went on.

"I swear I was *this* close to pulling over and taking my belt to her bratty buns at least half a dozen times while we were on our way over," she admitted, holding her thumb and forefinger less than an inch apart as her girlfriend glared pointedly at her, pouting just as much as Rhen was. "But I figured it'd be way more fun if we both had a blank canvas to work with, so I did my best to hold out until we got here."

"Little miss Abby getting grumpy because she's in trouble? Why, I'm shocked," teased Dana, watching on in mild amusement as the girl in question hopped around on one foot, attempting to undo her shoelaces. "Next you'll be telling me that she said Rhen was the one dragging her along against her will for their little hooky adventure."

"Oh wow, how'd you guess?"

Directing a meaningful look in the petite junior's direction, Dana chuckled.

"Hmmm… I wonder?"

"I mean, she *was* the one who texted me first," grumbled Abby, earning herself a pair of condescending smirks from the two older women as she added with far less confidence. "I just decided where we should go…"

"Actually, if you think about it, it's really our capitalist society that's at fault here," her partner in crime went on, picking up the bratting baton while the two of them shared an eye roll. "I seriously don't see how either of us can be held responsible for our actions when there's delicious coffee and *not* boring classes literally within walking distance of campus."

"Yeah!" affirmed Abby with an indignant nod. "It's positively criminal!"

"Lucky for you two then that I run a hot bottoms for all household," countered Dana without missing a beat, evaporating the tension among the four of them in an instant as they all shared a laugh.

Which, honestly, came as a huge relief to Rhen.

Even though she and her friend were about to be punished for their flagrant disobedience, she still took heart in knowing for sure that her partner and friends weren't actually upset with her. They'd just broken the rules was all, and now they were going to have to own up to that. No anger, no resentment, just the natural consequences of their actions coming back to bite (or in this case, smack) them on the butt.

Not that that's really going to be much of a comfort once we start feeling the burn... she mused to herself with a wry grimace while Courtney pressed on.

"So, what's the game plan here, Dana?" she asked. "You said you had something special in mind when we were on the phone earlier."

"Oh, yes, that's right!" replied the older woman, brightening as she turned and motioned for the three of them to follow her back into the kitchen. "Well, for starters, I thought we could kick things off with a good old-fashioned mouth soaping to take care of all those filthy fibs our little ladies have been telling us."

"Hah! I love that," beamed the TA, while her girlfriend and Rhen both raised their voices in adamant dissent.

"Oh my god, are you serious?"

"Aunt Dana, no, please!"

Neither of them were paid much attention, however, as they were ushered through the front room and into the kitchen.

"Have you ever washed someone's mouth out before, Courtney, dear?" Dana asked instead, addressing her fellow disciplinarian as she turned to lean against the edge of the island.

"Um... Not really," admitted the other girl, adding with a note of embarrassment. "Mom usually put some hot sauce on our tongue if she caught us swearing."

"A hot tongue to go with a hot bottom, eh?"

"Heh. Something like that."

"Well, don't you worry," the auburn-haired older woman went on with a reassuring smile. "It's remarkably easy once you get the hang of it, and Auntie Dana will be right there by your side to help guide you through it every step of the way."

"Oh joy..." mumbled Abby flatly, blowing out a puff of annoyed air.

"Yeah, we're totally screwed," commiserated Rhen. "Mouth soapings freaking *suck*."

"That's what makes them so effective, cutie pie," purred her partner, before pointing toward the tile floor at her feet. "Alright, you two, strip."

Adding with an impatient snap of her fingers.

"I want to see two naked butts, pronto."

"Wait, what? Why?" demanded Abby, reflexively tugging down on the front of her shirt as a strawberry flush crept its way up her pale cheeks.

"Because I said so?" suggested Dana, raising a brow.

"But… but…!"

Spluttering, the blonde looked to Rhen for support, only to find her already in the process of unhooking the straps on her shortalls.

"You didn't seriously think you were getting out of this with just a little ol' mouth soaping, did you?" taunted her partner, stepping in close and planting a quick kiss on her pouting lips. Abby remained undeterred, however.

"I was kinda hoping so, yeah," she deadpanned.

"Sorry, hot stuff."

Holding her emerald gaze with a viciously unsympathetic grin, Courtney reached down and began unfastening the front of her pants for her.

"But you know I can't go that easy on you," she went on, drawing down her zipper once her button clasp had been pulled free. "Not after the way you helped lead our poor, sweet, impressionable little sister astray."

"Humph. Impressionable, my ass," grumbled Abby, apparently deciding that if she were going to have her mouth washed out she might as well earn it.

"Oh, don't you worry," teased Courtney, her grin turning predatory as gravity whisked her girlfriend's stylish slacks down to her ankles. "I'll be making one hell of an impression on this sweet ass of yours soon enough."

Suiting actions to words, she reached behind the blonde and seized a great handful of cheek in either hand, squeezing tight and pulling her in close as she pressed her body to hers.

"Besides, I think you look great in just a button-up."

"No arguments here," agreed Dana with a lascivious grin, accepting her bride-to-be's shortalls and setting them aside on the island behind her.

"Ditto," chimed in Rhen, licking her lips with a mixture of nervousness and excitement as she slipped her bright pink Hello Kitty panties down off her hips and to the floor, teetering slightly as she stepped out of them before passing them along to her aunt as well.

Caught in a three-way attack of compliments about her caboose, Abby's pouting gradually gave way to a shy smile as the flush in her cheeks darkened to a cranberry red.

"Ugh, fine, whatever!" she finally groused, disentangling herself from Courtney and throwing her hands into the air in an obvious attempt to deflect attention away from her mounting embarrassment as her panties joined her shorts around her ankles, exposing a neatly trimmed patch of flaxen curls and a pair of round, full cheeks. "Can we just get this over with?"

"Yes, I suppose there's no time like the present," nodded Dana, absently folding her bride-to-be's own confiscated panties and laying them atop her shortalls before striding past the two bared brats in front of her and drawing out a pair of chairs from the kitchen table, spinning them around and positioning one behind each of them. "Alright, girls, have a seat."

Eager to cover their naked nates (even if just partially), Rhen and Abby each went scrambling for a chair with their hands clamped firmly between their legs.

"Sure thing!"

"You got it!"

While Dana watched on in obvious self-satisfaction, waiting patiently for the two of them to plonk down onto their respective perches before continuing on in a sugary sweet voice, bringing to bear every ounce of maternal condescension she possessed as she ruffled their hair affectionately.

"Well done, you two," she cooed. "Now you just go ahead and

tuck those hands of yours right beneath your buns and keep them there until I say otherwise, alright?”

“Yes ma’am…” came a chorus of less than enthusiastic replies from the two coeds this time as they shifted around in their seats to do as they were told, securing their fingers beneath the springy warmth of their bottom cheeks.

“Oooh, great idea!” commented Courtney with a surprised laugh. “I can’t believe I never thought of doing that before.”

“Mmhmm. It’s definitely a useful position,” agreed Dana, breaking out in a wicked grin of her own as she shifted over to stand behind Rhen, laying a hand on either shoulder. “Especially since it gives you access to all sorts of fun and interesting places without any pesky hands to get in the way.”

Demonstrating just what she meant, she leaned forward and seized hold of the hems of both the t-shirt and the thin camisole the petite junior wore underneath, dragging them both up to her collarbones to reveal her petite breasts for all to see.

“Eep!”

“Like here…” she chuckled, cupping one in either hand and giving their rapidly hardening nipples a firm pinch between thumb and forefinger.

“Ah!”

Which elicited a yelp of surprise from the shorter girl, followed by a whole host of involuntary giggles as she wriggled in her seat, just barely managing to keep her hands sandwiched beneath her buns while her fiancé fondled her.

“Or here…” the older woman went on a moment later, continuing to knead one breast while her other hand glided down along her smooth belly and in between her legs; wordlessly parting them and doubling her naughty niece’s squirming as her nimble fingers set to work playing with her clit and swollen lips, making her gasp and moan.

“I see…” drawled Courtney, making a show of rubbing her chin as if deep in thought while she closed in on her own girlfriend. “What do you think, babe? Should we give it a shot?”

Not actually bothering to wait for a reply, she circled around behind the huffy blonde and leaned forward, kissing her neck and fondling her full breasts through her shirt while her free hand slipped down between her obstinately pressed together thighs; producing much the same noises as those coming from Rhen just then as she found purchase there.

"Well, well, well," she purred a short while later, pulling away from her neck after one last, lingering kiss and holding up the index and middle fingers of her right hand for her mentor disciplinarian to see. "Looks like someone isn't quite as upset about her current predicament as she's led us to believe."

"Tsk, tsk," clucked Dana, feigning incredulous disbelief as she inspected her own glistening fingers after restoring Rhen's clothes to their proper position. "It's just fibs on fibs with these two, isn't it?"

"Noooo kidding."

The two of them shared an amused smirk then, before Dana brightened.

"Oh! That reminds me!"

Circling around to the other side of the island while distractedly sucking her fingers clean, she pulled open a drawer and retrieved from within two brightly colored bibs.

"Oh my god, Aunt Dana, no!" moaned Rhen as she caught sight of what the older woman held, wriggling in her seat and kicking her legs in protest as her face flushed twice as red as Abby's. "Where the heck did you even get those?"

"Why, at the supermarket, of course," replied her fiancé with an easy shrug. "They were on sale the other day, so I decided to grab a couple. Do you like them?"

"I mean, *yeah*," admitted the shorter girl with an exasperated grunt. "But that's, like, so not the point!"

"Duly noted, cutie pie. I'll be sure to make it up to you later."

"Humph. You'd better."

Then, turning back to Courtney with a very "What're you gonna do?" kind of look, Dana went on.

"Mouth soaping tends to be a rather drooly business, so these ought to help mitigate some of the spillover from these two once we get going," she explained, adding with a completely unashamed snicker. "Plus, well… They're just totally adorable, aren't they?"

"Hell yeah they are!" concurred the other girl, practically bubbling over with pent-up excitement. "God, I love playing with you Dana. You're always so creative!"

"Awww, why thank you, dear, you're too kind," demurred the older woman, feigning a blush before taking note of the sour look still evident on her naughty niece's face, as well as that of her friend, and adding with a raised brow. "Of course, if you'd prefer, girls, we can just as easily avoid this whole dribbling problem altogether by having both of you be naked for your punishment. Would you prefer we do that instead?"

"No ma'am!"

"No thanks!"

"Hmmm… Are you *sure*?" she pressed, her grin widening. "I really wouldn't mind, you know. Rhen and I can just play with these another night. I'm sure she'll give me a good reason to soap her out again sooner or later."

"Oh my god. Yes, I'm sure!" insisted Rhen, rolling her eyes while Abby nodded quickly beside her.

"Uh-huh, yeah. Totally fine with wearing one of those, ma'am!"

"Well…"

Dana let her lips bow into a mocking pout for a brief moment before they sprang back up into a triumphant smirk.

"Alright then."

After taking a bit more time to watch the two of them squirm, drinking in their obvious discomfort and embarrassed exhilaration as their thighs shifted together seemingly of their own accord, she turned her attention back to her soaping student and hefted a bib in either hand.

"So, flamingos or polka dots?"

"Flamingos, *definitely*," answered Courtney without a moment's hesitation, accepting the proffered bib and turning on her girlfriend with an amused gleam in her eye. "I'm pretty sure Abby has a pair of panties with this exact same pattern on them."

"Hah! Well in that case, you just feel free to take that home with you," laughed the auburn-haired older woman as she likewise circled back around behind her bride-to-be.

"Oh wow, that's so nice of you!" gushed the younger girl, pulling apart the velcro holding the neck of her bib together and securing it in place around her girlfriend before kissing her cheek. "Are you sure you don't mind?"

"Of course not," waved away Dana, likewise cinching Rhen's own rainbow polka-dotted bib around her neck before gliding past her on her way toward the sink at the other end of the room. "Now then, if you'll just step on over here, I'll show you how I like to get the soap ready."

"Ready?" echoed Courtney, trailing after her with a slightly confused expression on her face. "Don't you just need to, like, get it wet?"

"Well, technically speaking, yes," her mentor conceded with a self-deprecating laugh as she ducked beneath the sink and retrieved a pair of unopened boxes of Ivory. "But there *are* a couple extra things you really ought to do as well that might not be entirely obvious at first glance."

Passing along one of the boxes to the athletic TA, she tore open the side of her own and tipped its pristine bar of white soap out onto her waiting palm.

"For starters, it's best to take your time while getting ready and have the boy or girl you're about to discipline watch you prepare the soap. Doing so will give you a chance to calm down if you're peeved, and will give them ample opportunity to get into the proper headspace for what's about to happen."

"Hmmm... You don't say?"

Throwing a quick glance back over her shoulder, taking in the sight of Rhen and her partner in crime both alternating between sulking and nibbling nervously at their lower lips while fidgeting in their seats, Courtney couldn't help but smirk.

"Oh hey, yeah. I definitely see what you mean," she laughed. "It looks like if we gave those two a couple more minutes like this, they'd be just about ready to wet their pants… Assuming they still had any, that is."

"*Exactly.*"

"Humph!"

Fuming impotently at her partner's taunting tone and the smug, hummingbird smile on her surrogate older sister's face, Rhen summoned up her most powerful glower.

"Freaking bite me, you big jerk!" she mouthed at her, sticking out her tongue for good measure.

To which Courtney just winked and mouthed back.

"Ask your auntie first, you naughty girl."

Then, turning her attention back to Dana (who'd been watching their little exchange with an amused expression on her face), she asked, "So, what's next?"

"Why, getting it wet, of course," she grinned, starting up the flow of water from the sink and holding her fresh bar of soap beneath it, twisting it round and round in her hands as she continued to explain. "The aim here is to get it nice and bubbly, and to knock down any hard edges or sharp angles that might've been left behind from when it was molded by working it around between your palms. There's really no trick to this part other than to keep it moving, but you'll know it's ready once it's nice and smooth and has a good bubbly lather built up around it."

"Makes sense," nodded Courtney as she watched her work. "Is there any particular temperature I should be aiming for while I'm doing this? I'd imagine colder would be, I don't know… meaner, right?"

"Eh, not really," shrugged Dana, stepping aside to allow the younger girl access to the sink so that she could begin copying her movements with her own bar of soap. "The only person cold water is going to make uncomfortable is you, so I'd just stick to warm. It's a lot more pleasant to work with, and it also helps things soften up faster."

"I see…"

"Plus," she went on a moment later, her look turning devious as she flicked some suds from her fingertips. "Warm water is also very helpful for making soap sticks."

"Uh… Soap sticks?"

"Oh god…" groaned Rhen from somewhere behind them, lulling her head back in mortified disbelief.

Of freaking course she decides to bring those stupid things up now.

"Believe it or not, Courtney, dear, there are actually *two* places that you can use soap to discipline a naughty girl," her aunt elaborated in a lilting sing-song. "One is her mouth, of course, and the other…"

"The other?" pressed the TA, cocking her brows in amused curiosity.

"The other is between her cheeks," snickered Dana, miming the action with two fingers.

"Oh my god, *no!*" gasped the taller girl in horrified delight, breaking out into a fit of evil giggles. "Are you serious?"

"Mmhmm," confirmed her mentor with a triumphant tilt of her head. "First, you soften up a bar of soap in a bowl of warm water, and then once it's nice and malleable, you use a knife to cut it into strips just a bit wider than your thumb. From there, all you have to do is roll them around between your hands under some running water like you're doing now, and then once its ready, instead of using it to scrub out naughty words or fibs from a bratty girl's mouth, you bend her over and push it right on up her naughty little bottom hole and have her hold it there until you decide she's had enough. Or, even better, until it's completely dissolved."

"And, um… What happens then?" asked Courtney, swallowing excitedly as she sent a furtive glance in her girlfriend's direction.

"Hmmm, well…" mused Dana, pursing her lips as she picked her words before smiling enigmatically. "Do you remember how your tongue felt back when your mother used to put hot sauce on it?”

Not bothering to hide a grimace, the other girl nodded.

“Uh-huh.”

“Great…” came her mentor’s liquid reply, the corners of her mouth drawing back even further now as her eyes sparkled with grim amusement. “Now just imagine that same sensation, only it’s coming from inside your tush.”

“Oh, wow!” marveled Courtney with an exaggerated shiver. “That sounds *mean*.”

“Heh. Well, it’s certainly not nice,” agreed Dana, adding with an unrepentant wink. “But that’s what makes it such an effective punishment.”

Before throwing a look back over her shoulder toward her naughty niece.

“Isn’t that right, little girl?”

Flushing a hot shade of pink not all that dissimilar to the flamingo around her best friend’s neck, Rhen went rigid in her seat as if she’d just accidentally sat down on her punishment mat without thinking.

“Yes ma’am!” she hurriedly squeaked, cheeks clenching on reflex beneath her as humiliating memories of bubbles dribbling down between them flooded past her mind’s eye.

At least those stupid diapers are good for something…

“Hah! That’s awesome,” snorted Courtney, cutting off the flow of water from the sink with a shake of her head and turning a meaningful grin on her girlfriend. “Guess I know what I’ll have to try the next time *someone* decides she wants to give me a whole ton of attitude over what the chore wheel’s picked out for her.”

“Soap sticks definitely have a knack for instilling a spring in a naughty girl’s step,” agreed Dana as she led the two of them back toward their anxious partners at a leisurely pace. “Although, I still personally prefer enemas for that sort of thing. A backside full of hot, soapy water is an excellent motivator to get one’s chores done quickly. And, it has the added benefit of preparing the way for a thorough pegging afterward if you're in the mood to really show her who's boss."

"Huh."

That last bit seemed to have caught the taller TA's attention.

"And how, uh… How would one go about *doing* one of those, exactly?"

Smirking, Dana gave her a friendly pat on the shoulder.

"I'll send you some links later, dear."

Before taking up position just in front of her naughty niece, while her student adopted a similar stance before her own girlfriend.

"Now then, girls," she pressed on, brows arching as she gazed coolly down at the pair of them. "Do either of you have anything you'd like to say before we begin?"

Sharing a look of unease with one another, knowing full well that neither of them could do anything other than what they were told just then, Rhen and Abby both pushed their blushing cheeks out into a pout.

"Yes ma'am…" they answered together, deflating with a sharp huff as they rolled their eyes and shook out their respective heads of hair. "We're sorry."

Which at least made their partners laugh.

"So, how do we do this, Dana?" asked Courtney, hefting her bubbly bar of soap. "Just shove it in and start scrubbing?"

"That's the general idea, yes," nodded the older woman, before holding up a finger to forestall her. "But, again, there is a proper way of doing things that'll make the entire experience much more effective."

"Okay then. Lay it on me, sensei."

Turning back to lock eyes with her, Rhen's aunt's gaze grew decidedly more predatory.

"With pleasure."

Uh-oh… the twenty-one-year-old turned teenager thought to herself, wincing internally.

It never ended well for her whenever Dana decided to use her as an example in one of her "teachable moments".

Thank god it's just a mouth soaping!

The last thing she needed right then was for her to decide that she might as well throw in an impromptu crash course in how to administer an enema as well.

"Well, for starters," her fiancé continued to explain while she fretted silently to herself. "You want to make sure you get a good grip on the brat you're dealing with so that they can't wriggle free in the middle of their punishment. Luckily for me, Rhen has this oh so helpful little handle right back here."

Suiting actions to words, she leaned in close and wrapped the fingers of her free hand around the base of her ponytail, squeezing hard as she yanked her (quite literally) back to the present.

"Ah!"

"See? Now I have complete control over where she's looking, and she can't go anywhere I don't want her to," crooned Dana, tugging her head this way and that in demonstration. "You could always hold onto the back of their neck, of course, but I personally prefer to use a naughty girl's hair when possible. Just make sure you get a good, solid grip on a whole lot of it if you do, though. You definitely don't want to accidentally start yanking out small tufts of it once they start squirming."

"Yeah, that, uh… that wouldn't be good," agreed Courtney with a shiver as she followed the older woman's example and threaded her fingers through the back of Abby's thick flaxen tresses. "So, like this?"

"Ow! Geez, babe, careful!" yelped the blonde in question, glaring up at her with a petulant pout.

"Sorry, sorry," she apologized quickly, easing her grip but still maintaining a firm hold on the back of her head. "Better?"

At first Abby tried to nod, but when she found that her head was stuck, she instead huffed out an exasperated laugh.

"Yeah, that's fine."

"Remember, dear, you're aiming for firm and uncomfortable,

but not actually painful," cautioned Dana, smiling affectionately at the two coeds.

"Heh. Fair enough."

"Now then," she continued, turning her attention back to her own pouting princess. "The next step once you've gotten a good grip on your naughty girl is to order her to open her mouth. Usually this part is pretty straightforward, but some girls can be quite willful and refuse to do as they're told. In which case, all you really need to do is threaten to put them over your knee, or if you're in a hurry, just pinch their nose shut."

She then turned her head slightly to direct a withering glare at both Rhen and Abby, taking them in with cool, dark eyes.

"Of course, that won't be necessary today. Will it, girls?"

"No ma'am!"

"Nope!"

"Wonderful," she cooed, lightening up in an instant as she waved her sudsy bar of soap just beneath her bratty bride-to-be's nose. "Alright now, be a good girl for me and say 'ahhh', Rhen."

Suppressing the urge to literally say "Ah, Rhen" as she glared at her partner, the petite junior instead took in a resigned breath through her nose and then opened wide.

"Ahhhh- *Umph*!"

And immediately had her mouth filled with foul tasting, slippery soap.

Ugh. This part never gets any easier.

"You too, Abby, honey," her aunt chided gently a moment later when it became apparent that her friend was going to need some extra encouragement. "Come on now, no dilly-dallying. The sooner you open up, the sooner it'll all be over."

"Humph. Fine," groused the blonde, swallowing nervously before parting her lips. "Ahhh- *Umph*!"

And likewise having her face stuffed full of suds.

"Very good," sing-songed Dana, accompanied by a chorus of miserable moaning from the two soap-gagged brats in front of her as she nodded encouragingly at her student. "Now slowly start working that in and out of her mouth, alright?"

"R-Right!"

Sounding slightly less confident than she had just a moment earlier, Courtney still nevertheless did her best to maintain an air of control and authority as she set to work scrubbing out Abby's mouth.

"Like this?"

"Yes, that's absolutely perfect."

Making sure to keep one eye on her progress just in case she needed any help, Rhen's aunt then began doing the same. With well-practiced, firm but gentle movements, she started working the bar of soap in her mouth up and down along the length of her tongue. Painting a thick layer of bitter, slimy bubbles atop the taste buds there that immediately had her gagging and drooling as it mixed with her saliva and rushed in to fill every nook and cranny of her mouth before dribbling down her chin and onto her front.

Guess she wasn't wrong about the bibs... the thoroughly miserable twenty-one-year-old turned teenager couldn't help but think to herself with an internal huff as the absorbent material fastened around her neck soaked up the runoff from her mouth. Although, *I still don't see why she couldn't have just used a freaking washcloth or something. Humph!*

On the bright side, though, it seemed that her partner in crime wasn't having any better of a time than she was just then. In fact, judging by the muffled whining sounds she could hear coming from off to her left, Abby was regretting trying to lie to her partner just about as much as she was.

"How am I doing, Dana?" Courtney eventually asked after about a minute or so of scrubbing, pausing to look to her mentor for guidance.

"So far, so good," encouraged the older woman with a thumbs-up before leveling an expectant, motherly frown at the two bare bottomed girls sitting on their hands in front of her. "And how about you little sassmuffins, hmmm? Starting to think that maybe you should have just gone to class like you were supposed to?"

In response to her only partially rhetorical question, Rhen and Abby both nodded as much as they could as they gurgled out a reply that sounded somewhat like, "Yes ma'am!"

"Oh, you are? That's wonderful!" Dana cooed in turn, her tone positively dripping with patronizing sweetness before frowning once more in mock apology. "But I'm afraid you're just going to have to hang in there for a little while longer. I still need to teach Miss Courtney a thing or two about how to soap out a naughty girl's mouth."

Not bothering to wait for a response, she then turned her attention back to her student. Adopting a more brisk and businesslike tone as she did so.

"Right then. Once you've been going at the tongue for a while, your next target should be the insides of her cheeks and around her gums," she explained, demonstrating just what she meant by shifting the bar of soap in her niece's mouth around to her left cheek where she began gently running it back and forth along the base of her gums, before doing the same on her right. "This will help give you a more even and thorough distribution of lather along the surface area inside her mouth. And, if you're feeling *really* mean, or just need to make an impression, you can also take the opportunity while you're there to grind the soap against the sides and tops of her teeth as well."

"Her teeth?" pressed Courtney, unable stop herself from wincing as she ran her tongue across her own with a shiver.

"Mmhmm, that's right," confirmed Dana, chuckling darkly. "Doing that will get little pieces of soap embedded between them, and have her tasting bubbles *long* after she's had a chance to rinse."

That grim prospect alone managed to wring out a dual chorus of bubbly squawks of shock and terror from both Rhen and Abby as they shifted frantically in their seats. Gripping their naked cheeks for dear life as they tried to express how obedient they planned on being from that point on through only grunts and moans.

"But…" the older woman went on a moment later with a wink and a reassuring squeeze to her not-niece's ponytail. "I think we can safely skip doing that for tonight. Even with Abby's potty mouth earlier, I don't think either of them needs that big of a reminder about what they can expect the next time they try lying to us. We're doing a good enough job as is, aren't we, girls?"

Immediately she was bombarded by another matching pair of largely unintelligible moans and grunts that nevertheless had her and her apprentice disciplinarian grinning from ear to ear.

"Excuse me?" she teased, cocking her head to one side and leaning in to hear the two of them better. "What was that? Use your big girl words now, you two."

"No ma'amth!"

"I'm sorryth!"

Came Rhen and Abby's slightly more understandable responses, which, thankfully, seemed to be enough for their respective partners.

"Now that's what I like to hear!" cheered Dana, smiling fondly back at the two of them.

Then, seeming to sense that they were both about at their limit, and clearly not wanting either of them sobbing themselves to sleep that evening, she drew out the bar of soap from Rhen's mouth and eyed her and the blonde girl critically.

"Hmmm… I'd say that's probably about enough mouth soaping for one night, wouldn't you all agree?"

This time, she got three nods. One grudging, and two on the verge of panic.

"Great!" she chirped, shoving the bar of soap back into her naughty niece's mouth. "In that case, bite down on this for me, please."

Knowing better than to argue (and lacking the will to try even if she'd wanted to), Rhen did as she was told. Her teeth sinking into the soft soap far too easily for her liking as her aunt helped her back to her feet, Abby following shortly thereafter.

"Now then," she declared, taking hold of each of them by

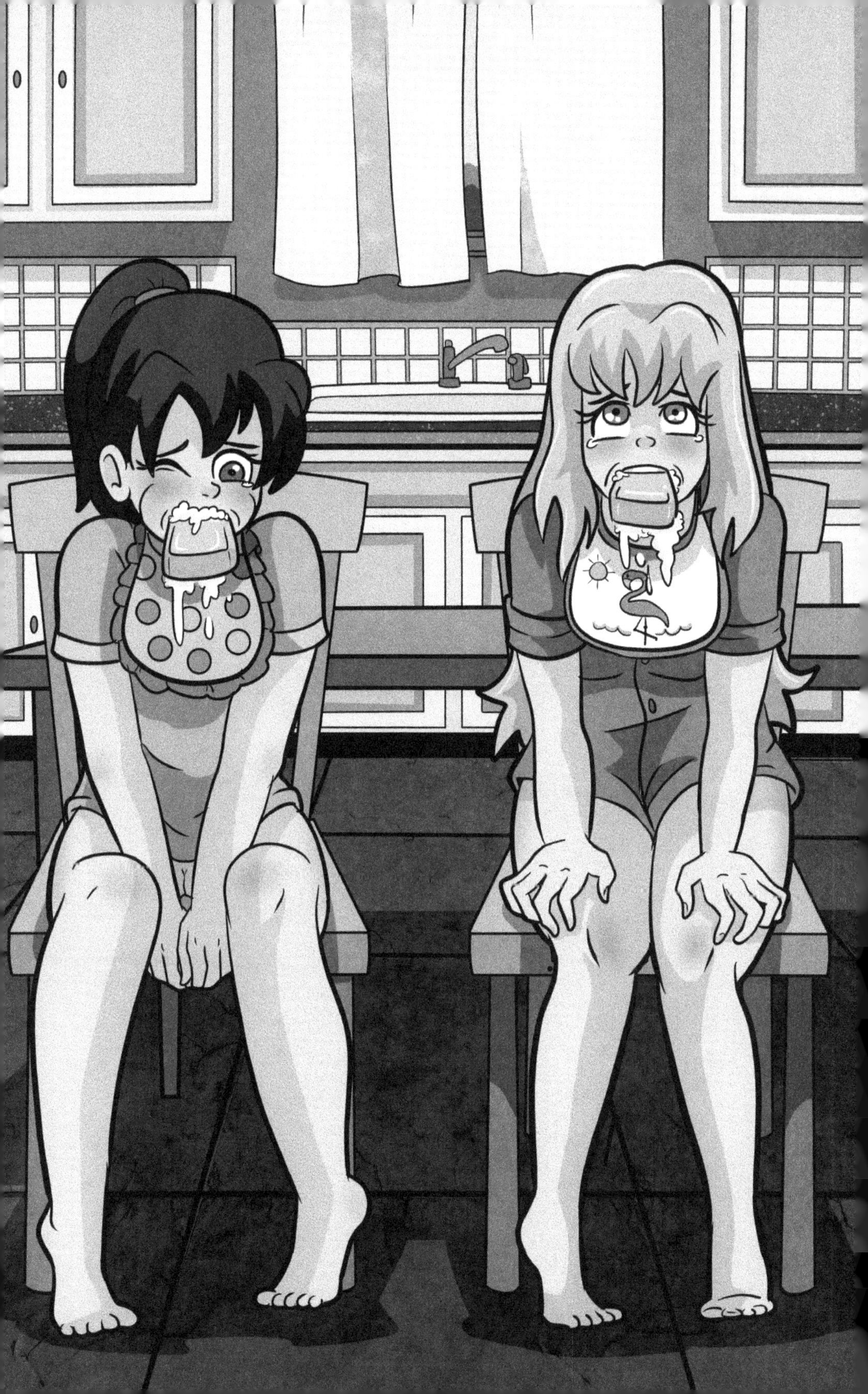

their upper arms and frog-marching them out of the kitchen.
"You two are going to stand in the corner with those bars of soap in your mouth and think about how you aren't going to be telling any more fibs for the next *ten minutes*."

Before seeming to take some small amount of pity on them as they entered the front room and adding encouragingly.

"Behave yourselves, and I'll make it five, alright?"

Not needing to hear any more motivation than that, both Rhen and Abby sped off toward a corner just as fast as their bare feet would carry them, taking up the position they each knew was expected of them in an instant.

"Alright, girls, the timer's running. Be good now, you hear?"

"Mmhmmth!"

"Yesth ma'amth!"

Chapter 21

Sizzling Seats and Summer Switches

True to her word, Rhen's aunt only kept her and Abby parked in their respective corners for a grand total of five(ish) minutes while she and Courtney made deliberately loud small talk over a couple of freshly brewed cups of coffee at the kitchen table in the other room. As if things weren't already bad enough with the seconds ticking by at an out of shape snail's pace while she and Abby did their best to will their brains to ignore the unhappy signals their taste buds were frantically sending them, they were *also* forced to endure the tinkling laughter of their partners drifting in to taunt them as they animatedly discussed the virtues of the particular blend that Dana had picked out for them and how delicious it tasted with just the right amount of cream and sugar.

It was positively criminal!

But, Rhen also had to admit, rolling her eyes as her fiancé made a point of smacking her lips after an extra-long sip, it wasn't entirely unexpected either.

Humph.

On the bright side, she could at least take solace in the fact that she and her friend didn't have to put up with their blatant teasing for very long.

Well... Sort of.

While it was definitely true that five minutes really wasn't all *that* long to stand in timeout for in the grand scheme of things (by now Rhen was well-used to staying parked in her usual corner for half an hour or more after she'd really worked her partner up into a tizzy), having to do so while biting down as softly as she could on a far too mushy bar of soap lodged between her teeth as a steady stream of bubbly drool dribbled its way down onto the front of her bib made the entire process feel a whole lot more like five *hours* instead.

Which, of course, was the whole stupid, freaking point.

Double humph.

"Alright, girls, you can come out now," Dana eventually announced, popping the mental (soap) bubble that Rhen had found herself floating along in as she strode back into the front room, silencing her phone's tingling timer as she did so.

"Oh thankth godth!"

With those five simple, beautiful words, any lingering annoyance or frustration that she or Abby might've still been harboring over their punishment immediately disappeared. Evaporating under the warmth of the auburn-haired older woman's smile as she watched the two of them turn and spit out their sudsy gags.

Before then being tackled in a rib-crushing double hug as they repeatedly chorused, "Thank you, thank you, thank you!"

"Oof!"

Laughing in spite of the rush of air that had just been knocked out of her, Dana held them close. Partially in a warm embrace, and partially in an attempt to keep herself from being toppled over.

"Well now, I'm glad to see there are no hard feelings, you two."

Adding with a wry smirk as her fingers walked their way down their backs to cup a handful of cheek in either hand.

"But, as much as I really do enjoy cuddling like this, I'd be remiss if I didn't mention that there are a couple of glasses of water with your names on them waiting for you in the kitchen."

Giving both of their seats a firm squeeze, she let them go and took a step back, hooking a thumb over her shoulder.

"So, if you don't feel like tasting Ivory with your dinner tonight, I'd get a move on."

Not needing to be told twice, the two bare bottomed brats immediately went scrambling toward the kitchen at top speed, each of them gratefully snatching up a glass of water from a smugly grinning Courtney as they tore off their bibs on their way to the sink for some much-needed rinsing relief. And, over the course of the next few minutes, the two of them focused exclusively on flushing out their foamy mouths while their partner's contented themselves with keeping up a self-satisfied running commentary behind them as they watched.

"God! The way they just keep waving those things at us is absolutely *scandalous*," huffed the athletic TA in mock-exasperation, crossing her arms in front of her with a pout as she stared fixedly between her girlfriend's partially splayed thighs while she bent over the edge of the sink to spit out another mouthful of water.

"I know," commiserated Dana, cradling her elbow in her opposite hand as she rested the side of her face against her palm, likewise following the sway of her naughty niece's hips with a hungry gleam in her eye. "It's enough to make you want to pounce on them right here and now, isn't it?"

"Tell me about it."

"Bedtime is going to be *so* much fun."

"Mmhmm."

Despite their obvious attempts to goad them into responding with something sassy that might give them a good excuse to get their hands on their naked cheeks, neither Rhen nor Abby paid the two leering women behind them much attention. Just then, they were both far too busy trying to eradicate every last trace of foul tasting soap from their mouths to really care about anything else.

Applying themselves with the same level of single-minded focus and fervor that they really should've been putting toward preparing for their finals that afternoon, the two of them repeatedly took in great mouthfuls of water. Swishing them around from cheek to cheek and spitting the entire mess back out into the sink in front of them, before starting the entire process over again from the beginning with a fresh gulp of water. It was grueling, desperate work to be sure. Even with her inexperience, Courtney had apparently managed to administer just as world-class a mouth soaping as Dana had. But, little by little and glass by glass, Rhen and her partner in crime gradually managed to purge every last bubble from their mouths. Until, finally, miracle of miracles, not even the faintest hint of bitterness remained.

"Holy shit, let's never do that again," panted Abby, drawing in a long, deep breath and letting it out just as slowly as she pushed her sweaty fringe out of her eyes.

"Yeah, no kidding," nodded Rhen, her relieved smile firming up just a bit at the corners with the ironic way her friend had chosen to express herself, knowing full well that had *she* been the one to speak like that just then they would've both been in for another round of soap scrubbing.

Sure must be nice being an "adult", she pouted silently, unable to really bring herself to be annoyed by the double-standard she was forced to live by as she caught sight of the adorable Hello Kitty panties beside her on the counter with the rest of her clothes. *Oh well… At least I totally rock the look.*

"Alrighty, you two, are you ready for the rest of your punishment?" her aunt spoke up then in a sugary sweet voice, drawing her and Abby's attention back to the matter at hand as she and her fellow disciplinarian swooped in and plucked their glasses from their hands.

"Oh boy, here we go again…" Rhen sighed, while Abby took a far less happy approach.

"Humph. *No*," she groused, rounding on the auburn-haired older woman with her arms folded beneath the generous swell of her chest, no longer seeming to care that she was naked below the waist.

Dana wasn't the least bit put off by her pouty attitude, however.

"Awww, what's the matter crabby Abby?" she cooed instead, still sounding saccharine as could be while Courtney just grinned. "Did you forget you still had a date with a sore bottom?"

"Ugh! This is, like, so not fair," harrumphed the younger girl with a frustrated toss of her honey blonde hair, taking the bait hook line and sinker. "Haven't we been punished enough already?”

“For the lying, you definitely have,” agreed her girlfriend without any hesitation, knocking her off balance by not arguing.

“But,” Dana continued on with a wink, wagging an admonishing forefinger at her. “We still have that little matter of you two skipping class to deal with, now don’t we, young lady?”

“I… I mean…”

“Yes, go on,” she encouraged, the corners of her mouth climbing ever higher. “If you have any more reasons you’d like to bring up for as to why you shouldn’t have that *very* naughty caboose of yours painted red, I’m all ears.”

Realizing that she was totally up a creek without a paddle (not that she’d even want one if she had it!), and didn’t even a pair of pants to shore up her arguments, Abby heaved out a dramatic sigh.

“Oh, never mind,” she harrumphed, sharing an exasperated look with her friend as her annoyance gave way to grudging acceptance. “What do you want us to do, Miss Dana?”

Heh. A little late to start kissing up now, Abby…

“Well, for starters, *you*, young lady, and Rhen,” the older woman replied with a stony expression, making it abundantly clear that the buxom coed was on thin ice, before warming once more as she nodded toward her bratty bride-to-be and pulled open a drawer beside her to retrieve a pair of scissors. “Can take these out back and trim us up some switches.”

“Switches?” squeaked Abby, going rigid as the petite junior beside her accepted the scissors with a resigned pout.

“Mmhmm. That’s right.”

Her smile broadening, Dana held up three fingers.

“I want three from each of you. Is that understood?”

This time it was Rhen’s turn to squawk in surprise.

“Three?” she demanded, spluttering with a mixture of indignation and no small amount of dread as a chill washed over her. “But that’s… that’s…”

“No more than you deserve, cutie pie,” her fiancé finished for her, laying a gentle hand on the shoulders of both her and her partner in crime and turning them toward the back door. "Now be a good girl and show your friend where the sassy shrub is, alright?"

"Yeah, yeah…"

SMACK!

"Ack! I mean, yes ma'am!" she amended in a rush.

"That's what I *thought* you said," sniffed Dana, propelling her forward with another, harder, swat.

SMACK!

"Now scoot."

"Okay, okay, I'm going!"

Bunny-hopping forward, the raven-haired younger girl sped toward the back door just as fast as she could while shielding her seat with her hands.

"And no running!" her fiancé called after her with a laugh. "You're carrying scissors, you silly goose."

"Oh! Uh, right. Sorry!"

Adjusting her pace down to a more reasonable fast walk, Rhen pulled open the back door to her house and hustled her way out onto the patio beyond with her best friend in tow just behind her. Their steps slowing even further as Courtney shut the door behind them with a far too friendly wave.

"Have fun, you two…"

However, now that they were both safely out of swatting range, it seemed that neither of them was in much of a mood to rush toward their doom anymore. Instead contenting themselves with putting off the inevitable for as long as they could as they dragged their bare feet across the sun-warmed patio concrete. Each of them warring with a stomach full of butterflies and a pair of wobbly knees brought on by anxiously exhilarating visions of what was to come all too soon.

"Ugh. It's this way," Rhen eventually declared with a pouty harrumph as they finally ran out of patio, pointing toward a tall crepe myrtle near the fence all the way at the other end of the yard.

"Uh… Okay. But, um…"

Realizing that she'd somehow left her friend behind after she'd made it a few feet out onto the grass, Rhen came to a stop and turned back to see what the holdup was all about.

"You good?" she asked with some genuine concern as she absently wiggled her toes between the soft blades of grass beneath her feet, enjoying the gentle breeze blowing past her with its soothing scents of laundry detergent and freshly mown yards. "It's okay to walk barefoot out here, you know. There're no rocks or anthills, I promise."

"That's, uh… Not really what I was worried about," mumbled her friend, tugging down on the front of her shirt once again as her eyes darted nervously from window to window above the fence line.

"Oh…"

Despite the fact that she was just as naked below the waist as her friend was, Rhen couldn't help but feel a small surge of smug pride.

Geez. I see someone's not used to having her panties privileges revoked.

"You really don't need to worry about anyone seeing your butt," she reassured her, matching her wry tone with an equally wry smirk. "The damage was already been done back when we were standing in timeout earlier."

"Ugh. I guess that's true…" grumbled Abby, at last stepping out onto the grass to join her, all the while still keeping her shirt pulled down in front as much as she could. "It still fucking sucks, though."

"Totally," agreed Rhen with a sympathetic pat to the other girl's shoulder, enjoying being the one (somewhat) in charge for a change. "But that's just the way it goes and there's nothing we can do about it. So, let's just get this over with, yeah?"

"Humph. Do we have a choice?"

"Not really."

Smiling in spite of her obvious embarrassment, the honey blonde coed gestured for the shorter girl to lead the way.

"After you then, bratty buns."

"That's *Miss b*ratty buns to you," snickered Rhen, turning with a mock-affronted sniff and guiding her friend the rest of the way over to the crepe myrtle she'd pointed out earlier. "So, uh… Have you ever cut a switch before?"

"Um… Not really," admitted Abby, fidgeting in the shade where she stood, apparently still not quite convinced that they weren't being spied on from all sides by the younger girl's neighbors. "My grandma threatened me with one a couple of times, but she never actually, like, did it, you know?"

"Lucky," smirked Rhen, wincing theatrically as a brief burst of memories of dancing under the lash of a freshly cut switch at the hands of her own grandma bubbled up inside of her. "Well, don't sweat it. It's pretty easy once you know what you're doing. I'll show you how it's done, alright?"

At the other girl's answering nod, she went on. Standing up just a little bit taller as she basked in the warm glow of being the one with the most experience with something for a change.

Even if that something was being a brat.

"Okay, so, first things first. You need to find one that's the right size," she explained, waving toward the thin, leafy branches of the shrub in front of her. "Too thick and it'll hurt like crazy. Well, *extra* crazy. And, too thin, and you'll have to go cut two more, which is definitely not fun."

"Yeesh. I'm sure," shivered Abby, looking to her for support as she let go of the hem of her shirt with one hand and tugged down on a whippy branch. "So… What? Should we go with one like this then?"

"Hmmm… That one's not too bad in terms of thickness, but it's a little on the short side," the twenty-one-year-old turned teenager dismissed with a shake of her head. "You want to go for one that's about as long as your arm."

Frowning thoughtfully at the tangle of long, supple branches in front of her, she stepped in a bit closer, rose up onto her tiptoes, and took hold of one just to the left of Abby's own.

"Like this one, see?" she continued, using the scissors her aunt had given her to cut it free from the shrub at its base. "It's the right length and about as thick as a pencil, which is perfect."

"Uh-huh…"

Abby didn't exactly sound happy about that as she watched Rhen start stripping off the leaves from the switch one at a time with her free hand, but she kept whatever complaints were rattling around inside her head to herself as her friend went on.

"So, once you've picked one out, the next thing you need to do is start pulling off all the leaves and stuff. Oh, and while you're at it, it's also a really good idea to try and trim down any big nubs that might still be there once you're finished with that," she said, demonstrating just what she meant by expertly cutting away several bumpy protrusions from the length of the switch with her scissors. "It's pretty much impossible to get rid of all of them, so don't bother trying. You'll just end up getting into even more trouble for taking too long to get ready."

"Great…"

"Yeah…"

Accepting the now fully prepared switch with a grimace, Abby gave it a couple of test flicks through the air beside her. Wincing all the more as it cut through it with a vicious *SWISH-SWISII! SWISH-SWISH!* that had the both of them clenching on reflex.

"Ugh. This is totally going to suck, isn't it?"

"Oh yeah."

Snorting gently, Rhen did her best not to look like she was *too* worried.

And failed spectacularly.

"Those two are going to straight up wear out our butts by the time they're finished with us."

"Well," smirked her friend, managing to smile in spite of the dire straits they now found themselves in. "Hopefully they'll kiss them better once they're done."

"Hah!"

Snorting again, some of the tension eased out of Rhen's shoulders as she shook her head.

"I think we can safely count on that after the way they were drooling over us earlier, yeah."

Then, brightening even more, she added.

"You know… If you want, you two are totally welcome to spend the night tonight. We could all hang out and play and stuff, and you and Courtney could just crash in my room."

"Oooh that sounds *awesome*!" exclaimed Abby, much of her usual exuberance bubbling its way up past her worry and embarrassment as she bobbed excitedly in place. "Are you sure Dana won't mind?"

"Psh, are you kidding?"

Blowing out a breath, Rhen gave her eyes an exaggerated roll.

"There's no way that lady's *not* busting out the strap-on just as soon as it's time for me to get into my jammies, and I know she'd love to have you two there as well."

Before adding with a sly grin.

"In fact, she was telling me just the other day that she's been dying to find a good excuse to get all three of us bent over side by side again like back when we were on vacation."

"Oh… Oh yeah?"

Now *that* managed to cement Abby's attitude squarely back into the bubbly, coaxing her into letting go of her shirt entirely as she ran her fingers through her long, flaxen hair in an obvious attempt to make herself look a bit more presentable.

"I definitely wouldn't say no to that. Especially if it also means getting *you* back on your knees between my legs, you naughty thing."

"I think that can definitely be arranged," crooned Rhen, matching her wicked grin with one of her own before turning her attention back to crepe myrtle in front of them with a slight blush. "Alright now, uh… Let's hurry up and get these stupid things cut and trimmed."

Jerking her head back toward the patio behind them where their partners now stood watching the two of them with predatory expressions and waving, she finished by saying.

"I don't know about you, but I'm sure as heck not willing to let those two canoodle with each other out of earshot any more than I absolutely have to."

"Yeah, noooo kidding," huffed Abby with a half-hearted attempt at a pout, turning to stick her tongue out at her girlfriend before accepting another switch from Rhen and beginning to strip it down just like she'd been shown. "Those two are a bad influence on each other, for *sure*."

—

With perhaps more trepidation than either of them would have liked to admit, Rhen and Abby turned and began slowly making the humiliating walk of shame back to their waiting partners once they'd finished collecting the remaining switches they needed for their upcoming bun blistering. Somehow, though, while they'd had their backs turned to it, the distance between the sassy shrub and the back patio seemed to have grown ten times as long as it had been originally. Which, much to their annoyance and unease, gave them both ample opportunity to ponder just how much the three freshly trimmed branches they each now held close to their chests were going to sting once they started snapping against their bare bottoms in just a few short minutes.

Needless to say, it *sucked*. But, even so, neither girl could truly say that she wasn't looking forward to it at least a little bit.

After all, half the fun of being naughty was getting caught.

And, judging by the looks on their partners' faces as they watched them awkwardly shuffle their way across the yard back to them, they knew it too.

"All done, girls?" Dana asked when they at last reached the edge of the patio where she and her fellow disciplinarian stood waiting for them, each with their hands planted firmly on their hips and their lips pressed into a thin line of mock-sternness.

"Uh-huh."

"Yes ma'am…"

"Well then, let's just give these a little look-see, shall we?" the older woman suggested, switching from strict to sugary sweet as she held her hand out palm up and gave her fingers an expectant wiggle.

Not willing to run the risk of being sent back out to collect even *more* switches, Rhen kept the smartmouthed reply struggling to break free from her just then under tight lock and key as she handed over the long, supple switches she'd collected (along with the pair of kitchen scissors) to her aunt.

"Hmmm…"

Humming pensively, Dana took her time giving each individual switch a few sharp test flicks. Whipping them through the air one by one and reveling in the grimace on her bride-to-be's face, before eventually nodding to herself, evidently satisfied.

"Yep. These'll definitely do the trick."

"And how," agreed Courtney from beside her, following her lead with the bundle of branches her girlfriend had given her.

*SWISH-SWISH-**THWIP!***

"Ah!"

And letting out a startled yelp, followed by a hiss of pain, as she caught the side of her bare leg with the tip of one of them.

"Holy cow, that stings!"

"Oh, does it?" simpered the huffy blonde in front of her, unable to quite wipe away the smug grin on her face as she watched her rub at the thin welt she'd managed to raise along the side of her calf. "That must be just so hard for you, babe. Really."

"Heh. Thanks for the concern, hot stuff."

Still snickering, Courtney countered the shorter girl's sass by tickling the tip of her button nose with the end of her switch, coaxing out a far more genuine smile from her this time.

"But I'd be way more worried about your smart little ass, if I were you."

Abby was just in the process of opening her mouth to fire back with something that was sure to exacerbate both her and Rhen's situations, when Dana intervened.

"Ahem. Why don't you two come on over here?" she half ordered and half suggested, clearing her throat as she gestured toward the glass and metal outdoor dining table that dominated one third of the cozy lounging space.

The very same table whose chairs had been moved aside, creating enough room for two bare bottomed brats to bend over while their respective disciplinarians stood to either side of them with switches in hand.

Uh-oh…

"Since it's such a lovely evening out," Dana elaborated further upon noticing the budding looks of concern on their faces, smiling in a way that made it abundantly clear that she knew *exactly* what she was doing. "Courtney and I decided that we might as well take care of your punishment out here where we can all enjoy the nice weather."

"What? Oh, come on!" demanded Abby, stomping a foot for added emphasis while Rhen just rolled her eyes sighed.

She'd had a feeling that something like this was going to happen.

It really was too nice of a night to stay cooped up inside, after all.

"But what if somebody sees?" her friend moaned, hands once again tugging down on the front of her shirt as she looked to her partner for support, only to find an amused, pitiless smirk on the darker-skinned girl's face.

"Oh, there's no need to worry about that, dear. Our neighbors have seen little Rhenny here getting it plenty of times before and it's never bothered them any," Dana reassured her, still all sunshine and saccharine sweetness as she moved to take up her position beside the table. "Besides, switches are nice and quiet. So, as long as you two don't kick up too much of a fuss, nobody should be any the wiser about what's going on back here. Isn't that right, Rhen?"

"That's certainly one way of putting it," harrumphed the younger girl, not bothering to hide her amusement at having the line her best friend had used to justify spanking her inside one of the changing rooms at Blush turned back on her so effectively as she moved to stand beside her fiancé.

Serves you right, you big dingus.

She definitely would've preferred to not also be about to get it, true. But, hey, beggars can't be choosers.

"Plus, doing it out here will make cleanup way easier," she added helpfully, deciding that she might as well attempt to ingratiate herself a bit with her auntie while she still had a chance to influence how hard she was going to swat her.

She seriously doubted that it would make much of a difference now, but at that point she was willing to take whatever she could get. That welt on Courtney's calf looked *mean*.

"Indeed it will," agreed Dana with an approving pinch to her left cheek, making her jump with a surprised squeak. "I'd rather not have to worry about finding little bits and pieces of twigs underneath our furniture for the next month."

"Well…"

Hard-pressed to argue with her there, much as she clearly wanted to, Abby was forced to reluctantly nod her head in agreement.

"Alright, alright, I guess I see your point," she grumbled to nobody in particular, sounding marginally mollified as she stepped up next to her girlfriend beside the table and gave her long blonde hair another toss for good measure.

"I wasn't really *asking* you, dear," Dana couldn't help but point out, her tone growing steely enough to make the other girl bite her lip, before adding with a playful smile. "But I do appreciate the cooperation nevertheless."

"I um…"

A visible shudder passed through Abby then as the tips of her ears lit up in a hot shade of pink, producing a pleasant wobble from her naked cheeks as she shifted awkwardly in place and looked away.

"Yes ma'am."

"Good girl."

With her point about who was the one in charge now made, Dana gave the table beside her a brisk couple of pats, once again all business.

"Alright, you two, hands flat, bottoms out, and feet together," she ordered, lightly flicking the backs of Rhen's thighs with her switch to get her moving. "Come on now, no lollygagging. We're burning daylight here."

"Pretty sure the sun doesn't set for, like, two more hours," mumbled Rhen under her breath, earning herself a much less friendly thigh flicking for her trouble.

THWIP! THWIP!

"Ah!"

"Save the meteorology report for later, cutie pie," her aunt admonished, her gaze hardening into a warning. "The only thing I want to see right now is a couple of full moons. You hear me?"

"Heh. Fine…"

With little choice other than to do as they were told, she and Abby shared one last long-suffering look with one another and bent over. Each resting their palms against the smooth, frosted glass tabletop in front of them with a pair of matching disgruntled huffs.

Which, unsurprisingly, did them no favors.

THWIP! THWIP!

"Yeowie!"

"I said bottom *out*, little girl!" Dana snapped, punctuating her reprimand with two more wrist-powered flicks of her switch to the centers of her naughty niece's cheeks this time. "If I have to tell you again, you and I are going to be taking a trip back inside for a soap stick."

"Okay, okay, okay!"

Face tingling with fresh embarrassment, made all the worse by her friends' snickering from right beside her, the thoroughly mortified twenty-one-year-old turned teenager hurriedly shuffled her feet backwards. Arching her back and pushing her cheeks further out behind her, she felt them part enough to allow the faint trace of a warm summer breeze to tickle its way down along their divide and in between her thighs, making it all but impossible for her to ignore just how wet she was right then.

"Ah, there we go. *Much better.*"

"Humph. If you say so…"

Ignoring her petulant pouting for the time being, her partner turned her attention away from her perfectly positioned posterior and toward her co-disciplinarian.

"Ready?"

"You'd better believe it," smirked Courtney, licking her lips as she eyed the alabaster curves of her girlfriend's heart-shaped caboose, idly flicking her switch back and forth beside her (making sure to keep its tip well away from her calves this time). "So, how many are we giving them?"

"Oh, honey," laughed Dana with a motherly shake of her head, while Rhen just groaned. "This isn't some big, formal paddling or anything."

Shifting half a step closer to her not-niece, she snaked an arm underneath the front of her waist, hoisting her up onto the balls of her feet in a preemptive effort to keep her from squirming around too much during what was to come.

"I never give a set number of swats when I'm switching a bratty backside."

"You, uh… You don't?"

Clearly Abby wasn't the only one who'd grown up never experiencing this particular form of down home discipline.

"Nope! That's the beauty of a switch, actually," chirped Dana, giving her bride-to-be's propped up backside a couple more light flicks. "You just keep swatting and swatting and swatting until it finally wears out. Then, you move on to the next one and start over again until you've ran out of switches."

"Ohhh!"

Face lighting up with understanding now, Courtney's grin took on a decidedly wicked edge to it.

"So *that's* why you told them to get three each."

"Precisely," confirmed Dana, looking just as impish as she matched the TA's smirk with one of her own. "We can't have the fun- I mean, *punishment*, winding down too quickly, now can we?"

"We sure can't," agreed the other girl, adopting a mock-serious frown as she too began *tap, tap, tapping* her switch against her girlfriend's round cheeks.

"Right then."

Gradually starting to build up the amount of force behind each of the flicks to the backs of her niece's thighs and bottom, Dana locked eyes with her co-disciplinarian and gave her a firm nod.

"Let's get cookin'!"

Before suddenly ratcheting up the intensity of her movements to full force as she began swatting in earnest.

THWIP! THWIP! THWIP! THWIP! THWIP!

"Ah! Oh! Owie! Ack! Ouch!" yelped Rhen, followed half a heartbeat later by a similar string of exclamations from Abby, their voices overlapping into a twin chorus of surprise and pain as a torrent of lightning-fast swats began to light up the backs of their thighs and cheeks.

"Oh my god, oh my god!"

For all of her earlier bravado, it had actually been quite a while since Rhen had last felt the snap of a switch against her bare skin, and she'd honestly forgotten just how much the darn things *stung*.

"Crap, crap, crap! Shoot, dang, ouch, *crap*!"

Oh, the first swat wasn't so bad. Nor was the tenth. Or even the twentieth for that matter. Individually, each snap of the switch was completely tolerable. It stung for a brief moment as it landed, cutting a razor thin line of heat across both of her cheeks (or thighs!), but that pain quickly receded a couple seconds later, leaving behind only the faintest hint of tenderness (and a livid pink welt) to mark its passing.

Unfortunately for her, though, her fiancé wasn't giving her *any* time to process each individual swat. And, with how light and flexible the switch was in her hand, she was able to **THWIP! THWIP! THWIP!** it practically nonstop with little to no effort. Which meant that by the time she'd completely worn out her first one some two or three minutes later, reducing it to a bent and floppy stub of its former self that she tossed aside without a second glance, her bottom and thighs were a throbbing mass of overlapping welts burning with a white hot fury that very nearly took her breath away.

And they were just getting started!

Ugh. No amount of free coffee points is worth this! Rhen found herself grumbling internally, cursing the Coffee Kate's loyalty program that had gotten her into this mess in the first place. *I swear to god, the next time we try doing something like this, I'm paying cash.*

Of course, given the amount of effort her aunt was clearly putting into teaching her a lesson she wouldn't soon forget, that hypothetical next time wasn't likely to be until well into next semester.

If not next year.

Or ever.

Ever was definitely seeming like the most likely candidate just then.

"Phew!" gasped Courtney as her own first switch finally fell to pieces, letting it go and pausing to massage her forearm while she admired her handiwork. "You really start to feel that in the arms after a while, don't you?"

"Mmhmm," agreed Dana with a low chuckle as she released her grip on her bride-to-be's waist and scooped up her two remaining switches, eyeing them both critically in an attempt to decide which she liked more. "It's a pretty good workout if I do say so myself."

"Yeah, no kidding," echoed Rhen and Abby in a simultaneous deadpan, before breaking down into a semi-hysterical fit of giggles upon realizing that they'd both said the same thing at the same time.

"Oh? Is there something funny about your punishment, little girls?" demanded Dana archly, the grin on her face belying her stern tone as she loomed over the pair of bubbly brats. "Do I need to go get the soap again so that you two have something to hold in all those giggles?"

"No ma'am!" the two of them replied in unison once again, going rigid at the threat while also cracking up at their unintended comedic timing.

"It sure doesn't sound like they're taking this very seriously to me, Dana," pointed out Courtney, matching her mentor's stern tone and amused expression.

"It sure doesn't," agreed the older woman with a put-upon sigh and an exaggerated roll of her eyes, settling finally on a switch and once more slipping her hand beneath Rhen's waist, sending the butterflies fluttering around inside her stomach into overdrive as she gave her pouting lips a reassuring pat before hoisting her back up onto the balls of her feet. "Guess we're just going to have to keep going then, huh?"

"Oh well," shrugged the taller girl as if she really were reluctant to keep tanning her girlfriend's hide. "If we *have* to…"

With that, Rhen and Abby's partners quickly fell back into their earlier switching rhythm. Once more plunging the two of them bottom-first into a fiery sea of searing agony as they effortlessly whipped their supple, green branches up and down with a ruthless efficiency that soon had them both begging for forgiveness as they struggled to hold on to what little of their dignity remained to them, no longer caring if anybody else heard them.

THWIP! THWIP! THWIP! THWIP! THWIP!

"Oh my god! Ah! Babe, *please*!"

THWIP! THWIP! THWIP! THWIP! THWIP!

"Owie, owie, owie! Aunt Dana- Oh! I'm sorry- Ack! I'm

sorry!"

But, try as they might to convince the older women that they'd learned their lesson, the switches continued to fall without mercy. And, before too long, their plaintive yelps and promises to be good had given way to a more generalized whining and less articulate cries of pain. The infernos being stoked in their bottoms and thighs pushing the two of them well past the point of grudging acceptance that they'd done something wrong and deep into genuine regret territory as tears began to prickle at the corners of their eyes.

"Now *that's* more like it," declared Dana with a grimly satisfied grunt as she turned her attention exclusively to Rhen's dancing thighs, working her switch all the way down from her sit-spots to just above the backs of her knees and up again.

Despite the relaxed atmosphere among the four of them just a few moments earlier, it was obvious that she wasn't at all happy about her skipping class (even if it was just a review day), and she was going to make sure it never happened again.

And that she and her friend would be remembering this punishment every time they stood up or sat down for the next *week*.

Oh crap, that's right!

Gasping with a sudden start, a cold shiver arced its way down Rhen's spine (doing absolutely nothing to cool her burning buns) as she remembered that she still had her Friday meeting with her academic adviser to go to that following afternoon.

Dang it, dang it, dang it!

Trapped as she was on the balls of her feet, she still nevertheless attempted to vent her frustration by stomping a foot. Which, rather than produce the satisfying thump she was looking for, instead only succeeded in momentarily exposing the inside of her right thigh to the tip of her aunt's switch for a trio of truly astounding swats.

THWIP! THWIP! THWIP!

"Aieee!"

"Watch that kicking, cutie pie," the older woman admonished, not slowing her swatting in the slightest as she tightened her grip around her middle.

"Ack! Yes- Oh! Yes ma'am."

Ugh. Maybe I'll get lucky and she'll let me off the hook with just writing lines or something? she grumbled to herself, knowing full well that that was just about as likely as her aunt *not* sending her to school wearing a pull-up tomorrow. *Humph!*

Face blazing nearly as hot as her bottom was just then, Rhen tried her best not to think too much about the deeply amused look that was sure to light up her professor's face when she got a good look at what she had on underneath her skirt.

Oh well… At least it'll help make things easier if she decides to use that stupid paddle of hers.

—

"Alright, girls, we're getting close to being just about finished here," announced Dana in a cheery voice some indeterminately long amount of time later once her second switch had finally become too short and floppy to be of any use, tossing it aside and picking up her final one from the table behind her. "Just one more to go, so hang in there a little bit longer, alright?"

Despite her cheery disposition, it was largely a rhetorical question, and they all knew it.

By that point, Rhen and Abby both were far too busy sobbing their eyes out (dribbling tears and an embarrassing amount of snot and saliva onto the tabletop beneath them) to really appreciate that they were nearing the end of their punishment. Which wasn't exactly surprising considering the fact that each of their bottoms was now a constantly throbbing mass of puffy dark red welts caked on top of one another from the tops of their cheeks down to just above the backs of their knees. Welts that continued to smolder and pulse with fresh heat in time with the beating of their hearts, even without their partners helping to stoke the flames.

Needless to say, the two of them would be sleeping on their

stomachs that night.

And sitting more than a little gingerly for breakfast the following morning.

But, even in the depths of their self-pity and remorse, neither of them could truly say that they didn't deserve every single stripe they'd collected so far. In that moment, they were no longer two supposedly mature college students nearing graduation, but instead just two naughty little girls who were being forced to face the music for their misbehavior whether they liked it or not.

And they wouldn't have had it any other way.

Unfortunately, though, no amount of personal reflection and acknowledgement of wrong-doing could lessen the burning in their bottoms just then. Or change the fact that they both still had an entire other switch to work their way through before this was all finally over.

Thank god we just stocked up on aloe vera. I'm pretty sure we're going to blast through an entire bottle of it tonight.

"Right then."

Nodding to her co-disciplinarian, wordlessly communicating that they needed to harden their hearts as they pressed on to the end, Dana lined up her final switch along the center of her naughty niece's carmine cheeks. Carefully inspecting them for any areas that looked like they might not be as well-reddened as the rest, before heaving out a sigh as she and Courtney began swatting once again.

THWIP! THWIP! THWIP! THWIP! THWIP!

—

When, finally, mercifully, the last of their switches were completely worn out (helped along in no small part thanks to the ones wielding them snapping them in half about a minute into their final round of swatting), Rhen and Abby both were completely spent and ready for a hug.

Which was something their partners were more than happy to provide them with.

"There, there, shhh…" soothed Dana, murmuring into the top of her bride-to-be's raven hair as she held her close, rubbing her back and scratching her just the way she liked between the shoulder blades. "It's all over now, cutie pie."

"That's right, I've got you, hot stuff," Courtney put in as well, cuddling her own girl and running her nimble fingers through her long, flaxen tresses, combing them out as she gently rocked her back and forth in place. "Easy now… Just let it all out, okay?"

Not needing to be told twice, the two of them continued to cry against the older women's chests for what felt like a very long time after that. (Though, in reality, it wasn't much longer than a few minutes.) Their comforting words and gentle caresses lifting them out of their haze of misery and pain and back into the light of day.

It really was amazing how quickly a bratty girl could recover when her bottom wasn't constantly being set ablaze. But, even so, it was definitely going to be a while before either of them was able to sit down, stand up, or wear a particularly tight pair of pants without experiencing a sharp reminder of the consequences of lying and skipping school.

Which, if Rhen was being totally honest with herself, was probably for the best.

Even if it totally sucked.

"How're you feeling, honey buns?" her fiancé prompted when her sobs had finally subsided to only the odd hiccup and occasional sniffle.

"Ugh. How do you think?" she groaned into her damp top, smiling despite the low simmer still radiating from her backside.

She could never bring herself to sulk for long after a spanking, and that evening was proving to be no exception.

"Sore and sassy?" Dana suggested, her voice a low, amused purr as she and Courtney chuckled to themselves.

"Lucky- Urk! Guess," huffed Rhen, the last word coming out as a grunt of pain as her partner gave her scalded seat a taunting squeeze, making her jump as she pulled her in close for a prolonged kiss before letting her go with a shameless smirk.

"Experience and intuition, my dear. Experience and intuition."

"Uh-huh."

If that were the case, you'd think I'd be better at avoiding getting my butt blistered by now, Rhen thought to herself with a rueful grimace, unable to resist the urge to reach back and carefully knead her achingly tender seat. *Geez, she really did a number on me this time, didn't she?*

Casting a glance over her shoulder, she was pleased to see that Abby too was massaging a strikingly crimson caboose. Hissing in sharply with each fresh squeeze as she shifted her weight from foot to foot.

Heh. Well, what do you know? It really is fun to watch a brat dance around after a spanking. Who knew?

"Mmmm…" sighed Dana, breaking the comfortable silence they'd all fallen into a minute or so later, stepping back and stretching her arms above her head as if she'd just wrapped up an intense workout and was now pleasantly sore. "I don't know about you three, but after all that, I'm *starving.*"

"Oh god, me too," echoed Courtney, likewise massaging her forearms and rolling her shoulders.

"Ditto," came Rhen and Abby's replies in turn as well, each still with their hands clamped firmly to their roasted rumps.

"Excellent!"

Beaming now, Dana eyed each of them in turn.

"As it so happens, we've actually got a bunch of steaks in the freezer. So, how about we have ourselves a little barbeque? It's been forever since I've had a chance to do some grilling."

This idea was met with a unanimous round of cheering from the gathered coeds, and Rhen quickly added.

"Oh! Hey, Dana, before I forget. Abby and I were talking earlier, and um… We thought maybe it'd be fun if she and Courtney stayed over tonight so that we could all, um…"

Even though she was standing there in her back yard naked from the waist down and not making any move to cover herself, she still couldn't stop a fresh splash of pink from working its way up to her forehead as she finished lamely.

"You know… *Play* and stuff."

"Oh you were, were you?" her fiancé teased, a crocodile smile spreading across her full lips.

"Yep!" chirped Abby, having far less trouble voicing her thoughts than her friend. "Rhen was mentioning something about how you wanted to get us all lined up like back when we were in California so that you could-"

"Abby!" yelped the shorter girl, rushing in to cover the blathering blonde's mouth before she could finish speaking, the blush on her face blossoming into a full on shade of stop sign red.

"What?" laughed her friend, dancing out of reach and circling around behind her partner for protection. "It's the truth, isn't it?"

"I mean, *yeah*," huffed Rhen, stomping a foot as she rolled her eyes. "But you don't have to, like, say it out loud and stuff, you know."

"Yes, I can think of a *much* better use for that lovely little mouth of yours, Abby, dear," agreed Dana, her smile widening even further as she shared a wink with her fellow disciplinarian. "What do you think, Courtney? I know it's technically a school night for you two, but a little sleepover fun sounds like just the thing to cap off our evening together, wouldn't you agree?"

"Hell yeah it does," nodded the taller girl, turning an equally lascivious look on her former student. "You're not too sore to sit on my face, are you, bratty buns?"

"I… I… I mean, um…"

Looking back to the now positively short-circuiting girl's partner, she added with a carefree shrug.

"And you really don't need to worry about keeping us up late, Dana," she reassured her. "We've still got all weekend to study, after all."

"Ah, yes, I guess that's true… Right then!"

With the matter now settled, Dana pointed toward the back door as she fixed Rhen and Abby in place with an eager, focused look.

"You two go grab the broom and a damp rag from inside and get to work cleaning up out here," she ordered, gesturing offhandedly toward the scattered bits and pieces of broken switch, and the two distinct damp patches they'd left behind on the tabletop. "Courtney and I will start in on dinner while you're doing that, and then once you're done with tidying up, you can start setting the table out here, alright?"

"Yes ma'am!"

Sped along by the prospect of both dinner *and* dessert, Rhen quickly nodded and turned to go while her partner in crime remained rooted to the spot where she stood, blushing.

"Um… Can we at least get dressed first?" she pressed, eyeing the wrought iron mesh seats of the patio chairs situated around the table.

Those definitely weren't going to be any fun to sit on.

"Nope," answered Dana and Courtney together, wearing identical evil grins.

"But," the older of the two of them went on, shushing the pair of protests the two bare bottomed brats were in the process of summoning with a fingertip to each of their lips. "If you two can show me that you can be good girls by getting your chores done nice and fast, I'll get you some pillows to sit on. Deal?"

"Deal!"

Sufficiently motivated now, the two of them turned and sped back into the house to do as they were told, chatting animatedly among themselves as they went. The lingering warmth in their tails all but forgotten. For, as humiliating and painful as their evening had been so far, neither of them could truly say that they hadn't enjoyed it.

Well, now that they were done being punished, that is.

And, best of all, they were just getting started!

Epilogue

– One Week Later –

Turning the page on the book she was reading, Rhen Mathews let out a long, drawn out yawn. Prompting the arm her sleeping partner had draped loosely over her waist to tighten reflexively.

And the pull-up she had on underneath her pajama bottoms crinkle audibly.

"Mmph, wassat?"

Oh crap.

Freezing in place, she held her breath for a five count as her lips twitched ever so slightly with a mixture of guilt and amusement. Waiting until she heard Dana's breathing return back to the steady in and out of light snoring before letting out a (much softer) sigh of relief as she willed her body to relax.

Phew! That was way too close...

According to the alarm clock on the nightstand beside her, it was just past two in the morning. And, much as she might deserve it, Rhen had to admit she really wasn't in the mood to have her bottom roasted for staying up way past her bedtime.

Again.

After the monumental bun blistering she and Abby had endured last Thursday, she'd been sure to stay on her very best behavior (aside from some casual disobedience here and there to help keep things interesting), and so far had managed to avoid taking any follow-up trips across her auntie's lap. Of course, that might've also had something to do with the fact that she'd been neck deep in finals for the last week and Dana had decided to take it easy on her. But, she liked to believe too that her partner's oft-quoted maxim about her ultimately being the one who decided whether or not her panties came down for a spanking was actually true.

Plus, having to sit on a pile of pillows to study at her desk all weekend had proven to be an *excellent* motivator to behave herself.

In the end, though, it had totally been worth it. She'd aced all of her exams, scoring near perfect marks on every single one of them. And, while that had basically been the expected outcome for her from the beginning, it was still immensely gratifying to see all of her hard work (and sore bottoms) actually pay off.

Doctor Holloway had been beyond delighted too at her results. But, somehow Rhen doubted that would lead to her winding up across her professor's lap any less come next semester.

Oh well… I can live with that.

It wasn't like she wasn't used to routine discipline by now anyway.

Honestly, I'm just surprised Dana hasn't found an excuse to get me back over her knee yet.

Granted, it *was* only Saturday (technically Sunday now). She was sure that before too long her grace period with her partner would come to an abrupt (and embarrassing) end. And, if not, well… She could always think of something to help push things along.

After all, relationships are built on teamwork, aren't they?

In the meantime, though, Rhen was just glad to be done with school for the time being. And, while it was true that her break between now and the start of fall semester in a couple weeks was absolutely pitiful, she still fully intended on making the most of it.

Like, for instance, finding a venue for her and Dana's wedding!

They still hadn't settled on an official date yet outside of the vague idea of "sometime next summer". But, they were both beyond eager to start nailing down some of the details.

I wonder if we could have two cakes instead of one at the reception? It'd be nice to have chocolate and vanilla as options so that nobody has to feel left out. I mean, they do it for chicken and beef dinner options, right? Then again, I guess that wouldn't really matter if we got a multi-tiered cake, would it? They can make those in alternating flavors, can't they?

Stifling another yawn as she stretched, Rhen decided that she could finish catching up on the latest adventures of her favorite duo of lesbian space pirates tomorrow night. It really *was* pretty late. Plus, it occurred to her as she rubbed one eye with the back of her hand, that she'd been reading and rereading the same paragraph for nearly five minutes now. And so, marking her place with the lacquered bookmark Dana had given her for her birthday, she laid her copy of *Draw of a Far-Off Nova* down on the nightstand beside her as softly as she could and switched off the light.

Then, wriggling her way deeper beneath the covers, she shifted closer to her partner. Turning her back and pressing her hips against her front as the older woman unconsciously wrapped her arms around her shoulders and pulled her close.

"I love you, Dana," she whispered, pressing a gentle kiss to the back of her hand as her eyes drifted closed.

"Mmmm… Love you… too… cutie pie," mumbled the older woman, her breath tickling the side of her face as she gave her a light squeeze and added with a groggy chuckle. "And you are *so* going to get it in the morning…"

Before falling back into the steady rhythm of sleep, snoring against the back of her hair.

"Heh. Fair enough."

Snuggling her teddy bear, happier than she'd ever been, Rhen allowed herself to be swept along into dreamland. Not sure what the next day might hold (other than a red bottom), but eager to find out together with the woman she loved.

THE END

More Books by Clarine Klein

(Available on Amazon)

Back to Her Teens
Clarine Klein

Back to Her Teens

Petite and oh so sassy college sophomore Rhen Mathews is being kicked out of her dorms to make room for new students, and is in desperate need of a place to live. And so, when Dana Johnson, her former boss from her brief stint as an assistant at a local daycare, offers to let her move in with her for free, she accepts without a second thought.

The only condition?

She has to do so as her thirteen-year-old niece from out of town.

What follows is a forced regression/ageplay novel filled to the brim with super embarrassing moments for Rhen and lots of much-needed spanking and discipline from her loving, but very strict, Auntie Dana.

Cat and Mouse
ATTITUDE ADJUSTER
Clarine Klein

Cat and Mouse

Cassidy Coleman is a sassy but introverted college sophomore out on her own for the first time in her young adult life. At the start of fall semester, she moves into an apartment with a randomly assigned roommate, Lauren Delaney. Lauren is a an outgoing and athletic economics major one year ahead of Cassidy in school, and is just looking for a place to live that doesn't also double up as a party house on the weekends.

Unfortunately, things start off more than a little awkward between the two of them at first, with Cassidy too tongue-tied by the captivating older girl to carry on more than a two sentence conversation before needing to flee to her bedroom. Eventually though, the two manage to bond over a mutual love of video games from their childhood, and overnight an instant and lifelong friendship is forged. From there friendship then blossoms into love when after pushing her roommate into a freezing pool on a chilly winter night, Cassidy suddenly finds herself being hauled across Lauren's ample lap for a bare bottom blistering they've both been dreaming of for weeks.

And it's only the beginning!

The Misty Bog

Clarine Klein
Leila Hann

The Water Nymph's Plaything

Fresh from her novice training as a sister of the Celestine Order, Sally Vinebrook travels the world in search of magical secrets to further her education in the arcane arts. Following up on a rumor, she comes across The Misty Bog, home to an ancient and powerful water nymph named Modan.

After begging for a chance to study with her for a time, and a very thorough spanking for being so disrespectful to her swamp upon arrival, she is shown a brand new world of magic unlike anything she's ever known!

Though by the end of her stay, she just might not be able to sit down ever again.

The SPANKING of Sally Marie

CLARINE KLEIN

The Spanking of Sally Marie

Sally finds herself in trouble once too often, and as grounding and other forms of punishment have had little effect on Sally's bratty behavior, her parents decide to spank their teenage daughter instead. It all begins when Sally stays up half the night playing around on her computer. Her dad is not pleased, and upends her for a bare bottom spanking. It is the first of many such spankings delivered by either Mom or Dad, and things get mega embarrassing for Sally when she's spanked in the Ladies Room in the mall, and in a side room at the local church during the Sunday service. Sally soon finds out the difference between 'attitude adjuster' spankings and the real thing, and her humiliation increases when her girlfriends find out she's still getting spanked - they even seize an opportunity to spank her themselves!

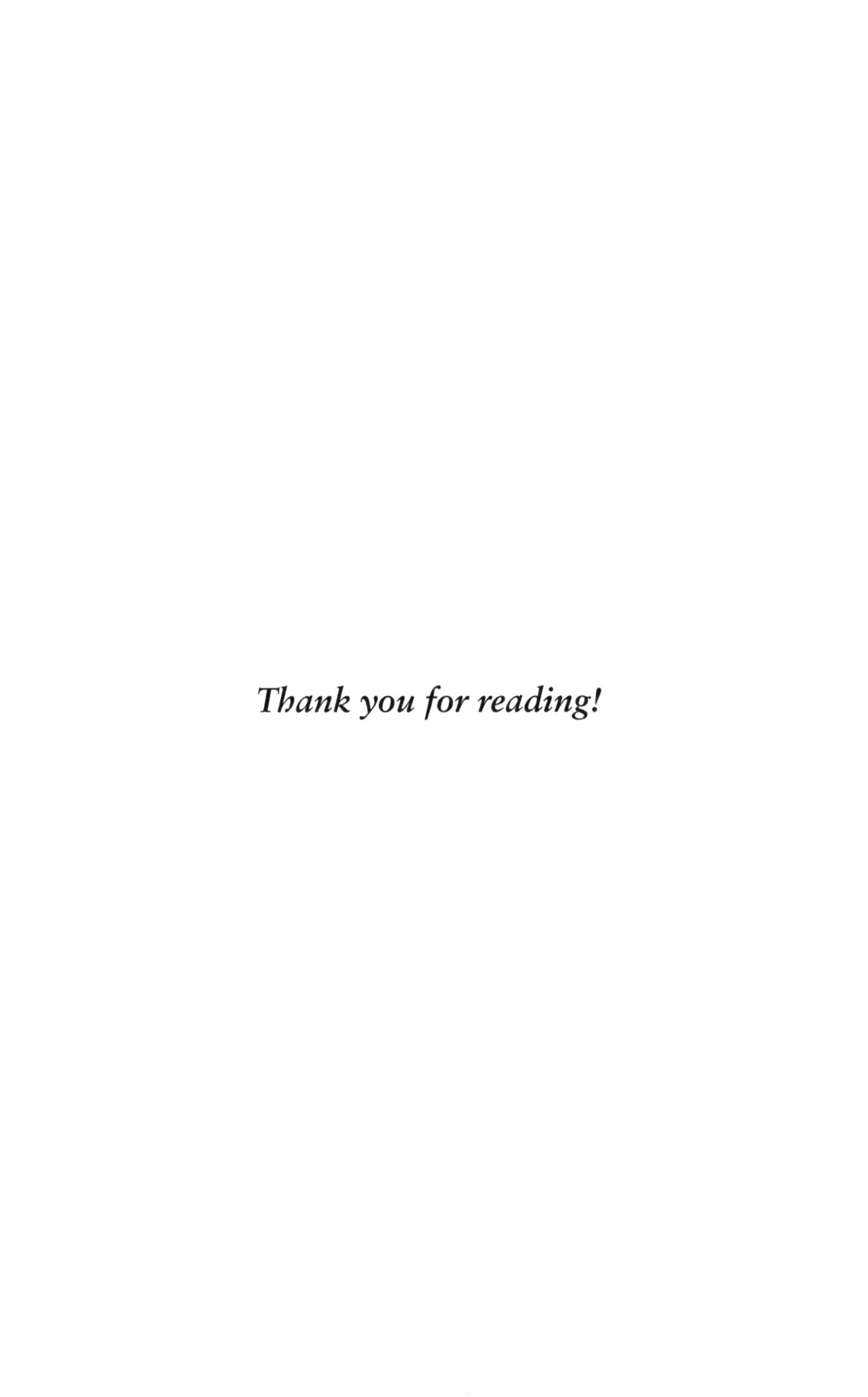
Thank you for reading!